'Throws light on an endlessly fascinating historical figure . . . making it feel so fresh and alive'
EARL SPENCER

'Lingers long after the last page is turned'
ELIZABETH FREMANTLE

'Will change everyone's preconceptions'
SUSAN RONALD

'Hugely enjoyable . . . Alison Weir knows her subject and has a knack for the telling and textural detail'
DAILY MAIL

'Enthralling'
SARAH GRISTWOOD

'I was gripped [from] start to finish'
MAVIS CHEEK

'Sparkling, gripping and word-perfect'
HISTORICAL NOVEL SOCIETY

'A fascinating insight into this period of our history'
SUN

ALISON W........ ....selling historical novelist of Tudor fiction, and the leading female historian in the United Kingdom. She has published more than thirty books, including many leading works of non-fiction, and has sold over three million copies world-wide.

Her novels include the Tudor Rose trilogy, which spans three generations of history's most iconic family – the Tudors, and the highly acclaimed Six Tudor Queens series about the wives of Henry VIII, all of which were *Sunday Times* bestsellers.

Alison is a fellow of the Royal Society of Arts and an honorary life patron of Historic Royal Palaces.

Praise for Alison Weir's
Tudor Novels

'A serious achievement'
THE TIMES

'Weir is excellent on the little details that
bring a world to life'
GUARDIAN

'This brilliant series has brought Henry VIII's six wives
to life as never before'
TRACY BORMAN

'A brilliant evocation of the period'
KATE WILLIAMS

'History has the best stories and they should
all be told like this'
CONN IGGULDEN

'Well researched and engrossing'
GOOD HOUSEKEEPING

'Alison Weir makes history come alive as no one else'
BARBARA ERSKINE

ALISON WEIR

HENRY VIII
THE HEART & THE CROWN

REVIEW

First published in Great Britain in 2022 by
HEADLINE REVIEW
An imprint of Headline Publishing Group

First published in paperback in 2024 by
HEADLINE REVIEW

1

Cataloguing in Publication Data is available from the British Library

ISBN 978 1 4722 7811 1

Typeset in Garamond MT by Avon DataSet Ltd, Alcester, Warwickshire

Printed and bound in Great Britain by Clays Ltd, Elcograf S.p.A.

HEADLINE PUBLISHING GROUP
An Hachette UK Company
Carmelite House
50 Victoria Embankment
London EC4Y 0DZ

www.headline.co.uk
www.hachette.co.uk

HENRY VIII
VIII
THE
HEART
& THE
CROWN

THE ENGLISH ROYAL HOUSE 1503

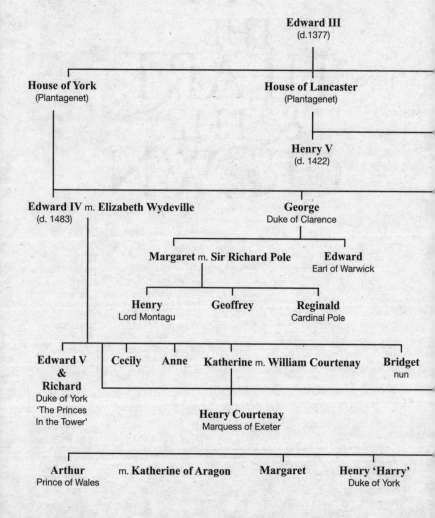

Edward III
(d.1377)

House of York
(Plantagenet)

House of Lancaster
(Plantagenet)

Henry V
(d. 1422)

Edward IV m. **Elizabeth Wydeville**
(d. 1483)

George
Duke of Clarence

Margaret m. **Sir Richard Pole**

Edward
Earl of Warwick

Henry
Lord Montagu

Geoffrey

Reginald
Cardinal Pole

**Edward V
&
Richard**
Duke of York
'The Princes
In the Tower'

Cecily

Anne

Katherine m. **William Courtenay**

Bridget
nun

Henry Courtenay
Marquess of Exeter

Arthur
Prince of Wales

m. **Katherine of Aragon**

Margaret

Henry 'Harry'
Duke of York

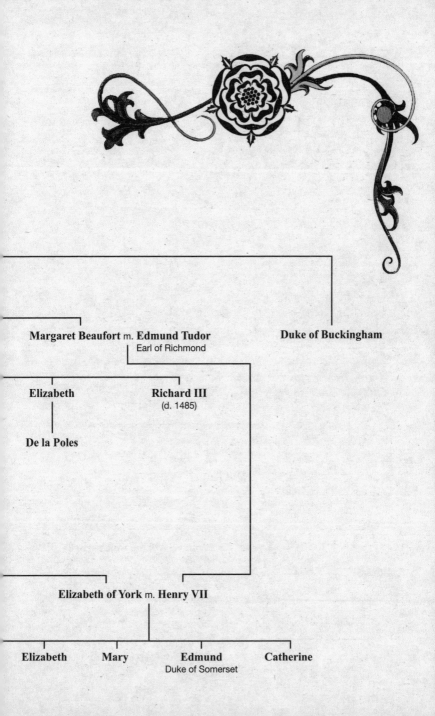

Margaret Beaufort m. **Edmund Tudor**
Earl of Richmond

Duke of Buckingham

Elizabeth

Richard III
(d. 1485)

De la Poles

Elizabeth of York m. **Henry VII**

Elizabeth   **Mary**   **Edmund**   **Catherine**
Duke of Somerset

To my beautiful daughter
Kate
to mark her marriage to Jason,
with all my love to you both.

Without discord
And both accord
Now let us be;
Both hearts alone
To set in one
Best seemeth me.

(King Henry VIII)

Whoever leads an auspicious life here and governs the commonwealth rightly, as my most noble father did, who promoted all piety and banished all ignorance, has a most certain way to Heaven.

(King Henry VIII)

Prologue

He was dying, he knew it. No one had dared tell him, and why would they, when to predict the King's death was treason? But he could feel it in his bones, in the bulk of his failing body – not so bulky now, since his flesh was hanging on him. He had not wanted food these past few days.

He tried to shift in the vast bed, but even that was beyond him. How much longer must he suffer this purgatory, he, who had ever shied from illness and death? He groaned aloud, but there was no one to hear him, only Will Somers, who was dozing in the chair by the fire. The diamond panes in the mullioned windows were rattling in the winds battering Whitehall Palace. Outside, the Thames might be freezing over.

He shivered, and not just from the chill in the room. It would not be long before he stood before the God he had so often invoked as his ally, and with whom he must soon make his peace. He had ever striven to be a virtuous man and keep the Commandments, but he had not been a good man. He saw that now, as the Day of Judgement approached ever nearer. It would be a long reckoning.

He wished that Kate was here beside him, but she was at Greenwich, where he had sent her, not wishing her to witness his final decline.

At least his councillors – vicious, quarrelsome, contentious knaves, all of them – had left him in peace for a space. This morning, he had roused himself sufficiently to discuss affairs of state with them, until the strength drained from him and they had gone away, bowing and whispering. They were like cats, poised to pounce. As soon as he was dead, they would seize power in the name of his son, and then God help England! But he had done what he could to safeguard the boy's

1

future. A rogue tear trickled down his cheek at the thought of his precious, beloved jewel, bereft and orphaned.

It was growing dark now. How the years had flown. He had not always been a prisoner of this unwieldy, diseased body. He had been a golden youth; he had known glory upon glory. The world had celebrated him. He had thought himself immortal. How God makes fools of men . . .

Not so long ago, it seemed, he had been young and full of hope, burgeoning with life and promise. And then tragedy had struck. Even now, remembering prodded the wound to which time had brought insensibility. From a distance of forty-four years, he could recall, as if it was yesterday, the soft velvet of his mother's counterpane, damp and spoiled beneath his cheek . . .

Part One

Spring

Pastime with good company
I love and shall unto I die;
Grudge who lust, but none deny,
So God be pleased thus live will I.
For my pastance
Hunt, sing, and dance.
My heart is set:
All goodly sport
For my comfort,
Who shall me let?

(King Henry VIII)

Chapter 1

1503

He had cried for hours. Mother, his dearest Mother, was dead. It had been the most hateful, dreadful news, broken to him by Mrs Luke, his old nurse. Not, thankfully, by Father, who was too broken by his own grief. Harry could not have coped with witnessing the King's distress. He had enough to bear. He had wept and wept on Mrs Luke's broad bosom, and now, aware that great boys of eleven were not supposed to give way to womanish tears, he struggled to compose himself and went to find his sisters, who were sitting desolately on the rug before the fire in Mother's bedchamber. He stared in horror at the bed, which had already been hung and draped with the black velvet of mourning. Mother would never sleep here again; he would never more hear her sweet voice, feel her gentle arms around him, her golden boy. How truly she had loved him; how desperately sad to think of the empty years ahead without her. He could not damp down the great swell of sorrow that was rising within him. He sank to his knees by the bed and buried his head in his hands.

He had loved her, revered her, adored her. Through her, he was the heir to the rightful royal line of England. She had been everything a queen should be: beautiful, kind, fruitful, charitable, open-handed and devout. She had taught him his first prayers and his first letters, soothed his childish ills and been a fount of wise advice and comfort. And now she was gone. He could not bear it.

His grandmother, the Lady Margaret, found him and lifted him up. Framed by her widow's wimple and black gable hood, her thin face was sad and drawn.

'Harry, you must rejoice that your dear mother is with God and be happy for her.'

'How can I?' he burst out. 'I need her! How can God be so cruel as to take her from me?'

'Hush, child! You must not question God's will.' She sat on the bed and drew him to her, as Mary, not quite seven and the beauty of the family, climbed on her lap and sat there, her lower lip trembling, and Margaret, thirteen years old and normally wilful and imperious, knelt at her feet, looking lost.

'Your lady mother is now in Heaven, looking down on you all and praying for you,' Grandmother told them. 'She would not want you to be sad. And she is with Arthur.' Even now, Harry felt the old familiar, resentful jealousy of his brother rising in him. Whatever Arthur had had, Harry had coveted, and when Arthur had died last year, at the tender age of fifteen, Harry had suddenly had it all. He was now the Prince of Wales and heir to the throne, and he was betrothed to his brother's enchanting Spanish widow. One day, he would be the King of England and Katherine of Aragon would be his Queen. But now, Arthur, in Heaven, had stolen one final march on him and was enjoying the greatest thing of all: their mother's presence.

'Why did she have to die?' Mary asked.

'God called her,' the Lady Margaret said.

'She died because she got childbed fever after having our sister Catherine,' Margaret elaborated.

'Would that Catherine had never been born,' Harry muttered.

'Never say that, Harry!' Grandmother chided, hugging him. 'She is an innocent, poor, motherless babe, and I fear that she herself is not long for this world.'

Harry wept again, as the reality of his loss sank in. He was motherless too. He leaned his head on the old woman's thin shoulder and howled.

Two days later, the Lady Margaret being of the opinion that lessons would help to take Harry's mind off his loss, he was back at his desk at Eltham Palace, labouring under the waspish eye of his tutor,

Master Skelton. Learned herself, Grandmother had always taken an active interest in the welfare and tutoring of her sweet children, as she called him and his sisters, and Mother and Father had always said they should be grateful for that, since she was a generous patron of scholars and the University of Cambridge. Like Mother, she loved books, and both women had inspired in Harry a passion for learning. It was a great source of enjoyment, a journey of discovery for a young mind avid for new information, and he had always been an apt and able pupil.

Three years ago, Lord Mountjoy, a scholar whom Father had appointed to mentor Harry, had arranged for a young lawyer called Thomas More to bring the celebrated Dutch humanist Erasmus to Eltham Palace. Harry and his younger siblings had received them in the magnificent great hall built by their grandfather, Edward IV, and he and Erasmus had conversed in an oriel window.

Harry had long revered Erasmus as a hero; even before he met the great man, he had read his books and been inspired by his understanding of the literature of the ancients and his studies of the Greek New Testament. He had been taught about the rediscovery of the classical works of ancient Greece and Rome, and knew that those who studied this 'new learning' were called Humanists. He had been honoured when Erasmus invited him to correspond with him in Latin, and elated when the great scholar praised his letters and said how impressed he had been to learn that they were all his own work. *I see you like to emulate my style*, Erasmus had written after the Eltham meeting. *You have the seeds of genius in you. You reach for the stars, and you could bring to perfection whichever task you undertake.* Harry had thrilled to his words.

Now, bent over a beautifully bound manuscript of Homer's *Odyssey*, he was finding it hard to concentrate, for his thoughts kept straying to his great loss. He was always an active child, and school-work could not distract him from his grief. He needed to be outside, running or riding or fighting with his friend Charles Brandon and the other boys seated at the adjacent desks, who seemed as fidgety as he was.

When he had been very young, there had been talk that he was to become a churchman. Fortunately, Father had changed his mind, for Harry had no inclination for the religious life. He wanted to fight battles and triumph at tournaments, woo beautiful ladies and perform feats of daring to win their love. Both his parents, especially Mother, had instilled in him a passion for chivalry and he wanted to be the new King Arthur. That role had been intended for his brother, who was to have ushered in the second golden age of Camelot, but Harry knew that he himself was far better suited to the task than Arthur would ever have been. Arthur had been skinny and sickly; Harry was bursting with health and energy. He was Lord Warden of the Cinque Ports, Constable of Dover Castle, Lord Lieutenant of Ireland, a Knight of the Garter and a Knight of the Bath; prior to becoming Prince of Wales, he had been Duke of York. He could not wait to feel the weight of the crown on his brow.

For now, however, he was relegated to the schoolroom.

'And what is so interesting outside the window?' barked Master Skelton, catching him daydreaming. 'To your books, Lord Harry! England has the right to expect much from a king who has been nourished on philosophy and the Nine Muses!'

'Yes, sir,' Harry muttered, failing as usual, for the life of him, to see why Erasmus had called crabby old Skelton – Skelinton, as he himself privately thought of him – an 'incomparable light and ornament of British letters'. More like the feared and hated scourge of his father's unsuspecting courtiers, whom the tutor targeted with derisory and contemptuous satires. It was not only Harry who had felt the lash of his tongue. Father had been angered by Skelton's barbs and had even clapped him in gaol for a short spell last year. Since then, Skelinton had tempered his criticisms and spoken of leaving court and taking up a rectorship in Norfolk. Harry had been gleeful to hear that, then realised he would miss him. He had his master's measure and knew how far he could push him. Better the devil you knew.

He caught Charles Brandon grinning at him across the room. Seven years his senior, Brandon had been chosen as one of his companions after Arthur's death. He was the son of Sir William

Brandon, who had been Father's standard-bearer at the Battle of Bosworth, but had been cut down by the Usurper, Richard III. Had Sir William not been guarding him, Father himself would have died. In gratitude, a few years after the victory that had won him the throne, Father had placed young Charles in Arthur's household and later made him a page. He was a boisterous boy, none too bright, but his love of jousting, chivalry and pageantry meant he and Harry had become inseparable.

Brandon hated Skelinton, who was often exasperated with him, but the tutor had Harry's interests at heart. Two years ago, he had written a book, *The Mirror of a Prince*, in which, with other improving advice, he had exhorted Harry to choose a good wife and prize her always. As if Harry would not do that! Ladies were to be worshipped and treated with reverence.

Trying not to laugh at Brandon's funny faces, he turned his eyes to the printed page before him, thinking of Katherine. His heart had been hers ever since he had welcomed her to London sixteen months earlier and escorted her to the altar in St Paul's Cathedral, where she was married to Arthur. He had been captivated by her fair prettiness, her long red-gold hair, her dignity and graciousness. Five and a half years his senior, dignified and serious, she seemed like a princess out of a legend and would surely be another perfect queen like his mother. How jealous he had been of Arthur. He had known even then that he himself would make her a far better and lustier husband. And now Katherine was to be his; in just over two years' time, when he reached fourteen, they would be married. He needed no advice from Master Skelton about prizing her.

The thought of his mother made him pause in distress. It was too painful to revisit his grief, but the sense of loss threatened to overwhelm him.

'Lord Harry, you have not turned the page this past quarter-hour,' the tutor rapped.

'How can you expect me to work when I cannot stop grieving for my lady mother?' Harry retorted plaintively, keeping his head down so that Skelinton could not see the tears in his eyes.

9

His master's craggy face softened. 'All right, my lord Prince, I understand. Maybe it would do you good to get out in the fresh air and practise your archery skills.'

'Yes, it would!' Harry cried, leaping up, desperate for a distraction.

'Be gone then. I will tell Master Dewes to come this afternoon, instead of this morning.'

'Thank you,' Harry breathed, hastening away. He liked Master Dewes, who taught him French, Latin and Italian, languages being a subject at which he excelled. At least that was one thing in which he pleased his father. But first, the great outdoors beckoned. After a few contests with his friends, he would ride and then practise at the quintain, and play tennis if there was time before lessons resumed. He loved nothing more than sport. Thankfully, Father had ordered that he be given instruction in all the exercises meet for a prince – horsemanship, skill with the longbow, fencing, jousting, wrestling and swordsmanship. And he excelled at them all!

Shrugging on his leather jerkin, he beckoned Brandon and his other young gentlemen to follow him out into the weak February sunshine, striding towards the butts, two Yeomen of the Guard trailing him. William Compton, one of the King's wards, hastened in his wake. Nine years Harry's senior, he came from a wealthy family, but Skelinton thought him a bad influence for his devil-may-care approach to life, which Harry knew masked an iron will and boundless ambition. One day, he would need men like Compton – and his own distant cousin Edward Neville, who, like Brandon, bore a marked resemblance to himself, and not just in their shared passion for jousting. Indeed, Brandon and Harry were often mistaken for brothers.

How different life would be if Harry had his own household, far from the King's watchful eye. At the thought of Father, he frowned. He felt sorry for him, for there was no doubting that he had loved Mother, and he could not but admire him, for he had won a kingdom after defeating the Usurper. And yet, there was no aura of glory about Father, no sense of greatness. The gaunt features, the wispy greying hair, the stooped, spare frame all betokened a clerk rather than a king. And always, it seemed to Harry, Father was saying no, or criticising.

Before Arthur died, Father had been planning to give Harry his own household at Codnor Castle in Derbyshire, and Harry had been beyond excited. By all accounts, Codnor was like a fortress out of legend, the ideal house for the chivalrous knight he dreamed of being one day. He had imagined himself hosting tournaments there, surrounded by dashing gentlemen and beautiful damsels, and one day bringing there a bride who would look just like Katherine. Best of all, he would be hundreds of miles from London and Father's eagle eye. Freedom had beckoned.

But then Arthur had died, and the King had abandoned the plan. 'I have already lost two sons,' he'd explained, as Harry stood before him, choking back tears of fury and disappointment. 'I cannot afford to lose you, the only one left to me. I sent Arthur far away to Ludlow, which I now regret, and I intend to keep you with me.'

Harry had barely been able to hide his resentment, which festered when he discovered that Father's idea of keeping him close meant his leading an almost cloistered life with his tutors, with nearly every moment supervised, even when he was out hunting. At every palace, he had been assigned a new bedchamber, which was only accessible via a door in his father's room. His contact with the court was strictly controlled, and he rarely set eyes on his future bride. He soon felt stifled.

When he dared to complain, Father had listened with unusual patience, then patted him on the shoulder. 'Quite simply, Harry, I keep you with me because I love you and could not bear to lose you. But that is not the only reason. You already have a royal demeanour, a pleasing dignity and courtesy, but I wish to improve you, and train you by example for the time when you will be king.'

'Could I not have a little more freedom, Sir?' Harry asked plaintively, thinking wistfully of Codnor.

'You are a prince. You live in luxury, thanks to my careful house-keeping in this realm. One day, you will be king and inherit immense riches, and marry one of the greatest princesses in Christendom.

Why are you not satisfied? You must serve your tutelage for these privileges.' Father's tone was severe, and Harry bowed his way out, quelled. When he grumbled to Skelinton, the tutor had been dismissive.

'Count yourself fortunate, Lord Harry. There could be no better school in the world than the society of such a father as King Henry.'

Only Mother had listened and understood. But Mother was not here now. She lay buried beneath the chancel of Westminster Abbey. Harry had not even been permitted to attend her funeral.

By June, Harry found his thoughts straying less to his recent loss, and more to the future. On a beautiful summer's day, having cast off his mourning and donned a splendid gown of white damask and crimson velvet, he rode with the King through London to the Bishop of Salisbury's house in Fleet Street, where he was to be betrothed to Katherine. Father had signed the treaty with Spain two days earlier.

Entering the upper chamber, where the sun was streaming through the windows, he took in his breath when he saw his future bride. She was wearing virginal white, with her golden hair falling loose as a token of purity. Her eyes were demurely lowered as she sank into a curtsey. Harry's heart swelled with pride.

They stood before the Bishop and made their promises. Afterwards, wine was served in jewelled goblets and Harry and Katherine smiled at each other as they tried to carry on a conversation in English, French and Spanish, neither being fluent in all three. But what Harry read in Katherine's eyes was kindness and sympathy, calling to mind dear Mother. It seemed that she was trying to comfort him for his great loss. Yet there was something else. Could it be that, like nearly everyone else he met, she was falling under his spell?

All too soon, Father made him bid her farewell, and they returned to the Palace of Westminster, while Katherine left for the Archbishop of Canterbury's house at Croydon, where she was staying.

'It is fortunate that I and the Spanish sovereigns managed to obtain a dispensation from the Pope for your marriage to take place,' the King said, as they trotted along the Strand, their small retinue clattering on the cobbles behind them. 'Because Katherine was Arthur's wife, and we were concerned at first that she might be carrying Arthur's child. We were assured that the Princess was still a virgin, but I thought it prudent to provide for the case as though the marriage had been consummated. A watertight dispensation is vital because the succession depends on the undoubted legitimacy of your union.'

'Why does it matter that the Princess is still a virgin?' Harry asked, nodding graciously at the people who had come running to cheer them.

Father reined in his horse. 'The Bible warns that a man who marries his brother's widow will be cursed with childlessness, but it also enjoins him to wed her and raise up children for his brother. I am informed by my bishops that the crucial issue is not Katherine's virginity, but whether she bore Arthur a child, which, of course, she did not. Had she done so, you could never have married her, Harry. But I wanted to cover all contingencies. It is just possible that the marriage was consummated and that Katherine did not realise it, or even that she was briefly pregnant and in ignorance of the fact. Only God can know the truth of the matter.'

Harry felt a sudden pang of jealousy at the thought of Katherine in Arthur's bed. Until now, he had assumed that they had lain there chastely together, with Arthur too ill to attempt anything. He could not bear to think that his brother had been there first.

'But she said she was still a virgin,' he protested. 'She wore white today.'

'Indeed, that is true,' the King said. 'She is a devout girl and I am sure she was telling the truth. You have nothing to worry about, Harry.'

1504–5

Harry had to wait until the following summer for the chance to spend more than a few minutes with Katherine away from his father's watchful eye. In August, Father invited her to join them at Richmond

Palace, and she came by river from Durham House on the Strand, which the King had now placed at her disposal.

Richmond was an earthly paradise, a great battlemented fantasy fashionably modelled on the palaces of the dukes of Burgundy. Harry could remember the old palace of Sheen burning down one Christmas during his childhood. In its place, Father had raised a masterpiece of red brick and stone, with vast expanses of bay windows, fairy-tale pinnacles, and turrets surmounted by bell-shaped domes and gilded weathervanes. There were fountains in the courtyards, orchards, and pleasant gardens containing shrubs, flowers and herbs shaped into the new interwoven patterns known as knots. They were intersected by wide paths and statues of the King's beasts. In the great tower housing the royal lodgings, the ceilings were painted azure and studded with golden Tudor roses. Above the gatehouse were blazoned the arms of Henry VII, supported by the red dragon of Wales and the greyhound of Richmond, after Father's former earldom.

This was a joyful time for Harry because he and Katherine were allowed to go out hunting every day. She rode well, easily keeping pace with him, and she was not too nice to be in at the kill. He found himself loving her more each hour, and she gave every sign that, although he was younger than her, she adored him too.

Harry was thirteen now; his body was changing, and he was beginning to understand what desire really was. He was broadening out, his flesh turning to muscle, his voice deepening and, down there, his sceptre, as he liked to think of it, had suddenly become unpredictable and ungovernable. He found himself responding to the sight of red lips, a breast exposed above a bodice, an ankle revealed as its owner ascended the stairs – and to Katherine in all her womanly glory. He longed to reach the age when they would be married, and he could do to her what Arthur (he profoundly hoped) had failed to do. Only ten months to wait. The time seemed endless. He was ready for marriage now, but the Church, for some unfathomable reason, had decreed that boys could not bed their wives until they were fourteen.

In the meantime, he made the most of his time with Katherine, who showed herself delighted to be drawn into the wider life of the court. They feasted and danced, went on long rides in Richmond Park, sang together with Harry accompanying them on the lute his father had given him, and thoroughly enjoyed themselves.

But, in the tradition of Spanish princesses, Katherine had a duenna, Doña Elvira. Father called her the Dragon because she had defied him when Katherine first came to England, refusing to let him see his son's bride unveiled. He had overridden her protests, and they had been enemies ever since.

Now Doña Elvira, who fiercely guarded her young mistress's honour, professed herself scandalised by the King allowing Katherine and Henry such liberty, and was concerned that Katherine might demean herself in the eyes of the English by associating freely with her betrothed.

'She has complained to me that you are encouraging the Princess to disport herself in public,' Father sighed, having summoned Harry to his study, where he sat behind a great pile of account books. Harry had long wondered why a king who could be out enjoying himself, with all the riches of the kingdom at his disposal, would want to waste his time checking those endless lists of figures. But he forgot about that in his indignation at the duenna's complaint.

'We've done nothing wrong!' he protested. 'And Katherine always conducts herself most virtuously. I have never even kissed her.'

His father harrumphed. 'Things are done differently in Spain, my boy.'

'But Katherine is in England now!'

'Nevertheless, I would not do anything to anger the Spanish sovereigns or jeopardise the alliance. I shall tell Katherine that she must continue to behave as her parents have commanded. She must keep to the same rules and seclusion here as she does in her own house.'

'But Sir—'

'Enough!' The King raised a hand. 'Next year, when you are married, Katherine will be subject to your governance. Until then, she will obey me.'

Harry left, simmering. He would find a way of seeing her, he was determined on it. But Fate played into the duenna's hands, for Katherine fell ill with an ague. When the King moved to Westminster, he insisted on taking her with him and leaving Harry behind. Harry was almost mad with fury and frustration. Why should he be treated like this when he had done nothing to merit it? What was wrong with wanting to spend time with your future wife?

He forgot his anger when word came that Katherine had been sent back to Durham House, seriously unwell. She was feverish, Father wrote, and had no appetite, although her physicians were confident that she would soon recover. The King was sending every day to ask after her health and had offered to visit her, but she was too ill to receive him.

It was terrible news. What if she died? Harry could not bear to contemplate it. She was to be his Queen; he wanted no one else. He spent the next few anxious nights imagining the worst.

To his huge relief, she recovered, but she did not return to court. Shortly before Christmas, news arrived from Spain of Queen Isabella's death. Harry's chivalrous heart went out to Katherine. He understood the pain of losing a mother. He wished he could be with her to comfort her. It seemed inhuman of Father to keep them apart at such a time. He hoped she would realise that his sympathies were with her; all his prayers were directed to that end.

And then Father sent for him. Harry stood resentfully before him, burning to voice his outrage at his parent's great unkindness. But Father's mind was on other matters.

'What I am about to say to you, Harry, is in the strictest confidence.' He regarded his son sternly. 'There is great mourning in Spain for the death of Queen Isabella, as well there might be, for that kingdom will once more be divided. King Ferdinand has no right to inherit Castile, and it will now pass to Isabella's heir, their eldest daughter, Juana. And we, my boy, are now bound in an alliance, not with a strong, united Spain, but with the far less important kingdom of Aragon. You understand what I am saying?'

Harry did – and wished he didn't. He stared at the King, unwilling to grasp the implications.

'The sad fact is,' Father continued relentlessly, 'that Katherine's status and political importance have been devalued at a stroke.' (God's teeth, Harry seethed, he talks like a tradesman, not a king!) 'Other, more advantageous marriages might be considered more appropriate for the heir to England.'

Harry did not hesitate. 'No. I want Katherine; no one else.'

'You will do as I say, boy, and know that I will do what is right for England.'

'But Father—'

The King held up a warning finger. 'Enough! I have decided. I am stopping Katherine's allowance and bringing her to live at court, so that I do not have to support a separate establishment for her. She will remain secluded with her servants and you will not attempt to speak to her without my permission. You will act as if your marriage to her is still going ahead. In the meantime, I shall consider other matches for you. Don't scowl at me, boy – it doesn't become you. Now go back to your studies.'

Harry went, clenching his fists in desperation. He could not bear the thought of his Katherine being treated so shabbily. He prayed she would never have cause to think he approved of his father's behaviour. If only he could be afforded an opportunity to cross paths with her, so that he could convey to her his love and his loyalty. Yet even after he learned that she had joined the court at Richmond Palace, he rarely caught a glimpse of her, and when he did, he was shocked to see her wearing gowns that looked worn and rubbed. Resentment against his father turned to anger.

But his fourteenth birthday was fast approaching. Father would surely make a decision before then, and Harry was willing him to honour the marriage treaty. But it soon became increasingly obvious that no plans for a wedding were being made.

He could not bear the uncertainty. One night, he knocked on his father's door and was admitted to the royal bedchamber. He found the King seated on the chest at the end of his bed, wrapped in a velvet nightgown and shuffling through a sheaf of documents.

'Yes, Harry, what is it?' he asked, amiably enough.

'Father, what of my marriage? It should be taking place soon. What is your intention?' He tried not to sound too accusing.

The King frowned. 'I have not yet decided. There are many factors to be considered, but Katherine is due a magnificent dowry, of which we have only received half. To be plain, I am reluctant to forgo the rest. There is no more advantageous or lucrative match to be had just now. My policy is to delay your marriage for as long as possible to see if one transpires.'

'But that's not fair on me or Katherine!' Harry protested.

'This is politics, boy, and you would do well to learn a lesson from it,' Father said mildly. 'We must keep our options open. On the day before your birthday, you will stand before the Bishop of Winchester and revoke the promises made at your betrothal, on the grounds that they were made when you were a minor and incapable under the law of deciding such things for yourself.'

Harry clenched his fists, appalled. 'But I did know what I was doing!'

'That's beside the point. I mean to ensure that, if a better match presents itself, there will be no difficulty in breaking your betrothal to Katherine. And you will keep these proceedings secret – that's a command!'

Harry could not credit that his father could be so cold, calculating and, yes, cruel. He was desperate to see Katherine, warn her what was afoot and explain that he wanted no part in it. He even thought of bursting into her lodging and blurting out the truth before anyone could stop him. But it would probably only make matters worse and, much as he hated his father right now, he also feared him. He knew that when the moment came to revoke his betrothal, he would have to do it.

In October, the King strode into his bedchamber. 'I have good news for you, my son. I have entered into secret negotiations with Queen Juana and King Philip for a marriage between you and their daughter Eleanor.'

Harry was momentarily speechless. Despite having been forced to revoke his betrothal, he still longed to claim his bride. 'But Queen Juana is Katherine's sister. Surely she will not agree to her being displaced?'

'I doubt she has had any say in the matter. It is her husband, Philip of Burgundy, who rules Castile, and his word is law to her. He resents Ferdinand's interference in Castilian affairs and sees this marriage as a means of exacting revenge. And I believe he will offer a great dowry.'

Harry's heart sank like a stone. 'But the Infanta Eleanor cannot be very old.'

'She is six, but at twelve she will be ready for marriage, and the time will soon pass. Remember, you can mould a younger bride to your will more easily than one who is older. You are but fourteen, and Katherine is nearly twenty. It would be more of a challenge to impose your authority as a husband. She has a strong will.'

Father had it all wrong. Katherine had never been anything other than submissive and deferential.

'Eleanor is a far greater matrimonial prize than Katherine,' the King said. 'Her mother is queen of Castile and the heiress to Aragon, and her father is heir to all the Habsburg territories and might one day be Holy Roman Emperor.'

But Eleanor was not Katherine. And Harry hated the idea of delaying his marriage for six years.

Father was implacable. 'You had best get used to the idea, boy. I intend to pursue this marriage.'

1506

As the new year began, Harry watched anxiously as his father turned near-disaster to his advantage. Having learned that Queen Juana and King Philip had been shipwrecked off the English coast on their way from Burgundy to Spain, King Henry moved with almost unseemly haste to assist them and welcome them to Windsor as his guests. And Philip, Father said, was no less eager to meet with him, for he was resolved to conclude the betrothal of his daughter to the Prince of Wales and drive a wedge between King Henry and King Ferdinand. The elements had played right into the hands of both monarchs.

Despite himself, Harry was impressed by Philip the Handsome, who embodied all the virtues and magnificence he thought a prince ought to have. He was less than enamoured of Juana, who held herself aloof from the celebrations, yet seemed to fawn excessively on her husband, who was clearly embarrassed by her overt displays of jealous affection. Ladies should not make such exhibitions of themselves, Harry thought.

Katherine was hastily summoned to Windsor for a short visit to see her sister. Father didn't want the sovereigns of Castile to know that he had been treating her with less than the reverence she was due and was falling over himself to give her a prominent role in the festivities. Harry was thrilled when she was seated next to him in a place of honour beneath the King's canopy of estate, but with Father invariably enthroned next to them, it was impossible to tell her what was in his heart, and he had to content himself with mere pleasantries. But he did his best to convey his sympathy for her and thought he could read in her eyes that she understood.

Father had bidden Katherine wear Spanish dress and dance with her ladies for Philip's pleasure. But Philip didn't look very pleased, and when she tried to persuade him to dance with her, he politely declined and resumed his conversation with King Henry. As they watched ten-year-old Princess Mary taking her place on the floor and sweeping the most elegant curtsey, Harry realised that Philip must not want to see Katherine accorded so prominent a place at court, especially as he was resolved to put his own daughter in her place. But that was probably Father's intention, to make Philip the more amenable to favourable terms; he was wily like that. Harry noticed that Katherine was not allowed to be alone with Juana for more than half an hour. Of course, the King would not want her airing her grievances, to be reported back to their father.

Philip made much of Harry, for whose benefit he exercised his famous charm. And Harry was drawn in. Philip was the son of the mighty Maximilian, the Holy Roman Emperor; one day, he would be master of all Spain and the Empire. It was as well to make a friend of such a prince and store up credit for the future. When Philip and Juana finally left England in April, Harry was sorry to say farewell, even as he felt relief that nothing had been decided about his marriage.

That autumn, the worst news he had received since the death of his mother reached England. Philip was dead. It was horrifying to think that so young and splendid a prince should be gathered to his forefathers at just twenty-eight. At the impressionable age of fifteen, the tragedy brought home to Harry the dread truth that all men were mortal and could be summoned by God at any time. He began to fear every slight ailment or hint of illness.

The immediate effect of Philip's passing was the improvement of Katherine's standing at court, giving Harry cause to hope that Father was not so keen now on a match with the Infanta Eleanor. If only King Ferdinand would pay the balance of Katherine's dowry, all might yet be well. But he was not bound to do so until the marriage took place, even though Father unjustly expected it. Harry wished Ferdinand would demonstrate that he really did have his daughter's interests at heart. It seemed all wrong that two old men should be able to interfere in the happiness of two young people!

Chapter 2

1507

Wherever they stayed, the King had taken to joining Harry in his bedchamber for late-night discussions about state affairs, which were effectively homilies on how his son ought to conduct himself as king and how he might best confound his enemies. Harry thought that Father was preaching the obvious, and was bored. He could think of much better things to be doing with his time. Brandon and Compton, bosom companions who shared his passion for war and sport, were often out roistering in the streets, getting drunk or bedding wenches. Heaven forbid that Father ever found out, for his friends provided the few excitements Harry had in life, even if he did enjoy them vicariously. He had never even had the opportunity to kiss a girl. He secretly longed to know what it felt like to be inside a woman, yet did not see how it could ever be accomplished, so heavily supervised was he. That was why he longed to be married. Part of him found his friends' boasts distasteful; they made it sound so base, so animalistic. It would not be like that with Katherine, he was sure. The act of generation must be different with someone you loved.

Tonight, Father had a shifty look in his eye. 'Harry, you should know that I am considering a marriage with Queen Juana.'

Harry was speechless. The implications were so vast. 'But I want to marry Katherine,' he stammered at length.

The King smiled. 'No, my boy, *I* mean to marry Juana. I was much struck by her beauty when she visited England, and the match would make me king of Castile. But to accomplish this, I need Ferdinand's goodwill and consent. It is this that has stopped me from breaking off your betrothal to Katherine.'

Harry found the prospect of his decrepit father wedding Juana shocking, although he knew that age rarely counted when it came to forging royal marriage alliances. He did not want to imagine Father lusting after the Castilian Queen; it was disgusting and seemed like a betrayal of his mother. And Juana, remote, intense and strange, did not seem to be fitted to be queen of England. But he made no protest. At least Father was showing kindness to Katherine, albeit because he wanted her to influence King Ferdinand in his favour. Yet that kindness did not extend to allowing her and Harry to spend time together, which seemed to Harry a great cruelty.

An exception was made, however, for his sixteenth birthday, when Katherine was permitted to grace the tournaments held in his honour. How he revelled in showing off his knightly prowess in the lists and demonstrating what a skilful horseman and jouster he was. He had grown tall – taller than his father – and strong, with gigantic, heavily muscled limbs, and knew himself to be a model of young manhood. Everyone showered him with praise and compliments, and the Spanish ambassador gushed to his face that there was no finer youth in all the world. He found himself beloved by the common people; whenever he showed himself in public, riding through London or the countryside, usually in his father's wake, they came rushing to see him. He discovered he could talk with them amiably and heed their concerns. It was a common touch that the King lacked; no one dared approach *him* so familiarly.

The age gap between Harry and Katherine seemed to have narrowed as he grew towards adulthood. The time was surely ripe for their marriage, yet still the King delayed coming to a decision – and Harry began to fear that he never would. It grieved him to imagine how distressing the constant delays must be for Katherine, who was now twenty-one and growing no younger. But all his protests had been to no avail.

He was bursting with eagerness to play his part in the world, to be older and free of his father's tutelage. He was weary of waiting to be king. He dreamed of war and glory and chivalry, as much as he dreamed of his beloved Katherine. Because of her, his political sympathies lay with Spain; how could they not, when he longed to conquer France, Spain's great enemy, and England's? A hundred and seventy years ago, his ancestor, King Edward III, had laid claim to the throne of France and won great victories in the Hundred Years War. Since then, English kings had quartered the royal lilies of France with the lions of England on their coats of arms and, nearly a century ago, King Henry V had vanquished the French at the Battle of Agincourt and made himself king of France. Harry never tired of hearing of these noble deeds of his forefathers, and had read all the histories in the royal library. He was filled with a burning desire to be a second Henry V and recapture the French throne, lost sixty years ago when the long war had come to an ignominious end. He could see himself in the cathedral at Rheims, where French kings were crowned, kneeling in glory to receive the coveted diadem. He would be the King who was remembered for regaining France and forever enhancing England's fame.

He could not understand why his father did not share his ambitions, nor why he would not let Harry lead his own army across the English Channel. Instead, during one of their nightly conferences soon after his birthday, the King laughed at the idea.

'Wars are costly, my boy,' he said, gathering his night robe around his thin frame. 'I can think of better and more prudent ways to spend my money. It is far more advantageous to have the friendship of other nations than to be at war with them. Besides, I dare not allow you to risk your life. I have no other sons. What would happen to England if you were to be killed in battle? There would be another civil war.'

Harry knew he was the living embodiment of the peace brought about by the marriage of his parents. Mother had been the heiress of York, and Father had been the sole male descendant of the House of Lancaster; their union had ended the long conflict between their rival families. Father would never admit to owing his crown to his marriage to Mother, for he had won it by right of conquest, but Harry was sure that the prior claim was hers.

Some of her relatives, it could be argued, had better claims to the throne than Father did. Her sisters, for example. Aunt Catherine was married to William Courtenay, Earl of Devon, who had been a prisoner in the Tower of London for years for abetting a pretender to the throne. Harry's childhood had been overshadowed by threats from pretenders – he could recall his mother hastening him to the Tower for safety when an invasion led by Perkin Warbeck, the most dangerous of them, was believed to be imminent – so he understood his father's concerns, even as he chafed against them.

Aunt Cecily, who lived with his grandmother, the Lady Margaret, had been banished from court for marrying beneath her; Aunt Anne was married to the Earl of Surrey's heir, Lord Thomas Howard, and Aunt Bridget was a nun at Dartford. But the aunts were all women, and women were not meant to wield dominion over men. Harry inwardly grinned when he imagined how England would fare under his tempestuous sister Margaret, who was now queen of Scots and doubtless leading her husband, King James, a merry dance. But it wasn't really funny because, if Harry died and she became heir in his place, James would seize England – and that could never be allowed to happen. The Scots, like the French, were England's ancient enemies, and Harry fully intended one day to bring them too under English rule.

'There would be a bloodbath if I died without an heir,' Father said, interrupting his reverie. 'There is no one else with a clear claim to the throne, discounting the women. But some have married and have sons – and ambitious husbands. Why do you think I have kept young Henry Courtenay in your household? It is so that I can keep an eye on him. Likewise, your cousins, the Poles. I have shown them favour to keep them faithful.' He rose and began stoking the fire.

'Courtenay would not be disloyal,' Harry observed. He liked his eight-year-old cousin, who followed him around like an adoring slave, always game for a prank.

'Any man might betray you if the prospect of a crown were dangled before him,' Father said severely. 'Why do you think I had to execute the Earl of Warwick?'

'He was a simpleton who was led astray by the pretender Warbeck.'

'He was also the son of your great-uncle, the Duke of Clarence, who was executed for treason, and there were those who would have made him king after Bosworth. I had no choice but to incarcerate him in the Tower. He grew up not knowing a goose from a capon, yet he remained a danger to me.'

'But he was the son of an attainted traitor, barred from inheriting the throne,' Harry countered.

'Acts of Attainder can be reversed,' Father said, grim. 'Do you think I wanted to put poor Warwick to death? Sometimes, Harry, kings have to make unpalatable choices. Treason must always be stamped out.'

'Indeed, it must,' Harry agreed, nodding emphatically. This was one thing on which he and Father were fully in accord. Treason was the most heinous of crimes because it struck at the sacred person of the monarch and subverted the divinely ordained order of the world.

'Princes,' Father went on, 'ought to be obeyed by the command-ment of God, and obeyed without question. A king is entitled to expect the same devotion and obedience from his people as he himself renders to God, for the King's law is God's law and the royal prerogative is the will of God working through the will of the King. Therefore, the King can do no wrong. This is why treason is the most serious of crimes, and why it has always been punished harshly, for the example and terror of others.'

Harry nodded again. He was aware of the terrible but just penalty the law meted out to traitors. They were dragged on hurdles from their prison to the place of execution, being deemed unfit to walk upon earth; they were hanged until they were not quite dead, then cut down, castrated and disembowelled, still living; finally, they were beheaded and their bodies chopped into quarters, the head and quarters being put on public display as a salutary warning to other would-be traitors. For peers of the realm, it was usual for the King to commute the sentence to beheading.

Harry was resolved that, when his time came, he would deal severely with treason. He had no intention of suffering the insecurities that had bedevilled his father's reign, or of allowing the extortions of

26

grasping men like Richard Empson and Edmund Dudley, who served the King so ruthlessly and did the Crown's reputation no service. He would overawe and subjugate his noble subjects so that they never dared to turn against him, and did only his bidding.

The King was seized with an attack of coughing. Harry had noticed lately that his face had become lined and drawn, while his eyes had a sad and haunted look. It had never occurred to him before that Father might be lonely. There had been talk that he had grown close to Warbeck's beautiful widow, Lady Catherine Gordon, who had served Mother, and before word had got out that he might marry Queen Juana, rumour had even claimed that he might wed Lady Catherine. But Harry placed little reliance on gossip. It would be the grave rather than the marriage bed that claimed the King, if looks were anything to go by. He almost felt sorry for him.

1508

Harry fidgeted as he sat at the council board, barely able to contain his frustration. Nothing further had come of Father's interest in Juana, but neither was he himself any closer to his own marriage. For the past few months, he had been required to attend these boring meetings so that he could learn how government worked, but the old men droned on interminably. If only they would hurry up and finish, he could be off to the tiltyard. It was too fine a spring day to be cooped up in this hot, stuffy chamber, where the fire had been built up because Father felt the cold. Harry was fighting off sleep.

Suddenly, his ears pricked up.

'Regarding the matter of the Prince's marriage,' the King was saying, 'relations with King Ferdinand have deteriorated badly, and I intend to reopen negotiations with the Emperor Maximilian for his Highness to wed Eleanor of Austria. My son is hardly much inclined towards marrying the Princess Katherine. Besides, their union would be of questionable validity anyway.'

Harry glared at his father. Hardly much inclined? Where had Father gained that impression?

He said nothing. There was no point, as the King would only overrule him. Instead, as soon as he was at liberty, he vented his anger in the lists, unseating one opponent after another. One day, he would be free to make his own choices.

One fine summer day, Gutier Gómez de Fuensalida, Ferdinand's new ambassador, sought Harry out as he was playing bowls with his young gentlemen. He broke away when he saw the dignified, portly Spaniard waiting for him, and they walked along the gravel path between the rose beds.

'Your Highness will be aware that King Henry appears to be in the last stages of consumption,' the ambassador ventured.

'I am,' Harry replied, although in fact he had not realised quite how ill Father was.

Fuensalida cleared his throat. 'This is a delicate matter, your Highness. My master feels it would not be worthwhile to press for your marriage to the Princess Katherine while the King lives, but I am to assure you of the great love King Ferdinand bears you. He has told me to say that you may command him and his realm in anything.'

Harry smiled. How very satisfying. If he was to conquer France, he would need the support of Ferdinand. But it was best to remain circumspect. 'I thank his Majesty for his friendship,' he said. 'I pray it will soon be sealed by my marriage.'

But there was Father, still alive, and still determined to have Katherine's dowry before committing his son. When Harry told him that Fuensalida had indicated that King Ferdinand was still eager for the marriage to take place, Father snorted. 'He has many crowns, but he hasn't the money to pay his daughter's dowry! And what business of Fuensalida's is it to be discussing the matter with you? I make the decisions in this kingdom!'

Harry turned away, seething. He could not see the King ever allowing him to wed. And yet, it was clear to him, from what he heard at court and what his friends told him, that the English nobles wanted Katherine as their future queen. Apparently, a deputation of them had knelt before their sovereign and pressed him to agree to the marriage. But nothing had come of it. And Father, coughing his lungs up, was still clinging on to power. Why could he not see that Harry was man enough to be wed, and that it was a political imperative, since the kingdom stood in danger through having only one heir?

Harry could bear it no longer. He was seventeen, a man now, but Father was keeping him under as much supervision as if he were a young girl. He was allowed no royal responsibilities, unlike Arthur, who had presided over the Council of the Marches at Ludlow Castle while serving his apprenticeship for kingship. Harry was not even permitted to leave the palace unless he used a private door that led from the King's apartments into the gardens, and always he had to be attended by companions appointed by his father. He was constantly watched, to the extent that few dared to approach him or speak to him. He had given up trying to gather an affinity at court and found it easier to withdraw into himself, not speaking a word in public, unless it was to respond to Father.

Every conversation in his presence touched on virtue, honour, wisdom and chivalrous deeds; nothing that could move him to any vices was ever said, and this could only be on his father's orders. It seemed the King did not trust him to choose a virtuous path by himself, and Harry burned with the injustice of it. As if he had the opportunity to behave licentiously! He would still be a virgin when he died if Father had his way! When he thought of what his friends were getting up to . . .

Isolated, and chafing against his invisible bonds, he had taken to spending most of his time in his room beyond the King's bedchamber. He kept up his studies, voraciously reading books by Thomas Aquinas, the Church Fathers and ancient classical writers, and making copious notes in the margins. Learned men, even Erasmus and Thomas More, had praised his scholarship, but what he craved most was just one word of praise from his father. Yet a gulf of resentment lay between them, and Harry struggled to understand what he had done wrong. Was it because he was not Arthur? Well, he couldn't help that. Sometimes he thought his father hated him. Certainly, he never showed him any affection.

One day in high summer, he decided to challenge his tormentor.

'Yes, Harry.' Father looked up from his account book. 'What is it?' He was busy and obviously did not welcome being interrupted.

Harry felt defeated already. 'I will not trouble your Grace now,' he said, turning to leave.

The King laid down his quill and sighed. 'No, no, stay. What can I do for you?'

Harry took a deep breath. 'I wish, Sir, that I could play a greater role in government. Why will you allow me no power?'

His father frowned. 'As our ancestor, William the Conqueror, once said, it is not my custom to strip until I go to bed. It is I who rule here and, while I reign, you will do as I say. I do not think you are ready to assume power. Your boredom in the council chamber is obvious to all. You would clearly rather be out playing sports than learning statecraft. You cherish romantic notions of marriage, when your head should be ruling your heart. For now, therefore, you must show me that you have it in you to watch and learn from those wiser than yourself.'

'That's unfair!' Harry protested, raising his voice. 'You allowed Arthur responsibilities, and he was much younger than me.'

'And had more gravitas!' Father said cuttingly.

'Is that what you call it? He hadn't got it in him to be a king!' As soon as the words were out, Harry regretted them. Father's face had turned puce.

'Arthur understood that rashness and glory-seeking in a king are undesirable qualities,' he said, his tone scathing.

'You wouldn't have described Henry V thus!' Harry retorted, losing his temper. 'Was it rashness and glory-seeking that won him France? When I am king—'

'You are not king yet!' roared his father.

'More's the pity!' Harry countered, quivering with anger.

'Get out of my sight before I kill you,' the King hissed, rising, reaching for his dagger, then bending double in a sudden fit of coughing. 'Go!' he choked.

Harry needed no second bidding. For a moment, he had really believed that Father was going to stab him. He must indeed hate him. Well, the feeling was mutual!

Back in his chamber, he tried to still his raging breast and pulled a book on astronomy roughly off the shelf. The study of the movement of the heavens had long absorbed him, and it would help now to take his mind off what had just happened. He threw himself into a chair, his hands shaking, and opened it. The words and diagrams danced before his eyes, having no meaning and offering no refuge.

And then he had a moment of revelation. Of course. Father was afraid of him, and jealous too! He was aware of Harry's capabilities and strengths, and probably feared that allowing him too much power would prove dangerous to himself in the end. It was entirely credible, for who among the King's subjects would not prefer a golden, accomplished young man bursting with the desire for victories to an ailing monarch with his nose stuffed deep inside his ledgers?

He could not endure this tutelage much longer. Next June, he would be eighteen and attain his majority. God grant that Father would then realise he could not treat him like a child any more.

When they met again, in the council chamber, the King was cold towards him. It was as well that many lords were present, otherwise their quarrel might have resumed, for Harry was still feeling ill done by, and clearly he had grievously offended the King. No longer did he join Harry in his bedchamber for confidential talks. When they met in the court, his manner was distant, unbending. Harry was grieved by this, but not bowed. If Father thought he would apologise, he had a long wait ahead of him. The grievance was all Harry's.

31

Slowly, as the months passed, the King's attitude became more relaxed and relations between him and Harry mellowed to the point where, if they were not warm towards each other, they could at least carry on a civilised conversation. At least Father was not continually haranguing him or remarking sarcastically on his shortcomings.

It was as well that matters had improved between them because the King was in an obvious decline. His robes hung on him and his cough racked him pitifully. Yet still he would not let go of the reins of government, and Harry dared not risk asking if he could shoulder some of the burdens of state.

A new Spanish ambassador, Luis Caroz, had arrived in England in place of Fuensalida, who had been recalled. In April, Caroz waylaid Harry in Richmond Palace, as he was making his way to supper.

'Your Highness, forgive me for approaching you, but I have tried to obtain an audience with the King without success. They told me he is too ill to see me.'

Too ill? Was it imminent at last, the moment Harry had long awaited?

He would not pump the ambassador for information. It would be humiliating for a foreign dignitary to realise that the heir to the throne was unaware that his father was now gravely ill. 'Can I help you instead?' he asked, assuming a solemn expression.

'I thank your Highness. It is about your marriage to the Princess Katherine. My master King Ferdinand is desirous of it taking place as soon as possible.'

'That is my desire too,' Harry said. 'Be assured that I am doing everything in my power to bring the wedding plans to fruition.' And he would, as soon as he was king. 'When my father is feeling better, I will pass on your message.'

'May I, on behalf of my master, wish his Grace a happy recovery?' Caroz asked.

'I thank you, my lord ambassador,' Harry replied, and walked on, feeling like a king already.

Two days later, as he sat in his chamber late in the evening and worked on his design for a massive bombard he hoped one day to use against the French, Harry was uncomfortably aware of increased movement and noises in the King's bedchamber next door. For more than twenty-four hours now, his father had been suffering the agonising pangs of mortality, enduring the final assaults of his illness. This morning, Harry had been appalled to see him looking grey and skeletal, and to be told by the royal doctors that it could not be long now. Within him, a sense of freedom and triumph had stirred, but he had suppressed it. This was not the time for exultation.

He had stayed as long as was fitting, desperate to be out of that chamber of sickness and decay, until Father had waved him away, bidding him go and pray for his deliverance from his pains. Harry had gone into his oratory, a dutiful son, and made his intercessions, then he had returned to his chamber and done his best to distract himself.

Now he looked up as Thomas Wolsey, his father's chaplain, was announced.

'My lord Prince, the King your father is asking for you. Come quickly, for he is *in extremis*.'

'Why was I not called sooner?' Harry asked. 'This touches me more than anyone.'

'I am sorry, Sir, but his Grace has suffered a sudden deterioration. Let us make haste!'

The King's candlelit bedchamber was now crowded. Lords, councillors of state, household officers, clergy and physicians were clustered around the bed, and the air was stale with illness and encroaching death. Henry shrank from approaching the emaciated figure panting for breath in the bed, yet his father's bony fingers were reaching out to him, like claws.

'Harry, my boy!' he rasped. 'Heed me!'

Harry knelt unwillingly beside him and took his hand. 'Father?'

'I am dying, my son. Soon you will be king. My councillors have sworn to ensure a smooth succession.' The hoarse voice grew fainter.

'Before I go to meet my Maker, I expressly command you to take in marriage the Lady Katherine.'

'I will, Sir,' Harry promised. In this matter, the King's will and his were finally at one. But his words went unheeded, for his father was seized by a violent paroxysm of coughing followed by a ghastly spouting of blood from his mouth. When it subsided, he lay gasping. John Fisher, Bishop of Rochester, chaplain to the Lady Margaret, held a jewelled crucifix before the dying man's eyes, and Harry watched, moved, as Father reached out feebly for it and beat it against his chest.

'Into thy hands, O Lord, I commend my spirit,' his confessor recited, 'in the name of the Father, the Son and the Holy Spirit.' By the time he had uttered the words, Henry VII had dropped the crucifix and fallen still.

Everyone in the room knelt in respect for the passing of a soul. Bishop Fisher made the sign of the Cross over the body. 'Eternal rest grant unto him, O Lord, and let perpetual light shine upon him,' he intoned. Harry stayed on his knees, head bent.

'Amen,' he said when the prayer was finished, and rose to his feet, wishing to be away from the presence of death and forget the horror he had just witnessed. Then he realised that all those kneeling had shifted around to face him.

'The King is dead,' the Earl of Surrey said. 'Long live the King!'

'Long live the King!' With one voice they echoed him.

Part Two

Summer

I hurt no man, I do no wrong
I love truly where I did marry.
Though some saith that youth ruleth me
I trust in age to tarry.
God and my right and my duty,
from them shall I never vary,
though some say that youth ruleth me!

(King Henry VIII)

Chapter 3

1509

Resplendent in cloth of silver and the midnight-blue velvet of royal mourning, Harry rode to the Tower of London, through streets lined with cheering crowds. He had just been proclaimed king, and paid his respects to his father's corpse, now lying in state in the Chapel Royal at Richmond Palace, whence it would shortly be taken to Westminster Abbey for burial. As Harry raised his hand in greeting, his new subjects cried out their acclaim, hailing him as their deliverer, the one who would usher in a golden world. It was becoming abundantly clear that few mourned his father's passing. The dead King might have brought peace and firm government to England, but he had been despised as a miser and an extortionist. Harry knew that the contrast between his father and himself could not have been greater. He was nearly eighteen and bursting with youth, zest and vigour, and no one could deny that he embodied all the knightly virtues.

He had Father to thank for two things, though. He had left England with a reputation in Europe so impressive that all Christian nations were eager to forge alliances with her. He had also left the treasury full of the riches he had accumulated over the years, and in this wealth lay England's strength and security. Grandmother, bravely stifling her tears, had told Harry that people had always underestimated the late King's greatness.

'They saw him as infinitely suspicious, a miserly and grasping schemer, a dark prince who was not to be trusted,' she said, her thin face framed by a black wimple and veil. 'They should have recognised him as the wise founder of a strong dynasty and the guardian of peace. Instead, they rejoice that he is gone.' Her tone had been bitter.

Harry had nodded in sympathy. He had been resentful when told that his father had appointed the Lady Margaret to act as unofficial regent until he himself reached his eighteenth birthday, but he had reasoned that it would not be for long: just a few short weeks. Whatever Grandmother thought, he was going to dissociate himself from his father's unpopular policies. Today, he was having a universal amnesty proclaimed – and he had already ordered the arrests of the old King's most hated advisers, Empson and Dudley. Their heads would seal his popularity. He would never allow his ministers to practise such wicked extortions. His mouth set in virtuous determination.

Tower Hill was packed with happy crowds, all waving and calling down blessings on him. The Constable of the Tower came forward with the keys to the fortress, and Harry rode through the great Lion Tower and into the outer ward, where the Yeomen Warders were struggling to keep the people back. When he entered the royal palace, where the court had assembled, the state chambers were crammed to bursting point, with everyone straining to catch sight of him or present a petition. He was the fount of honour and patronage now; he could make or break men as it pleased him. It was a heady prospect. But he must use his power wisely. A good prince cultivated those who could be useful to him and rewarded those who gave good service.

Bowing to left and right, he moved through the throng, preceded by the Yeomen of the Guard, his personal bodyguard. He ascended the dais to the throne, which stood beneath a rich canopy of estate embroidered with the royal arms of England, and paused briefly to savour the moment. Seating himself tall and straight, one hand on his hip, chin held high, he addressed the company, speaking the words he had long rehearsed in his head.

'My lords, welcome! We thank you for your warm greetings, and we wish you and all men to know that we mean to rule over you wisely and well. We are a lover of justice and goodness, and bear much affection to the learned, who will always be welcome at our court. Avarice will be expelled from this realm and extortion put down; our liberality will scatter riches with a bountiful hand. Know that we do not desire gold, gems or precious metals, but virtue, glory and immortality!'

Watching their joyous faces and hearing their ovation, in which the voices of Brandon and Compton rang louder than anyone else's, he was again seized with elation. He was making a good beginning, there was no doubt of it; he had started as he meant to go on, leaving no one in any doubt as to who ruled here.

He rose, raising a hand in acknowledgement of the cheers, then withdrew to his privy chamber. There was to be a solemn feast tonight in the great hall of the Tower – no levity, of course, for the court was in mourning – and he must appear at his most splendid. To be a great king, it was essential to look the part and make a display of your magnificence.

And he *was* magnificent; in his person, he was the embodiment of kingship. He knew, without being boastful, that among a thousand noble companions of his own age, he would stand out as the tallest, being more than six feet in height. His body was majestic and strong; there was fiery power in his eyes and beauty in his face. Standing before a mirror of Venetian glass, a masterpiece bought by his father at great cost, he saw a narrow-waisted, broad-shouldered young giant with fair skin and auburn hair, worn chin-length and straight in the French fashion. He had the same broad face, penetrating eyes and small, sensual mouth as his grandfather, Edward IV, albeit with a high-bridged nose – fittingly imperial, he thought. Many had told him that he was the handsomest prince they had ever seen.

Thomas Wolsey, smooth, reliable and deferential, seemed always to be at his elbow these days, or never far away. Harry liked the man, admired his energy and brilliance, and his willingness to do his new master's will. He was quickly realising that, if he wanted something done, Wolsey was the man to ask. And he knew that, when Wolsey called him 'our new Octavius', it was not mere flattery.

'England has cause to rejoice in your Grace!' Wolsey declared, after Harry's first council meeting. There had been no occasion for boredom that morning. Harry felt he had demonstrated a good grasp of affairs, showing himself masterful and confident. The chaplain had followed him out to the gallery, his jowly face alive with admiration. 'We are blessed to have a prince who behaves wisely, loves justice and goodness, and bears such affection to learned men. It is no wonder that the whole kingdom is rejoicing in the possession of so great a king.'

'Amen to that,' murmured the Earl of Surrey, but Harry did not miss the cold stares that he and the Duke of Buckingham bestowed on Wolsey. It did not trouble him. He was resolved to promote men not on account of their noble rank, but because of their abilities – and their congenial companionship. New men for a new age. He saw that Wolsey could be very useful to him. And there would be others.

Wolsey seemed oblivious to the hostility of the lords. 'I think your Grace is most prudent to defer making any decisions until you have slept upon the matter.'

Harry beamed at him. 'You will find, Thomas, that, once I do make my mind up, I judge myself to be in the right, as a divinely appointed king.'

'Invested with a wisdom beyond ordinary mortals,' Wolsey observed.

'By St George, you speak truth!' Harry clapped an arm around the older man's shoulders. Yes, he liked this Wolsey! And Wolsey clearly liked him, knew him for a simple, honest man who loved virtue and lived by the ideals of chivalry. If only Father could have been more like Wolsey.

Harry had been staggered to learn just how much his father had left him in the overflowing treasury. Few kings had started their reign in possession of such a fortune. He was full of plans for spending lavishly on enjoying himself and creating the most magnificent court in Christendom; and there would be ample left to fund his other ambitions. He was burning with a zeal for war. Nothing now stood in the way of his realising his dream of victory over the French – certainly not the old greybeards on his Council. He raised the topic at their next meeting.

'Your Grace,' protested the elderly Thomas Howard, Earl of Surrey, the most influential nobleman on the Council, speaking, it seemed, on behalf of them all, 'the late King left this realm flourishing in an abundance of wealth and riches and enjoying the benefits of peace after thirty years of conflict. Why waste money on another war?'

Harry placed a hand on his hip and fixed his steely gaze on them. He was finding that the habit of authority came easily to him. Where was their sense of glory and renown? Dried up and desiccated, no doubt!

'My lords,' he said, 'when you are attending my coronation at Rheims, I will remind you of your misgivings!' He raised his hand. 'Nay! I will hear no more protests.' That silenced them. Even Grandmother, sitting mute at the other end of the board, regarding him with dismay, knew better than to try to dissuade him.

He changed the subject. 'Let us talk about my coronation at Westminster.'

Elaborate plans were already in hand. Harry was determined that it would be the first of many displays of splendid pageantry to delight the people and bolster their love for him. 'I expect my lords to put on a fine display,' he said. 'Make sure that we order sufficient fabrics for new liveries for all the royal servants.'

'Sire, is that not an extravagance?' ventured William Warham, the ageing Archbishop of Canterbury. 'The old liveries would surely serve, seeing that your Grace has your father's initials.'

'This is a new reign and a new era, my lord Archbishop,' Harry said, rising. 'They will have new liveries. See to it, my lords.'

With that, he departed. He had made it his policy not to linger at the council board for hours upon end, but to hasten through business speedily, so that he could be free to go hunting with his young gentlemen. They were the people with whom he shared his pleasures and zest for life, the friends who populated days that were now full of laughter and jesting. They too were keen to prove their valour in the fields of France. Let him just be crowned and come of age, and then he would formulate his plans!

Before then, however, he must marry. A king's first duty was to get himself an heir. It seemed that everywhere he looked in his court, he saw scions of the House of York, outwardly loyal, but inwardly – who knew? He had resolved to keep them close and favour them, his kinsmen, to keep the spectre of civil war at bay. Meanwhile, he must get himself a son – and soon.

Once his father had been consigned to his grave in Westminster Abbey, Henry took his court to Greenwich Palace. There, standing before the magnificent windows that afforded spectacular views of the River Thames, he announced that he intended to revive Edward III's ancient claim to the throne of France, that he would win back that realm and have himself crowned at Rheims, a latter-day Henry V. There was much cheering. He hoped the naysayers were listening.

He was now ready to cement the alliance with Spain with his marriage to Katherine. His lords were urging it, and King Ferdinand was promising to pay the rest of the dowry punctually.

The Earl of Surrey was hottest for the marriage. Of all the old men who served him, Harry liked and respected Surrey the most. He was a man of the utmost wisdom, solid worth and loyalty, and very popular with the people of England. His father, the Duke of Norfolk, had died fighting for the Usurper at Bosworth, and Surrey, who had fought with him and been wounded, had been attainted by King Henry. Harry had often heard the tale of the old King asking Surrey why he had supported Richard, and Surrey staunchly replying, 'He was my crowned king, and if Parliament set the crown on a stock, I will fight for that stock. And as I fought then for him, I will fight for you.' Who could not admire such a man? Father certainly had, and Surrey's integrity, his tenacity and his abilities as a soldier and administrator had enabled him gradually to regain royal favour and some of his lands. No doubt he was also hoping to recover the dukedom of Norfolk. Well, he was going the right way about it.

But then old Warham, having craved a private audience, spoke out against the match. 'Has your Grace considered that you might be committing a sin in marrying the widow of your deceased brother?' he asked.

'The Pope issued a dispensation,' Harry reminded him.

'I am aware of that, Sir.' Warham frowned. 'But was it sufficient to cover all eventualities? What if the marriage was consummated and the Princess was with child, then lost it?'

Harry flushed. It felt unseemly to be discussing such things with a man of God. 'Surely she would have known?'

'Ah, but it is not always possible to be certain. Young people are often ignorant of these matters. I beg your Grace to think seriously before taking this irrevocable step.'

He left Harry feeling as if a carpet had been pulled from under his feet. He had thought that the matter had been remedied by the dispensation. Surely the Pope had known what he was doing! He was a higher authority than Warham, and infallible.

When Harry confessed to his councillors that his conscience was nagging at him, most did their best to reassure him. Only Warham and a few other churchmen counselled prudence. Then Caroz sought him out.

'Your Highness need not have any doubts!' he declared. 'The dispensation is sufficient, and this marriage will bring peace between England and Spain. I am certain that you will enjoy the greatest happiness in your union with the Princess and leave numerous children behind you.'

Next, he brought word from King Ferdinand himself, having evidently wasted no time in informing him of Harry's misgivings. 'His Majesty loves your Highness like a son,' the ambassador gushed. 'He would be a true father to you and offer you advice in all things.' Harry noticed his councillors exchanging frowns at that. 'The Princess will be able to help foster an understanding between your two kingdoms.'

'And Spain will govern England at one remove,' Harry heard the Duke of Buckingham mutter. He glared at him. Now was not the time to offend Ferdinand's representative. Did they not think he had a mind of his own? He would never allow a wife to rule him. Women were not fashioned to meddle in politics.

* * *

It was now early June, and the coronation was looming. At the end of the month, Harry would be eighteen, and of age. It was time, his councillors said, overruling the dissenters, to proceed to his marriage.

'Your Grace could find no lady to equal the Princess Katherine!' Surrey declared. 'She is the image of her mother, Queen Isabella, and possesses the same wisdom and greatness of mind that wins the respect of nations. As for your Grace's doubts, we have the Pope's dispensation. Will you be more scrupulous than he is?'

Harry sat at the head of the table, looking from one eager face to another. He had made his decision and knew it was the right one. 'I agree, there are many good reasons for the marriage, not least that I desire the Princess Katherine above all women; I love her and long to wed her.' He thought of her long red-gold hair, her fair skin, her dignity, her lineage and her graciousness. 'Everything about her proclaims her a fit mate for the King of England. Her kind disposition, her learning, her humility . . .' There was more to it than that, of course. Honour demanded that he marry her, for in doing so he could rescue her from penury and dishonour, like a knight errant of old, and win her unending love and gratitude.

He stood, beaming, to receive the congratulations of his lords, noticing that Warham and his supporters had held their peace. Then he settled down in his study (from which all the piles of ledgers had now been cleared) and wrote to tell his future father-in-law that he had rejected all the other ladies in the world who had been offered to him, thereby demonstrating the love he bore to Katherine, his very beloved consort – for so he already thought of her.

He dressed with care, in black silk. Wanting to surprise her, he stilled her usher with a gesture, opened the door to her chamber himself and bowed.

Katherine was playing a board game with one of her Spanish maids. She immediately rose and sank down before him in the deepest curtsey, her fair cheeks flushed, her gentle grey eyes raised towards his. Her hair rippled down to her hips. To him, she seemed the most beautiful creature in the world.

He waved away her attendants. Once he was alone with her, he raised her and kissed her hands as she gazed at him adoringly.

'Katherine, my lady,' he said. 'We must talk.'

She was momentarily speechless when he proposed to her. 'Yes!' she breathed, her eyes wet. 'Yes! Oh, yes!' Then she surrendered to his kiss. He had long dreamed what it would be like to kiss a woman. It was exquisitely sweet, and so easy.

Too easy. When he thought about it later, he was conscious of a sense of deflation. He had wanted Katherine for so long, kept faith with her through all the difficult years and claimed her as soon as he could. Yet, flattered and gratified as he was by her response, he felt she should have made him pursue her a little. In the hunting field, it was the anticipation of the chase that thrilled him, the build-up to a conquest. And so it should be with women.

He knew, though, that she had not been brought up to flirt in the manner of young English girls; she had been reared to duty and modesty. He should be glad of that, for a virtuous woman was a prize beyond rubies; old Skelinton had drummed that into him. And he *was* glad of it, he assured himself as he lay down to sleep in the bed that Katherine would soon be sharing with him. He had achieved his heart's desire.

In the days that followed, he tried to suppress his doubts. He reminded himself that the five-and-a-half-year age gap did not matter. At twenty-three, Katherine was still young, still beautiful, still ripe for bearing children – and for bed sport. So what if her chin was rather heavy – how had he not noticed that before? – and her adoration too obvious? It did not matter!

Katherine was joyful when, soon afterwards, he took her and the court to Greenwich Palace, where they were to be married. The gardens were in lush bloom, the fountains playing and the orchards heavy with fruit; in their midst, the turrets of the palace rose majestically skywards. Harry loved Greenwich; he had been born here, and he enjoyed hunting in its vast park. He led Katherine up the tower and showed her the opulent apartments that had been prepared for them, revelling in her exclamations of delight at their luxury and the views over the river. After the years of penury his father had forced her to endure, it must seem as if she had attained Heaven.

Kissing was one thing; the act of procreation, as Skelinton had coyly called it, was quite another. What Harry now desired more than anything was to impress Katherine on their wedding night. Heaven forbid that he should fumble things and make a fool of himself!

What he needed was a woman who could initiate him into the joys of love. But who? With the exception of the Spanish ladies, who stayed secluded in Katherine's apartments and whom he would never dare touch, there were no women at court apart from his laundress, and he found himself eyeing even her. But she was too plump, too old. He shrank from the prospect of those work-roughened hands touching his flesh. Once again, he cursed his father for keeping him so cloistered.

His young gentlemen had bragged of their prowess in the stews of Bankside and Southwark, on the Surrey shore of the Thames. Men could hire whores there for just a few pennies. But he didn't want a raddled old tart, and he didn't want to catch anything unpleasant; he had heard of the dreaded French disease. Yet there would be no harm in going to see for himself what – or who – was on offer.

Late one night, he wrapped himself in a lightweight cloak, pulled the hood down over his face, evaded his guards and slipped down the spiral stair to the ground floor. Then he made his way out of the palace, keeping within the shadows cast by the buildings. At the jetty, he hailed a boat and directed the boatman to take him to Southwark. He found himself enjoying the journey, seeing the lights of London – his capital city – glimmering ahead. What would its citizens think if they could see him now, alone and unattended, seeking forbidden pleasures? He smiled at the thought.

The boatman grinned as he dropped him off. 'I should try the Cardinal's Hat, guv'nor,' he said. 'The girls there are clean and it's well run.'

'Thanks,' Harry muttered, gathering his cloak around him.

The Cardinal's Hat was one of a row of brothels. Rough men and sailors were hanging about in the street making lewd comments to girls leaning out of the windows, and Harry, who had never lacked for courage, felt momentarily daunted. But he strode up to the door and pushed it open. The bawd sitting inside looked at him speculatively.

'What's a fine gentleman like you after?'

'A girl,' he muttered. 'Clean. Healthy.'

'All my girls is clean and healthy. Want a virgin? That'll be extra.'

Harry knew from his friends that virginity was often faked in these places, but he nodded. The crone rose and disappeared through a door. When she returned, she had with her a rosy-cheeked girl with fair hair who looked as if she had just come up from the country and couldn't have been more than fifteen. Harry stared at her, not believing his luck.

And yet, not half an hour later, he found himself rolling back on the dirty sheets, his face burning with shame, his sceptre soft as a rotten pear. When it came to the point of penetration, he had failed. He had been too excited, too much in a hurry, and his bolt had shot before it met its target.

Mortified, he pulled on his clothes, crashed out of the room and hurried into the night air.

Harry and Katherine knelt together in the Queen's closet at Greenwich as Archbishop Warham said over them the sacred words that made them man and wife. The court was still in mourning for the late King, so there were no official celebrations, and Harry had made it very clear that there would be no public bedding ceremony either. The getting of royal heirs, for all that it was a matter of interest to his subjects, was to be a private business between him and Katherine alone.

Now that the moment of possession was approaching, he found himself consumed by jealous fears that Arthur had been there first, and even more pressing fears that he would play the husband no better than he had served the whore. Yet he need not have worried.

As he lay with his bride in the huge bed with its gold and silver canopy and silken hangings, he was not in as much of a hurry as he had been that first time, and Katherine was so adoring, so sweet. She cried out something in Spanish as he entered her, her fingernails digging into his shoulders. Then she relaxed and it was beautiful, far more joyous and pleasurable than he could ever have anticipated. His Kate, as he now called her, was everything a lusty man could want. He had never dreamed that love could be so beautiful.

He was surprised to see that there was no blood on the sheet the next morning; its absence made him pause. But, he reasoned, cursing his ignorance, there might not necessarily be blood. So he pushed his unworthy doubts aside and felt himself blessed to have attained such wedded bliss.

If I were still free, I would choose Katherine for my wife before all others, he wrote to King Ferdinand that morning, sitting in his nightgown by the open window. Then, going over to the bed, he bent and kissed his new Queen and picked up his mother's missal, which he had gifted to her before their wedding, having inscribed it: *I am yours, Henry R., for ever.* There had been tears in her eyes as she read that.

'It is fitting you should have this,' he told her. 'You will be as perfect a queen as my dear mother was. It was you I wanted all along, Katherine. And now I have you; by God's good grace, I am blessed indeed!'

He looked at her intently. He had to ask. 'I must know. Did Arthur ever . . . ?'

'No, Henry. He was too ill, the poor boy.'

'Then all their carping was for nothing,' Henry muttered.

'What carping?'

'Oh, Warham and a few of my councillors, bleating on about our marriage being forbidden in Scripture.'

'But we have the Pope's dispensation!' she cried.

'So I told them. Do not worry, my sweet. All is well. Think you I would have married you if there had been the slightest doubt? I would not have risked your future, or mine. But the Pope has given us his blessing, and now you are my wife in the eyes of God.' And he began kissing her fears away.

He could not bear to be apart from Kate. Every afternoon, he was to be found in her apartments, discussing politics, theology or books, or just enjoying being with her. He often stayed for supper, and he always joined her for Vespers. His chief desire was to please her.

Every night, they were lovers. Once awakened to the joys of sexual union, Harry could not get enough, and Kate was a willing partner, responding joyously to his lustiness. He was now enchanted by how much she adored him. 'My Henry', she liked to call him. He had never known such contentment. And soon, God willing, their happiness would be crowned with God's gift of a son.

Three weeks into June, the court moved to the Tower of London, for it was traditional for sovereigns to lodge there before being crowned. When the royal barge drew up at the Queen's Stairs beneath the Byward Tower, the sun was blazing down and cheering crowds lined the riverbanks. The Constable of the Tower bowed low as Harry ascended the stairs, which were lined with Yeomen Warders in their ceremonial livery of scarlet. Before him, a fanfare sounded.

The Constable escorted the King and Queen along the outer ward of the fortress. To their left, the great White Tower soared above them, as mighty today as when it was built by William the Conqueror centuries earlier. Ahead lay the King's Hall and the ancient royal palace. Harry had ordered that it be refurbished for his coronation and its chambers hung with tapestries and painted cloths of red, green and white, the Tudor colours. A distant throaty roar reminded him that the Tower housed the royal menagerie; even the lions were making him welcome!

For all the pageantry and splendour of his reception, and the fortress's long and illustrious history, Harry did not like the Tower, with its unhappy associations. In the bedchamber Kate was occupying in the Queen's Lodgings, Mother had passed away. It was six years ago now, and still he felt her loss keenly. And there were sinister memories here too. His great-uncle, the Duke of Clarence, was said to have been drowned in a butt of Malmsey wine within these walls. And, eight years before he himself was born, his mother's brothers, the famous Princes in the Tower, had been murdered so that their uncle – another great-uncle, the Usurper Richard – could seize the throne. Father, of course, had avenged their deaths at Bosworth, but their bones had never been found. Despite the heat, Harry shivered a little to think that they were probably still hidden somewhere nearby.

Enjoying a rare moment of privacy before the feast that was being prepared, he inspected his surroundings with distaste – the thick stone walls, the crudely painted murals of angels and heraldic beasts, the ancient, musty smell of the place (by St George, was that whiff of refuse coming from the moat?) – and decided that he would not visit again unless he had to. He had inherited many great houses, most of them far more fitting for a modern monarch.

The next day, London afforded its King and Queen a state welcome, as Harry and Kate processed in a glittering column through Cheapside, Temple Bar and the Strand to the palace of Westminster. The buildings along the route were hung with tapestries, and the conduits flowed with free wine. Above Harry's head was a rich canopy borne by the barons of the Cinque Ports. Beneath his robe of crimson velvet furred with ermine, he wore a doublet of gold embroidered with precious stones, and across his shoulder was slung a baldrick of rubies. Not far behind him, Katherine, in white satin and ermine, followed in a litter hung with white silk and cloth of gold, her ladies, clad in blue velvet, riding behind on matching palfreys.

In Cheapside, Harry doffed his bonnet to the Lady Margaret, who was watching the spectacle from a window, weeping for joy. Exultant crowds packed the streets, hailing him as he went. On, on he rode, the bells of St Paul's and over a hundred City churches ringing out in salute, and then he was on the Strand, passing the grand houses of the nobility.

Not until late afternoon did the great procession arrive at the sprawling palace of Westminster, his chief residence and the seat of royal government since time immemorial. As the King and Queen entered the vast Westminster Hall, trumpets sounded and the assembled court made its obeisance.

Here, as in the Tower, the royal apartments reflected the faded splendour of a bygone age. When Harry entered the cavernous Painted Chamber, he was assailed by memories of his father, whose bed with its depictions of Paradise still stood there, the bed in which, in all probability, he himself had been conceived. It was strange to think that his parents, who had come together in love to create him, were now reunited in Heaven.

On the wall above the bed was an ancient mural in still-vivid colours of red, blue, silver and gold. It depicted the coronation of Edward the Confessor, England's royal saint, whose jewelled shrine stood in Westminster Abbey, opposite the palace. Harry had a special affection for the Confessor, who had been the embodiment of a wise and merciful ruler, one he meant to emulate. He would be crowned tomorrow within a stone's throw of the shrine, as if St Edward himself were hallowing the occasion. The knowledge left him feeling so exalted that he felt quite dizzy.

All through the feast that evening, his mind was on higher things. He had been chosen by God to rule his people, and tomorrow the Church would confirm him in that high honour, and he would receive the crown of his forefathers. Looking at Kate, sitting solemnly beside him at the high table, he knew that she too was thinking of the immense significance of what lay ahead.

Until four in the morning, the two of them knelt, keeping vigil in the chapel of St Stephen, watched over by images of angels, saints and a great mural of King Edward III and his family. As his eye lighted on Edward's son, the renowned Black Prince, who had won famous victories during the Hundred Years War, Harry vowed that he would be worthy of his illustrious ancestors; he too would bring glory to the English crown.

Chapter 4

1509

It was Midsummer Day. From his window in the palace, Harry watched the crowds gathering. Workmen were trying to keep the press of people back so that they could lay a striped carpet from the door of Westminster Hall to the Great West Door of the Abbey. He felt a frisson of excitement and awe. He was ready, spiritually and in every other sense, dressed resplendently in royal robes of crimson furred with ermine. Despite his lack of sleep, he felt wide awake and invigorated.

When he entered Westminster Hall, everyone fell to their knees and he stood there for a marvellous moment, smiling at them. Then there was a flurry as they all took their places for the procession to the Abbey. Wolsey was nearby, talking to John Fisher, Bishop of Rochester, Grandmother's saintly confessor.

'This day consecrates a young man who is the everlasting glory of our age,' Wolsey exulted.

'Aye,' smiled the gaunt-faced Fisher. 'This day is the end of our slavery, the fount of our liberty, the beginning of joy. Watch how the people, liberated, run before their King with bright faces!'

Harry reached out and grasped each of them by the hand.

'Thank you,' he beamed.

Suddenly, there was Kate, golden-haired and beautiful in her crimson mantle and white satin gown, smiling at him like a Madonna in a church. Leaving the two clergymen, who smiled after him indulgently, he hastened to take her hand as their retinues gathered around them. Then, preceded by the nobility in furred gowns of scarlet, they walked to Westminster Abbey to deafening cheers.

He had been acclaimed by the peers. He had sworn his coronation oath, vowing to defend his realm, uphold the Church and administer justice fairly. He had been anointed with holy oil and made different to ordinary mortals, invested with an insight into the subtle mysteries of state denied to them. He was set apart now, hallowed as God's deputy on earth, called by divine right to hold dominion over his subjects. As king of England, he had no superior but the Almighty.

Seated in the ancient coronation chair in this state of grace, he stared straight ahead as Archbishop Warham placed the crown of St Edward on his head. At that wonderful moment, when he felt his soul lifted to a higher plane, the trumpets sounded and the choir burst into the *Te Deum*, their voices sounding more divine than human. Then all the bishops came forward and led Harry to his throne to receive the homage of his chief subjects.

He watched Kate's face shining as she too was crowned, and then took her hand and led her, both smiling with happiness, out of the Abbey. As the crowds roared, the organ and trumpets sounded, drums thundered and bells pealed out, proclaiming to the world that King Henry VIII had been gloriously crowned to the evident joy and comfort of all his realm.

The coronation banquet in Westminster Hall was greater, Harry wagered, than any the Caesars had known. When he was seated at the high table, a fanfare sounded, and the Duke of Buckingham and the Earl of Shrewsbury rode into the hall on horseback to herald the arrival of the first sumptuous dishes. The palace kitchens had been working at full stretch for days. There were fine and succulent meats in abundance, and every kind of delicacy. After the second course, the King's Champion, Sir Robert Dymmock, observed the tradition of parading up and down the hall on his courser before throwing down his gauntlet with the customary challenge to anyone who dared contest the King's title. Of course, no one did, even though Harry was watching all those Yorkist cousins closely. Beaming, he rewarded Dymmock with a gold cup.

After the banquet, he led the entire company outside for a

tournament that lasted until midnight. Still filled with elation, he found it hard to sleep when finally he did get to bed – alone, since Kate was exhausted and he did not feel he should visit her on this of all nights. In the end, he rose, taking care not to disturb the gentleman who slept on a pallet at the end of his bed, and donned his velvet night robe and slippers. With a nod to the guards outside his door, he slipped down the spiral stair to his walled privy garden, and made his way through a wicket gate to the gardens beyond, which led down to the river. Behind him, torchlight glimmered through the palace windows. He savoured the pleasure of being alone for once. He wanted to reflect on the marvellous day that had passed and grasp the reality of the great change that had taken place in his life.

The celebrations continued for several days. Harry delighted in the jousts and tourneys that were held in the grounds of the palace of Westminster. Sitting in a pavilion covered with tapestries and hung with rich cloth of Arras, he fervently wished he could join the gallant young lords and knights taking part. But on this, his councillors had stood firm. Without an heir, he must not put himself at risk. But it would not be for long, he was sure. He was doing his husbandly duty – and pleasure – nightly now, and soon, surely, Kate would be with child. Next year, all being well, he would be the one in the plumed helm, leading the challengers in the lists.

At least they hadn't banned him from going hunting. In honour of Diana, goddess of the hunt, deer were herded into a miniature park and castle that had been created in the tiltyard, and there chased and slaughtered before their bloody carcasses were presented to the Queen and the ladies.

In the midst of the festivities, Harry was summoned urgently to the bedside of his grandmother at the house of the Abbot of Westminster. The Lady Margaret had lived to see him attain his majority and now, finally, was ready for her eternal rest. Harry arrived just in time to hear her weakly exhort him to take as his mentor her confessor, the devout Bishop Fisher.

'He is the most holy and learned prelate in Christendom,' she gasped. 'There can be no better man to guide you, my sweet King.' Harry bowed his head in acquiescence. Another old man, much to be admired, but of what use to a young man was a cleric who wore a hair shirt beneath his episcopal robes, slept on hard straw matting, scourged himself regularly and ate mainly bread and pottage? Still, he need not pay too much attention to him.

He grieved for the Lady Margaret, for she had been a constant and loving presence all his life. He ordered that the church bells toll for six days to mark the old lady's passing. Bishop Fisher paid tribute to her virtues in a homily preached at her funeral at Westminster Abbey and prevailed upon his friend Erasmus to write her epitaph. With her passing went the last of the adults who had wielded authority over Harry in youth. Now there was no one left of his close kin to gainsay his will.

Now he began to rule his kingdom.

Thanks to his father and Skelinton, he was well aware that on his shoulders lay the entire responsibility for England's government. Parliament, the Privy Council, the officers of state, the judges, the sheriffs and the mayors all exercised authority in his name. He was also the fount of honour and, in times of war, the nation's military leader.

He was not daunted by the weighty task that lay ahead of him, but consumed with resolve. He could hear his father saying, 'Kings govern by the grace of God.' But God would be Harry's ally. If no one else kept faith with him, the Almighty would prosper his affairs.

It was important, therefore, to enhance and maintain his prestige and that of the monarchy. A king needed not only to be visible and in touch with his subjects, but also to impress them and foreigners with displays that would dazzle the beholder. Even Father had understood this, insisting that elaborate ceremonial attend every aspect of the lives of himself and his family, and employing pageantry and symbolism calculated to enhance the royal image. Harry intended to take things further and build or beautify palaces to serve as settings for his princely magnificence. After he let it be known that architects, artists, musicians and scholars were welcome at his court, talented men began flocking to it, enhancing his own prestige. An army of workmen were set to constructing, painting, restoring, gilding, glazing and carving, as he embarked on a busy building programme. He decided to style himself 'your Majesty', in the continental manner, although most people still continued to use the traditional titles of 'your Grace' or 'your Highness'.

Not for nothing had Harry imbibed humanist teachings on sovereignty. He had read that the perfect ruler should be a prince of splendour and generosity, giving freely to everyone. Old Skelinton himself had enjoined him to be bountiful, liberal and lavish. And he would, he resolved – he was rich enough! His court would be the most magnificent in English history. He would outshine even his European rivals, the King of France and the Holy Roman Emperor.

He knew he looked every inch the King, with an air of authority and assurance that came naturally to him, and he had heard people predict that, in the future, the whole world would talk of him. Everyone expected marvels of him, and he was determined not to disappoint them.

He was happy to delegate power to his ministers, leaving them to work out the details of his policies, but made it clear that he remained very much in control, and kept his own counsel. He managed to control his temper – most of the time – although he saw red when his councillors protested against his determination to send Empson and Dudley to the block, and silenced them with a snap of his fingers.

'If anyone dares cross me,' he threatened, 'there is no head in my kingdom so noble but I will make it fly off!' He regretted the outburst later, yet still felt it right that he had put them in their places.

Little escaped his scrutiny. He was grateful now for his encyclopaedic memory and an education that had provided him with a vast store of knowledge, advantages when it came to briefing ambassadors and dealing with state affairs. He delighted in amazing his councillors with his command of information.

He clashed with them once more when he again raised the subject of war with France. Kate had just told him that she was with child, and he had spun her around in joy, thrilled at the prospect of having an heir – and exultant that no one could now say he had not provided for the succession.

'I am resolved to play a prominent role in Christendom,' he told them, 'and reclaim what is mine by right.'

'Your Grace may be lusty for glory,' Surrey cautioned him, 'but remember that the King of France is richer in resources and manpower than you are.'

'Did that deter Henry V or the Black Prince?' Harry countered. 'By St George, they didn't have to contend with old women like you pouring scorn on their endeavours! Besides, King Ferdinand is my ally.'

The faces around him looked dubious.

'Is your Grace sure that Ferdinand is not using you to fight his wars for him?'

'The Queen's got at him,' he heard someone mutter.

He stifled his annoyance. He knew some believed that Spain was ruling England at one remove. It was true that Ferdinand's letters were always full of good advice, much of it undoubtedly to his own advantage, and that Kate naturally took her father's part, but, dammit, Harry was not to be taken for a fool, and he could make up his own mind.

'May I remind you,' he said icily, 'that my interests and Ferdinand's are one and the same in this matter of conquering France? France is his ancient enemy as she is mine. With her vanquished, we will both be the stronger.'

'But you can't both conquer France,' Surrey's son, Lord Thomas Howard, pointed out. He had a face like granite, with thin lips and a high-bridged, aristocratic nose.

'We can portion it out between us,' Harry said, summoning his patience. 'Divide and conquer – haven't you heard of that? I know I have the right. My people want war. They want victories like Agincourt.'

'Sir, that may be so,' Warham put in, 'but I counsel patience. You do not yet have an heir. If you were to die in battle, this kingdom might once again be plunged into civil war, since there would be many with a claim to succeed you. It is prudent to delay any offensive against the French until you are in a strong position dynastically.'

'You sound just like my father!' Harry flung back. 'Always urging caution. But I will soon have an heir. And let me tell you, my lord Archbishop, and you, my lords, that great victories were never attained by being cautious! No, I will not wait!'

They sat there, shaking their heads as if he were a recalcitrant child.

'I will not wait,' he repeated, and stalked out.

Wolsey came to him when he was working in his study; Wolsey, who was making himself indispensable.

'Your Grace, it has come to my knowledge that some of your councillors have written in your name to King Louis, offering friendship and peace. I thought you should know.' He handed over a transcript.

Rage rose in Harry's breast. There it was. They had dared to usurp his prerogative. It was not to be borne!

'Summon them!' he barked, then began pacing up and down, working himself into a frenzy.

He was still incandescent when, half an hour later, he strode into the council chamber.

'Who wrote this letter?' he shouted, waving it about. No one spoke; no one would meet his eye.

'I ask peace of the King of France, my enemy?' he roared. Again, he was met with silence, so he stormed out of the room, calling over his shoulder for Wolsey to attend him.

'Find the French ambassador,' he instructed, striding fast along the gallery. 'Invite him to watch the jousts this afternoon. I intend to take part and display my martial prowess.'

'Is that wise, your Grace?'

'Are you going to forbid it too? No, Thomas, my mind is made up. Make sure there is nowhere for the ambassador to sit. Let him feel the blast of our enmity towards his King. Then, when he has learned what it is to feel conspicuous and embarrassed, you may provide him with a cushion.'

'Your Grace, it will be seen as an insult.'

'That,' Harry smiled grimly, 'is the intention.'

Watching from behind his visor as he rode in the lists, he took pleasure in seeing the discomfiture of the French ambassador, and in the amused reactions of his courtiers. It meant everything to him to know they shared his sentiments about England's ancient enemy. After the jousts, in which he covered himself in glory and escaped without a scratch – take heed, Surrey! – he walked along the lines of spectators, chatting and laughing with them, here clapping a man on the shoulder, there chucking a woman under the chin. He could see that they adored him. It was as if he was not a person of this world, but one descended from Heaven.

'Your Grace shows himself more of a companion than a king,' Wolsey observed, materialising at his side as he walked back to his tent. 'You understand the value of being accessible to your subjects.'

'I want to see them, and be seen by them,' Harry said. 'They are welcome to come into my palaces to watch tournaments and court entertainments. And I mean to go on progress annually to be accessible to my subjects, especially those who live farther off in my kingdom.' He did not mention that he had now gone into London in disguise several times to mingle with the people and hear their opinions, which were often freely voiced in taverns. No one had guessed that the tall, genial young man who had so readily stood them a round of drinks was their King. Fortunately, none had said anything unfavourable about him; love for him seemed to be universal among them. And he rejoiced to know it.

Wolsey's voice brought him back to the present. 'Sir, since the Queen is with child, and the campaigning season ends in October, it might be best to defer the French venture until next year. You will need time to prepare well, if it is to succeed. And by then, you will have your heir.'

'Hmm.' Harry thought about it. It was wise advice and offered in a far more constructive way than his councillors had done. He was liking Wolsey more with each passing day, and admired his brilliance. He knew the man came from humble origins, and that his father had been an Ipswich grazier and wool merchant, but he recalled Father saying that Wolsey had been an outstanding scholar at Oxford and had deserved his rapid rise to prominence. He was handsome, learned, eloquent and indefatigably able, and he was highly regarded by the new men on the Council too. Harry was coming to understand that he could always rely on Wolsey to give him excellent advice. Yes, France would have to wait.

The golden summer that followed the coronation was spent in continuous festival, as Harry presided over jousts, hunting and hawking. He was eighteen, young and lusty, disposed to pleasure and laughter, and not minded to apply himself to the affairs of his realm. He was so busy enjoying himself that he would only work during Matins in the Chapel Royal, or late in the evenings – unless he had something better to do. He had soon found that being in charge of meetings of the Council had not made them any less tedious, so he had asked his councillors to report back to him after their business had been concluded.

They made their disapproval plain. Pointed comments were muttered about how dedicated and careful his father had been in addressing matters of state. Harry did not see why they were complaining, for they were all experienced men who were perfectly capable of governing the country in his name.

Richard Foxe, Bishop of Winchester, the Lord Privy Seal, was his most outspoken critic, and as foxy as his name, in Harry's opinion. 'Your Grace seems not to care to occupy yourself with anything but the pleasures of youth,' he remonstrated, after Harry had turned up an hour late for a council meeting, having been engrossed in a game of tennis. 'All other affairs you neglect.'

Harry scowled. He resented being taken to task, even by venerable bishops. He was the King now, not a trodden-down prince.

'Sir, we are concerned lest the abundance of riches you now possess should move you in your young years to a riotous forgetting of yourself,' Foxe continued relentlessly. 'We must insist that you be present with us, so that we can acquaint you with the government of your realm, with which, I regret to say, you obviously cannot endure to be troubled.'

Harry glared at him. How dare he harangue his royal master as if he were just a naughty schoolboy? 'I might find council meetings less tiresome if you gentlemen did not take so long to deliberate on affairs,' he snarled. He forbore to say that he hated being cooped up for hours on end in the company of greybeards, preferring to surround himself with young people. 'And,' he added, truthfully, 'writing is to me somewhat tedious and painful. It gives me headaches.'

The lords sat there, shaking their heads. 'Sir,' Foxe said wearily, 'such excuses are not worthy of you. A king must be seen to be diligent. Only yesterday, the Milanese ambassador complained that you had put off an audience because you were in a hurry to go and dine and dance afterwards. Now, your secretary has some diplomatic documents for you to peruse and sign. We respectfully ask that you do so tomorrow morning.'

Harry grudgingly agreed. But when the next day dawned bright and fair, he decided to go hunting instead. He leapt out of bed, shouting at his snoring esquires to wake up and attend him. As a Yeoman of the Wardrobe brought his freshly brushed clothes to the door of the privy chamber, the esquires dragged themselves from their pallet beds next door and hastened to dress him in his fresh, clean body linen, which was lifted from the chest smelling of the herbs with which his laundress had sprinkled it. He stood impatiently as his gentlemen completed his robing, one of their fiercely guarded privileges, and his barber shaved him and trimmed his hair and beard.

At last, at last, he was ready. He left his secretary a message to say that he was attending Matins and made his escape.

On his return hours later, all spattered with mud from the chase, he found the man waiting for him.

'Is your Grace ready to go through these papers?' he asked, eyeing his master's hunting clothes.

'No,' Harry said, 'for it is dinner time.'

It was evening before he finally agreed to look at the reports. Bishop Foxe had clearly been told, for he was cool towards Harry at the next council meeting. But Harry did not care. Besides, Foxe and old Warham were hardly in a position to criticise him. Career churchman both, they had long neglected their ecclesiastical duties to further their political ambitions.

But he had his own man now, someone who was on his side and far more congenial to him than his disapproving councillors. Wolsey was sympathetic towards him.

'After your Grace determines or approves policy,' he said smoothly, as they walked in the palace gardens one afternoon, 'it is your councillors' duty to implement it. I don't know what they are complaining about. It is natural for young people to want to pursue their pleasures. Sir, if ever there is anything I can do to lighten your burden, I am willing to do it.'

Harry beamed. 'I want you to be my Lord High Almoner, Thomas,' he said. 'You shall distribute my charity to the poor. I know you will serve me well and work hard.'

'Your Grace does me great honour,' said Wolsey, bowing.

'And I will remember your offer to ease me of my burdens, Thomas. I need a man like you to rely on.'

'I understand your Grace very well,' Wolsey smiled.

The next time his secretary produced a sheaf of papers to be gone through, Harry took them without protest or excuse, promising to digest them and give his opinion by the next day, much to the man's surprise. Then he took them straight to Wolsey, who returned two hours later, full of sound advice, allowing Harry to hand them back to his surprised secretary the following morning.

Meanwhile, a grateful Harry had enjoyed a fruitful afternoon with the Master of the Revels, planning an evening of pageantry to entertain the court and impress foreign visitors. He himself was going to take part, relishing this opportunity to show off his talents.

Chivalry, he had decided, was to be the watchword of his reign. He had resolved to host annual jousts each May and June, and at every court festival. They would provide his courtiers – and himself – with honourable and healthy exercise before the hunting season began, and help to keep his men in peak condition in peacetime. He was not minded to see young gentlemen lacking expertise in martial feats, especially when they would soon be going to war. Tournaments, of course, were not just military rehearsals; they had become glittering social events that afforded Harry and his courtiers the chance to show off their wealth and expertise before foreign ambassadors.

And the world was taking notice. He knew he was being favourably compared to his unpopular father, that he was fast gaining a reputation as a magnificent, liberal and talented prince. Staging sumptuous court entertainments could only enhance his fame. He had appointed the talented genius and composer William Cornish, Gentleman of the Chapel Royal, as Master of the Revels, with instructions to put on pageants for the courtiers and performances of plays and concerts by the Children of the Chapel Royal, who sang like angels.

Harry loved music and dancing; Kate liked to dance too, but could no longer do so because of her condition. She was happy to watch him leaping like a stag as the court whirled around him. He was so proud of her, and thrilled that God had smiled so soon on their union.

He was in love with life. The world lay at his feet and the future looked golden. He was young, he was healthy and he was loved. With Wolsey to help him, he could enjoy all the glorious pleasures of youth.

Harry laid down his quill and surveyed his surroundings, relaxed in the company of his twelve friends and former boyhood companions who had been appointed gentlemen of his Privy Chamber. It was important to make the distinction, for the Privy Chamber was not just the suite of rooms he occupied as king, but also the chief department of state, a power base to rival the greybeard Privy Council, whose members were distrustful of the mischievous influence his gentlemen could exert on their young sovereign. But Harry cared not a fig for their concerns. His father had set up the Privy Chamber to look after the private needs of the monarch and provide him with a retreat from public life. Small wonder there was rampant competition for places, for the King's gentlemen had daily contact with him; they had his ear. That made them highly privileged and powerful, controlling access to his presence and exercising extensive patronage. He knew that they profited from those who bribed them to seek favours from him.

Some were young men whom Harry had promoted just because he liked them and enjoyed their company. Stiff-backed Buckingham, who considered himself royal even though he was only descended from the youngest son of Edward III, had dared to say he preferred his King not to give out offices and rewards to boys rather than noblemen, but he was just jealous. Why, Harry thought, would I want to spend my days in the company of a pompous aristocrat who thinks he is my equal?

But he made his friends work for their privileges and insisted on their absolute discretion. They had to show a vigilant respect to him at all times, and study him to see how they might do his pleasure. They waited on him hand and foot and guarded his lodgings when he was absent, whiling away the time playing cards and dice. They were forbidden to tattle about what was said or done in the privy chamber, or to ask where the King was, or where he was going. When relaxing in his company, they must be ready to turn their hands to making music, singing, dancing or acting.

Today, Harry was absorbed in one of his favourite leisure pursuits, composing songs. He was writing one to celebrate the pleasures of his new life, honest pleasures he could now enjoy without constraints.

> Pastime with good company
> I love and shall unto I die
> Grudge who lust, but none deny
> So God be pleased thus live will I.
> For my pastance
> Hunt, sing, and dance
> My heart is set:

> All goodly sport
> For my comfort,
> Who shall me let?
>
> Youth must have some dalliance
> Of good or ill some pastance;
> Company methinks then best
> All thoughts and fancies to digest,
> For idleness is chief mistress
> Of vices all; then who can say
> But mirth and play
> Is best of all?

Casting about in his mind for the words for another verse, Harry's gaze fell on William Compton's handsome, dissolute face. Compton was now the Chief Gentleman of the Privy Chamber, rejoicing also in the title of Groom of the Stool, for it was his privilege to attend the King in the royal privy – where the intimacy of the occasion lent itself to confidences. Now one of the most powerful men at court, Compton ran the Privy Chamber and was Keeper of the King's Privy Purse, which funded Harry's everyday expenses.

Four of Harry's gentlemen were Esquires of the Body, knights who watched over him day and night, helped him dress and informed the Lord Chamberlain, the head of the King's household, if he needed anything. Their true business was keeping his secrets. Not, Harry could have said honestly, that there were many to keep. His life was a model of virtue; he had no vices. All he asked was the love of his wife, and the company of his closest friends, the dashing gallants with whom he hunted, play-acted, gambled and made merry each day. With them, he could forget the responsibilities of state, and be just a young man bent on having a good time.

He had made Brandon, his closest friend, an Esquire of the Body. He was struck again by how Brandon, sitting there, strumming a lute, looked so like him. He had been amused to hear speculation that he was his bastard brother – as if Father had ever been a ladies' man! Brandon had grown into a handsome fellow who dazzled the ladies with his charm and courage, and he had long been a star of the tiltyard. It pleased Harry to shower him with lucrative offices and privileges; Brandon was like the big brother Arthur had never been. He was steadfastly loyal and always willing to please his master, and while he might not be Harry's intellectual match, he made up for it with his sporting and martial accomplishments.

It bothered Harry slightly to think of his friend's complicated love life. Brandon had long had a reputation as a womaniser; seduction seemed to come effortlessly to him. Some years ago, he had promised marriage to Anne Browne, a maid-of-honour to Harry's mother, and got her with child. Then he had abandoned her and married her rich old aunt, Margaret Mortimer. Immediately, he had sold all Margaret's property, had the match annulled, then abducted and married the long-suffering Anne, who had by now borne him two daughters. Margaret Mortimer was still complaining that the annulment of her marriage was invalid, and she would not be silenced. Harry thanked God that his own love life was so straightforward – as it should be.

The words had come to him; he had the final verse. He resumed his scribbling.

> Company with honesty
> Is virtue, vices to flee;
> Company is good and ill,
> But every man hath his free will:
> The best ensue,
> The worst eschew.
> My mind shall be
> Virtue to use
> Vice to refuse,
> Thus shall I use me.

The suave, genial Sir Thomas Boleyn was another Esquire of the Body. He had long been at court, but had not formed part of the little band of companions who had attended Harry when he was Prince of Wales. Yet Harry had noticed him, become aware of his abilities and known that he could prove useful. Boleyn was more fluent in Latin and French than anyone else at court, and he was an outstanding performer in the lists, an essential requisite in gaining royal favour. He came from a rising, socially aspiring family that had risen from trade to gentility thanks to a succession of brilliant marriages. Boleyn himself was married to Surrey's daughter, Elizabeth Howard.

Harry watched him as he played cards with Compton. At thirty-two, Boleyn was shrewd, able and greedy for power, wealth and advancement. It was no secret that he would sooner act from interest than from any other motive. Yet Erasmus thought him outstandingly learned. He had all the qualities that made a good diplomat and a shrewd politician. Harry could do with more new men like him.

He beckoned to the thickset Henry Guildford, another lusty gallant and long-standing jousting partner whom he well liked. 'Have you heard from Erasmus lately?' Guildford, like himself, was a cultivated Humanist, and regularly corresponded with the great scholar.

'Not this week, Sir. But I've been too busy to write to him. Fitzwilliam and I have been practising for the tournament on Saturday.'

'Aye,' said William Fitzwilliam, Harry's cupbearer, who had been brought up with him and shared his love of the chase. 'But I doubt we'll beat you, Sir!' He grinned. He understood Harry better than most. If there was any task to be done, he was the one to ask. He was a dependable, solid young man, refreshingly free from the rapacious acquisitiveness of most courtiers.

'Thanks to your Grace's kindness, my father will be able to watch the jousts.' Henry Courtenay smiled. His cousin Harry was more his hero than ever now that he had released Courtenay's father, the Earl of Devon, from the Tower, where he had languished under suspicion of treason for eight years. But there had been no real evidence against him, as Harry remembered his mother saying as she comforted his aunt, her sister, the Countess Katherine, and the Earl's children, whom Father had taken into the royal household to be brought up with her own.

Courtenay was one of Harry's few aristocratic companions. The old King had mistrusted the nobility and barred them from maintaining private armies of retainers. It was such affinities, he'd told his son, that had made the late wars possible. But Harry was aware that, since feudal times, the nobility had served the King in a military capacity; that was their function. They had, therefore, to be given a new purpose in life, and what better than aiding him in the conquest of France? That should channel their martial energies and give them something useful to think about, instead of skulking on their estates, muttering about their power having been curbed, or plotting against the Crown. No wonder the aristocracy in general had hailed his accession!

But would going to war be enough? He discussed the matter with Wolsey over a private supper that evening, and confided his fears. 'Some of my lords have royal blood and might be covetous of my throne.'

Wolsey, as ever, gave him sound advice. 'Keep them busy with affairs at court and in the shires, and reward them handsomely, to keep them faithful. Take care to identify their interests with your Grace's own.'

Harry nodded; yet still he was not satisfied. 'They are jealous of the new men I am promoting. They think it their time-honoured right to act as my chief political advisers, but I regard good service as being as important as high birth. And I am determined, as my father was, to re-establish the dominance of the Crown over the nobility. It was greatly weakened during the late wars.'

'That is essential, Sir. Even so, in this realm, power has long been the privilege of the nobility. They will not give it up lightly. But your Grace has the ability to redefine what it is to be noble.'

Harry rose and started pacing up and down, like a caged lion. 'How do I do that? The privileges of the nobility are laid down in Magna Carta and are defined by long tradition.'

'Sir,' Wolsey smiled, 'you, the sovereign, are the fount of all honour. Only you can create a peer. You can also unmake them, and they are aware, I promise you, that their status and wealth depends on your goodwill and their conduct. You are setting a precedent in establishing a magnificent court. Might I suggest that you encourage your lords to emulate your example – I think they will need little persuasion. Every one of them wants to show off his wealth and his grand houses. It will distract them from any thoughts of warmongering. What you have, they will want, and the effort to keep up with you will either fully occupy and focus them, or it may lead them to ruin, which will result in a loss of power and independence, further impeding their ability to become involved in the kind of subversive activities you so fear.'

Harry smiled at Wolsey's genius. If the likes of Buckingham and Surrey heard this conversation, they would have apoplexy!

'Excellent,' he said.

He let it be known that his nobles should come to court if they wished to take their rightful place in society. He was amused to witness the scramble to attend on him, and their eager attempts to re-create in their own stately piles the splendours they were seeing at court.

But the older nobility remained disparaging and resentful, Buckingham being the most outspoken among them. Collaring Harry as he emerged, hot and sweating, from a long game of tennis, he insisted that he speak to him about the 'new men' surrounding their King, spitting out the term disdainfully.

'Your Grace should know that it is the nobility of this realm who should be your natural counsellors, not jumped up johnny-come-latelies with no lineage and no experience. It is an insult to see them flaunting themselves as if they were landed aristocracy and affecting manners, dress and lifestyle way above their station!' He was bristling with outrage.

'I understand your concerns, cousin,' Harry said evenly. 'Walk with me and I will explain. But first, tell me, what defines a gentleman?'

Buckingham was in no doubt. 'Noble blood, of course!'

'Surely there is more to it than that? It is not just the ability to live at ease without doing manual labour!'

Buckingham looked down his nose at him. 'Of course it isn't! It's about military prowess, liberality, honour, courtesy and chivalry – and the benefit of centuries of serving the Crown.'

'So gentility lies in action rather than the intellect?' Harry was enjoying this. 'This is the age of the written word. We have printed books; people are becoming ever more literate, diplomacy is developing. Many of these new men you despise are scholars, able to be of service to their prince in practical ways. But few of my nobles have been near a university, nor do they have any intellectual interests. I was horrified recently to hear one lord, come up from the country for the coronation, say that he would sooner see his son hanged than have him reading books.'

'We're not all like that,' Buckingham retorted.

'No, there are honourable exceptions.' Harry sat down on a bench and mopped his brow and neck. 'But, faced with the choice, cousin, who would you choose to serve you? An earl whose family goes back to the Conquest, but who knows only warfare and nothing of the modern world; or a man of ability and letters who can get things done, whatever his background?'

Buckingham snorted. 'The nobility of England have served their kings since time immemorial, and there is no reason why they should not go on doing so. You can leave clerking to churchmen like Master Wolsey!'

Harry looked up, shielding his face from the sun. 'The world is changing. The Humanists argue that true nobility lies in the intellect rather than in blood. I think it essential for any gentleman who wishes to succeed at court to be literate, learned and musical, and to have some knowledge of law and theology, and an understanding of art. I am sure that you, my noble cousin, being the premier peer of England, can comprehend the importance of that.'

Buckingham glared at him. 'I don't hold with this new-fangled Humanist nonsense.'

'That, cousin, is really immaterial,' Harry retorted, losing patience and rising to his feet. 'It is coming to something when the greatest noble in my realm is so dismissive of my wishes in this important matter. Look at you! You own vast lands in twelve counties, you serve on my Privy Council and you are High Steward of England. You could be one of my closest advisers, but you never will be if you oppose me. I do not wish to fall out with you, cousin. You are a fine jouster, and that counts for a lot with me! But this overweening pride in your lineage and your tendency to rail at me do you no favours.'

The Duke had flushed a deep red. Haughtily, he stared at his sovereign. 'I hear what you say, Sir. But remember, my father gave his life to make your father king. Such loyalty should weigh more heavily in the balance than being able to write a letter or strum a lute!'

Harry swallowed. It was true: the last Duke of Buckingham had been beheaded by the Usurper for rising on behalf of Father. 'And I will always owe a debt of gratitude for it. But that is not the argument, and I fear we will keep going around in circles. Try to see things from my point of view, cousin, then I am sure we will get along better.' With that, he bowed and walked off towards the palace.

It would not do to make an enemy of Buckingham. He was too near the throne for comfort. Best to keep him close and accord him the precedence and rewards that were his due, to stop him complaining, just as Wolsey had advised Harry to manage those other kinsfolk who had royal blood. It was wise to keep a watchful eye on his relations, as his father had done. However, where the late King had been ruthless in suppressing his unwanted relatives, Harry thought it politic to treat them well and keep them loyal. And it was easy to do so, for he was fond of them, especially Henry Courtenay and Margaret Plantagenet, sister to the late Earl of Warwick and widow of Sir Richard Pole. She was a delightful woman and one of Kate's close friends. In fact, most of the old 'White Rose' families were members of Kate's circle. Their high lineage and conservative outlook appealed to her Spanish pride. Harry too was friends with them all.

All except the Earl of Suffolk, whom his father had incarcerated in the Tower three years ago on account of his nearness to the throne; and Suffolk's hot-headed younger brother Richard, a notorious traitor, who had fled abroad and was now beyond Harry's reach. But his potential rivals, for the most part, had been contained. They posed no real threat to him.

Chapter 5

1509

It was a heady summer, perfect for the sports Harry loved. He hunted, played tennis, wrestled and defeated all comers with his heavy two-handed sword in mock combats. People said he could draw a bow with greater strength than any man in England. He was proud of his athletic physique and sheer masculine vigour, proof that, by exercise, the health of a man was preserved and his strength increased.

Well satisfied with life, he departed with Kate on a progress that took them north to Lincolnshire. Everywhere he rode, the people came running to see him, calling down blessings, and he felt as if his heart would burst. All this fair kingdom was his!

Kate was over the sickness she had suffered in the early weeks of her pregnancy, and the two of them were very merry together. Harry fussed over her like an old nurse and insisted that she rest and eat hearty food, for she was inclined to fast over-much on holy days, thanks to the injunctions of her confessor, Fray Diego, a man Harry had never liked, but had tolerated for her sake. Never had she looked more beautiful to him than now, carrying his child.

On their return, they took up residence at Richmond Palace, where they celebrated Harry's first Christmas as king. It was marked by a joust before the palace gates, where many notable feats of arms were performed. The court was packed, and the palace was decorated with holly, ivy and bay, and filled with the scent of spices and oranges. The people were invited inside to watch the gorgeous mummeries, while in the great hall, a mighty Yule log crackled on the hearth, and carols were sung and danced to, to Kate's delight.

As custom demanded, the twelve days of festivities were directed by a Lord of Misrule; this year, it was a fellow called Will Wynesbury, who took evident pleasure in ordering his sovereign about, much to the mirth of the court.

''Tis very expensive being the master of merry disports,' he announced, striding up to the high table in the middle of a feast, just as Harry was tucking into his seasonal spiced brawn. 'Will your Grace be so good as to pay me five pounds on account?'

There were splutters among the guests, and Compton and Brandon were splitting their sides laughing. But Wynesbury was relentless.

'If it shall please your Grace to give me too much, I won't give you any back,' he warned. 'But if you give me too little, I will ask for more!'

Harry chuckled. 'Give the man some money,' he instructed Wolsey, whom he had seated near him.

He loved the solemnity of Christmas, the majesty of Matins in the Chapel Royal, with himself participating and the choir singing 'Gloria in Excelsis'. He loved the sacred mystery of it all, the sense that something wonderful and supernatural was happening. He delighted in being showered with gifts by his courtiers on New Year's Day. He revelled in the sumptuous feast that marked Twelfth Night, when the cake contained a bean, and whoever found it would be King or Queen of the Bean for the evening and hold sway like the Lord of Misrule. (He suspected that the recipients were selected in advance, just to ensure that they would not be too riotous.) Then there was the private banquet on Twelfth Night, when the choir of the Chapel Royal sang as the wassail cup containing spiced ale was presented to the King and Queen and passed around the table. Finally, there was the ceremonial offering of gold, frankincense and myrrh on the Feast of the Epiphany. It was his favourite time of year.

1510

One of the things Harry loved best was a disguising. That January, he and his friends gleefully dressed up as Robin Hood and his outlaws, donning short coats of green Kentish Kendal with hoods that concealed their faces. Having armed themselves with bows, arrows, swords and bucklers, they burst into the Queen's chamber.

Kate and her ladies leapt up in genuine alarm.

'May it please your Grace, Robin Hood and his merry men are at your service,' Harry cried. 'We outlaws crave the pleasure of dancing with the ladies!'

Kate looked suspicious, but she graciously consented, and her musicians struck up a tune. Harry held his hand out and she took it, then everyone entered into a pavane and the ladies began to enjoy themselves. Suddenly, when they were all laughing, Harry gave the signal and the men threw back their hoods. Grinning at the look of astonishment on Kate's face – she hadn't guessed! – he swung her into his arms and kissed her, to much clapping from his fellows, then called for wine. It was a very merry morning.

That week, Harry jousted in public again, ignoring the advice of his councillors to avoid the lists until he had his heir in his arms. But they wouldn't know anything about it, as he was going in disguise, in full armour. He felt rather pleased with himself for evading their strictures. At the outset, he and Compton locked in combat on foot, fighting across a wooden barrier with swords, as Lancelot and other knights of olden times had done. Then followed the tourney, fought out on horseback, and finally the dramatic tilt between mounted knights with lances couched, thundering towards each other on either side of a wooden palisade. Harry revelled in the exhilaration of the rush; he had high courage, a good eye and a fine sense of timing. He was well aware of the risks he was taking, because men sometimes did get killed or injured, but achieving honour in the joust was almost as prestigious as attaining glory in battle. Today, the fighting was fast and furious, and Compton, in combat with Edward Neville, was thrown and lay in the dust unmoving, bleeding. As the heralds ran to aid him, Harry deemed it wise to leave the field.

As he rode away, he heard someone cry out, 'God save the King!'

Discovered! But it did not matter now. He was safe, and he had acquitted himself well. Laughing, he pulled off his helm, and was gratified to see the spectators looking utterly amazed – as well they might be, for kings rarely participated in tournaments. He cantered to his pavilion to rousing applause.

As soon as his armour had been removed, he hastened to see Compton, fearing to hear the worst. The doctors were just emerging from the tent.

'How is he?' he called.

'Your Grace has no need to worry,' they reassured him. 'He is a little dazed and has a flesh wound in his shoulder, where the armour pinched it, but he will recover.'

Harry dived into the tent. 'I hear you'll live,' he said, relieved to see Compton sitting up on the couch, rubbing his head and looking rueful.

'You wait till I get you in the lists again,' he warned Edward Neville, who was standing anxiously by. 'I'll have my revenge!' He gave Neville a playful cuff.

'I see you are better,' Harry observed, 'and will live to fight another day.'

'As will your Grace! You were the star of the day. You cannot stay away from the lists now.'

'Tell that to the ancient fathers on my Council,' Harry snorted. 'Not that I will let them dictate to me.'

But they tried.

'Your Grace,' Surrey remonstrated when Harry faced them the next morning, 'you must have more care for your person. Has it not occurred to you that you might be injured or even killed?'

Harry sighed, exasperated. 'Your confidence in my jousting skills is touching!'

'Sir, even experienced jousters take falls – look at William Compton.'

Harry groaned. 'If it makes you happy, I will use hollow lances to reduce the impact. But I'm not giving up jousting. My subjects were thrilled to see me taking part yesterday. And I have no fear of anyone in the world.'

Reluctantly, they agreed. When it came to it, they could not gainsay him. He was the King.

Freed from their constraints, Harry began training daily. His favourite opponents were Compton, Neville, Buckingham and, above all, Brandon, for whom he ordered jousting clothes to match his own. Without vanity, he knew himself to be the most assiduous and the most passionate participant. And, if he was not taking part, he never missed the opportunity to watch the combats. Kate enjoyed them too. He had feared she might join the chorus of protests from the council board, but she had nothing but admiration for him and showed herself thrilled when he wore her favour on his lance.

'You look like St George in person,' she called to him once, in her prettily accented English, as he entered the lists, gallant on his destrier. And for three hours, she sat there engrossed as he outshone all others, shivering many lances and unhorsing several of his opponents.

Life was not all heroic pleasures. Later that month, Harry donned his crimson and ermine robes of estate and walked in procession beneath a canopy carried by the monks of Westminster Abbey to open his first Parliament. He was preceded by mitred abbots, bishops, heralds, Archbishop Warham, Garter King of Arms, the royal mace-bearer, and the Duke of Buckingham and his son bearing the Cap and Sword of Estate. In the Abbey, he sat enthroned as Mass was celebrated, before proceeding into the Parliament Chamber, where he put on the Cap of Estate, then nodded to the Lord Chancellor to address the assembly in his name. This was what it was to be a king.

He was eagerly anticipating the birth of his son and heir, and longing for the child to be born so that he could get on with his plans to invade France. He had ordered a new cover for the baptismal font and linen towels to be used at the christening. A sumptuous cradle of estate padded with crimson cloth of gold embroidered with the royal arms stood ready in Kate's chamber. There was new linen for her bed and swaddling bands in which to wrap the baby, and a groaning chair for the delivery, upholstered in cloth of gold. Harry did not like to dwell on the process of childbirth, being squeamish about such matters, which were best left to women and from which he would be barred anyway, for when Kate took to her chamber to await the birth, men would not be admitted, and her women would take on the duties of her male officers.

She had not yet retired from public view; there were some weeks to go, but Harry could not wait. He saw himself teaching the young Prince Henry – the child would be named for him, of course – to ride his first pony and play with toy swords and shields, making a soldier of him. He would engage the finest tutors, for his son was to be the best-educated royal heir in history. He would create him Prince of Wales and have him invested in a splendid ceremony at court. When the time came, he would give him his own household; his heir would never have to experience the frustration that Harry had suffered under his father's strict tutelage. His head was bursting with plans. And soon, God willing, there would be brothers, more princes for England, and sisters, who could make dazzling marriages with foreign princes. By then, of course, he himself might be king of France!

Kate smiled to hear him talk. She shared in his excitement.

'Above all, my Henry, I just want to hold our babe in my arms,' she said. They were sitting in her chamber, cosy together by the roaring fire, as the winter winds whistled outside and rattled the window frames.

'It will not be long now,' he said fervently, squeezing her hand. He wished he could touch her, hold her naked in his arms and make vigorous love to her. But that was forbidden; the doctors had warned that there might be some risk to the child, so he had abstained from her bed. It was torture for him. They had had such a short time to be lovers, and he was finding it hard to control himself. Other husbands, he knew, took their pleasure elsewhere, but he was not of that stamp. He could not be unfaithful to his Kate. And so, every night, he kissed her tenderly and left her and her precious burden to get the rest they needed.

He was awoken by Brandon hissing urgently in his ear.

'Harry, you must wake up! The Queen is in labour.'

He was instantly awake, quivering with alarm. 'But it's too soon.'

'Not too soon for the child to survive. Make haste!'

'Help me dress.' Harry was out of bed like a deer in the chase, tearing off his nightgown and reaching for the clean shirt his laundress had left out for him. Gathering its folds between his legs, he pulled on his hose, his fingers trembling as he tried to lace the points of his codpiece. Oh, God, oh, God. Let Kate be all right. Let the child live.

The worst of the waiting was not being able to be with her. He flew to her apartments, but the door to her privy chamber was firmly closed, even to him. Yet he could hear her screams, and knew she was in great distress, which tore at his heart. She, who was normally so calm, so dignified.

And then – silence. The screaming had stopped. Not knowing what was happening was agony.

After an age, a woman emerged, carrying a bundle swathed in white linen. He gasped – his son at last – and then he saw her face. She was crying. Panicking, he reached out and pulled away the material, reeling in horror at the sight of the tiny grey corpse with raw, unformed hands and ugly red veins marking its bald head. It was a girl.

'Take her away,' he croaked, covering the little face, choking back tears.

His heart broke when he saw Kate lying there, weeping and full of guilt because she had failed him, and fretting for fear of what her father might say. They wept together, and he assured her that he thought nothing the worse of her, and that they could try again as soon as she was well. She cried more piteously at that and begged him not to make their private tragedy a public one. So nothing was said about it. The court – and the world at large – would draw its own conclusions. So many babies were lost in childbed; it was not a rare event. And yet, it had been a huge event in Harry's life, and it made him realise how precious each child was, and how grievous a blow this loss had been. Their little daughter had never drawn breath, and the sight of her had shocked him, yet she had been the flesh of his flesh and he mourned her deeply, as did Kate, who was inconsolable for weeks. In fact, it affected Harry more than his disappointment at having to defer once again the French venture. His councillors, despite being sympathetic to a man, had insisted on that.

When Kate had been churched, he visited her bed again, but it was not the same as before. She was unresponsive and tearful, and not really interested in lovemaking. He swallowed his disappointment. He reminded himself that she had been through a painful ordeal. He did all he could to cheer her. And then he had an excellent idea about how to lift her spirits.

Shrove Tuesday was approaching. He was to host a banquet for all the foreign ambassadors, and afterwards, he decided – remembering how Kate had enjoyed that Robin Hood mummery – that he would stage another disguising and take part himself!

When the day came and dusk fell, he led Kate and his nobles into the Parliament Chamber at Westminster, where the ambassadors were waiting. He himself showed them to their seats before taking his place next to Kate at the high table. He was soon up again, walking around the boards and chatting with his guests. Then he slipped away and joined his kinsman, the Earl of Essex, in the pages' chamber. There they dressed up in Turkish costume, while six other gentlemen donned Prussian attire.

By the light of torch-bearers blacked up as Moors, they all sallied back into the Parliament Chamber, brandishing scimitars, much to the astonishment of the company. Harry strode up to the dais and extended his hand to Kate, who looked at him doubtfully, but took it. Then the other players invited ladies on to the floor and the dancing began. When it ended, Harry bowed and handed Kate back to her seat, after which he departed again and changed into a short doublet of blue and crimson, slashed with cloth of gold, which showed off his fine, muscular legs. More dancing followed, and he suddenly saw in Kate's eyes that look of desire he had longed to revive. He kissed her, there in the middle of the floor, in front of everyone, to resounding applause. Then he danced with his sister Mary, now nearly fourteen and drawing all eyes because of her budding beauty. He saw Brandon gazing at her, smitten, the rogue – and him with a wife!

As he took his seat at the high table, he was smiling. Never before, surely, had a monarch performed in front of his court or received such acclaim. It would, he resolved, be the first of many such occasions.

St George, the patron saint of England and of the Most Noble Order of the Garter, had been Harry's hero ever since he had been dubbed a Knight of the Garter when he was four. Every year on 23 April, St George's feast day, it was customary for the King to hold a chapter of the Order and a banquet; last year's had been a muted affair because Father had just died, but this year, clad in the blue velvet mantle of the Order with a silk garter embroidered with Tudor roses around his leg, Harry presided over the chapter in all its pageantry and splendour.

At the feast, the tables were laden with rich dishes. Everyone was seated in order of rank and served with great ceremony. Harry's cupbearer and food taster remained kneeling beside him throughout the proceedings. The choicest food was brought to him and, when he had helped himself and eaten his fill, what remained was passed down to lesser mortals as a mark of favour. Along the walls stood great oak buffets and court cupboards groaning with gold and silver plate reflecting the dancing lights of the hundreds of candles that illuminated St George's Hall.

The traditional May Day celebrations soon followed, always the occasion of cheerful merrymaking at court. That morning, Harry rose early, donned a suit of white satin and went a-Maying, he, Kate and their courtiers venturing into the woods and meadows around Greenwich to fetch in the may boughs and shoot with bows and arrows. There were sports, horse races, jousts, and dances around the maypole. Later, as Harry sat in the greenwood eating cream cakes, with the sun shining above and a gentle breeze playing, he smiled at Kate, thinking of the secret hopes they were cherishing. It was early days yet, but he was almost certain that their prayers had been answered. He was in a buoyant mood when they all returned to the palace, every man sporting a green bough in his cap, for his head was bursting once again with plans for invading France,

Nearly every day that month, Harry amused himself in the tiltyard, running the ring, jousting and participating in tournaments on foot, determined to be in peak condition for war. Kate was suffering the sickness of early pregnancy and keeping to her chamber in the mornings, but some of her ladies came to sit in the stands and watch the contests, among them Buckingham's two married sisters, Elizabeth, Lady FitzWalter and Anne, Lady Hastings.

'Are they not a pair of beauties?' Compton grinned, as he, Harry and Brandon waited on their mounts for the tourney to begin.

'Too grand for the likes of you!' Brandon ribbed him.

Harry barely heard them. His eyes were fixed on Anne Hastings' striking dark looks and inviting eyes; she was smiling boldly at him. Leavening his joy at Kate's pregnancy was the prospect of more long months with no bed sport. Was this to be the pattern of his life from now on? A few short weeks of pleasure followed by an eternity of enforced celibacy, year in, year out? He had waited long enough to experience the delights of love and did not want to waste his youthful vigour any more. What harm would a little dalliance do? Kate need never know, and what she did not know could not hurt her. As for Lord Hastings, he need be none the wiser.

'Wake up, Harry!' Brandon said.

'Where were you?' Compton put in. 'Dreaming of the fair Lady Hastings?'

'As a matter of fact, I was,' Harry admitted.

'Ho, ho!' Brandon crowed, slapping him on the back.

He flushed. 'Would that I could contrive a meeting – secretly, of course. No one must know.' It was important to show himself to be a virtuous prince.

'I could arrange it,' Compton offered. 'I could pretend to pursue her myself.'

'Do you think she would be willing?' Harry asked.

'To oblige her sovereign? Ha! If you let it be known that you're game for some dalliance, the ladies would be queuing up!'

'You could have your pick of them,' Brandon added. 'You're the King! Crook your little finger and they'll be on their backs in a trice!'

Harry chuckled. He could do this. He needed to do this. 'When can you arrange a meeting?'

Compton was as good as his word – and Anne Hastings more than willing. Before the week was out, Harry found himself mounting her in the narrow bed in Compton's lodging, much to his satisfaction. By St George, it was liberating being able to indulge himself physically without having to go through all the folderol of a courtship. Both of them knew what they wanted, and they had fallen on each other, not even bothering to remove all their clothes the first time. And he had performed wonders . . .

Then, just hours after he and Anne had crept out of the apartment, Compton appeared in the privy chamber, unusually agitated.

'I must speak to your Grace in private, now!' he muttered.

They moved into Harry's closet, a cosy panelled room he used as a study.

'What's the matter?' he asked.

'I've just been to Anne Hastings' apartment, keeping up the pretence that I am paying court to her. But Buckingham was there. He called me a scoundrel and warned me not to go near her. He used very hard words. He said his other sister was concerned about my seeing her and warned him and Lord Hastings.'

'But you have done nothing wrong,' Harry protested. 'Even the most chaste married ladies have devoted servants paying court to them.'

'Buckingham thinks it has gone beyond that.'

'Even so, I will not have him reprimanding one of my closest friends in such a manner. Leave this with me!'

Seething, feeling guilty because Compton was being blamed unjustly, and angry because his little idyll had been so nearly discovered, Harry summoned the Duke to his closet.

'How dare you impugn Compton's honour!' he raged. 'He had no evil intent towards Lady Hastings.'

'I know what I know!' Buckingham countered, puce in the face.

'Then you know wrong! And you will apologise to Compton.'

'Apologise to a pimp? Never!'

Harry drew in his breath. Buckingham knew. Or had he just guessed? 'You will do as I command,' he hissed.

With gross discourtesy, Buckingham turned and stamped out. Harry followed him into the privy chamber and stood there glowering as the Duke barked out an apology to a startled Compton – an apology that sounded like an insult.

That night, the Duke left the palace. The next day, Compton told Harry that Lord Hastings had carried off his wife and shut her up in a convent.

'It's my belief that she confided in her sister, who warned Buckingham and Lord Hastings.'

'Then Lady FitzWalter shall know my displeasure.'

'Harry, be warned. People may talk. There could be a scandal.'

Harry ignored him. He ordered that Lord and Lady FitzWalter be banished from the court.

Later that day, one of Kate's pages presented himself in his privy chamber, saying that her Grace was asking to see him. Harry bristled. No doubt she was going to complain about being deprived of her ladies-in-waiting and would be asking awkward questions. Very well, let her ask!

He burst into her chamber and waved away her ladies, regarding her with a steely gaze. If he showed himself sufficiently outraged, she might believe he was the injured party in this matter.

She did not waste time. 'Sir, why has Lady FitzWalter been banished?' He detected a tremor in her voice, her Castilian accent becoming more pronounced in her distress.

'Because she has been telling lies,' he snapped.

Kate looked at him accusingly. 'She told me that you and Lady Hastings were too close, and that Sir William Compton was pretending to court the lady to divert suspicion from you. Henry, I must know: is it true?'

'Of course not!' he shouted. 'She had no business to be saying such things to you. It was a mere flirtation on Compton's part.'

'Then why did Lady Hastings tell her sister it was you?'

'Because she is a foolish woman who likes to think I fancy her! Kate, I will not have you question me like this.'

'You are my husband, Henry, and owe me fidelity.'

'I have been faithful! But even if I had not, it is a wife's duty to be silent.'

'I have no intention of being silent!' Kate countered, looking much as he imagined her formidable mother, Queen Isabella, must have looked when confronting the Moors. 'You should have taken greater care not to get into a situation that was open to more than one interpretation.'

Harry felt himself reddening. How dare she speak to him thus! 'Who are you to tell me what I should and should not do? I have honoured you with my marriage and I expect unquestioning obedience. You have no right to criticise me – I am the King, the Lord's Anointed!'

'Which is why you should ensure you are above suspicion! And don't shout – my ladies will hear you, and they gossip!'

'Let them! Let them hear how you forget your duty to me!'

'My Henry . . .' Kate grasped his arm, but he pushed her away. 'Henry, please – I must know. Has there been anything between you and Lady Hastings?'

'No! Do you doubt the word of a prince?'

'No,' she said, her eyes filling with tears.

'Good! Then I'll leave you to reflect on a wife's proper duty to her lord!'

There was an atmosphere between them for days; almost all the court knew they had been vexed with each other, and Kate could not conceal her hurt, or her ill will towards Compton. Harry was furious because he had been found out. He cringed to think of his shameful secret being exposed, especially after he had gone to such lengths to maintain the utmost discretion. He was angry with Kate, who should have preserved her dignity and avoided a mortifying public row; she should have shut her eyes to the matter and been grateful that he had not shamed her by flaunting his mistress.

He had been very ill done by, yet it was Kate who was acting as if she were the one with a grievance. He found himself living under a cloud of her disapproval.

The frostiness between them thawed in July when she finally apologised and he willingly forgave her. They were at Windsor Castle on the first stage of their annual progress. Harry threw himself into daily exercise, shooting at the archery butts, wrestling with his gentlemen and challenging them to feats of strength. The evenings were devoted to dancing, singing and practising on the lute and the virginals, which he tried to do daily. He composed several ballads, and set two Masses to be sung in his chapel. And he wrote a love song for Kate.

> Now unto my lady
> Promise to her I make:
> From all other only
> To her, I me betake.
>
> Adieu, my own lady,
> Adieu, my special,
> Who hath my hart truly,
> Be sure, and ever shall.

As he sang to her in his high tenor voice, strumming his lute, their eyes met and he poured his soul into the words, belatedly aware that he had hurt her, and feeling guilty because she was carrying his child and should not have been upset. And then she smiled – and the world came to rights again.

Chapter 6

1510

From Windsor, their progress took them to Woking Palace, where Harry participated in a series of tournaments. Woking had been one of the chief residences of his grandmother, the Lady Margaret, and he almost expected to see her gaunt, black-robed figure pacing slowly down the chapel aisle or kneeling at the prayer desk in his bedchamber. He missed her. He had loved her, and she had doted on him.

He devoted the rest of the progress to hunting, hawking, shooting – and praying for the safe delivery of a son. Even on days when he went hunting, he heard three Masses – five on other days – and he always joined Kate for Vespers and Compline in his private closet.

She was now great with child and, thanks be to God, in the best of health. That autumn, when they returned from the progress, Harry gave orders for the preparation of a nursery. He appointed a Lady Mistress, Elizabeth Poyntz, to take charge of the birth and care for the infant and had the Queen's bedchamber adorned with new hangings. The royal tailor was set to making a purple velvet mantle with a long train for the Prince to wear at his baptism.

Harry willed matters to progress normally this time. Everything must be done properly and the observances laid down by his father for his mother rigorously observed. Kate's bedchamber was furnished with sumptuous tapestries, which covered the walls, ceilings and windows.

'But it will be very dark,' she protested, looking around the room.

'One window will be left uncovered,' Harry said, 'so that you can have light when it pleases you. Notice that the tapestries depict pleasant scenes from romances, so that the child is not frightened by figures that stare gloomily.'

Kate laughed. 'I doubt it will have the wits to notice!'

'Nevertheless, darling, precedent must be followed.' Harry was firm. 'Six weeks before the child is due, you will take to your chamber, and you will remain in seclusion until after the birth.'

'I will miss the Christmas celebrations,' she reminded him.

'I know, but the safe delivery of our son is more important.'

'Of course.' She squeezed his hand. 'But I want to give birth in bed, not in the groaning chair.'

'Very well. I will order that a pallet bed be placed next to your state bed, and made up with a fine tester and bedding. And you'll need smocks of Holland cloth for the delivery.'

'Thank you, my Henry. You think of everything!' She kissed him.

'Anything for you and our son, darling. I'm having the great font from Canterbury Cathedral brought here specially, in case the child is weak and needs immediate baptism. Not that I have any reason to fear that he will be,' he hastened to assure her, 'but it's best to be on the safe side. Now you must rest and not worry about a thing.'

Nevertheless, after what had happened last time, he himself could not stop fretting. Childbirth was a hazardous business, and many mothers and babes were lost, like his own dear mother. The future of his dynasty depended on a happy outcome.

He diverted himself with tournaments, throwing himself into the action and breaking more lances than anyone else. Then it was November and time for the court to move to Richmond, where Kate took to her chamber. Harry spent an anxious Christmas, praying that all would go well.

1511

On New Year's Eve, he received word that Kate's travail had begun. He was grateful that the Abbot of Westminster had lent her Our Lady's Girdle, one of the Abbey's most precious holy relics, which had been worn by the Virgin Mary herself when she gave birth to her Son. It would surely offer Kate protection against the perils of childbirth.

He was awoken by Brandon in the early hours of New Year's Day.

'Your Grace, the Queen is safely delivered of a prince!'

Harry sprang up, instantly wide awake and filled with jubilation. Before dressing, he gave orders for a royal salute to be fired from the cannon on Tower Wharf, and for all the church bells to peal out in celebration. England had her heir, and all must share in the rejoicing.

Donning his damask night robe, he hastened to the Queen's apartments, where he waited impatiently in an antechamber until Mistress Poyntz arrived and placed his son in his arms. What a prince he was! He had his father's red-gold hair and the bluest eyes, which stared at him serenely, unblinking. The tiny fingers gripped his thumb with surprising force. Tears filled Harry's eyes.

'Here's a fine king in the making!' he exclaimed, as his gentlemen and Kate's attendants crowded around admiringly. 'He looks like me. Greet the future Henry the Ninth!'

Everyone began showering him with heart-felt congratulations, but the one person he wanted to see was Kate – Kate, who, thanks be to God, had survived her ordeal and given him this great and precious gift. She was recovering well, they assured him, and in high spirits.

Rules be damned! 'I will see her,' he said.

The women began protesting, but he waved them aside. 'On such an occasion as this, no one may gainsay me!' With the child still in his arms, he pushed aside the heavy curtain and opened the door – and there was Kate, lying propped up on her pillows, holding out her arms to them both. Love and gratitude overflowed in him.

All over the land, *Te Deums* were sung by the clergy; in London, there were triumphant processions. Harry ordered that bonfires be lit in the streets and commanded the Lord Mayor to provide free wine for the citizens to drink the Prince's health.

His son looked very tiny indeed in the vast new painted cradle, which was trimmed with silver gilt and had buckles on either side to secure his swaddling bands. Little Henry lay wrapped up tight, under a coverlet fringed with gold and a scarlet counterpoint furred with ermine. When he was displayed to foreign ambassadors and important visitors, he was placed in an even bigger state cradle upholstered in crimson and gold, with the royal arms above his head.

Harry sat with Kate as she lay in her great bed, wrapped in a mantle of crimson velvet; together, they received guests and well-wishers. He watched as she wrote letters to the nobility and her chief officers, formally announcing the birth. She had to lie in for forty days before being churched and returning to her daily life. Harry could barely wait. He longed to hold her in his arms again and reclaim her. Together, they would make more lusty sons – a whole quiverful of them!

When he was five days old, the little Prince of Wales was carried to his christening. Harry had chosen as godparents Archbishop Warham, the Earl of Surrey, and the Earl and Countess of Devon, while the King of France (unsuspecting that he would soon be overthrown!) and Margaret of Austria, Duchess of Savoy, daughter of the Emperor Maximilian, had both agreed to be sponsors and sent expensive gifts of gold plate.

Harry was terrified lest any ill befall his precious heir. The nursery staff had been chosen with the utmost care. The wet nurse was of excellent moral character, and all her meals were assayed for poison. A physician supervised every feed to make sure that the child was getting enough sustenance and was not being slipped any unauthorised foods. Forty people had been appointed to the Prince's household, and Harry had already designated a room in the palace of Westminster as his son's council chamber. One must always look to the future.

He could not stop thanking God for the great gift of a son, and made a pilgrimage to the shrine of Our Lady of Walsingham in Norfolk to give thanks, for Our Lady of Walsingham was famous for granting the prayers of those who longed for children. Dismounting a mile away at the Slipper Chapel, he removed his shoes, like all the other pilgrims, and walked barefoot to the shrine, where he lit a candle and offered a costly necklace. He also arranged to donate new stained-glass windows for the chapel at the priory. Then he rode home, dreaming of victories in France. There was nothing to stop him planning his campaign now.

When he returned to Richmond, Kate was sitting up in her chair. He kissed her, admired the Prince, who had surely grown bigger while he was away, and took the seat opposite.

'You must be churched as soon as possible, Kate, so that we can leave for Westminster. I'm planning a magnificent tournament to celebrate the birth of our son.'

'And the Prince – he will come with us?'

Harry shook his head. 'I would not risk our precious jewel, even for your sake. Here at Richmond the air is purer and there is less risk of infection.'

'But I cannot bear to leave him! He is so tiny! He needs his mother.' Kate looked tragic. 'Let me stay here, Henry, I beg of you!'

'Sweetheart, your place is at my side. People will expect you to be there. Little Harry is in good hands – never child had better or more loving nurses. You have done your duty – now enjoy the applause. And after we have celebrated, you can come back to Richmond and see him. It is not so far away.'

In the end, she ceased protesting and accompanied him to London, but he was aware that her heart was at Richmond. When he dressed for the opening joust on the twelfth day of February, cladding himself in green satin and crimson velvet, he was feeling a little grieved that she was spoiling what was supposed to be a joyous and triumphal occasion. He was feeling quite sorry for himself when some of his councillors waylaid him and his companions on the way to the tiltyard.

'Your Grace,' Archbishop Warham pleaded, 'we beg of you, cease putting yourself at risk. You will lose no honour by presiding over the tournament from the royal stand.'

'No,' Harry said firmly, outraged that they should carp on this of all occasions, and aware that Brandon and Neville were listening intently. 'You will not gainsay one of my courage.' He strode on defiantly.

Kate did not grace the jousts with her presence that day. She could not help having a bad headache, but Harry still felt, irrationally, that she was spoiling things for him. But when he got back to the palace, he found her lying in a darkened room with a damp flannel across her brow, looking pale and drawn. Instantly, he felt contrite. He had been unfair to her.

He would make it up to her. Over the next two days, he was planning to stage the most lavish tournament ever held in England; and it would be in her honour – and for her delight.

He was relieved to find that she was much restored the following morning. He watched from his pavilion as she took her place in the royal stand that had been specially erected for her and hung with sumptuous cloths of gold and purple velvet embroidered with their initials and their badges of pomegranates and roses. She seated herself beneath the cloth of estate, her ladies about her, carrying herself elegantly, despite retaining some of the plumpness of pregnancy.

Harry had dressed to please her, as *Coeur Loyal* – Sir Loyal Heart – with the name embroidered in gold on his clothes and his horse's caparisons. The Earl of Devon was *Bon Valoir*, Thomas Knyvet was *Bon Espoir* and Edward Neville was Valiant Desire. Course after course was run in the lists, with Kate bestowing the prizes, and there was great applause when Harry won the challenger's prize.

'My lady!' he cried, beaming at her. 'The mother of my son!'

That night, he and Kate were lovers again. She seemed a little reluctant, but he was gentle and soon she relaxed. He was a little dismayed to find her breasts less firm than he remembered, but it did not really matter, nor did it bother him that she had put on weight with her pregnancy – he liked plump, buxom women. What mattered was that they were one again, and that they could once more enjoy the lusty business of getting sons.

The tournament continued on the second day, and that night there was great revelry in the White Hall, where a short play was performed by the gentlemen of the Chapel Royal in honour of the Prince. Then there was another pageant, 'The Garden of Pleasure', in which Harry again appeared as *Coeur Loyal*, wearing a purple satin suit adorned with gold Hs and Ks. A pageant car had been constructed for the occasion, decked out as a forest with rocks, hills, dales, trees, flowers, hawthorns and grass, all fashioned from velvet, silk and damask; a golden castle stood in its midst, within which Harry and his companions concealed themselves. He could not wait to see Kate's face when he emerged, wearing her favours. Drawn by men dressed as a lion and an antelope, the car was trundled into the tiltyard, carrying four foresters in green velvet and a gentleman making a garland of roses for the Prince. When it stopped before the Queen, the foresters sounded their horns, and Harry and his fellows burst out of the castle and presented their shields to a delighted Kate. Then they danced with her ladies, who were wearing gowns of green and white, the Tudor livery colours. There was much applause, especially from the far end of the hall, where the common people had been admitted to watch the festivities.

As Harry led Kate in the dancing, he heard Luis Caroz observe that the initials he wore must be of base metal.

'Nay!' he cried, wishing to boast of his wealth. 'They are real gold!'

But the ambassador still looked dubious, as did Surrey and several others standing nearby.

'I will prove to you that they are gold!' Harry cried, laughing. 'Come, everyone – pull them off me and see for yourselves!' He took Kate's hand and whirled her about the floor. One by one, the courtiers came forward, hesitantly at first, then with increasing boldness. Harry chuckled as they plucked the initials from his clothes and stared at them in amazement. Then, suddenly, the common people were rushing forward, yelling, 'Largesse! Largesse!' They barged into the dancers and began divesting the King and his courtiers of their finery, grabbing and pulling as they went. At first, Harry thought it was funny, realising that the rabble had mistaken his challenge as a generous invitation to help themselves to his riches. He laughed to see his courtiers' discomfiture.

But matters were quickly getting out of hand. Clothes were being ripped, jewellery tugged off without care for any injury to its wearers, and some gentlemen had been wrestled to the floor by greedy assailants bent on booty. It was like a mêlée! Harry saw the shock on Kate's face as two rough men pulled off his gown and stripped him to his doublet and hose. His bases torn, he stood there laughing helplessly, for his good commons were now setting about his lords and divesting them too of their finery. It was so funny to see the looks on their faces!

Katherine took refuge with her ladies on the dais, where Harry belatedly hastened to join her.

'Shouldn't they be stopped?' she cried, but he just laughed.

'Let them have their largesse in honour of the Prince!' he said. 'I will cry it! Largesse! Largesse! Mother of God, look!'

Katherine raised her eyes to where he was pointing, to see Sir Thomas Knyvet, the Chancellor of the Exchequer, shinning up a pillar to escape the rapacious hands of the mob. He was stark naked and affording the ladies a comprehensive view of his manly parts. Harry felt himself blushing, but he could not help guffawing.

'They have gone too far, for shame!' Katherine protested, rising to her feet as the milling crowd began edging towards the dais. Harry saw the look of horror on her face as two beefy varlets began tugging at her ladies' gowns, provoking a lot of squealing.

'Enough!' he cried, in a voice like a trumpet, and signalled to the Yeomen of the Guard. Suddenly armed pikemen were in the midst of the throng, pushing the people back towards the doors and ejecting them from the hall, leaving Harry and his tattered courtiers staring at each other. Someone threw poor Knyvet a torn gown. Then Henry let out a roar of laughter. There was a pause, and others followed suit, until the rafters were echoing with the sounds of mirth.

'Well, that was one hell of a pageant!' he cried, passing the whole thing off as a joke. 'Let our hurts be turned to laughter and games! Come, my lords and ladies, let us to the banquet – as you are!'

Grabbing Kate by the hand and marching ahead to his privy chamber, he gave them no time to complain. And soon – as he had expected – his merry, bedraggled courtiers came hastening after him, gabbling and chuckling, and no doubt ribbing poor Knyvet mercilessly about losing all his clothes.

Tables had been set out with the best and rarest sweetmeats and fine wines.

'Help yourselves!' Harry called, signalling to the servitors to depart. Then he took a plate and helped himself to suckets, marchpane, jellies, biscuits, comfits of sugar fondant and syllabub.

'Don't eat too much, Harry,' Compton murmured with a wicked grin. 'They're all aphrodisiacs!'

'The Queen will be most appreciative,' Harry chortled, picking up a spice plate piled with apples with caraway seeds and sugared spices.

Compton grabbed a sweetmeat. 'Your cooks have excelled themselves tonight.'

Harry could barely hear him; the babel of chatter was deafening. Courtiers were laughing and drinking, some staggering a little as they wove their way around the room. He wanted the evening to go on for ever. And then he would take Kate to bed. He could feel a certain stirring that made him wonder if Compton had been right about the aphrodisiacs. It prompted him to sing some of his love songs to her, before the admiring company. He barely noticed Surrey approaching until the Earl bent to his ear.

'Forgive the intrusion, your Grace, but there is news from Richmond.'

It was the hoarse note in his voice that alerted Harry. Something was amiss. Excusing himself, he led Surrey through the royal apartments and into his study. There on the desk lay the plans he had been drawing up that afternoon for a new palace. His scissors, compasses, drawing irons and steel pen were lined up neatly.

'Richmond? Is it the Prince?' His voice tailed away as he saw Surrey's face.

'Your Grace, I fear to tell you that the Prince is departed to God.' The Earl's voice cracked.

'No!' An unearthly howl broke from Harry. 'No! He was healthy! God would not be so cruel . . .' He collapsed into his chair, weeping.

The door quietly opened and a hand rested on his shoulder. It was Wolsey. 'And God shall wipe away all tears from their eyes; and there shall be no more death, neither sorrow, nor crying, neither shall there be any more pain: for the former things are passed away. Blessed are they that mourn, for they shall be comforted.'

Harry looked up. He had barely registered the words of solace. The world had crashed down on his shoulders and nothing would ever be the same again. His son, his little son – the hope of England – was gone. He had lived for just six weeks! Kate would be devastated.

'Why?' he asked. 'Why?'

'It was a fever, such as carries off so many infants,' Surrey told him. 'The physicians were summoned at once, but there was nothing anyone could do.'

'The Queen,' Harry blurted out. 'Does she know?'

'Not yet,' Wolsey said gently. 'We thought it best for your Grace to break the news to her. I will bring her to you. Then you and she can share your sorrow together in private.'

Harry swallowed. How was he ever going to find the words to tell Kate the terrible news?

She arrived, looking bewildered. 'Henry, our guests are wondering where you are . . .' Her voice tailed away as she saw his face in the light of the candles he had lit, his hands trembling. She shook her head.

'No! No!'

He reached out to her. 'Kate.' His voice broke. 'Our boy is dead.' He would never forget her screams as he folded her in his arms.

He did not know how to summon the words to comfort her. Not since the death of his dear mother had he felt such grief. It was beyond pain. He lay with Kate on her bed, trying in vain to soothe her cries.

'He did not suffer,' he wept. 'His soul is now among the innocents of God. We can have other children.' But nothing helped. They were floundering in sorrow, not knowing how to rise above it.

'We must not question the wisdom of God,' he murmured. 'A sudden chance like that, a chill – he was so young.' His voice threatened to break again.

'I wish God had taken me!' Kate wailed, piercing him to the heart. 'I cannot face life without him. I cannot bear the pain. My little babe . . .'

Harry did his best to hide his own misery. He stayed with her through the darkest days, holding her through every storm of weeping, and trying to divert her with music and pastimes.

'There will be no court mourning,' he decreed. But he wore black on the day the little Prince was brought in great state from Richmond and buried in Westminster Abbey, and spent a fortune on the funeral. All that pomp – vigils, candles and torches – for one tiny babe; but it was fitting that the King's son be laid magnificently to rest among his forefathers.

Harry made no further outward show of grief, although in private he had all to do to succour Kate. He threw himself into state affairs with a determination that surprised his councillors. Pope Julius – and Kate, before tragedy struck – had been pressing him to join the Holy League, an alliance between the Vatican, Spain and Venice against King Louis, who had aggressive territorial ambitions in Italy; and that accorded well with Harry's own ambitions. That Easter, the Pope bestowed on him a Golden Rose he himself had blessed, which symbolised the Passion of Christ – a token of high apostolic favour. Yet Harry's pleasure in it was dimmed when he thought of that tiny body lying beneath the floor of Westminster Abbey.

He summoned his courage and wore a smile. At night, when he could not sleep, he lay planning campaigns in France. He celebrated May Day as usual, and jousted with Brandon, Thomas Howard and Edward Neville for three whole days, taking on all comers. He then took Kate on a summer progress through the Midlands, visiting Nottingham and Coventry, where they watched the famous cycle of mystery plays, performed by local guildsmen. He indulged in sports, dice and cards. He made sure his life was full of distractions.

Wolsey helped. He was now Harry's right-hand man, his unofficial secretary, always ready with sage fatherly advice and priestly words of comfort. Many were the stimulating sessions they spent together in Harry's study, discussing the affairs of the realm and the world at large – for Wolsey took an international view of things – and sometimes mundane domestic matters. The almoner knew everything that went on at court, who was at odds, who was in love, who was behaving unfittingly – all useful knowledge to have at hand. Recognising his worth, Harry appointed him Dean of Hereford and Lincoln, Prebendary of York, canon of Windsor and registrar of the Order of the Bath. He had happily granted Bishop Foxe's request to give Wolsey a seat on the Privy Council. And Wolsey showed himself flatteringly grateful. Harry was not unaware that he was proud and acquisitive, and had ambitions above his station in life, but it did not bother him. He liked Wolsey's charm, wit and convivial manner. The butcher's son served his King well. Why should he not be rewarded?

Chapter 7

In October, Harry joined the Holy League. He could now say that he was embarking on a holy war against France. Priding himself on being a good son of the Church, and wishing to please his Holiness, he commanded his courtiers to curb their extravagance and dress soberly – albeit with limited success; he even forbade the nobility to wear silk, another order that was largely ignored.

'Instead of wasting money on outward show, my lords,' he told his councillors and his courtiers, 'you should be spending it on weapons and horses for our crusade against the King of France.' He practised what he preached, putting away his rich garments and wearing plainer clothes. That December, he opened Parliament in a long grey gown cut in the Hungarian fashion.

But he soon got bored with austerity. He kept Christmas at Greenwich in a princely manner, hosting great revels and a throng of guests, and spent a king's ransom on New Year's gifts and pageants. He was in his element. When he saw Kate enjoying herself, clapping with delight, it did his heart good. If only he could get her with child, life would be perfect.

For Twelfth Night, William Cornish, the Master of the Revels, had devised an entertainment called a masque, something not seen before in England, but popular in Italy. Harry and eleven other gentlemen disguised themselves, appropriately, as Italians, in garments, visors and caps wrought with gold. They appeared masked in the presence chamber after the evening's banquet and invited the ladies to dance, a thing that had never happened in pageants. Some looked askance, not wishing to perform before the court, but most were easily persuaded. Harry had been practising for days, and led his partner effortlessly in steps requiring skill and agility. She was a pretty little thing, fair-haired and sweetly spoken, and he almost regretted his resolve never to stray from Kate again. But then he saw his wife watching him lovingly from the dais, and knew where his heart really lay. But it was good to be the king, to be twenty years old and the centre of the world's attention, and to have all the young ladies competing to be noticed by him. He revelled in it all, and in the wild applause that erupted when the dancing was over, and he and his companions revealed themselves. He would have more of these masques, he vowed.

1512

In March, Pope Julius withdrew King Louis' title of Most Christian King and bestowed the kingdom of France upon Harry. All he had to do was win it.

'There will be no more delays,' he told his councillors. 'I am going to war.'

Seeing their alarm, he banged his fist on the table. 'I'll brook no opposition. We invade France this summer.'

'I will put preparations in train, your Grace,' Wolsey said smoothly, as the others glared at him. 'But might I suggest that, given everyone's concerns about your safety and the succession, the expedition be led by some noble commander on your behalf? If he is victorious, the triumph will still be yours.'

It was not what Harry wanted, but he saw the wisdom in it.

Kate added her pleas to Wolsey's. 'I am all for this war,' she said that afternoon. 'My father has also declared war on King Louis, and he urges you to win praise and glory in reclaiming what is rightfully yours; but, my Henry, I care more about your safety.'

In the end, Harry capitulated. But the invasion would go ahead; that was what mattered.

* * *

Harry closed the lid of his writing desk, a beautifully fashioned box of walnut and gilded leather painted with his arms and Kate's amid a riot of cherubs with trumpets, figures of Venus and Mars, and antique decoration. At last, he had finished his letters. It was a bright late-April morning, and he was eager to be out of doors. But there was Wolsey, framed in the doorway, looking unusually agitated.

'Your Grace, the palace of Westminster is on fire!'

'What?' Harry was horrified. 'Is it bad?'

'Everyone is doing their best, but I fear it is out of control. The messenger said it started in the kitchens.'

'Have my barge brought to the jetty,' Harry ordered. 'I will see for myself.' He could not begin to contemplate the loss of the ancient palace, his chief seat of government, which dated back to the days of St Edward the Confessor. But after the barge passed the ships moored by the Isle of Dogs and rounded the bend in the river, he could see billowing black smoke in the sky some way ahead. By the time he reached the City of London to see flames leaping high, he knew, with a sinking heart, that he should fear the worst.

The bargemen could not approach too near the burning palace because of the fierce heat, so Harry had to watch from the Thames as it was slowly consumed. Desolately, he gave the order to return to Greenwich, unable to bear witnessing its complete destruction.

Wolsey returned that evening, as Harry and Kate were picking at their supper. 'The fire is out, Sir, but I fear that, despite the strenuous efforts of those who fought it, much has been lost. Yet they managed to save Westminster Hall, the Painted Chamber, the crypt of St Stephen's Chapel and the Jewel Tower.'

It was like grieving for an old friend. 'So the royal lodgings are destroyed?'

'Yes, Sir. I have seen the devastation myself, and they are past restoring, as are the service quarters. Will your Grace rebuild them?'

Harry tried to think straight. 'Sit down, Thomas. Have a goblet of wine. You look as if you need it.'

Kate smiled at Wolsey and poured his drink, for which he thanked her profusely.

'I will have to give this some thought,' Harry said. 'It will take years to rebuild. In the meantime, Westminster Hall can still house the law courts and be used for ceremonies of state. But I will need an official residence in London.'

'There is Baynard's Castle,' Wolsey suggested. 'It is the Queen's own property.'

'It is beautiful,' Kate said. 'I stayed there with Prince Arthur.'

Harry frowned. He did not like to be reminded of that particular wedding night.

'It was the London seat of the House of York,' he said. 'But it's now used chiefly to store her Grace's wardrobe stuff. It's too cramped for a court and there is no room to expand.'

'There is always the Tower of London, Sir. Your late father built splendid lodgings there and raised others for the officers of his household.'

'It's also too small, and outdated. I will sleep on the matter.'

In the morning, Harry realised that he had to compromise. If he could not live comfortably in London, he could live near it in royal style at Greenwich or Richmond, or Eltham Palace. All were a short boat ride from the capital. And Westminster – what was left of it – could remain the seat of government.

His decision made, he conveyed it to his Council at their meeting that afternoon. Then he went out riding with Kate in Greenwich Park.

'My chamberlain wishes to retire,' she told him.

'The Earl of Ormond? He must be pushing seventy.'

'He's older than that and has given good service. I wonder, my Henry, if I might have Lord Mountjoy in his place. As you know, he is married to one of my ladies, and I'm sure he will serve me well.' She looked so fine on her palfrey, tendrils of her golden hair whipping around her face, that Harry would have given her the world in that moment. And Mountjoy was a good choice.

'By all means,' he said heartily. 'Mountjoy is famed all over Christendom for his learning. He is a most enlightened man. Did you know that Erasmus was one of his tutors?'

'*You* told me! He is friends with Thomas More and other humanists, and they correspond in the Latin of the ancients – and he has a long record of loyalty to the Crown.'

'You don't need to persuade me, Kate,' Harry laughed. 'I'm keen to encourage the appointment of such men to high office. It enhances the magnificence of a prince to be surrounded by scholars. Their presence demonstrates how much I love learning and adds lustre to my fame.'

'It needs no added lustre,' Kate said loyally.

He leaned across in the saddle and kissed her.

'I wish everyone approved of the new learning,' he said. 'Some of my bishops regard the Scriptures and the works of St Thomas Aquinas and the Church Fathers as the only authorities and resist any attempts to reinterpret them. I like Aquinas, but I also admire Erasmus and More and their fellows, who want people to take a broader view of the universe, and a less pessimistic view of man's humanity. They have no equal, even in Italy, the very cradle of Humanism. They would be the founders of a new commonwealth.'

'And they want an end to war,' Kate said, giving him a wry glance, 'and for the rich to consider the needs of the poor.'

'Ah, now there, I am not entirely in agreement, darling. War is sometimes necessary to enforce a rightful cause, if diplomacy has failed. But one must always be charitable to the poor, and I never stint in my alms-giving.'

They had reached a clearing and reined in their steeds, for a table had been set up there, laid with a cloth and gold and silver plate, and servitors were setting out platters of cold meats, bread, cheese and fruit.

'A banquet all to ourselves,' Harry smiled as they sat down, while their attendants withdrew to a discreet distance.

'You know, even Erasmus has his critics,' he went on, 'and he is one of the greatest minds of our age. He's a brilliant writer and a passionate advocate of truth, yet some accuse him of presumption for daring to rewrite the Gospels.'

'My mother would not have approved.' Kate sipped her wine. 'But I admire him. We correspond regularly. I loved his book, *In Praise of Folly.*'

'I too! And what a privilege it will be to read the Scriptures in the purest translation. What I like about Erasmus is that he has a high opinion of England – and of me! More told me he called me a universal genius.'

'Well, you deserve it.' She smiled at him. 'I would have liked to ask him to dinner, but we're a long way from Cambridge. We could invite Thomas More, though. He is lonely, I fear, since his wife died.'

'A capital idea!' Time spent with the wise and witty lawyer was always a joy. 'He wasn't going to marry, you know. He intended to take holy orders, but decided he could not renounce the pleasures of the flesh, or give up his promising legal career and his studies; he already had a reputation as a brilliant classical scholar. So he married and became a Member of Parliament, and had all those children.' Harry's voice sounded wistful. Why hadn't God been as bountiful to him?

'His wife was only twenty-three,' Kate said sadly. 'Yes, let's have him to dinner.'

Wearing a plain black gown, Thomas More seated himself at table, professing himself overwhelmed at the honour being shown him.

'Nonsense, Thomas,' Harry replied, clapping him on the shoulder. 'The pleasure is all ours. It is not often we enjoy the company of such a renowned scholar.'

'But your Grace's court is packed with men of learning!'

'And none has such a reputation as your good self!'

'We hear you have just remarried,' Kate said.

'Yes, your Grace.' More smiled. 'My children are young and need a mother. Alice is a widow, older than me, plain-spoken, and certainly no scholar, but she is an excellent housekeeper and I believe I shall come to love her.'

Harry served his guest some choice slices of meat. 'I have heard that your house in Bucklersbury is not only a meeting place for scholars, but breathes happiness.'

'I like to think, Sir, that that is because I run it on Christian principles, in emulation of Plato's academy. All my children, even my daughters, are enjoying a classical education. They learn Latin, Greek, logic, philosophy, theology, mathematics and astronomy. And yet their lives are not all learning. I find time to make merry with them, and we keep several wild animals as pets, and an aviary of birds.'

A radiant smile lit up his face as he spoke of his children. Harry could see why men called him the laughing philosopher. And yet he knew More for a man of staunch faith who would never compromise his principles, and there was still something of the ascetic about him. He was deeply pious, and it was rumoured that he wore a hair shirt next to his skin. You would never have known it. Far from appearing uncomfortable, he was charming and courteous, with an earthy sense of humour.

'I read your translation of the life of Pico della Mirandola,' Harry said over a dessert of jelly made with hippocras. 'It's a vivid portrayal.'

'Thank you.' More bowed his head, acknowledging his sovereign's praise. 'Italian Humanists ought to be better known in England.'

'That's exactly my own opinion!' Harry agreed. He was finding More's company stimulating and thinking that he actually preferred it to that of young men lost in luxury or gold-chained nobles, and even women, although Kate was the honourable exception.

'The culture and art of Italy are incomparable,' More said. 'I applaud your Grace for bringing over Pietro Torrigiano to sculpt your father's tomb.'

'It was my father who introduced me to Italian art. He was given Raphael's painting of St George and the Dragon, and he commissioned Guido Mazzone to make a bust of me as a child. It's very lifelike, as it shows me laughing. But Torrigiano . . .' Harry's voice tailed off. 'The man is a genius, but he has a fiery temper. In Italy, he quarrelled with Michelangelo and broke his nose. I wanted

Benvenuto Cellini to assist him with the tomb, but Cellini would not be associated with a man of so violent a temper, nor did he wish to live among the English. He called us beasts!'

More smiled. 'Maybe your Grace ought to be satisfied with just one volatile Italian!'

'Kate, we ought to have our children educated on Humanist principles,' Harry said later, after More had departed and they were sitting in the royal library, leafing through some of the exquisite illuminated manuscripts that Harry had acquired or inherited.

Sorrow briefly shadowed Kate's face, but then she was smiling again. 'I agree, my Henry. And we should ask Master More for his advice. I am sure he will give it readily.'

'A capital idea, darling! Let us hope that it will not be too long before we are having those conversations.'

The Marquess of Dorset had been chosen to lead the French campaign. He was a seasoned soldier and an able strategist, and Harry felt confident that he would soon trounce the enemy.

King Ferdinand had insisted that the best way to take France was from the south, and so, that June, Harry sent his army down to occupy Aquitaine, which had long ago been in English hands. Some of his councillors had advised against it, believing that an attack from the north would be more effective.

'Your Grace should consider that King Ferdinand is thinking of his own interests. With your army in Aquitaine acting as a barrier, the northern border of Spain is protected from a French invasion.'

'But Ferdinand has promised to send troops to help me conquer Aquitaine,' Harry protested. 'He can hardly march them through France. No, it makes sense to attack from the south.'

Kate said the same. Her father was committed to helping Harry achieve his dream and she begged him not to listen to his councillors. He was so enraptured with the imminent prospect of being crowned at Rheims that he heeded her unthinkingly.

But, as the weeks passed, the promised troops from Spain did not arrive, and in August the English force was still camped in Aquitaine, ravaged by dysentery and growing alarmingly short of supplies.

Word came from Dorset that Ferdinand had pressed him to assist with the conquest of Navarre, north of Spain.

'That was not part of your agreement!' Surrey thundered in Council.

Harry had to concede that it was not. He was burning with frustration, furious with Ferdinand, who had made a fool of him, and with Kate, who had made so many empty promises on her father's behalf.

When the English forces mutinied against Dorset, Harry summoned him home in disgrace, then stumped around in a temper for days, snarling at Kate, impervious to her tears. When Dorset presented himself at court, looking gaunt and terrified, Harry shouted at him for the best part of a quarter-hour.

It was Wolsey who stepped in and calmed the waters. 'Sir,' he said, hastening after Harry as he crashed out of the council chamber, 'all is not lost. The Emperor Maximilian is joining the Holy League, hot against France. King Ferdinand miscalculated in trying to take Navarre before France, but it would be unwise to make an enemy of him, for he is still your friend. Next year, it will be a different story. We will raise a greater army – and you will lead it yourself!'

1513

Wolsey was correct. As the new year dawned, Harry and his allies in the Holy League were again poised to go to war against France, and the almoner was indefatigable, undertaking a multitude of tasks with good humour and efficiency. Harry was amazed at the sheer volume of his work. It would have overwhelmed lesser men, and yet his friend – for that was what Thomas was now – seemed to thrive under the pressure.

Harry was relying more and more on Wolsey these days, though he was aware that the man's growing power alarmed others. The nobility still considered him an upstart, while the gentlemen of the Privy Chamber, especially Compton, resented his influence over the King.

'There are those,' Brandon said one day, as they practised at the archery butts, 'who would see Wolsey toppled.'

'I am aware of it,' Harry muttered.

'Buckingham complains of his ruthlessness and his desire for self-aggrandisement. Compton is just jealous.'

Harry stole a glance at Brandon, but there was no sign of jealousy there.

'Wolsey is the most earnest and readiest of all my councillors to advance my will and pleasure,' he countered. 'He disburdens me of much weighty and troublesome business. He shares my tastes in art and building and so many other things. He's a good friend, Brandon, and no threat to my other friendships. Love is not finite!'

'Others do not see it that way. I suspect Bishop Foxe sees himself being eclipsed by a man he advanced.'

'I don't think so,' Harry replied, drawing his bow. 'Foxe is not in the best of health these days and hopes for a peaceful retirement spent looking after the spiritual needs of his diocese, which he has much neglected.'

'Ha!' Brandon guffawed. 'A bishop seeking holiness? What is the world coming to? But at least you'll be rid of one of the greybeards who oppose the war.'

Foxe and his ageing fellows on the Council were not Harry's only gainsayers. On Good Friday, John Colet, the Dean of St Paul's, was invited to preach before him at Greenwich. Harry admired Colet, who was a member of Thomas More's circle and a great scholar who had just founded a school at the cathedral, and he was much looking forward to hearing his homily, settling happily into the royal pew in the Chapel Royal.

'In the name of Christ, amen,' Colet began, then surveyed the congregation, which was full of young gentlemen all avid to prove themselves in a war that was now only a few weeks away. 'My brethren, all good Christians should follow the example of our Lord Jesus Christ, the Prince of Peace. For they who, through hatred or ambition, fight each other, slaughtering one another by turns, are warring under the banner, not of Christ, but of the Devil!'

Harry stirred in his seat, unable to believe his ears. Of course, the humanists hated war, but this was going too far!

'It is a hard thing to die a Christian death,' Colet continued. 'Few enter a war unsullied by hatred or love of gain; can you not see how incompatible a thing it is, that a man should feel that brotherly love without which no one would see God, and yet bury his sword in his brother's heart? I exhort you, follow the example of Christ, not that of a Julius Caesar or an Alexander the Great! An unquiet peace is preferable to a just war.'

Harry looked about him, seeing faces full of dismay and bewilderment. By God, the Dean had overstepped himself! What if his men, whom he was on the point of leading into battle, should feel their courage gone because of this diatribe?

As Colet left the pulpit, a buzz of murmuring broke out.

'He has betrayed the Holy League, the Pope's own alliance!' Compton growled. Even some of the bishops were shaking their heads.

Old Surrey lumbered over. 'Your Grace should take Dean Colet to task!'

'Indeed, I will!' Harry seethed.

He summoned Colet to Greenwich the next day and received him in the garden of the adjacent convent of the Observant Friars. He was surprised to find him looking as amiable and cheerful as ever, and felt somewhat disarmed.

'Let us speak without ceremony, Mr Dean,' he said. 'I have not sent for you to disturb your sacred labours, which have my entire approval, but that I may unburden my conscience of some scruples and, with the help of your counsel, may better discharge the duties of my office.'

It was the right approach, and he now saw why Wolsey had counselled him to adopt it.

'I have offended your Grace, I know,' Colet said, as they began strolling along the pleached paths.

'I must confess I was surprised to hear your homily against war,' Harry admitted. 'But we are at one upon all points, save only that I would have wished you to preach against war at some other time.'

'For Christians, no war is a just one,' Colet said. 'That is a universal truth for all times.'

'Yes, but I am committed to a just cause in France and I have to think of my captains and my soldiers, who must not be put off their duty. You do understand my position? King Louis and his forebears have taken what is rightfully mine, and this war I must undertake is purely defensive, *and* it is in the nature of a crusade, sanctified by his Holiness himself.'

Colet bowed his head. 'I understand perfectly, and I will undo any damage I have done to your Grace's cause. Let me preach at court again, I pray you, and I will speak with such eloquence on the right of Christians to wage war as to inflame even the spiritless and timid.'

'Bravo!' cried Harry, clapping him on the back. 'Let it be done – and now let us go and drink to your health!'

He gestured to his gentlemen, who had been keeping a discreet distance. 'Bring some wine.' When they had done his bidding, he raised his goblet. 'Let every man choose his own doctor. This is mine!'

Harry clenched his hands in anger and glared at his councillors through narrowed eyes. 'Suffolk? So Louis thinks to undermine my throne, to save him the need to engage with me in battle! How craven!'

Surrey spread his hands. 'Sire, I think he will fight you if he must. But by recognising the Duke of Suffolk as the rightful king of England, he means to distract you at this time.'

'But he certainly intends to support him,' Buckingham growled.

'Well, he shall support a king without a head!' Harry snapped. 'Suffolk's family have ever been a thorn in the crown and I will suffer it no longer. He shall go from the Tower to the block. My father had him attainted years ago, but spared his life. I do not mind to be so merciful. The Act of Attainder still stands. He shall die, and I would mete out the same sentence to that traitorous brother of his, but for the fact that he is in France and beyond my reach. See to it!'

Suffolk perished, and Harry found himself all the richer for it, for the Duke had owned many estates and a fine manor house at Ewelme in Oxfordshire, which Harry planned to convert into a beautiful palace. But that would have to wait. First, he was for France, at last!

On a blazing June day, Harry left Greenwich for Dover with Kate by his side. He had appointed her Regent of England in his absence to demonstrate his trust in her. She had wanted to come and wave him farewell, and he had been eager for her to see the splendour and pageantry of his departure, so here they were, riding at the head of a great cavalcade that included a score of peers, not to mention Wolsey on his humble mule. Heralds and trumpeters rode before them, announcing their presence to the crowds who flocked to see them as they wended their way along the leafy roads of Kent.

Harry swung around in the saddle, waving at the people and gazing with pride on the six hundred archers of the Yeomen of the Guard, in their green and white liveries, who marched behind him. He had brought also three hundred servants, his great bed of estate, several suits of armour, brightly coloured tents and pavilions and the choir of the Chapel Royal. The French were not only going to be conquered – they were also to be astounded at his magnificence! He could not wait to board his ship.

There was another, secret reason for his buoyant mood. Kate was with child again, and his head was filled not only with dreams of his coronation at Rheims, but also with joy at the prospect of having a son to succeed him, both in England and France. And now he could see the mighty fortress of Dover ahead, high on the cliffs overlooking the English Channel.

In the ancient keep, he formally invested Kate with the regency, and commanded Archbishop Warham and Surrey, now seventy and too old to go campaigning, to act as her advisers. On the last day of June, he bade her a hearty farewell on the quayside at Dover, kissing away her tears and promising he would stay safe; then he bounded aboard his flagship, leaving the gallant Surrey to comfort her and escort her back to Greenwich.

The French who lined the roads gasped in awe at the sight of Harry riding proudly at the head of his magnificent army. They had probably never seen anything so glorious! It was fitting that they were impressed by their rightful sovereign.

When they met, he thought the Emperor Maximilian was suitably stirred to see his ally with such a formidable fighting force. Resplendent in gold armour, Harry had cantered across the field where their armies were drawn up and greeted the Emperor warmly with a firm handshake, taking in his gilded black armour, prominent hooked nose and sardonic grin.

'Welcome, your Highness!' Maximilian said.

'It is a pleasure to meet your Imperial Majesty!' Harry replied. 'I trust in God that we shall do great things here in France.'

'That is my hope too. Let us go to my tent and discuss our strategies.' The Emperor laid a gauntleted hand on Harry's shoulder in the most paternal fashion. 'It is a shame that King Ferdinand cannot be here, but I know he shares our joint objectives.'

Joint? Harry had been under the impression that Maximilian was supporting his cause because the French were encroaching on the Empire's borders. Harry was to aid him in neutralising that threat, then Maximilian and Ferdinand would assist him in the conquest of France. But probably the Emperor was merely expressing solidarity with Harry; after all, he would benefit from having an ally on the French throne.

Matters moved frustratingly slowly after that first meeting, but finally Harry and Maximilian laid siege to the town of Thérouanne, which threatened neighbouring Burgundy, one of the Emperor's chief territories. Harry set up camp to the east of the walls, surrounding himself with heavy artillery. He took quarters in a wooden cabin flanked by colourful tents, each bearing painted wooden statues of the King's heraldic beasts. Ignoring the foul wet weather, he entertained Maximilian to a feast in a gallery hung with cloth of gold. Since they were constrained to sit and wait for the town to fall, they might as well enjoy themselves.

Infuriatingly, the French managed to get food and other supplies to the besieged townsfolk. Never again, Harry vowed, and moved his headquarters to the tower of Guinegate, where he would be better placed to keep an eye on all comings and goings. While there, he received intelligence that a French army was approaching. They had even attempted diversionary tactics to lure the English forces away. Well, he would put paid to their impudence! Now it truly could be said that this war was defensive.

Riding back to Thérouanne, he gave his captains the order to draw up thousands of soldiers in battle order, ready to face the enemy. He would have led them himself, but his councillors, hovering nearby like clucking hens, fretted that it was too dangerous; he should direct operations from the sidelines. Harry wanted to argue, but Maximilian said it was wise advice, and he did not wish to offend his ally, who clearly had his interests at heart.

Frustrated, itching to be in the midst of the action, he watched as the English bowmen, famed and feared for centuries throughout Christendom, launched a volley of arrows. The French, seeing themselves overwhelmingly outnumbered, began to retreat. Harry could scarcely believe it. It had been so easy! Was all France to fall to him in like fashion? Excitement welled in his breast. It was happening; it was really happening. His dreams were on the cusp of coming true. He looked on, thrilled, as his commanders ordered the English army to charge after the fleeing French, gratified to see that Maximilian's troops were descending on their other flank. In evident panic, the craven enemy soldiers spurred their horses and cast their weapons, horse armour and standards to the ground, thundering away as if the hounds of Hell were after them, with their pursuers chasing them into the distance in a cloud of dust.

'We must send troops in after them and outflank them,' Maximilian said.

'I will lead them!' Harry cried, desperate to be a part of the battle – and cover himself in glory.

'No, *I* will lead them,' the Emperor said firmly, 'and send my men in.' He wheeled his horse around and shouted the order to charge, leaving Harry speechless. Trembling with anger, he saw the Imperial army gallop after the French, saw the French cavalry turn as if they would meet them, and then flee after their fellows.

When they had disappeared from sight, Harry rode back to Guinegate, knowing that the allies had scored a great victory. And it was *his* victory, even though he had not taken part, for it had been he who had drawn up the English forces that had routed the French. The battle had been won before Maximilian made the rash charge that Harry would find hard to forgive. But he was cheered when reports began to filter in, recounting how the French had been pursued for three miles, and that several high-ranking prisoners, among them the valiant Chevalier Bayard and the Duke of Longueville, had been taken. His good mood restored, he thought gleefully of the ransoms they could command.

Brandon and Sir Henry Guildford appeared, smiling broadly. Brandon was serving as marshal of the royal army, and had led the vanguard, and Harry had seen for himself how valiantly he had acquitted himself, while Guildford had proved his worth as the King's standard-bearer. Brave men, both; men to be proud of.

Six days later, Thérouanne surrendered, and Harry rode into the town in triumph to receive the keys, expecting the citizens to welcome him as a saviour. Instead, he was met with a sullen silence from those who had slunk from their houses to stare at him as he passed by. They looked pinched and starved. Well, serve them right! They should have surrendered at the outset. Aware of the hatred in their faces, he felt chilled.

'Set the soldiers to work pulling down the walls,' he ordered. 'Then burn the town, but turn the people out first. They shall not stay to harass the Emperor's territory another day.'

'His Holiness has sent your Grace his congratulations,' Wolsey said a week later, as Harry and Maximilian sat at table, the remains of a fine repast between them. Harry threw a glance at the Emperor.

Had Pope Leo sent *him* congratulations too?

If Maximilian was put out, there was no sign of it, but Harry had learned that, with him, you never knew. The old fox just sat there, smiling.

'Oh, and Sir, the Queen has written again, desiring news of you. She asks after your health and trusts in God that you will come home shortly with tidings of another great victory. Your Grace, she says she can take no comfort or pleasure unless she hears from me.'

'I will write to her,' Harry promised. 'Is she keeping well?' He needed to know that her pregnancy was progressing satisfactorily.

'It seems so.' Wolsey smiled. 'She says she has been horribly busy making standards, banners and badges to send to us.'

'We will have need of them,' Harry said, 'for my next objective is to take Boulogne. With that and Calais in our hands, we can command the Channel and use the ports as a bridgehead for bringing over more soldiers.'

'First, I think,' Maximilian said, 'we should go to Lille to see my daughter, the Regent. She has followed our campaign with great interest, and would be delighted to receive your Grace.'

Harry had never met the Archduchess Margaret, but he had often corresponded with her, ruler to ruler, and was repeatedly surprised to find himself dealing with a woman on equal political footing – *and* admiring her abilities, for she governed the Netherlands and Burgundy with wisdom and integrity. It was against the natural order of the world for a woman to rule. Women had not the capacity of men; they were inferior creatures, weak and emotional. Yet there were rare honourable exceptions – Kate's mother, Queen Isabella, for example, and this Archduchess Margaret. His own grandmother, the Lady Margaret, had been another such.

'Might I suggest,' said Maximilian, 'that you take the town of Tournai, which is near Lille, and consolidate our supremacy in the east.'

'But what of Boulogne?' Harry thought his plan was better.

'We march there afterwards!'

It could only be a short delay, Harry told himself. There were weeks of the campaigning season left before winter set in.

They arrived at Lille early in September, just as Harry's army was surrounding Tournai. The Regent afforded them a lavish welcome, receiving them with every honour. After the feast that evening, Harry showed off his musical skills, playing the lute, harp, lyre, flute and horn in succession for the company, to great ovation, then, nimble as a stag, dancing until dawn.

Three days of festivities and merriment followed. The Burgundian nobility had hastened to pay their respects to him, showering him with praise, and the ladies fawned all over him. He was supposed to be taking his ease, but he took pleasure in astonishing everyone with his energy. He jousted before the Archduchess and her thirteen-year-old nephew, the very solemn Infante Charles, the heir to Castile, whose heavy Habsburg jaw was so misshapen that his mouth seemed permanently to be open. Harry felt sorry for the boy, whose father, Philip of Burgundy, had died young and whose mother – Kate's sister, the beautiful, tormented Juana – was said to be mad and had been shut up in a convent, with Ferdinand ruling Castile in her name. Harry wondered if it were true. He could easily imagine that old villain Ferdinand putting it about that Queen Juana was insane, just to gain control in Castile. And yet, there had been talk that Juana had refused to relinquish her husband's body for burial and had dragged it around Spain for months, opening the coffin and kissing the corpse. No sane person did that.

He wished Charles would unbend and enjoy life, because he was betrothed to Harry's beautiful sister Mary, and Harry wanted Mary to be happy in her marriage. Then he forgot about the boy in the excitement of running many courses against Brandon and the Emperor's champion, Guillaume de Ghislain, and breaking numerous lances, to deafening acclaim.

The next afternoon, Harry showed off his skills in archery, competing with the Duke of Longueville, then danced with Margaret and her ladies in the evening. It was so hot beneath the myriad candles that he threw off his doublet and shoes and continued around

116

the floor in his unlaced shirt and stockinged feet, aware that the Archduchess was sneaking admiring glances at the golden hairs on his chest. He smiled to himself. In youth, Margaret had been married to Kate's brother, the ill-fated Infante Juan, who had died young, like Harry's brother Arthur, of consumption. It had been widely rumoured that his lusty bride had worn him out in the marriage bed.

Other eyes were on Margaret. Brandon, a widower these two years, had hardly taken his eyes off her. When there was a break for refreshments, Harry returned to his seat on the dais and beckoned his friend over.

'I see you've taken a fancy to the Archduchess!' he teased.

Brandon flushed. 'Is it that obvious?'

'Yes. I reckon everyone here is gossiping about it,' Harry smirked. 'She's a comely woman!'

'And her father is giving you the eagle Habsburg eye. It would not benefit Anglo-Imperial relations if you cause a scandal.'

'I had no intention of doing so,' Brandon retorted, sounding injured. 'I had something far more honourable in mind.'

Harry whistled. 'By God, Charles! You aim high.'

'Would you object?'

'I might remind you that you are precontracted to Elizabeth Grey.'

Brandon snorted. 'Betrothals can be broken. I'm sure there must be some proof of consanguinity.'

'No doubt there is. And if you could extricate yourself honourably, I would smile on a match with the Regent. It would be to my advantage to have my greatest friend entrenched at her court, upholding England's interests.'

Brandon smiled. 'You can count on me to do that.'

'I would miss you,' Harry told him.

'Then we'd have to visit each other. I imagine you will be in France often.'

'Indeed, I will. I have resolved to divide my time between my two kingdoms.'

'Then I will not be far away. Harry, I will be forever in your debt.

I am smitten with the lady – and not just with her royal birth and riches.'

'Then go, my friend, and woo her!'

'Watch me!' Brandon said.

The guests of honour were being summoned to a banquet in a pleasure house set in the palace gardens amid damask roses. As sweetmeats and drinks were being served, Harry led Brandon over to where the Archduchess was talking to two noblewomen, who curtseyed low as he appeared.

'My lady, allow me to introduce my great friend, Sir Charles Brandon,' he said. Brandon bowed low.

Margaret's heavy features relaxed into a smile. She gave him her hand to kiss. 'Any friend of yours, King Henry, is a friend of mine too. I trust you are enjoying our little entertainment, Sir Charles?'

'All the more for being in the presence of so great and fair a lady,' Brandon replied, gazing at her intently.

Margaret blushed, looking more like a young maiden than a stateswoman. 'I am told that you distinguished yourself at Thérouanne,' she said.

'I will leave you to tell her Highness of your wondrous exploits,' Harry said. 'If you will excuse me, Madam, I think your father would like to speak to me.'

Maximilian had not been looking his way at all, but Harry thought it a good idea to leave Brandon to work his magic on Margaret. Not that he would have to work too hard, he thought, amused. He was right. As he and the Emperor discussed siege tactics, the couple remained together, talking in the most animated fashion.

The next day, as Harry and Maximilian rode to Tournai to see how matters were progressing, Harry noticed that Brandon was looking mightily pleased with himself. That was fast progress, he thought; but then Brandon always had enjoyed success with the ladies. This might be the beginning of something beneficial to them all.

But all thoughts of nuptial intrigues were swept from his mind by news from England. Taking advantage of his absence, James IV, who had naturally allied himself to King Louis, had crossed the Scottish border with an army of eighty thousand men and invaded England. Surrey had hastily raised an army and was already marching north. Kate had written to say that she herself was on her way to Buckingham to rally the troops. Clearly, she had inherited the martial spirit of her mother.

Harry was in a fever to be back in England. He should not be here trying to take a small town when his throne was under threat. The Scots were England's ancient enemies, and fierce too, and it was only fitting that he should be riding at the head of Surrey's army to deal with them as they deserved. He spared a thought for his sister Margaret, whose loyalties must be cruelly torn at this moment. Father had never envisioned this when he married her to James; their marriage was supposed to herald perpetual peace. Ha!

Maximilian was supportive. 'Your Highness must do whatever is necessary,' he said. 'It would be a shame to abandon the siege, since there are signs that the resolve of the people of Tournai is weakening. But you must decide where your priorities lie.' He placed a comforting hand on Harry's sleeve.

Harry's head began to ache as he debated what he should do. Wolsey was of the opinion that, if he took his army home, he might arrive too late to trounce the Scots. The councillors were of the same opinion.

'By the time your Grace returns, Surrey will be in the north. He is a great soldier. Put your trust in him. With luck, God may give you the victory over both your enemies.'

In the end, the decision was made for him. Surrey had vanquished the Scots in a great battle on Flodden Moor in Northumberland, leaving James dead on the field, alongside the flower of the Scottish nobility and ten thousand of their countrymen. Harry stood in his tent, staring at Kate's letter, his head in turmoil, knowing that Flodden was a far more important victory than anything he would achieve this year in France. Scotland could never recover from this defeat. Its new King, young James V, was a mere infant whose realm would be ruled by a council of regency – and everyone knew how treacherous and quarrelsome the Scottish lords were. Not for nothing did the Scriptures say, 'Woe to thee, O land, when thy King is a child.'

Yes, it was a resounding victory, and he owed a huge debt of gratitude to Surrey, and to Kate, for all her valiant efforts. Yet he should have been there, leading the English army. But James, treacherous, perfidious James, had stolen a march on him.

He was still feeling injured and cheated days later, when another letter arrived from Kate, who was still exulting in the great victory that God had sent Harry's subjects in his absence. He drew in his breath as he read it. *To my thinking,* she had written, *this battle has been to your Grace and all your realm the greatest honour that ever could be, more than should you win the crown of France.*

Enclosed with the letter was a piece of the Scottish King's blood-stained coat, which Kate had sent as a trophy. She explained that she had wanted to send his body, but the Council would not allow it. She prayed that God would bring Harry home shortly, for without him she could take no joy in life. In the meantime, she was going on pilgrimage to Our Lady of Walsingham. He understood then that there had been no mishap with her pregnancy and that she was going to pray for a son, an heir to England, to crown these victories.

All was as it should be. The Scots were vanquished, the French trounced for now. Tournai fell to Harry as easily as a leaf from a tree. It had been a year of victories, and he ought to be jubilant. But he could not banish Kate's words from his mind. She had belittled his success, setting it at naught against her own. And there was no time to make an assault on Boulogne and strike a victory that would make him feel better, for it was now autumn and the end of the campaigning season. Harry and his allies signed a treaty pledging themselves to launch a combined invasion of France before next June. Under its terms, the marriage of Mary and the Infante Charles was to take place by May. Harry stayed on in Burgundy, where the Archduchess arranged three weeks of jousts and revels to celebrate the treaty. Brandon was still manoeuvring around her, making his interest plain, and she seemed to be enjoying the flirtation. Then, late one night, at a banquet, he produced a gold ring and pushed it on her finger, drawing off one of hers at the same time, and placing it on his own hand. She stared at him, then started to giggle.

'That was presumptuous of you, Sir Charles! People will think we are betrothed.' She did not look displeased.

Harry stepped forward. 'I heartily recommend this good knight as a husband, Madam!'

'Is that so?' she replied. 'As you see, I still wear black for my dear late Duke of Savoy. I have not thought of wedding again. However, I might be persuaded to change my mind if the right match presents itself.' With a dimpled smile, she moved away.

But there was Maximilian, glowering at both Charles and Harry. 'Wait, daughter!' he barked. 'What are you thinking of? Habsburg princesses do not wed low-born knights.' Harry winced at the slight to Charles, who had fought so bravely for him and the Emperor.

Margaret smiled. 'Sir, any rumours about me and a certain gentleman are base lies.'

People were staring at them, listening avidly. Harry felt he ought to intercede. 'Madam, I apologise for any annoyance that my friend's jesting may have caused.'

'It is nothing,' Margaret smiled. Maximilian nodded. If Brandon were to press his suit, he would face an uphill climb, with little hope of reaching the summit of success. Yet he seemed determined on making the ascent.

The festivities continued in a whirl of feasting and dancing. One evening, Harry and Brandon slipped away and changed into costumes of cloth of gold, then returned to the great hall and performed a masque, in which they danced and sang for the company. Afterwards, they cast off their outer garments and distributed them amongst the ladies. Harry handed his cap to a laughing young brunette who had stumbled into his path. Her sallow face was flushed with wine, although she could not have been much more than twelve years old.

'And who are you, fair maiden?' he asked, rather drunk himself.

'Your Grace, I am Anne Boleyn,' she said, executing a very elegant curtsey. 'My father, Sir Thomas, serves you as ambassador.' She tipped her golden bonnet at a jaunty angle on her head above a pearl-netted caul.

'It becomes you!' he said. 'Will you do me the pleasure of dancing with me, Mistress Anne?'

She curtseyed again, and he led her in a lively *branle*, both of them leaping and kicking as the courtiers formed a circle around them and clapped.

'Bravo!' cried the Regent, who was standing close to Brandon.

'Bravo, Harry!' echoed Brandon.

As the music drew to a close, Harry bowed, thanked Anne Boleyn and turned away. Across the room, among the Archduchess's ladies, he noticed a much prettier blonde girl with pouting lips whose eyes lit up invitingly as he approached. He bowed and held out his hand.

Her name, she told him, as they paced across the floor, was Etiennette de la Baume, and she was the daughter of a French nobleman. She was quite enchanting. Three dances later, they were still together, and Harry was loath to end it.

Why not? he asked himself. No one need be any the wiser, and Kate would never find out. Her condition was common knowledge now. Given the demands the regency had made on her, it was a miracle that she was still with child, for which they owed very much to God. Even if he was in England now, he could not touch her. But he was a man with needs.

At the end of the next dance, a saltarello, his eyes met Etiennette's, and he bent and kissed her on the lips. And everything led from there . . .

Etiennette was not just a responsive lover. Harry found himself enjoying talking to her. She was witty and realistic, asking nothing from him but the pleasure of the moment.

To facilitate their secret trysts, Etiennette disguised herself as a page, binding up her hair and pulling her cap down so that it hid her face. In such a guise she bedded with Harry, amid much suppressed laughter lest the guards outside the door hear them.

'My father is looking to find me a lordly husband,' she told him as she lay in his arms afterwards, her fair tresses tumbling over the pillow.

'Marriage can be a beautiful thing,' he murmured in her ear. 'The love and companionship between husband and wife are blessings to be cherished. I tremble when I think of how God has entrusted my Queen to me, and how I must use her so that, when God demands His own again, I return her to him as pure as when I received her.'

'I have never heard of a man speak of his wife like that,' Etiennette replied. 'You clearly love her, so why are you here with me?'

'Because you are here, and she is across the sea, and I like you, and I cannot live like a monk.' He pulled her close. 'I am not using you, my little page. You are very dear to me, and I care what happens to you. When you marry, you must let me know, and I will send you ten thousand crowns towards your marriage portion.'

'You would do that for me?' She sat up, amazed. 'How will I explain it?'

'You may say that I took a paternal interest in you and other young ladies when I visited the court here. Now, come and thank me properly!' He drew her down into the bed beside him and proceeded to tickle her.

Chapter 8

1513

Late in October, Harry's fleet made port at Dover and, taking just a small company with him, he galloped towards Richmond, passing cheering, waving crowds. 'Look at them! Love for your Grace is universal with all who see you,' observed Wolsey, riding beside him. 'To them, you are not a person of this world, but one descended from Heaven!'

Harry smiled broadly. His hand was weary with waving, his face muscles aching with smiling, yet still he must acknowledge his subjects' acclaim, for their love was very necessary to him.

He raced the final miles to Richmond, longing to see Kate. He could not wait to lay at her feet the keys of the cities he had taken. But first, here was Surrey, come to be congratulated. The old man knelt before him in the archway of the great gatehouse, but when he raised his face to his sovereign, his expression was nothing like that of a conquering hero; in fact, he looked stricken.

'What is it, my lord?' Harry barked.

'Your Grace, a word in private, please.' He led Harry into the guard chamber and closed the door. 'Forgive me for being the bearer of bad tidings. The Queen's son came early and lived only a short while. We thought you should be told, Sire, before you see her. I am so very sorry.'

Harry stood there, reeling. All his hopes dashed a third time. Was he ever to have an heir? Had he offended God in some way?

He shook his head, bewildered. 'Excuse me, my lord. I am not myself. This has come as a shock.'

Surrey laid a grizzled hand on his. 'I know what it is to lose a child, Sire. I have lost four sons myself.'

'But you have others – a large family!'

'Yes, your Grace. I counsel patience. God will grant you an heir in His own good time.'

'I wish I could believe it,' Harry replied miserably. 'The meanest peasant in my realm has a son to inherit his cooking pot and his pig, yet I, the King, have none, and I have most need of an heir! But I must go to the Queen and comfort her. She must not think I blame her.'

'I fear she does, Sire. She is very anxious about it.'

'Then I'll try to allay her fears.'

Kate was waiting in the great hall, her ladies around her. Harry folded her in his arms, and it was such a loving meeting that everyone around them rejoiced and applauded. But he could feel the tension in her. As soon as he could, he dismissed everyone and sat down by the fire, pulling her on to his lap and kissing her soundly.

'I fear I have overburdened you with duties, Kate,' he said gently. 'They told me what happened. I am very, very sorry.' He drew her closer.

She was trying not to cry, he could see it.

'It is the will of God,' he said, near to tears himself. 'All I care about is that you are all right.'

'I am much restored,' she told him. 'The sight of you, my Henry, is all I needed to return me to perfect health.'

'God be thanked! Kate, we must not mourn, for this is a time to be joyful. Come, let me greet the ladies!'

He lay with her that night, even though she was still bleeding slightly. Her breasts and belly were slacker than before, three fruitless pregnancies having taken their toll on her body. He tried not to show his dismay. He took his pleasure as passionately as usual, but gently, mindful of her comfort. Afterwards he kissed her and lay beside her, his arms curled around her.

The next morning, he met with his Council and formally thanked Surrey and everyone else who had worked to counter the threat from the Scots.

The next matter on the agenda was the war with France.

'It has cost one million pounds so far,' Archbishop Warham said, 'and your Grace has taken two small towns to the benefit mainly of the Emperor.'

'Graceless dogholes, they're calling 'em,' observed Lord Thomas Howard.

Harry bridled. That they should dare to belittle his triumphs! To return home in glory – and now this?

'They were important strategic victories,' he protested, feeling like banging his fist on the table.

'I beg to disagree with your Grace,' Surrey countered. 'Tell him, Master Almoner.'

'The fact is,' Wolsey said, 'that your Grace need not have gone to war at all. We have learned that King Louis made peace with Pope Leo before you even left England.'

Harry drew in his breath, mortified. He had been made a fool of! 'And neither Maximilian nor Ferdinand knew anything of it? I find that hard to believe.'

'Evidently not, Sir,' Wolsey replied. 'They have been wrong-footed as much as your Grace has. And both are fully resolved to invade France with you next year.'

'Good! Louis shall answer for himself then! As for his Holiness, words fail me. He is as crafty as any Borgia!'

'Alas, the Holy See is not as holy as we might wish,' Wolsey observed. 'The Pope is a prince like any other, and protective of his landed interests.'

'Well, he too shall be taught a lesson about fidelity,' Harry said, his mouth setting in a prim line. He would not be deterred, even by the Vatican! He had acquitted himself well in France and, by St George, with the help of his allies, he would conquer it within a twelvemonth!

Harry found himself liking his hostage, the Duke of Longueville, who was also the Grand Chamberlain of France. Anxious to comply with the rules of chivalry, he lodged him in a fine apartment in the palace of the Tower of London and treated him as an honoured guest, often inviting him to court. When Kate, at his behest, entertained the Duke to a feast at the palace of Havering in Essex, a masque was performed for his pleasure, followed by dancing, during which the noble guest managed to partner most of the ladies, charming them all, especially pert Jane Popincourt, one of the Queen's maids-of-honour, whom Harry rather fancied himself. Afterwards, Harry gave handsome gifts to the Duke and his attendants.

'Your Majesty is most kind.' The Frenchman smiled. 'I might be tempted to stay in England for ever.'

'And we would be glad if you did. But I fear that France needs you.'

'France will have to wait, your Majesty!' A look of sadness briefly clouded the Duke's swarthy face. 'My family have a great ransom to raise.'

Harry was seized with a generous impulse. 'Then I shall pay half of it, even though it is to my advantage in all respects to keep you here.'

The Duke gaped at him. 'Your Majesty is most bountiful!'

Harry was about to reply when he espied his seventeen-year-old sister Mary making sheep's eyes at Brandon – and not for the first time. He frowned.

'Have I offended your Majesty?' the Duke asked, looking bewildered.

'Not at all,' Harry assured him, collecting himself. 'If you will excuse me.' He bowed and sped over to where Mary was surrounded by a group of adoring gallants, all vying with each other to win her smiles, for she was a paradise to behold. Tall and graceful, with red-gold hair and the fairest of complexions, she had a charming, lively manner and all the courtly graces. Tonight, she was in her element, revelling in being the centre of masculine attention, yet still her gaze kept straying to where Brandon stood laughing with Compton.

The men bowed as Harry joined them. 'A word,' he murmured in Mary's ear.

'Excuse me, good sirs,' the minx dimpled. 'Yes, brother dear?'

He drew her away. 'I've seen you looking at Brandon, and I just wanted to say that he is not for you.'

She pouted. 'There's no harm in looking! Since I am doomed to wed that miserable Infante, you can at least allow me the pleasure of admiring a man who knows how to treat a lady.'

Harry paused. 'How do you know how Brandon treats ladies?'

'By his very demeanour, of course.'

'I hope he has not presumed to pay any addresses to you!'

'Not at all. He is always respectful.'

Harry suspected that there had been some dealings between them. Was that rogue pursuing his sister as well as the Archduchess? 'Are you sure he has not courted you in any way?'

'Of course not!' But a telltale blush had risen to Mary's cheeks.

'If he ever presumes too far, you are to tell me!'

She winked at him. 'As if I would not!' She tripped away to rejoin her gallants, leaving Harry fuming, aware that she could always run rings around him.

Harry kept Christmas at Greenwich, laying on lavish revels to cheer his nobles. Guildford and Brandon put on a mumming play, in which Nicholas Carew, one of the young gentlemen who had been brought up with Harry, took part, with his pretty wife Elizabeth. Carew was a lot younger than Harry, being only seventeen, but was already a fearsome opponent in the lists as well as being excellent company. But it was Elizabeth who drew Harry's attention, with her wanton eyes and her low-cut gowns. He sought her out in the dance, taking care to partner other ladies so that Kate would not think he was favouring one too much. Elizabeth was the daughter of the Queen's vice-chamberlain, and it would not do to cause any scandal, especially after what had happened with Buckingham's sister. Besides, this was a holy season and not the time to be contemplating fornication. Reluctantly, he bowed to Elizabeth, resolutely ignoring the invitation in her eyes, and rejoined Kate on the dais.

Soon after Christmas, Harry felt feverish. His head hurt so badly he could barely see straight.

'I'm aching all over,' he told Dr Chamber, one of his physicians.

The doctor tested his urine. 'Has your Grace vomited?'

'No, but I'm damned tired.'

'Please remove your shirt.' Chamber peered at his body, both front and back. Harry could sense him tensing. 'Hmm. A rash is developing. I fear it is smallpox, your Grace.'

'Smallpox? Dear God!' Terror gripped him. He had not reigned for five years yet! And he had no son to succeed him. Even worse, he had never conquered his abhorrence of disease and what it could do to a man.

With an immense effort, he summoned his courage. It would not do for a king to look craven. 'Will I die?'

'Not if I can help it, Sir,' Chamber replied. 'Now your Grace must go to bed and rest.'

Harry lay delirious, burning up, yet icy cold, huddled in fine lawn sheets and woollen blankets, having unwittingly tossed off his fur counterpane. His bolster was sodden with sweat. He was dimly aware of the doctors around him, their probing fingers and their anxious voices. Then a woman spoke.

'Is he in danger?' she asked. He could hear the catch in her voice. It was Kate. Or was it his mother?

He did not hear the reply. He existed now in a twilight world in which the days and nights ran into each other. He had never felt so ill.

And then he came to himself.

'Your Grace has made a miraculous recovery, thanks be to God,' Dr Chamber told him, looking rather smug. 'We feared for your life, but you will mend now.'

Harry crossed himself. It was horrifying to learn that he had been close to death. But the life force in him was strong. He tried to sit up. 'I think I owe thanks to you too, my good doctor. By St George, I stink,' he sniffed. 'Ask them to bring scented water and a clean nightshirt. I never could bear to be dirty.'

He made a rapid recovery. By the beginning of February, he had risen from his bed, fierce against France and eager to start campaigning again. At Candlemas, after High Mass, he created Brandon duke of Suffolk and restored to the valiant Surrey the dukedom of Norfolk. The ceremony of ennoblement took place in the great chamber at Lambeth Palace, the London residence of Archbishop Warham. Kate and her ladies were present, with the Duke of Longueville and the peers who were in London to attend Parliament.

As Harry processed down the chamber afterwards, he was aware of an undercurrent of disapproval. His advancement of Brandon was not popular; many considered it surprising, and Buckingham, who had not troubled to hide his fury, was nowhere to be seen. He and most of the older nobility considered Brandon an upstart for his lack of noble lineage. But Wolsey had urged his ennoblement.

'Your Grace might render him more meet a husband for the Regent Margaret,' he had argued. Harry had known there was an ulterior motive. As soon as Wolsey knew that Surrey was to be restored to his father's dukedom, he had determined to counter-balance his influence and Buckingham's on the Council, with Brandon as his advocate. Harry saw the wisdom in this. New blood and new men were what he needed!

Brandon – my lord of Suffolk now – emerged from the presence chamber in Harry's wake, resplendent in his velvet robes and ducal coronet. Harry had granted him the estates confiscated from the previous Duke of Suffolk, and he was now one of the richest peers in the realm. His resemblance to his master remained so striking that he looked like a second king. But he was taking it all in his stride. Harry had seen no one bear so great a rise with so easy a dignity.

'Well met, my chief nobleman of England!' he cried, clapping Suffolk on the back, ignoring the barely concealed anger of some watching lords.

'The King has turned a stable boy into a nobleman,' one muttered.

Harry swung around, glaring, but could not identify the culprit among the false smiles.

He made a point of congratulating Norfolk warmly. 'In recognition of your victory at Flodden, I grant you the right to display the royal arms of Scotland beside your own, with the Scottish lion impaled with an arrow, as King James' heart was. And I am confirming you as Earl Marshal of England, the office your ancestors nobly bore.'

The old man had tears in his eyes. 'That I should live to see this day, Sir. I thank your Grace from the bottom of my heart.'

'A toast to you, Father!' Norfolk's son, Thomas, now earl of Surrey, raised a goblet. He too had fought bravely at Flodden. His first wife had been Harry's aunt, Anne of York, who had died young; now he was married to Buckingham's fourteen-year-old daughter Elizabeth – and he forty-one, the old goat! Harry knew that the blue-blooded Howards had little love for Suffolk and were poised to destroy him should the chance arise, but he needed to keep them sweet, for they served him well. He raised his glass and joined in the toast.

He had not forgotten the man who had worked so hard to make the French campaign a success. Wolsey was now bishop of Lincoln.

'We should drink to you too, my friend!' he said, turning to the new prelate, who bowed and smiled. Again, the vultures of the court looked ready to swoop. But Harry ignored them. Good service deserved to be rewarded, and he needed men like Wolsey and Suffolk and Boleyn. They were proof that an ancient pedigree was not necessarily a prerequisite for advancement at court.

'What?' Harry roared, his voice ringing through the council chamber. He could not quite grasp that there was such duplicity in the world. 'Are you telling me that Ferdinand and Maximilian – my allies – have gone behind my back and signed secret treaties with Louis?'

'I fear it is true, your Grace,' Norfolk said. A frisson of outrage was palpable among the councillors. 'We have the reports here from your agents.'

'Then I have been made to look a fool!' Harry snatched them and read quickly, clenching his fists and tasting bitter gall in his throat. He sat there, speechless, devastated at their desertion. He had trusted them, thought them men of honour. Well, he would never be so trusting again.

'The ramifications of this alliance breaking down are manifold,' Warham observed. 'The Princess Mary's marriage to the Infante Charles cannot now go ahead, for Maximilian's council has refused to accept her as his bride.'

Another body blow. Mary had been destined to become queen of Spain and – God willing – Holy Roman Empress, a glorious future that augured well for England's prosperity.

'But preparations for the wedding are well advanced!' Harry cried. 'They are to be married in May, and I have spent a king's ransom on the Princess's trousseau, jewellery, furnishings and plate. Her retinue is drawn up.'

'Sir, there will be no wedding,' Norfolk said gently.

Harry was about to explode again when Wolsey spoke. 'Your Grace, there is an advantageous way to counteract this misfortune. You yourself might consider an alliance with France.'

Everyone stared at him.

'But we are at war with France!' Harry protested.

'Wars never brought prosperity,' Wolsey continued. 'Peace with France will save England's face and bring many benefits. And I hear that King Louis is looking for a wife.'

'No,' Harry said. 'France is mine and I mean to win it!'

'But without allies, it will be a costly struggle.' Wolsey leaned forward. 'I am not advocating abandoning your Grace's ambitions in that direction. I merely advise postponing the enterprise until you are in a position to pursue it. The Princess may yet be a queen – and I think Louis will be eager to come to terms.'

A few councillors nodded sagely. Harry glared at them, disgusted. Old greybeards, always urging caution. They had never wanted war in the first place. They had forgotten what it was like to have martial blood running in your veins, to be impelled to pursue the right, and be determined on victory. He could not abandon his dream of the French crown. He would not!

'You can all forget that idea,' he said brusquely. 'As for the perfidy of Ferdinand and Maximilian, I will sleep on the matter and advise you tomorrow.'

Someone must pay for this, he fumed, as he stalked down the gallery to the royal apartments. He had been grossly misled! And who had misled him? Kate. She was the faithless Ferdinand's daughter and she had abused Harry's trust by urging him to ally with her father, promising him the world!

'Your father has deceived me!' he roared, crashing into her chamber.

'I will not believe it!' she cried. 'He loves you.'

'Ha! You are an innocent, Kate – or so you pretend! I have been duped and made a fool of in the eyes of Christendom. Hear this: Ferdinand and Maximilian, who are supposed to be my allies, have signed secret treaties with King Louis, leaving me to fight France alone. No, hold your peace, you will hear me out before you spring to your father's defence, for it is clear now that neither of them ever had any intention of helping me to win the French crown. The worst of it is that Louis had agreed with them beforehand that I should be allowed to take Tournai and Thérouanne so that I would go home satisfied and leave them all to pursue their devilish ends.'

Kate stood there, mute and shamefaced. As he ranted at her, she began to cry, but he was in no mood to take pity on her.

'This is your fault!' he shouted. 'For years you've been urging me to take your father's advice, and now see where it has led me! And *you* must bear the responsibility for your father's desertion!'

She tried to protest, but in vain.

'I heeded you, fool that I was,' he raged. 'Now I find myself wedded to the daughter of a man who was my enemy all along.'

'It does not matter who my father is,' she wept, deeply distressed now. 'What matters is the love and trust we have between us.'

'Don't talk to me of love and trust!' Harry spat. 'That has been betrayed, and in future, Madam, I will not be listening to you!'

Hot with rage, he stormed out of the door and slammed it behind him.

'I want a divorce!' he demanded of Wolsey, having summoned him to his closet. 'Can it be accomplished? I will pay the Pope's price.'

The normally urbane Wolsey was clearly shocked. 'Your Grace, I urge caution. There are no grounds.'

'She has betrayed my trust and she is barren! Are they not grounds enough?'

'Not in the eyes of the Church, Sire.'

'But is not her barrenness a sign that God does not smile on my marriage?'

'Her Grace has borne two sons; that they died is not her fault. And you are both young yet. There is plenty of time.'

'You're one to talk,' Harry snarled, pacing up and down like a caged lion. 'You advocate a peace with France, so why should you champion one who is a friend to Spain?'

Wolsey held his gaze. 'Because of the great respect and love I have for the Queen, Sire, and because putting away such a great lady will bring down the wrath of Spain and the Empire on you. But if you are bent on a divorce, I will put out discreet feelers as to how the matter would be viewed in Rome.'

'See to it!' Harry commanded.

After several sleepless nights and an agony of indecision, Harry was gradually coming around to favouring a French alliance. It was chiefly down to Wolsey's excellent powers of persuasion. His friend was now his chief councillor; even Suffolk did not enjoy as much influence. Harry still loved him above all other men, but Suffolk had been bested by a far more able rival.

If Suffolk strove to hide his resentment, there was open mutual hatred between the Howards and Wolsey. Aged as he was, Norfolk was determined to unseat the man he called a low-born upstart and was relentless in trying to poison Harry's mind against him. And Wolsey, in turn, was doing his best to unseat the Duke.

Harry was learning fast that it was essential to maintain good relations with everyone who served him well, and to keep the peace between his councillors. It was fortunate that most of them actually often found themselves in agreement with Wolsey's policies and were ready to set aside their prejudices and work with him. Yet there were those like Buckingham who opposed everything he did on principle.

Buckingham made no secret of the fact that he loathed Wolsey; he was his greatest enemy. Those aggrieved lords who felt that the butcher's son was usurping their traditional privilege of being chief advisers to the King had rallied behind the Duke. There came the day when Harry sat down to dine with Wolsey in his privy chamber and it was Buckingham's turn to have the honour of presenting the golden basin for the King to wash his hands in. After Harry had finished, Wolsey smiled at his rival and dipped his fingers in the same water.

Harry would not forget the look of outrage on Buckingham's face, or the water that somehow splashed out of the basin, soaking Wolsey's shoes.

'You did that deliberately, my lord!' Wolsey snapped, scowling.

'I, my lord Bishop? It was an accident.' Buckingham smirked.

'And I am supposed to believe that?'

'Gentlemen, please!' Harry intervened. 'I'm sure his Grace of Buckingham will apologise.' He looked up expectantly at his cousin.

'I apologise,' the Duke muttered, with ill grace.

Why could the man not realise that, his hatred of Wolsey apart, it was his overweening pride, his aloof manner and his sheer incompetence that prevented him from rising to the kind of eminence Wolsey enjoyed? But he was too stupid. Instead, he had to parade his bitterness at being excluded from the royal counsels.

Now the insufferable fellow was standing stiffly to attention, reeking of disapproval, as Wolsey proceeded once more to enumerate to Harry all the good reasons why he ought to make peace with the

French. He must be furious that Harry was not including him in the conversation or asking for his opinion, but Harry had no need to. He was well aware that, like most of the older nobility, Buckingham hated the French, England's traditional enemy, and on principle would never bring himself to approve of Wolsey's foreign policy. Deep in his heart, Harry felt the same, but he could see the wisdom of Wolsey's advice and took a mischievous pleasure in discomfiting the Duke.

'Very well,' he told Wolsey, 'I will extend the hand of friendship to Louis. See to it, Thomas.'

Buckingham looked as if about to suffer an apoplexy.

'As your Grace wishes,' Wolsey said smugly.

To mark the coming of May, Harry held a tournament in the new tiltyard he had built at Greenwich. He and Suffolk appeared in the lists disguised as hermits, Harry in a white velvet habit with a cloak of leather and cloth of silver, Suffolk in black. Before the jousts began, they threw off their disguises and tossed them to the Queen and her ladies, who were seated in the magnificent viewing gallery between high octagonal brick towers with pinnacles. As Harry bowed in the saddle to her, Kate smiled at him for the first time in weeks, for there had been a coolness between them after their quarrel. But, as his anger abated, he had found himself missing her company and her caresses. Tonight, he told himself, he would return to her bed. England needed an heir, and it would be good to lie in her arms again. He had decided not to pursue his inquiries about an annulment; he would tell Wolsey to countermand his instructions to the agents who had been sent to Rome.

Three weeks later, Harry emerged from the Bishop's Palace by St Paul's Cathedral, wearing robes of purple satin chequered with gold flowers, a jewelled collar worth a well full of gold and a cap of purple velvet with jewelled rosettes, and mounted his beautiful black palfrey. Thousands had come to watch him ride in procession to the cathedral to receive the signal honour conferred upon him by Pope Leo, who had been offended by the duplicity of Ferdinand and Maximilian and wanted to reassure Harry of his friendship and retain his goodwill as an ally.

At the great doors, Harry dismounted and walked to the high altar, where the Papal envoy waited with a sword and cap of maintenance consecrated by his Holiness. As the King knelt, two noblemen girded him with the sword and placed the cap on his head. It was of purple satin, a foot high, with an embroidered brim and pendant tails of ermine. Then he stood up and made an entire circuit of the vast church, so that everyone in the congregation could see the Pope's gifts. As he departed, the crowds were thronging outside to watch him return to the Bishop's Palace carrying the cap on the tip of the gilded sword.

He was in a high good mood when, in June, dressed in cloth of gold with a whistle on a gold chain around his neck – the insignia of the supreme commander of the navy – he travelled in his state barge with Kate and Mary from Greenwich to Erith, where a new warship lay in dock, ready to be launched. Sitting in the statehouse with the windows open and the breeze from the river ruffling his long hair, he felt exhilarated. The sea was in his blood; ships were a passion with him. He had been steadily building up his navy, determined to make England a power to be reckoned with on the high seas.

And there she was, his finest ship yet, the *Henry Grace à Dieu*, which people were already calling the *Great Harry*. She had no equal in bulk, towering high above the royal barge with five decks and an incredible array of more than two hundred cannon. Bounding aboard, with his courtiers scrambling after him, Harry stood on deck and waited impatiently while she was blessed at a special High Mass, before conducting a guided tour of the ship, proudly pointing out her advanced features, and taking care to blow his whistle loudly at every opportunity.

Everyone congratulated him, but Mary was subdued, and Harry knew why. Wolsey's negotiations with France had progressed most satisfactorily, and King Louis had asked for Mary's hand.

'But he is so old!' she had protested. 'And he is ailing. I don't want to marry him.'

'You will be a queen,' Harry had reminded her. 'No English princess has ever been queen of France. And, from what I hear, Louis is no cold fish like the Infante Charles. He is an eager bridegroom, ready to lavish affection and riches on you.'

Mary had begun pacing the floor of her chamber. 'I will not marry an old man!'

She was still fighting tears when they reboarded the barge to return to Greenwich. She seemed bent on spoiling this wonderful day.

'What ails you, sister?' Harry asked testily.

'Nothing,' she said, turning away to look out of the window.

He shrugged and picked up his tidal almanac of Europe. He knew more about French tidal waters than the experts did, and his admirals had already learned to trust his encyclopaedic knowledge of naval matters.

'I won't do it,' Mary said suddenly. 'I can't. I love another!'

Harry grabbed her hand. 'You are not free to love where you choose. You are a princess and must marry to the advantage of this kingdom.'

'But I love Charles!' Mary was weeping now.

'Suffolk! I trust he has not been encouraging you!' Harry thought of his friend's ways with women. 'By St George, if he—'

'No, I swear. He has told me there can be nothing between us.'

'Thank God someone has some sense in this matter! Now cease your complaints and do as you are told – for me, and for England.'

That summer, at the royal manor of Wanstead, Essex, Mary formally renounced her betrothal to the Infante Charles. A week later, peace with France was proclaimed, and it was announced that Mary was to marry King Louis himself.

Harry could not sufficiently thank Wolsey for negotiating such a satisfactory settlement, one that would restore his own greatness in Europe. Immediately, he made him archbishop of York, and wrote to the Vatican, urging Pope Leo to appoint him a cardinal.

At once, Wolsey set about making lavish improvements to York

Place at Westminster, the ancient London residence of the archbishops of York.

'Thanks to your Grace's bounty, I can transform it into a fine palace where I can entertain you in princely style,' he enthused. And Harry, who loved beautifying his old residences and building new ones, was pleased to see the project progress, and glad to know that his faithful Thomas had been amply rewarded.

In August, the whole court gathered in the great banqueting hall at Greenwich, which had been hung with cloth of gold embroidered with the royal arms of England and France. Today, the Princess Mary was to be married by proxy to King Louis. With Kate enthroned beside him, looking very fine in silver satin with a gold Venetian cap, and carrying her high belly proudly, for she was pregnant again, Harry watched as the bride made her entrance, wearing a chequered gown of purple and gold, which matched the robes of the Duke of Longueville, who was standing in for the King of France. They stood and exchanged vows, rings and a kiss before Archbishop Warham, who then conducted the nuptial Mass. After the wedding feast, Harry and Buckingham led the dancing, throwing off their long gowns and strutting about in their doublets. Later, when the feasting had gone on for too long and Harry was becoming bored, he amused himself by throwing sugar plums at the guests, laughing at their discomfiture. Mary started giggling and soon everyone was joining in the laughter and the fruit fight.

When darkness fell, the company proceeded into a chamber where a great bed had been prepared. The new Queen of France appeared in a sumptuous nightgown and lay down, baring one leg to the thigh; Longueville, having removed his hose, lay beside her and touched her naked leg with his own.

'Now we may deem the marriage consummated,' Harry declared, smiling at Wolsey. 'Let us all rejoice!'

He had opened his coffers to ensure that his sister went to France sumptuously attired. Merchants of every nation had been summoned to the palace, and Mary now had thirty gorgeous gowns. In addition, Harry had supplied her lavishly with jewels and furnishings.

She was also to take with her a large entourage. Louis had approved every name on the list save that of the alluring Jane Popincourt, whose reputation had suffered after she became the Duke of Longueville's mistress. Mary wept, but was mollified when she received Louis' bridal gift, a huge diamond with a great pendant pearl called the Mirror of Naples. Harry stared at it covetously, thinking that he ought to own such a jewel. When his jeweller informed him that it was worth sixty thousand crowns, he felt sick with jealousy.

Deep inside, he was sad at the prospect of losing his sister. They had always been close, and he felt protective towards her. Not that he feared that Louis would be unkind to her – the French King was, he had heard, a perfect gentleman and an eager bridegroom. He would just miss Mary, and he knew that Kate felt the same.

But soon, God willing, Kate would hold their son in her arms. She was blooming with health, and Harry allowed himself to get a little excited at the prospect of finally having an heir.

Just then, out of the blue, he received a letter from Etiennette de la Baume, with whom he had dallied in France the previous year. Enclosing a screw of paper containing some medicinal roots of great value (he was impressed that she had remembered his telling her how he enjoyed concocting his own remedies), she reminded him of his promise to her of ten thousand crowns when she married. Now, she was to be wed.

His first instinct was to burn the letter. Kate must never find out; she must not be upset in her condition. Then he realised he should do the honourable thing and send the money he had promised. But what if Etiennette kept demanding more? The matter preyed on his mind all through his summer progress through Berkshire and Surrey. In the end, he sent the money, deciding that it was the safest course, but he enclosed no note. Etiennette would know who had entrusted it to her servant. It was some weeks before Harry began to relax in the likelihood that she would trouble him no more.

The beginning of October found him embracing Mary at the waterside at Dover.

'There is one thing I would ask, brother,' she murmured in his ear. 'I beg this favour of you. King Louis is a sickly old man, by all reports. If he dies, will you give your promise that I may choose my next husband?'

'It's a fine thing to be going to your wedding and thinking of widowhood,' Harry chuckled. 'Very well, I promise.' He kissed her cheek. 'Now I commend you to God and the fortunes of the sea, and the government of the King your husband. God speed you, sister!'

Escorted by Norfolk, Suffolk and Longueville, Mary embarked on the ship that would take her to France. Katherine pointed out a fair-haired young girl at the end of the train of ladies who followed her, who was looking nervously at the churning sea below.

'It looks as if that little maid doesn't want to board,' she said.

'That's Boleyn's daughter, Mary,' Harry told her. 'She's new to court.'

'He has two daughters, doesn't he?'

'Yes. The younger one is at the court of the Archduchess Margaret in Brussels. He secured her a place as maid-of-honour when he was on an embassy there. I met her at Lille. She is very accomplished.'

They watched, smiling, as Boleyn hastened to coax his daughter aboard the ship. But tears blurred Harry's vision as the fourteen stately vessels sailed out of the harbour, carrying his darling sister away, then gathered speed as they reached the open sea and the wind filled their sails. He blinked and turned, mounted his horse and rode up to the castle.

Chapter 9

1514

After they returned to Greenwich. Kate remained well and in good spirits. In a few weeks, she would be taking to her chamber for the birth. Harry ordered a new cradle upholstered in scarlet, and linen and curtains for the nursery. God willing, they would soon be in use.

The October nights were growing chilly. Most evenings, Harry commanded the Knight Marshal to bring his cards and dice in a silver bowl. His gentlemen and the Queen's ladies partnered him in games of mumchance, click-clack, imperial and primero, or clustered around, watching the play.

Carew's wife Elizabeth and her friend Bessie Blount were often present. Harry and Suffolk had long flirted with the pair of them, and Suffolk had even written from France to ask him to remind them to reply to him when he sent them love tokens – and this from the man on whom Mary had set her heart!

'You are very remiss not to respond,' he reproved the young ladies, with a twinkle in his eye.

'Ah, but your Grace, a lady should play hard to get!' Elizabeth smiled.

'And you, Mistress, will you not be kind?' Harry asked plaintively.

Bessie Blount dimpled at him. She had come to court as maid-of-honour to the Queen the previous year; her father had fought for Harry's father at Bosworth, and Lord Mountjoy was her kinsman. She was sixteen and very beautiful, with corn-coloured hair and eyes that reminded Harry of periwinkles, and she was less bold than Elizabeth Carew.

'I would be kind to a man I loved, Sir,' she said, folding her hands demurely over her stomacher.

Harry laid down his cards. 'Then you do not love my lord of Suffolk?'

'Sir, I was speaking of another.'

Harry signalled to her to bend to his ear. 'And who might that be?'

'That is for him to discover, Sir.' She smiled at him.

By St George, she had been well schooled in the game of love! His interest was piqued. He saw himself unlacing her gown, uncovering those pert breasts and kissing those lovely lips. He had been too long without a woman in his arms! He had resisted all temptation this time for Kate's sake, but virtue made a cold bedfellow.

'Let us finish the game and have some dancing,' he said. 'I think the victory is mine?'

'No, Sir, it is mine,' Elizabeth said, laying down her cards. Harry groaned. He had lost hundreds of pounds – again.

'Very well. The Knight Marshal will settle with you.'

He forgot about his losses in the delight of dancing with Bessie. She was a graceful, skilful partner and their bodies seemed to move in unison, as if they were made for each other.

Kate was watching them from the dais, smiling and clapping. Harry often invited her ladies to partner him, but two dances was the limit – any more, and she might wonder. He bowed to Bessie.

'It has been a pleasure, Mistress.'

'Thank you, Sir.' A faint tinge of pink spread across her cheeks as she curtseyed – very becoming, Harry thought approvingly.

He sought Bessie out after that, taking care to be discreet. He walked with her and the other maids in the gardens, chatted with her during gatherings in the Queen's chamber, or bade her play for the company, for she was accomplished on the lute. She was not just a pretty face; she was bright and intelligent, and restful company. He found himself liking her more and more.

Suffolk returned as winter set in, and Harry bade him share a ewer of wine in his closet, himself stoking up the fire. The Duke reported that Mary's wedding to King Louis, and her coronation at Saint-Denis, had been conducted with great magnificence.

'The French King was very taken with her,' he related. 'After their wedding night, he boasted that he had performed marvels.' Did Harry imagine a note of jealousy in his voice?

'I very much doubt it,' he said, ignoring it.

As the wine flowed, and the evening wore on, he felt the need to confide in his friend. 'I will tell you a secret, Charles. I have become enamoured of Bessie Blount.'

'Harry, you old stag!' Suffolk guffawed, elbowing him in the ribs. 'Has she succumbed to your charms?'

'Not yet,' Harry admitted. 'She is too often with the Queen; I can never see her alone. And I dare not do anything that will give rise to gossip, with her Grace so near her time.'

'Then let me help.' Suffolk grinned. 'Let it be thought that I am courting her. I will secrete her in my lodging and you may dally with her there.'

'Capital!' Harry cried, slapping him on the back. 'I knew you would come to my aid.'

But would Bessie play along?

Two days later, Suffolk arranged for her to be in his lodging at midnight. The situation had been explained to her and, to Harry's delight, she had consented. It was then that Harry bedded her, and found it so sweet a pleasure that he wanted it never to end.

Harry dismounted, and ordered his huntsmen to carry the deer he had shot to the game larder. Then he saw the Queen's vice-chamberlain, Sir Thomas Bryan, approaching him across the cobbled stable yard, bowing.

'Your Grace, could I have a private word with you?'

'Of course. Walk with me.' He began striding back in the direction of the palace, with Sir Thomas striving to keep up. 'What is it?'

'Sir, some of the Queen's servants have complained that her confessor is having affairs with women, here at court, notably the

Queen's laundresses, Thomasine Haverford and Cecily Swan. I felt it my duty to inform you.'

That pesky Fray Diego! Harry had never liked him. He had made trouble for Kate before their marriage, setting her at odds with his father, and there had been talk then of his hold over her. That had all ceased when she became queen, for Harry had made it plain that he would not brook undue influence over his wife. Yet Kate could see no wrong in the friar; she had been too innocent to realise that her devotion to him might be a source of gossip. Harry had remained uneasy. Aware that she was longing for a living child, Fray Diego was now encouraging her to fast as often as she could, in order to purge her sins and win God's favour. As if all that fasting would do her health any good!

'I will speak to the Queen,' he said, thinking that this might be a Heaven-sent opportunity to be rid of the man.

Fray Diego stood before Harry and Katherine, his swarthy face reddening angrily when he heard what had been said against him.

'I deny it, Sir!' he growled.

'Then you are saying you have been badly used?' Harry replied.

'I certainly am. And if I am badly used, the Queen is still more badly used!'

Harry could not believe his ears. Surely the friar could not be referring to Bessie? Even if he wasn't, he was being grossly impertinent.

'You had better explain yourself,' he said, 'and be careful what you say. I would not have you impugning anyone without good cause.'

Fray Diego looked mutinous. 'I meant, your Grace, that you had best take a look at my accusers before paying heed to them. I know who they are, and that they resent me for refusing them absolution. They should be dismissed from her Grace's service. One is a perjurer and traitor, one has a bastard son, and one leads an unclean life.'

'Then you have never had any connection with Mistress Haverford or Mistress Swan?'

Fray Diego started in surprise. His hot denial came after too long a pause, and Harry pounced.

'Ah, but you did meddle with them, you cur, didn't you?'

'No, Sire, I did not!' barked the friar.

'I don't believe you,' Harry said, 'and I cannot allow any taint of scandal to stain the honour of my Queen. You are forthwith dismissed from her service and will return to Spain.'

Katherine looked as if she was about to protest, but Fray Diego forestalled her.

'Your Grace, that is unjust. For nine years I have served the Queen faithfully. I have endured many evils for her sake, even a lack of meat and drink, clothes and warmth. Your Grace has called me a fornicator. By the Holy Gospel, I swear this charge is false. Those who complained of me are my enemies and disreputable rogues. Yet I am willing to forget all this unpleasantness, and I am prepared to remain in her Grace's service if you desire it – but only on condition that I be heard by honest judges.'

No one had ever spoken to Harry in such a condescending manner. He felt a hot, furious flush rising.

'*You* are prepared? *You* are willing to forget . . . ? Do you question my justice? Am I a dishonest judge?' He was almost spluttering in rage. 'You will be tried by an ecclesiastical tribunal. Now get out. Go!'

'As your Grace pleases.' Fray Diego's voice shook. 'Wherever I go I shall pray that you have sons.' He bowed to Katherine. 'God go with you.'

Kate looked distressed, but there was nothing she could say. A virtuous queen could not be tainted by scandal in her household. (Of course, Harry thought uncomfortably, she was tainted, all unwittingly, by what he was doing with her maid-of-honour, but at least he was being discreet about it.)

He made sure that Wolsey chaired the tribunal.

'I have been an impartial judge, Sir,' Wolsey said afterwards. 'The evidence was incontrovertible, and we found him guilty of fornication. What sentence would you like me to impose?'

'I will pass sentence,' Harry declared, and strode ahead of Wolsey into the chamber where the tribunal was sitting. Everyone rose to their feet. The friar was staring at him malevolently.

'Fray Diego Fernandez,' he said, 'you shall be deported immediately to Spain.'

'Your Grace's justice is a travesty!' the friar roared. 'Never, within your kingdom, have I had to do with women. I have been condemned unheard by disreputable rogues.'

Harry was trembling with rage. 'Take him away!' he hissed. 'And be grateful, wretch, that I do not deal more severely with you.'

He was still smarting with rage when he returned to the privy chamber. To think that he had allowed that viper to minister to his Queen!

Kate had not yet taken to her chamber at Greenwich when her travail began, but everything was in place in the royal nursery. Harry had again arranged for the loan of the silver font from Canterbury Cathedral for the christening.

The hours dragged on in an agony of suspense. He could settle to nothing. Surely this time God would vouchsafe him an heir?

When they told him that his son had died within minutes of his birth, he broke down.

'What have I done to deserve this?' he cried, devastated. 'How have I offended God?'

In his heart, he knew the answer. This was his punishment for all those nights of forbidden joy. And yet, he had been a faithful husband when Kate lost her first child, so how could it be his fault? Was it hers?

Just to be on the safe side, he decided he would not sleep with Bessie again. He confessed his sins and performed the penance imposed by his confessor. Yet even absolution did not banish a lingering sense of guilt. His son was dead, and it might have been his fault. In the end, he felt so wretched that he sought comfort in Bessie's arms once more, for Kate was distraught with grief and had nothing to give him. Yet return to her bed he must, to impress his reluctant flesh into service, for England needed its heir.

When he did, he realised, with a sense of shock, that he was no longer in love with Kate. Six years of wedlock and four dead babes had done their worst. He was beginning to understand the difference between loving someone and actually being in love with them. He loved Kate, he always would, but there was no passion left between them. He wondered if she knew it too. Yet she never seemed to waver in her adoration for him.

Christmas was approaching and Harry was planning a pageant. He told himself that it would cheer himself and Kate, but he had an ulterior motive. Bessie was to feature prominently in it, alongside Elizabeth Carew and others. On Christmas Day, they dressed up in blue velvet gowns, gold caps and masks, and were rescued from danger by four gallant Portuguese knights, played by Harry, Suffolk, Carew and the Spanish ambassador. Kate was so delighted with their performance that, before they removed their masks, she invited them to dance again before her in her chamber. There, Harry partnered Bessie, and there was much laughter when the dancers flung off their masks and their identities were revealed.

Kate rose. 'Thank you, my Henry, for this goodly pastime!' She reached up and kissed him. He smiled down at her, feeling awkward because Bessie was watching and he did not want her to think that his love for his wife precluded his having feelings for her.

1515

As the new year dawned, Harry walked around in a dream, cherishing thoughts of Bessie. How she came to him so tenderly and gave herself so completely. How lovely she was, and how charming. How she loved him without artifice or any mercenary motive.

He took care to hide his feelings, and reined in his desire until the nights when they could lie together in Suffolk's bed. Creeping, cloaked and hooded, down the privy stair from his apartments only lent spice to the affair.

But Kate noticed a change in him.

'My Henry, you seem preoccupied,' she said, as he tried to focus on a game of backgammon, aware that Bessie was sitting chatting with the other maids behind him.

Quickly, he collected himself. 'I was just calculating how much I might lose if you win,' he smiled.

'Is that all? You have been with me, but not with me, these past days. Is something troubling you?'

'Not at all, sweetheart. I have been enjoying the season. I was not aware of being distant with you. How could I be, my dear wife?'

She smiled at him. 'No matter.'

But it was enough to sound alarums in his head.

By popular demand, the pageant was to be staged again on Twelfth Night.

'It is best you do not appear,' Harry told Bessie as they lay together in the small hours of the next morning, both sated with rich food, dancing and sex. 'The Queen must never suspect us. I will find someone to take your place. Boleyn and his son George are arranging a disguising in the watching chamber and you can take part in that. If anyone asks, you can say that they asked for you.'

Bessie smiled and went along with it. She was so kind, so undemanding, always alive to his needs and wishes.

Bessie was momentarily forgotten when Suffolk returned from an embassy in Paris. King Louis was dead, and there was a new monarch in France, his late Majesty's cousin, the Count of Angoulême, now King Francis I. Harry frowned when he learned that the new French King was three years younger than he and, by all reports, looked set to rival him in magnificence and martial valour. But Suffolk assured him that he was a great deal more handsome than Francis.

'He looks like a satyr with his dark hair and the long Valois nose,' the Duke grinned.

'I hear he is a notorious lecher, and that his court is licentious,'

Harry said, primly pursing his mouth. He was worrying about Mary, a beautiful widow who was now at Francis' mercy.

'I saw little of that, for they are all in mourning.'

'Did you see my sister?'

'No. She has retired into seclusion at the Hôtel de Cluny. Francis is on edge, waiting to see if she is with child by the late King.'

'Ha!' Harry laughed. 'I'd like to see his face if she is. He'll be king no more!'

'Well, she might be,' Suffolk said, pouring them some wine. 'They say she led Louis a merry dance. The poor man was quite worn out.'

'I can believe it,' Harry chuckled. 'She was, quite literally, the death of him.'

He was not smiling when rumours drifted across the Channel that Francis was thinking of divorcing his pregnant wife, Louis' daughter Claude, and marrying Mary. Then there were frantic letters from Mary, who feared he had designs on her virtue. Worst of all was the report that he was trying to negotiate a marriage between Mary and the Duke of Savoy, which Harry did not want. She could make a more advantageous match elsewhere.

'Suffolk, you are to go to France to bring the Princess home,' he ordered. 'I should say that I know how matters stand between you and her.'

'Harry, it is her fantasy—'

Harry cut him short. 'Nevertheless, I want your promise that you will not propose marriage to her.'

'You have my word,' Suffolk declared.

'Your Grace, I must speak with you.' Wolsey had appeared at Harry's side as he shot at the butts on an unseasonably warm day in March.

'Can't it wait?' Harry raised his bow and drew his arm back.

'No, Sir.'

The arrow sped to the bullseye.

'Bravo!' the watching courtiers cheered, clapping their hands.

'Very well,' Harry said. 'Gentlemen, continue without me. I will be back later.'

As they walked through the budding gardens to the palace, Harry saw that Wolsey was looking deeply troubled, which was unusual, for rarely did anything disturb his customary urbanity. 'What is wrong?' he asked.

Wolsey frowned. 'Sir, Queen Mary has married the Duke of Suffolk.'

'What?' Harry could not believe his ears.

'I've just received a letter from the Duke in which he confesses his offence and begs me to solicit your forgiveness. He wrote that the Queen would never let him rest till he had agreed to marry her.'

'I'll have his head for this!' Harry seethed. 'How dare he! We must have it annulled.'

'Alas, Sir, I fear it is too late for that, for he says he has lain with her and thinks she may be with child.'

A red mist of rage descended on Harry. That wicked little minx – how she had betrayed him!

As soon as he reached the palace, he bawled out an order for the Council to convene at once. Its members were as outraged at Suffolk's presumption as he was, old jealousies surfacing fast.

'He should be executed, or at least imprisoned, for he has committed treason by marrying a princess of the blood without royal consent!' Norfolk thundered, and the other lords nodded their agreement.

'Gentlemen, gentlemen,' Wolsey intervened, 'can we all calm down? Given his Grace's love for Queen Mary and his affection for Suffolk, may I propose that he demands a large fine as punishment?'

There were rumbles of disagreement, but Harry's anger was cooling and he could see the wisdom in Wolsey's solution. He was furious with Mary, but he did love her, and Suffolk was closer to him than any of his other friends.

'Yes,' he said slowly, 'a fine would compensate for the usurpation of my prerogative and the loss of an opportunity to marry the Queen to England's advantage. I think that twenty-four thousand pounds should be sufficient.'

There were sharp intakes of breath all along the table.

'That is a huge sum,' Buckingham said. 'Even Suffolk, with all his new-found riches, won't be able to afford it.'

'They can pay it in instalments,' Harry said. 'They can sell some of the Queen's jewels.' His eyes gleamed as he recalled the fabulous Mirror of Naples. 'Better still, she can surrender to me all the jewels and plate Louis gave her, in part payment.'

'I will write to her Grace and the Duke immediately,' Wolsey replied, rising.

Mary and Suffolk accepted the terms with such alacrity that Harry realised they must have been expecting a far worse punishment. Greatly placated, he graciously consented to receive them back into favour, ignoring the barbed comments of those who felt that Suffolk had got off too lightly.

By the end of the month, Harry had the Mirror of Naples in his hand. Francis had asked for it to be returned, arguing that it was the hereditary property of the queens of France, but Mary had told him she had sent it to her brother as a peace offering, and Harry refused to give it back, provoking a diplomatic row. Francis offered him thirty thousand crowns for it, but Harry insisted on keeping it; it was worth more to him than that.

On May Day, he arranged a wondrous pageant to impress the new Venetian ambassador, Sebastian Giustinian. He rose early, had himself dressed entirely in green velvet and dispatched two of his lords to conduct the ambassador to Greenwich. Then, mounting his favourite horse, the mighty Governatore, he and Kate rode into the great hunting park that surrounded the palace. Kate was richly dressed in the Spanish style and attended by twenty-five damsels, all mounted on white palfreys with embroidered gold caparisons and wearing dresses slashed with gold. Harry tried not to stare at Bessie, but could not help himself, for she was by far the most beautiful of them all. Beside her, Kate, now in her thirtieth year, appeared ever more middle-aged and faded. He felt disloyal to think that, at only twenty-three, and bursting with vigour, he was tied to an older wife who had become over-pious and staid. Yet her face lit up, as it always did, the moment she saw him.

When they arrived in the woods, Harry could barely contain his excitement, for there were many delights in store for their pleasure. The Venetians were waiting in a clearing, clearly impressed to see him surrounded by two hundred archers of his guard, all in green livery with bows in their hands. One was got up as Robin Hood and stood with a boy dressed as Maid Marion in a red kirtle. A hundred noblemen on horseback were in attendance.

Robin Hood bowed before Kate.

'Would your Grace and your damsels like to enter the greenwood and see how we outlaws live?'

'I wonder that the Queen would dare venture into a thicket with so many outlaws,' Harry cried.

She smiled at him. 'Where you go, my husband, I am content to go.' As trumpets sounded, he took her hand and led her through the wood. They came to another clearing where some carefully constructed bowers had been decorated with flowers, herbs and boughs and filled with singing birds that carolled most sweetly. Within the bowers, tables had been set for breakfast.

'Sir,' Robin Hood addressed the King, 'outlaws eat venison for breakfast, and you must be content with such fare as we enjoy.'

Harry beamed at him, sitting down with Kate and the visitors, as the archers served them great platters of game and flagons of wine. In another bower, they could see triumphal chariots containing musicians, who provided the sweet accompaniment of organ, lute and flutes throughout the feast.

Harry could not sit still. Goblet in hand, he made his way around the tables, chatting to his guests and pressing them to eat the delicacies that were being served, even handing them out himself. The Venetians were staring at him open-mouthed, doubtless marvelling that a king could be such a good fellow. He remembered that they had been in Paris before coming to England, and his curiosity was piqued.

'Talk with me awhile,' he said to them. 'The King of France, is he as tall as I am?'

'There is but little difference. Your Majesty,' one of the envoys replied.

'Is he as strong in body?'

No, he was not.

'What sort of legs has he?'

'Spare, your Majesty.' Harry beamed. Pulling aside the bases of his doublet, he slapped a hand on his thigh. 'Look here! I have also a good calf to my leg.'

The visitors clapped their hands delicately.

When the tables had been cleared, Harry mounted Governatore and began making the horse curvet and perform great feats, which the Venetians applauded wildly.

'I fancy I am looking at the god Mars!' Giustinian exclaimed.

Harry bowed in the saddle, then dismounted and invited them to take part in an archery contest, which he easily won.

That afternoon, Harry and Compton won resounding ovations in a tournament, Harry having exerted himself to the utmost, knowing that some of the Venetians would be departing for France in the evening, and determined that they should be able to tell King Francis how magnificently he had acquitted himself. He was aware of both Kate and Bessie watching him from the gallery, which drove him to even greater feats.

All that week, the May sun shone down and the jousting continued. Nicholas Carew and his rake of a brother-in-law, Sir Thomas Bryan's son Francis, joined Harry in the lists, and he lent them horses and armour, wishing to encourage all young men to seek deeds of arms. He found his match in Carew, an outstanding jouster renowned for his fearless daring. He was so expert at horsemanship that he entered the lists with his steed blindfolded, so that it should not rear in fright when three men carried into the tiltyard a tree trunk twelve feet long and balanced it on Carew's lance rest. Harry's jaw dropped as he watched Carew ride the length of the tiltyard, couching the tree like a lance, as the crowd held its collective breath, then burst into delighted applause.

The next day found Harry relaxing in the park with his gentlemen. A table had been placed under the trees, set with cloth and plate, but they were all lying on the grass in their shirtsleeves, having thrown off their doublets and tired themselves out with bouts of wrestling.

'I think I'm the all-round winner,' Francis Bryan boasted.

'Nay, it was Harry here,' said Compton.

'He speaks truth,' Harry said. 'I'm the King – I have to be the winner.' He grinned and downed the dregs in his goblet.

'Yes, like you do at cards and dominoes!' Bryan jested.

Harry groaned. 'Don't remind me.' His losses the previous evening had been severe.

'Never mind!' His cousin Henry Courtenay, now earl of Devon after the death of his father, clapped him on the arm. 'You excelled in the lists.'

'This is the life,' Bryan sighed, chewing a blade of grass. 'No court, no wars, no show, no courtesy. All I need is a pastoral idyll, a soft bed and a hard harlot.'

The others laughed.

'That would never be enough for you,' Carew said. 'You're always on to the next thing. You'd be bored in five minutes.'

It was true, Harry thought. Bryan was full of pent-up energy, ever ready for an adventure. He might be a hell-raiser, a viciously witty, incorrigible intriguer who was two-faced and promiscuous, but he was a clever man of letters who had also distinguished himself as a soldier and had irresistible charm.

Yet he was not Suffolk. Harry had missed his old friend, but Mary and Suffolk were due back in England any day, and he could not wait to be reunited with them. Of course, he would put on a show of displeasure at their great transgression, but he would soon allow himself to be mollified and forgiving. And presently the first instalment of that fat fine would be in his coffers.

Chapter 10

1515

Mary knelt before him, more beautiful than ever, with unshed tears sparkling in her blue eyes. And there was his beloved Suffolk, head bent in shame and abasement, craving his pardon, knowing that he was lucky to have that head still on his shoulders. How could he resist them?

'You have grievously offended me,' he said sternly. 'I could have sent you both to the Tower and charged you, my lord, with treason. Yet . . .' He allowed his voice to trail off, to prolong their suspense. 'Yet the love I bear you both has constrained me to mercy. Rise, and let us be reconciled.' As Mary stood up, he held out his arms and she went into them, weeping with relief. Then it was Suffolk's turn to be embraced and received back into favour. Harry observed the faces of the watching courtiers, saw the false smiles and knew they were rejoicing at Suffolk's discomfiture and thinking that he deserved a lot worse than this.

'You shall be married in public,' he told the couple. 'I cannot have my sister wed in secret. Our father would be turning in his grave, and there would be those to say it was no marriage.'

'Harry, that would be wonderful!' Mary cried, reaching up and kissing him. 'Thank you! God has blessed me in sending me such a kind brother!'

The wedding took place in the church of the Observant Friars at Greenwich. The bride wore a black velvet gown studded with pearls and a halo-shaped French hood, a fashion that drew much scandalised comment because it exposed her hair – and she already a married woman!

The whole court attended, but the celebrations were muted because Harry was painfully aware that his subjects generally did not approve of the marriage, and that among the guests were some who had pressed for Suffolk's execution. He had heard the doggerel doing the rounds, which proclaimed that cloth of frieze should not be so bold, even though it was matched with cloth of gold.

Wolsey, of course, was delighted that everything had turned out well, and not only for Mary and Suffolk. Harry now saw that the Archbishop had, through his intervention, reduced the Duke, a potential rival, to the status of a client seeking his patronage; Suffolk would now have to learn to work amicably with him. Yet, to counterbalance that, he had become the King's brother-in-law. Honour and respect had to be paid to him. After Wolsey, he had the second seat on the Privy Council, even though he rarely attended, for he was busy elsewhere, Harry having deputed him to looking after royal interests in East Anglia, which of course suited Wolsey very well.

Out of affection for his sister and his friend, Harry graciously reduced their fine. Soon after the wedding, Suffolk was able to afford to build a splendid brick residence, Suffolk Place, on his ducal estate by the Thames in Southwark. He was also busy making improvements in the new antique style to his country seat, Westhorpe Hall in Suffolk, where Mary was royally attended by fifty servants. The Duke was frequently at court, but, to Harry's disappointment, Mary preferred the country, although she did visit from time to time, taking precedence, as Queen Dowager of France, over all other ladies except Kate.

Summer came, and Harry went on progress to the west, visiting his towns and castles and hearing the complaints of his subjects. As he journeyed, he took every opportunity to hunt, and liberally gave away the venison.

At Woking, in the middle of September, Kate came to him in the privy garden and told him that she was with child again.

'That is the most welcome news!' he cried, drawing her to him and kissing her. 'Darling, are you feeling well?'

'Never better, my Henry!' She smiled. 'I have been cherishing my hopes for some time, but I did not want to say anything until the babe moved in my womb.'

Harry's spirits soared. His head was suddenly full of plans for his son's nursery and household, the honours and titles he would heap upon him, the fine education he would receive. He would be called Henry, of course . . .

Later that day, Wolsey arrived with his own good news.

'Word has just come from Rome, your Grace. I am to be made a cardinal.'

Harry grasped his hands. 'Thomas, I am heartily pleased for you. No man deserves such a high honour more. And your advancement reflects well upon me and upon England!'

'I am not deserving, Sir,' Wolsey protested.

Harry slapped him on the shoulder. 'Nonsense, man! No prince ever had a better counsellor. So what's next for you, eh? The Papal throne?'

He fully expected Wolsey to say that, no, he did not aspire to be Pope, and was astonished to see the gleam in his eye.

'Oh, no,' he said, 'I could not bear to lose the ablest man in my kingdom, and my good friend. What would I do if you went to Rome?'

'You would be very well served, Sir, with an Englishman sitting in the seat of St Peter. To my knowledge, there has only been one English pope, and that long ago. Most popes serve only their own interests. But, were I to be elected Pontiff, I would put yours and England's first, and continue to serve you in every way I could.'

'Hmm. Well, that day may come, but I would rather have you here! Tell me, how is work on that new palace of yours progressing?'

'Hampton Court? Slowly, Sir! You know how workmen are.'

'Oh, I keep a close eye on those working for me,' Harry said. 'I often ask for plans or reports while works are going on, and I make a point of visiting a site to make an inspection. I'll abide no slacking!'

'Your Grace is lucky,' Wolsey said, warming his hands by the fire. 'You can impress any workman, be he carpenter, mason, plumber or labourer, even if he is engaged upon another project.'

Harry sat down. 'True – and I often do. I know they think me demanding. But I'm impatient to see my houses finished. I set a completion date and, if necessary, I have the men working through the night by candlelight in order to keep to it. Do you know, at Bridewell Palace, I've even had tents erected over scaffolding so that work can continue during bad weather. But I think of the men's welfare too. If they're standing deep in mud, digging foundations in wet weather, I provide beer, bread and cheese.'

'Methinks I must take a leaf out of your Grace's book,' Wolsey smiled.

Harry grinned at his friend. 'I'm happy to be of service. After all, you are building yourself a palace to outrival any of mine!' It was said only half in jest. Deep inside, he was jealous. If anyone in England owned such a wondrous palace, it should be he, the King. But, having raised Wolsey to dizzying heights and made him the most powerful man in the kingdom, he could hardly blame him for aspiring to a lifestyle fitting to his position.

'My dear mother used to stay at Hampton Court when Lord Daubeney owned it,' he recalled. 'She was there shortly before she died.' As ever, he felt a pang when he remembered his loss.

'I fear that the old house has now been pulled down,' Wolsey told him. 'I've saved the clock from the tower, though. The new palace is being built in the Burgundian style, of red brick with two courts. There will be luxurious apartments for your Grace and the Queen, for when you honour me with a visit. I shall spare no expense in making you welcome.'

'Be assured I shall visit often!'

'That would only be fitting, for it is thanks to your Grace's munificence that I am able to enjoy such an abundance of riches.' Wolsey seated himself at the table. 'Now, Sir, maybe you would like to see these reports of the French advance on Milan. King Francis is determined to conquer the duchy, but, as you know, it is occupied by the Swiss. I have asked our envoys in Italy to keep your Grace informed of events.'

* * *

Late that month, a French envoy bowed before the King.

'Your Majesty, my master King Francis has sent me to inform you that he has won a great victory over the Swiss in a battle at Marignano. He has vanquished those whom only Caesar vanquished.'

Harry drew in his breath. How could the new French King, still green about the ears when it came to the business of ruling, have achieved such a triumph when he himself had been denied the chance of conquering France?

'I find this hard to believe,' he said at length.

'Maybe your Grace would like to read this letter in his Majesty's own hand.' The envoy handed it over.

As he read, Harry struggled to contain tears of mortification. It was true. Francis was basking in his victory; was a king to be reckoned with.

'Your Majesty does not seem glad to hear of my master's success,' the envoy commented. Damn the fellow!

'On the contrary, I send him my warmest congratulations,' Harry managed to say, in a strangled tone.

He was still simmering with resentment a month later, when, dressed in a sailor's coat and breeches of cloth of gold, he launched another new ship, *The Virgin Mary*, at Greenwich. She was a huge vessel with a hundred and twenty oars, two hundred and seven guns, and the capacity to carry one thousand men, and seeing her looking so mighty and battleworthy, he began to feel happier. He'd wager anything that Francis had no ship like this!

Accompanied by Kate, the Suffolks and the whole court, Harry himself piloted the ship down the Thames to the open sea, blowing his large gold admiral's whistle as loudly as a trumpet. After Mass had been celebrated on board, the Queen formally named the vessel, and Harry hosted a great feast on deck. He was in his element again, never happier than when he could feel the swell of the deep beneath him.

There were more celebrations in November, when Wolsey's red cardinal's hat arrived in England and was conveyed to London with such triumph that you would have thought the greatest prince of

Christendom had come into the realm. Harry had arranged for Wolsey to be invested with it in a glittering ceremony in Westminster Abbey, which was conducted with the kind of pomp that normally attended a coronation.

He was aware that Wolsey's elevation had made him more unpopular than ever. The common people hated him. When he rode abroad on his mule, wearing red silk robes and fastidiously holding an orange stuck with cloves to his nose to mask the stink of the watching crowds, they stood sullen and resentful, and some booed.

The nobility still looked down on the butcher's boy who had made good, deeply jealous of the power he wielded, power that should have been theirs. Even Archbishop Warham had several times clashed with Wolsey.

'Your Grace, might I speak to you?' he asked, as Harry was about to leave a council meeting.

'What is it, my lord?'

The old man looked pained. 'Alas, Sir, I am weary of public life and wish to retire to my diocese. I must confess, I am finding it increasingly difficult to assert my authority as Lord Chancellor in the face of the Cardinal's superior power and his hostility towards me. I therefore crave your permission to resign.'

'I don't see why you and Wolsey can't work amicably together,' Harry said testily.

'Oh, but Sir, we could, if I were to agree with him in every respect. But I fear I cannot compromise on some issues, and I am tired of the constant wrangling.'

'Very well,' Harry said. 'If you feel like that, I will accept your resignation. But I will be sorry to lose you, for you have been a good servant to me.'

'And will continue to be,' Warham assured him. 'I am still your Archbishop of Canterbury, and I still have a seat on the Council and will support you in every way I can.'

'I am grateful for that, and for all you have done for me.'

Secretly, Harry was pleased that Warham was resigning. For some time now, he had been thinking that matters would run far more smoothly if Wolsey was Lord Chancellor. And thus it was that, on Christmas Eve, at Eltham Palace, he bestowed the honour on the Cardinal and delivered to him the Great Seal of England. The lords stood around, barely concealing their animosity.

Deep down, he could understand it. No subject had ever before held so many high offices in both Church and state, nor commanded an income that enabled him to live like a king. But Wolsey worked hard for his rewards, ruling everything with consummate ability and prudence, lifting so many of the burdens of kingship from Harry's shoulders. It was now well known that it was essential for anyone, be he councillor or official, to speak first of all serious matters to the Cardinal, and not to the King. Visitors had to kiss Wolsey's hand before they sought an audience with Harry.

Only Suffolk had the temerity to express his concerns, raising the matter one day over Christmas, when he and Harry were out hunting and taking a rest to eat their noon pieces, their breath steaming in the cold air.

'Harry, I must speak to you about the Cardinal. Your lords find themselves disempowered. Often, they cannot even obtain an audience with him. He dominates the Privy Council and the household; he even exercises royal patronage on your behalf. In fact, he chooses to interfere in everything.'

Harry regarded his friend sadly. 'So they've got at you too. Suffolk, I have complete confidence in Wolsey. I marvel that men overlook his abilities and his industriousness.'

'They resent his power, which he seems to exercise to the exclusion of everyone else. And they resent his lavish mode of life. He lives like a king! He is attended by a thousand servants wearing velvet, like lords! Even his cook wears damask, silk or velvet, with a gold chain about his neck. And when the Cardinal goes forth in procession, he is accompanied by a large entourage, preceded by silver crosses and pillars, poleaxes, a mace and what-have-you, and nobles bearing the Great Seal on a cushion and his cardinal's hat, raised up like some holy idol. He dresses not as a man of God, but in robes of silk, velvet and ermine . . .' His voice tailed off as he saw Harry's face.

'That's enough,' Harry said, angered by his friend's candour. 'I raised Wolsey, and if he enjoys the fruits of his high offices, he does it with my blessing. You're all jealous – but not one of you can do for me what he does.'

'So it does not bother you that this worldly churchman, this paragon, never visits his diocese. That he dances and hunts for his pleasure and keeps a mistress who has borne him two children. Mary tells me that Queen Katherine deplores his voluptuous life and abominable lechery. And, when crossed, he can be ruthless and violent: he actually hit the Papal nuncio and swore at him. For God's sake, Harry, it's inappropriate for a man of the Church!'

'And so we are to believe that all bishops, nay, all in holy orders, lead virtuous lives and never lose their tempers?' Harry retorted.

'Some do, and one such as Wolsey, who holds high public office, should take care to keep his nose clean.'

'But he does not flaunt his mistress.'

'Only his wealth and his power and his overweening pride!'

Harry finished the last of his pigeon pie and wiped his lips with a napkin. 'If I, your King, do not resent the splendour in which my servant lives, then no one else should. Remember, it reflects well upon my greatness to have such a distinguished counsellor. And you need not worry, Brandon. I do not intend ever fully to relinquish my power to Wolsey. I am happy for him to shoulder administrative affairs and routine state business for me, but everything he does is by my authority. All important decisions are made by me.' He walked over to the trees where the horses were tethered. 'If I do not agree with his actions, I intervene. I keep a grasp on affairs, for I can rely on him to keep me well informed. He labours hard for me. He rises before dawn and sits at his desk for twelve hours without stopping once to eat or relieve himself. Which of you other councillors does as much, eh?' He glared at his brother-in-law.

Suffolk had the grace to look away.

Harry put his arm around him. 'Charles, you are my friend. Wolsey is my friend. It grieves me that you resent him so much, for I have done as much for you as I have for him, and you both do me excellent service in your different ways. Remember that I have good cause to value the Cardinal beyond the ordinary. When he tells me that my realm, God be praised, was never in such peace and tranquillity as it is now, I know who I have to thank.'

Harry spent Christmas with Kate at Eltham, which, with its happy memories of childhood, was still one of his favourite palaces. He had designated it one of his greater houses and used it frequently. He had even had a hill flattened to improve the view from his windows.

He was in high spirits, glad to see Kate so great with child and so happy. He could not but love her for she was carrying his heir, even though he had spent many nights during the long months of her pregnancy with Bessie – Bessie, whom he loved in a different way, for she was so young and full of life. As he watched her sitting with the other maids-of-honour and laughing unrestrainedly at the Chapel Royal's performance of the comedy *Troilus and Pandarus*, he wished he could be seated beside her, sharing the hilarity. Instead, he was in his chair of estate next to Kate, who was smiling, but probably, even after fourteen years in England, unable to understand all the jokes. On Twelfth Night, he broke through her Spanish reserve by catching her unawares and popping jellies in her mouth in front of the whole court. She smacked his hand lightly and kissed him.

1516

Harry paced his privy chamber at Greenwich, unable to settle to anything. His gentlemen kept looking up at him concernedly from their interminable games of cards and dice, but he barely heeded them, his thoughts being with Kate, who had laboured for hours now. He was thankful that he had obtained for her the holy girdle of her patron saint, St Catherine, to cling to during her pains; hopefully, the blessed martyr would alleviate them.

When the door opened and the Queen's chamberlain appeared, Harry's throat constricted in fear.

'Your Grace, the Queen has borne a healthy princess.'

A girl. Not the son he was longing for. All the same, he almost ran to her apartments, as his guard hurried ahead of him, crying, 'Make way for our lord the King, make way!'

Harry beamed at Katherine and the infant in her arms.

'God be praised!' he cried, hastening over to kiss her. Then he lifted up his snugly swaddled daughter, her little red face all he could see of her under her tiny white bonnet. His heart melted and tears sprang to his eyes. This was his child, flesh of his flesh, a gift from God. He ought to be disappointed because she was not the male heir he desired, but he could only feel thankful for this miracle he and Kate had been vouchsafed.

'A right lusty princess!' he declared, his voice filled with emotion. 'May God bless and preserve you all the days of your life, my little daughter!' He looked at Katherine. 'You have done well, Kate, very well,' he said. 'She is a beauteous babe. I do trust that all is well with you?'

Katherine smiled up at him. 'I am tired,' she said, 'but so thankful that all went well. I would have been yet more pleased had I borne you a son.'

Henry shook his head. 'What matters is that you have come through your ordeal safely and that we have a healthy child. We are both young; even if it was a daughter this time, by the grace of God sons will follow. We will name her Mary, in honour of the Blessed Virgin. Does that please you?'

'I could not think of a better name,' Katherine smiled, well content. 'And it is also in honour of your sister.'

'We will have a splendid christening in the Observant Friars' chapel,' Henry said. 'Lady Salisbury must be one of the godmothers. But we can talk about that later. For now, you must get some rest. Where is the nurse?' A woman stepped forward and he laid the baby in her arms. 'Put her in her cradle and see she is rocked to sleep gently.'

He stood up. 'Bless you, Kate,' he said, stooping to kiss her tenderly. 'I will visit you when you are rested.'

When she was three days old, the Princess Mary was christened in the church of the Observant Friars. The silver font had again been brought from Canterbury Cathedral, costly carpets were laid along the processional route, and the church was hung with tapestries. Harry remained with Kate in her bedchamber as the godparents escorted the baby to the church. He had chosen Wolsey, his aunt Catherine, Countess of Devon, Lady Salisbury and the Duchess of Norfolk. When the ceremony was over, they carried the Princess back to the King and Queen, to receive their blessing.

Afterwards, there were jousts to celebrate her birth. But, in the midst of them, a letter arrived from Spain.

After Vespers, Harry made his way to Kate's chamber, dreading having to tell her the news. She looked up from her book and smiled when she saw him. Beside the bed, Mary slept peacefully.

Harry sat down and took Kate's hand. 'I trust you are feeling stronger today, darling.'

'I am,' she told him. 'I'm not bursting into tears at everything, thank goodness. Hopefully I'll be allowed to get up soon. I am longing to be back to normal.'

A lump rose in his throat. 'Kate, there is some news that I can keep from you no longer. Your father has died, God rest him.'

He held her as she wept, moved himself. His bitterness against Ferdinand had long dissipated, and a new accord had recently been established between them. It was sad that the old fox was no more. And now the Infante Charles was king of all Spain – that cold little boy, who must now be sixteen years old, whose measure Harry had yet to discover.

When Kate was up and about again, she made a pilgrimage to Our Lady of Walsingham to give thanks for her safe and successful delivery, and to pray for the soul of her father.

Mary was placed in the care of a Lady Mistress, the widowed Lady Margaret Bryan, mother of Francis Bryan and Elizabeth Carew. Harry had created for his daughter sumptuous nursery apartments at court and appointed an army of servants. He enjoyed showing her off to courtiers and ambassadors, proudly carrying her about in his arms and praising her sunny nature.

'This child never cries!' he told them. 'She is the pearl of my realm.' Already, she was bright as a button, her intelligent blue eyes fixing enquiringly on everything.

There was further cause for joy when, in March, the Suffolks' first son was born. Harry was named godfather and attended the lavish baptism, where the child was christened Henry in his honour. As he held the lusty boy at the font, he could not help thinking wistfully that he should have been holding his own son, and wishing that God had seen fit to send him one. But he was thrilled with his daughter, relieved that Kate had borne a healthy child and confident that they would have a boy soon.

Chapter 11

1516

Hampton Court was well on the way to completion, sufficiently finished for Wolsey to invite Harry and Kate to stay there. When Harry saw the vast red-brick palace, he gasped.

'By God, it's a wonder! I have nothing like this, and I'm the King!' A sharp pang of envy smote him. As he rode through the imposing gatehouse, there was Wolsey, bowing and waiting to greet him. 'Don't tell me he's going to welcome me to his humble abode,' Harry muttered to Kate, who was riding beside him.

'Your Grace, welcome to my humble abode,' Wolsey beamed, but Harry barely heard him, for he was staring ahead at the vast courtyard surrounded by fine lodgings. He dismounted and embraced Wolsey, reminding himself that it was his own patronage that had made his friend rich enough to build such a palace. Kate's eyes met his; he read indignation in them. She must be thinking that only the King should live like this. But he loved his Thomas and could not begrudge him the fruits of his unparalleled service, even if he could not help feeling envious.

'This accommodation, Sir, is for my household and guests,' the Cardinal told him, waving an expansive hand around. 'I keep two hundred and eighty beds with silk hangings made up in readiness for visitors.' He led the way through a second imposing gateway to another courtyard. 'Here you see my great hall, the banqueting chamber and the chapel.' Harry looked up at the large mullioned windows, the turrets, the tall chimneys, the sculpted new-fashioned antique work and the stone cherubs supporting Wolsey's coat of arms above the gateway.

'It's all inspired by the architecture of Italy,' Wolsey explained. Harry could see that. His father had patronised Italian artists and sculptors, and he himself had done so on occasion. He owned some architectural pattern books from Italy. He knew how important a display of the sophisticated arts of that country could be to a monarch who desired to be at the forefront of world affairs, and how useful it could be in enhancing his magnificence. In future, he promised himself, all his palaces and banqueting houses would be adorned with antique ornament.

Wolsey escorted Harry and Kate into a tower housing the special lodging he had built for them. 'There are apartments on each floor for your Graces and the Princess,' he told them. Everything was new and luxurious, more than fit for a king. But Harry's eyes widened when he saw that Wolsey's own apartments were even more sumptuous. He felt sick with envy, burning with the desire to own such a palace himself. Fortunately, the one he was building at Bridewell, near the Blackfriars monastery by the Thames, was coming on apace, although not fast enough for his liking. It too was of fashionable red brick and built around two courtyards; the royal lodgings were on the first floor, in the French style, and would be accessed by a processional stair, a novelty in England. Men were working around the clock to build a long gallery, a tennis court and terraced gardens fronting the river. Already, Harry had spent a fortune, and now he was bursting with new inspiration and determined to lay out far more money to make Bridewell a rival to Hampton Court.

In May, he rode to Tottenham, north of London, to welcome his sister Margaret to England. It was thirteen years since he had seen her, and a great deal had happened since then. After King James had been killed at Flodden, she had taken a second husband, Archibald Douglas, Earl of Angus, a match that had proved unpopular with the Scottish nobles, who had chosen the Duke of Albany to be regent in Margaret's place and seized custody of the young King James V.

Great with child, and desperate for aid against those who had stolen her son from her, Margaret had fled south to England and given birth to a daughter, whom she named after herself. She had been ill for a long time afterwards, but reports Harry had later received suggested that she was more interested in the beautiful clothes he had sent her than in her baby.

Now she had ridden south with the child, and he knew she was going to beg him to restore her to the regency.

Margaret had grown plump during her years in Scotland, and her prettiness had faded, but she was as imperious as ever.

'Oh, brother, I am desperate!' she cried, as she threw herself into Harry's arms. 'The Scots have behaved so cruelly! They have seized my son, and he so little to be deprived of his mother.'

Harry comforted her as best he could. He had feared she might resent or hate him as the man whose forces had deprived her of the King her husband, but she was treating him as if he were her saviour. He was not sure if it would be politic for England to become involved in Scotland's internal squabbles. Margaret had made a fool of herself by marrying Angus for love, without first seeking the approval of the lords, and by all accounts the marriage had proved tempestuous. But he welcomed her warmly and escorted her in state into London, she riding a white palfrey sent by Kate. He had arranged for her to lodge at Baynard's Castle by the Thames, which had once been their mother's London residence.

At Greenwich, Harry and Kate formally received Margaret, and there was an emotional reunion with her sister Mary. Harry saw her gaping at the splendour of his court, heard her gasps of delight at the gowns and gifts he showered upon her. It pleased him to know that the Scottish court could not compare with his in magnificence.

He was much taken with his niece, little Marget, as he called her.

'She must be brought up at court with the Princess Mary,' he said. 'They are near in age and will be fit companions for each other. Indeed, Meg, Marget is my next heir after Mary. She must have the best!'

Margaret beamed. She was looking less drawn. Gracing the tournaments and festivities held in her honour, she began to relax and enjoy herself. During two days of jousts, in the presence of the three queens, every man did well, but Harry excelled them all, winning applause when he unhorsed Sir William Kingston, a tall, strong knight whom few had beaten.

Soon afterwards, Wolsey arranged for Margaret to take up residence at Scotland Yard, the ancient London residence of the kings of Scotland, hard by York Place. She kept little state there, but spent her days praying and scheming for her husband Angus to join her in England.

Harry deemed it best not to intervene. He did not want to become embroiled in the turbulent politics of Scotland, nor did he have any intention of giving Margaret military aid. She was not fit to be regent. Better by far that Albany was in charge.

It was quiet up on the leads of Greenwich Palace and the sky above was twinkling with stars. Harry stood gazing upwards, with Thomas More beside him, pointing out the courses, motions and operations of the stars and planets. Astronomy was one of the many interests they shared. He was glad that he had persuaded More to come to court and serve him as his unofficial secretary. He knew that the lawyer was reluctant to leave his quiet family life at Chelsea, his studies, and those clever girls he had afforded the same education as his son. Harry envied him his idyll. If only he could have been so blessed. Sometimes, he thought he would have preferred being a private man with a fine house and time to write and indulge his intellectual interests. He had long respected More for his learning and wisdom, and envied him his international reputation. Now, he could enjoy his company and wit daily, and benefit from his opinions.

Only this evening, More had dined privately with him and Kate, and they had made merry and enjoyed a lively discussion about subjects as diverse as geometry and theology. They had not been king and subject, but two men of like mind, tossing about ideas. There had been laughter too, and Harry had teased him about his dislike of the court.

'I know you came here much against your inclinations,' he had said, grinning.

'Your Grace would hardly believe how unwilling I was,' More replied, with a self-deprecating gesture.

'Most men would kill for the honour,' Harry reminded him.

'Alas, Sir, I am not like your courtiers. I perceive the superficiality of court life; I do not seek the trappings of wealth and power.'

'Many are motivated by greed,' Harry concurred. 'They embrace the frivolity, luxury and idle pastimes, but these are just light distractions. Think you I do not know that my court is a cauldron of frustrations, resentment, intrigue, treachery and backbiting? How can there not be when there is intense competition and rivalry?'

More had nodded, smiling at Kate, who was listening while she peeled an orange. 'A courtier has no choice but to compromise his moral principles and his honesty in order to survive.'

'You speak truth,' Kate said. 'Many men here buy friends and sell women; they betray friendships for profit and pretend to be virtuous.'

'But how can I stem the tide?' Harry asked.

'You won't, Sir,' More told him. 'It is the way of the world. Be grateful you have some men of integrity and wise counsellors around you.'

'Wolsey?'

More hesitated. 'He is a most able man.'

'I sense you do not fully approve of him.'

'I get on well with him, Sir.'

'That's not what I asked you!' Harry elbowed his friend in the ribs.

More's swarthy, sensitive face assumed a wary expression. 'I think no evil of anyone. The Cardinal serves you well. I am happy to work with him.'

'You think him too worldly?'

'*I* do,' Kate said.

'Each must account for himself to God,' More observed, and would not be drawn further.

When they returned downstairs from the roof, Kate had retired, so Harry ushered More back to the table, poured more wine for them both and picked up the book his friend had brought for him.

'*Utopia*,' he said. 'You have published it at last. Congratulations!'

'It has been a long labour, but one of love.'

'And it describes the ideal state.'

'Hence "Utopia", which means "nowhere" in Greek! But yes, it is based on Plato's republic, with Humanist laws. I hope your Grace will approve, for it is somewhat critical of modern governments.'

'Do you think I cannot brook constructive criticism, my friend? Without it, there can be no change, no progress. I will read it at once.'

He started on it that very night, reading in bed by candlelight. He was so gripped that he was still absorbed hours later. He understood now why More had looked nervous. *Utopia* was a powerful critique of the political system in England and the vicious machinations of monarchs and courtiers. He winced when he read about idle monarchs and nobles seeking to increase their wealth and power at the expense of the people, leaving them in poverty and misery. Yet it was well founded and just, and the eloquence of the Latin prose was impressive. Books like this one changed the world and how people thought; it had certainly made him think again about how he ruled his kingdom. He was sure it would win praise everywhere, and deservedly. He knew himself blessed in having such a servant. He would promote More to the Privy Council.

In June, Harry celebrated his twenty-fifth birthday. He looked in his mirror with some satisfaction. He had heard himself described as the handsomest prince in the world, and he liked to think it was not mere flattery. His complexion was fair and there was no streak of grey in his auburn hair. His face, he had been told, was so very beautiful that it would become a pretty woman, although no woman ever sported such a fine Roman nose or such a bull of a neck. His shoulders were broad, his waist trim. He looked every inch a king.

That summer, he was present in Canterbury Cathedral to honour the translation of the relics of St Thomas Becket to a new shrine, kneeling in reverence before the congregation, amazed at the press of people. Outside, the souvenir sellers were doing a roaring trade with their crude pilgrim badges depicting the saint. Harry wondered if it was right for people to make money in this way. But, if it encouraged others in their devotion, then he supposed it was not to be despised.

He and Kate set off on their summer progress, which took them to Winchester and then to the Vyne, a fine house built by the amiable Sir William Sandys, one of Harry's Knights of the Body. Sandys gave him a lavish welcome; he had even purchased a great bed hung with green velvet for his master. Harry admired the impressive long gallery with its linenfold panelling embellished with the royal arms, and the glorious chapel lit by windows depicting himself, Kate and his sister Margaret, all of them kneeling at prayer with their patron saints.

That evening, after dinner, he summoned a new musician to play for the company. Friar Dionysio Memmo had been organist at St Mark's Basilica in Venice. Hearing of his reputation, Harry had invited him to England to wait on him in the privy chamber. When Memmo had begun playing on his portable organ, he had sat open-mouthed in rapture and promoted him at once to chief musician, knowing he would never weary of listening to him. Now Memmo was playing a new song he had composed, which had everyone laughing, for its lyrics contained a strong hint that he might appreciate an increase in salary.

Harry roared with mirth. 'Very well, Friar! I can take a hint. You shall have a lucrative church living for your pains!'

1517

That Christmas saw the usual lavish festivities at Greenwich and was graced by the presence of the three queens. Wolsey murmured to Harry discreetly that Margaret had come to him, embarrassed because she was unable to afford New Year's gifts. 'Do not concern yourself, Sir; I gave her some money to pay for them.'

'I am most grateful.' Harry was feeling distracted. Even Wolsey did not know that Kate had recently lost a baby, in her fifth month. He was starting once more to fear that God would never send him a son.

'You should go to Our Lady of Walsingham,' he urged her, as

they lay abed one night in early January. 'Take rich gifts, and she will surely hear your prayers this time.'

'I will, my Henry,' Kate agreed, but she sounded depressed. When he bent to kiss her, she turned away. 'I do nothing but pray,' she whispered, and he realised she was weeping.

'I know,' he said. She was becoming more devout with every passing year. With the loss of each child, she had turned increasingly to her faith for solace. She no longer participated so enthusiastically at court revels, but often withdrew early, and although she always made a good show on state occasions, he could not overlook how she was ageing and growing stouter.

'I will go to Walsingham when the weather is better,' she promised. 'In the spring.'

'Good. And, in the meantime, God has sent us a surer way to get a son. No, Kate, don't cry. Come to me.' And he pulled her into his arms, sad that the fire that had once flared between them burned no more.

On May Day, Harry and his train of courtiers rode into the woods at Kensington to bring in the May. They were engrossed in their pastime when they saw Wolsey riding towards them on his mule, his brow furrowed.

'Your Grace,' he called breathlessly, as soon as he came within earshot, 'there are riots in the City. The apprentices have risen against the foreigners.'

Harry's anger flared. 'By God, how dare they? For years I've been encouraging foreign merchants to set up trade in London, yea, and seen they were made welcome.'

'Aye, Sir, and they have prospered.'

'And England has prospered because of it,' Harry said. 'How dare these knaves attack those under my special protection! I will leave for the City at once. Send my guards ahead, and tell them to bring the rioters under control as quickly as possible.'

Wolsey sped away and Harry hastened back to the palace with Kate and his courtiers. Then he was gone, riding like fury to London.

* * *

Harry sat enthroned at the top of the steps at the end of Westminster Hall. Beside him sat Kate, with Wolsey standing behind with the lords of the Council. Before him knelt four hundred apprentices wearing halters around their necks. Crowded at the other end of the hall were their families and many wailing mothers, all in terror lest their sons meet the same fate as the ringleaders of the riots, who had been hanged.

Harry had been all for hanging the lot of them as an example to show those who were guests in his kingdom that he was determined to protect their interests. But Wolsey had objected.

'They are mere boys, most of them. They were probably led astray by those hotheads. I urge you, Sir, not to put them to death. I think it would enhance your fame to pardon these silly youths.'

'Hmm.' Harry's anger having cooled somewhat over the past three weeks of meting out summary justice, he found the idea of appearing all-merciful appealing. 'But how would it look to the world at large?'

'Everyone would applaud you. Sir, let the Queen and myself publicly plead for the lives of these wretches. Then you can show mercy without any loss of authority.'

Harry had agreed. Now he rose and addressed the quaking apprentices before him. 'You have disgraced this kingdom,' he said sternly. 'Rioting and attacking foreigners is not the way to settle your grievances. You are supposed to be learning a trade, in obedience to your masters, so that one day you too can become prosperous. But you chose to risk everything.' From the back of the hall came the sound of hysterical sobbing. Some of the apprentices were weeping too.

'You have deserved death,' Harry went on, 'and that is the sentence I must pass on you.' He turned to Kate and a look passed between them.

'Sir,' she said, dropping to her knees before him, 'for the sake of Our Lord Jesus Christ, and His Holy Mother, who knew what it was to lose a son, I beseech you, pardon these boys. They know they have done wrong, but I am sure they have learned their lesson. I beg of you, set them free to return to their loving families.'

As she raised her hands in supplication, Wolsey knelt too. 'Your Grace was ever a merciful prince. I too crave the lives of these youths, who have suffered sufficiently to atone for their crimes.'

Harry looked down at them both, frowning. Then his eyes ranged around the hall, seeing faces turned imploringly up to him. He smiled. 'How can I refuse such heartfelt pleas? I graciously pardon you all. You are free to leave.'

There were great shouts of exultation as the apprentices threw their caps in the air for joy, and their mothers, pushing through the throng to embrace them, called down blessings on the King.

There was little time for rejoicing, for the dread illness known as the sweating sickness had once again visited England; already there were several cases in London. Harry was a brave man in most ways, but he remained terrified of disease, especially the plague, of which there were outbreaks most summers in the hot, crowded, dirty capital. But the sweat, as it was called, could kill with even more devastating speed.

Dr Chamber had described it to him. 'One has a little pain in the head and heart; suddenly, a sweat breaks out, and a physician is useless, for whether you wrap yourself up much or little, in four hours – sometimes within two or three – you are dispatched without languishing.' Harry wished he hadn't asked the doctor to elaborate; he'd rather not have known this.

'Most people succumb on the first day,' Chamber had continued, oblivious to the fear in his monarch's eyes. 'A man can be merry at dinner and dead at supper. But once twenty-four hours have passed, all danger is at an end. Of course, the numbers of cases are always exaggerated. One rumour can cause a thousand cases, for people suffer more from fear than from the sweat itself.'

Even so, Harry thought, too many people were dying of it, and some were saying it was a judgement of God. It had first appeared in the year of Father's accession, and then again when Harry was fifteen, although that had been a mild outbreak. But why should God visit it upon England now?

It was not as if the country was being infected by heresy, as was happening in Germany, where a monk, Martin Luther, had nailed to the church door at Wittenberg a list of ninety-five theses, attacking abuses in the Church. Harry knew that the Church needed reform. Too many clergy lived immoral, venal lives. It was wrong to sell indulgences that could buy forgiveness from sin. The Vatican was corrupt, everyone knew that. But rejecting Papal authority, as Luther had, as well as pilgrimages, holy relics, penances and clerical celibacy, was plain wrong.

Harry was shocked to learn that Luther advocated praying directly to God rather than through the Virgin Mary, the saints and the clergy – and that he acknowledged only two of the seven sacraments: baptism and the Mass. Worse still, he had asserted that the consecrated Host did not miraculously become the actual body and blood of Christ, but merely symbolised it. Faith alone, rather than ritual, ceremonial and good works, was the foundation of his new religion. As a good son of the Church, Harry could only abhor such heresies – and wonder why divine displeasure was being visited on his kingdom.

There was no cure for the sweat. He liked making up his own remedies, but even he could find no clue in the works of the ancient Greeks as to what might prove efficacious. The truth was, no one had any idea of what to do. The only thing his doctors agreed upon was that the patient should be kept awake. Thus the mere mention of the sweating sickness was so terrible to Harry's ears that his first instinct was to flee from any place remotely near where it had appeared. Anyone he encountered might bring death to him, so it was essential to see as few people as possible.

Ordering that no one who had been in contact with any infected person was to come to court, he gave the order to remove to Richmond, and thence to Greenwich, having dispatched Mary and her attendants to Beaulieu in Essex. But by August, the sickness had crept too near for comfort, so he sent home most members of his household and moved to Windsor, where he shut himself up with Kate, Friar Memmo, Compton, Carew and six physicians. All but the most necessary government business was being held in suspension.

'Wolsey can deal with it,' he told Kate. 'He's had the sweat four times in the past.'

But the news Wolsey sent from York Place was grim. *Multitudes are dying around us*, he wrote. Harry immediately abandoned his plans for a summer progress, for who knew where the sweat might appear next? It was rampant in Oxford and Cambridge now, and the universities had sent their students home.

Windsor, with its stout walls keeping the world out, seemed like a safe haven, until some of the pages who slept in his chamber sickened and died. Ill with fear, he fled with his small entourage to one remote house after another, trying to escape the contagion; but he was never quite ahead of it. Some of those who worked in the royal kitchens and stables caught the sweat and perished, as did Harry's Latin secretary. That was too close to home by far. To make matters worse, there were reports of civil disorder in London, and Kate miscarried another child. Harry wished he could seek comfort on Bessie's ample bosom, especially since Kate was spending such long hours on her knees in chapel. But Bessie was far away – and, please God, still with the living.

He too was seized with the need to appease the Almighty, fearful that he had truly offended Him. He became more assiduous at his devotions, attending Mass and receiving communion more frequently than usual. He kept terror at bay by hawking, or making music with Friar Memmo. He made another attempt to concoct a remedy for the sweat, an infusion of sage, herb of grace and elder leaves. But he had little faith in it working.

By December, there were fewer cases of the pestilence, yet Harry was too wary to keep Christmas as usual. His provisions were running low, and he had no wish to purchase goods that might be contaminated, so he and his companions rode to Southampton, where they waited for Flemish ships to offload food supplies. It was a dismal Yuletide.

The sweat lingered through the winter. Harry continued on his travels, keeping in touch with Wolsey by messenger. In March, when he visited Abingdon, he began to relax a little, since there were no new reports of any deaths. But he restricted the numbers attending court at Easter.

After that, with the situation so improved, he was all for returning to London, but Kate was reluctant. Instead, after the St George's Day celebrations, the small court moved to Woodstock Palace near Oxford. There was excellent hunting, and Harry felt exhilarated to be riding to the chase with the wind blowing through his hair and the horns sounding ahead. But his optimistic mood was shattered when he received reports of plague nearby, which sent him galloping to Ewelme, and thence to Bisham Priory, Greenwich, Richmond and Esher.

In August, he stayed as Buckingham's guest at Penshurst Place in Kent. The sweat had at last died out, Kate was with child again, and he was in a more ebullient frame of mind. He departed on a hunting progress, and when he was reunited with Kate at Woodstock, he was delighted to see her belly so high.

'I must have been further along than I thought,' she said, as they embraced. 'And the child has quickened and is lively.'

'A lusty son, I hope!' he replied.

'I pray so.' She looked anxious. 'But the doctors say that all is well.'

'Then you must not worry. It is bad for the babe. Come, let us go in to dinner. I'm starving after being in the saddle all day. I hope you have some news of Mary for me. Is she well?'

'She is bursting with health,' Kate told him, her eyes lighting up at the thought of their daughter.

Out of the corner of his eye, Harry saw Bessie staring at him with undisguised joy. He quickly looked away, promising himself that later, with Kate forbidden to him, he would send for her. And then, by God, they would make up for lost time!

* * *

The court had reassembled in its entirety at Bridewell, and Harry was glad to be working again with Wolsey. In May, the Cardinal had been appointed Papal legate and given unprecedented authority over the Church in England, even surpassing that of the Archbishop of Canterbury. When he went abroad in procession, two crosses were now borne before him, and he carried himself with great pride. Yet still Harry did not begrudge him his greatness.

It seemed now that Wolsey's dream of becoming Pope might come true. To make that happen, he needed the backing of King Francis or the Emperor Maximilian, who would no doubt have their own candidates when the time came. Harry knew that Wolsey's determination to play an international role was not just to his master's benefit, but also aimed at making himself indispensable to those two great princes. Nothing would please Wolsey more than to become the arbiter of Christendom. He had just negotiated a treaty between England, France and the Papacy, its aim being to persuade Maximilian and the Infante Charles to agree to maintain peace in Europe. Harry made sure that he himself took the credit for bringing about this ambitious alliance, even though he suspected that most parties knew that Wolsey had done most of the negotiating.

To cement the concord with France, the Princess Mary was to be betrothed to the Dauphin Francis, the French King's heir, and Harry was to meet with Francis the following year – a prospect that filled him with overweening curiosity and jealousy.

'You are going to be a queen, Mary,' he told his daughter, dandling her on his knee. She was two now, an exquisite, bright, joyous child with red hair like his, a snub nose and a determined little chin. 'Would you like that?'

She smiled up at him, revealing pearly baby teeth.

'She hardly knows what it means.' Kate's eyes were on the altar cloth she was embroidering.

'She will make a great queen, and all France will love her. Show me how you curtsey, Mary.' Harry stood her on the floor and she executed a perfect bob. 'Excellent! You have taught her well, Kate.'

'Lady Bryan must take some of the credit.'

Although the birth of their child was imminent, Kate was not happy. It was obvious that she hated the idea of her precious child being married off to France, Spain's ancient enemy, and plain that she resented Wolsey for brokering the alliance. No doubt she was angry with Harry too, for signing the treaty. But even she could not deny that peace in Europe was preferable to war. And it was a great achievement on his part! She should be proud of that.

There were lavish celebrations in London. In September, a French embassy, headed by the Admiral of France, accompanied by eighty fashionably dressed noblemen and their entourages, arrived in England. When the King received them in audience, the Princess Mary was brought in for their inspection. Catching sight of Friar Memmo, who was sitting in a corner quietly strumming a lute, she piped up, 'Priest! Priest! Play "Jolly Foster" for me!' Harry caught her up in his arms as the friar obliged, much to her delight. The Admiral bowed to his future Queen and professed himself enchanted.

Early in October, Harry signed the treaty in St Paul's Cathedral, watched by a vast concourse of nobles and dignitaries. Wolsey celebrated High Mass with splendid solemnity, and the King's secretary, Richard Pace, delivered a long oration praising his master, who sat beaming before him on a throne upholstered in cloth of gold. If Wolsey thought that Harry had unfairly appropriated the glory and praise, he gave no hint of it.

Afterwards, Harry hosted a dinner for the ambassadors in the Bishop's Palace next door. That evening, at York Place, now a magnificent palace, Wolsey gave a sumptuous supper, the like of which, the Admiral said, had not been given even by Cleopatra or Caligula. When the feasting was over, Harry and his sister Mary – here on a rare visit to court and visibly happy with Suffolk – led out twenty-four masked dancers, among them Bessie Blount, Suffolk, Neville, Bryan, Carew, Guildford and Henry Norris, a young gentleman recently appointed to the Privy Chamber. Harry cherished a high opinion of him; Norris had all the qualities he looked for in those who attended on him daily – diligence, wit, charm and the ability to anticipate his needs – and he had quickly been accepted into the inner circle of royal companions.

After the masque, large bowls brimming with gold coins and dice were brought to the tables so that the company could settle down to some serious gambling. Then there was dancing until midnight, when Harry retired to steal a few precious hours alone with Bessie.

Two days later, at Greenwich, the Princess Mary was formally betrothed to the Dauphin in the Queen's great chamber in the presence of her parents, her godfather, Cardinal Wolsey, the Papal envoy, Cardinal Campeggio, the ambassadors and the lords and ladies of the court, all decked out in their finery. Mary looked exquisite in a gown of cloth of gold with a black bejewelled hood; already, she had learned to manage a court train without falling over. The Admiral stood proxy for her future bridegroom, as Wolsey held her in his arms and placed on her tiny finger a great diamond ring that was much too big for her.

'Are you the Dauphin of France?' Mary asked the Admiral. 'If you are, I want to kiss you!' The august company rocked with indulgent mirth.

'That will have to wait a little!' Harry chuckled. 'No, sweeting, the Dauphin is in Paris, tucked up in his cradle.'

After the two cardinals had blessed the little bride-to-be, she was carried off to bed. Harry led his guests into the presence chamber for the betrothal feast, at which he was served by the dukes of Norfolk, Suffolk and Buckingham. The latter, much to his master's irritation, did not trouble to conceal his disapproval of the alliance with France. Harry was vexed with Kate too, who had barely smiled all day, and who excused herself after the first course, saying that she was tired. He watched her go, feeling resentful, then forgot about her as the wine flowed and he remembered that there would be celebratory jousts and a pageant tomorrow. His good mood restored, he carried on carousing until two o'clock in the morning. And when the Admiral admired his long gown of gold brocade lined with ermine, he magnanimously threw it off and told him to keep it.

Chapter 12

1518

The child was born in November. Harry was bitterly disappointed to be told that it was a girl and could not hide his despondency when they placed the tiny, mewling creature in his arms. He knew she would not live; her cries were so weak. She did not even survive to be baptised.

Eight children, all dead except one. Why? he kept asking himself as he lay in bed the night after the burial, wondering yet again what he had done to offend God, that He should deny His faithful servant the blessing of an heir. Kate thought that He was punishing her, and maybe both of them were to blame. The thought was chilling.

He must visit Kate's bed and try again. She was thirty-three now, well into middle age, and looked it. He feared she might never bear a son. What would he do without a male heir to succeed him? What would happen to England? If he dropped dead tomorrow, his kingdom would be at the mercy of those sprigs of the House of York who mayhap thought they had a better claim to the throne than he did. It would be the wars of the two roses all over again.

There was Mary, of course, his heir presumptive. King Francis would doubtless seize the chance to press her claim and make his son king of England, but Harry could not bear the thought of his kingdom becoming a province of France, and the English would never tolerate being ruled by their ancient enemies.

He turned over, trying to get comfortable, wishing he could sleep. He was weary of agonising about a future that did not include him. He had maintained the peace in his realm, won victories, achieved great successes in diplomacy. But it could all be torn apart without his firm hand.

He knew Kate's views without asking her. Her mother, Isabella, had ruled Spain jointly as queen alongside Ferdinand. She had led armies; her fame was legendary. Kate clearly believed that Mary could be another like her. Yet, God had intended men to govern nations. Women had not the strength nor the mental capacity, which was why the law deemed them infants. Look at Kate's sister Juana, the rightful Queen of Castile – a raving lunatic thankfully locked up in a castle in Spain. And the English did not take kindly to queens. Back in the twelfth century, they had sent the last one packing before she could be crowned.

What to do? What *could* he do? Apply to the Pope for an annulment and take a younger wife? But that would break Kate's heart. He did not desire her as he once had, but he still loved her.

He was too tired to worry about it now. If only Bessie was here in bed with him. He yearned for the comfort of her lusty embrace, her undemanding company, her gentle touch. Dare he summon her? She would be sound asleep in the maids' dorter by now. No, he would wait until tomorrow night.

She came to him the following evening, pink and white in her rose-coloured gown trimmed with rabbit fur. There was a new bloom about her, a comely plumpness that he put down to too much indulging in good food. He liked that in a woman.

Scarcely had she let fall the latch than he pulled her into his arms.

'Sweetheart,' he murmured, 'I have longed for you!' His hands were feeling for the laces of her bodice.

'Oh, Harry, we mustn't,' she giggled.

'Why not? Have your courses come?'

Her face widened in a lovely smile. 'Not for a long time. Harry, I'm with child!'

Oh, joy! He stared at her as if she were the Virgin Mother incarnate. 'Oh, my darling!' he breathed. 'That is the best news you could have given me.' Tears welled in his eyes; he felt choked. It was

185

wonderful – but it was bittersweet too. It seemed all wrong that his mistress should be carrying his child while his wife was all but barren.

Yet he found his spirits soaring on wings when he thought of the child growing beneath Bessie's stomacher. She was well, she said; everything seemed to be as it should. Of course, she could not remain at court when her pregnancy began to show, so he confided in Wolsey, who made discreet arrangements for when that time came. Bessie would stay at Jericho, a secluded, peaceful house in Essex that Harry had bought from the nearby priory of St Laurence. Kate could be told that the girl was needed at home in Shropshire to be company for her mother, who was ailing. That was far enough away for no one to discover the truth.

Bessie went willingly enough, relieved to be able to hide her shame and escape public censure. Harry watched her go from his window, desperately wishing that things could be otherwise. He would miss her sorely.

1519

In the new year, word reached England of the death of that old fox Maximilian. A new Holy Roman Emperor would now have to be elected. Harry immediately put himself forward and sent the ever-diligent Richard Pace to Germany to campaign on his behalf, while he himself rode down to Beddington Park in Surrey to spend a week as Sir Nicholas Carew's guest. His friend's house had a lofty great hall with a splendid hammerbeam roof, and Harry resolved to build one like it at one of his palaces.

Each evening, after a good day's hunting, he sat up late by the fire, chatting with Carew, as the musicians played softly in the shadows.

'Compton asked me for permission to propose marriage to the Countess of Salisbury,' Harry recounted. The widowed Margaret Pole, a sprig off the old Plantagenet tree, was his second cousin, a saintly, and very rich, lady whom he much admired.

'He has an eye to a fortune,' Carew observed. 'It can't be love. He's been committing adultery for years with Lady Hastings, ever since her husband released her from that nunnery.'

Harry felt his cheeks flush. Compton had made his move with almost indecent haste after he himself had been obliged to cease pursuing Anne Hastings in the wake of Kate's tantrums. 'I think Lady Salisbury is aware of that. She turned him down. If he's not careful, he'll end up before an ecclesiastical tribunal for living openly in sin with a married woman.'

'Him and half your court!' Carew chuckled.

Harry frowned. Wolsey had been complaining for some time that the conduct of some of his young gentlemen was bringing the court into disrepute. He had winced at that, wishing to be seen as a virtuous prince, but he was also aware that Wolsey and his colleagues on the Privy Council were jealous of the influence wielded by the gentlemen of the Privy Chamber, who were effectively rivals for the King's ear. The lords had a motive for wanting to curb their influence.

After St George's Day, Harry moved to Greenwich, and it was there that the Cardinal declared his hand, in Council.

'Your Grace, we are all agreed that the Privy Chamber should be purged of those young minions who behave in a manner not in keeping with your dignity and honour.'

For once, heads were nodding in unanimous agreement with Wolsey. Harry said nothing, torn between loyalty to his friends and the desire to protect the reputation of his court. It must never become the cesspit over which King Francis presided!

Wolsey spoke again. 'I am speaking of Sir Nicholas Carew, Francis Bryan, Sir Edward Neville and Sir Henry Guildford, to name but a few.' Thank God he had not named Compton! 'They give your Grace evil counsel. They encourage you to gamble away large sums; they are too familiar and forget themselves. You patiently suffer these things, but because of your gentle nature, you neither rebuke nor reprove them.'

'These men are my friends,' Harry declared. Secretly, he too had become concerned about the overfamiliarity, although he had permitted and even encouraged it. Yet he did not want to dismiss his close companions.

'Alas, Sir, they are not good friends. You may not be aware that recently, during a diplomatic mission to Paris, Neville and Bryan publicly disgraced themselves when accompanying King Francis as he rode in disguise through the streets. They were throwing eggs, stones and other trifles at the people.'

Harry flushed, remembering the times when he and his friends, all incognito, had visited taverns in London and got drunk and foolish. He prayed that Wolsey had never heard about that.

'I fear that, back home, they are now all French in their eating, drinking and apparel, and French in their vices,' Surrey sniffed.

'It's true, Sir,' Norfolk chimed in. 'They sneer when they compare your court with that of France; they poke fun at older courtiers and household officers, and generally comport themselves in a reprehensible manner.'

'Aye, Sir,' chorused the other councillors, even Sir Thomas Boleyn.

'We ask your Grace to put a stop to their behaviour, since it reflects badly upon you,' Wolsey demanded.

Harry squirmed in his seat; it was like being a youngling again, with Father telling him off. Yet, resent it or not, he knew what he must do. 'Very well,' he said. 'My Lord Chamberlain, you will summon them all and dismiss them from their posts, then order them to leave court. But they can still make themselves useful to me. Carew and Neville can go to Calais to help man its defences; the rest can attend to their duties in their own counties.'

He rose and left them to it, not wishing to dwell on how grieved his friends would be to be sent away. And he soon missed them; life had become much less lively. But when, as the days passed, he saw that their removal was little mourned at court, he began to feel justified. A king, after all, should not behave like a fool; he must have dignity, gravitas.

In place of those who had been dismissed, Wolsey brought into the Privy Chamber some older, more sober knights whom Harry liked, even though he knew they were the Cardinal's men. Thankfully,

Henry Norris was allowed to remain, for everyone thought him trustworthy, thoughtful and discreet. No doubt Wolsey, Norfolk and the rest were hoping that, freed from the influence of his friends, Harry would lead a new, more mature mode of life, paying less attention to revelry and pastimes and more to state business.

Despite this brief accord against the Privy Chamber, the councillors' resentment of Wolsey was livelier than ever. Norfolk in particular was jealous of that fine palace at Hampton Court. He was now the patron of old Skelinton and it was probably he who had bidden Harry's former tutor to compose some waspish doggerels attacking Wolsey, which were still causing much mirth among the courtiers. Skelinton had evidently taken pleasure in sneering at the Cardinal's shameless ambition and greasy genealogy.

> Why come ye not to court?
> To the King's court, or to Hampton Court?
> The King's court should have the precedence,
> But Hampton Court hath the pre-eminence.

Wolsey had been so wrathful when he read this that he had ordered Skelinton's arrest, but the old man had fled into sanctuary at Westminster Abbey. Harry would have gone after him too, for Skelinton had dared to attack him in a morality play called *Magnificence*. Harry had expected it to be laudatory, but instead he found himself heavily censured for immoderate indulgence in pleasure and advised to seek a compromise between showy display and frugality. The play showed him dismissing a wise minister and giving a foolish one too much power, a none-too-subtle message that he found quite unpalatable. Had his old tutor not been skulking in sanctuary, he would have clapped him in the Tower for a spell.

With his friends gone, he absorbed himself in more solemn matters. Just now, he was planning his tomb. Torrigiano had sculpted a glorious monument for his parents in Westminster Abbey. When he gazed on their golden effigies, it was like looking on their living selves again: Father, as dull and severe as ever, and Mother in all her sweetness and beauty. He had thought that Kate would be her image in all things, and that was true to a certain extent, yet Kate had failed where Mother had succeeded, for she had not given him a son.

He wanted an even more imposing tomb for himself, one that would reflect the magnificence of his person and his achievements – an enormous sepulchre of white marble and black jasper, crowned with a triumphal arch bearing a statue of himself on horseback and surrounded by dozens of life-sized gilded figures.

When he was not drawing up plans for his memorial, he spent time in the lists or in the company of his new astronomer, Nicolaus Kratzer, whom he had persuaded to leave his native Germany to enter royal service. Kratzer was brimful of wit and on good terms with Erasmus and Thomas More.

On a warm day in late spring, he brought to Harry's study his design for a sundial. Normally, Harry would have been riveted, but today he was distracted. The results of the Imperial election were expected at any time, and he was awaiting them with impatience.

In the end, he could contain himself no longer. 'Alas, Master Kratzer, state business calls,' he said. 'We will discuss your design another time.'

'Is there any news?' he asked for the umpteenth time, bursting into Wolsey's closet.

'No, your Grace, not yet.'

'Do you think I stand a good chance of being elected?' It was his constant refrain; he could not bear the thought of being passed over.

'I am quite optimistic,' Wolsey replied. 'But I don't think we will get the result this week. Why don't you go hunting, Sir?'

Harry went, his head full of plans for what he would do if he became emperor. He saw himself in Rome, kneeling before the Pope to receive the crown of Charlemagne, or travelling the length and breadth of Christendom, with all nations bowing before him, or ensconced in the great palaces of Burgundy, Germany, Austria, Hungary and Italy. *Henricus Imperator!* What a ring it had!

He was being lavishly entertained once more by Buckingham at Penshurst Place, and enjoying a game of tennis, when Richard Pace's arrival was finally announced. Harry hastened to receive him in the garden, where they could not be overheard.

'Well?' He was bristling with anticipation.

'Your Grace, I fear it is not the news you wish to hear. The Infante Charles has been elected emperor.'

'That stripling?' Harry exclaimed, appalled. 'By God, he won't be up to it!'

But it would not do to parade his crushing disappointment in public. At all costs, he must not lose face. 'Well, I'm sure the electors knew what they were doing.'

'Your Grace can have no idea how much money Charles spent bribing them,' said Pace, with a look of disgust.

'Then I am right glad that I did not win the election, if the Empire is so corrupt,' Harry replied, grateful to his secretary for making it easier for him to swallow his dismay. 'Now, my friend, I insist that you take supper with me.'

As they walked back to the hall, he turned his thoughts to the future. 'I wish I had not got so caught up with the Imperial election, Richard. I should have been meeting with King Francis, but now it must wait until next year. I know he is as keen for the summit as I am. We have both agreed not to shave until we meet, hence this beard. The Queen does not like it.' He grinned.

'I think it suits your Grace very well,' Pace complimented him. Harry agreed. The fine golden beard made him look very distinguished. But Kate persisted in waging war on it.

'I hate beards,' she protested. 'I love you the way you look normally, clean-shaven. I beg of you, get rid of it, for my sake!' She made such a clamour that Harry, preferring a quiet life, capitulated. Then he had to write to King Francis, explaining what had happened and feeling rather a fool. But Louise of Savoy, Francis' mother, neatly averted a diplomatic incident, declaring that the love the two kings bore each other was not in the beards, but in the hearts. Harry smiled at that. How easily lies became politic currency.

Inwardly, he knew he should not have given way to Kate. There had been an escalating distancing between them, at least on his side.

The five-and-a-half-year age gap was becoming ever more obvious. One glance in his mirror showed Harry that ambassadors were not exaggerating when they said he was far handsomer than any other sovereign in Christendom. He was still fair, still admirably proportioned. Nature, people said, could not have done more for him. Next to him, Kate looked faded, the marks of disappointment and sorrow etched on her face, which only became illuminated when her eyes lighted upon him – a middle-aged woman looking like a green girl. Harry's sense of chivalry had been outraged when he was told that King Francis had called her old and deformed – when he hadn't even set eyes on her – yet it wasn't far from the truth. That firm, jutting chin did look deformed, there was no denying it.

He missed Bessie – Bessie, whose pregnancy was progressing well, according to the reports sent by her midwife to Wolsey. As spring turned into summer, he became increasingly excited about the impending birth and anxious lest anything should go wrong. And then, one glorious day in June, Wolsey came to his closet, beaming.

'Your Grace has a healthy son. I have just had the news from Jericho.'

A son! A healthy son! But a bastard who could not inherit the crown. Harry's joy was tempered with frustration. How could God be so cruel, when He knew that the thing Harry most desired, and needed, was a boy to succeed him?

'I trust that Mistress Blount is well?' His heart was filled with gratitude towards Bessie, and bitter regret that she was not his wife.

'She is very well and in no danger. And I am told that the child has the beauty of both its father and mother.'

'I shall visit them soon.'

'I advise your Grace to be discreet.'

'No,' Harry said.

'No, Sir?'

'I see no reason for discretion.' Suddenly, he wanted to punish Kate for failing to bear him a son. He wanted to say to her, and to the world, 'Look what I can do! The fault does not lie in me!' Never again would he fear that his lack of a male heir was a slur upon his manhood. 'The child shall be called Henry Fitzroy – son of the King! And I mean publicly to acknowledge him, so that everyone will know that I am capable of siring boys, if any ever doubted it! You shall be godfather, Thomas, and be responsible for his care. While he is young, you may leave him with Mistress Blount. And I insist that she be called and honoured as "the mother of the King's son".'

Wolsey was frowning. 'Alas, Sir, I fear she may not be treated honourably, unless she makes a good marriage.'

Harry stared at him. 'But I want her back at court. The King of France has *maîtresses-en-titre*, who openly consort with him. Why should I not have the same?'

'Because this is England, Sire, and your subjects will not tolerate it. The Queen is much loved. By all means, continue to honour Mistress Blount with your attentions, but I pray you be discreet. Let a respectable marriage be a cover for your affection.'

Calmer now, Harry saw the wisdom in Wolsey's advice. The Cardinal never failed him.

'Very well,' he said.

Wolsey worked quickly. He arranged for Bessie to be speedily married to one of his wards, a wealthy young gentleman called Gilbert Tailboys, who had estates in Lincolnshire and Somerset. Parliament was persuaded to assign her a handsome dowry. Much to Harry's disappointment, she left court, to live with her new husband, but Wolsey arranged for her to visit in secret, and she and Harry resumed their affair.

Their shared love for their son brought them closer than ever before. Harry delighted in the little boy, who was the very image of himself. If only, *if only*, this child could succeed him! He could never look at him without wishing that things were otherwise.

Kate said nothing, made no mention of Henry Fitzroy, even though the court had been buzzing with gossip. She must know what had happened, yet she continued to show a loving countenance to Harry. In fact, no one openly criticised him. It was Wolsey who was targeted, as his enemies gleefully accused him of encouraging immorality in the young by the well marrying of Bessie Blount. And that gave Harry an opening to bring back the friends Wolsey had had dismissed.

'Well, my lord Cardinal, you can't have it both ways,' he taunted him, as they walked in the gardens one day.

Wolsey looked at him blankly.

'Ha!' Harry laughed. 'You dismiss my minions, as you were pleased to call them, for their misconduct, yet you openly make a mockery of marriage, or so your opponents say.'

'But I helped you, Sir.' The Cardinal could not hide his dismay.

'You did, and I am grateful. But I am recalling my friends. I will not have it said that you are a hypocrite. And in doing that, I am helping you.' He grinned.

'Alas, Sir, you have outfoxed me,' Wolsey said ruefully.

1520

On a cold February morning, Harry attended the wedding of his distant cousin, William Carey, an up-and-coming gentleman of his Privy Chamber, and Sir Thomas Boleyn's daughter Mary. Mary had been in France for several years, having gone there in the train of Harry's sister and stayed to serve the Queen of France. Given what Harry had heard, she was lucky to have secured such a fine husband. The words 'soiled goods' came to mind, and it was even rumoured that King Francis had boasted of having ridden his English mare. But Boleyn was a clever operator; somehow, he had managed to sell his daughter to Carey. Looking at her, all pert dimples and soft flesh, Harry could see why the young man was so smitten. As he bent to kiss the bride, he felt a twinge of envy – and lust.

After leaving the bridal party to their revelry, he summoned Wolsey to his closet. The time was fast approaching for his meeting with King Francis, for which the Cardinal was overseeing every detail involved in transporting five thousand people across the English Channel to Calais, England's last remaining possession in France.

Wolsey arrived with a sheaf of plans and lists. 'Now, Sir, it has been agreed that the meeting will take place six miles from Calais in a place called the Val d'Or, which lies in the open countryside between your Grace's town of Guisnes, where you will be based, and Ardres, where King Francis will stay. I fear, however, that Guisnes Castle is too small for a sufficient display of magnificence. Might I suggest, therefore, that we build a temporary palace at the meeting place?'

He laid a set of elaborate designs before Harry, who stared at them, impressed.

'It will be a palace of illusions,' Wolsey elaborated. 'Not even Leonardo da Vinci could improve upon it. It will be built of timber on stone and brick foundations and covered with canvas painted to look like brickwork or masonry. The dining hall is to have a ceiling of green silk studded with gold roses, and a floor covering of patterned taffeta. There will be a King's Side, a Queen's Side, a suite for my humble self, and one for your Grace's sister, the French Queen. Senior courtiers will be accommodated in Guisnes Castle; the rest can stay in tents. I have ordered two thousand, eight hundred of them. Now these pavilions . . .' He unrolled a page covered with colourful designs for tents of green and white, blue and gold, and red and gold, all adorned with the King's badges, beasts and mottoes. 'They will serve for entertainments and banquets. Your Grace will have your own dining tent of cloth of gold.'

'You have done marvellously, Thomas,' Harry beamed.

Wolsey smiled. 'I have ordered in great quantities of livestock and foodstuffs. We must spare no effort or cost to impress the French.'

Harry nodded. He was determined to outshine Francis. He had been lukewarm about the visit, but now he found himself looking forward to it. 'It is a mighty enterprise,' he observed.

'Everything is under control, Sir. Many other items are being shipped abroad, including tapestries, furnishings and everything needful for tournaments. We have fifteen hundred spears from the Tower arsenal, one thousand Milanese swords, and a great number of horses. I am moving the armourers' steel mill at Greenwich in its entirety to Guisnes, for the repair of armour and weapons.'

It gave Harry great pleasure to think of the French jealously tracking the English preparations. Wolsey's spies had reported that they had no wish to outlay as much money. There would be no prefabricated palace for the King of France; instead, the French court would be housed near Ardres in a little town of tents. Already, they were calling it the Field of Cloth of Gold.

Paramount was the question of etiquette. Wolsey had taken it upon himself to resolve the numerous disputes that arose and laid down the rules governing precedence.

'It has been agreed that, in order to preserve the honour of both nations, neither your Grace nor King Francis will take part in any joust or combat against the other.'

Harry frowned. He had envisaged himself vanquishing Francis in the lists, even unhorsing him, and winning all the prizes.

Wolsey had noted the frown. 'It would not be politic, Sir. All things must appear equal, for your purpose is to forge a lasting peace. The very terrain is being flattened so as not to give either side any advantage.'

Harry supposed that Wolsey was right. All the same, he would have loved to have bested his rival. For they *were* rivals; all the diplomacy in the world could not disguise that. France might have been England's friend for the past six years, and little Mary might be France's future Queen, but ancient enmities died hard.

Nonetheless, he decided to regrow his beard in Francis' honour. Kate, joining him for supper one evening, bristled like a cornered cat. 'You shaved it off for me!' she cried.

'Sometimes, Kate, it is politic to put up with things we do not like.' He had been anticipating a quarrel and was on the defensive.

'You know I have no reason to like this alliance, and you should not either. France will never be your friend; the French will betray you, as they have many times before. Their King is a lecher and I fear he will not keep faith. It would be to your advantage to seek a rapprochement with my nephew, the Emperor Charles. That way, you would win the friendship of Spain and all the Empire. Against that, France is nothing!' She snapped her fingers.

Harry was about to protest on principle, but he could see that she had a point. Charles *would* make a far stronger ally. He nodded. 'You may have the sow by the right ear, Kate. It would be wise to keep all my options open.' He drained his goblet. 'He will soon be leaving for Spain, after his coronation in Aachen. I shall invite him to visit us here, before we leave for France.'

Kate's eyes filled with tears. 'Oh, my Henry . . . You will not regret it, I promise you.'

He held up his hand. 'We are still going to France. Francis remains my ally, and I want you to show him a smiling face.'

'I will do it for your sake,' she promised.

Wolsey was not pleased when Harry told him he was meeting the Emperor. He had ever favoured the French, and Harry suspected he feared the Queen's influence.

'But preparations are so far advanced,' he protested, shuffling yet another pile of papers.

'I'm not calling the French visit off,' Harry assured him. 'They will not be wasted.'

'Yes, Sir, but, with respect, there is no point in all this extravagant outlay if you are thinking of breaking faith with King Francis.'

'I did not say I was. There is no harm in inviting my wife's nephew to visit England.'

'The French might not see it that way.' Wolsey looked deeply troubled. He had invested a lot in this coming summit.

'Then we will disabuse them of any doubts when we arrive,' Harry said breezily.

Chapter 13

1520

All the arrangements were in place. Norfolk was to remain in charge in England during the King's absence, and the Princess Mary, now four, would be left in the care of Lady Salisbury, who had recently been appointed her governess, and keep royal state at Richmond, where she was to receive some Venetian envoys. Harry knew that she was so well schooled by Kate that she would play her part to perfection. She had uncommon poise for one so young.

In May, Harry and his vast entourage left Greenwich and proceeded in stately fashion through Kent. They stayed first at Archbishop Warham's palaces at Charing and Otford, and then at Leeds Castle, before arriving in Canterbury, where they were to receive the Emperor Charles. When Harry was informed that his guest had docked at Dover to a thunderous salute from the English fleet, and been met by Wolsey and conducted to Dover Castle, he mounted his horse and galloped overnight to the port, just in time to greet Charles as he arrived downstairs in the morning.

Charles had grown to manhood, but even at twenty he looked immature and ponderous, and that gaping mouth was a tragedy. Still, he had a royal bearing and – as Harry discovered as they conversed, riding side by side to Canterbury – a will of steel and a strong sense of honour. An ally to be proud of!

In Canterbury, the people, who made no secret of their hatred of the French, gave Charles a rousing welcome, for much of England's trade was done with the Empire. Mass was celebrated with great pomp and ceremony in the cathedral, and then both King and Emperor knelt in prayer at the shrine of Thomas Becket. Afterwards, the Abbot showed them precious relics of the saint: his hair shirt, his broken skull and the sword that had split it. Harry reverently kissed each one, reflecting on how shocking the sacrilegious murder of the holy martyr had been.

When he arrived with Charles at the Christ Church Gate by the Archbishop's Palace, Kate was waiting for them, looking very regal in cloth of gold and violet velvet trimmed with ermine, with ropes of beautiful pearls around her neck. At the sight of her nephew, she wept with joy.

'You are so like your mother, my poor sister,' she told him, drawing him into her embrace. 'How does she fare these days?'

Charles had shown a little warmth at her welcome, but he now looked uncomfortable. 'She is still somewhat crazed, but the nuns are looking after her very well.'

They dined privately, having been joined by the French Queen. Harry saw Charles' admiring gaze fix upon Mary, remembering no doubt that she had once been his affianced bride and that all that beauty could have been his, but for the perfidy of Ferdinand and Maximilian. And Mary would now have been empress. But there was her husband, Suffolk, presenting the basin of scented water so that they could wash their hands.

In the afternoon, Ferdinand's attractive widow, Germaine de Foix, Dowager Queen of Aragon, arrived in Canterbury with a train of sixty ladies. At a banquet that evening, the three queens sat with the King and the Emperor at the high table, and there was much merriment when the Spanish Count of Cabra got so amorous with one of Kate's ladies that he fainted and had to be carried from the room. Even the elderly Duke of Alva entered into the spirit of the occasion and led the company in some Spanish dancing. Henry danced with his sister, but Charles just sat and watched.

'Did you notice something going on between Charles and Queen Germaine?' Mary asked, as Harry spun her around the floor.

'Really? That's rather incestuous, isn't it?'

'It's like having an affair with your grandmother,' she smiled, 'except that Germaine is only twelve years older than he is.'

'Well, well. He needs a wife!'

'I imagine that the kings of Europe are throwing their daughters at him,' Mary giggled. 'There is no greater prince in Christendom. Yourself excepted, brother,' she added hastily, seeing his grimace. 'But you must have noticed that he has set himself to charm us all – not that he has much charm to speak of!'

'I did notice. He would far rather I made an alliance with him than with Francis.'

'That odious man. You'd do better with the Emperor, Harry.'

'I'm thinking about it.' He was, seriously, especially after learning that Charles was keen enough to award Wolsey a handsome pension and a promise that, when Pope Leo died, he would help him secure the Papacy, in return for brokering an alliance with England. Harry had had to drag the information out of Wolsey, who was still determined to pursue the friendship with France.

'It would be a shame not to go to Calais, though,' Mary said, executing a graceful curtsey as the dance ended. 'I've bought so many new gowns.' She smiled at him wickedly.

'Let's just say I'm keeping my options open,' he told her, bowing. Her comment about Charles needing a wife was echoing in his mind. He had a daughter too . . .

Before Charles departed for Sandwich, he asked Harry to meet with him at his town of Gravelines, after the summit with Francis, and Harry agreed.

Kate was ecstatic. 'He is seeking your friendship, my Henry,' she said, after Charles and his train had disappeared from sight and they were walking back into the palace. 'I beg of you, do consider it. Think of the advantages!'

'I am weighing up all my advantages.'

'You would not regret it. Oh, I was so dreading this trip to France, but now I feel I can go with a lighter heart and bear it.' She reached for his hand and squeezed it.

Harry stared in wonder at the gateway to the temporary palace at Guisnes, which was decorated with a scallop-shell pediment, the royal arms, two large Tudor roses and a golden statue of Cupid. On the lawn in front of it stood a gilded pillar topped with a statue of Bacchus, the god of wine, and a fountain in the ancient Roman style. From this flowed white wine, Malmsey and claret, free to all comers, day and night. Chained to the fountain were silver drinking cups.

He dismounted and allowed Wolsey to escort him inside. The Cardinal was eager to show him the spacious chambers decorated with gilt cornices and furnished with gorgeous tapestries, hangings of cloth of gold, Turkey carpets and buffets laden with gold plate. The glass windows had diamond-shaped panes and the chimneys were of stone. He walked into an exquisite chapel painted blue and gold and hung with cloth of gold and green velvet; on the altar stood a great gold crucifix, ten candlesticks, large gilded statues of the twelve Apostles and many holy relics. Inside and out, the palace was skilfully decorated with Tudor roses, antique work and heraldic devices. Even the pitched canvas roof was painted to look like slates.

'This place is a marvel!' he exclaimed. 'The French have nothing like it. You have done well, my lord Cardinal.'

It seemed as if the whole world was here, crammed into the English camp. Everyone was wearing their richest attire and most sumptuous jewels. Harry reckoned that the outlay must have ruined some of his courtiers.

In his bedchamber, his gentlemen were laying out his clothes for the evening's feast. He had brought with him numerous changes of attire, designed to be more dazzling than anyone else's. For months, he had been importing great quantities of rich fabrics, cloth of gold, velvet silk and damask. Kate was kitted out as no queen had ever been kitted out before, although Harry had been dismayed at her insistence on bringing Spanish headdresses, which would not be a welcome sight in France. But it was too late now to change them, and she had absolutely insisted that she would never be seen dead in a French hood. Fortunately, Mary invariably wore them, which Francis would take as a compliment. She would slay the French again with her beauty and her elegant clothes.

* * *

At a prearranged time on the Feast of Corpus Christi, cannon fire boomed out simultaneously from Guisnes and Ardres, and the two kings, accompanied by a host of courtiers, rode forth to meet each other. They came in battle array, with a show of strength, as if each feared the other side would attack. Attended by the Yeomen of the Guard, Harry rode a bay horse hung with jangling gold bells and cut a dashing figure in cloth of gold and silver, heavily bejewelled, with a feathered black bonnet and his Garter collar. Francis, in equally gorgeous attire, was flanked by his Swiss Guards.

At the perimeter of the Val d'Or, the sovereigns paused, then, to the sound of trumpets and sackbuts, they galloped alone towards each other, doffed their bonnets and embraced while still on horseback, eyeing each other speculatively even as they expressed their joy at meeting.

'Brother!' Harry cried, noting the cynical, saturnine smile, the long Valois nose, the sensual features and muscular strength of the younger man. But not that much younger – there were fewer than three years between them.

Dismounting, they linked arms and entered Francis' sixty-foot pavilion of gold damask lined with blue velvet embroidered with fleurs-de-lis, which was guarded by a statue of St Michael, the special protector of the kings of France.

'It is the greatest pleasure to me to see your Majesty at last,' Francis declared, as if he really meant it.

'I have been longing for this moment,' Harry told him.

Hippocras was served and they sat down. All afternoon they talked, discussing everything from Harry's calm sea crossing to the entertainments that had been planned for the next fortnight. They ended up laughing and joking, as the wine flowed and they began to relax together. Harry found himself warming to Francis, even as he deplored so much about him and was jealous of his greater wealth. He liked his wit and his evident appreciation of art and building. Outside, they could hear their respective retinues drinking toasts to each other, English and French together, as if they were good friends. Altogether, it was a most satisfactory beginning.

Three days later, Harry rode to Ardres to pay his respects to Queen Claude, as Francis came to visit Kate. Having impressed on Kate the importance of showing a smiling face to her visitor, Harry knew that, when it came to it, she could be relied on not to let him down, so he was entirely at ease when he entered the French Queen's pavilion. Claude was a plain, plump woman with a squint and a limp, and heavily pregnant, yet she rose and greeted him graciously. He kissed her hand and bowed, noticing that the gowns of her ladies were scandalously low cut. He averted his eyes.

'I see that congratulations will soon be in order,' he smiled, but he was inwardly bitter. This little lady had borne two healthy sons and several daughters, and he felt ill done by that Kate had not.

'If God wills,' she said. She sounded tired and did not look well. 'Shall we sit down?'

They talked for an hour, by which time the awkward silences were becoming longer. 'I will not tax you further, Madam,' Harry said. 'You must rest, and I shall look forward to seeing you soon.'

He rode back to Guisnes, feeling sorry for her. When he returned, he found Kate fuming.

'That man is the greatest heathen there ever was! No woman is safe with him.'

Harry frowned. 'I trust he did not behave dishonourably to you, Kate?'

'Only in that he ignored me when his eye lighted on one who pleased him better. Poor Mistress Carey was quite embarrassed. He kept staring at her.' She shuddered, as if shaking off some insect. She was still grumbling when they sat up late, sipping wine in her sumptuous apartment. 'My face ached with smiling through that banquet. And Francis was rude. When my ladies were presented to him, he kissed them all, save those who were older and not fair. Oh, my Henry, we have days of this to come.'

Having begun to enjoy himself and relishing the prospect of all the wonderful festivities that had been arranged, Harry did not need Kate damping down his enthusiasm. 'Just remind yourself of the benefits this friendship will bring to me and my realm,' he said tersely.

'What benefits?' she retorted.

'Our daughter will be queen of France, for a start!'

'She could be empress and queen of Spain! It is a greater destiny.'

They stared at each other. He had thought much on this too. It irritated him that Kate had been the one to raise the subject.

'We will speak of this later,' he said. 'Now is not the time.'

There followed a seemingly endless round of feasting, jousting, dancing and games, in which the two courts vied for supremacy. The Val d'Or resounded with happy, excited voices, but Harry was becoming weary of the constant rivalry and Francis' condescension, and he was aware that not all the English looked kindly on the French. Clearly Francis knew it too.

'I fear your Englishmen even when they come bringing gifts,' he observed as he and Harry helped themselves to candied fruits at a banquet. His smile did not reach his eyes.

Anger rose in Harry. 'No one in my train has any evil intent towards you. We come in peace and friendship.'

'But our kingdoms have long been enemies.'

'I trust that will end now,' Harry countered, barely containing his fury. The fact was, he and Francis were not at peace, and never would be. There was too much history, rivalry and jealousy between them. Their cordiality now masked their mutual hatred.

Great tournaments were held in the huge tiltyard, which had been built to Harry's design. The jousts were organised by Suffolk and Admiral Bonnivet, and the rules of protocol had been agreed by a committee of English and French knights. Only blunted swords and lances were used, and even the design of armour had been agreed beforehand by the two kings.

Two trees of honour thirty-four-feet high, bearing Harry's emblem of the hawthorn and Francis' raspberry leaf, were set up at the end of the lists, and each day the challengers and defenders hung their shields on them. Harry insisted that his shield and Francis' be placed on the same level to demonstrate their equality, and they contrived to run the same number of courses – although never against each other – and break the same number of spears. Their combat was so fast and furious that sparks flew from their armour; Harry's horse was killed beneath him, which grieved him no end, and he sprained his hand, while Francis sustained a black eye. But, to Harry's gratification, many Englishmen, especially Suffolk and Carew, gave gallant accounts of themselves.

Harry and Francis were still taking care to observe every courtesy towards each other. Hearing an English herald read out a proclamation beginning, 'I, Henry, by the Grace of God King of England and France,' Harry raised a hand to silence him and turned to Francis.

'I cannot call myself king of France while you are here, for I would be a liar,' he smiled, as Francis looked suitably pleased.

Later, Harry regretted his magnanimous gesture and, after watching a wrestling match between the Yeomen of the Guard and some Frenchmen, and forgetting that he was not supposed to be entering into any contest with Francis, he challenged him to a fight. Instantly, he saw the gleam in Francis' eye. Ho, ho, the French King was as keen as he to show his prowess! Mouths agape, the courtiers looked on avidly. Harry saw the two queens clasp each other's hands, dismay in their faces.

Taking care not to look in Wolsey's direction, Harry stripped to his shirt and breeches, then faced Francis. For several seconds, they grappled with each other, but Harry realised from the first that they were unequally matched. Strong he might be, but Francis was leaner and more agile. To his horror, he found himself thrown to the floor, to a collective gasp from the spectators.

His cheeks burning, he scrambled to his feet. Honour required that he demand another round. 'Again!' he said.

'I think not,' Francis replied, looking as smug as a cat that had cornered a bird.

Harry saw red. He was shaking with mortification. But, as he made to lunge at his rival, Kate and Claude quickly stepped forward and pulled them apart. He was furious at being deprived of the chance to avenge himself, and only calmed down when he won an archery contest later that day. He was still smarting the next morning when he woke to find Francis standing over him.

'Brother, what do you do here?' he asked, instantly awake. 'Have you ridden all the way from Ardres?'

'I have come to serve as your valet and help you dress,' Francis answered cheerfully.

Harry was stunned, and inordinately pleased to be shown such a signal mark of respect, which was clearly intended to make him feel better about being ignominiously thrown yesterday. Clearly, there was more to Francis than he had realised. 'Brother, you have played me the best trick ever played,' he told him. 'You have shown me the trust I should have given you. From now on, I am your prisoner.' Leaping out of bed and opening his jewel chest, he drew out a fabulous collar of rubies and presented it to his guest. In turn, Francis handed him a bracelet that must have been worth twice as much. Honour was now satisfied.

The weather turned stiflingly hot. Strong winds blew dust into faces and over clothing; the gusts were so powerful that the jousters could not couch lances, and some of the tents, including Francis' vast marquee, were blown away. Local peasants and beggars invaded the Val d'Or to guzzle the free wine, and Harry deplored the distasteful sight of them lying comatose by the fountain. One day, ten thousand people turned up to watch the jousts.

Fearing what might happen if they too became inebriated, Harry and Francis agreed that persons having no business in the Val d'Or should be ordered to leave, on pain of hanging. Yet still the people kept coming, and the Provost Marshal of the Field was powerless to stop them.

Saturday, 23 June, saw the final public event. The tiltyard had been converted into a temporary chapel and there, at noon, Wolsey, assisted by five other cardinals and twenty bishops, celebrated a solemn Mass before both courts. The choir of the Chapel Royal sang alternately with its French equivalent, La Chapelle du Musique du Roi; then Richard Pace gave a Latin oration on peace. The only hitch occurred when a firework in the shape of a salamander, Francis' personal emblem, was accidentally set off during the service, causing a brief panic.

After the thanksgiving, the two kings watched as Wolsey laid the foundation stone of a chapel to Our Lady of Peace, which they had agreed to found on the site of their meeting. The ceremony was followed by an open-air feast, a final round of jousts and a spectacular firework display. Some were already calling the summit the eighth wonder of the world.

After taking leave of Francis and Claude, Harry moved his court to Calais.

'Well, that was a triumph,' he observed to Wolsey, who was riding on his mule beside him. 'I am as pleased with this meeting as if I had gained a great realm.'

'Indeed, your Grace. It will bear abundant fruit, I am certain.'

But Kate was of a different opinion. As soon as they were in bed in the Exchequer Palace that night, she tackled Harry. 'What did that whole costly charade actually achieve? Very little, I imagine!'

'That's unfair,' Harry protested.

'No, tell me exactly what good will come of it?'

He found himself floundering, remembering that barely a word had been said about Mary's marriage, even though he had raised the subject several times, and that there had been tensions between the English and the French. As for Francis, he was definitely not to be trusted. Any fool could see that. Resentment rose in him. Kate was right.

'That remains to be seen,' he said at length.

'I thank God we are meeting with the Emperor in a fortnight,' she said, plumping up her pillows.

'Yes, I think we might have cause to,' he agreed.

* * *

Charles had brought his aunt, the Regent Margaret, to Gravelines, and both greeted Harry warmly, expressing their goodwill and showing intense interest in the summit with Francis. Harry escorted them to Calais, where he had built a temporary banqueting house of canvas painted with heavenly bodies. Unfortunately, when they arrived, they found that the strong winds had blown it down, so Harry and his courtiers, resplendent in their masquing attire, came to the Emperor's lodging instead. As he chatted amiably with Charles and danced with the Regent's ladies, Harry kept smiling inwardly to think how angry Francis would be when he heard of this visit. Later, he was positively gleeful as he imagined him learning that Harry and Charles had signed a new treaty agreeing not to make any new alliances with France for the next two years. He returned home a satisfied man.

Chapter 14

'I have some concerns about the Duke of Buckingham,' Wolsey said, when Harry returned from his late-summer progress.

'What has he done now?' Harry asked, leaning back in his chair. They were sitting in his closet, catching up on business.

'Your Grace may be aware of speculation that you might name Buckingham your successor.'

'Never! I wouldn't inflict that on England.'

'Very wise! But it has also come to my notice that some believe he might attempt to seize the crown for himself. I took the precaution of making discreet enquiries among his servants. Some have heard him comment several times on his proximity to the throne. He has even predicted that your Grace will have no sons and that he himself will be king one day.'

'How dare he!' Harry was seething, for Buckingham's pretensions had touched a raw nerve. Of course he would have sons one day! He had not ceased his efforts in that direction. He had not given up hope.

'I have been keeping a close watch on him,' Wolsey continued, 'but he has taken himself off to his castle at Thornbury. Naturally, I have planted my spies in his household. I will not cease to be vigilant. Even if his intentions are not treasonable, he has certainly acted with a worrying lack of discretion.'

'He is very wealthy and can command a large affinity. He could pose a very real threat to me.' Harry was struggling to suppress his alarm.

'Do not fear, Sir,' Wolsey said, smiling. 'I have him under observation.'

It came to Harry that Wolsey was pleased about Buckingham's indiscretions – if that was all they were. Their great enmity had not cooled. Who could blame the Cardinal if he wanted the Duke brought down? But Harry knew he could trust Wolsey to do what was best for his master, and for England; and if that happened to coincide with his own inclinations, so be it!

1521

At New Year, Harry was surprised to receive a golden wine goblet from Buckingham, engraved with the words *With humble, true heart*. His fears were somewhat allayed, but not for long.

'Buckingham is mobilising troops,' Wolsey murmured in his ear, coming upon him one day in March when he was waiting to take his turn at the archery butts.

Alarums sounded in Harry's head. 'Carry on,' he told his gentlemen, and led Wolsey a little way off. 'What is he up to?'

'Ostensibly, he needs them to protect him when he tours his estates in Wales, where he is not popular.'

'But he might use them against me!'

'We cannot discount it,' Wolsey said. Even he looked worried. 'I fear he is plotting treason. One of my sources – who may not be entirely reliable – states that he has sworn to assassinate your Grace. He means to gain audience with a knife secreted about his person, and when kneeling before you, he will rise and stab you.'

Harry could almost feel the thrust.

'His servants all say he has purchased a large amount of cloth of gold and silver and will use it to bribe the Yeomen of your Guard to gain access to you.'

Fear gripped Harry. 'Enough! He must be stopped. Have him arrested.'

'Sir, until we have more substantial evidence than malicious gossip, I advise you not to proceed against him.'

'No! I've heard enough. He might be stupid, but he is dangerous.

No, my lord Cardinal, I will brook no more arguments. I will bring down this over-mighty subject!'

Reluctantly, Wolsey summoned Buckingham to Windsor and had him apprehended on the way.

'He has been taken to the Tower and charged with imagining and compassing the death of our lord the King,' he informed the Council, as Harry gripped the arms of his chair, reflecting on what a lucky escape he had had.

The sentence of the peers who tried Buckingham was death.

'The chief evidence against him was the testimony of his own officers,' Wolsey told Harry after the trial. 'But your Grace may rest assured that justice has been properly served.'

Four days later, the Duke was beheaded. Not for a long time had such a prominent noble – and one with royal blood, at that – been sent to the scaffold, and there was a great stir.

'All London is lamenting his end,' Suffolk reported, sitting down at Harry's bidding in the window seat of the King's closet. 'It is believed that the Cardinal brought him down out of pure malice.' And the Londoners weren't the only ones blaming Wolsey for Buckingham's fall; fingers were pointing at him all over the court. It was being whispered that a butcher's dog had killed the finest buck in England.

Harry was left so shaken by Buckingham's treachery that he deliberately shunned those members of the older nobility who had blood ties to the Duke, lest they be tainted by his treason. Ignoring Kate's protests and his daughter's tears, he dismissed Lady Salisbury from her post as governess, for her daughter was married to Buckingham's son and she was herself too close to the throne for comfort. He sent her eldest son, Lord Montagu, to the Tower for a brief spell, as a warning not to dabble in treason, while the younger sons, Geoffrey and Reginald, felt the draught of royal displeasure.

Meanwhile, despite feeling sick and feverish with malaria, Harry was busy dividing up Buckingham's extensive landed property, which had been forfeited to the Crown. He reserved some for himself and distributed the rest among those lords and courtiers whose loyalty he felt he could depend on. As they scrambled for the spoils, the rumblings of discontent at Buckingham's fate died a quick death.

Not even Harry's illness could dampen his pleasure in the seven great houses he had seized from the Duke, among them Penshurst Place, Kimbolton Castle and Bletchingley Manor. But the greatest prize was the palatial Thornbury Castle, which was only partially completed. It had been modelled on Richmond Palace and had beautiful gardens. He could use it when he was on progress in Gloucestershire.

When his fever lifted, he decided, good son of the Church that he was, to go on pilgrimage to give thanks for his safe recovery. But, as he rode to Walsingham, something was preying on his mind. He grieved that the Church to which he was devoted was under threat. Despite being condemned by the Pope, Martin Luther had refused to be silenced. He now attracted a strong following, especially in Germany, where the controversies he had stirred were provoking civil disorder.

Like most right-thinking people, Harry deplored the fact that Luther's heresy was quickly contaminating Christendom. Both Wolsey and More agreed with him that it was one of the most serious threats, not only to the Roman Catholic Church, but to the unity of Christendom as a whole. And these heresies were spreading alarmingly. On his return from Norfolk, Harry read in Wolsey's reports that Lutheranism was now infecting England. Banned subversive tracts were being circulated, even though the penalty for heresy was death by burning.

'I cannot afford to let this blasphemy take root,' he declared, slamming the papers on Wolsey's desk. 'It encourages divisions, sedition, even revolution, and undermines the very body politic of Church and state. Think of it, Thomas: by one man's disobedience, many are made sinners. These new ideas rob princes and prelates of all power and authority. They threaten the established order and hierarchy in a Christian society.' He was pacing up and down now, unable to contain his fury. 'Religious doctrine is a matter for those best qualified to understand and interpret it, not the common man!'

'I absolutely agree, Sir, but it is difficult to root out all subversives. All heretical books have been banned, and seized and burned when found. To date, your Grace has not enforced the heresy laws, but they remain in existence and can be used.'

'What's needed is the discrediting of Luther,' Harry growled. 'And I mean to be the one to do it.'

'Your Grace?' Wolsey looked up, curious.

'Yes, Thomas. The Emperor and the King of France have had special titles bestowed on them by the Pope. Charles is "the Most Catholic King" and "Protector of the Holy See", and Francis is "the Most Christian King". I have been hoping that the Pope might bestow one on me too. But now I see I must earn it, by becoming the champion of the Church against this weed, this dilapidated, sick and evil-minded sheep! But how?'

Wolsey rested his chin on his steepled fingers, thinking. He smiled. 'There is no prince to equal you in scholarship. Why not use your talent to write a book defending the Church against Luther's heresies?'

'By St George, you have the sow by the right ear, Thomas!' Harry was instantly fired up by the idea. 'I'll make a start today, right now.'

He wrote and wrote, pouring all his outrage and passion into his words. Richard Pace gave advice, and Thomas More assisted in collating his random arguments into a cohesive narrative, while he and Bishop Fisher offered the benefit of their knowledge of the Church Fathers. Yet the book was, from first to last, Harry's own. He gave it priority over state affairs and even hunting expeditions.

What serpent so venomously possessed this man who called the Most Holy See of Rome 'Babylon' and the Pope's authority 'Tyranny' and turns the name of the Most Holy Bishop of Rome into 'Anti-christ'? he thundered, the quill flying furiously over the paper.

'Sir, might I suggest you tone down that passage,' More urged, leaning over his shoulder. 'The Pope is a prince as you are, and there may one day be some conflict between you. I think it best therefore that his authority be more slenderly touched upon.'

213

'No, it shall not,' Harry argued. 'I am so much bound to the See of Rome that I cannot do too much honour to it.'

'Very well, Sir.' More retreated.

In May, the book was finished. Harry called it *A Defence of the Seven Sacraments against Martin Luther*. In his introduction, he explained that it was the offspring of his intellect and erudition, and that he had felt it his duty to write it so that all might see how ready he was to defend the Church, not only with his armies, but with the resources of his mind.

Wolsey displayed the manuscript at Paul's Cross on the day he had Luther's works publicly burned. It was printed, and thirty presentation copies were sent to Rome; one, beautifully bound in cloth of gold, was for Pope Leo, to whom Harry dedicated it in his own hand.

He was elated to learn that his Holiness had thanked God for raising up such a prince to be the champion of the Church and expressed astonishment that Harry had found time to write a book, a most unusual thing for a king to do. And he was thrilled to be asked what title he would like.

He consulted the Cardinal and the bishops.

'"Most Orthodox",' suggested one.

'"Angelic",' offered another. Harry did not miss the raised eyebrows and suppressed a smile. Even he did not see himself as angelic.

'I like "Defender of the Faith",' he said, to a chorus of approval.

The book was selling faster than the presses could print it when Pope Leo died in December. When the news reached England, Wolsey could not conceal his excitement.

'The loss of his Holiness is a tragedy for Christendom. He was a man who strove for peace. But now we must look to the future – and a new pope.'

Harry did not need to be told that Wolsey expected it to be himself. The Cardinal had gone against his political instincts to promote an alliance with the Emperor, if only because Charles had promised to help make him Pope.

When the news came that he had backed another candidate, Wolsey was furious.

'I should have known he would favour his old tutor!' he seethed.

'My envoys report that he preferred him because he is hot against Luther,' Harry said, sorry for his friend's disappointment, but secretly pleased that he would not be losing him to Rome.

1522

The following February, a Papal legation came to England formally to present Pope Leo's bull to Harry, and he was proclaimed Defender of the Faith at Greenwich. He went in procession to High Mass, the trumpets sounding a joyous fanfare.

But Luther was not a man to be cowed by a mere king. In his incensed response to Harry's book, he accused him of raving like a strumpet in a tantrum. *If the King of England arrogates to himself the right to spew out falsehoods, he gives me the right to stuff them back down his throat!* he had written. Worst of all, he suggested that the book had not been Harry's own work at all.

Harry was furious, but would not stoop to answer Luther's scurrilous arguments. That task he delegated to More and Fisher. He had knighted Thomas More in reward for his help with the book and appointed him under-treasurer of the Exchequer. More expressed his gratitude, but Harry knew he felt he was being drawn increasingly along a path he did not want to follow. It was rare – and pleasing – to find a man with so little ambition. He knew where he stood with More, knew that the man would give him service and sound advice without any ulterior motive.

Wolsey, meanwhile, was unwillingly tying up the new alliance with the Emperor.

Charles had finally weaned Harry away from Francis with promises of a joint invasion of France, the partition of any conquests and his recognition of Harry as King of France.

'Francis will never offer me that,' Harry grinned, as he sat by the fire with Wolsey on a chilly late-February morning, going over the terms. 'And Mary will be empress!'

Wolsey gave him the semblance of a smile. 'Alas, not for some time.' It was true. Mary was six, Charles twenty-two. They could not be wed for six years. But they would be betrothed.

Kate, sitting at her embroidery and ecstatic at this new friendship between her husband and her nephew, looked up. 'My lord Cardinal, I was betrothed to Prince Arthur when I was just two. The Imperial crown is a prize worth waiting for.'

Watching her, Harry remembered how beautiful she had been in her youth, and felt a deep pang to see her looking so old at thirty-six, while he, at thirty, was in the prime of his manhood. He still visited her bed, for duty called him there, but she had not conceived in more than three years, and he now doubted that she ever would again.

Increasingly, he was becoming convinced that their marriage had somehow offended God. He remembered the objections that had been put forward against it all those years ago. What if the matter had not hinged on Kate bearing Arthur a child? What if the sin lay in his having married her when she had been his brother's wife? There might be more than one way of interpreting Scripture.

Tormented by doubt, he raised the matter with his confessor, Dr Longland, the Bishop of Lincoln. 'Tell me, Father, is my marriage cursed?'

To his dismay, Longland took him seriously. 'My son, the Book of Leviticus warns that a man who incestuously marries his brother's wife will be punished with childlessness.'

'But Pope Julius granted a dispensation.'

'Whether he had the power to do so is debatable.'

'I was told that her Grace was free to wed me because she had not borne my brother a child.'

'Was their marriage consummated?'

'She denied it. But . . .' He thought back to his wedding night. 'There was no blood when first I took her to wife. Recently, fearing that we have offended God, I have been wondering if she told the truth.'

The Bishop hesitated. 'I cannot believe that such a virtuous lady would lie. No, Prince Arthur probably did leave her *virgo intacta*. In which case, your marriage is lawful.'

'But why have I no sons?' Harry burst out. 'Eight children she's conceived, and only one girl lives. Is it a judgement on me? Could it not be that I have sinned just by taking my brother's wife in wedlock?'

'My son, you must not distress yourself. The dispensation is very likely sound. God will provide for the succession.'

Granted absolution, Harry sat in the royal pew in the deserted chapel, his head in his hands. He was not reassured. It was all very well for Dr Longland to mumble platitudes about God providing, but he wasn't a king who bore the responsibility for leaving his realm peaceful and stable.

Yet what could he do? The churchmen would probably all say the same as his confessor. The Pope, if bribed enough, might grant an annulment; popes were usually most accommodating to monarchs in such circumstances. But he could not bring himself to set Kate aside. She was much loved by his subjects and was a good woman for whom he still retained a deep affection. Moreover, she loved him – her eyes still lit up with joy when she saw him. Above all, he did not wish to prejudice the Imperial alliance by putting away the Emperor's own aunt. So he did nothing. Yet still his doubts continued to eat away at him.

Bessie Blount had faded amiably from his life. She had borne him a daughter, passed off as her husband's, and he had never acknowledged the child. He had no need to, the legal presumption being that Tallboys was her father. The hiatus of Bessie's second pregnancy had sounded the death knell of Harry's passion for her; that, and the knowledge that another man was sleeping with her.

But there was someone else. Of late, his eye had been drawn to Mistress Carey, the former Mary Boleyn, who was often to be seen at court, where she shared her husband's lodging. Having heard tales of her naughty exploits in France, Harry had expected her to be an easy conquest, but no. When he partnered her during a dance and murmured in her ear that she looked very beautiful and he would like to see her in private, her eyes had widened in astonishment.

'Oh, Sir, I couldn't possibly,' she had stammered. 'I could not betray my husband.'

He had retreated then, bowing, and tried to forget her. But it was no good. His interest was piqued. His blood was up for the chase.

Early in March, at the jousts in honour of the Emperor's ambassadors, he appeared in the lists on a horse trapped in silver caparisons embroidered with the motto 'She has wounded my heart'. One glance at Mary, seated among the spectators, showed him that the dart had struck home. Her pink, creamy complexion was flushed a becoming crimson.

When, two days later, on the night of Shrove Tuesday, the envoys were Wolsey's guests at York Place, Harry took part in a pageant, 'The Château Vert'. On the pageant car stood a castle with three towers. On each flew a banner: one showed three broken hearts, another a lady's hand holding a man's heart, and the third a lady's hand turning a man's heart. Harry had persuaded Master Cornish to adapt the pageant to his chosen theme, and if Cornish had suspected it was a ploy to win a lady, he had given no sign of it.

The castle was occupied by eight young ladies, all masked and (in theory) unknown to Harry and his seven companions. Each wore a gown of white satin and Milan lace and had her name embroidered in gold on a matching gold-encrusted bonnet: Beauty, Honour, Perseverance, Kindness, Constancy, Bounty, Mercy and Pity. Crouching beneath the fortress were seven more ladies whose names were Danger, Disdain, Jealousy, Unkindness, Scorn, Sharp Tongue and Strangeness; they were dressed like Indian women and wore black bonnets.

Harry and the other gentlemen entered, all in disguise and wearing cloth of gold and cloaks of blue satin. They bore the names Love, Nobleness, Youth, Devotion, Loyalty, Pleasure, Gentleness and Liberty. Cornish went ahead in the guise of Ardent Desire, resplendent in crimson satin with burning flames of gold. The ladies pretended to be so awed by his appearance that they offered to surrender the castle, but Scorn and Disdain insisted they hold the fort. The gentlemen thereupon stormed it, to a great report of gunfire, while the ladies defended their citadel, throwing rose water and comfits at them. The besiegers responded with a hail of dates, oranges and other fruits until, inevitably, the castle was taken and Lady Scorn and her companions fled. Harry enjoyed that part immensely, and he had even more pleasure in taking the hand of Kindness, as the lords led the ladies out as prisoners, bringing them down to the floor and dancing with them, to the delight of the envoys and the company.

Harry knew that Mary Carey was Kindness, but he expressed himself suitably surprised when, after the dancing, everyone unmasked themselves. And yet there was no mistaking the reluctance in her eyes.

'I think you are playing with me, Mistress Carey,' he said, bowing over her hand.

'I beg your Grace's pardon.' The blue eyes brimmed with tears.

'What's this?' Harry murmured, concerned. 'Am I so unappealing to you?'

'Oh, no, Sir, you could never be that,' she whispered. 'But I have my reputation to think of.'

People were staring at them. Harry's sister Mary, one of the dancers, was frowning; and a dark-eyed brunette with a graceful bearing and slender figure was regarding Mary Carey with something like alarm. He recognised her sister Anne, recently returned from the French court, who had just been appointed a maid-of-honour to the Queen.

'We cannot talk here,' he said to Mary. 'I will come to you later. Wait for me in the little banqueting house by the tennis courts.'

'No, please, Sir,' she hissed, but he left her and returned to the high table where Kate and Wolsey were chatting to the Spanish envoys, Kate in the most joyful fashion, Wolsey studiedly courteous, for all his lavish hospitality.

Harry led Kate to the chamber where she was to host a lavish banquet for the ambassadors. Helping himself from the hundreds of tempting treats on offer, and chatting animatedly to the Cardinal and his guests, he betrayed no sign of interest in any other lady present. With his usual courtesy, he heartily kissed Kate good night, thanked her for her hospitality and left her.

Too restless to sleep, he paused in the gallery above the hall where the revelry was continuing, and watched the dancers on the floor. There was Anne Boleyn again, partnering her brother George, who was one of Harry's pages. There was something about her. She wasn't beautiful, but she had poise and an air of sophistication. French mannerisms too. That had put off Kate, who had not wanted to take her, but Sir Thomas Boleyn had been persuasive, and Harry had insisted, knowing that Boleyn would not let up where self-interest was concerned, and that the girl had impeccable credentials. Her father had used his diplomatic influence to secure places for his daughters in Burgundy and France. Anne had been a maid-of-honour to Queen Claude and then to King Francis' sister Marguerite, but the recent deterioration in relations between England and France had obliged her to return home, along with other English subjects.

Harry slipped downstairs and entered the throng, much to the delight of his courtiers. He danced with Carew's wife, but his eye kept straying to Mary Carey, who was with her husband. She was far prettier than her sister, fair and rounded, where Anne was dark and thin-faced. It would surely not be difficult to overcome her reluctance.

He saw his sister Mary chatting to Suffolk, and held out his hand. 'Will you do me the honour, Mary?'

She smiled and let him lead her onto the floor as the musicians broke into a lively galliard. As they danced, Harry contrived to pass Mary Carey.

'I will see you anon,' he whispered. She looked startled before William Carey whirled her away, unsuspecting. Harry wondered if she had heard him aright. Would she be there?

Cloaked and hooded, he stole out of the privy garden and made his way to the rendezvous. In the moonlight, he could see her waiting there for him. She looked scared, like a cornered animal.

'There's nothing to be afraid of, Mistress,' he said, as he drew level with her. 'I mean you nothing but kindness, as I hope you intend to show to me.'

'Your Grace, forgive me.' She looked distressed. 'If I have misled you, I'm sorry. But it was not I who chose that name.'

'Who then? Master Cornish?'

'Well, yes, but . . .'

'You must have known what message that would send.' He grinned, his blood up in the excitement of the chase. 'If you were not willing to play the game, you could have insisted on another name. I think you are teasing me.'

'No, Sir, I would never do that.' Her lip trembled.

'Mary, I do desire you,' Harry breathed, pulling her into his arms. 'Come.' He felt her resist, trying to wriggle away.

'No, Sir! Please!'

'I will not hurt you, sweeting,' he assured her, and bent to kiss away her qualms. 'Besides, it is cruelty on the part of a lady to promise much and then withdraw.'

'I promised nothing,' Mary quavered.

'But I can give you much!' he murmured, pulling off her hood. 'There is no shame in becoming the King's mistress. It is an honour. And I will not forget your kindness to me.'

He sensed her surrender, and took her there in the banqueting house, with the latticed windows closed against any prying eyes, and his cloak wrapped around them both to keep out the cold. It was sweet and satisfying, and all the better for the secrecy.

He carried on seeing her. He felt as he had eight years earlier, in the heady early days of his affair with Bessie. He could not resist the excitement, the thrill of seduction, the quest to make Mary love him. She was gradually opening up to him, and sweet it was to see her giving of herself.

Kate knew nothing, he was certain. She was wholly preoccupied with the Emperor's coming state visit to England to mark the signing of the new treaty and his betrothal to the Princess Mary.

In May, his ships docked at Dover, and Wolsey conducted him to the castle. Harry welcomed his future son-in-law warmly. He could not wait to show off his warship, the *Henry Grâce à Dieu*, and himself gave Charles a tour of it. Afterwards, they were rowed around the harbour in a little boat, the Emperor marvelling at the well-armed English fleet.

The royal retinues then rode to Gravesend, where thirty barges waited to convey them upstream to Greenwich. All the ships on the Thames had been decorated with streamers and banners and, as the royal barge passed, every gun fired a salute. When they arrived, Harry escorted Charles into the palace, where, at the hall door, Kate was waiting with Mary and their ladies, eager to welcome her nephew. He knelt for her blessing.

'It is a great joy to see your Majesty again,' he told her, 'and especially my dear cousin Mary.' He bent to kiss the Princess's hand and complimented her on the brooch pinned to her breast, which bore the legend *The Emperor*.

She had been well schooled in the courtesies. 'I am heartily pleased to receive your Imperial Majesty. I have some gifts for you, horses and hawks. I hope you will like them!' Prettily, she took his hand and led him through the palace and out to the mews, where she almost danced up and down in excitement as he admired her presents and thanked her.

That evening there was a great dinner, followed by dancing, during which Charles solemnly led out his diminutive betrothed. Harry saw Kate looking misty-eyed as she watched them.

'This is a dream come true, my Henry,' she said to him.

He nodded, but the sight of his daughter with her future bride-groom had brought home to him, even more forcefully than before, the fact that he had no son to succeed him. When he died, England would become absorbed into the Empire, to be ruled by foreigners.

That night, he summoned Mary Carey and tried to lose himself in her voluptuous embrace, craving oblivion.

The next day, he put on a brave show as he escorted Charles to London, where the guilds and the German merchants residing in the

City accorded him a lavish welcome, mounting wonderful pageants. They welcomed this alliance, given their lucrative trade with the Empire, and there was much cheering from the crowds who were crammed into the narrow streets. Sir Thomas More made a speech formally welcoming the Emperor to London, and the citizens presented Charles and Harry with finely crafted swords.

Charles and his suite were then conducted to the priory of the Blackfriars, where they were to lodge. Over the next couple of days, Harry took pleasure in showing his guest around Westminster Abbey and Westminster Hall, although they had to fend off an enthusiastic crowd who were desperate to see and touch them. Charles looked alarmed, but Harry shrugged it off; he knew his people loved him and had no fear of them.

At Bridewell, he and Charles played tennis – there was no ban on competitiveness here, as there had been in France. Harry shuddered when he recalled the false bonhomie of that extravagant charade and the money wasted on it. But now there was just a good, honest contest, with the Emperor and himself well matched, for they drew even after eleven games.

On and on went the round of entertainments, until it was time to move to Windsor for the signing of the treaty. During the Mass that followed, Charles wore his Garter robes, and he and Harry both swore on the Blessed Host to remain in perpetual amity. That evening, the court gathered in St George's Hall to watch a disguising in which a proud horse representing King Francis was tamed and bridled by an allegorical figure called Amity.

The next few days were given over to the pleasures of the chase. Then, on 19 June, the Emperor and Mary were formally betrothed. Kate wept for joy as she saw her daughter's tiny hand being placed in Charles' outsized one, but Harry could only feel dread for the future. All the time he and Charles were out hunting, or feasting in Winchester Castle beneath the great Round Table of King Arthur, which had been repainted in honour of the Imperial visit with a prominent Tudor rose in the middle, he was thinking of the day when Mary would leave these shores and become imbued with an alien culture and customs. Then the ancient royal line of English kings would die with him. It made him feel an utter failure.

It was a relief when, after nearly two months of celebrations, Charles sailed from Southampton, escorted by thirty of Harry's ships, which were then detailed to reconnoitre along the French coast.

At Windsor, preoccupied with mortality, Harry had been dismayed to see that Pietro Torrigiano had made very little progress in building his tomb. On his return, he sought out the Italian and berated him.

'I'm paying you well. The least you can do is keep to the terms of our contract!'

Torrigiano's temper flared. 'I am an artist and I work to my own schedule, when the Muse takes me – that is the way to achieve a masterpiece. I will not be dictated to, even by princes.'

Harry was speechless. No one ever spoke to him like that. 'Then this prince will not employ you any longer. You can leave England and find some other patron.'

He saw the fury in the sculptor's eyes and remembered that this was the man who had broken Michelangelo's nose. He watched as the fellow unclenched his fists, clearly thinking better of taking a swipe at a king. 'Get out!' he said.

Torrigiano threw all his tools into a large dusty bag and stamped off, leaving Harry to contemplate the unfinished sepulchre. Wolsey, who had followed him into St George's Chapel, stepped forward. 'A pretty mess, Sir,' he said. 'You were right to dismiss him.'

'Yes, but now there is no one to finish the work.'

As usual, the Cardinal came to the rescue. 'On the contrary, I have in my service a Florentine, Antonio Toto, who is very good, and skilled at architecture. He may be able to help.'

'Thank you, Thomas.' Harry was calming down now. 'I will speak to him. Have this cleared up, will you?'

Chapter 15

1523

In February, they celebrated Mary's seventh birthday.

'It is time for her formal studies to begin,' Harry decreed, as he and Kate watched their daughter playing blind man's buff with her little maids, all of them squealing with excitement. 'I want her to have the best education we can give her.'

Kate gazed fondly at the child. 'I want that too. My parents had me and my sisters taught to the same high standard they did my poor brother. My grandmother disapproved. She said that too much learning was bad for women and might encourage light behaviour.'

'Many people still think that, alas, but Mary is my heir and must be properly prepared for her position as England's sovereign queen and Charles' consort. And we can best prepare her by affording her an excellent classical education in the Humanist tradition.'

'We should consult Sir Thomas More,' Kate smiled. 'His daughters are outstandingly learned, and virtuous too. No one is better placed to advise us.'

They invited More to dine with them, and the evening was as merry as they had come to expect when in his company. Only when the remains of the roast meats and pies had been cleared away, and a flagon of Malmsey had been placed on the table, did Harry ask More for his opinion.

'I can only applaud your Graces' aims,' he said. 'Fortunately, attitudes towards female education are beginning to change. I see erudition in women as a reproach to the idleness of men. It is appalling to deny the fair sex the pleasures and advantages of learning.'

'Your daughters are an example to us all,' Kate said. 'They are rightly famed for the breadth of their knowledge. We want that for the Princess.'

'And I will do all in my power to help, Madam,' More promised. 'Yet it is important not to lose sight of the feminine virtues. After all, marriage is a woman's highest vocation. I have always insisted that, alongside their studies, my daughters be trained in the traditional domestic skills; and, bearing in mind St Paul's injunction that women should learn in silence from their husbands, I have never allowed them to show off their academic achievements outside the home.'

'Quite rightly,' Harry commented. 'At present, my physician, Dr Linacre, teaches Mary Latin and rudimentary grammar, but he is old and ailing. Can you recommend anyone suitable to replace him and give her the kind of schooling we want?'

More sipped his wine, giving the matter some thought. 'Might I suggest the Spaniard, Juan Luis Vives? He is reader of rhetoric at Corpus Christi College in Oxford, and a finer scholar and advocate of women's education you could not find. I met him three years ago in Bruges and was very impressed with his ideas.'

'I am acquainted with his scholarship,' Kate said. 'Last year, I granted him a pension and asked him to dedicate his translation of St Augustine's *City of God* to his Grace here. I had thought of consulting him about Mary's education, so I am glad that you have suggested him. He is my countryman too, which is most fitting if he is to school the future Queen of Spain and Holy Roman Empress. Do you not agree, my Henry?'

Harry nodded. 'Vives is the perfect choice.' But, as ever, he was shrinking inside at the thought of England being subsumed into Charles' empire. 'Kate, as Mary's mother, you should make the approach.'

'I will do it gladly,' she replied, her eyes aglow with purpose.

Two weeks later, Harry was sitting by the fire in Kate's chamber, looking over the curriculum Vives had drawn up.

'Do you think it is a little severe for a child of seven?' she asked him.

He read it, praising it heartily. 'No, I do not,' he said. 'Mary is a clever girl. By God, she will be the best-educated woman in Christendom!'

'Fortunately, she is bright,' Kate observed. 'It would not suit every child. But Master Vives has borne in mind that she is no ordinary princess. He sees the need to instil in her the highest moral standards.'

'She needs no tutor to do that when she has you,' Harry said.

Kate smiled. 'She is by nature a virtuous soul and, to preserve and maintain that, Master Vives recommends that she reads only the best classical and scholastic authors. He mentioned Cicero, Seneca, Plutarch, Plato, St Jerome and St Augustine, *and* Erasmus and More.'

'I agree that she should eschew romances or idle books that might lead to wanton behaviour,' Harry remarked, perusing the curriculum. 'Educated or not, women are feeble-minded and easily corruptible – present company excepted, of course. And I also agree that Mary should not be taught rhetoric. Silence is an admirable quality in the fair sex.'

Kate nodded. 'Master Vives also believes that theology, philosophy and mathematics are beyond a woman's intellectual capabilities, although I'm not sure I agree. I think it's more a case of women not being given the opportunity to learn these subjects. Who knows, they might excel at them.'

'Well, we can leave that aside for the present,' Harry said, not wanting to dispute with her, and feeling sickened at the realisation that, if Mary had not the capacity to comprehend these things, she would never be able to grasp the mysteries of statecraft. Of course, she would have no need to; Charles would be ruling for her. His mind set off again on its tortuous dance . . .

'We must appoint some companions to share Mary's studies,' he said.

'That's what Master Vives recommended. He said they could all be taught Latin, French, Italian, Greek, grammar, music, dancing, household management and good manners; and they should read selected passages from the Bible every day. He himself is willing to instruct Mary in Latin. We discussed who should teach the other subjects, and decided upon my old chaplain, Father Fetherston, who is kindly and will wield the carrot rather than the stick. I will continue to read regularly with Mary, and I can help with her translations. By the way, Henry, I have asked Master Vives to write a treatise on female education. He says he will dedicate it to me.'

Harry wondered, not for the first time, why Kate was so unconcerned about the fact that they had no son and spoke as if a woman ruling England was no rare and unpalatable thing. The subject lay like a sword between them these days, never mentioned, but ever present in his mind. But he knew his own subjects; they would not tolerate a woman on the throne, however well educated and virtuous she was. Dear God, why could he not have a legitimate son? He thought of little Fitzroy, growing up away from the court, a sturdy, forward boy – just what England needed. If only there was a way to declare him legitimate. But the people would no more endure a bastard on the throne than a woman. Everyone whom Harry had consulted had said the same.

'Henry, are you all right?' Kate asked. He stared at her, seeing that Vives' lists had fallen from his lap to the floor, and he all unheeding of it.

'My head aches,' he lied. 'I think I will retire.' He could not face bedding her tonight; he was too down, too worried. Getting an heir would have to wait until another day. What was the point anyway? His efforts were all futile.

'Kiss me!' Harry demanded. Mary Carey giggled and flung herself on top of him. They had ridden out with a hunting party on a blazing summer day, left everyone else behind and found a shady copse in the woods where they could dally undisturbed.

Harry gazed hungrily at Mary's full, creamy breasts. He had unlaced her bodice and her clothes were now somewhere around her waist. He fondled her and pulled her to him, rolling her over on the grass and grappling to free his member from his codpiece. By St George, what a woman! He could not get enough of her.

Afterwards, he lay sated as she rearranged her clothes, opened the basket of food and bit into an apple. 'You could be Eve,' he said, twirling a tendril of her hair around his finger and drawing her lips to his. 'You're as bad a temptress! And to think you weren't willing when I first courted you.'

'I am not only willing now, but eager,' she told him.

He sat up and poured some wine for them both. 'I think we should drink to your father and your blissfully ignorant husband.'

'To Father and Will!' Mary chuckled, raising her glass. 'And they should be toasting us too. They've done very well out of us. All those grants to Will . . .'

'And your father is now a wealthy man thanks to the stewardships I've heaped on him. He is Treasurer of the Household and a Knight of the Garter.'

'My family has much to thank you for.'

'Nay, Mary, it is I who should be thanking you. You have made me happy.' It was true. With her, as with Bessie, he could forget politics and the succession for a short while.

They tidied themselves and walked back to where their horses were tethered, then cantered across the park. Nearing the palace, Harry saw a couple strolling beneath the trees, hand in hand.

'There's my sister,' Mary said. The couple turned at their approach, but hastened away behind a hedge.

'Who was that with her?' Harry asked.

'I . . . I don't know.' She was lying.

'Well, it's not the Butler lad, for certain,' Harry said. 'You'll know that I gave my approval for her to wed the heir of the Earl of Ormond, to settle the dispute over who should have the earldom.'

'It's my father's by right,' Mary said.

'Possibly, but the argument had to be resolved in a way acceptable to both claimants. I've been wondering why the marriage hasn't taken place.'

'I don't know,' Mary said. 'Anne's very headstrong. If she doesn't want to marry him, she won't.'

'Won't she?' Harry bridled. 'I would never allow a daughter of mine to be so disobedient.'

'Oh, Anne can wrap our father around her little finger. I wouldn't dare try.'

'And that's why I like you best!' he grinned.

He parted from her there, before curious eyes could see them from the palace windows. As he rode to the stables, he kept puzzling as to the identity of Anne Boleyn's companion. He had looked familiar, but Harry couldn't place him at that distance. It was time, anyway, to meet with the Council to discuss a recent abortive campaign Suffolk had led in France, and presently he forgot about it.

'Your Grace, might I speak to you for a moment?'

Harry looked up and saw Wolsey standing at the door of his closet. Wolsey knew he never had to wait to be announced. He was one of the few people who could approach his sovereign directly, with impunity.

Harry replaced his pen in the inkwell. 'Yes, Thomas. What can I do for you?'

'A problem has arisen concerning Lord Henry Percy, the Earl of Northumberland's heir.'

Harry realised now who he had seen with Anne Boleyn. 'Really?'

'I feel responsible, Sir, for he is one of the young gentlemen of my household. Regrettably, he has presumed to contract himself to Boleyn's younger daughter.'

'By God, how dare he! He is already precontracted to the Earl of Shrewsbury's girl, a match to which I gave my hearty consent.'

'I shall reprimand him soundly, Sir, and send for his father to take him up north and make immediate arrangements for his marriage. And I will send that foolish girl, Mistress Boleyn, home.'

'With my blessing!' Harry growled, angry with young Percy. 'What are things coming to when the sons of the nobility take it upon themselves to wed without royal permission?' He spread his hands in despair, then turned back to the deeds to Ampthill Castle, his latest property acquisition. 'Thank you, Thomas.'

'There is another matter,' the Cardinal said, lingering at the door. 'Reports from Rome suggest that his Holiness is dying. This might be my chance to become pope, with your approval.'

'You know you have it,' Harry said warmly, 'even though I would hate to lose you to Rome. And I'm sure the Emperor will back you this time, in view of our alliance.'

But the Emperor did not. When Pope Adrian passed away, not a single cardinal voted for Wolsey, and Charles put his weight behind an Italian, Giulio de' Medici, who was elected Pope Clement VII.

Wolsey could not hide his bitter disappointment at seeing the triple tiara fade once more from view. 'He is in his prime and may live for many years,' he lamented. 'I will never be Pope now.' He did not voice his anger at what he clearly saw as the Emperor's betrayal, not when Charles was Harry's friend, but Harry was aware of it and feared that Wolsey would never forgive Charles for letting him down a second time. If the Cardinal had loved the French before, he loved them doubly so now, and did not trouble to conceal it.

1524

The new suit of armour, made to Harry's own design by the Greenwich workshops, shone in the spring sunshine, drawing much admiration as he made his way to the lists and mounted his horse. Eager to try it out, he had arranged a tournament in which Suffolk was to be his chief opponent.

He would have liked Mary Carey to be here, admiring his armour and his prowess, but she had gone home to Hever to have her baby. Harry wondered if the Careys had an idea that the child was not Will's; for that matter, could he himself even be certain that he was the father? He missed Mary, but her condition had placed her at a distance for months now, and his passion had cooled. He doubted he would take her back. When the child was born, the world – and the law – would deem it her husband's. It was better that way. He could not bear to think he might have another son born out of wedlock.

A hush fell on the crowded stands as, lances couched, Harry and Brandon galloped towards each other. Suddenly, people were screaming, 'Hold! Hold!'

Startled, Harry realised, too late, that he had forgotten to pull down his visor, and that Suffolk was racing towards him unheeding, his lance pointed directly at Harry's exposed face.

'Hold! Hold!' Harry yelled, pulling on the reins, as the spectators roared warnings, but the Duke carried on, seemingly oblivious. Harry braced himself for the impact as Suffolk's lance struck him on the brow under the guard of his helmet. The collision was so momentous that the spear broke into splinters and pushed Harry's visor far back.

For a moment, he reeled in the saddle, his head exploding with flashing lights, but he managed to maintain his balance and, within seconds, his vision righted itself.

'Holy Mother of God!' Suffolk cried, pulling off his helm, visibly shaken. 'Oh, my God, Harry, are you hurt? I am so sorry, deeply sorry.'

Harry smiled at him, determined to make light of the accident. 'I am unscathed,' he declared, ignoring the pain in his head, which he was sure would abate very soon, for it was just a knock. He waved to the crowd. 'I have taken no hurt!' Everyone cheered.

'My God, my God!' Suffolk kept saying. He was shaking with shock. 'I swear I will never run against your Grace again.'

'Nonsense,' Harry said, as they turned their horses around and trotted back to the pavilions. 'No one was to blame but myself. Your heavy helmet prevented you from hearing the people crying out, and I should have remembered to close my visor. Now, forget it, my friend, for I mean us to run six more courses just to prove that I am not injured.'

'That will be a great joy and comfort to all your subjects here,' Brandon said. 'I must confess, though, I am not happy jousting against you after that.'

Harry grinned. 'It's like falling off a horse. The best thing to do is get back in the saddle again.'

Kate had not been watching from the royal stand, being indisposed with a cold, but she was horrified when she heard what had happened.

'You could have been killed!' she cried, when Harry visited her chamber later that day to ask after her health.

His councillors were equally aghast. 'With no son to succeed your Grace, England came perilously near to civil war this morning,' Wolsey said when they convened late in the afternoon.

'To be plain, there are those who might dispute the right of the Princess, a little girl, to succeed.' That was Surrey, who would surely soon succeed his ailing father as duke of Norfolk. He was a martinet, tough and blunt, and lacked the geniality of his sire, but Harry saw his point, remembering his kinsmen with Plantagenet blood, any of whom might attempt to enforce their claim to the throne.

He sat at the head of the board, his head aching, feeling defeated. 'I agree. The problem of the succession must be settled, and soon,' he said. 'I will be candid with you, my lords. It is five years since the Queen's last pregnancy. She is thirty-eight now, and her courses are becoming irregular. I fear that, despite doing my duty and praying devoutly, there will be no more children – and no son to inherit the throne.' He raised his eyes to them, letting them see his utter dejection.

The lords looked uncomfortable, glancing at Wolsey, doubtless for once glad to leave the problem to him.

'I know that I speak for us all, Sir, when I say that, should anything befall your Grace, we will ensure the smooth succession of the Princess,' the Cardinal said comfortingly. Harry looked away. No, there had to be a better solution. He must think of one.

'Thank you,' he said, rising abruptly and leaving them.

He sat opposite Kate at supper. He had no appetite for the orange pie that was one of his favourite dishes, for he was thinking that the age gap between them had never been more obvious. The pretty girl he had married was now a dumpy middle-aged matron who increasingly sought solace for her disappointments in religious observances. It was almost impossible nowadays to feel desire for her, to coax his manhood to do what it must to get a son. He was still pressing it into service, hoping against hope that, even at this late stage, God would answer their prayers.

'I took my barge to Syon Abbey today,' she told him, as he carved some meat for her. 'Enjoying the peace there made me desire a more tranquil life than the one I now lead. You know, my Henry, if I had to choose between extreme adversity and the great prosperity I enjoy, I would prefer the former, because those who are prosperous can easily lose their spiritual integrity.'

'Are you saying I have lost mine?' he countered.

'How could I say that about you, my Henry? Your piety can never be in doubt.'

He smiled at her, having suddenly seen a way out of his dilemma. 'Kate, if you felt you had a vocation for the religious life, I would never stand in your way.'

'No!' Her response was passionate. 'I have no vocation. God made me your wife and I can think of no higher calling. I was only saying that I love the peace of Syon.'

He nodded, disappointed. 'I thought you were trying to tell me something.'

'No.' She began to eat her meat, saying no more.

Norfolk clung on to life until May, when the doughty old warrior ceded his last battle and his son Surrey inherited the dukedom. Harry mourned his faithful friend, who had served him so well. He did not much like the new Duke. Norfolk was fifty-two. A martyr to rheumatism and indigestion, he was constantly grumbling or sighing, but he was an efficient and often ruthless military commander, and an able and polished courtier. Like his brother-in-law, Sir Thomas Boleyn, the guiding factor of his life was self-interest.

'With Buckingham gone, Norfolk regards himself as the chief of the older nobility,' Wolsey said, as he and Harry were inspecting the new building works at Greenwich. 'He has no time for new men.'

Harry grunted, sidestepping to avoid a bucket of plaster. 'You men, continue with your tasks and stop gawping!' he ordered, and turned to the Cardinal. 'When I made Suffolk a duke, Norfolk told me that a prince may make a nobleman, but not a gentleman. He was most put out.' He grinned at the memory.

'He has no love for the clergy either,' Wolsey said, 'and he hates me. In that, at least, he is at one with Suffolk.'

Henry bent to inspect some brickwork. 'For all his faults, he is useful to me. You must work with him.' He beckoned to the foreman. 'That pointing needs seeing to. Have the men work late to redo it, under canvas if it rains. My lord Cardinal, see that ale, bread and cheese are brought to them.' He led Wolsey away from the site. 'Ah, see who comes! Talk of the devil.'

It was Norfolk himself, with his handsome dark-haired nephew George Boleyn in tow, carrying bows and arrows and clearly on their way to the archery butts. They bowed when they saw Harry.

'Good day to you, my lord Duke, Master Boleyn,' the King said. 'I see you are making the most of this fine weather.'

'An hour at the butts, Sir, and then we'll be off hunting,' Norfolk replied, ignoring Wolsey. 'Anything to get this lad's nose out of a book. I never did hold with all this learning.'

'I doubt his Grace would agree with you, Uncle.' George Boleyn smiled. 'We should all profit from the example of a learned king.'

Harry smiled, acknowledging the compliment.

'Work is coming on apace over there.' Norfolk nodded in the direction of the palace.

'More slowly than I would have liked,' Harry said. 'I hear that you are rebuilding Kenninghall. I must come and visit you in Norfolk when it is finished.'

'I will be honoured,' Norfolk said proudly. 'I'm having it done in the antick style. It will be a showplace when it's finished.'

'It's strange,' Wolsey observed, as they parted company, 'how a man with such old-fashioned views can favour modern architecture.'

'Like most of my nobles, he is keen to emulate me,' Harry said. 'As you once told me, it keeps them all out of mischief.'

'Young Boleyn is a promising chip off the old block,' Wolsey said. 'One to watch, Sir.'

'He is to be married soon. I gave permission for him to wed Lord Morley's daughter Jane. I'm giving them a manor in Norfolk as a bridal gift. I wish her joy of him. He's promiscuous, I hear.'

Wolsey lowered his voice. 'My gentleman usher, Cavendish, keeps his ear to the ground at court. He tells me that Master Boleyn is something of a beast. Deflowers widows and virgins at will, whether they be willing or no.'

'Is that so?' Henry's expression darkened. He would not brook blatant immorality at his court. Men should be discreet in their amours, as he was himself, and as the code of chivalry dictated. No one knew that Mary Carey had just had a daughter who was probably his. At least it was not another boy. He could not have borne that.

'It may be pure gossip,' Wolsey was saying. 'He's as proud as the rest of his family. But for that, he'd be more popular, for he is intelligent and witty, and something of a poet. And he may be useful to you, for he speaks fluent French.'

'I will bear that in mind.' Harry said.

At Christmas, he planned to stage a great pageant, 'The Castle of Loyalty'. An army of carpenters had been set to building a wooden fortress twenty feet square and fifty feet high, to his own design, in the tiltyard at Greenwich, where jousts were to form part of the entertainment. But when he came to inspect the finished structure, he was appalled to see how badly the men had interpreted his plans.

'It's completely contrary to what I ordered!' he shouted. 'It won't stand the slightest assault. And it's too late in the day to do anything to remedy it. We'll have to abandon the pageant. Begone, the lot of you!'

It was infuriating, not least because, at thirty-three, he was finding that he had less appetite than before for pageantry, and this was to have been his play-acting swansong. But he could still recapture the heady days of youth, for the tournament could yet go ahead. It began with Kate seating herself in what remained of the flimsy model castle.

Then Harry and Suffolk, disguised as two ancient knights, came before her, craved her leave to break spears and ran several courses, to great ovation.

When they bowed to her, she praised their courage. 'It is rare to see gallant knights performing such feats of chivalry at your advanced age,' she said, whereupon Harry and Suffolk threw off their disguises and Kate showed herself suitably astonished. It was a charade they had played too many times before, and it had lost its appeal. In fact, it reminded Harry that they were all getting older, and that life was short.

Chapter 16

1525

Charles' messenger, with the Imperial eagle blazoned on his livery, knelt before Harry, breathless and mud-stained. 'Your Grace, the Emperor has defeated the King of France in battle at Pavia in Italy, and taken him prisoner.'

Harry nearly whooped for joy. His rival had been vanquished and humiliated!

'I am instructed to tell your Grace that your great rebel, Richard de la Pole, called the "White Rose", fell fighting for the French.'

'All the enemies of England are gone!' Harry exulted. 'My man, you are as welcome as the Archangel Gabriel was to the Virgin Mary!' He sent the messenger to the kitchens for food and commanded that he be rewarded for his pains. Then he summoned Wolsey and ordered that bonfires be lit in the streets of London and free wine distributed to the citizens.

In March, he went in state to St Paul's to give thanks for the Emperor's victory. Then he commissioned a painting of the Battle of Pavia to remind him of this great triumph. He was still gloating over the capture of King Francis and the disarray in which France found herself, when Master Fermour, a merchant of Calais, brought a young fellow called Will Somers to Greenwich.

'You should receive him,' Wolsey said. 'I've never seen a funnier jester.'

Somers, who looked older than his thirty years, was lean, hollow-eyed and stooped, with a Shropshire burr and a little monkey. He didn't look promising.

'Well, fool, let's see what you can do,' Harry said, settling down in his chair, prepared to be underwhelmed.

He was wrong. Will Somers was a born comedian. He soon had Harry and his courtiers in fits of laughter as he capered around the room, diving behind the tapestries and thrusting a comical face through a gap between them. Then, with his monkey on his shoulder, he minced around the presence chamber, rolling his eyes, as the animal performed tricks. He then fell to telling jests, laughing uncontrollably at the punchlines, and impersonating to the life all sorts of characters, from high-and-mighty nobles to innkeepers.

'Believe me, Harry,' he said to the King, 'you have many frauditors, many conveyors and many deceivers, and they take all for themselves!'

Harry roared with mirth. He too took a dim view of his auditors, surveyors and receivers. He liked this fool and his wicked sense of humour! There was an instant rapport between them. And he did not mind the familiarity; jesters were allowed to take liberties forbidden to others.

'Come and be my fool,' he said, when Somers had made his final bow.

'Ah, Harry, that I will! And we shall do well together,' Somers replied, making another face.

'Enough!' Harry gasped. 'Or I shall die laughing.'

He soon realised he had added a new jewel to his crown. He had had fools all his life, but none had made him so merry. Somers had appeared at a time when Harry most needed light relief from worrying about the succession. His cheery prattle was the perfect diversion and his company strangely soothing.

Harry was out hawking in Hitchin in Hertfordshire. The weather might be chilly, but the sun was shining and he was enjoying himself. Just as he released the jesses and his falcon took flight, his horse suddenly halted, nearly throwing him. Clinging to its neck, he saw that the silly creature had baulked at crossing a wide ditch. Well, he would not wait for it to gather its courage, or for his companions to catch up with him. Dismounting, he cast an eye about the surrounding farmland, spying a barn. There, propped against the wall, were some wooden staves. One would serve as a pole vault. Pushing it deep into the mud below the waters of the ditch, he launched himself across, but immediately there was a sickening crack as the stave snapped and he found himself cast head-first into the stream. As his head hit the bottom and stuck fast in the clay, below the water, he tried to lever himself out, but the suction was too strong, and he realised in panic that he could not breathe and would surely drown.

Then there was a mighty splash and strong arms laid hold of him, tugging hard, as he pushed yet again with all his might to get free. He felt himself being pulled to the surface and, gulping in God's good air again, spluttering and spitting foul, brackish water, he clutched his rescuer as he strove to stand up.

It was one of his footmen, Edmund Mody. They stared at each other.

'You have saved my life,' Harry said, shuddering from the shock and the cold water. 'I could have died here.'

'I am just glad that I was coming up and saw your Grace fall,' the man said. He too was shaking.

'I thank you – and England too has cause to thank you this day. You shall be well rewarded.' Harry was recovering his equilibrium now.

'I don't want a reward, Sir. It was an honour to rescue your Grace.'

Harry put an arm around the man's shoulders and they walked back to find the hawking party, who were horrified when they related their tale. As he rode to Knebworth, where he was staying as a guest of the Lyttons, who had served his father well, Harry could not help grimacing when he thought of the near-escape he had had. God had certainly been watching out for him today. But the accident made it plain to him, more forcibly than ever, that the problem of the succession must be solved as a matter of urgency.

Of late, he had taken to visiting Kate's bed only occasionally, for form's sake. He would rather have stayed away, for she was suffering from some persistent female complaint that produced a repellent discharge. As she was definitely now past the ways of women, it was a relief not to feel pressured any more into getting her with child. He would bid her a courteous good night, or they might talk for a bit, and then he would lie as far as possible from her, burying his nose in the sheets.

At Knebworth, he summoned Wolsey and told him what had happened at Hitchin.

'I know now that the Queen will never bear me a son,' he said. 'The galling thing is that I do have a healthy son.'

'That is a most regrettable situation, Sir,' Wolsey commiserated. 'My godson is a fine boy, one to be proud of.'

Harry locked eyes with him. 'Is there any way that I could name him my heir?'

Wolsey drew in his breath. 'Bastardy is a serious bar to inheritance, Sir, but natural children can be legitimated in certain circumstances. Yet before your Grace embarks on such a course, the first step would be to bring the boy to court, where he will be in the public eye. Then you will be able to judge whether or not he would be acceptable to your subjects.'

Harry began pacing the floor. 'He is six. His tutors say he is way-ward and doesn't concentrate. They fear his mother has spoiled him.'

'A firm hand is all he needs, Sir,' Wolsey soothed. 'It is time for him to be given into the care of men. But he is a charming boy and will win hearts. A little boisterousness is only natural in one so young.'

'I will take your advice,' Harry said.

Henry Fitzroy was duly brought to Windsor in time for the chapter meeting on St George's Day, when he was made a Knight of the Garter. Kate had long been aware of his existence and showed no rancour towards him. She even came to watch the ceremony from her closet above the high altar in St George's Chapel. Harry was touched to see her there, for his son was a living reproach to her for her failure to bear an heir; it could not be easy for her. But if she accepted Fitzroy, others would too. He was pleased that the boy was conducting himself well – he had had a stern word with him before-hand – and proud that his son was now sitting beside him in the second stall on the sovereign's side of the chapel. His gaze travelled over the faces of the lords and clergy in the congregation. There was not a hint of disapproval in any one of them; in fact, many were smiling indulgently at the boy. Were they thinking what he was thinking?

Vastly encouraged, he decided to make his intention plain.

'I am going to create Fitzroy a duke,' he told Wolsey. 'I am giving him two royal dukedoms, those of Richmond and Somerset. My father held the earldom of Richmond before his accession, and he made my brother Edmund duke of Somerset, a title that was once borne by my Beaufort ancestors. These titles will proclaim to the world my son's high status and royal blood. And look, I have designed a coat of arms for him.' He pushed a parchment across his desk to Wolsey.

'I have been taking soundings,' the Cardinal said. 'Many fear a disputed succession; they would like to see the matter settled. I think they might accept Fitzroy as your heir.'

'We shall see how his ennoblement is received,' Harry murmured.

The investiture of those chosen to be ennobled took place in June in the presence chamber at Bridewell Palace. It was intolerably hot and, standing under his cloth of estate, attended by Cardinal Wolsey, the dukes of Norfolk and Suffolk, and the earls of Arundel and Oxford, Harry was sweltering in his velvet and ermine robes. The room was packed with courtiers and stank of sweat.

A fanfare sounded and Henry Fitzroy entered the chamber. He knelt before his father, and Harry clothed him in a crimson and blue mantle, and gave him the sword, the cap of estate and the coronet of a duke, as the patent of creation was read out. Then the child took his place beside his father on the dais, taking precedence over every other peer in the room, despite looking very small beside them. The message was loud and clear: he was now next in rank to His Majesty and might, by the King's means, easily be exalted to higher things.

Next came forward Harry's nephew, Henry Brandon, who was created earl of Lincoln; his cousins, Henry Courtenay, Earl of Devon, who was made marquess of Exeter, and Thomas Manners, who became earl of Rutland; and lastly Sir Thomas Boleyn, bursting with self-importance at being elevated to the peerage as Lord Rochford.

Kate kept her composure through the ceremony, but she would not look at Henry or speak to him as they sat together at the feast held to mark the ennoblements and the disguisings that followed. When Harry joined her for Vespers, she was decidedly frosty, but when he next visited her, she made no reference to young Fitzroy and held her peace, much to his relief.

But his sister was not so reticent. 'If you think your people will accept your bastard as king, think again!' she said tartly, when she came to Harry's chamber to bid him farewell, just before she left court. 'I tell you, they never will.'

'Then what do you suggest I do about the succession?' Harry growled.

'You have an heir!' Mary retorted. 'There is no reason why the Princess should not make a great queen.'

'My subjects will never accept a woman as their monarch. This is not Spain.'

'They will not accept a bastard either!'

'I will hear no more of this,' Harry snapped, and strode away.

'Kate thinks Wolsey put you up to this,' she called after him. 'Wolsey hates her because she is Spanish and the Emperor's aunt. He will do anything to have his revenge on Charles for failing to make him pope!'

'Enough!' Harry barked over his shoulder. 'Hold your tongue, Sister!'

When he had calmed down, he had to admit that Mary was right. Wolsey was no Imperialist; he always favoured the French, so it was not surprising that Kate distrusted him. His political dominance remained unchallenged, and Harry still relied heavily on him; indeed, the Cardinal was indispensable. But he was becoming aware that he himself was now a mature man with a changing outlook on life, and that part of him was uncomfortable about sharing his power with one he had raised high.

Even so, he still resented others criticising Wolsey. Norfolk was never backward in voicing his views. Only last week, at York Place, he had expressed them forcefully.

'With respect, your Grace, he's become too autocratic for his own good. I can remember a time when he'd say, "His Majesty will do so and so." Then it was "We shall do so and so." Now it is "I shall do so and so."' His gaze swept the magnificent chamber with its rich tapestries that Harry knew were changed once a week, and the sideboard groaning with plate. 'Sir, this Cardinal is king, and in flaunting his wealth, he shows he holds your honour in small account.'

Himself somewhat overawed by the splendour of York Place, Harry was gazing with envy at the paintings, the fine furniture, the bedstead of alabaster bearing Wolsey's arms, and the delightful gardens beyond the window. Norfolk's words had touched a tender spot. Bridewell was sumptuous, but it lacked the magnificence and expanse of Wolsey's palaces; the site was too small, hemmed in by other buildings. Discontent and jealousy consumed him.

But at supper that evening, he could not but enjoy Wolsey's scintillating company, as he enthused about Cardinal College, his new foundation at Oxford, and the fine tomb he was having built for himself at Windsor, in the small chapel that had been meant to house Harry's own tomb. That unsatisfactory structure had now been dismantled, and Harry had made the chapel available to Wolsey.

'I am honoured that the Queen's Grace has taken an interest in my college,' Wolsey said, as they ate from plates of solid gold. 'She told me how pleased she was to know that it would draw students from all over England, and that students and masters alike would pray for her welfare.'

Mention of Kate brought another, less congenial matter to Harry's mind. Kate was no friend to Wolsey; they both knew it. 'I understand that there has been some unpleasantness concerning her Grace,' he murmured.

'I fear she blames me for the advancement of Fitzroy,' Wolsey replied, looking grieved. 'Three of her Spanish ladies have been encouraging her to make a fuss about his recent elevation. I immediately had them dismissed.'

'I know,' Harry nodded, thinking that Wolsey must have spies even in Kate's household – or someone had overheard gossip. 'She has asked me to rescind the order, but I refused and told her to submit and have patience.' He winced to think of the pained look on her face.

'I am sorry to have caused trouble for her Grace,' Wolsey said.

Harry frowned. If reports from Spain were anything to go by, Kate would soon be even more isolated at his court. For a coolness had been developing between himself and his ally.

It was true, what he had both suspected and feared. The Emperor had jilted the Princess Mary. Offered the chance of marrying the beautiful Isabella of Portugal, who would bring with her a dowry of nearly a million ducats, he had decided that he did not want to wait for Mary to grow up.

Harry blustered and raged at the slight to his daughter, even as his rational self was telling him that he would have done the same had he found himself in Charles' position. Kate wept, her dream of a Spanish marriage for Mary in tatters.

Harry took his fury out on her. 'Now that Mary is not going to Spain, she must be prepared for queenship,' he told her. 'You say she has what it takes, that she is Queen Isabella to the life. Well, I hope you are proved right.'

'Mary *will* make a great queen!' she assured him. 'I have no doubt of that.'

'We shall see.' He would not concede more. 'I do not intend formally to create her princess of Wales, but that role she shall have. You will recall the precedent set by my father and grandfather, who sent their heirs to live at Ludlow—'

'No, Henry,' Katherine interrupted. 'Please, no!'

'But Kate, it is the best apprenticeship for princes. I wish I had

245

been afforded the opportunity, but I was only the younger son, so Arthur was sent. This is how Mary will best learn to rule. She is nine, an apt age to begin, and I intend for her to stay there until she marries.'

'Henry,' Kate cried, 'you must know what this means to me! I had counted on keeping her with me, my only child, until she is twelve. She is so young to be parted from us. She needs me, her mother.'

'It is for her good. I am her father. Do you not think I have her interests at heart?'

'I know you do, of course you do, but what of me? I have no other child to console me in her absence. I cannot bear to part with her. Send her to Ludlow if you must, but let me go with her! I know Ludlow, I was there with Arthur, and I could be a help to her.'

Harry was immovable. 'Your place is with me, as my Queen. You have a role to perform here at court. My mother did not go with Arthur; she knew her duty.'

Kate was frantic. 'Henry, I am begging you!' She fell to her knees and clutched his hands. 'Let her stay with me until she is twelve.'

'No,' he said, disentangling his fingers, not looking her in the eye. 'Lady Salisbury shall go with her as her governess. Let that be a comfort to you.'

Kate put on a brave face, as befitted Isabella's daughter. She summoned Mary and told her she was to go to Ludlow because she had to learn how to be a great queen. Mary's eyes lit up at that. Later that day, Kate dictated to Wolsey a long list of instructions for Lady Salisbury regarding her daughter's upbringing, and showed them to Harry.

'Most fitting,' he commented, for she had covered every aspect of Mary's well-being. He congratulated himself on having handled the matter so well. But he had known that Kate's ambition for her daughter would prevail over her personal heartbreak at being separated from her.

Harry had plans for young Richmond too. He sent him to the north, having appointed the six-year-old boy Lord High Admiral,

Warden General of the Northern Marches and Lord Lieutenant of England, with command of all military operations north of the Trent, offices Harry himself had held before his accession. In Yorkshire, Richmond's household was established in Sheriff Hutton Castle, one of eighty manors Harry had granted him.

No one could be in any doubt now that Harry was grooming the boy for kingship. He was being well brought up as the King's son and kept the state of a great prince, holding court from a rich chair of cloth of gold set under a canopy of estate, and being addressed as royalty. In Yorkshire, he acted as nominal president of the old Council of the North, now known as the Council of the Duke of Richmond. And Harry was toying with the idea of marrying him to another rich Portuguese princess.

He cherished his son like his own soul. The child was his worldly jewel, and it was a joy to know how he loved and revered his father. As soon as Richmond, belatedly, mastered the skill of writing, they began to exchange regular letters.

Harry had to smile at one the boy sent him. *My most dread and sovereign lord, I send you my duty and make my most humble intercession for a harness to exercise myself in arms. I think Julius Caesar would have smiled on my request. I crave your blessing. Your luving son, Harry Richmond.*

How could he resist? It thrilled him to learn that his boy had martial instincts, and that he was absorbing the new learning and the classics. The harness was promptly dispatched north, along with a lute, for his son had also inherited the family talent for music. Kate made no secret of her dissatisfaction with his treating Richmond as royalty. She plainly feared that Mary would be displaced.

In late August, when Hampton Court was finally completed, Harry went to see it. Hearing Wolsey boasting about its thousand rooms and pointing out the new medallions of Roman emperors carved by the Florentine sculptor Giovanni di Maiano, he could not resist a dig. 'You know, Thomas, my palaces are nowhere near as splendid as yours. All this' – his hand moved to encompass the lofty great hall with its oriel window – 'belongs to a subject. Not that you do not deserve to be well rewarded for your labours.'

Wolsey was quick to take the hint. He was ever one for the grand gesture, especially when it was politic to make it. 'Your Grace, without your favour, I am nothing. All I have is yours. It would give me the greatest pleasure to present Hampton Court and all its contents to you.'

Harry had not expected such speedy munificence. He clapped Wolsey on the back. 'Was ever king so beholden to a subject? Thomas, I did right to raise you high, and you have rewarded me a thousand-fold. Thank you for your gift. But I cannot take it without giving something in return.' He thought for a moment, but his head would not clear because he was too busy looking around him at the treasures he had just acquired. 'I will give you in exchange Richmond Palace,' he said, aware that it was nowhere near as big or magnificent as Hampton Court. 'But you are welcome to make use of Hampton Court whenever you wish, especially for official entertaining.'

Wolsey bowed his head in gratitude, not quite managing to hide his consternation at having made that impulsive gesture.

They walked through glorious gardens in the sun and strolled along the paths between the flower beds, breathing in the scent of lilies, violets, primroses, gilliflowers, columbines, lavender and herbs. Across the wide expanse of lawn, Harry spied some of Kate's maids-of-honour playing ball amid squeals of laughter, looking like flowers themselves in their graceful gowns.

They had seen him. The ball was dropped as they sank into curtseys.

He strode over. 'Rise, ladies. No ceremony on this beautiful day.'

He and the other men watched appreciatively as, at his nod, they resumed their game, self-consciously at first, and then with increasing abandon.

He became aware of a pair of dark eyes regarding him boldly, and held their gaze. It was Anne Boleyn, back at court after her brief spell of disgrace. And where, until now, he would not have seen anything remarkable in that narrow face and sallow skin, it struck him that here was beauty beyond the ordinary. It was in her eyes that seemed to invite conversation, in her slender form, in her French mannerisms and smiling lips. In that moment, he was struck by Cupid's dart of love – but it was more like a thunderbolt.

Chapter 17

1525

The tables had been cleared and removed, for there was to be dancing in the presence chamber that night. As the musicians began playing, Harry stood up, bowed to Kate and led her out in a stately pavane, with the courtiers joining them. He noticed Anne Boleyn among the throng, dancing with Thomas Wyatt, Clerk of the King's Jewels and the Boleyns' neighbour in Kent. Other heads were turning, for she was an extraordinarily accomplished dancer, leaping and jumping with infinite grace and ability, and even inventing new figures and steps. By St George, she could trip and go!

Tom Wyatt was a charming, intelligent man, a poet and dreamer who preferred country life to the court. He was tall and good-looking, with curly fair hair, and a dashing performer in the tiltyard. Women found him compellingly attractive, and he had a well-deserved reputation as a philanderer. The only woman who didn't fancy him, it seemed, was his wife, Elizabeth Brooke, who was notoriously unfaithful.

Harry had long favoured Wyatt for his talent as a poet; the young man also had potential as a diplomat. But now, seeing him chatting animatedly with Anne Boleyn, who was clearly enjoying the flirtation, he felt raging jealousy rise within him.

When the dance ended and Anne returned to wait with the other maids behind the Queen's chair, Harry made his move.

'Will you do me the honour of dancing with me, Mistress Anne?' he asked.

There was a slight pause before she lowered her head and gave him her hand. He took it, thrilled at the touch of her skin, and escorted her to the floor.

They danced in silence. She would not meet his eye.

'You are very quiet tonight, Mistress Anne,' he said, as they set the pace in a *basse* dance. 'Usually, I have noticed, you have a lot to say for yourself.'

'I am a little tired, your Grace,' she said coolly.

He gripped her hand. 'Why won't you speak to me?' he growled.

'I? Sir, it was never my intention to offend you.'

'You seem to be doing your best to ignore me,' he muttered. 'Am I not pleasing to you?'

'Sir, the King's condescension is pleasing to everyone, including me. I fear you have misunderstood my awe at being in your presence for rudeness, and I am heartily sorry for it.' The words were courteous, yet her manner belied them.

'Mistress Anne, I am relieved to hear that,' he said. 'Yet it is I who am in awe of you. I have been watching and admiring you for some time. If you could find it in your heart to show a little kindness, it would be a great happiness to me.'

She gave him a hard look. 'How could I not be kind to my sovereign?'

'You mistake my meaning,' Harry murmured, as they moved closer in the dance. 'I am struck with a dart, Mistress Anne, and do not know how to tear it out!'

Their eyes met again, but she looked away quickly.

'Sir,' she said, 'since you are married to the Queen, my good mistress, I know not how to answer you.'

'You know well enough how to answer Master Wyatt!' Harry flared.

'He is not the King of England,' she faltered, 'and he is married, but I am not afraid of reproving *him* for his pursuit of me. Sir, I am jealous of my good name. I cannot risk tangling with one who is forbidden to me, however well I think of him.'

'But you are not above dancing with Wyatt.'

'I have known him since childhood, Sire. I danced with him as a friend.'

251

Harry relented. 'Will you dance with your King as a friend too?'

'Sir, how could I do otherwise, when your Grace has been so generous to my father?'

'I have been glad to show favour to your family, and he has served me well,' Harry said. 'I am prepared to be more generous still.'

'As you were to my sister?' Her voice was low, he could not be sure she had been so candid.

He was taken aback. 'I was fond of your sister,' he muttered, 'but these things end . . . It ran its course.'

She gave him a look. 'From what I heard, there was less fondness than force at the start!'

'Anne!' he said urgently. 'Do not let Mary poison your mind against me. She came to me willingly enough.'

'She told me your Grace gave her no choice!'

Harry's cheeks were hot. 'Is that really what she told you? Well, as a gentleman and a knight, I will not gainsay her. But I pray you will not think ill of me for taking only what I believed was offered freely.'

'Offered so freely that she was distraught and in tears afterwards! I know – I was there.'

The music had stopped. Hastily, Anne curtseyed, as Harry bowed.

'I pray you, dance with me once more,' he invited. 'I would make things right between us.'

'Sir, forgive my boldness, but there can be no "us", and there is no need to make anything right.'

'Then I will escort you back to your place,' he said in his steeliest voice.

It was a novel experience for him to be left dangling in suspense by a woman. All those he had pursued – except Mary Carey in the beginning – had been eager for his attentions and his favour; he was the King, after all. Of course, he had played the courtly game of love first, as was expected of him, and because he enjoyed it. He was a hunter by nature and the pleasure was all in the pursuit. It was familiarity that often bred boredom and contempt.

He could not be angry with Anne for long. Her virtue and her loyalty to her sister were admirable. When next he paid Kate a visit, he smiled at Anne and asked her to play her lute for them.

'You play very well,' he complimented her.

'Not as well as your Grace,' she said, giving the expected response – an olive branch, he hoped. And there was Kate, smiling at them both.

Christmas brought its customary revelry and good order was turned on its head; all ceremony was forgotten and the Lord of Misrule reigned supreme. There was a game of hoodman blind, when the Master of the Revels, blindfolded, chased the shrieking courtiers through the royal apartments. Harry's face darkened when he saw Anne running hand in hand with Tom Wyatt towards an arras, behind which they concealed themselves with a lot of fumbling and giggling. Why could she not be like that with him?

He would have to resort to subterfuge. There was to be a disguising, which suited his purpose admirably. He dressed himself as the Green Man, hiding his face behind an elaborate mask of leaves, and caught Anne from behind under the kissing bough suspended from a roof beam above the doorway. Twisting her around to face him, he kissed her heartily on the lips. How sweet it was! She broke away and ran from him, disappearing around a corner. He followed her, as the sounds of merriment faded into the distance and all was quiet and in darkness. Then he saw her, frozen at the end of a gallery, and hastened towards her.

'Anne!' he cried. 'Do not fear me. I am no rapist, as your sister alleges. For weeks now I have been unable to think of anything but you. I come to you as a supplicant, hoping you will take pity on me.'

Was that a smile playing about her lips? 'Sir, I am flattered to receive the attention of so great a king, but in truth I do not know how I can help you.'

He tore off his mask, placed his hands on her slender shoulders and gazed into her eyes. She felt so small and vulnerable under his touch. 'Anne!' He could not hide the catch in his voice. 'You have cast an enchantment on me! I do not know how to explain it. It seems presumptuous to use the word love, but I know what I feel. I do not sleep at night; I see only your face before me. I am in torment!'

'Sir!' she protested. 'I have cast no enchantment! I am your good subject, nothing more.'

He let his hands encircle her waist and drew her to him. 'I want you, Anne,' he murmured. 'I want to be your servant, and I want you for my acknowledged mistress. Venus, that insatiable goddess, has brought me to this pass, but I pray that you, sweetheart, will be kind to me!'

'Sir!' She went rigid in his arms and he let her go, standing back and looking at her, knowing she must see the naked longing in his face.

'May I have time to think on this?' she asked. 'Your Grace has so overwhelmed me that I do not know what to say to you.'

'Of course, Anne!' he agreed, jubilant that she was finally playing the game.

1526

After Christmas, Wolsey joined Harry at Eltham, where they drew up a list of ordinances for the reform of the royal household.

Wolsey had prepared well. 'My aim is to save money, and eliminate waste,' he said.

'I have long felt the need for these changes.' Harry nodded. 'They are necessary. The war with France has drained my treasury.' All that gold inherited from his father had disappeared, spent on palaces, entertainments, kingly display and war. Matters had reached the point where some servants would have to be pensioned off and hangers-on ejected from the court. Harry knew he had been over-generous in granting positions to his favourites and their clients; now he would have to be more careful.

Predictably, Wolsey seized this second chance to counter the threat to his authority from the Privy Chamber, the one centre of power at court over which he lacked influence.

'Your Grace,' he said, in his most paternal manner, 'those who surround you should lead an example as your courtiers. They should be eloquent, learned and well informed, and thus able to influence their master in a beneficial way. They ought to be the epitome of chivalry and courtesy, lovers of the arts and expert in martial exercises and sports. But these virtues are not apparent in the Privy Chamber. It is full of pride, envy, indignation, mocking and derision. There is more malice than moderation, and there are too many young men of a martial bent with time on their hands.'

Harry knew that Wolsey was right. Those who surrounded him were greedy to feather their own nests and averse to giving place to anyone else. But he did not want to admit that there was a problem. 'I provide them with outlets for their energy and aggression,' he declared. 'There are many opportunities for sport and feats of arms and entertaining diversions. I've built tiltyards, houses of pleasure for playing at chess, backgammon, dice, cards and billiards, and bowling alleys, archery butts and goodly tennis plays.'

But Wolsey remained implacable. In the interests of economy, Harry's gentlemen were reduced from twelve to six. Convinced that Richard Pace was working against him, Wolsey saw to it that he was ousted from his post as secretary and sent to Spain on a demanding diplomatic mission. Many people left court burning with resentment, chief among them Wolsey's enemies, Compton, Bryan, Carew, Rochford and George Boleyn, all vowing revenge upon the Cardinal and determined to recover their former positions.

Harry missed his friends. He wondered why he had again allowed Wolsey to persuade him that their removal was for the best. He had insisted on retaining as chief nobleman of the Privy Chamber his cousin Exeter, who was no lover of the Cardinal. To counter his influence, Wolsey quickly brought in his own adherent, the one-eyed Sir John Russell, an ambitious courtier, soldier and diplomat. The charming and polished Henry Norris, who had once again escaped the cull, replaced Compton as Groom of the Stool and head of the Privy Chamber; he was close to Harry and eminently fitted for this most confidential of court offices.

* * *

On Shrove Tuesday, Harry hosted a tournament at Greenwich. In a bullish mood, he had summoned his banished friends back to court, telling a disapproving Wolsey that he had need of them. In truth, he wanted to assert himself.

But he was not thinking of his companions in arms as his attendants dressed him in a magnificent jousting costume of cloth of gold and silver with the motto 'Declare I dare not' embroidered on his breast beneath a man's heart engulfed in flames.

Would she notice? Would she even care? Since that encounter at Christmas, he had barely seen her, and still she had given him no answer. Had she been avoiding him? He had feared so, but once or twice, when their paths had crossed and others were present, she had bestowed a dazzling smile on him and flashed those fascinating eyes. It had left him bewildered.

He could not stop thinking about her. Her face came between him and his kingly duties. He would sit in Council dreaming of her, then realise he had not the faintest idea of what his councillors had been discussing. Today, therefore, he was going to declare himself – in the most subtle way, of course, for secrecy was one of the rules of the game. But she would know: he felt certain of it.

He peered through the opening in his tent, looking across to the tiltyard gallery.

Yes, she was there, seated with the other maids-of-honour, near the Queen. Beside her, Kate – indeed, all of them – looked insignificant.

Fanfares sounded and the jousts began. Harry lifted the flap of his tent and watched the opening courses, thrilling at the thundering hooves of the mighty steeds and the clash of lances. And then a terrible cry rent the air. Sir Francis Bryan was down, howling in the dirt and clutching his eye.

Harry threw a cloak over his costume, raced forward with the rest and knelt beside his friend. 'Call a doctor!' he shouted. In the stands, the spectators were on their feet, straining to see what had happened. Some ladies were shrieking.

'My lance splintered,' Compton said, shaking. 'It caught him in the eye.'

'It was an accident,' Suffolk assured him.

'It was,' Harry concurred. 'You are not to blame. We all know the risks.' He laid a hand on Bryan's shoulder. 'Hold on. Help is coming.'

When Dr Chamber arrived and pulled Bryan's hand away from the wound, all that could be seen was a gaping, bloody eye socket. 'Be grateful that God gave you two eyes,' he said, as the wounded man was laid on a stretcher.

The accident cast gloom over the day. As Harry watched his friend being carried away, he risked a glance in Anne Boleyn's direction. Even she, normally so composed, looked shaken.

'The jousts will continue!' he cried, marching back to his tent.

Mounted on his horse, he trotted to the lists. At the sight of him, as well as cheers, there was a buzz of murmuring from the crowd. Kate was staring at him with a puzzled smile on her face. Surely she was not thinking that his motto and the blazing heart were for her? Those days were long gone.

But the one for whom they *were* intended was not there; she had simply vanished. He felt inordinately crushed, and angry – he was the King, after all!

The next morning, immediately after Mass, he went to Kate's apartments, hoping he would see Anne, and surprised her as she walked into the antechamber. As she paused, startled, to curtsey, he closed the door. She put her hand up to steady her French hood and as the hanging sleeve she affected fell away, he noticed that she had a rudimentary sixth nail on her little finger. At once, she pulled down her sleeve and covered it. He understood. Ignorant people might think the deformity a sign of inner corruption or divine disfavour, or even a witch's mark, but he was not one of them. He took that hand and kissed it, even as he felt her instinctively tug it away.

'Mistress Anne, you have cast an enchantment on me.'

'Like my sister did?' she retorted. Was she never going to forget that?

'It was nothing like this,' he said gravely, willing her to understand his passion and his need of her.

'And it would end up as nothing if I gave in to your Grace's desires.' By God, she was cruel!

'I am not asking you to bed with me,' Harry protested. 'I would be your servant and have you for my mistress, to wield mastery over my heart.'

'And have the world think me your harlot!' she cried.

'Never that!' he said vehemently. 'I have far too much regard for you. In fact, I came in the hope of seeing you. You left the tournament yesterday.'

She drew her hand away. 'I am recovered from my headache, thank you, Sir. I have yet to recover from seeing you publicly proclaim your feelings! Truly, that was unfair of you.'

He was immediately contrite. 'Anne, I cannot live without you. I have never been this powerfully attracted to any other woman. Help me, please! Give me some crumb of affection.'

'Alas, Sir, you are not free, so it would not be proper. How is Francis Bryan?' Very deftly she had changed the subject!

He grimaced. 'His eye is gone, but he will otherwise recover.'

'I am relieved to hear it. Forgive me, Sir, her Grace is waiting, and I shall get into trouble if I am late. Fare you well!' She pushed open the inner door and hurried away, her skirts rippling behind her.

He had thought himself in love with Kate in the beginning, and with Bessie, and to a lesser extent with Mary Carey, but it had felt nothing like this searing desire to possess. He was mad for Anne, desperate for her body, for a kiss, a kind word even. But she continued to evade him. When he did contrive an encounter, she was charm itself, deferential and fizzing with wit, but she was holding back on him, he knew it, and it left him intrigued, entranced and anguished.

Mary Carey had said that Anne drew men to her, but that she could not understand why, as she was not one of the handsomest women in the world, but that was probably sisterly cattiness, as Mary did not sparkle socially in the way Anne did. Anne was always at the centre of a group of young people, most of them gallant gentlemen like Tom Wyatt, who was still mooning around her, Harry noted jealously. It was true: she was not conventionally beautiful, but there was loveliness in her graceful figure, long neck, small, neat bosom and wide mouth – and in those glorious black eyes that she used to great effect. No wonder she had so many men paying court to her. It ate at Harry to realise that he was just one of several suitors – and that she was showing him no special favour.

Well, he would make her notice him! One spring evening, he caught up with her in the gardens and pressed into her hand a pouch containing four expensive gold brooches: one represented Venus and Cupid, the second a lady holding a heart in her hand, the third a gentleman lying in the lap of a lady and the fourth a lady holding a crown. The symbolism was unmistakable, he hoped.

He waited to see how she would respond. Most ladies would be falling over themselves to thank him for such a gift, eager to capitalise on his favour. But not Anne Boleyn, it seemed. She just walked away.

One morning, gazing out of his window, brooding on what her silence betokened when he should have been signing state papers, he spied her in the orchard, alone. His feet seemed to grow wings as he sped out of his apartments, down the privy stair and out into the palace grounds, ignoring the astonished glances of courtiers surprised to see him unattended. He slowed down as he entered the orchard, as if he were merely enjoying a summer stroll there, and came upon Anne as if by accident.

'Good day, Mistress Anne!' he said.

If she was surprised to see him, she did not betray it. 'Your Grace,' she said, and swept him an elegant curtsey. 'I was just enjoying a few cherries. They have such a short season.'

'They are my favourite fruits,' he said, his heart beating furiously at being so near to her. 'Those, and strawberries. We have some coming along beautifully in the orchard garden.'

Anne popped a cherry in her mouth. 'Mm. So sweet!'

'You have been avoiding me,' he said.

'I? Oh, no, your Grace. I have been overwhelmed by the favour you have shown me and have not known quite how to express my thanks. The brooches are beautiful, but I do not know how I should interpret such a gift.' She pulled the brooch with the crown from her pocket.

'It is symbolic of your holding the love of a king,' he told her. 'You do like them?'

'They are beautiful, Sir, but I am unworthy of them.'

'Nonsense!' he declared. 'Even though they can only be eclipsed by your beauty, they will enhance it. You need no adornment, but I should like you to wear these tokens of my love for you.'

'Then I must wear them in private,' Anne said, 'or people will wonder how I acquired such costly jewels.'

'Let them!' he cried.

'I dare not,' she protested. 'I'm not sure I should even accept them, sensible though I am of your Grace's generosity.'

'But you must, Anne. I commissioned them for you. Please wear them, and think of me when you do.'

'Very well,' she said doubtfully. 'Thank you.'

'And will you give me something in return?' Harry asked. 'I beg only for a small token.'

'I have none,' she said.

'Yes, you do!'

'No!' she cried.

'Grant me just one token,' he pleaded. Reluctantly, she drew a ring from her finger and gave it to him. It was a trifle, of little value, but he kissed it with reverence and pushed it down to the first joint of his little finger.

'That which is not freely given is worthless,' she sniffed, and walked away.

The ring *was* worthless, a trifle really, but he had it resized and wore it all the time. He noticed, however, to his disappointment, that she never wore the brooches.

* * *

He was not angry or offended. On the contrary, Anne's coolness merely served to inflame his ardour to fever pitch. It was a piquant, even humbling situation for a great king, and it fuelled what had burgeoned into a raging desire.

He could think of nothing but Anne. He was enraptured by her sophistication, vivacity and wit, and her independent spirit. In other ladies, he would have deplored that, but Anne was no ordinary woman. No one dressed as elegantly as she did; on her, the fashions of France looked wonderfully becoming. Every day, she made some change in the style of her garments. You might have taken her for a Frenchwoman born! She sang like a second Orpheus, accompanying herself on the lute or a clavichord she had decorated with green ribbons. Harry had heard her on several occasions when he visited Kate's chamber. His eyes narrowed when he found Wyatt there, watching Anne play the virginals, singing a song she had composed, or reciting one of her poems.

He did not doubt that, had Anne's ambitious father known of his interest in her, he would have put pressure on her to show herself amenable. But he did not want her to be coerced. He wanted her to love him willingly.

Summer was blazing forth in all its golden glory, and Anne had still not given Harry the answer he craved. The more evasive she became, the more ardent was his pursuit.

'Be mine!' he kept urging her. 'I want to hold you and love you.'

'I cannot love you!' she told him, again and again. 'Not only on account of my honour, but also because of the great love I bear the Queen. How could I injure a princess of such great virtue?'

'She would not know,' he hastened to assure her. 'I would handle things with the utmost discretion.'

'No!' Anne cried. 'I will not be your leman!'

'Please!' Harry pleaded, his hand stealing around her waist. 'It will not be like that. I will love you and honour you. There will be no limit to what I would do for you. You can have whatever you want – riches, houses, jewels – if you will only consent to becoming my mistress.'

Anne shook him off and moved away. 'Is that your idea of discretion? Surely your Majesty speaks these words in mirth to prove me sincere, without any intent of degrading your princely self. And to spare you the labour of asking me any such question again, I beseech your Highness most earnestly to desist, and to take my refusal in good part. I would rather lose my life than my honesty, which will be the greatest and best part of the dowry I shall bring my husband.'

It was as if she had slapped him.

'Well, Mistress Anne,' he said, 'I shall live in hope.'

She rounded on him. 'I understand not, most mighty King, how you should retain such hope! Your wife I cannot be, both in respect of my unworthiness, and also because you have a queen already. Your mistress I will not be! And now, Sir, I beg leave to return to my duties.'

'Anne!' groaned Harry. 'Don't do this to me! Go if you must, then – leave me to my torment!'

He was a man possessed. Anne's refusal to sleep with him made her infinitely more desirable.

'Why these excuses?' he asked plaintively. 'I would not make you do anything against your will, sweetheart, much as I desire you. But if you will consent to be my mistress, and let me be your chosen servant, forsaking all other, then I will respect your virtue and humbly do your will.'

She was silent for a long pause. 'Sir, I will be your mistress, but on two conditions,' she told him. 'One is that you do nothing to compromise my honour. The other is that this remains a secret between us. I do not want the world thinking I am your whore.'

'Anything, anything, darling,' Harry agreed, tears shining in his eyes. 'You have made me the happiest of men! Let us seal our love with a kiss.' And he bent his lips to hers and kissed her properly for the first time, as if he would devour her.

Throughout that summer's progress, he channelled his raging

desire by throwing himself into the pleasures of hunting, travelling from place to place, dispensing alms on the way, shooting venison for his hosts and being entertained in the evenings by Will Somers and his other fools. The court was diverted by gossip about an acrimonious rift between Anne's uncle of Norfolk and his wife, Elizabeth Stafford, Buckingham's daughter.

'I hear that the Duchess has moved into her dower house,' Harry observed to Kate, as they were returning from the chase.

Her eyes flashed. She was close to the Duchess. 'Yes, and left the Duke free to install that churl's daughter, Bess Holland, at Kenninghall. She was a washer in their nursery. The Duchess turned her out when she became the Duke's mistress; she refused to have her in the house. In retaliation, the Duke became abusive and cut off her allowance. The Duchess told me that recently Bess and her friends tied her up so tightly that blood poured from the ends of her fingers, and they sat on her chest until she spat blood. But the Duke never punished them. Indeed, he dragged her by the hair from her bed when she had just given birth and wounded her in the head with his dagger.'

Harry had heard rumours about Norfolk's violence, but he was shocked. Some men were brutal towards their wives, but such behaviour disgusted him. Never had he raised a hand to Kate, although it was perfectly permissible for husbands to chastise their spouses. 'That is no way to treat a lady,' he growled. 'But is it true?'

'Of course, he has denied it all,' Kate said. 'He accused her of slander. But he is so far in love with that woman that he regards neither God nor his honour.'

Harry drew in his breath. She might have been speaking about *him*. Was it a subtle reprimand? He thought not. He had never flaunted his mistresses and he had been so discreet these past months that surely no one could know about his pursuit of Anne.

'I think the marriage was breaking down long before Bess Holland came along,' he said.

'That's as may be, but it's no excuse for his cruelty, or his poisoning their children's minds against their mother. The two eldest are siding with their father. Now the Duchess fears that, if she goes home, she will be poisoned.'

As Kate prattled on, Harry wondered what she would say if she knew what was going on in his mind. She could not be aware that it was filled with thoughts of Anne – or that he was now finding the prospect of an alliance with France more desirable by the day. He still burned with bitterness against the Emperor and meant to make his displeasure clear to the new Spanish ambassador, Don Diego Hurtado de Mendoza, whom Charles had sent to smooth over the troubled waters between himself and Harry. Kate, Harry knew, was hoping they would become friends again. The new Empress was her niece, and although she was disappointed that Charles had rejected Mary, she was more understanding than Harry.

There was a frosty nip in the December air when Harry suggested a game of bowls to Suffolk and Francis Bryan, who nowadays looked like a pirate with his silk eyepatch. Harry was not best pleased when Bryan brought Wyatt with him, for Wyatt was still sniffing around Anne, but they played amicably until both Harry and Wyatt rolled their bowls to a stop near the jack.

Pointing with the hand on which Anne's ring was prominently displayed, Harry called, 'The game is mine, Wyatt! It is mine!' He was not just talking about the bowls.

Wyatt was riled, he could see. 'Might I have permission to measure the distance, Sir?' he asked. Harry nodded, sure from where he was standing that his bowl was nearer. Then Wyatt drew a locket from inside his shirt and used the chain as a measure. 'I hope it will be mine,' he said pointedly.

Harry recognised the locket as one of Anne's. Fury rose in him. It was bad enough that Wyatt was his rival in love, so he was in no mood to be beaten by him in a game. 'It may be so, but then I am deceived!' he hissed, and stalked off, leaving Suffolk and Bryan standing there nonplussed.

He tackled Anne as she was taking a brisk walk along the lime avenue at Greenwich, accompanied by her maid. It was a fine day, the sun shining, the air crisp.

'Why is Master Wyatt flaunting your jewel?' he demanded to know.

'He took it from me some months ago,' she said, clearly startled. 'He would not give it back.'

Harry was not mollified. 'I was playing bowls with him just now. The winning cast was mine, but he disputed it. He measured the distance with the lace on your jewel. He almost waved it in my face!'

'Sir, I assure you, I have no feelings for Tom Wyatt beyond friendship. As I told you, he is married. It would be out of the question.' She looked at him pointedly.

He gripped her arm. 'You assure me there has been nothing between you? He seems to think otherwise!'

'Let go, Sir! You are hurting me. Of course there has been nothing! I have never encouraged him.'

He let her go. 'Forgive me, sweetheart, I did not mean to doubt you. It's just that you are so precious to me that the thought of your loving another is unbearable.'

'Then all is well,' she said.

Harry was not surprised when, soon after Christmas, he learned that Wyatt had attached himself to Sir John Russell, who was leading a diplomatic mission to Rome, and left England. Clearly the fellow knew himself bested in love. Good riddance, he thought.

Chapter 18

1527

At the end of February, an important embassy arrived from Paris to negotiate another new treaty. It had been brokered by Wolsey – who was in his element again, being convinced that England would be better off allied to France – and was to be sealed by the marriage of the Princess Mary to the Duke of Orléans, the second son of King Francis. Harry was painfully aware that everyone believed Orléans would one day rule England as Mary's consort. It was not a satisfactory solution to the problem of the succession, but it was the best he and Wolsey could think of – unless Harry legitimated Richmond. But he remained uncertain of how that would be received.

During these weeks, Harry had barely had time to see Anne, for he was busy playing host and engrossed in long private talks with the ambassadors. He had to content himself with snatched meetings that left him dissatisfied and depressed, for it seemed not to bother her that they were so often apart.

Early in May, when the negotiations were completed, the French envoys made their way to Greenwich for the signing of the treaty and the elaborate celebrations. Harry had ordered the construction of a grand banqueting house and a theatre, which had hastily been built at either end of the tiltyard gallery. Both were lavishly embellished with carvings of the royal arms, antique busts and *trompe l'oeil* paintings of mythical beasts. Nicolaus Kratzer had designed a complicated cosmographical ceiling, and Master Hans Holbein, a German artist who had been recommended to Harry by Thomas More, had painted it. Holbein had also designed two triumphal arches and executed portraits of those who had collaborated with him – and very fine they were too, Harry thought, when he came to inspect the works; much better than any portraits ever produced in England.

When the French envoys arrived, he had them conducted along a gallery hung with tapestries depicting the story of King David and dominated by a massive buffet with a glittering display of gold and gem-studded plate. Holbein's triumphal arch was at the far end of the room, and above it a large painting Harry had commissioned from him of the victory at Thérouanne. Wolsey had warned that it was a tactless choice, but Harry had been unable to resist the opportunity of reminding the French of his conquest. He rather regretted it, however, when they were visibly offended – not a good start to their visit, he realised. But he would make up for it by entertaining them lavishly.

The treaty was signed in the new banqueting house, in the presence of the Queen and Harry's sister Mary. Kate was putting on a brave face, but Harry knew she deeply disapproved of the new alliance and found the prospect of her daughter marrying a French prince intolerable.

The next day, he was unable to participate in the tournament he'd planned because he had injured his foot playing tennis. It was Sir Nicholas Carew who triumphed that day in the lists, as his master looked on, frustrated, from the gallery. After a lavish banquet came a recital by the Gentlemen and Children of the Chapel Royal in the theatre, which boasted tiered seating around three of its walls, a floor carpeted with silk embroidered with gold lilies, and a huge proscenium arch adorned with terracotta busts and statuary. Holbein had designed it, again proving not only useful, but exceptionally skilled. Yet his greatest achievement was the ceiling, which depicted the earth surrounded by the sea, like a map; beneath it was suspended a transparent cloth, painted and gilded with the signs of the Zodiac and glittering with stars, planets and constellations. It was stunning, and Harry could not take his eyes off it as the music soared heavenwards.

He had arranged for Mary to make her appearance at the masque that followed. Eleven years old now, but small for her age, she was decked out with jewels, and looked very pretty. Wearing black velvet slippers because of his injured foot (and having commanded every man present to follow suit), Harry led her out in the dance and could not resist pulling off her netted caul and letting her profusion of red-gold tresses cascade about her shoulders for the benefit of the French envoys, who were loud in their praises.

The celebrations continued for several days. As Harry and Kate watched fondly from their thrones beneath the canopy of estate, Mary appeared dressed as a Roman goddess in cloth of gold studded with precious stones. Then Wolsey staged a play celebrating the alliance, which was performed by the Chapel Royal, and gave a feast at Hampton Court.

The next day, he and Harry sat down with the envoys to discuss the finer points of the treaty. All proceeded well, but Harry was aware that the Bishop of Tarbes, the head of the French embassy, seemed ill at ease.

'Something is troubling you, my lord Bishop,' he said.

The lean-faced cleric hesitated. 'There is one rather delicate matter on which King Francis will need some reassurance from your Majesty.'

Harry frowned. 'What reassurance?'

Wolsey raised his eyebrows. 'I thought we had covered everything, my lord.'

'Yes, your Eminence, but I have received further instructions. Doubts have been raised about the Princess's legitimacy.'

'Doubts?' Harry echoed sharply. This touched too rawly on his own doubts about his marriage, doubts he had voiced to no one except his confessor, who had repeatedly urged him to seek clarification from the Pope. But he had not taken that step because he was aware it would look as if he was questioning the authority of Pope Julius to dispense in such a case, which was a very grave thing indeed; and he shrank from impugning his beloved child's legitimacy. And yet he was increasingly tempted to discover if there was a way out of his marriage.

The Bishop looked embarrassed. 'My master has learned that the legitimacy of your Grace's marriage was queried at the time. I would refer you to the Book of Leviticus in Scripture.'

Harry pulled himself together and put on a smile. This alliance must not founder on a doubt. 'Let me reassure you then that Pope Julius issued a dispensation for my marriage, which he pronounced entirely lawful.' He only wished he believed it. 'The injunction in Leviticus did not apply.'

'I thank your Grace for confirming that. King Francis will be delighted to hear it.'

Harry nodded graciously. 'Well, gentlemen, are we finished? If so, we have another pageant for you.'

But his heart was not in the dancing and feasting and disguising now. He kept brooding on the Bishop's words.

'This doubt has been eating at your Grace for a long while,' Dr Longland said, as Harry knelt in confession beside him. 'It must be resolved for the safety of your soul. Talk to Archbishop Warham and the Cardinal. They will know how to obtain the assurance your Grace seeks.'

Assurance? That his marriage was sound and he was bound to Kate for ever? In his heart, he knew that was no longer what he wanted. What he sought was confirmation that his marriage was incestuous and invalid – and an annulment. Then he would be free to marry again. He would be free to take Anne as his wife. As he could not win her by wooing, he would offer her marriage – and he had little doubt that she would accept.

Monarchs, he knew, did not normally marry commoners, but there was a precedent: sixty years ago, his own grandfather, King Edward IV, had married Elizabeth Wydeville, a knight's widow, for love. All his instincts urged him to follow his heart in this crucial matter. If he stirred up controversy, it mattered not a jot.

'I will take your advice, Father,' he told Dr Longland.

His confessor placed a hand on his shoulder. 'I am relieved to hear it, my son. There is so much at stake, and I fear your doubts may be well founded. And, until the matter is resolved,

I must warn you to abstain from the Queen's bed, for the avoidance of sin.'

Harry bowed his head, relief coursing through him.

He summoned Wolsey to his closet. It was a hot day and the Cardinal was red-faced and sweating in his robes despite the breeze coming from the open lattice window.

'Thomas,' he began, 'I need your wise opinion in a delicate matter.'

'Your Grace can unburden yourself to me,' the Cardinal said, urbane as ever.

Harry cleared his throat, aware of what he might be unleashing. 'For some time now, my conscience has been troubling me in regard to the validity of my marriage. I have always tried to be a good son of the Church, but I have come to believe that I have sinned in marrying my brother's wife, and I am convinced that my lack of a male heir is proof of Almighty God's displeasure.'

Wolsey looked doubtful, probably remembering that Harry had raised the matter before. 'Sir, the Pope issued a dispensation.'

'Yes, but was it sufficient? The Book of Leviticus warns of the severe penalty God inflicts on one who marries his brother's widow: "And if a man shall take his brother's wife, it is an unclean thing: he hath uncovered his brother's nakedness; they shall be childless." Thomas, I *am* as good as childless, lacking a male heir. God does not smile on this marriage!'

Wolsey's face had taken on a pasty pallor. 'The law as laid down in Leviticus only applies where there are children of the first marriage, and clearly there were not; indeed, Prince Arthur left her Grace a virgin. And the Book of Deuteronomy enjoins a man to marry his brother's widow and raise up children in his name.'

'Deuteronomy is ambiguous! Thomas, I know in my bones that my marriage is unlawful, and I mean to have it dissolved, so that I can take a wife who can give me sons!' There, he had said it! He had voiced his inmost desire.

Wolsey shocked him by falling to his knees in a swish of silks.

'Sir, I beg you, consider well before you take this matter further. To call into question Pope Julius' dispensation would be to undermine the authority of the Church at a time when she is under attack from the heretics. It would injure a most gracious queen and will surely arouse the wrath of the Emperor, her nephew. And it could call into question the status of the Princess, your only heir, although if you both entered into the marriage in good faith, believing it was lawful, then she might still be deemed legitimate. Even so, there is the French alliance to consider; King Francis will not marry his son to one of doubtful birth. Sir, I urge you to take this no further. The consequences could be grave and far-reaching.'

'No, Thomas,' Harry said, envisaging Anne in his bed and a son in his arms. 'My mind is made up. I want an annulment. Will you approach Rome for me?'

Heaving himself back into his chair, Wolsey looked ashen. Rarely had Harry seen him at such a loss for words. 'You know you can rely on me to do your bidding,' he said slowly, pondering; then his face brightened a little. 'And something good may come of this. If your Grace's union is deemed invalid, then the French alliance can be cemented with your marriage to a French princess. I am sure King Francis will see the advantage in that, and it will hopefully provide you with a solution to the problem of the succession.'

Harry sealed his lips. He thought Wolsey was probably aware of his passion for Anne Boleyn, but he was not ready to share with him his true intentions; he had not even spoken of them to Anne, the person most closely concerned. He would have to play it carefully there. But (and he smiled inwardly to himself) let Wolsey think that a French marriage was his goal, and he would pursue an annulment with his usual zeal. Harry was suddenly glad he had confided in him.

The Cardinal seemed to gather himself together. 'As Papal legate, I will convene a secret ecclesiastical court at York Place. Archbishop Warham can preside with me.'

'Can you yourself pronounce on the validity of my marriage?' Harry asked eagerly.

'No, Sir, not without Papal sanction. This is a very difficult, sensitive matter. But I will consider the evidence formally and make suit to Rome.'

Having made up his mind to marry Anne as soon as he was free, Harry sent her a note asking her to meet him in the Chapel Royal at midnight. He was there first, waiting for her in the dimness in the royal pew. When she arrived, he bade her sit in the Queen's chair, hoping that she would soon be occupying it by right.

She looked uncertain, for once. 'What has happened?' she asked.

'Anne, I have to talk to you,' he said. 'I am in turmoil, and I do not know whether to rejoice or weep. The Bishop of Tarbes has raised the question of the Princess Mary's legitimacy.'

Her shock was unfeigned. 'But how can that be, Sir? You have been married to the Queen for . . .'

'Eighteen years,' he finished. 'And never did man have such a faithful, virtuous and loving wife. Katherine is nearly everything a queen should be.' The memory of his mother came suddenly to mind. 'But she has failed to bear me a son, and she is past the ways of women.' He buried his head in his hands. 'I have not told anyone this, darling, because it touches the Queen too nearly, but I can never convey to you how much I have agonised over not having a son and how to resolve the problem of the succession.'

'But, Sir, the Princess is forward for her years and graced with all the virtues. Why should she not rule after you?'

He stared at her, amazed that she had said the same thing as Kate. 'A woman rule England? It is against Nature! No man would heed her. And who would lead our armies into battle?'

'The Queen's own mother did in Spain,' Anne reminded him.

'So Katherine keeps telling me,' he sniffed. 'But Anne, this is England, and our people would not tolerate it. There was a queen, years ago, who attempted to rule and became a byword for infamy. Memories are long. I have a son, as you know, but he is baseborn, and I'm not sure my subjects would tolerate his succeeding me either. Now it has been put to me that my sole heir may be a bastard too. And if she marries into France, then I might well be the last king of

England, for the French will rule here in her name after I am gone. So,' he ended, turning to her, 'you can see why I am in turmoil.'

'I understand very well,' Anne said. 'But why did the Bishop question the Princess's legitimacy?'

Harry sighed. 'On the grounds that, all those years ago, the Pope had no business to be issuing a dispensation allowing me to marry my brother's widow. The Queen was married to Prince Arthur before, you know.'

She nodded, those enticing black eyes holding his gaze.

'There were those who expressed doubts at the time, but my Council overruled them, and I was determined to have Katherine for my wife. It was a brilliant marriage alliance, and I loved her. Besides, I was assured, by her, and by her father, that she was still a virgin. But if the Bishop has these doubts about my marriage, others may too. I've talked to my confessor. He fears I may well be living in sin, and, to avoid God's displeasure, I have asked for the Cardinal's advice. Anne, I mean to have my union with the Queen declared invalid.'

Anne started. 'Your Grace would go so far? You would divorce such a devout and beloved lady?'

'I must think of my kingdom, and what will surely ensue if I die without an undisputed heir. There would be civil war, make no bones about it. God knows, I have enough relations of the old Plantagenet royal blood ready to stake their claim, and some may not do me the courtesy of waiting till I die. I must have a son, Anne, and to do that I need to take another wife.'

'But the Queen? What of her? She will be devastated. She loves you so much.'

'She will understand that these doubts must be resolved, and that I need an heir. But, God help me, I don't know how I am going to face breaking this to her. For now, Anne, you must say nothing of it to anyone.'

He put his arm around her slim shoulders and drew her to him, aware that his cheeks were wet with tears. 'Anne, I did not ask you here just to talk about my marriage. You have said that you will not give yourself to me, and I respect that. But when I am free, will you marry me?'

She drew in her breath, clearly stunned, and he searched her face intently for some sign that his proposal was welcome to her. 'Maybe I should not have spoken at this time, since I am not yet free, but Anne, I love you truly; I am mad for you, and I can think of no woman I would rather marry!' He seized her hands and kissed them. 'Tell me I may hope!'

'I am not worthy,' she said. 'I am a commoner.'

'You have the soul of an angel and a spirit worthy of a crown!' he declared, squeezing her hands. 'None could deny it. My own grandmother was a commoner. My grandfather, King Edward, married her for love. There was a lot of fuss, of course. The nobility resented her and said *she* was not worthy, but she proved a good queen – as you will, my darling, I have no doubt of it! You are not of ordinary clay. Besides, it seems the only way I can win you is by marrying you!'

He expected her to laugh or make some witty remark, or at least to look joyful. But her face was registering only dismay.

'Sir, these doubts you have – they are not on account of me, I trust?'

'No, Anne, of course not. Had I never met or loved you, I would still have them, and still be wanting an annulment. I have to provide for the succession. It is my duty as king.'

He watched her considering, weighing up her answer. The suspense was unbearable. She had to say yes. Dear God, let her say yes!

A distant bell struck, heralding the watchman's cry: 'One o'clock and all's well!'

'It's late, Sir,' she said. 'I must go to bed. I beg you, do not think me insensible of the high honour you do me in asking me to be your wife and queen. In truth, my mind cannot quite compass it. I pray you, grant me time in which to consider, for this is not a matter to be undertaken lightly.'

Harry strove to hide his terrible disappointment. 'Take all the time you need, sweetheart,' he murmured, and drew her into his arms, pressing his lips on hers. This time she did not resist.

The next he heard, she had left court and gone home to her mother at Hever Castle. From there, she sent him a jewel, fashioned in gold as a solitary damsel in a ship tossed by a tempest. Nothing could better have conveyed to him her inner turmoil and her hopes that her ship would come safely to harbour. A harbour, he hoped, that she would find in his arms. He sent her an impassioned letter, thanking her and assuring her that henceforth his heart would be dedicated to her alone, and that he desired fervently that his body could be as well. Her reply was swift: she would be his Queen. His heart leapt in exultation.

Summoned in May to appear before the secret ecclesiastical court convened at Westminster, Harry seated himself before Wolsey and Warham, with ranks of senior clergy on either side.

'Your Grace,' Wolsey intoned, 'you have been asked here to account, for the tranquillity of your conscience and the health of your soul, for having knowingly taken to wife your brother's widow.'

Harry bowed his head. 'I admit the charge. I confess I have had doubts of conscience about my marriage for a while.' He looked up to see that the lords spiritual were all hanging on his every word, and took his time explaining why he had those doubts. 'I ask, in all humility, for a decision to be given on my case,' he concluded.

'We thank your Grace,' Wolsey said briskly. 'Now we will confer and debate the matter.'

Harry withdrew to his library, seeking to find solace in books. But the words danced before his eyes. Walking to the window, he looked down to see Mary playing ball in the garden with her puppies, and Lady Salisbury seated on a bench, keeping watch on her. His heart contracted. That which he had set in motion could well have a shattering impact on this child he loved so dearly. He could not divert from his course, but he could protect her. He sent for his secretary and gave the order for her to be sent with her household to

Hunsdon House in Essex, far away from the storm that was about to break.

Late in the afternoon, Wolsey appeared as he thrashed out his anxieties in a game of tennis. He flung down his racquet and hurried over to the net that divided the tennis play from the spectators' gallery.

Wolsey leaned in and spoke in a low voice.

'Your Grace, we find that there is a case to answer, and the matter has been referred to Rome for judgement. The messenger has just left.'

Harry picked up his towel and his doublet and walked to the door, motioning to Wolsey to follow him, and wishing that the Cardinal had won the Papal election. What would he not give now to have his friend in the Vatican?

'What happens next?' he asked, as they emerged into the sunlight. 'What shall I do about the Queen?'

'On no account must she learn what is going on. Forewarned is forearmed. There must be no open rift between you.'

'I have no personal quarrel with her,' Harry said, striding along the gravelled path to the privy garden. 'She has been a good wife, loyal and devoted.'

'And that is how your Grace must play it. You love the Queen; it will pain you to leave her, but you must do what is right and have a care to the salvation of your soul. While awaiting his Holiness's decision, you should appear together in public, dine and be of company in private, and show each other every courtesy. But on no account can you bed with her Grace.'

'It is rare for me to do so these days, and then only for form's sake,' Harry confided, feeling his cheeks flush. 'Nothing passes between us. She has a female disorder that makes it . . . er, unpleasant.'

Wolsey nodded sympathetically, batting not an eyelid. In every way that mattered, he was a married man himself, and no doubt Joan Lark, the mistress whose existence was an open secret, had suffered her share of women's ailments.

'Then her Grace will surely not realise that something is amiss,' he said. 'Above all, she must not be allowed to confide any fears or suspicions to Mendoza. I will block any attempt she makes to see him in private. We do not want any hint of this matter reaching the ears of the Emperor. I have impressed on his Holiness the need for discretion until a decision is given.'

Harry beckoned Wolsey through the wicket gate that led into the sanctum of his garden and found a seat in an arbour shaded from the sun.

'The Queen must be watched,' he said.

'Sir, several of her women are already in my pay.'

So Wolsey had indeed set spies on Kate, without so much as a by-your-leave. Harry stared at him, but the Cardinal was unperturbed.

'I will ensure that every letter her Grace sends or receives is scrutinised,' he added.

Guilt, and the need to appear as if everything was normal, drove Harry to sup with Kate that night. She was as pleasant and welcoming as ever, and he was sure she suspected nothing. But, one day, maybe soon, he would have to tell her what he had done. Time was when they had meant the world to each other, when they had sorrowed together over the loss of seven children. For the sake of what had been, he would not hurt her for the world. If only he could find a way to make this easy for them both – or, rather, if she would put his needs first, as she always had, and make it easy for him.

Then, like a fool, he made a stupid blunder. 'I am thinking of making Richmond king of Ireland,' he said.

Kate's eyes flashed. 'Is that a preliminary to naming him your heir?' she cried.

'No, not at all,' he lied. 'I have a mind to marry him to the Infanta Maria of Portugal, and raising him high will make him a more desirable match.'

'He will be turned down,' she retorted angrily. 'She is my niece Eleanor's child, and the niece of the Emperor, and Habsburgs and Trastamaras do not marry bastards.'

'We'll see about that,' Harry blustered, grabbing his napkin and wiping the meat juices from his mouth. 'The marriage will go ahead whether you approve or not.'

Harry was in turmoil, but the seemingly endless round of celebrations had to continue. He wished they could be at an end, and that time would race forward, bringing with it the Pope's decision on his suit. He could not bear the waiting. At thirty-six, he could not afford to delay much longer in siring a son, and he wanted to live long enough to prepare that son for kingship.

He had invited the French envoys to yet another feast and seated them in the places of honour next to him and Kate at the high table, where the wine flowed freely and the conversation sparkled. But he was in no mood for pleasantries.

Then Wolsey appeared from behind the arras, and hastened over to him, looking as if the sky had fallen on him. 'Your Grace, there is dreadful news. Rome has been sacked by mercenary troops of the Emperor.'

'What?' Harry was appalled, while Kate burst into tears. The envoys were looking at each other in horror and all conversation in the hall had ceased. 'Tell us all what has happened, my lord Cardinal.'

Wolsey was trembling. 'The report I received states that terrible atrocities have been committed in the holy city itself. Nuns have been raped, men murdered in cold blood, churches desecrated. The entire Papal guard was massacred on the steps of St Peter's. I will spare the ladies further details, but the carnage is appalling. It is thought that half the city may have perished.'

'What of his Holiness?' Harry cried.

'He has fled and is now a prisoner in Castel Sant'Angelo.'

'And the Emperor? Could he not control his troops?'

'He was not there. It is said he too is appalled by the violence, and by the way his forces have made the Pope captive.'

'Perhaps he sees it is to his advantage to have his Holiness in his power, for he may wrest the territory he wants and other advantages from him,' the Bishop of Tarbes observed. 'It strikes me that his Imperial Majesty has got the Pope exactly where he wants him.'

Harry saw then, quite clearly, what the sacking of Rome would mean for him. As Kate sobbed quietly beside him, and Wolsey related more information to the envoys and lords who had clustered around him, he sat staring into an uncertain future. What hope was there now that Clement would grant him an annulment? Kate was the Emperor's aunt, and Charles was unlikely to allow his prisoner to dissolve her marriage.

He stood up. 'My lords and ladies, in the circumstances, all festivity must now cease. Please return to your lodgings.' He took Kate's hand and led her out of the hall, both of them – along with the whole world, no doubt – in shock. When he left her at the door to her apartments, he was seized with the need to comfort and be comforted, and took her into his arms. She cried again, for the poor people of Rome, little realising that he, Harry, was as much a victim of the mercenaries as they were.

The French envoys quietly returned home. By Harry's order, the banqueting house and theatre were briefly opened to the people, who came in great numbers. Then the buildings were stripped of their decorations, which were carefully stored away, poignant reminders of those golden days.

Wolsey believed that the Pope would soon be free and that all was not lost. He was departing for France, confident that he could persuade King Francis to join them in pressing for Clement's liberation and to support Harry's bid for an annulment. Especially, Wolsey said, if it freed Harry to marry a French princess and enabled him to break his ties to Spain.

'In time, your Grace, you may win your case. But you may have a battle on your hands. It would be politic to obtain the Queen's co-operation. If she supports the nullity suit, it has a better chance of succeeding, for even the Emperor cannot complain if she herself wants any doubts resolved.'

Henry's heart plummeted like a stone. 'You mean I should break it to her.'

'I do. Somehow, it has become public knowledge that you are

seeking an annulment. The matter will soon be notorious. Better that she hears about it from your Grace.'

Harry was shaking when he strode into Kate's chamber. As she sank into a deep curtsey, he bade her be seated. Even now, he had no idea what he was going to say to her.

'I trust you are well.' He attempted a smile.

'I am in health, thank you, and all the better for seeing you.' It sounded like a reproach, for he had not visited her for some days.

They spoke of Mary for a space, then Harry gathered his courage. 'Kate, I need to talk to you. Of late I have been troubled – much troubled – in my conscience about the validity of our marriage, and . . . well, I am sorry, but I have reluctantly come to the resolution that we must separate.'

She turned as white as a corpse. 'Who has put these words in your mouth?' Her voice broke.

Harry explained, as gently as he could, about the concerns raised by the Bishop of Tarbes and how his conscience was troubling him.

'Are you sure it is not the Cardinal who has encouraged you to have these doubts?' Kate cried. 'He would love to be rid of me. Now that you have agreed this French alliance, it is no longer an advantage for you to have a Spanish queen.'

'No, Kate, that is not so. Wolsey knows of my doubts, but from the first he has been against my acting upon them, although he is as anxious as I am to have them allayed. It was he who advised me to ask the Pope to resolve them.'

'There is no need to approach the Pope!' Kate cried. 'We have a dispensation!'

'But the Bible warns that God will inflict a severe penalty on a man who marries his brother's widow. You know what Leviticus says, Kate! "They shall be childless." Believe me, I have studied the matter at length, and I am convinced that we have broken a divine law. Surely a marriage that causes me such fear and torment of conscience cannot be lawful!'

'Henry, it *is* lawful! The Pope said so! How can he be wrong?'

Harry began pacing the floor. 'The evidence of God's displeasure is there for all to see. All our sons died soon after they were born. That is our punishment.' He turned to her and spread his hands in supplication. 'For a long time now, I have felt that I am living under the awful displeasure of the Almighty. Now I know why – and I dread His wrath if I persist in this marriage. That is why, out of regard for the quiet of my soul, and the need to ensure the succession, I must have these doubts resolved.' He found himself near to tears.

Kate looked as if she were witnessing the end of the world.

'Have you talked to your confessor?' she asked.

'Yes. He was the first person I spoke to. He urged me to seek Warham's advice, and Wolsey's. Kate, I'm sorry this brings you grief, but it has to be resolved.'

'On what grounds are you doubting our marriage? I came to you a virgin. Arthur and I never consummated our marriage.'

'But you bedded together at sundry times, you lived at liberty in one house—'

'Are you saying I lied to you, that I am lying still?' she cried.

'No, I mean . . . I do not know! And maybe you don't either. You were an innocent, maybe it happened, and you didn't realise it.'

'Oh, Henry! You think I wouldn't know? It was painful the first time with you.'

He shook his head. 'That's all beside the point. Leviticus might well apply whether your marriage to Arthur was consummated or not.'

'I don't see how!' Kate was becoming exasperated too. 'The barrier to the second marriage only exists if there were children born of the first, which there were not. What else do I have to say to reassure you? The Pope examined all the evidence over twenty years ago. He would not have issued a dispensation if there had been any doubt. Henry, there is no cause for these scruples of conscience. You have not offended God – and we have not lived in sin these eighteen years!'

Harry glared at her. 'The Pope had no right to issue that dispensation.'

'No right? He is invested with the authority of Christ. Are you challenging that? Are you saying he had no power to dispense at all in our case?'

'That is what I am saying.' He knew it sounded almost blasphemous.

'It is heresy, no less. Do you not realise that? Oh, my Henry! Do not do this thing, I beg of you.' To his horror, she fell to her knees before him, raising her hands in supplication.

'Kate!' He grasped her wrists. 'Do not do this to me. I am moved only by a scrupulous conscience, and because I despair of having a son.'

She was weeping. Harry stared at her, moved by her grief. He let her hands drop and she knelt there for a moment, then rose and sat in her chair. 'And if the Pope rules that our marriage is unlawful? Which he will not, I assure you.'

'Rest assured, Kate, you will want for nothing, not for riches, honour or love. You can have any houses you want.'

'And our daughter? Have you thought of what this will do to her? She is your heir.'

'And, as our marriage was made in good faith, she will remain so, until I have sons.'

Her face registered shock. 'You want to remarry. Why don't you just say so?'

He felt himself flush. 'It's not like that. I've told you, I need to set my conscience at rest. But if the only way of doing that is by an annulment, then yes, I must take another wife to ensure the succession and the quiet estate of my realm. It is my duty, no less.'

He could stand no more of this. He stood up and walked to the door, then turned back to her. 'All will be done for the best, I assure you, Kate. I ask you not to speak of this matter to anyone, for I fear that the Spaniards in your household might make some demonstration, and I don't want to provoke the Emperor.'

Kate remained silent, her face working. Suddenly, she burst into wails of distress. It was terrible, seeing her so out of control, howling and beating her breast.

'Oh, God, oh, Holy Mother!' she keened. 'Please help me!' She sank to her knees once more and buried her face in her hands. 'What did I do to deserve this?' she sobbed.

'Kate, don't,' Henry pleaded, not knowing how to make her cease. 'Please, stop crying. Stop it!'

But she just knelt there, rocking in misery, weeping her heart out. Quietly, he made his escape and summoned her women.

Chapter 19

1527

Harry departed with Kate on progress, hunting every day. Each night, at supper, he entertained Anne's father, Rochford, and her uncle of Norfolk, with Suffolk and Exeter. His nullity suit was being whispered about at court now, and naturally Norfolk and Boleyn were privately vocal in their support, eager for the honours to come when Anne was queen. Harry did not want to confide in Exeter or Suffolk just yet, for both their wives were close to Kate. Inevitably, he knew, the matter would divide opinion.

Kate was not present at these suppers, but she and Harry put on a united front when they visited Mary at Hunsdon, and they rode forth together to Beaulieu. And there Anne was waiting for them, having rejoined the court from Hever. She looked more alluring than ever, with her graceful figure and dark, inviting eyes that were regarding Harry with a new intimacy. He was in raptures, past caring about secrecy now, or sparing Kate's feelings, and he took Anne hunting daily, and supped with her in private every evening.

She was wonderful, witty company, but she made it very clear that she was not prepared to anticipate their marriage. When he became passionate, she drew back and stayed him. After a month, she went back to Hever, leaving him in misery, sending her letter after letter, begging her to return, desperate to know if she had any real feelings for him. He was like a man possessed, not caring that they were becoming the subject of gossip and scandal.

* * *

'Harry!' Suffolk said sharply, interrupting his reverie as they sat sharing a flagon of wine in one of the little banqueting houses at Hampton Court. 'Are you well?'

'Perfectly,' Harry replied, trying to forget his torment over Anne's absence.

'Sir, you must know that your Great Matter is the talk of the court – and the whole kingdom, I shouldn't wonder. People are saying that, if you can obtain a divorce, you will end by marrying Rochford's daughter. That will not go down well with the French when you are seeking their support in Rome!'

'It's a mere flirtation,' Harry protested, hating himself for dissembling to his old friend.

'I've seen you together, and it looks like more than that to me,' Suffolk growled, stroking his beard. 'Your sister isn't happy. She says Anne Boleyn is trouble – she served Mary in France.'

'What did she mean by that?' Harry hissed. He would not believe any ill of his darling.

'She did not elaborate. I think she is inclined to criticise her because she has long loved the Queen and feels for her. She says her Grace is in great distress.'

'I know, I know. But the matter has to be tried. My doubts of conscience must be resolved. I trust I have your support in this, Charles?'

Suffolk sighed. 'Yes. But I would not flaunt La Boleyn. It seems to me that her influence has increased during the Cardinal's absence in France.'

'Why should that worry you? You've never liked Wolsey.'

'I admit it, and I think it would be no bad thing to see his monopoly on power weakened. In that, I am at one with Norfolk and Rochford and many others.'

Harry was surprised at his brother-in-law's candour. Not so long ago, he would have leapt to Wolsey's defence. But Anne too had spoken out against the Cardinal. She had said – more than once – that he had usurped too much of Harry's power. It galled her that Wolsey was working to marry his master to a French princess. He would not be making such strenuous efforts to put *her* on the throne, she had pouted. It still rankled with her that he had once called her a foolish girl, when he broke her betrothal to Henry Percy. Now she was pressing Harry to make his true intentions known to Wolsey, so the Cardinal would know that the foolish girl would soon be queening it over him. Harry had been shocked to see how much anger she had nurtured against him.

'Wolsey has ever been a good, loyal servant – the best,' he said now to Suffolk. 'But he has no monopoly on power. I am still king here.'

Dusk was falling outside, and Suffolk's face was in shadow. 'My advice, Harry, is to keep a curb on Mistress Boleyn. Your courtiers are beginning to seek her patronage. She shows herself determined to advance her family and friends. She grows haughty and proud. Have you seen how she decks herself out with jewels? Did you give them to her? That could be misconstrued!'

'Actually, I did not, or not all of them,' Harry protested. 'I think her family supplied them. As for hauteur, I do not see it. With the Queen, her behaviour is circumspect and courteous.'

It was Kate who shot the barbs, he reflected. She would not upbraid him; she saved her venom for Anne, whom she suffered to have about her for his sake, he supposed. After that long-ago falling-out over Anne Hastings, she had never again ventured to rebuke him for his infidelities. But only this week, she had been unable to resist jibing at Anne. They had all been playing cards with Suffolk, and Anne had turned up a king. To be fair, she had smiled at Kate provocatively, whereupon Kate had quietly observed, 'My lady Anne, you have the good luck to stop at a king, but you are not like the others – you will have all or none!' There had been an embarrassed silence.

Harry knew that Anne would not tolerate playing second fiddle to Kate or Wolsey for long. He feared to cross her, lest she take herself off again and put him once more through the agony of wondering if she had left him for good. In his worst moments, he suspected that it was a crown, rather than himself, she coveted.

* * *

They were at Richmond when an usher announced that Wolsey had returned from France and craved a private audience to discuss his mission.

'He wishes to know where he should meet with your Grace,' the man said.

'I must go to him,' Harry said, as Anne's voice rang out: 'Tell him he may come here, where the King is.' She turned to Harry. 'A servant must wait upon his master, and not the other way about,' she murmured, quite audibly. Harry nodded at the usher unhappily. It seemed a gauntlet had been thrown down. He sensed that this was the beginning of a bitter power struggle and prayed he would not have to choose between his lady and his loyal servant.

It did not help that the hoped-for support from King Francis was not to be forthcoming. It would all be grist to Anne's mill.

'I fear that even the lure of a French marriage for your Grace did not break his resolve to remain neutral,' Wolsey said, looking discomfited, when, later, they were alone.

'That is perhaps as well,' Harry said slowly, girding his loins to tell the Cardinal the truth. 'For I have resolved to marry Mistress Anne Boleyn as soon as I am free.'

Wolsey gaped at him, shocked. 'Your Grace, you cannot!' His mouth was working in distress.

'No one tells me what I can or cannot do,' Harry said sternly. 'Kings are answerable only to God.'

'But kings do not marry their mistresses – they marry for policy! And they marry those of royal blood. Mistress Boleyn, whatever her virtues, is a commoner.'

Harry clenched his fists, anger rising in him. 'She is not my mistress. And my grandfather married a commoner, who proved an excellent and fruitful queen.'

'Nevertheless, Sir, I beg of you to reconsider. You have not asked her yet, I trust?'

'I have, and she has accepted. And that is an end to the matter, my lord Cardinal. Do not offend me by trying to dissuade me. My mind is made up.'

Wolsey uttered no reply. His face said it all. And, in that moment, something broke in Harry. He had regarded the Cardinal as a second father, a friend who would never fail him. Not any more. Wolsey had failed him in this one, crucial thing.

'You will continue to support me in this matter?' It was more of a statement than a question.

'I am your Grace's humble servant,' Wolsey replied, mustering a weak smile. 'You can rely on me.'

1528

That winter was exceptionally bitter – even the sea froze in some parts. Harry kept Christmas at Greenwich, but Anne had insisted on going home to Hever. She made him wait until March before she returned to court, then she brought her mother with her as chaperone, to give the lie to all the nasty gossip about her. She looked like a vision in carmine velvet when she dismounted from her horse at Windsor, and Harry could not wait to be alone with her. But there was Lady Boleyn, never very far away. It was maddeningly frustrating.

Every afternoon, they went hunting or hawking in Windsor Forest, or walked together in the Great Park. In the evenings, they amused themselves with cards, dice and dancing, played music and recited poetry. One day, Harry ordered a picnic, and they feasted on plovers, partridges, larks and rabbits, as well as puddings with lashings of cream, a gift from the park-keeper's wife.

It thrilled Harry to have Anne riding pillion behind him on his mount, feeling her arms tightly wound around him and her body pressed to his, rendering his excitement almost uncontainable. He knew others were looking on with slightly scandalised expressions, but he had cast all caution to the four winds.

He was not feeling himself, though. He had begun to suffer feverish headaches and aches and pains, which he put down to growing older – he was thirty-seven, after all – and there was a sore on his leg that would not heal. Awareness of encroaching middle age alarmed him. What if he died leaving no son? His Great Matter must be resolved soon. Yet his case still languished in the Vatican. The Pope was free now, but apparently still terrified of provoking the Emperor. Wolsey warned that it might be some time before a decision was given. But Harry didn't have time for delays. Again and again, he put pressure on the Cardinal and his envoys in Rome to explain to Clement that a decision was needed right now, for the sake of the succession and the continuing peace of the realm. Surely his Holiness could understand the urgency!

Anne came to him as he sat in his study, bringing a book for him to read. It was William Tyndale's *The Obedience of a Christian Man*. Harry recognised it as one of the heretical works Wolsey had banned. He wondered where she had got it and was a little perturbed that she was reading such a book with impunity. But then she fell to her knees before him and explained that it had been sent to her from abroad and that she had been struck by the arguments it contained. She had lent it to one of her maids, whose betrothed had snatched it from her, but been caught with it and taken before the Cardinal. Wolsey had said he would report the matter to the King, but Anne had now got to Harry first.

'Sir,' she urged, 'I recommend that you read this book, which should never have been banned.' Another barb aimed at Wolsey. 'I should love to hear your views on it.'

He read it that night in bed, impressed by Tyndale's criticisms of the Papacy and his emphasis on the authority of monarchs. By St George, he concluded, this is a book for me and all kings to read! Let Wolsey complain if he wished! He would not listen.

After that, he allowed Anne the freedom of the royal library, where he kept for reference other books that had been banned in England. Doubtless there were more circulating illicitly at court, despite efforts to suppress them.

She urged him to remove Tyndale's book from the banned list, but he refused. 'It is not suitable for commoners,' he decreed, and would not relent.

* * *

Then came the most welcome news – the Pope was sending a legate to England to hear the King's case. He had chosen Cardinal Lorenzo Campeggio, who had been the Papal protector of England since 1523, and whom Harry had made bishop of Salisbury. It was an excellent choice, and Harry was confident that Campeggio would rule in his favour. He was desperate with impatience for him to arrive.

But suddenly it seemed that Fate might snatch from him that which he most desired, for in May the dreaded sweating sickness broke out again. Gripped with fear, he dismissed most of his courtiers and fled to Waltham Abbey in Essex, taking Kate and Anne with him.

The reports that reached him from London were terrifying. There were forty thousand cases there. Parliament had to be adjourned and the courts ground to a halt. At Waltham, George Boleyn and a few others sickened, but mercifully recovered. When one of Anne's maids fell ill, Harry sent his beloved home to Hever, then fled to Hunsdon, where he shut himself up in a tower with his physicians, and dosed himself regularly with physick, in a fever of anxiety lest Anne succumb to the sweat. But no news was good news, and he began to relax when no one else in his small household fell prey to it.

Then the blow fell. Anne had sickened. Shaking at the prospect of a world without her, Harry dispatched his second physician, the learned, urbane Dr Butts, to attend her. Impatiently, he waited for news, unable to settle to anything. Thanks be to God, Butts was soon back at Hunsdon with the cheerful tidings that Anne had recovered. Harry had never felt such relief in his life.

Yet the sweat was still raging, obliging him to move from one house to another almost daily, until at last he came to Tittenhanger, one of Wolsey's residences. He gave orders for it to be purged daily by fires and preservatives such as vinegar, and had the windows enlarged to admit more fresh air.

'I will stay here for the time God allows me,' he told Kate. 'We cannot go on running.' She looked at him almost reproachfully, as if the sweat was his fault. He suspected she believed it was God's judgement on him for seeking to end their marriage. He thrust the thought away. If it had been so, why had the Almighty allowed Anne to live? Even so, his conscience stirred. What if he were summoned soon to his Maker to face divine judgement?

He was riven with perplexity. To be safe, he kept Kate at his side. He was assiduous at his devotions, attending Mass, taking communion more frequently than usual and going to confession daily. He saw hope in Kate's eyes, and there was a new kindness between them, but he knew deep inside himself that it could not last. As soon as this was over – if God had not struck him dead first – he would be summoning Anne.

News came of the deaths of his old friend Compton and Will Carey, Anne's brother-in-law. Compton, Wolsey wrote, had been lost through negligent servants letting him sleep at the onset of the sweat. He had left no heir, and there was a stampede for his vacated offices. Even young Richmond wrote to Harry urging that some be given to his beloved master of horse, Sir Edward Seymour. Harry was too grieved to care. The arrival of a package of the items bequeathed to him by Compton had upset him deeply. The little chest of ivory filled with jewels, the chessboard and the backgammon set all brought back poignant memories of a shared youth. His eyes blurred with tears.

Pulling himself together, he granted the wardship of young Henry Carey to Anne, the boy's aunt, and ordered a reluctant Rochford to take the widowed Mary Carey under his roof. Then he assigned Carey's vacant place in the Privy Chamber to Sir Francis Bryan, as a reward for befriending Anne. Bryan's advancing years had not sobered him; he was still a profligate libertine. But Harry liked him. He remained good company and a worthy opponent at gambling, bowls and tennis. Bryan was here now, at Tittenhanger, and Harry liked to pass the time with him at cards. They were often joined by Francis Weston, one of the King's pages, a gifted lute player and a superb athlete. He was such a pleasant young man that Harry often chose him to sleep on the pallet bed in his bedchamber at night.

As the summer wore on, the sweat began to abate. Harry decided to move to Ampthill, and then deemed it safe to lodge at other places. What had begun as a flight from the plague turned into a progress, but he was careful to visit shrines and religious houses for the health of his soul.

By the autumn, he was back at Greenwich – and there was Anne. After the long months of separation, Harry caught his breath at the sight of her, his ardour greater than ever. All doubts of conscience had fled. God willing, Cardinal Campeggio would be in England imminently and wedding bells would soon be ringing out.

The pestilence had swept through Europe, but even so, Campeggio seemed to be taking his time.

'He should have been here by now,' Harry fumed, almost dancing with impatience.

'He suffers from gout, I am told, and has to make the journey in slow stages,' Wolsey told him, looking vexed.

'By St George, I hope Clement didn't send him on that account, hoping I'd give up on my nullity suit,' Harry flared.

The Cardinal shrugged, his expression grim. 'Let us hope not.'

'All this delay has given the Queen leisure to marshal support,' Harry grumbled. 'Bishop Fisher is foremost in her defence, and that chaplain of hers, Thomas Abell. Even Warham thinks my marriage valid.'

'Yes, but he will support you.' Wolsey sounded weary; it was obvious that his heart was not in this.

Harry looked hard at him, noticing the veined cheeks, the pasty countenance and the sagging jowls, and realised that his friend was growing old. Anne kept complaining that Wolsey was not working as hard as he could to secure the annulment. Why would Wolsey exert himself to make his enemy queen, when he knew she was just waiting to destroy him? But it could not be denied that he was labouring day and night to give Harry what he wanted. Nevertheless, it was sad, but true: Harry no longer felt the same affection for the

Cardinal. At times, he felt resentful towards him for not expediting matters quickly enough. It was irrational, he knew, and he hated to admit that he had been swayed by a woman, but he adored Anne, wanted to please her and craved her approval. Favouring Wolsey in the old way would not win him that. Her love for him was too tenuous for him to risk testing it, and so he put her first in all things. If that meant the Cardinal was no longer received at court as graciously as before, so be it.

'Wolsey has overreached himself and forgotten who is king here,' she'd said the other day while they were out hunting. 'Let him jostle for supremacy with everyone else.'

'Darling,' Harry said, for the hundredth time, 'he is doing his best for us. He means well.'

'How can you be so blind?' she'd cried, and urged her horse into a canter, dark hair flying out behind her. Harry spurred his own mount and galloped after her, vexed because she just would not see his point of view. But then she turned and gave him a dazzling smile, and his heart melted. For her, he would do anything; yes, even sacrifice his old friend.

With the Boleyns and their supporters riding high, Wolsey seemed aware that he was teetering on the edge of a precipice. He was doing his best to sweeten Anne with gifts and entertainments and redoubling his efforts to obtain an annulment. Relations between them were outwardly cordial, but that deceived no one.

It had become obvious that Anne could no longer go on serving Kate, so Harry installed her in the palatial surroundings of Durham House on the Strand, as befitted a future queen. But when he visited her there, he found her in a petulant mood.

'This place hasn't been refurbished for years,' she complained, waving a hand to indicate her surroundings. 'The gilding needs replacing, the paint's faded and there are cracks in the ceilings.'

Harry looked around him, wondering what was so bad about the lofty chambers and magnificent wainscoting. 'Very well, darling, I will move you elsewhere. Just give me a few days.'

She kissed him sweetly. 'You are so good to me, Harry,' she murmured, squeezing his hands. How could he resist her?

He was now spending up to four hours each day poring over heavy books on theology, seeking for arguments and precedents to lay before Cardinal Campeggio. The legate's journey had taken for ever, it seemed, but at last, late in October, came the joyful news. He was in England.

Harry was ready to lay on a lavish welcome in London, but Campeggio took to his bed as soon as he arrived, and it was some days before he was well enough to meet with Harry and Wolsey in the King's privy closet. Harry greeted him as warmly as if he had been the Saviour Himself.

'Let us not waste time, my lord Cardinals,' he said. 'I am keen to have my doubts resolved and a decision given on my nullity suit.' He looked at Campeggio, eagerly expectant.

The older man took his time in answering. 'Your Grace, this is a difficult matter, one to which his Holiness has devoted much thought and prayer. But he has asked me to assure you that your doubts are unfounded and to bring about a reconciliation between you and the Queen.'

It was as if an abyss had opened up before Harry. He had staked his hopes on Campeggio bringing instructions from Pope Clement to annul his marriage – not pushing for a reconciliation!

'Am I hearing correctly?' he asked. 'I have long been tormented by doubts of conscience. Doctors and scholars have assured me I have a case to answer. It's there in the Bible itself, man!' He was beside himself now. 'Yet you come all this way to tell me, glibly, that my doubts are unfounded? Or is it that his Holiness is afraid to provoke the Emperor?'

Campeggio raised his hands defensively, looking pained. 'Your Majesty, rest assured that his Holiness has not allowed worldly considerations to influence his position. The truth is that the law of Leviticus only applies when a child has been born of the first marriage. The Queen and Prince Arthur had no children, so there was no bar to your union.'

'Not so!' Harry retorted, impassioned. 'Leviticus warns that if a man marries his brother's widow, he has uncovered his brother's nakedness, and they will be childless. There's nothing ambivalent about that.'

Campeggio shifted on his bench and held up his hand again. 'Before we enter into further debate, his Holiness did suggest another way out of your predicament. He asked me to persuade the Queen to enter a convent, which would free your Grace to remarry.'

Harry sat up. 'That would solve everything. Her Grace could bow out gracefully, our daughter's legitimacy need not be challenged, and I would be free. But she has refused to countenance the idea.'

'Indeed,' the legate agreed. 'I have already seen the Queen and she made it very clear that she has no vocation for the religious life. She insists that she is your Grace's true wife, and nothing would make her say otherwise.'

'But that is very much in doubt,' Wolsey chimed in. 'I trust you made her understand that this is by far the best solution for everyone?'

'Go to her again,' Harry intervened. 'Tell her I'll have her made an abbess; she can keep great state, like a queen, see the Princess whenever she wishes, and be free to come and go as she pleases. What has she got to lose? I no longer share her bed or play the husband. But I am more than willing to treat her most honourably as my sister-in-law. And Mary can keep her place in the succession after any sons I have with a future wife.'

'His Grace is being most generous,' Wolsey said.

'I see that,' Campeggio replied.

'Admit it, the marriage is invalid,' Wolsey persisted. 'That will settle the matter.'

The legate looked distressed. 'Alas, I have explained that the matter is a difficult one, with serious implications for the Church.'

'That would appear to contradict his Holiness's objective view of the case,' Wolsey challenged. 'Clearly, he will not admit that his predecessor was not infallible!'

'Your Eminence should try to understand my position, but I feel

I am speaking to a rock,' Campeggio said plaintively. 'Remember, I am trying to help.' He turned to Harry, who had been listening in increasing dismay. 'Sir, there is a third way. To settle the problem of the succession, his Holiness is ready to grant a dispensation for a marriage between the Princess Mary and the Duke of Richmond.'

Harry stared at him, aghast. 'But they are half-brother and sister. It would be incest! How could a pope sanction it? And you worry about the Church being brought into disrepute!'

'I do!' Campeggio countered. 'And so does his Holiness. Pope Julius' dispensation was sound; challenging it could compromise the integrity of the Holy See. It's as simple as that.'

Harry was ready to explode with rage. 'The integrity of the Holy See is not best served by one pope granting a dispensation on dubious grounds and another encouraging incest!'

The legate looked equally angry. 'Nevertheless, the marriage is valid, and I came to set your Grace's mind at rest. Yet you persist in your belief that it is unlawful, and if an angel were to descend from Heaven, I fear even he would not be able to persuade you to the contrary. For it is obvious to me, and to his Holiness, what impels your Grace to seek this annulment. We are aware that there is a certain young lady whom you wish to marry. It has been reported that you see nothing or think of nothing but her, and that you cannot do without her for an hour; that you are constantly kissing her and treating her as if she were your wife. I am assured that you have not proceeded to any ultimate conjunction, but Pope Clement fears that this passion has clouded your judgement.'

Harry was so shocked at Campeggio's plain speaking that he was momentarily speechless. 'My intentions towards Mistress Boleyn are entirely honourable,' he said at length, 'and the matter of the succession is pressing whether or not I intend to marry her. I cannot live any longer under God's displeasure! I looked to his Holiness for a remedy, but he has failed me abysmally.' Temper seized him. 'I warn your Eminence that if this annulment is not granted, I will annihilate the authority of the Pope in this kingdom!'

Campeggio was stunned into silence. Wolsey, looking desperate, leapt into the breach. 'Sir, I too have legatine powers, and I promise you that I will work with Cardinal Campeggio to reach a solution.'

Campeggio stared down his long, thin nose at him. 'Let us all pray that God shows us the right path to take.'

Harry went away smarting from Campeggio's candour and burning with resentment against Kate. Why couldn't the infuriating woman enter religion? She spent half her life on her knees, so how could she say she had no vocation? She must know she had lost him, and that she was no longer of any use to him, now that she could bear no more children and England was allied to France. What was the point of clinging on?

Maybe she would relent when she saw how generous he was prepared to be. But no. Even after the cardinals had spelled it out, she remained as obstinate as ever. His heart hardened against her.

Chapter 20

1528

Anne was still complaining about Durham House and demanding a more fitting residence. It was Suffolk who came to Harry's rescue.

'Suffolk Place is at your disposal,' he said, warming himself by the fire in the privy chamber. 'We rarely use it these days as Mary is often in the country and I'm at court. Mind you, it needs some work done.'

'I will pay for it,' Harry said eagerly, aware – and hurt – that his sister no longer came to court because she could not bear to see Anne playing the queen. 'I am most grateful to you.' He knew what it would cost Suffolk to make the gesture.

The works were completed quickly – he would not brook any tardiness – and Anne was soon in residence, in a suite of rooms of impressive splendour. Here, she kept great state, attended by her own ladies-in-waiting, train-bearers and chaplains. Whatever they thought of her, most courtiers came hastening in droves to pay their respects, eager to gain the favour of the ascendant star, while Kate's chamber, once the hub of courtly entertainments and gatherings, was deserted.

Even so, Harry was aware of a strong undercurrent of resentment among them, for Anne and her family were not liked. Jealousy – that was all it was! – and a misplaced loyalty to Kate. It was the same with his subjects at large, most of whom seemed to side with their beloved Queen, when they should be supporting their divinely appointed sovereign! When he had been out hunting with Anne, people had sometimes hooted and hissed at her, and once someone had yelled at him, 'Back to your wife!' Not to be borne! If he'd seen the fellow, he'd have had him clapped in the stocks, at the very least.

Was ever man so beset? There was Kate, stubborn in her belief that she was right. And there was Anne, complaining that Harry was still dining regularly with Kate and spending time in her company.

'It's essential, sweetheart, that I show myself a devoted husband who will be grieved to have to part from a beloved companion.' But his sweetheart wasn't impressed.

'It's a bit late for that now!' she retorted, her dark eyes flashing.

That November, as Harry and Kate were walking along the river gallery at Bridewell Palace, a large crowd outside began cheering the Queen. Harry looked down on them aghast, as Kate raised a smile and a gracious hand in acknowledgement. Indignation and fear coursed through him. The love of his subjects was the breath of life to him; he could not allow it to be usurped or compromised.

He summoned the Mayor, the aldermen and the leading citizens to the palace, and addressed them in the great hall.

'I assure you all, my good people of London, that I have instigated nullity proceedings only to set my mind at rest in regard to some doubts of conscience, and that, were I to choose again, I would take Queen Katherine for my wife above all others.'

There were nods and cheers of approval, and he relaxed, beaming at them. He had them in his hand.

Feeling more confident, when Kate visited Mary at Richmond in December, he took advantage of her absence and installed Anne at Greenwich in a very fine lodging near his own, letting it be known that he expected people to pay court to her daily as if she were already queen. And they came – courtiers and supplicants, all seeking her patronage.

The atmosphere was tense during the Christmas celebrations. Kate presided with Harry over the revelry in the great chamber, and twelve-year-old Mary was there too, charming everyone. Meanwhile, Anne kept open house in her own apartments. Harry knew that Kate was putting on a brave face, but it was painfully clear that she found it hard to look cheerful. He ignored her misery; she did not have to suffer like this. With a single word, she could end all this unpleasantness.

After Christmas, Campeggio and Wolsey began preparing for the hearing of the nullity suit.

'You will need your own counsel to represent you,' Harry told Kate, during one of his increasingly rare and acrimonious visits to her apartments. 'Might I propose Archbishop Warham and Bishop Fisher?'

She agreed, ever the obedient wife. He left, feeling he had been fair. Both were men of principle, and he was confident that they would steer her in the right direction.

It was almost June by the time everything was ready, and Harry had long suspected that Campeggio had again been resorting to delaying tactics. But Wolsey was in a good mood as he went over the final arrangements with Harry and showed him how the great hall of the priory of the Blackfriars had been turned into a legatine court.

'I am confident of a happy outcome,' he smiled.

'Do you think the Queen will obey the summons?' Harry wondered.

'It would be in her interests to do so,' Wolsey replied severely. 'Let us hope there are no demonstrations in her favour.'

'That's a vain hope,' Harry said, gazing at the two thrones, one on each side of the hall, the chairs set on the dais for the legates, the rows of benches, and the tables stacked already with legal papers. 'Opinions are running high. And I have never heard or read of a king and queen being summoned before a court in England.'

'Small wonder there is great interest in the proceedings. But set your mind at rest, Sir. I think Campeggio will deliver the verdict you desire.'

'I pray so!' Harry said fervently, hoping that, very soon, Anne might be lying in his arms, in his bed, his lawful wife at last. He was missing her terribly, having sent her home to Hever, thinking it politic while the court was sitting. But it would not be long, he was sure, before she was back with him.

* * *

'King Harry of England, come into the court!'

'Here, my lords!' he replied in ringing tones.

Then Kate, seated in a lesser chair opposite, was formally called. Harry started as she rose and crossed the court with her ladies following. Ignoring the legates, she made her way towards him and – to his horror – fell to her knees before him. He was so thrown, so consumed with mortification, that he could hardly take in her words. She was pleading with him, begging him to spare her the extremity of the court, protesting that she had been a true wife to him, and that when they had married, she had been a true maid, without touch of man. Then she raised her eyes to his. 'And whether it be true or not, I put it to your conscience.' He looked away, embarrassed; it was not proper for her to be speaking of such intimacies in public.

If he would not heed her, she concluded, she would commit her cause to God. There was a long pause, and he knew she was waiting for him to say something in response. But he could not, would not, and it was foolish and ill judged of her to expect it. In the end, she rose, curtseyed and, leaning on the arm of her receiver general, left the court, ignoring urgent calls for her return. Harry could hear the crowds outside, cheering and clapping her.

He thought he could detect a certain sympathy in Campeggio's face, but the legate still declared her contumacious.

'We will proceed without her Grace,' he decreed, to Harry's relief.

Harry did not attend the court during the days that followed, but relied on Wolsey to keep him informed of its proceedings. The weather was hot and the Cardinal often arrived perspiring and uncomfortable after long hours of sitting on his high chair.

'Another day of interminable depositions and heated discussions,' he reported, after a month had gone by and Harry's temper was becoming so frayed that he was like a lion at bay with all who approached him.

'We are getting nowhere,' he fumed.

'I fear so,' Wolsey agreed, looking grey and drained. 'Much of the evidence relates to whether Prince Arthur consummated his marriage. We've had a whole host of lords lining up to boast that they were capable of it at his age, which really is immaterial.'

'But the case is going my way?' Harry could not disguise his anxiety.

'I think so. Much of the evidence is heavily weighted in your Grace's favour, though Bishop Fisher did not help when he stood up in court and insisted that no power, human or divine, can dissolve your marriage.'

Harry was crestfallen. He had counted on Fisher. 'But that's just the view of one man.'

'Indeed, and I do not think that many gave credence to it.'

'What about Campeggio?'

'He gives nothing away, but I sense he is sympathetic. I do not think your Grace should be concerned.'

But it was impossible not to be, as the weeks went by, June turned into July, and still the case dragged on. And then, with August only days away, Wolsey came to Harry, wearing a triumphant smile.

'Your Grace, you might wish to attend the court today. Campeggio has hinted that he is ready to give a decision.'

His heart singing, Harry made his way across the river gallery to the Blackfriars and seated himself on his throne. Kate's remained empty; she had not attended the court since her dramatic appeal.

Campeggio rose. 'Having listened to both pleas, and heard all the evidence, I find that I am unable to pronounce sentence. I hereby adjourn this case to Rome, to be tried by his Holiness himself.'

There was a shocked silence as Harry tried to take in the import of his words. Adjourned to Rome . . . That could mean weeks, if not months, of more delay. He saw Anne slipping away from him, himself getting older, his hopes of an heir shattered . . .

A fist banged down hard on a table. It was Suffolk, his face red with anger. 'By the Mass, it was never merry in England while we had cardinals among us!' he shouted.

Harry looked at Wolsey – Wolsey, who had led him to believe that all would be well. The Cardinal looked as appalled as everyone else, doubtless because he knew that the adjournment might mean his ruin. Harry watched him fix his gaze to Suffolk.

'Of all men in this realm, my lord, you have least cause to be offended with cardinals. For if I, a simple cardinal, had not come to your aid when you married the King's sister, you would have no head upon your shoulders.'

By St George, the arrogance of the man! It was not the moment to refer to the power he had long wielded and enjoyed, thanks to the munificence and misplaced trust of his King, whom he had failed grievously. Harry seethed inside. This was what Wolsey had brought him to, everyone staring at him as he stood there, his humiliation exposed for all to see. Rage welled in him. He would not brook such treatment, even from the Pope, who owed him a great debt of gratitude for championing the Church against Luther.

Clement must be forced to see the error of his ways, Harry resolved, as he stalked out of the hall, looking to neither right nor left. If he did not, there would be a chill wind coming his way from England.

Anne had hastened back to court for the judgement. She was incensed at the adjournment, as well she might be. Kate was no doubt rejoicing in the solitude of her apartments, while Wolsey was skulking in disgrace. When Harry took Anne with him on his summer progress, he ensured that she kept state like a queen. She, Norfolk, Rochford and the rest of their faction urged him incessantly to be rid of the Cardinal for good. But, angry though he was with Wolsey, Harry found that he could not just cast him away. It would take more than one disappointment to kill a friendship that had lasted for more than twenty years. What he felt now, weeks having passed since the court rose, was not so much anger as grief.

They were at Grafton, near Northampton, when the two legates arrived, so that Campeggio could take his official leave of the King before returning to Rome. Anne, of course, was against Harry receiving Wolsey, but he insisted on observing the courtesies.

Wolsey looked full of trepidation as he entered the crowded

presence chamber and knelt before his master. Seeing him looking so miserable and diminished, Harry felt a sudden upsurge of his old affection for him. Smiling, he raised him and led him to a window embrasure, as the courtiers stared. No doubt someone would be speeding on their way to Anne to tell her how warmly Harry had received her enemy, but he was determined to show her that Wolsey could still prove useful to them.

'Your Grace, forgive me,' Wolsey murmured. 'I did everything I could to persuade the legate to grant your suit. I strongly suspect he had orders to adjourn the case before he even left Rome. If there is anything I can do to make amends, I shall not hesitate to do it.'

Harry placed an arm around his shoulder. 'I am sure there is a way through this impasse. Let us work together to find it.'

The gratitude in Wolsey's eyes was a joy to behold.

'We will meet in the morning to discuss the matter,' Harry said. 'Now, you must be hungry. Go to dinner and I will see you tomorrow.'

Anne was incandescent. Seated opposite Harry at table, she ranted and wept and upbraided him.

'How could you entertain, for one moment, a man who has done you and your realm so much ill?' she shrilled. 'Let alone spend the morning closeted with him!' She was so beside herself that Harry began to fear that she might take herself off to Hever again.

'We were going to see that new hunting park tomorrow,' she pouted. 'I'm not wasting the day waiting for you to talk to Wolsey.'

'But, darling, I have business to discuss with the Cardinal.'

'You have no business with traitors!'

She won the argument, as she always did. Miserably, in fear of losing her, Harry agreed to ride out with her to the hunting park.

Just as they were mounted and ready to leave, the two cardinals entered the courtyard. Harry registered the dismay in Wolsey's face.

'My lord Cardinal,' he called from the saddle, 'I fear I have no time to talk this morning. Fare you well!' And he rode off with Anne, who threw a triumphant smile at Wolsey over her shoulder.

She had ordered a lavish picnic and saw to it that they were away all day. When Harry returned, Wolsey and Campeggio had left, for the legate had a long journey ahead and could not afford to tarry.

Harry soon became aware that Kate now had a staunch champion in the newly arrived Imperial ambassador, Eustache Chapuys, a fellow humanist and a friend of Erasmus. The Emperor had chosen well. Aged forty, Chapuys was a highly efficient canon lawyer and judge from Savoy, able, astute and – as Harry quickly learned – never afraid to speak his mind. His zeal for the Queen shone forth. It irritated Harry, but he genuinely liked Chapuys; in other circumstances, they would have been friends. Anne and her family loathed him, of course, and the antipathy was mutual.

'The new ambassador has been complaining about Mistress Anne's religious sympathies,' Suffolk told Harry as they stood in the autumn chill, shooting arrows at the butts.

'She but favours the reform of the Church, and God knows it needs it,' Harry said. 'It's no more than Erasmus advocates.'

'Chapuys has been saying that she and her family are more Lutheran than Luther himself, and that they support his heretical doctrines and practices. He claims she is the principal cause of the spread of Lutheranism in this country.'

'By God, I'll have him muzzled,' Harry exploded.

'To be fair,' Suffolk said, flexing his bow, 'Mistress Anne's support of reformers who are openly challenging the traditional teachings of the Church might be giving the wrong impression.'

Harry had been troubled by that. He wished Anne would desist. But she was on a mission, leading her own personal crusade to reform a church that sanctioned the sale of indulgences, obscenely wealthy clergy – and a pope whose rulings (or lack of them) were dictated by political considerations. And how could he argue with that?

In the days and weeks that followed, whenever Harry spoke up for Wolsey, or of enlisting his formidable capabilities in his cause, Anne reacted so passionately that he backed down, hating himself, but dreading to hear her say that enough was enough. She even accused the Cardinal of witchcraft. She would not be satisfied, she declared, until he was made to pay for having schemed to bring about her ruin. In vain did Harry protest that that was not true, that Wolsey had worked himself almost into the grave to secure an annulment. But Anne was having none of it.

In the end, he agreed that the Cardinal be indicted under the Statute of Praemunire.

'What's that?' Anne asked, looking suspicious.

'It prohibits Papal interference in English affairs without royal consent. Wolsey cannot deny that he received bulls from Rome without my knowledge.' Harry dared not admit to Anne that he had trusted Wolsey so implicitly he had given him leave to deal with the Holy See as he thought fit.

He agonised over how to deal with the Cardinal. In October, he stripped him of his office of Lord Chancellor, and sent Norfolk and Suffolk to collect the Great Seal from him at Esher. Aside from that, he was resolved to be merciful. When, in November, Parliament arraigned Wolsey on forty-four charges, Harry refused to proceed against him. Instead, he allowed him to retire to his diocese of York.

He had not anticipated the effects of Wolsey's fall, or the wave of anti-clerical feeling it unleashed, which was fuelled by Norfolk, Suffolk and the Boleyns. Years of pent-up resentment and jealousy drove other lords to support them. It left the Privy Council and the nobility more powerful now that they had no rival.

Harry's own feelings towards Wolsey were mixed. He missed him, yet he enjoyed the autonomy of ruling without him. He seized York Place and three more of Wolsey's most desirable houses, along with their priceless contents. He ordered that building works continue and had Wolsey's coats of arms torn down and replaced with his own. But, early in November, when he, Anne and her mother went to look around York Place, he was overcome by a sense of loss and guilt, seeing the Cardinal everywhere, in all his old familiar places. He watched Anne looking over the inventory of goods that Wolsey had left, and eagerly inspecting the piles of gold plate set out on trestles in the presence chamber and the sumptuous hangings in the long gallery, and could not help feeling a treacherous resentment towards her, quickly suppressed.

'I like this house,' she declared, taking his hands and spinning him around before the startled eyes of their attendants. 'It has no apartments for the Queen, I can share it with you alone. And there is plenty of accommodation for my family.' She was full of plans.

Harry now lived in fear that his nullity suit might drag on indefinitely. He returned to Greenwich feeling dejected and was in no good mood when he learned that his recently appointed secretary, Dr Stephen Gardiner, and his almoner, Edward Foxe, had just returned from a mission to Rome and were requesting an audience.

He knew it would be bad news. He had hoped that the swarthy, arrogant and irascible Gardiner, an able Cambridge man who had served Wolsey and held conservative views, would have made some headway with Clement, for Gardiner staunchly believed in the absolute power of kings and was hostile towards Kate for defying it. That had been enough to endear him to Harry, but today he was not in the frame of mind for Gardiner's strident dogmatism, or for yet another disappointment. Wearily, he agreed to see him and Foxe, and was surprised when they arrived with a short, moon-faced cleric he had never met before. As he raised his eyebrows, Gardiner ushered the man forward.

'Your Grace, this is Dr Thomas Cranmer, whom we both knew at Cambridge and fortuitously encountered on our way back from Rome. We think you will be interested to hear his views on your Great Matter, given that his Holiness will do nothing for you.'

Harry seized on his words; he had expected nothing from Clement. He felt his mood suddenly lighten. He was desperate for any counsel that might bring his case to a speedy and satisfactory conclusion. 'Yes, Dr Cranmer, we are listening,' he said.

Cranmer seemed nervous, but he cleared his throat and spoke up. 'Your Grace, I have studied this matter at length and come to the conclusion that it is a theological issue that cannot be dealt with under canon law. I respectfully suggest that you canvass the universities of Europe, where are to be found the greatest experts on theology, and seek their opinion. That will give weight to your case.'

It was as if a flame had been kindled. Harry beamed at him. 'By St George, this man has the sow by the right ear!'

They talked at length and Harry ended by asking Dr Cranmer if he would write a treatise on his views, which could be sent to the universities. Then he sent for Rochford, who was keen to see his daughter a queen and readily agreed to take Cranmer into his household as his chaplain while he wrote his tract. Harry was impatient for him to finish it. He had great hopes that this, at last, was the solution to his troubles.

At Hampton Court, he began building a new lodging for himself, the Bayne Tower, so called because it was to house his bathroom, and while work was in progress he lodged in Wolsey's old apartments, again feeling pangs of guilt and regret. He stifled them, planning a great programme of improvements at the palace to make it a fitting setting for Anne when she became queen. He was going to transform the chapel, build royal apartments in the latest style and remodel the vast great hall.

He had been determined to manage his own affairs from now on without relying on anyone else, but the novelty soon wore off. It was a heavy duty, more onerous than he could ever have dreamed. At first, he thought that Wolsey had left everything in such a chaotic state that he would have to work day and night to set everything in order. Yet it quickly became clear just how many burdens of state the Cardinal had shouldered, and Harry soon lost patience with his councillors, even shouting that Wolsey had been a better man than any of them for managing matters, and stamping out of the council chamber in disgust at their incompetence.

Gradually, though, he found himself gaining a new confidence and authority and relying more and more on his own judgement and political instincts. He was devoting less time to hunting and more to paperwork, personally correcting letters drawn up by his secretaries, and drafting several versions before he was satisfied. His Great Matter was still the burning issue of the day, and he was more certain than ever that he was in the right.

He promoted Norfolk and Suffolk, making them joint presidents of the Council. But who could be Lord Chancellor in Wolsey's place? Harry immediately thought of Suffolk, and consulted Norfolk for his view.

'He has enough power,' the Duke stated jealously. 'How about Sir Thomas More?'

It was typical of Norfolk to put forward one of his friends, with an eye to his own interests, but Harry leapt at the idea. More was a man of principle, renowned throughout Christendom for his integrity. If Harry could persuade him to accept the office, and More could be brought to support his Great Matter, then many waverers might come around to Harry's point of view. But More had held strangely aloof from the debate, and looked anything but overwhelmed with gratitude when Harry offered to appoint him Lord Chancellor.

They were walking in the gardens of More's house at Chelsea. Through the open windows of the house wafted the sound of laughter as the family prepared for dinner, and the inviting smell of roasted meat.

'I was hoping for a more positive response,' Harry said, a little put out.

More's sensitive face creased in distress. 'Alas, Sir, I wish I could accept this great honour you extend to me, but I fear I do not wish to become embroiled in your Great Matter.'

Harry frowned. 'Is it that you do not support my suit, Thomas?'

'Not at all, Sir. I just would rather not be involved. It is a very complex matter, too obscure for the likes of poor laymen like me.'

Harry was disappointed, but not unduly so, being confident that he would in time persuade More to change his mind. 'I understand, my friend. Set aside your doubts. Accept the office. You need play no part in the nullity proceedings. I assure you, you can look first unto God and, after God, to me. I know for a fact that there never was nor will be a chancellor as honest and so thoroughly accomplished as you will be.'

More reluctantly bowed to Harry's wishes. Harry dearly wanted to win his support, but he had given his word not to press the matter. He wished too that More would demonstrate some awareness of the eminence of his new status. But he was making it plain that he cared nothing for the pomp and show of his high position, and that he hated wearing his gold chain of office.

'He dresses like a parish clerk!' Norfolk complained. But More was unmoved. He had greater matters weighing on his mind. Harry knew he was hot to root out the Lutheran heresy that was spreading alarmingly throughout England and determined to preserve Christian unity in Europe. He naturally resisted any attempts to reform the Church and dealt severely with heretics, determined to save their souls.

A new order was in power, yet above everyone was Anne. Harry now kept her constantly at his side. She sat in the Queen's chair at feasts and wore rich gowns of purple, a colour reserved for royalty. He had showered her with lengths of velvet, satin and cloth of gold, furs, fine linen and jewels, gold trinkets to sew on her gowns, biliments of gems and pearls to edge them, heart-shaped head ornaments, diamonds to wear in her hair and even a golden crown.

These days, Kate kept mostly to her own apartments. She showed herself loving and friendly on the rare occasions when Harry visited her, but sometimes the effort was too great. When he was dining with her late in November, her guard fell and she reproached him bitterly for having neglected her of late. Harry bore it patiently, not wishing to embroil himself in another quarrel in which she would tie him in knots. As soon as he decently could, he made his escape and fled to the comfort of Anne's arms, but she was unwilling to listen to his complaints.

'I've told you that you should not argue with the Queen! She is sure to have the upper hand. I don't know why you keep visiting her. She's not your wife and it's because of her obstinacy that the Pope is delaying a decision on your case. And here am I, endlessly waiting and wasting my youth to no purpose, when I could have made some advantageous marriage and be a mother by now! In fact, I'm tempted to ask my father to arrange a match for me, seeing that I might be waiting for ever for you!'

By St George, she knew how to twist the knife! Her words left Harry in terror lest she leave him, which was his greatest fear. He drew her to him and kissed her reluctant lips.

'Do not say such things!' he pleaded. 'If you knew how they hurt me, you would desist. I would give you the world if I could.' Then she did one of her mercurial about-turns and suddenly they were clawing at each other, mouth on mouth. How he controlled himself he did not know. It was ever the same: their quarrels invariably ended in a passionate reconciliation.

Chapter 21

1529

Anne was still devouring banned books, constantly seeking out arguments to bolster Harry's case. She showed him one by a lawyer, Simon Fish, who had fled into exile after falling foul of Wolsey. Fish had argued the case for translating the Scriptures into English so that all could read them. It left Harry thoughtful, but he would not remove the book from the banned list, despite Anne's pleas.

She too was passionate in her belief that the Bible should be read in her mother tongue. Harry was not opposed in principle to it being translated into English, but he disapproved of the reformist versions in circulation, convinced that they encouraged heresy. Anyway, it was the office of those in holy orders – and kings, who were sanctified with wisdom denied to ordinary mortals – to interpret the Scriptures for the laity.

What Anne's critics did not realise was that she was orthodox in the observance of her faith. She liked the images and ritual of the Church. She believed, unlike the Lutherans, that she would attain Heaven through good works as well as by faith. Her devotional books were traditional. Harry smiled when he remembered the loving couplet she had written to him in her Book of Hours: *By daily proof you shall me find, to be to you both loving and kind.*

Her embracing of the cause of reform had brought about a further realignment of factions at court. Those who supported Kate were now likely also to favour traditional religion, while the supporters of Anne were invariably committed to reform. In this climate, in November, Harry summoned Parliament.

The Boleyns now reigned supreme. In December, Harry created

Rochford earl of Wiltshire and Ormond, and the new Earl's daughter became the Lady Anne. At her request, her brother George, now Lord Rochford, was admitted to the Privy Chamber. At the lavish triumphal banquet Harry hosted to celebrate Wiltshire's ennoblement, Anne sat in Kate's chair, next to him, taking precedence over his sister Mary. The French Queen could barely conceal her fury.

At Christmas, though, Kate once again presided with Harry over the splendid festivities at Greenwich, while Anne was conspicuous by her absence. Taking advantage of that, Harry sent Wolsey an intaglio portrait of himself as a sign of goodwill, hoping Anne would never find out. After the celebrations, he dispatched Kate to Richmond and took Anne to York Place to see the designs for improvements he had had drawn up to please her.

Twelve days later, Wiltshire was appointed Lord Privy Seal and promoted to the Privy Council. Harry was conscious that he had elevated the Boleyns and their allies so high that they now dominated the court and the government, but was content that it should be so. It only showed Anne how much he was prepared to do for her and her family.

1530

In January, Dr Cranmer had finished his treatise and Harry sent it to every university in Christendom, asking for their views.

Through Anne, he had learned a great deal about Cranmer, chiefly that he was, like her, a keen advocate of reform.

'I suspect he might be leaning towards Lutheranism,' she confided, 'but you don't know that.'

Harry didn't care. Cranmer was proving too useful to him, and he liked the man. He frowned, however, when Anne revealed that he had been expelled from his Cambridge college for getting married when he had taken holy orders. Harry held strong views on clerical celibacy.

'She was a barmaid called Black Joan,' she related, snuggling up in furs beside the fire. 'She died in childbirth, and then he went to Germany for a time. He has hinted that he married again, but would not be drawn when I pressed him.'

'As long as he keeps quiet about it, I'll turn a blind eye,' Harry said. Deep down, he sensed that Cranmer's views were more radical than he had at first thought. But what he didn't know, he could not object to.

There was a vacancy on the Privy Council. Today, Harry was interviewing a former servant of Wolsey of whom he had received many excellent reports from the Cardinal. Thomas Cromwell stood before him. He was forty-five years old, a thickset, portly man with heavy jowls, a small, severe mouth and porcine eyes. But his unappealing looks belied his hearty manner and his wit. As they talked, his reserve gave way to jovial banter and animated expressions; he came across as a man of good cheer, gracious in words and generous in actions.

Harry was in no doubt of his abilities. Wolsey would not have employed a lightweight.

'Tell me something about your early background,' he commanded.

'I'm a commoner, Sir, like my former master,' Cromwell said, without any trace of diffidence. 'My father was a blacksmith in Putney. I travelled in Italy in my youth and learned much about banking. I also read the works of Machiavelli. Does your Grace know of them?'

'Indeed, I do,' Harry replied, pleased by Cromwell's broad experience.

'I fear I was a ruffian in my young days,' the man said, with a rueful smile that told Harry he had no regrets. 'But when I returned home, I settled down. I worked as a lawyer, a merchant and a moneylender before I entered the Cardinal's service in 1514.'

'He spoke of you as efficient and astute,' Harry recalled, and saw a shadow cloud Cromwell's bullish face. It was well known that he had remained loyal to Wolsey after the latter's fall and had wound up his affairs. Harry was impressed by that.

'Tell me what you achieved,' he said.

'I assisted the Cardinal in the suppression of some minor religious houses to raise funds for his college at Oxford, but most of my duties were administrative and financial.'

'Yes, I have heard that you are a genius in those fields.' Cromwell, Harry knew, was hiding his light beneath a bushel. Wolsey had once said that the man was formidable – pragmatic, knowledgeable, hard-headed, and ruthless when necessary. Above all, he was industrious and a good manager. He got things done with the minimum of fuss. Already, Harry had decided that no one would be better fitted to filling the space left by the Cardinal. He appointed Cromwell to the Privy Council and soon had cause to be well pleased with his choice. As Cromwell proved his worth time after time, Harry favoured him more and more. He was infinitely useful. He spoke Latin, French, Italian and even some Greek, and could hold his own with humanists like Nicolaus Kratzer and Dr Butts, who were both regular guests at his table.

Cromwell's hospitality was becoming famous. His wife and daughters had died of plague, a tragedy he never spoke of, and he had not remarried. He lived alone, with his promising son, Gregory, and entertained frequently.

Anne and her family wasted no time in taking up Cromwell. She approved of his reformist views and saw that his considerable abilities and increasing power could be used to her advantage. Like Harry, she was confident that this brilliant man would be able to work with Cranmer and bring the Great Matter to a happy conclusion.

It had been three years now, three frustrating years of waiting, hoping, and worrying about the succession, and sometimes it seemed to Harry that there would never be an end to it. His longing for Anne was a torment to him; he had not had a woman in all that time, and his thirties were flying by. Anger towards Kate was lively in him, and he was constantly on the watch for anyone who had the temerity to support her. He was growing ever more suspicious of people's motives and finding it harder to trust anyone.

He was as certain as ever that he was right to pursue his chosen course. He had been furious when he heard that Luther had said of him that he wanted to be God and do as he pleased. He would have strangled the man had he been within reach. It galled him that so many people failed to see the wider issues at stake. He had put himself out to defend the Papacy from attack, but was now regretting it. Why defend an institution that had authorised a marriage that should never have been allowed, or a church that was riddled with corruption? Anne and the reformers had it right!

Well, he would no longer be so nice. If need be, he would be ruthless, if it got results. He had made his mind up, and he would go the whole length.

Sometimes he would pick up a book or hear a tune and be reminded with a swell of regret of the young, idealistic humanist with liberal ideas about kingship he had been twenty years ago. He could still be that man. He was affable and accessible – he greeted even Chapuys with an affectionate hug – and his sense of humour was yet lively, if a trifle touchy. But these days he preferred to show himself as the masterful model of royal authority. He wanted his majestic presence to arouse both respect and fear. And that wasn't difficult, because he was finding it increasingly hard to control his temper. He was always ready to erupt. Kate had done that to him, and Clement, and the Emperor. Tears came readily too; he could not help finding it hard to hide his feelings. Anne complained that he was always sighing and that he overreacted to little things.

He also found himself experiencing an increasing desire for privacy. When he was on show, he was on show, but everyone wanted something from him and sometimes he just needed to get away from the clamour. Working behind the scenes, maintaining a distance, he could be more effective. And he could live a more secret existence, without the world knowing what he was doing and making a scandal of it.

He began to order the building of rabbit warrens of privy lodgings in some of his palaces, which would be accessed by covered galleries or stairs from private watergates, so that he could move from house to house without being seen by his subjects. These apartments were to be laid out on the first floor of his residences, like those of King Francis. Visitors would climb a processional stair and then emerge into the magnificence of the great hall – and be suitably awed. Then, if they had business with him, they would enter the watching chamber, where the Yeomen of the Guard and the Gentlemen Pensioners, his personal bodyguards, stood to attention along the walls. From there, they progressed to the presence chamber where he sat enthroned. Beyond that lay the door to the privy chamber, through which only the very privileged might pass. With the addition of more chambers and closets, he could withdraw completely from public life if he so desired.

He showed Anne the plans and took her to see the various building works as they progressed, pointing out the Queen's side, which would mirror his apartments and be connected by a door or secret stair.

'Some of my palaces are now out of date,' he said, as they skirted the scaffolding at Hampton Court. 'I don't feel inclined to modernise Richmond or Eltham, and Bridewell was always too small.'

'There are foul smells from the Fleet River,' Anne said.

'I have decided to lend it to the French ambassador as his official residence. No, sweetheart, Greenwich might be my chief residence, but I mind to make York Place an even greater palace. To be plain, though, I never realised how much work was involved in organising all these renovations. Wolsey used to take charge of them.'

But he was enjoying it. So what if he was spending more money than he ought? There was no one to caution him about the cost. And he would rather outlay lavishly on his houses than on expensive court entertainments. These days, he preferred to spend his leisure in private, being entertained by his musicians and fools, or gambling with his gentlemen.

He still enjoyed manly exercise, though, still sat his horse well, wielded the spear, threw the quoit, and drew the bow admirably. He could still slam his opponent at tennis. If he did not joust as often as he once did, he retained his passion for hunting and hawking. He still was building tennis courts, bowling alleys and cockpits at his palaces for the pleasure of himself and his courtiers.

It was a good life, but it would be a hundred times better if Anne were his queen and there was a prince in the royal nursery.

In February, Wolsey's physician was arrested, after one of Cromwell's agents heard him saying that the Cardinal was corresponding with the Pope. Under questioning, he revealed to the Council that Wolsey had asked Clement to excommunicate the King and lay an interdict on England if he did not dismiss Anne and treat the Queen with proper respect.

Anne flew into a rage when Harry told her, but he himself was not satisfied that it was the truth. He even wondered if Anne and Norfolk had briefed the physician, striving to bring about the Cardinal's ruin.

But Anne gave a convincing display of being shocked. 'Harry, how can you let this pass? It is treason, no less. I told you all along that Wolsey was working against you. It is he who is the cause of these interminable delays! It is because of him that I worry about time passing me by, and the loss of my honour. You know what people say about me! There she goes, the great whore! I do declare I will leave you if it goes on for much longer!'

As ever, she knew exactly where to twist the knife. In terror at the prospect of losing her, Harry threw himself to his knees by her chair. 'Darling, don't say such things, I beg of you! Without you, I cannot live!' He was crying now.

She turned on him. 'Then arrest Wolsey!'

'No, darling. Do not ask me to do that. The evidence is unsafe. I fear that physician was suborned.'

Something fleeting in her eyes told him he was right.

'But you will investigate the matter further?'

'I will,' he promised.

The Council could find nothing to corroborate the man's story. In the end, a relieved Harry formally pardoned Wolsey and confirmed him as archbishop of York, which left him ranking second only to the Archbishop of Canterbury.

'You should have had him arrested for treason!' Anne spat. And she was vile to Sir John Russell, who had merely uttered a few words in the Cardinal's favour.

'Darling, you cannot just refuse to speak to him, or insult him in my presence,' Harry remonstrated.

Anne knew how far she could go. She smiled suddenly. 'Very well, then. I will forgive him, for your sake.' She held out her arms.

Harry sat at table with Norfolk, Suffolk, More, Cranmer and Cromwell – an ill-assorted bunch indeed, thinkers and soldiers, and never the twain would meet, still less agree. Yet More and Norfolk were good friends, for all that More was a scholar and Norfolk a blunt military man who did not hold with book-learning. Suffolk would get on with anyone for a quiet life, and Cromwell was adept at cozening them all – except, perhaps, More, who was wary of him.

Harry signalled to Suffolk to pass around the wine flagon. It was a spring evening, and the days were drawing out; it was light outside the latticed window.

'Do you remember the time when we all embraced Humanism?' Harry looked at More wistfully.

'Aye, Sir, we thought we would change the world. In fact, I rather thought we had.'

The others laughed.

'It's so much more complicated now,' Harry sighed. 'Many now associate the new learning with reform. The Humanists are at odds among themselves.' It was, in no small measure, a consequence of the Great Matter. The partisans of both himself and Kate had been pressuring famous scholars for their support. Bishop Fisher, like many of the older generation, openly supported the Queen. Harry suspected that More was with him in that, but More was a dark horse and would never be drawn on his views. The younger element, led by Cromwell and Gardiner, championed Harry.

'It's true,' More agreed. 'Humanism attracts many radicals, if not outright heretics. We must be watchful.'

'It is sad,' Harry reflected, 'that the climate of intellectual freedom we enjoyed is changing to one of intolerance.'

'It makes no difference to me,' sniffed Norfolk.

'Luther has divided opinion,' Cromwell said. 'And the Great Matter – everyone is taking sides, and championing the Queen is seen as reactionary and anti-reform. I notice that your Grace's Yorkist relations support her.'

Harry nodded glumly. 'The Poles do, and I have long suspected that Exeter is torn.'

'His wife certainly is,' Cromwell said, draining his goblet. 'I am watching her.'

'She's half Spanish,' Norfolk commented, 'so she's bound to support the Queen.'

Harry was pensive. 'There is one Yorkist who might help me, Lady Salisbury's son, Reginald Pole. I paid for his education because he is outstandingly gifted, and he's recently completed his studies in Italy. Cranmer, you'll recall that I sent him to canvass the Sorbonne in Paris. Well, I have a mind to recall him and offer him either the archbishopric of York or the bishopric of Winchester. I think I can count on him as my man.'

'A capital idea,' Suffolk applauded. 'Where one of that faction leads, the rest will follow.'

At Harry's invitation, Reginald Pole came home and presented himself at court. His mother, apprised by the King of his intentions, was overjoyed, and Harry thought he might even win her around too. But when the scholarly, lean-faced Pole stood before him, Harry could sense the antipathy emanating from him, and almost refrained from holding out before him the great prizes he had to offer. But he made the gesture, thinking it would break his cousin's reserve.

'York or Winchester,' he repeated. 'The choice is yours, Reginald.'

'Your Grace, I am sensible of the high honour you do me,' his cousin said, cool as brass. 'But I fear I have no taste for public office.'

Harry blinked. Nearly anyone else would have been scrambling for the honour. 'Could it be that you fear being drawn into the debate about my Great Matter?'

'I do, Sir. And you should know that my sympathies are with the

Queen. Your marriage is valid. There is no doubt of it.'

'So you think you know better than all the learned doctors I have consulted?' Harry's temper was rising. 'Even the Pope is in doubt, otherwise he would have found for the Queen long since.'

'If he has not, it is for fear of offending you when he needs your friendship. That is the word in Rome.'

Harry was seething now. 'And is that how a pope should exercise his authority? By St George, man, he is Christ's vicar on earth and should not be bound by politics!'

'Nevertheless,' Pole countered, the heat rising in his cheeks, 'he is the Pope, and his office should be above reproach.'

Harry stepped forward and glared at him. 'And thus it is with kings! I know in my soul that my marriage offends God. Yet this Pope offers me no remedy! He leaves me to languish in sin. What kind of example is that?'

'Your Grace has no idea of how difficult things are for him—'

'He is Christ's mouthpiece! And you, cousin, are barely qualified to comment!'

'I have been in Rome, unlike yourself!'

Harry saw red. Who was Pole to speak to him thus? Instinctively, he raised his fist to punch his arrogant face, but restrained himself before he lost control. 'Get out of my sight!' he hissed. Pole hastened away.

When Harry had calmed down, he summoned him back. 'I did not mean to be so harsh with you,' he said. 'You can have no idea of the strain under which I labour, the anxiety I live with daily over who will succeed me when I am gone.'

Pole's demeanour had softened. 'The Princess Mary will make an admirable queen.'

Harry remembered that Kate and Lady Salisbury had once fondly hoped that their children would marry – another union of the red and white roses, sure to be popular with the people. But Harry did not want the Plantagenets in power again. He wanted a son of his body to reign after him, and he would move Heaven and Hell to have one. Besides, Pole was in holy orders.

They parted friends, however, and Reginald took himself off to the London Charterhouse to retreat into quiet contemplation and pursue his studies. The gardens there would be in bloom now. Harry almost envied him.

He was out riding with Suffolk, enjoying the May sunshine, when they came to a clearing and dismounted for a cooling drink of ale, then flung themselves down on the grass to rest awhile.

'I pray we hear from the universities soon,' Harry muttered. It had been four months now. Why did scholars take so long to make up their minds?

'They will be seeking for precedents, which may help your case.' Suffolk stretched out, resting his head on his hands. He was about to say something, but hesitated.

'What is it, Brandon? Spit it out.' Harry seemed to be impatient with everyone these days.

'God, I hardly know how to say this to you,' Suffolk said, sitting up.

'Say what?' Harry feared his friend was about to confess to some heinous offence.

'I want to urge you to reconsider marrying the Lady Anne.' The Duke's face was puce with embarrassment.

Harry jumped to his feet, shocked. 'By St George, why?'

'I fear she is unfit to be queen. You ought to know that she has had criminal relations with a courtier she loves very much, who is now on a mission overseas.'

'Wyatt!' Harry remembered how jealous he had been. 'That's arrant nonsense!' he spat. 'She would never condescend that far.' She certainly hadn't with him, and he couldn't bear to think of her doing so with Wyatt – or anyone else.

Suffolk looked so miserable that Harry felt sorry for him. 'I wrestled with my conscience for days before telling you,' he confessed.

'But who told *you*?' Harry still didn't believe it.

'Wyatt himself, before he left for France recently.'

Harry stood still as stone.

'He wanted to tell you in person, but dared not, so he asked me to. He assured me he could prove what he said.'

'He's a bold villain who cannot be trusted,' Harry flared, 'and you should know better than to heed him!' Without waiting for Suffolk to answer, he mounted his horse and galloped away. I don't believe it; I won't believe it, he said to himself, jolting up and down in the saddle.

As soon as he returned to Greenwich, he crashed into Anne's apartments. 'Leave us!' he commanded, and those who had been making music with her scurried away, taking their beribboned lutes and goblets with them.

Anne rose. She was wearing a gorgeous gown of crimson velvet, a rich gable hood and a heavy gold collar that proudly bore her initials. 'What in Heaven is the matter?'

'Is it true?' Harry grasped her wrist. 'Did you sleep with Wyatt?'

'You're hurting me!' she hissed. 'And I will not lower myself to answer such a question. How could you believe that of me?'

His heart overflowed with relief. 'Darling, I am sorry. Forgive me.'

'Who has been spreading this calumny?' She was justifiably indignant, painfully aware that her reputation at court and in the kingdom at large was dismal. He had seen her face when people called her 'the great whore' as she rode by in the streets. He had done what he could to still the slanders, but Cromwell's desk was littered with reports of them. And now this! He had only added to her mortification.

'Who was it?'

'My lord of Suffolk. He said he had it from Wyatt himself.'

'My God!' She rounded on him. He had rarely seen her so angry. 'Harry, you must recall Wyatt and ask what he has to say for himself. And I want to be there!'

As he hastened away to do her bidding, eager to allay her rage, he told himself that a woman who had something to hide would never expose her lover to such scrutiny. And yet, lying wakeful in bed that night, he could not suppress his unworthy suspicions. She had not actually denied having anything to do with Wyatt. She had, he feared, skirted around the subject.

He had always thought her chaste, believing that, if she had held him off, she must have held off her other suitors too. She had made a great issue of saving herself for marriage. Had that been just a bait to hook him in? She knew how he prized virtue in ladies. And yet she had been in France for many years, in the most licentious court in the world. He had heard it said that no wife or maid ever left it unsullied. Certainly it was there that she had learned her coquettish ways; God forbid she had learned other practices too! And what of Percy? Had she given herself to him? They had betrothed themselves to each other, and for many couples that was all the formality they needed before jumping into bed together.

God knew, she had had plenty of opportunities. But he would have sworn on his life that she had never succumbed to temptation – until now. He was burning to speak to Wyatt.

The poet stood before him, young, handsome and plainly terrified. They were alone in Harry's closet.

'Is it true what you told my lord of Suffolk about the Lady Anne?' Harry growled.

Wyatt would not meet his gaze. 'No, your Grace. He misunderstood me. It was but a fantasy. As you know, I did love her once.'

A fantasy! Could he believe that? His eyes narrowed. 'He seemed to think it a most serious matter!'

'We were drunk, Sir. I said some stupid things and he believed them. But I would happily swear on oath that they were not true.'

'Do not dare to repeat them again, on pain of severe punishment,' Harry barked, and let him go.

Anne remained furious with Suffolk. 'He has insulted me!' she cried. 'You will not let that pass, will you?' The dark eyes glittered. 'And anyway, who is he to cast the first stone? He has seduced his son's betrothed, a girl of eleven!'

Harry caught his breath. Not his old friend Charles! 'I don't believe it.'

'It's true. Send him away, Harry, for my sake!' She sank into the chair and began sobbing – and he was lost.

Suffolk was most indignant. 'That is a lie!' he roared.

'I'm not banishing you for that,' Harry muttered, hating himself for having to exile the Duke from the court. 'It's for slandering the Lady Anne.'

'I've explained that – it was a misunderstanding.'

'And one that led to a lot of unpleasantness.' Harry was implacable.

'For Heaven's sake, Harry! She's overreacting.'

'Get out!' Harry had had enough. Secretly, he too thought that Anne's response had been immoderate, but he did not dare to tell her so.

'With pleasure!' Suffolk snapped, and stumped off.

Harry shook his head, wishing he could summon him back. God only knew what his sister would say when the Duke arrived home at Westhorpe and told her what had happened. He knew that her hatred for Anne was the reason why she never came to court these days. Harry suspected that Suffolk too sympathised with Kate. He was in a difficult position, torn by divided loyalties.

'I'll let him stew at Westhorpe for a couple of weeks,' he told Anne at supper later.

'You're not recalling him so soon?' she challenged.

'Darling, be reasonable. He is my oldest friend and was acting only in what he thought were my interests – and he is useful to me. He's one of the premier dukes of my realm. Two weeks is punishment enough, surely?'

Anne frowned. 'I suppose so.' But she didn't look happy, and it took a lot of effort on his part, and the gift of a jewel, before she would unbend.

The strain of the prolonging of the Great Matter was telling on her too. She was indefatigable in her endeavours to move things ahead, doing her best to force courtiers to abandon the Queen, and openly threatening to have them dismissed if they did not. She assigned to two of her friends, William Brereton, a groom of Harry's

Privy Chamber, and Thomas Wriothesley, one of the royal secretaries, the task of obtaining the signatures of lords and courtiers for a petition to the Pope, urging him to grant the King an annulment without further delay.

Chapter 22

1530

On a cold day in early November, when Harry took his seat at the head of the council board, he noticed that the lords were unusually silent and caught one or two exchanging glances. Then Norfolk pushed a paper in front of him.

'Your Grace, here is evidence that the Cardinal has committed treason,' he said triumphantly.

Harry saw the old familiar handwriting. He read the letter, the words dancing in front of his eyes. Wolsey had written to the French ambassador, praying he would urge King Francis to speak in his favour to Harry.

'It is treason for a subject to appeal to a foreign prince,' Norfolk said.

'But that is not all, Sir,' Rochford added. 'We have further testimony of the Cardinal's presumptuous, sinister practices. He has again urged the Pope to excommunicate your Grace if you do not put away the Lady Anne. He hopes thereby to cause an insurrection through which he would recover power.'

'And, forgetting the kindness and mercy your Grace showed to him,' Suffolk chimed in, 'he still sends the Pope and other princes letters reproaching you, and stirring them to avenge his grievances against you. In consequence of which your nullity suit will drag on.'

'And I spared him,' Harry said bitterly. Such breathtaking ingratitude! Suddenly the ties of affection snapped. 'It is not fitting to let him continue any longer in his malicious and proud purposes. Order the Earl of Northumberland to go to Cawood and arrest him.'

Anne would be pleased that the man Wolsey had once forbidden her to marry would be tasked with this duty.

It was a sunny December day and Harry was taking his sport at the archery butts at Hampton Court when he saw Master Cavendish, Wolsey's gentleman usher, leaning against a tree looking pensive, clearly waiting to speak to him. Handing his bow to Anne, Harry walked over to him and clapped a hand on his shoulder.

'I will make an end of my game, then I will talk with you,' he told him, anticipating that, with his master under arrest, Cavendish was looking for a post at court.

Later that afternoon, when Harry was sitting by the fire in his privy lodgings, wrapped in a gown of russet velvet lined with sables, Sir Henry Norris brought Cavendish to him.

'What can I do for you?' he asked.

'Your Grace . . .' The man's face crumpled. 'I bring heavy news. The Cardinal is dead.'

Harry had been incandescent at Wolsey's treachery. He had lain awake at night raging against him, had resolved to have him clapped in the Tower and tried for treason as soon as Northumberland brought him south to London, and was ready to sign his death warrant. But now, faced with this stark news, grief swept over him. He could only remember all the long years of friendship, Wolsey's diligence and incomparable service, his fatherly advice.

'Tell me what happened,' he said, collecting himself and pouring some wine to numb the pain. 'Sit down and drink this.' He handed a goblet to Cavendish, who looked devastated, for he had been close to his late master.

'My lord of Northumberland came to Cawood to arrest my lord Cardinal,' he related, gratefully sipping the wine. 'I was permitted to accompany him on the journey south. We were met on the way by the Constable of the Tower, Sir William Kingston, with his men. My lord knew, when he saw him, what his fate would be, but he was already very sick, and when we arrived at Leicester Abbey to stay the night, he collapsed.' Cavendish took a moment to master his emotions. 'He was clearly dying, and he did not last the night.'

Harry crossed himself. He thought of all that greatness, brought to naught. And he had done this to his friend. Had it all been contrived? He knew that Norfolk and the Boleyns had never ceased openly pursuing their quarry, but had they secretly colluded to bring him down? Instead of allowing himself to be blinded by rage, he should have probed further and questioned the evidence. He hated to think that he had been their puppet. But he dared not risk offending Anne by making accusations.

'Did he have any final message for me?' he asked at length, willing Cavendish to say that Wolsey had forgiven him at the last.

Cavendish would not meet his eye. 'Alas, Sir, I cannot utter it.'

'Tell me, man!' he commanded, shivering despite the furs.

It came out as a whisper. 'He said, "If I had served God as diligently as I have done the King, He would not have given me over in my grey hairs."'

Harry hung his head. He had deserved it. He could do penance all his life and never atone properly for his treatment of Wolsey. 'Tell me about his last days,' he said, and then spent an hour quizzing Cavendish on his late master's life in Yorkshire. It seemed that the Cardinal had made up for all the years of neglect by looking after his diocese like a good shepherd.

'I wish he had lived,' he confessed, when Cavendish had run out of reminiscences. 'I would give more than twenty thousand pounds to have him back.'

When she heard the news, Anne was jubilant, and all Harry's pleas could not prevent her from staging, for the edification of the court, a farce showing the descent of Wolsey into Hell. It was in the worst possible taste, he argued, but she would not listen. He could have commanded her, but feared to provoke her temper, which seemed more volatile these days. And he could understand it, for the interminable delays were making him prone to lashing out verbally.

Anne needed to be mollified anyway, because Harry had decided that he ought to preside with Kate over the Christmas celebrations at Greenwich, and bring Mary to court. Kate was pathetically grateful, and he could see that she was making a huge effort to be cheerful company, but nothing she said or did now could move him. His heart was at Hever with Anne. As soon as he decently could, he summoned her back to court for the New Year festivities.

1531

He had kept his grief for Wolsey to himself, as he knew Cromwell did; Cromwell, who had loved Wolsey, but was nevertheless ready to help Harry assert his authority over the Church in England. It was Cromwell who urged that he indict fifteen of his senior clergy for having recognised Wolsey's unlawful ecclesiastical jurisdiction.

On the one side, Cromwell, and on the other, Anne, both urging him that the Church needed reforming.

'And not only the Church,' Cromwell declared, as he lingered with Harry after a good dinner, a ewer of fine wine on the table between them. 'England should be a sovereign state supported by Parliament, the law and an efficient administration. What you have now is unwieldy and inefficient. I could overhaul things for you.'

'Then do it!' Harry commanded, impressed by the man's genius, his vision and his ability to get things done.

'Your Grace could go further and set yourself up as the temporal, or secular, head of the English Church.'

'What, break with Rome?' Until now, Harry had concluded that was a step too vast, too immense and too far.

'Not at all. I am not suggesting that you challenge the Pope's spiritual authority.'

'Such as it is!' Harry's tone was bitter. He had lost all respect for Clement.

Cromwell gave a grim chuckle. 'Anyone who believes that the Holy See is particularly holy is either mad or a fool. Even Archbishop Warham thinks that your Grace should wield jurisdiction over the

Church in your realm. He suggested that you take the title of Supreme Head and Protector of the Church of England.'

Harry was impressed. A whole vista of possibilities was opening out before him . . .

The idea being born, Harry embraced it with zeal.

'I like what you propose,' he told Cromwell, refilling their goblets. 'I could appoint my own bishops without recourse to Rome.'

Cromwell smiled. 'You could.'

'And I would be responsible for the souls of my people?'

'No, Sir. That would remain with the clergy. I fear that, if your Grace pressed that point, you would meet with fierce resistance. Bishop Fisher has already urged that the title of Supreme Head be qualified by the words "as far as the law of Christ allows".'

'Fisher!' Harry interjected. 'He would oppose me on principle!'

'His word carries great weight with some. But he has not opposed your assuming the role of Supreme Head.'

'Well, we shall proceed without his approval, if need be. I want these plans implemented without delay.'

In February, Harry convened a convocation of the bishops, whom he indicted for having upheld the temporal authority of the Pope in England, in contravention of the law. For this, he imposed an enormous fine, having ignored protests that they had merely been following ancient custom. Then he demanded that the assembled clergy recognise him as Supreme Head of the Church of England in secular matters, as far as the law of Christ allowed. It was obvious that they did so against their will, but he ignored that. He was the King, and they must obey him. And maybe, when Clement heard of this, he would pull himself together and realise what might be at stake if he did not do the right thing by his most faithful servant.

Spring came and went, with still no word from Rome. It was nearly two years since Harry's case had been revoked to the Papal court, an unconscionable time to keep him waiting. What was Clement doing? Hoping he would go away or give up?

As the weeks passed, his patience dwindled. If he didn't get a decision soon, he would go mad.

He was painfully conscious of time flying by. He was forty that June, and still he lacked a son; if Clement had his way, he'd still be waiting for a decision when he was a hundred. But he did not look old. He was still handsome – a glance in his mirror showed him that. He now wore his auburn hair shorter, and a beard, neatly trimmed. He stood tall, upright and muscular, with a noble bearing and an air of majesty – a perfect model of manly beauty. But his face also bore the marks of strain. Sometimes, he wished he was someone else.

That summer, he indulged in an orgy of hunting with Anne, trying to forget his impossible situation. He might have his new title, but nothing had really changed. He and Kate were still making a point of visiting each other every few days for the sake of appearances, and he made the effort to treat her with respect; occasionally, he even dined with her, much to Anne's fury. But now, he decided, all that had to end. He would show Kate what happened to those who defied him. They must separate for good.

He could not bring himself to tell her face to face or say farewell. One Friday in July, he rode out from Windsor with Anne and went to Woodstock, leaving her behind. He left orders that she was to move with her household to the More, one of Wolsey's former residences. She was not to write to him – or see Mary. That, he told himself, would bring her to her senses!

He allowed her to retain the trappings of queenship, and continued to pay the expenses of her household, but once he had made it clear that he did not look kindly on those who resorted to her court, few went to pay their respects.

He sent Mary to Richmond. She was fifteen now and very pretty, but seemed to be continually suffering from one ailment or another. It was hard on her, this rift between him and her mother, he knew that, but he suspected that, although she loved him and was dutiful, she secretly supported Kate. This was another reason why he refused to allow them to meet. Heaven forbid, they might plot against him!

He soon realised he had been right to send Kate away. Her departure undermined the influence of her supporters. The balance of power at court was further shifting. As the ascendancy of the Boleyns and Cromwell waxed, so that of Norfolk and Suffolk waned. The two dukes had now realised that they had brought down Wolsey only to have another common upstart take his place, rather than themselves, and they were implacably hostile towards Cromwell. They never spoke evil words of him to Harry; they did not have to, for their hatred was writ plain on their faces. Yet they were wise enough to establish good working relationships with him.

Cromwell was no fool. 'My lord of Norfolk would have my head if he could,' he told Harry, after the Duke had been especially dismissive of him in Council.

'Well, he can't,' Harry countered, grinning.

'He is one who can speak as fair to his enemy as to his friend,' Cromwell went on, sifting papers, 'and young Surrey, his foolish son, likes to call me a foul churl.'

'Crum, you are not the only person who is out of sorts with Norfolk,' Harry said, feeling exhausted just thinking of it. 'He has crossed swords with the Lady Anne several times of late. And he and Suffolk are now at odds.'

'Then I am in good company,' Cromwell observed, a smile replacing the grimace that had appeared when Harry called him Crum. By St George, the man should be honoured to have his sovereign speak so familiarly with him!

The atmosphere at Greenwich that Christmas was subdued. People were saying that there was no mirth because the Queen was absent, but Harry knew that his own morose mood was to blame. Anne had wanted to queen it over the festivities, but he had sent her home to Hever, being intent on impressing the new French ambassador, who might not approve of his mistress flaunting herself, but might yet obtain King Francis' support for him.

If only Anne were his mistress, in deed as well as in name! It had been more than six years now. Thwarted desire like that did something to a man, made him bad-tempered and restless and robbed him of any interest in other women. The only one he wanted was Anne, the one he could not have. At this rate, his sceptre would shrivel up into uselessness, and he could say goodbye to siring a prince. By St George, Clement had much to answer for!

1532

At New Year, Anne returned to court and delighted Harry with a gift of ornamental spears in the Biscayan fashion; in return, he gave her a set of rich hangings of cloth of gold and crimson satin, lavishly embroidered, and a bed hung with cloth of gold and silver. He had sent a gift to Mary, but not to Kate, so he felt angry and embarrassed when a messenger was admitted to his study bearing a beautiful gold cup.

What business had Kate to be sending him a gift? She was not his lawful wife!

'Take it away,' he commanded. 'I will not receive it.'

As soon as the man had bowed his way out with the offending article, it occurred to Harry that he might just return later in the day to present it in front of the whole court. It was the kind of thing Kate might have asked him to do. So, feeling something of a fool, he recalled the messenger, took the cup and had it discreetly placed among his other gifts on a sideboard in the presence chamber. Only in the evening did he return it, with the command that she was not to send him gifts in future.

This could not go on! He was heartily sick of the Pope's procrastination.

'It is bringing the Church into disrepute,' he thundered to his Council. 'I am beginning to think that I should break completely with Rome.' He watched the faces of the lords as he said it, saw the radicals nodding their heads in approval and the conservatives looking shocked.

He banged his fist on the table. 'The Holy See is not popular in England.'

'It never has been, Sir,' Warham observed.

'Indeed, and it's easy to see why! There is bitter resentment against the tithes it exacts, tithes that are being paid to a Church that is already fabulously wealthy – and corrupt. If I broke with Rome, the revenues of the English Church would be mine, and my power and jurisdiction would increase immeasurably.'

'It is a huge step to take after a thousand years of unity,' ventured Warham.

Harry began to waver. Inwardly, he baulked at taking such a step. Even after all this time, the Pope might pronounce in his favour.

'Your Grace should know that Reginald Pole has gone to Italy,' Cromwell said.

'Without my leave?'

'Sir, you can imagine why. He does not wish to face a conflict of loyalties. His mother is a friend of the Queen.'

'It's a pity that all her friends don't run off to join him,' Harry snorted.

After the meeting ended, Cromwell came to see Harry. Never ostentatious, he was wearing a sober gown of the finest quality and cut. His tastes were modest and middle class, compared with those of the Cardinal; he lived in a well-appointed house in London, enjoyed hunting, bowls and gambling and gave generously for the relief of the poor. So far, he had avoided the kind of criticism that had been levelled at his late master. He did not enjoy Wolsey's monopoly on power for he had to share it with Anne and her faction, yet he had speedily risen above everyone else, and Harry had come to value him highly. He knew it was being said that there was now no one but Cromwell who did anything, but Harry did not allow him to make all the decisions. It was he, the King, who shaped policy, and Cromwell who implemented it.

'What can I do for you, Crum?' he asked, as they walked in his private gallery.

'Sir, I was thinking of what you said about breaking with Rome.'

Harry paused beside a portrait of his father, who had never had to contend with such troubles as he faced. 'I may have been a little premature.'

'Even so, Sir, it might be politic to bring in measures to further limit Papal power in England. It could bring your Great Matter to a satisfactory conclusion. To begin with, Parliament might legislate to deprive the Pope of his dues from English parishes.' He smiled mischievously. 'Squeeze him gently, and he will be in fear that you might squeeze him hard!'

The man was brilliant!

'A capital idea! How shall we broach it?'

'Your Grace may safely leave that to me,' Cromwell beamed.

Harry had long cherished a special devotion to the Observant Franciscans whose friary stood adjacent to Greenwich Palace. He had been baptised in their church, as had his daughter Mary. His sister Mary had been married there. But, of late, he had sensed a coldness on the part of the friars, and it was not hard to comprehend why, for they had long enjoyed a happy relationship with Kate. There had been no open hostility or rift, but Harry no longer felt welcome at the friary.

At Easter, wishing to restore good relations, he invited William Peto, the provincial minister of the Observant Friars, to preach before him and the court. But he was outraged when Father Peto frowned down from his pulpit at Harry and Anne and thundered that any marriage between them would be unlawful.

'If, like Ahab in the Scriptures, your Grace commits such a dire sin, the dogs will one day lick your blood, as they did Ahab's!' he ranted.

Furious, with Anne's outraged clamour ringing in his ears, Harry ordered one of his chaplains to preach a retaliatory sermon the following Sunday, but the chaplain was heckled by another Observant friar, Father Elston. His patience exhausted, Harry had Elston and Peto arrested.

As if he had not troubles enough, his sister Mary, on one of her rare visits to court, made it very plain to anyone who would listen precisely what she thought of Anne. It had already provoked a fight between the retainers of Suffolk and Norfolk, and one had been killed in the fray, having been dragged out of the sanctuary at Westminster Abbey by an enraged Suffolk. The court was in an uproar. Too late, the Suffolks retired to their estates, but their followers were still in a riotous mood, and Harry and Cromwell had to intervene to prevent any further trouble.

Soon afterwards, trying to build bridges, Harry visited Mary and Suffolk at Westhorpe, braving his sister's tart tongue – she seemed to forget that he was king – and using all his powers of persuasion to make the Duke return to his duties at court. He was exhausted by the time he returned to York Place.

Despite the strain, Harry and Cromwell now had a bullish Parliament in the palms of their hands. When the assembly threatened to remove the autonomy of the church courts – another of Cromwell's inspired ideas – the convocations of Canterbury and York nearly fell over themselves to surrender them into the King's hands, hastily conceding that they held their authority at his pleasure.

Gardiner alone dared to protest. Harry gave him short shrift and sent him scurrying back to his diocese of Winchester, where he was now bishop.

The stress was telling on Harry. Almost daily, he was troubled by headaches. Sometimes, he could not think straight. He found himself wondering what had happened to the carefree, ebullient young man he had once been. Frustration was his constant companion, unbearable at times: bitterness at the Pope for delaying a decision on his case for what could only be political reasons; anger with the Church that had sanctioned his marriage; and exasperation with Kate for obstructing him at every turn. He was enraged at those of his subjects who had the temerity and ingratitude to support her and desperate at being thwarted in his attempts to provide for the succession. And he was still consumed with longing for Anne; would he never hold her in his arms and make her his? How much deprivation could a man take?

And now Sir Thomas More was abandoning him. The very day after the convocations had submitted, he resigned the office of Lord Chancellor.

Harry knew what had prompted it. It wasn't just the curbing of the power of the clergy. A few days before that, Harry had visited More at Chelsea. As they walked in the gardens in the chilly spring sunshine, he had broached the subject that had been very much on his mind.

'Thomas, it grieves me that you will not give me your support in this matter of my marriage,' he said, casting a sideways glance at his lean-faced old friend.

More hesitated. 'Your Grace was good enough to say you would not press me on it.'

Harry turned to him. 'Yes, but things have moved on since then. You are my Lord Chancellor. I need your approval. You have one of the finest and most respected minds in Europe, and your support would add immeasurable weight to my case.'

There was a long pause. 'Alas, your Grace,' More said, looking as if the weight of the world had just fallen on his shoulders, 'I wish I could give it, but I cannot.'

'But why?' Harry cried.

'Do not press me, Sir, I beg you. This is between me and my conscience.'

'And the whole damned world!' Harry flared. 'Your deafening silence speaks volumes! Everyone knows you do not agree with me.'

'No one knows what I think,' More countered, looking pained. 'No one has heard me express an opinion.'

Harry snorted. 'I'm a plain man, Thomas, and have no time for your sophistry. Either you're for me or against me – which is it?'

More's expression was anguished. There were tears in his eyes. 'Alas, Sir, I wish with all my heart that I could go with you along this road. But I cannot.'

The sun had gone in and the breeze was cold.

'Lady More will be waiting to serve dinner, Sir,' More said, rubbing his hands.

Harry had rounded on him. 'How can I sit at meat with one who persists in defying me? Give her my apologies and tell my gentlemen to attend me at my barge.' And he had walked off, leaving More standing there.

Now the man had resigned. He never had desired worldly glory or riches. Harry could picture him surrendering the Great Seal with relief, looking ahead to a peaceful existence with his family and his books. Anger burned in him. It was all very well for More, just swanning off to Chelsea and leaving him in the lurch. He had a son, and a wife he loved. He had no idea how Harry was suffering, and now he had just made things worse.

Harry conferred with Cromwell. He needed a replacement for More, someone who would be loyal to him. Cromwell suggested one of his lawyer friends, Sir Thomas Audley, the Speaker of the Commons.

'He is your man through and through,' he said. 'Your Grace will have no trouble with him.'

Harry sought solace in his building projects. He ordered the embellishment of the chapel of King's College, Cambridge, with a superb rood screen, organ loft, and stalls carved by Italian craftsmen, who were instructed to incorporate Harry and Anne's initials and emblems. He visited Hampton Court, where a new great hall was rising on the site of Wolsey's old one. It was to be the first of the royal apartments, crowned by a magnificent hammerbeam roof: a room designed to impress and overawe visitors.

And yet, as he raised his eyes to where the roof would soon be in place high above him, he was aware that great halls were becoming out of date. In his growing desire for privacy, he had ordered some at his other houses to be demolished and replaced by first-floor apartments inspired by those in King Francis' palaces.

He had acquired the old leper hospital of St James, which stood in open countryside near York Place, and had the old buildings demolished. Now he was building a magnificent house there for Richmond and the children he hoped to have with Anne. It was to be known as St James' House. A great hunting park surrounded it, which he planned to stock with deer for his own pleasure.

With the summer came a resurgence of his optimism. The opinions of the monasteries, secured at great cost in several cases, had proved largely favourable to him, and Dr Cranmer was becoming cautiously excited. Soon, the Pope would have to bow to the weight of scholarship in Harry's favour and he would not need to break with Rome; Anne would be his, and England would, God willing, have an heir.

He gave orders that the palace of the Tower be refurbished for Anne's coronation, and Cromwell took charge, spending lavish sums on having the old royal apartments gutted and decorated in the antick style. A new Queen's lodging was created, with a presence chamber, a dining chamber, a bedchamber, a gallery that led to the King's apartments, and a private garden. Harry took Anne to inspect the works and felt elated as she looked around approvingly.

'You never stay here,' she observed, watching one of the painters gilding the ceiling battens.

'My lodgings are too dated and uncomfortable,' he replied. 'But yours will be sumptuous, fitting for my Queen!'

'If only I was,' she said sharply, and he regretted having said it. 'Yes, they are going to be beautiful. All the same, I would rather be staying elsewhere.'

'It's the custom for kings and queens to lodge in the Tower before they are crowned,' Harry reminded her, stepping over a roll of carpet. 'And it won't be for long.'

'All that outlay for such a short stay!' she smiled, then shivered. 'I don't much like the Tower. It's more like a fortress than a palace, and I can't forget that it's a prison.'

'I will be with you, darling,' he said, and took her hand, raising it to his lips and kissing it.

* * *

When they returned to Hampton Court, Harry joined Anne in her chamber, where her friends gathered daily to amuse themselves and courtiers came to show support for their future Queen.

Today, a handsome young groom of the Privy Chamber called Mark Smeaton was playing the virginals and singing a song that Anne's brother Rochford had composed. It was very good, and Mark had a melodious voice. Wolsey had spotted his talent and found him a place in his choir; after the Cardinal's fall, Mark had transferred to the Chapel Royal, a heady advancement for the son of a carpenter, but then both Wolsey and Cromwell had risen from similar humble beginnings. It was ability that mattered, Harry reflected, not pedigree, although Norfolk would be sure to disagree!

Anne clapped when the song ended, but kept on chatting to her ladies. Harry caught the look of disappointment on Mark's face. He had been hoping for praise, or even to be noticed. Well, he might wait for ever. Even Harry sometimes found himself waiting to be noticed. Oh, she was a mercurial woman! He never knew where he was with her.

Chapter 23

1532

They spent another summer in hunting and disports. The French ambassador, Monsieur de la Pommeraye, joined them, having come to conclude a new treaty of friendship between Harry and Francis. It was agreed that Harry would again visit France, and he was hoping that, when they met in person, he would finally be able to persuade Francis to intercede on his behalf with Pope Clement. He therefore made a point of extending great favour to the ambassador, personally showing him the improvements he had made at the houses they visited, singling him out as his sole companion on hunting expeditions, inviting him to partner Anne in archery contests and seating him as guest of honour when they feasted.

He played the genial host, and although he was feeling far from well, suffering from chronic toothache and sinus trouble, he tried not to let these complaints interfere with his pleasures or his plans for the French visit. He was in an optimistic mood. Most of the universities had declared for him, and he was confident that pressure could now be brought to bear on Clement to give a decision in his favour.

In August, old Archbishop Warham, ever a lukewarm supporter of Harry's plea for an annulment, spoke out against it. Harry angrily threatened him with the same fate as Wolsey, but was told that the Archbishop was too ill to leave his bed, and past worldly considerations.

Now he was dead, and Harry could choose in his place someone who would prove more amenable. And he knew exactly who that would be.

'I should be mourning the old man, but he's of more use to God than he ever was to me,' he told Anne, feeling revitalised by this new hope. 'No one can say no to us now, darling! I'm nominating Cranmer to the see of Canterbury this very night. I shall go through the motions with Rome, so that no one can challenge my new Archbishop. Cranmer will not hesitate to declare my union with Katherine invalid, and he will zealously push through the religious reforms we want.'

Anne smiled radiantly, looking every bit as alluring as she had done seven years before, when he had fallen in love with her. It could be only a matter of weeks now before she would be wholly, finally his. He caught his breath at the thought. He had yearned for her for so long, had ached to possess her, and could not now imagine how glorious the reality would be.

Her eyes met his, and in them he read both invitation and promise. Barely comprehending, he took a step towards her, and she went into his arms.

'I love you, Anne,' he breathed, his face in her hair. 'Be mine, darling! There is nothing to stop us now.'

'Would your Grace like to see me in that beautiful black night-gown you bought me?' she murmured, looking up into his eyes.

'Darling!' His voice trembled. He could hardly speak.

'I will wear nothing underneath,' she promised.

Unable to believe that this was happening, Harry slid the silk nightgown from Anne's shoulders, then stood back so that he could gaze on her body, revealed to him in its entirety for the first time. His eyes raked the small breasts, the narrow waist, the triangle of dark hair hiding her secret places.

Dear God, she was so thin without her clothes! He could see her ribs. There was nothing of the buxomness he usually admired in women. His member, which had been painfully erect, suddenly subsided, and he was thankful that he had not yet stripped. He swallowed. To fail at such a moment, after all these years! He caressed her breasts and bent to take a nipple in his mouth, a sure way to rekindle desire, but it didn't work tonight, even though she was arching her back in pleasure. He pulled her down beside him on the bed, opening his codpiece and gripping his manhood, thinking of the lewd Italian woodcuts he kept locked in a drawer in his study. That did the trick and he entered her, breathing heavily, thrusting frantically. It was all over very quickly.

Slick with sweat, he lay with her in his arms, shamed and perplexed. Was that it, the great consummation he had anticipated and imagined a thousand times and more? He could have sobbed. If only he could feel something. This was Anne, his Anne! What was wrong with him?

He held her for a long time after they had made love.

'I love you,' he said, again and again. 'Thank you for giving your-self to me.' The words sounded all wrong in this strange, confused world he now inhabited.

Unable to bear it any longer, he rose from the bed and pulled on his gown.

'I'm going to write Cranmer's nomination, sweetheart. I will return as soon as it's done. I hate to leave you, but I want to get it off to Rome tonight.' He kissed her hand and made his escape, hating himself. The letter was an excuse; he prayed she had not guessed. He didn't think she had. She lay there watching him with a triumphant smile, as if to say, 'You are mine now.' Thank God she was clearly innocent of the ways of men. She had no idea that anything was amiss. He sighed with relief. It would be better next time. He had been deprived for too long, far too long. Clement had much to answer for!

He returned to her bed an hour later, but he barely slept. He was too aware of her lying beside him, the nearness of her, the sound of her breathing.

When dawn broke, he got up. He dared not risk another failure. He was pulling on his nightgown when her eyes opened.

He bent and kissed her. 'Good morning, sweetheart!'

'Good morning, Harry!' She smiled.

'I wish I could stay, but I must go,' he said. 'I ride to Hunsdon this morning.'

'To Hunsdon? Why?'

'I had planned to visit Mary.'

Anne sat up, no longer smiling 'I marvel that you show her such favour, considering how disobedient she has been in opposing you.'

Harry bent to put on his slippers. 'At heart she is a good child, and loving. I would bring her around with gentle words.'

'It's more than she deserves!' Anne snapped. 'She's sixteen and should know her duty better. If I were her father, I would have her whipped, and put an end to this nonsense.'

'Darling, give me a chance! I would speak with her.'

'You've spoken with her before, to no effect! I had thought you would spend this day, of all days, with me.'

Harry squeezed her hand. 'I promise I will not stay long. I'll be back by evening, and then, sweetheart, we can be together again.' He contrived to look as if he was longing for it.

'Very well,' she said, 'but bring her to heel. She could prove every bit as dangerous as her mother, inciting disaffection and the sympathy of the Emperor.'

'I am her father,' Harry said. 'She will obey me, you'll see.'

At Hunsdon, he tried in vain to win Mary around. Her button mouth set in a determined line, her chin jutted in obstinacy, just like her mother's, as she told him, weeping, that she could never consider herself baseborn. When he rode back, he was seething at her defiance, while trying to make sense of his feelings for Anne. Perversely, once he had left her, he found himself wanting her again. He loved her, he was in no doubt about that. Yet he could not shake off a terrible sense of disappointment. Her body had failed to move him. He had expected their coming-together to be sublime, and it had not been. He wished he understood why.

A treacherous little voice in his head kept telling him that it was because all cats were grey in the dark, that Anne was just a woman like the many others he had had – had and abandoned, to be blunt.

But she was not like the rest. She was special! And she was, she was!

Tonight, it would be different – and so it proved, to his utter relief. As she wound her arms around him and her robe fell open, he was suddenly his old virile self, and the world began turning again on its axis. Relieved and unutterably thankful, he took her with fervour, knowing that this was what he wanted and that there would never be anyone like Anne for him.

Harry was becoming more confident that Anne would soon be queen, but, lying beside her in the darkness thinking of all the setbacks he had suffered, he dared not allow himself to be over-optimistic. What would happen if he got her with child and then some new obstacle was put in their way? He must take measures to protect her. And he must elevate her to a rank that would enable her to be received by King Francis.

By the time dawn broke and he turned to take her in his arms again, he had decided to honour her as no Englishwoman had ever been honoured before.

Sunday Mass was over, and Harry was seated beneath the canopy of estate in the presence chamber at Windsor, waiting for Anne's procession, his courtiers packing the room and the French ambassador standing in the place of honour beside him. He watched her advance between their ranks, wearing a gown of crimson velvet covered with costly jewels, her hair loose about her shoulders. She was escorted by the countesses of Rutland and Sussex; following behind was Norfolk's daughter, Lady Mary Howard, carrying a crimson velvet mantle and gold coronet.

Anne gave Harry a triumphant smile, then knelt before him. He took the mantle and draped it over her shoulders, then placed the coronet on her head, as Bishop Gardiner read out the letters patent creating her Lady Marquess of Pembroke – a noblewoman in her own right. He could hear murmuring among the throng; some had perhaps noticed that the reference to the new peeress's male heirs in the patent of creation was missing the usual words 'lawfully begotten', overturning the law under which a bastard could not inherit. But they would be silenced soon, those gainsayers. Cranmer had it all in hand.

Anne rose, curtseyed, thanked Harry for the favour shown her and retired as the trumpets sounded.

Harry was determined that Anne should be at his side throughout the visit to France, a queen in all but name. He demanded that Kate surrender the official jewels of the queens of England, so that Anne could wear them, and was furious when he was informed that she had indignantly declared she would not give up what was rightfully hers to adorn a person who was a reproach to Christendom and was bringing scandal and disgrace upon him. There was more in the same vein, provoking Harry to insist that she send him the jewels without further prevarication.

Anne was determined to have all the trappings of queenship. She had her chamberlain seize the Queen's barge and have its coat of arms burned off and replaced with her own. Harry had known nothing of this and was deeply embarrassed when Chapuys made an official complaint about it, leaving him with no choice but to castigate the chamberlain. When he remonstrated with Anne, she became angry, accusing him of taking Kate's part.

She had ordered gowns in the French fashion for the visit, as a compliment to King Francis. They were cut low and left her shoulders nearly bare, and Cromwell – whose spies now seemed to be everywhere – warned Harry that people were criticising her for wearing wanton fashions unfit for a chaste woman.

Harry prided himself on being a virtuous man, and he did not think Anne looked wanton in the gowns. He was sure the French would love them. Ironically, the item of clothing they would not see – the black satin nightgown banded with velvet – was modestly cut.

After Anne's grand preparations, she and Harry were appalled to learn that no French royal lady would agree to receive her. They had not expected Francis' second queen, Eleanor of Austria, to do the honours, for she was the Emperor's sister, but Harry was shocked that Francis' own sister Marguerite, whom Anne had once served, refused to meet his whore, as she bluntly put it, and even more horrified when it was suggested that Francis' mistress, the Duchess of Vendôme, should stand in.

'There is nothing for it, darling,' he told a seething Anne. 'I would not for the world have you publicly humiliated. You will remain in Calais, and I will travel alone to meet Francis.' Of course, that provoked a storm, but Anne had calmed down by the time they embarked at Dover, accompanied by a retinue of more than two thousand persons, among them Harry's son Richmond, now a gangling and disorganised boy of thirteen, Norfolk and a reluctant Suffolk, whose wife had refused to accompany him because Anne was going.

The wind was fair, and they were in Calais by mid-morning. Waiting to receive them was the Mayor and Lord Berners, the King's Deputy. They rode in a torchlit procession through the autumnal mist to the church of St Nicholas to hear Mass, then settled into their lodgings at the Exchequer Palace, which had been enlarged for their visit. Harry's bed had been sent ahead from England, set up in his lodgings and hung with green velvet. A connecting door linked Anne's bedchamber to his. The nights would be theirs. Being away from England, from the hostility of Kate's supporters and the cares of state, made the trip feel like a holy day, and taking Anne to bed made it seem like a honeymoon too. He had her accompany him everywhere, as if she were queen already.

'Why can't we marry here?' she asked.

'We must marry in England,' Harry replied, pulling her into his arms and thinking how becoming she looked in her green damask gown. 'I want it to be done properly. Let us wait on Cranmer; he said that everything was nearly in place for us.'

He did not tell Anne of his concern that, when it came to it, Cranmer might not have the courage to take such a provocative step as annulling his marriage. He feared yet another outburst of her increasingly uncertain temper. Maybe it was just Cranmer's lugubrious manner and the natural timidity of the man that made him jittery. No, Cranmer would deliver the right verdict; he had said as much, and Harry must have faith in him.

Always, since their first night together, Harry had taken the initiative in their lovemaking, as was proper. But on their second night in Calais, when he reached for Anne, she astonished him by pushing him back on the bed and trailing light kisses down the length of his body; then, to his shock, she used her mouth to pleasure him, something no woman had ever done to him before. He gasped and spent himself almost at once. As he lay there panting, she returned to his side and held him.

'I wanted to please you,' she whispered.

He could not answer her. He was too stunned.

'Where did you learn how to do that?' he asked at length. He would have liked to ask who had taught her.

'At the French court there were books in circulation, showing people making love in different ways,' she replied, then laughed. 'I have never done it! I just remembered and thought to please you.'

He did not know what to say to her. He would have liked to express his outrage that a woman who claimed to be virtuous would stoop to such a lewd act. He could not begin to imagine Kate descending that far. But he feared to spoil this new intimacy they were sharing.

'Darling,' he said, deciding to be tactful, 'if we are to get a son, that is not the way to go about it. The Church frowns on practices like that. But I appreciate your wanting to please me. You do that best when you allow me inside you.'

'Then I am your Grace's to command!' Anne said, sounding a little chastened.

He kissed her, satisfied that he had expressed his displeasure without being confrontational.

Harry and Francis had agreed that their meetings were to bear no resemblance to the Field of Cloth of Gold. There was to be no lavish display, no extravagance. Each would be attended by his household only and six hundred men-at-arms, and the cost of the entertaining was to be borne equally. But Harry had almost immediately broken his own rule and spent a fortune on new clothes and hospitality.

In the middle of October, the two kings embraced each other at Saint-Inglevert near the border of the English Pale. Harry was secretly pleased to see that Francis, at thirty-eight, had not aged well. He looked foxier than ever with his long nose and coarsened, puffy features. Harry grew prim as he recalled all the rumours he had heard about the promiscuous life Francis led in his wanton court. It was said that no woman ever emerged virtuous from that den of iniquity. For an uncomfortable moment, he thought of Anne and the unseemly practices she had learned of there. He prayed that was all she had learned. It troubled him now that there had been no blood on the sheets when he first took her.

For a mile, he and Francis rode hand in hand, then stopped near the French border to drink a toast. At Boulogne, where Francis was staying, the Dauphin Francis and his two younger brothers were waiting to meet them. Harry took one look at the three sturdy boys in black velvet edged with silver and felt a visceral pang of jealousy. Why could he not have such fine, strapping sons? Steeling himself, he bent down and kissed and embraced them fondly. With a thousand cannon sounding a deafening salute, the royal procession entered Boulogne.

Harry was satisfied with the suite of chambers Francis had assigned him in the abbey of Notre-Dame. They were hung with cloth of silver and tapestries depicting scenes from Ovid's *Metamorphoses*. However, the rivalry between the two men soon came into play again. Harry was annoyed to see that Francis and his train had also ignored the agreement and provided themselves with such splendid attire that they far surpassed the English. Not to be outdone, Harry appeared in an outfit Francis had given him, a crimson satin doublet encrusted with pearls beneath a long gown of white velvet embroidered in gold.

He was ready to offer inducements to secure Francis' support for the annulment, or, better still, his agreement to approach the Pope on Harry's behalf. Clement might well listen to him, and, even at this late stage, Harry would have given much to have Rome rule in his favour. If he could avoid a rift, he would. But at their first meeting, Francis was full of his plans for a joint crusade against the Turks. That was all very well and noble, and ordinarily Harry would have liked nothing better than to cover himself in glory fighting the Infidel, but he had other priorities.

Finally, after dinner was over, and he and Francis were walking in the cloisters, he managed to raise the subject of his Great Matter, deciding that it was probably best not to mention what Cranmer was planning.

Francis smiled, but his eyes had narrowed. He was probably calculating what advantage, if any, there might be in this for him. But he was now Harry's ally and would be counting on his friendship.

'Brother,' he said at length, 'I will use my influence with his Holiness to help you achieve a favourable outcome. This very day, I will send two cardinals to Rome to inform him of our alliance and assure him that he need no longer fear the Emperor because we will use our joint might to protect him, should the need arise.'

Harry relaxed and started to enjoy himself. Francis truly was his friend.

The weather being fine for the season, he watched the French princes playing tennis. The next day, he offered at the shrine of Our Lady of Boulogne and entertained Francis' nobles to a sumptuous feast. He lavished gifts on his host – pure-bred horses, mastiffs, falcons and jewels – and gave the Dauphin and his brothers great bags of gold crowns. Francis looked slightly embarrassed at not being immediately able to match such munificence, but the following morning he presented Harry with six horses and even gave him his own bed, hung with crimson velvet.

That day, Harry escorted Francis to Calais, where young Richmond was waiting to greet him.

'He is a goodly prince,' the French King declared, 'and a handsome one.'

Harry's chest swelled to hear his son so praised – and called a prince. Privately, he had decided that, if Anne bore him no son, he would have Richmond legitimised and proclaimed his heir, and be damned to anyone who opposed him.

Three thousand guns sounded a deafening salute as the royal cavalcade rode into Calais through streets lined with English soldiers, and Francis was conducted to his lodgings in the magnificent Staple Inn, the headquarters of the merchants of the town. That evening, Anne was delighted to receive a costly diamond, which he had sent her as a token of his esteem.

The following day, Harry hosted his brother monarch at a lavish dinner in the banqueting hall of the Staple Inn, which had been hung with silver and gold tissue adorned with gold wreaths sparkling with precious stones, reflecting the light from twenty silver chandeliers. A seven-tier buffet creaked under the weight of the gold plate displayed upon it. Harry appeared in purple cloth of gold with a collar of fourteen rubies, the smallest the size of a goose's egg, and two rows of pearls, from which hung the famous Black Prince's ruby. The French appeared suitably awed at the sight.

After supper, Anne and seven other ladies, all masked and wearing cloth of gold and crimson tinsel, danced before the two kings. Then, amid much laughter, they led out the gentlemen, Anne herself taking Francis' hand. Henry could not resist pulling off her mask to show him who his partner was, and Francis rose to the occasion superbly. After the dance had ceased, he drew Anne to a window seat and spent an hour chatting with her.

Four days later, Harry held a chapter of the Order of the Garter, which Francis attended in his Garter robes. Both made a solemn pledge to go on crusade against the Turks, although Harry had no idea when he would find time for it. Afterwards, they watched wrestling matches between the English and French champions, then Francis invited Richmond to visit his court to complete his education. It was agreed that the boy and his friend and close companion, Norfolk's son, the Earl of Surrey, should accompany him into France.

When the visit ended, Harry escorted Francis back to French soil, and there they bade each other a hearty farewell. This time, unlike at the Field of Cloth of Gold, a strong rapport had been established between them, and Harry was confident that Francis would prove a supportive friend.

After he returned to Calais, violent storms began lashing the Channel coast, and he and Anne were obliged to remain at the Exchequer for nearly two weeks. When the tempest had abated, fog set in, but Harry insisted on sailing back to England, and they took ship at midnight on 12 November. After a leisurely progress through Kent to Eltham Palace, they made a state entry into London and Harry gave thanks at St Paul's Cathedral for the success of the visit and his safe return.

1533

Harry was surprised to see Anne waiting for him when he emerged from the council chamber. There was an air of excitement about her.

'I need to speak to your Grace,' she said, ignoring the staring lords behind him.

'Of course, sweetheart,' he agreed. 'Gentlemen, we shall meet again at the same time tomorrow.'

He led her into the deserted chapel, and closed the door.

'I'm with child!' she burst out.

It was like the Annunciation; a sign from above. He could barely believe it.

'Thanks be to God!' he cried, crossing himself and bowing to the crucifix on the altar. He crushed Anne to his breast and kissed her soundly. He would have swung her off her feet, yet he feared to harm the precious life budding inside her. 'This is the best news you could have given me.' He gazed down at her, his future Queen, the mother of his son. How right he had been to pursue his arduous course. Truly, God was smiling on him! 'You know what this means, Anne? It is a vindication of all I have done! Our marriage will be truly blessed. Oh, my darling, I am so proud of you!' He bent and kissed her again. 'You must take care. You carry a precious burden. Thank you, Anne, thank you! You cannot know how much this news means to me.' He laid his hand on her belly. 'A son – an heir to England, and her saviour, no less. Now we will be free from the threat of civil war.'

'I am the happiest of women!' she cried. 'I shall choose "The most happy" for my motto as queen, to remind me of this precious moment.'

'We must be married without delay,' Harry said. 'I'll go and talk to Cranmer at once. We will keep this wonderful news to ourselves for now. But we should make plans anyway. Our son must be born in wedlock.'

It was still dark, and the palace was silent when Harry took his place in the Chapel Royal at York Place. It was the feast of the conversion of St Paul, the twenty-fifth day of January. Awaiting him was a priest Cromwell favoured, Dr Lee, standing in full vestments in the sanctuary, and behind followed the witnesses, all sworn to secrecy: Sir Henry Norris, Thomas Heneage and William Brereton, all of the Privy Chamber.

Harry had donned cloth of gold; only the best would serve for this long-yearned-for day.

And now, here was Anne, attended by two ladies, who divested her of her cloak to reveal a gorgeous gown of white satin. She wore her hair loose, in token of the symbolic virginity of a queen, and curtseyed gracefully to Harry, who took her hand and kissed it. 'You look so beautiful,' he said. Just as he had always imagined she would. They knelt together before the altar, and Dr Lee began intoning the words of the Holy Sacrament of marriage.

'I, Henry, take thee, Anne . . .'

'I, Anne, take thee Henry . . .'

His eyes never left hers as they took their vows.

'Those whom God hath joined together, let no man put asunder!' Dr Lee intoned, and pronounced them man and wife.

Part Three

Autumn

Then some discuss that hence we must
Pray we to God and Saint Mary.
That all amend and here an end.
Thus saith the King, the VIIIth Harry!

(King Henry VIII)

Chapter 24

1533

For the present, they kept their marriage secret, but Harry could not resist dropping hints, and soon the court was a-buzz with speculation.

He sent Kate to Ampthill Castle with a reduced household, as a warning of what her future might be like if she continued to defy him. He did not like to think about how she would react when she heard he had married Anne without waiting for the Pope to pronounce on his case – or what the Emperor Charles might do. It was essential, therefore, that Kate make no protest. Effectively, he wanted her muzzled, and now was the time to set about doing it.

At the end of March, Cranmer was consecrated Archbishop of Canterbury. He took the traditional vow of allegiance to the Pope, but added that he would not be bound by any authority that was contrary to the law of God or of England. Harry was aware of how much Cranmer was sacrificing in accepting this great office, for the quiet cleric would greatly have preferred a life of study to one at the centre of public affairs. He had no love for pomp and ceremony, but was a simple, charitable man with a high regard for the truth, a zealous reformist unswervingly loyal to his King yet vulnerable to the vicious machinations of his enemies on the other side of the religious divide. He was probably aware that there were many who would have destroyed him.

Harry had informed Cranmer of his marriage to Anne, and Cranmer had declared himself ready to put it on a legal footing, whatever the Pope might rule. To this end, Parliament quickly passed the Act in Restraint of Appeals. Harry himself had had a hand in drafting its introduction, which majestically proclaimed that the realm of England was an empire, governed by one Supreme Head and King who owed submission to no one but God.

'Your Grace does realise that this is a direct challenge to the Pope's jurisdiction over the English Church,' Cromwell had warned.

'Yes,' Harry had replied. 'But, thanks to this new law, appeals in spiritual matters will now be heard in England, not Rome, and I will henceforth enjoy entire power, authority and jurisdiction here. My church will be independent, with myself as its governor.' He shivered with exultation as he spoke. 'This Act effectively prohibits the hearing of my suit by the Pope and bars the Lady Katherine from appealing to Rome against any decision that an ecclesiastical court in England might take.'

Now he sat at his desk, thinking of the enormity of the step that had just been taken. No English sovereign had ever before been granted such power. He had been exalted above all other mortals, not only as king, but as the spiritual leader of his people, strong in virtue and righteousness. It was a vindication of everything that he had striven for during these last years, and he allowed himself to bask in the certain knowledge that both God and Parliament were on his side.

He stood up and walked over to the window. Below, in the privy garden, Anne was sitting in the April sunshine, deep in conversation with her brother George. He hoped she was sensible of what he had done for her. She had been chafing against the secrecy, but everything was in place now.

On Easter Eve, Anne appeared in public as queen for the first time. Glittering with diamonds and preceded by trumpeters, she came to Mass in the Chapel Royal, attended by sixty ladies. From the royal pew above, Harry watched his astonished nobles closely, determined to see that they were paying her the respect due to her rank. When the service was over, he waited by the door and urged each man to go and pay court to their new Queen. Some seemed taken aback by her sudden elevation; others looked as if they did not know whether to laugh or cry.

Harry had commanded that on Easter Sunday, in churches all

over the land, Anne was to be publicly prayed for as queen.

'Some of your subjects might be a little bewildered,' Francis Bryan observed that morning over a game of cards in the privy chamber. 'Many remain under the impression that your Grace is still married to the Lady Katherine.'

'Hmm,' grunted Harry, not in the mood to jest about it. He had been keeping an eagle eye open for any sign of dissent or opposition, but few had spoken out in Kate's favour. Even Fisher and More had been strangely silent. He wondered what they were saying in private. Only Kate's former confessor, Friar John Forest, dared openly to challenge Anne's right to be queen – and found himself promptly clapped in the Tower. And when Sir John Gage, Harry's rather unworldly Vice Chamberlain, dared to voice similar misgivings, Harry banished the silly fool from court. But theirs were lone voices among a silent majority.

Anne revelled in being queen. Her badge of the white falcon with a crown and sceptre had replaced Kate's pomegranate in all the royal palaces, on every available surface. She wore jewels displaying her initials, to exalt her family, who were now enjoying unprecedented influence. She was lavish in her charities, as a queen should be, and sponsored scholars, among them Wolsey's bastard son, which touched Harry deeply.

In the presence chamber, Harry watched, eyes narrowed, as Anne's new household of two hundred persons took their oaths of allegiance, but all seemed sensible of the honour of having been appointed to her service; in fact, there had been a frantic demand for places. He noted that the chaplains she had chosen were all reformers, and applauded her for having bidden them exhort her servants to embrace Christ's Gospel. He did not mind that she was defying the law and keeping Tyndale's English Bible in her apartments for all to read; she was quite open about it and enjoyed discussing its contents with him over dinner. There was no doubting her zeal for her faith. In public, she was rarely seen without a book of devotions in her hands.

'Katherine does not have a monopoly on piety,' she had said. 'I too will be setting a virtuous and devout example.' Harry sensed her determination to outrival her predecessor and give the lie to those who believed she was of bad character. He approved of the new rules she imposed. Her officers were to be honourable, discreet, just, and thrifty in their conduct; they had to attend Mass daily and display a virtuous demeanour. On pain of instant dismissal and perpetual banishment from court, they were forbidden to quarrel, swear or frequent brothels. The ladies were expected to be above reproach.

Anne's friendship with Cromwell, who sometimes joined them at the dinner table, pleased Harry. They were natural allies, sharing religious and political views. Harry knew that Cromwell was helping Anne to assist reformers who had fallen foul of the law and sought her protection.

Anne was at Harry's side when he kept St George's Day at Greenwich with great solemnity. The court was packed with people agog to see their new Queen. Soon afterwards, he attended the wedding of his niece, Suffolk's daughter Frances, to young Henry Grey, Marquess of Dorset, at Suffolk Place. But Anne would not go. The Duke and Duchess of Suffolk were hosting the event, and she did not want to run the gauntlet of the Duchess's hostility.

Harry was shocked when he saw his sister. Mary, whose beauty had been famed far and wide, had aged far beyond her thirty-seven years. She seemed to be holding herself stiffly, and he feared she was in pain. Her manner towards him was civil, but lacking in warmth. On any other occasion, he guessed, she would have had something tart to say to him, and he was sad to part from her on such chilly terms. He was not surprised when a worried-looking Suffolk informed him that she had gone home to Westhorpe, feeling unwell. He hoped it was just an excuse not to be at court.

That month, Archbishop Cranmer convened an ecclesiastical court at Dunstable Priory. There, he pronounced Harry's union with Kate null and void. Five days later, he declared that the King's new marriage was valid and lawful.

Tears welled in Harry's eyes when they brought him the news. He could not believe that, after all these years and the interminable procrastinating, he had been granted his greatest desire.

'Now you are truly my wife!' he told Anne, kissing her soundly and avoiding crushing her against him lest he hurt the babe, now a visible mound beneath her girdle.

'I can hardly believe it,' she breathed.

'All we need to crown our happiness is our son!' he added joyfully, patting her belly and feeling the little knave tumbling inside. 'Ha! It's a fine warrior you've got in there, darling!'

He drew her down on the window seat next to him. 'Now you can go to your coronation! I have ordered that it be more splendid than any that have gone before. It will be as if you are a queen regnant in your own right.'

The triumph was to be Anne's alone. He would not be taking part, so he was not present when she was borne along the river to the Tower amid much pageantry. Instead, he was waiting for her as she alighted from her barge, wearing cloth of gold and looking radiant. He kissed her and, in full view of his lords and bishops, and the Lord Mayor, sheriffs and aldermen, openly cupped her pregnant belly with his hands. Then he escorted her to the sumptuous apartments that had been prepared for her, where she could rest before the evening's feasting began.

Two days later, he watched her procession leave the Tower. Today, she was to make her ceremonial entry into London, travelling in procession to Westminster in a litter draped with white cloth of gold. There would be pageants and tableaux and fountains spouting free wine for the citizens. He hoped they would turn out in large numbers to see and cheer her.

That evening, she joined him at York Place.

'I trust you had a warm reception, darling,' he said, taking her into his arms.

She looked near to tears. 'It was more like a funeral than a pageant. There were large crowds, but few doffed their caps or cried "God save the Queen!" My fool yelled at them, "I think you all have scurvy heads, and dare not uncover!" And then, seeing our joint initials in the decorations, some dared to laugh, "HA! HA!" Oh, Harry, it was awful.'

Anger seized him. How dare they treat her like that! She was their Queen and deserved respect, and, by God, he would make them respect her!

'Think nothing of it, Anne. I care not a fig for those oafs. We will turn it into a triumph. Now, let us eat. You must be starving.'

'I just want to sleep,' she said. 'I am so tired. I just hope that tomorrow will be better.'

'It will,' he assured her, wishing he felt more optimistic.

On Sunday 1 June, Harry thrilled at the sight of Anne dressed for her coronation in a kirtle of crimson velvet and a traditional sideless surcoat of purple velvet furred with ermine, with a caul of pearls beneath the rich coronet on her head. He watched as she left Westminster Hall, walking beneath a cloth of gold canopy, with the Dowager Duchess of Norfolk carrying her train, as she went in procession to the Abbey opposite, attended by thirteen mitred abbots, the monks of Westminster, the entire Chapel Royal, the bishops and clergy, and the lords in their robes of estate. He looked in vain for Sir Thomas More and the Exeters; he had willed them to be there, especially More, knowing that their presence would be seen as an endorsement of Anne's queenship, but they were conspicuous by their absence. He could have wept with disappointment and chagrin.

But there was no time to fret, for he had to make his way by a private route to the Abbey, to view the ceremonies from a latticed closet, unseen by the congregation. As the crown was placed on Anne's head, he felt vindicated, certain that the child under her stomacher would be a son and heir, a reward for his taking the righteous and virtuous path to this moment.

By the time it was all over and Anne, wearing her crown, returned to Westminster Hall, Harry had seated himself in another latticed closet in the cloisters of St Stephen's Chapel, which afforded him a good view of the coronation banquet. He watched as the eight hundred guests were seated, with Anne sitting in his throne at the high marble table on the dais, served by nobles and attended by two countesses. He saw her wave away dish after dish, saw the ladies holding a rich cloth in front of her face and suspected she might be nauseous. By St George, he should never have agreed to such prolonged celebrations when she was six months gone with child. But he had wanted to honour her as no woman had been honoured before, to show his subjects how worthy she was of such reverence. Now he could not wait for it to be over, for her sake.

At last, at long last, the service of food ended and the Lord Mayor presented Anne with a gold cup full of hippocras. She sipped from it, took some of the spices served to her, then thanked the company and left the hall. When she returned to Harry at York Place, she was exhausted.

'Go to bed,' he commanded. 'From now on, sweetheart, you must take things easily and get plenty of rest.'

She smiled up at him. 'At least they did not jeer me today.'

The courtiers were diligent in paying their respects to Anne, but Harry suspected it was not because they wanted to, but because they felt obliged to comply with his wishes. Well, that would suffice for now. Once Anne had borne him a son, things would be different.

He ordered jousts in honour of the coronation in the new tiltyard at York Place, but one of his headaches came on, so he left Nicholas Carew to lead the defenders. He was well enough to preside over the banquet that followed, however, and felt a lot better by the time he could get out in the fresh air and go hunting.

It was a summer of feasting and revelry. There had been no word from Rome, and Harry was beginning to hope that the Pope had seen the wisdom in Cranmer's judgement and decided not to challenge it. He relaxed, and took his pastime in Anne's chamber, where there was music, gambling and dancing and everyone was bent on pleasure. She was great with child now, and in robust health.

Watching her engaged in sparkling conversation with Norris, Francis Weston and other gallants, Harry was confident that their child would be healthy. He could not wait for it to be born.

One afternoon, as he was relaxing at Anne's side, listening to an Italian consort playing the viols, Suffolk was suddenly at his elbow.

'Harry,' he murmured, 'I've just had word from Westhorpe. Mary is very ill, and I crave your leave to go to her.'

Harry's joyous mood dissipated. 'She is in danger?'

'I fear so. My chamberlain has warned me not to tarry.'

'Then go at once. And take her a message from me. Tell her I am sorry that there has been a coolness between us. Tell her I love her dearly and never wished to hurt her. Say I wish only to be in perfect love and friendship with her again.'

'I will,' Suffolk promised, and vanished.

Harry stared at Suffolk's letter. Mary was dead.

Tears filled his eyes as he read on. She had received his message warmly and sent him her blessing even as she lay on her death-bed. The words blurred before him and he sank into his chair, giving way to grief, remembering the times they had played together as children, Mary's unique way of wheedling him to do as she wanted, the beauty that had once radiated from her – and how he had adored his little sister. Now she was gone from him for ever.

When he broke the news to Anne, he was dismayed at her lack of sympathy.

'I will not be a hypocrite and mourn her, for she had no love for me,' she said. 'And she opposed you for years.'

'Anne, she was my sister. I loved her.'

'I am sorry for you. But don't expect me to grieve for her loss.' She left him then and returned to her merrymaking. It continued uninterrupted, with Mary's passing making barely a ripple in the life of the court.

July came, and still no word from Rome. Harry now girded his loins to do battle with Kate. He sent her former chamberlain, Lord

Mountjoy, to Ampthill to inform her officially of his marriage and order her to relinquish the title of queen.

He was on edge as he waited for Mountjoy to return. When Cromwell took him to Bridewell Palace and showed him a splendid double portrait of the French ambassadors painted by Hans Holbein, he was impressed, but found it hard to concentrate as Cromwell explained the significance of the objects in the painting.

'If you stand to the side, Sir, a skull will appear, a *memento mori* – a reminder of the transience of life. It's an anamorphosis – a distorted perspective – and very clever. You can only see the true picture from one vantage point.'

'I have rarely seen such a fine work,' Harry commented, wondering how long it would take Mountjoy to get to Ampthill and back. 'Holbein is a talented fellow.'

'A genius, Sir. I paid him to paint my portrait, and now it seems he is in demand. Everyone at court wants one. Your Grace might like to commission him to produce something for you.'

'I will think on it,' Harry said.

'It occurred to me,' Cromwell pressed on, 'that Master Holbein could be useful in another way too. It is easy for him, as an artist, to obtain entry into the houses of those whose loyalty might be suspect. Sir, I need information on certain people – those who I fear have no liking for Queen Anne.'

Harry made himself listen. 'And you think Holbein has the wits and discretion to obtain this information?'

'Undoubtedly! He desires her Grace's continuing patronage. He was overjoyed at being asked to design that new triumphal arch for her coronation and is eager to do her service in any way he can.'

'Then let him,' Harry said. 'Now, Crum, I must catch the tide and get back to Hampton Court.' With any luck, Mountjoy would be there, waiting for him.

He was, but Harry could tell from his demeanour that he did not bring good news.

'Tell me everything,' he commanded, sitting down at his black leather desk.

Mountjoy looked distressed. He had been a great favourite of Kate's, and of Harry's too, back in the early days when they had all shared a passion for Humanism and the new learning. 'When I conveyed your Grace's message to the Lady Katherine, she insisted that she was your true wife, and absolutely refused to renounce the title of queen, even when the lords of Council warned her that she might be indicted for treason. She expressed the view that Queen Anne is influencing your Grace against your true nature to set her aside. I am sorry to be the bringer of such news.'

Harry's fist crashed on the table. 'I will not brook her defiance! She will obey my laws or she will suffer for it.' Beside himself with rage, he dismissed Mountjoy and began pacing the room, aware that underlying his fury was fear that Kate might incite the Emperor to make war on him. He was so agitated that he summoned Cromwell and told him what had transpired.

'The problem, as I see it,' Cromwell said, 'is that, if the Lady Katherine is not your wife, then she is not your subject and owes you no obedience.'

'She is living in my kingdom and must obey my laws!' Harry raged. 'She must be made to see the error of her ways. I'll not stand for her defiance.'

He resolved to send her to some meaner house. Ampthill was too good for her. He settled on Buckden Towers in Huntingdonshire, further from the court, and again reduced her household. He would not have her making mischief when Anne was soon to bear his child. Nothing must be allowed to spoil the arrival of his son.

It could not be long now. That July, Harry set off on his usual progress, but did not stray far from London because he wanted to be at hand for the birth. All was progressing well.

Then came the news from Rome. It was grave. Even Cromwell's hand was trembling as he handed Harry the letter.

The Pope, having learned of the King's remarriage, had threatened to excommunicate him if he did not repudiate Anne by September.

Harry's first thought was that Anne must not know. He dared not upset her at this time. Suppressing his rage and trepidation, he told her he was going hunting, then hastened to York Place to meet with his councillors.

'I will not be intimidated,' he told them. 'I will not respond to this threat.'

They looked worried and he suddenly found himself in a long discussion as to how he could counteract the effects of the Papal command.

'My feeling,' Cromwell said at length, 'is that your Grace should use your progress to win over those who may have become disaffected by recent events. Honour them with a visit. Gain their support.'

It sounded like good advice, and Harry took it. He visited his cousin Exeter at his house at Horsley in Surrey, where, over a lavish banquet, he dropped heavy hints that he was ready to shower honours on those who showed their support for his Queen. Exeter listened politely, nodded, and declared that he would always be Harry's loyal subject. Harry next descended on Sir John Russell at Chenies in Buckinghamshire, where his host made a similar declaration of support. He left with the strong impression that he had won over two waverers.

Late in August, he rejoined Anne at Windsor and they travelled to Greenwich, where she was to take to her chamber to rest before the birth. She had a very high belly now and the babe was active. She was peevish, though, wanting her confinement to be over and fretting that something might go wrong, being painfully aware of the importance of bearing a healthy son.

Harry was understanding. He bore her complaints with patience. It was unwise to cross a gravid woman. Privately, though, he wished she would cease and be grateful for what he had done for her. She had the best care and attention, and her child would be born in luxury. He had ordered that a magnificent bed that had been part of the Duke of Longueville's ransom be taken from his treasury and placed in Anne's bedchamber.

Once he would never have imagined that he would look at another woman, but the long months of celibacy were beginning to tell.

Abstinence was not good for him at his age. He felt his virility dwindling, and that could never be allowed to happen, for he wanted many more sons to safeguard the succession.

Most nights, he lay wakeful. He had ceased sleeping with Anne even just to be close to her, for she was restless and suffering in the summer heat. He had no wish to add to her discomfort, so he stayed away, remembering how he had strayed whenever Kate was pregnant. Of course, he had strayed at other times too, but then he had not loved Kate as passionately as he loved Anne.

When he did sleep, he was troubled by lascivious dreams. In the end, he could bear it no more. He sought out Carew's wife Elizabeth, whom he had bedded years ago. She was still beautiful, and willing. He led her in the dance, with the whole court watching, and later he tumbled her in bed. Too soon, he became aware that there was gossip about them, and Elizabeth told him that Chapuys and others were encouraging her to pursue the affair to discountenance Anne. Harry was furious. Nothing must upset Anne now, at this crucial time!

Somehow, Anne found out.

'Is it true what my ladies are saying about you and Lady Carew?' she asked one day, when he arrived in her chamber with some new season's apples for her.

His good mood evaporated. 'I danced with her, that's all. What do you take me for?'

'You were seen kissing her!' she cried, fierce as a lion. 'And the gossip I heard accuses you of more than that. Do you deny it?'

'I do deny it!' he flared.

'Then you are lying!' she accused. 'I have it on good authority that you have bedded with her.'

'You would believe gossip rather than my word? By God, Anne, you try me!'

'I have good cause – admit it!' she shrieked, beside herself with fury. 'You pride yourself on your honour, but what price honour when your rod governs your royal will?'

He would not let her speak to him thus. 'Remember your dignity! When I think of what I have done for you – how I fought the whole world to have you and honoured you with my marriage! How I have showered you with gifts – look at that great bed I gave you! By God, Anne, you would not have it now, having used such words to me! You are my wife, and you must shut your eyes and endure as more worthy persons have done.'

She looked as if he had slapped her. 'Then you admit it!'

'Madam,' he said icily, 'you ought to remember that it is in my power to humble you again in a moment, more than I have raised you.'

He stalked off, aware that he should not have spoken to her like that, not in her condition. But *she* should not have upbraided him thus!

For three days he did not visit her. When she came upon him at the archery butts, he greeted her coldly. She waited until he had finished shooting, then walked back with him to the palace. He did not want her there, but he would not risk her making a scene in public.

'A year ago you were my loving servant,' she muttered. 'That man would never have spoken to me the way you did the other day.'

'We are married now,' he said. 'A husband is not a servant. As my wife you owe me obedience, and it is not your place to criticise me. I will not brook it!'

The coolness between them persisted until the day Anne took to her chamber. He could bear it no longer. He could not let her go through the ordeal to come without making this right between them. Before the ceremonies began, he bent and kissed her.

'I will come to see you, and I will pray constantly that God will send you a happy hour,' he said.

Her eyes filled with tears.

'All will be well,' he reassured her.

'What will you do while I'm in seclusion?' she asked.

'I'll be hunting hereabouts. I won't be far away. I've had letters to the nobility prepared, announcing the birth of a prince.' He tilted her chin up and kissed her again. 'Anne, I love you. Never forget that.'

Once she was immured with her women, he began planning jousts, banquets and masques to celebrate his son's birth. For the twentieth time, he consulted his physicians and astrologers, and all assured him once more that the child would be male. He had not yet made up his mind whether to call the boy Edward or Henry, but had asked the French ambassador to hold him at the font at his baptism.

At last, on 7 September, Anne's travail began. Harry could not contain his impatience or settle to anything. Too much hung upon what was happening in that bedchamber.

Almost too late, he remembered that Suffolk was getting married again today and that he had promised to attend. Clapping on his feathered bonnet, he hastened to the Chapel Royal, leaving word that he was to be summoned immediately if there was any news.

He was grateful that Anne was otherwise occupied, for she strongly disapproved of Suffolk's new marriage. He himself had mixed feelings about it, since it was mere weeks since Mary's death. Yet he understood the Duke's pressing need to remarry and beget another son to ensure that his blood inherited his considerable estates, for he was now nearing fifty, growing fat and no longer the splendid knight who had once excelled in the tiltyard; and his only son was sickly.

It was Suffolk's choice of bride that perturbed Harry, for Brandon had snatched his son's thirteen-year-old betrothed, Katherine Willoughby. It wasn't her age that troubled him, though; rather that she was the daughter of the Spanish Lady Willoughby, one of Kate's staunchest and most strident friends. Having suffered a conflict of loyalties during his marriage to Mary, Suffolk had now placed himself in an even more challenging situation, especially with his new mother-in-law. There was no accounting for what lust did to a man, Harry thought grimly. No doubt the wags would be saying that the Duke had done a service to those ladies who were reproached for marrying again immediately after the death of their husbands!

He could not concentrate on the ceremony. As soon as it had ended, he bestowed a kiss on the little bride's cheek, slapped Suffolk on the back and hurried to his privy chamber. And there was Anne's chamberlain, Lord Burgh, waiting for him.

'Your Grace, the Queen has been brought to bed.'

He knew at once that the news was not what he had been hoping for. 'Does the child live? What is it?'

'A healthy princess, Sir.'

His first thought was that God had abandoned him entirely. His disappointment was unbearable. How could those doctors and astrologers have so confidently predicted it would be a son? By St George, they would hear about this!

Then he remembered Anne, who must be feeling as crushed as he was. 'How is the Queen?'

Lord Burgh smiled. 'Well, Sir. It was an easy travail.'

'I must go to her,' Harry said.

Making his way to her apartments, he reasoned to himself that the child was strong and healthy and had birthed easily. That augured well for the future, didn't it?

Anne looked terrified. She was shaking.

'Darling!' he said. 'Thank God you are come through this safely.' He bent over the bed and kissed her, then peered into the cradle. 'Hello, little one,' he said, and picked up the sleeping infant, tenderly kissing the little head. She had the Tudor red hair, his Roman nose and her mother's narrow face and pointed chin. 'May God bless you!' He could sense the palpable relief in the room. What had they all expected – that he would deny his own child?

'Sir,' Anne faltered, 'I am so sorry I did not bear you a son.'

'You have given me a healthy child,' he said. 'You and I are both young, and by God's grace, boys will follow.'

She started to cry.

'Darling . . .' Harry gave the child to the midwife and took Anne in his arms. 'I am proud of you. I would rather beg from door to door than forsake you.'

'Thank you!' she sobbed, laughing and crying at the same time.

He let her go and reclaimed the infant. 'We will call her Elizabeth, after my mother,' he said.

'By a happy coincidence, it's my mother's name as well,' Anne said. 'The perfect choice!'

Harry kissed the child and laid her back to sleep, nodding to the rockers to come forward. 'Now I will leave you to rest, darling. I have the christening to arrange.'

'What of those letters you had prepared?' Anne asked.

'There is room to amend "prince" to "princess",' he said. 'They will go off tonight.'

'When will you hold the tournament?'

'I've decided not to.' He couldn't face it; it had been too closely associated in his mind with the birth of a prince. 'But we will have a splendid christening. Until we have a son, Anne, Elizabeth is my heir, and all must recognise her as such.'

When she was three days old, Elizabeth was carried in a splendid procession to her christening in the church of the Observant Friars at Greenwich.

Harry was determined that the world would acknowledge her as his heir until such time as she had a brother. In October, a deputation of lords was sent to inform his daughter Mary that she must no longer style herself princess. If she proved obedient, she could retain her household and her beloved governess Lady Salisbury.

He was shocked when his councillors brought back a letter for him, in which she defiantly refused to relinquish her title and censured him in such strong terms that even Chapuys, he felt, would say she had gone too far.

Harry was incandescent. He ordered that Mary leave Beaulieu, a house she loved, and move to Hertford Castle. Lady Salisbury wrote, pleading for him to be merciful. Mary was under great strain. Her health was declining. She was plagued by headaches, toothache, palpitations, depression and women's ailments. Harry closed his mind to these excuses. If Mary was suffering, it was her own fault. She had but to obey her father and her King, as was her duty, and all would be well. Her fate lay in her own hands.

He found distraction in the wedding of his son Richmond to

Norfolk's daughter, Lady Mary Howard. The bride was a member of Anne's household and a staunch advocate of reform, and Richmond was close friends with her brother Surrey. Anne had brokered this marriage; it was a triumph for her, allying her blood once more with that of the royal house, and a slap in the face for the Duchess of Norfolk, who had opposed it and was stout in her support of Kate.

Watching the young pair making their vows, both of them just fourteen, Harry was glad he had commanded that they wait a couple of years before consummating their union. He had never forgotten the fate of his brother Arthur, whose death he now believed had been hastened by overindulgence in the marriage bed – even though Kate had always denied it. He was taking no chances. His son was too precious to him.

For all that Anne had secured this great match for her uncle's daughter, there was little love lost between them these days. The Duke had clashed with her on several occasions and waxed vocal about what he called her insufferable pride. Last month, he'd complained to Harry that she had used more insulting language to him than one would to a dog, obliging him to leave the room before he exploded. He was so offended that he was seizing every opportunity to heap abuse on her in public; he had even called her 'the great whore' in Cromwell's hearing. Harry was vexed with them both. Once, he would have leapt to Anne's defence, but he had to admit that she was becoming increasingly overbearing, and Norfolk was not the first courtier she had offended. But he had too much to preoccupy him to engage in a battle over who had said what to whom.

'I have a great gift for you.' Anne gave Harry an arch smile as she seated herself at the dinner table in his private closet. 'I am with child again!'

'Anne!' He rose and pulled her up into his arms. 'You are certain?'

'Oh, yes. And this time, we must pray, it will be a boy!'

'A son for England!' He kissed her tenderly on the lips, willing it to be so.

'It is early days,' she cautioned. 'Let us keep this precious news to ourselves until I have quickened.'

'Of course, darling,' he agreed. He would have given her the moon had she asked for it.

In December, when Elizabeth was three months old, Harry set up a large household for her at Hatfield in Hertfordshire. Lady Margaret Bryan, who had had charge of the Princess Mary in infancy, was appointed her governess. Anne was stoical about being parted from her baby, and content to receive regular reports of her progress.

'We can visit her whenever we wish,' Harry said. 'Hatfield is not too far north of London. And it is fitting that my heir has her own establishment.'

There remained the problem of his other daughter. Mary was still refusing to give up her title of princess. She would not give place to Elizabeth or acknowledge her as their father's successor. Nor would she recognise Harry's marriage to Anne. Well, she must be taught a lesson!

Harry commanded that her household be disbanded; Lady Salisbury was dismissed, and Mary was sent to live with her half-sister. A new governess was appointed, Anne's aunt, Lady Shelton, and Anne made it very clear to her that she was not to spare the rod.

When Mary fell ill, it tugged at Harry's heartstrings, but he would not allow her mother to visit her. Instead, he sent his own physician. He himself would not see Mary when he went to visit Elizabeth, not while she was being so disobedient, and he shut his mind to the misery she must be feeling. After all, it was her own fault!

Chapter 25

1534

It had been, despite everything, a merry Christmas and Harry kept a great court. At New Year, Anne presented him with an exquisite fountain of gold, studded with rubies, diamonds and pearls, from which water spouted from the teats of three naked women.

'Master Holbein designed it,' she told him, kneeling on the bed in her nightgown as he admired his gift. He would have liked to tumble her then, but dared not do so for fear of hurting the child.

'Thank you,' he whispered hoarsely. 'You make me very happy.'

Nothing must be allowed to prejudice the coming heir's right to the throne. In March, Parliament passed an Act settling the succession on the Princess Elizabeth and formally disinheriting the Lady Mary.

At Harry's insistence, every loyal subject, when required, was to swear an oath recognising him as Supreme Head, Anne as his Queen and Elizabeth as his heir; and commissioners were sent out to administer it to all who held public office. Most people took the oath.

Kate and Mary both refused.

'You should send them to the Tower!' Anne cried, shrill.

'By St George, I would, but for the fact that the Emperor might declare war.'

Anne pushed aside the baby bonnet she was embroidering. 'Charles won't make war on you. He has his hands full fighting off the Turks on his eastern borders.'

'Who knows what action he would take in defence of his own blood? In his eyes, Mary is the true heir to England. He sees me as the Antichrist. And he has great resources and many generals who could lead an invasion. No, Anne, I will not use force!'

Anne opened her mouth to protest, but, to Harry's relief, Cromwell was announced.

'Your Graces.' He bowed to them both. 'Sir, I am sorry to tell you that Sir Thomas More and Bishop Fisher have declined to swear the oath.'

Harry rose and strode over to the window, trying to master himself. He had expected Fisher to refuse. But More – More had been his friend. He was known throughout Christendom for his integrity. Where he led, others might follow. It was a terrible betrayal. Nevertheless, Harry had to admit he had constrained him to it. He had promised to leave him alone and not press him on his Great Matter. But More's silence had been more than he could countenance.

'What reason did they give?' he asked at length.

'What reason *can* they give?' Anne sniffed.

Cromwell shrugged. 'The Bishop reiterated what he has said all along, that your Grace's marriage to the Lady Katherine is valid and he cannot swear it to be otherwise. Sir Thomas would not say why he refused the oath. He said only that he is your Grace's faithful subject. He says no harm, he thinks no harm, he wishes only good to everybody. And he said that if this was not enough to keep a man alive, in good faith, he longed not to live.'

Harry swallowed, feeling sick. 'Then the law must take its course. Let them be committed to the Tower. And Crum, question them both. See if you can make them see reason.'

'There is still no moving Fisher,' Cromwell reported two weeks later. 'He is mired in his views and stubborn. He declares that your Grace is not, and can never be, the Supreme Head on earth of the Church of England. And he refused to acknowledge your marriage to Queen Anne. His defiance can only be construed as treasonous. But Sir Thomas . . . We've interrogated him several times now, Norfolk, Cranmer and I, and all we get from him is silence.'

Seated at his desk, Harry sank his head in his hands. He had prayed constantly that More would come with him. His support would be immeasurably valuable.

'Does he say nothing at all?'

'He comments on the fine weather. He did say he has always looked first upon God and then upon the King, according to the lesson your Grace taught him when he first entered your service. Otherwise, he sits there mute.'

'His silence speaks volumes!' Harry hissed. 'It might as well be a battle cry for those who oppose me.'

'We have warned him that he is being disloyal. Norfolk told him in no uncertain terms that it was perilous to strive with princes. He was unmoved.'

'Keep the pressure on,' Harry instructed. 'Do whatever it takes. I want him on my side.'

The Pope, he learned soon afterwards, was most definitely not on his side. Even Cromwell's hands shook as he showed him the Papal bull pronouncing sentence. Harry could barely take it in. *The marriage always has stood, and still does stand, firm and canonical, and the aforesaid Henry, King of England, is and shall be bound to the matrimonial society and cohabitation with the said Lady Katherine, his true wife.* He was forbidden to remarry on pain of excommunication.

'It's a declaration of war,' he said, forcing a grim smile. 'A gauntlet thrown down. Well, if Clement thinks to make me bow to his will, he can think again. His bulls have no force in England now. There will be no turning the clock back.'

Brave words, yes. But they concealed the dismay he was striving to suppress. Because there was a part of him that had been hoping that, even now, all could be mended between himself and Rome. Yet Clement, the fool, had decided otherwise.

'This will have repercussions,' Cromwell said darkly. 'It will lend strength to the Lady Katherine and her supporters and leave England open to the Emperor's wrath.'

'Charles will not invade England, not for his aunt,' Harry said, more bullishly than he felt.

'He may change his mind if the Pope excommunicates your Grace. That could leave you isolated and friendless, shunned by the rest of Christendom.'

For a moment, Harry felt chilled. The prospect of being cut off from God and the consolations of his faith would at one time have struck terror into him. But it could not affect him now or weaken his resolve.

'Then I'll have to make friends with the Protestants in Germany!' he jested.

He was determined to show a righteous face to the world, resolved to demonstrate that he cared not a fig for Clement's sentence, and that his kingly will was not to be opposed.

There was a nun of Kent, one Elizabeth Barton, who, for all her lowliness, had been a thorn in his side for some time now. She claimed to have angelic visions and had repeatedly prophesied doom for him and Anne. She was crazed, of course, but foolish people heeded her, and he could not allow that. He'd had her brought before Cranmer to be examined. She'd been warned not to incite the people with her so-called prophecies, but she ignored the command, and was hauled before the Archbishop again. That time, she admitted she had never had a vision in her life. Harry had sent her and her associates to the Tower and made them do public penance at Paul's Cross before being returned to prison.

And that, he had thought, was the end of the matter. But no. Freed from the Tower, Elizabeth Barton had continued to make her treasonable prophecies. So he had her arrested again. His patience had run out and he meant to make an example of her.

'Put her on trial,' he commanded Cromwell. 'By pretending that she works miracles, she has seduced the Princess Dowager and the Lady Mary into believing in her nonsense, and incited them to disobedience.' Actually, there wasn't much proof of that, but he was convinced it was true. Cromwell had done his best to draw from the nun whether Queen Katherine had had any doings with her, but she would admit to none.

Convicted of treason, Elizabeth Barton and her associates were drawn on hurdles to the gallows at Tyburn, where, before huge crowds, she was hanged until dead, then beheaded. The men suffered the horrors of hanging, drawing and quartering.

Harry was aware of the shocked reaction, not only at court, but in the country at large. This was the first blood spilt as a result of his Great Matter, and it was the blood of a religious. It might not be the last. Let the people tremble. They now knew where opposition to the King would lead.

Anne was radiant with health. The doctors and astrologers were predicting a healthy son. Harry knew better than to rely on their forecasts, but he shared their optimism. It must be a prince this time. There would be such rejoicing that no one would ever think of questioning his legitimacy.

To mark this auspicious pregnancy, he ordered a medal of Anne to be struck, inscribed with her portrait and her motto, 'The most happy'. He had commanded that every care be taken of her. When she complained that her morning rest was being disturbed by the screeching of his peacocks and the pelican that had been a gift from the Americas, he persuaded Sir Henry Norris to remove them to his house near Greenwich Palace.

At Eltham, where Harry had spent so much of his boyhood, the Queen's apartments were being converted into a nursery with a great chamber, a dining chamber, a dressing chamber and a bedchamber. He commissioned his goldsmith to make a silver cradle to Holbein's design, adorned with Tudor roses and golden figures of Adam and Eve, and made up with bedding embroidered with gold. A cloth-of-gold layette was stowed away in a chest, awaiting the Prince who would wear it.

Harry had been planning another visit to Calais that July, but decided to postpone it because Anne's pregnancy prevented her from accompanying him. Instead, he went on a progress. It took him to Guildford, where she joined him. And it was there that the child came early.

It was all over within two hours. When they told him that his son was born, he waved them away and hastened to Anne's chamber, joy bubbling up inside him. At last! At long last!

He was shocked to find her racked with sobs, huddled in the bed. He knew at once what it betokened and could not hide his devastating disappointment or an irrational sense of betrayal. If this got out, he would lose face entirely in the eyes of his enemies.

'I am so sorry!' she sobbed. 'He came too early.'

'Where is he?' Harry demanded.

'Here, your Grace.' The midwife nervously handed him the shrouded bundle and he pulled the covering aside to reveal the still little face beneath. The babe was so beautiful, so perfect.

'Oh, God, my son, my little son,' he murmured brokenly, tears streaming down his face. 'Take him.' He thrust the body back into the midwife's arms, mastered himself with an effort, then bent his gaze on every soul in the room.

'None of you will speak of this to anyone, on pain of severe punishment,' he commanded. 'If you are asked, you must say that the Queen miscarried. Do not reveal that it was a son. Do you all understand?'

The women nodded fearfully.

'I will leave you to rest,' Harry said to Anne.

He did not want to be with her. He left Guildford and rode towards Woodstock, wondering why he had moved Heaven and earth to have a woman who could not bear him the son he needed. And after all he had done for her! What a fool he had been.

Anne mended quickly. By the end of July, she was able to rejoin Harry on the progress, yet he could not warm towards her, or lust after her in the old way. He returned to her bed because it was his duty. It was a joyless experience that left him feeling bereft. How had his passion died? What had happened to it?

Still feeling betrayed and ill done by, he sought solace in the arms of a maid-of-honour, Joan Ashley. Love had nothing to do with it, just pure physical need.

Frustration and resentment made him even more determined to justify himself to the world and crush any opposition. That autumn, he suppressed the Observant Friars, who had often spoken out against his nullity suit and the royal supremacy. The friary church at Greenwich where he and Kate had once worshipped was converted into a mill for the royal armoury.

Harry's enemy, Clement, was dead. He felt not a pang; the old fool had had much to answer for. All he knew of the new Pope, Paul III, was that he was an ageing reprobate with dubious morals and a clutch of bastards – the kind of cleric who had given the Church of Rome a bad reputation. Again, he was filled with a sense of righteousness, for having delivered his people from such iniquity.

In November, an Act of Supremacy was passed by Parliament, enshrining in law Harry's title of Supreme Head of the Church of England and finally severing the latter from the Church of Rome. For it was clear now that there was to be no agreement with the Holy See. Clement had not gone so far as to excommunicate Harry, but he had threatened it. It remained to be seen what Pope Paul would do. Let him do his worst! Harry seethed. See if he cared! Now that he had broken with the Vatican, the mouthings of the Bishop of Rome – as the Pope was henceforth to be known in England – no longer held any force in his realm. Henceforth, it was he, Harry the King, who would be in control of church matters and religious doctrine. He was God's deputy on earth, a latter-day King David or King Solomon, responsible for both the temporal and spiritual welfare of his subjects. He was leading his people out of darkness into the light. Now the word of God was to obey the King, not the Bishop of Rome. He preferred to forget that he had once written a tract defending the latter's authority.

Anne, Cranmer, Cromwell and all those who had pressed for reform applauded what he had done.

'Any bishop who shows himself reluctant to accept the change shall be made to do so,' Cromwell assured Harry one evening over dinner – Cromwell, whose jurisdiction over spiritual affairs was now second only to his master's, and who was zealous in implementing the new laws. 'My men are watching,' he grinned and poured more wine into Harry's goblet. 'I know some think me an emissary of Satan, but I will not brook anything that smacks of Popery.'

Harry helped himself to more roast beef. 'There are those who would have me take an even harder line. A few would have me abolish the Order of the Garter and do away with St George as England's patron saint, but I will never go that far. I am a devout Catholic; I deplore Luther and his Protestant heresies. But I have to maintain a balance between the radicals who are urging more sweeping reforms and creeping ever closer to heresy, and the conservatives who want to turn the clock back.'

'It is important to be consistent,' Cromwell advised. 'Your Grace needs to make it clear where you stand.'

'Crum, there are things I will never change because they are unchangeable and the essence of our religion. I will never deny that the bread and the wine become the actual body and blood of Christ during the Mass, as the heretics do. I believe in Purgatory and that those in holy orders should be celibate. I will maintain the Latin rituals and ceremonies. I am no iconoclast, and I intend to keep the images in my chapels. But I am not in favour of extreme unction, individual confession or the mystery attached to ordination to the priesthood. If I must, I will punish unrepentant Lutherans for heresy and Papists for treason. I will never cease to proclaim my zeal for the faith with all the resources of my mind and body. As for consistency, see this.' He held up before Cromwell's eyes the gold chain around his neck, which bore the Latin inscription *I prefer to die rather than change my mind*.

He could see from Cromwell's expression that the minister was not happy. Doubtless he would have had him go further. 'So religious observances are to remain largely unchanged, Sir?'

'Yes, Crum, but I want to see more emphasis on preaching. The right kind of preaching. Cranmer must ensure that preachers new to the court avoid controversial issues and speak for no more than one and a half hours.'

'Be assured that I will use every resource at my disposal to promote and glorify this New Monarchy your Grace has fashioned. The whole realm will give thanks for being blessed with the noblest King who ever reigned in England.'

Harry smiled. He wanted his subjects to see him as he saw himself: the father of the English nation, a man of princely goodness and honour, through whose virtue, learning and courage his kingdom was being newly brought from thraldom to freedom.

He knew he could rely on Cromwell. He was aware that Master Secretary had begun to manipulate the machinery of government to ensure that Parliament was packed with those sympathetic to the new order, so that there would be little opposition to the momentous changes being introduced. He had wrought such a close alliance of the monarch, the peerage and Parliament that protest would be virtually useless.

On the table, there sat a small bag of new coins; Cromwell had brought them to show him. They bore an image of the King as Roman emperor. And Harry's new Great Seal showed him seated on an antique throne as Supreme Head of the Church. An Imperial crown was being added to the royal arms to signify that he recognised no higher power than his own, save God.

He applauded Cromwell's brilliant idea to revive the cult of King Arthur. From boyhood, Harry had thrilled to the tales and exploits of his famous ancestor, and had tried, when he was young and devoted to romance, to model himself on England's hero. But now, Arthur was to be hailed as the forerunner of the New Monarchy.

'Arthur owned a seal proclaiming him emperor of Britain and Gaul,' Cromwell had informed Harry. 'In assuming the imperial mantle of this realm, your Grace is merely reviving his ancient title and dignity, as is your right. For a thousand years, England's sovereignty has mistakenly been subjugated to Rome by your royal predecessors; now you have redeemed it.'

Harry's heart had swelled with pride at that. He had freed England from bondage. It was being made clear in the flood of tracts and pamphlets proclaiming his heroic virtues and moral superiority; that was Cromwell's work too. The minister was recruiting preachers, artists, craftsmen, writers, poets, playwrights and historians to use their talents to advertise and glorify the New Monarchy. They were to portray the King as semi-divine, the image of God upon earth. Harry's subjects must be taught that he was not a mortal man, but a being of much higher estate, in whose presence one could not stand without trembling.

'I am indebted to you, Crum,' Harry said now. 'You have helped to make it possible for me to realise my full potential as a ruler. But let us not forget to thank God, who has not only made me King by inheritance, but has given me, in abundance, the wisdom and other graces necessary for a prince to direct his affairs to his honour and glory.'

He drew from his doublet a small, exquisite miniature showing Solomon receiving the Queen of Sheba. 'Holbein presented this to me today. I commissioned it. The figure of Solomon represents myself. See, above the throne, the words I chose: "Blessed be the Lord thy God, which delighteth in thee to set thee on His throne, to be King for the Lord thy God". The Queen of Sheba kneels in homage; she symbolises the Church of England.'

'It's very fine, and says it all,' Cromwell declared. 'Holbein is a genius. Gardiner will love it!'

They smiled at each other. Gardiner was no longer the firebrand who had been so zealous in pursuing Harry's nullity suit, but a staunch conservative opposed to the new order. Indeed, he had allied himself with Norfolk, who had told Harry in Council, in no uncertain terms, what he thought of the recent changes. 'I have never read the Scriptures, nor never will,' he'd declared. 'It was merry in England before this new learning came up. For my part, I would that all things were as they were in times past.'

Harry had let it go. Norfolk was loyal, through and through, even though Cromwell thought him a pernicious influence and was making every effort to oust him from court. Norfolk represented the old feudal order, and there could never be anything but rivalry between him and the man he regarded as an upstart. But Harry would not dismiss him. After Master Secretary, Norfolk was the most experienced and respected member of the Council.

It was he whom Harry chose, in November, to receive King Francis' special envoy, the Admiral of France, who had come to help restore good relations between England and France, which had deteriorated since Henry's break with Rome, for the Most Christian King had felt unable to support his brother monarch.

Harry ordered that the Admiral be lodged at Bridewell Palace, entertained by Norfolk and Suffolk, and invited to dine with the King.

But there was Anne, at his elbow. 'The Admiral is acquainted with me. We met in Calais in 1532. Yet he has not followed the practice of previous ambassadors and sent me a courteous message of goodwill. And I had planned to give a banquet in his honour!'

Harry sighed. Anne was always complaining these days. He was weary of it. But he would not have his Queen slighted. When he next saw his guest, he dropped a heavy hint that he should pay his respects to her. The Admiral took the hint, but he was chillingly correct in her presence and did not participate in the dancing and tennis she had arranged for him. Instead, he struck up a friendship with Chapuys, which alarmed Anne greatly.

Worse was to come. Harry could not believe his ears when the Admiral proposed a marriage between the Lady Mary and the Dauphin, ignoring Elizabeth entirely.

'Your master would wed his heir to a bastard?' Harry retorted.

The Admiral held his gaze, unflinching. 'If your Majesty does not agree to the match, my master will marry his son to the Emperor's daughter.' He smiled, showing that he knew, as well as Harry, that such an alliance would leave England isolated in Europe at this critical time. Harry was mortified, and dared not contemplate how Anne would react.

'Then let him,' he said, anger surging through him. 'Maybe he would like to betroth his son Charles to the Princess Elizabeth.'

The Admiral was unmoved. 'I think not, Sir,' he replied.

* * *

'The King of France is no longer my friend!' Anne railed, when Harry related this to her afterwards, having steeled himself to do so. He watched her ranting at Francis and wondered again what had become of the young woman who had bewitched him all those years ago. No wonder he was still turning to Mistress Ashley for comfort. She was pretty and pliant, and knew how to pleasure a man – and when to keep her mouth shut.

He was growing weary of the whole arrogant Boleyn tribe. When Anne's sister Mary appeared at court noticeably pregnant and revealed that she had married – for love, if you please – a landless nobody called William Stafford, Harry was ready to bow to Anne's demand that both be banished from the court. But he would not permit Wiltshire to abandon his daughter to penury and insisted that he support her. And there was Anne, complaining again . . .

It was hard to show a hearty manner to the world. The tensions in his marriage now seemed to dominate the court. No longer was it a haven of chivalry and revelry, but a tilting ground for religious disputes and factional rivalry. It was partly his own fault, of course, but the reforms he had introduced had been necessary, even if they had cost him dearly. His treasury was alarmingly depleted. Was ever man so beset?

When he sent for Joan that night, thinking to lay his cares on her soft bosom, his usher came racing back up the secret stair to his bedchamber. 'I found the lady packing her gear, Sir,' he reported.

'Packing?'

'Yes, Sir. She said Lady Rochford had told her that the Queen had commanded her to go home.'

Anne knew! How dare she interfere!

Harry pulled on his furred night robe and barged through the door that led from his lodging to hers, beside himself with rage. When he charged into her bedchamber, thrusting aside her women, he saw the smile on her face fade.

'You ordered Mistress Ashley to go home,' he flung at her.

'Yes,' she answered defiantly. 'I will not tolerate your slut in my household.'

Henry felt himself flush. 'Remember, Madam, it is I who decree who shall, and who shall not, be in your household. Do not forget what I have done for you, with so little by way of reward. You have good reason to be content with that for, were I to begin again, I would certainly not do as much, and you ought to consider where you came from and how high I have raised you.'

Anne drew breath to complain, but he forestalled her. 'I'm banishing Lady Rochford from court.'

'You should not be punishing me and my kin!' she hissed. 'You're the adulterer!'

'I am the King and you will respect me as such,' Harry shouted and stormed out of the room. His temper simmering, he took his revenge by inviting a number of beautiful ladies to a feast in the Admiral's honour, among them Joan Ashley. Let that be a lesson to Anne! When they were all gathered, he saw Anne stiffen as she caught sight of her maid-of-honour. Later, when he paused to speak to Joan, he heard his wife's hysterical laughter ringing out and turned to see their guest staring at her with astonishment. Then she was speaking in his ear and looking Harry's way. By St George, what was the woman doing now? Appealing to France for help? He would not put it past her.

Chapter 26

1535

'The church of which your Grace is now Supreme Head possesses untapped wealth,' Cromwell said, steepling his hands on his desk. 'Make me your vice regent in spiritual matters and I will make you the richest monarch England has ever seen.'

Harry raised his eyebrows. 'And how will you do that, Crum?'

'By suppressing the monasteries.' Cromwell smiled. 'Your Grace looks askance, but it is no new thing. Your illustrious ancestor, Henry V, did it a century ago, and Cardinal Wolsey closed down some small religious houses. Even the Pope once professed himself willing to sanction the closure of some of our English abbeys. Sir, the monastic orders are in decline: no new house has been founded since Syon Abbey more than a century ago, apart from six friaries of the Observant Franciscans.'

Untold possibilities were opening up in Harry's mind. Already he was itching to find out how much profit he would acquire from these closures.

'I take it you are suggesting closing down only the smaller houses,' he said, fingering his beard.

'To begin with.' Cromwell's smile was impish. Harry caught his drift.

'It would be politic not to declare your true intentions too soon,' the secretary advised.

Harry rose and walked over to the mullioned window, looking out on the snow-covered gardens. 'So how do we go about this?'

'I will order a survey of all the religious houses in England in order to discover any abuses within them, and – more importantly – to establish the possessions of each.'

'Capital!' Harry applauded.

It was going to take a long time; the survey must be completed before the closures began. The results of the visitations were being recorded in a great book called the *Valor Ecclesiasticus*. Harry could barely contain his impatience.

Cromwell kept him informed of the progress that was being made.

'Your Grace's commissioners have exposed much laxity and several cases of fraud, with so-called holy relics being proved fakes. We've had reports of monks and nuns fornicating, or living worldly lives, against the Rule, and sad cases of houses being too poor to justify their existence. Some religious recite by rote Latin prayers that they do not understand. And several communities clearly oppose the royal supremacy. They're hotbeds of Papistry.'

Harry was standing at the window. The reports were all grist to the mill, but a disquieting inner voice was questioning whether the commissioners had found what they had been told to find. But that could not be, for some had written of holy lives being led and good husbandry and financial management. Generally, however, the findings of the visitations appeared to support Cromwell's arguments for suppression.

When Harry told Anne of his intentions later, over supper, he was surprised to find her opposing them. 'Why shut down the abbeys? Reform is a better alternative than closure.'

'Reform will not fill my treasury,' Harry retorted, unable to forget that Cromwell had promised to make him the richest of kings. With the wealth and vast lands of the monasteries in his possession, he could not only replenish his treasury, but also reward those who had shown their loyalty to the new order. 'Besides, I will not brook lightness and misconduct in the religious houses.'

Anne said nothing, but he had the sense that battle lines were being drawn.

They had quarrelled again recently when she had pushed her cousin Madge Shelton in his path and he'd taken the bait. He knew why she had done it: if he was unfaithful, better by far that it was with one who would stay loyal to her. But the frivolous creature had started giving herself airs and graces, and Anne had quickly grown resentful and taken to upbraiding him again. She was now going about playing the virtuous wife, with an air of suffering he was determined to ignore.

Early in May, the Boleyns were out in force at Tyburn to witness the first executions of those who had refused to swear the Oath of Supremacy. Among the condemned were the Prior of the London Charterhouse and a monk of Syon Abbey; both were renowned throughout Europe for their learning and integrity, but it did not save them from the dreadful sentence of hanging, drawing and quartering. Harry would have liked to be present, and had considered going masked, like some of his courtiers, but thought better of it. Afterwards, he was glad he had not been there to witness the angry reactions of the bystanders.

Anne shrugged when he came to her chamber and told her of the day's proceedings. 'They could have spared themselves the agony,' she observed.

He noticed she had been reading Miles Coverdale's new English translation of the Bible, which had been dedicated to them both. She was keen to see the ban lifted on English Bibles, but Harry was not ready to sanction it. Yet, when he took the book from her and saw its frontispiece, which was clearly Holbein's work, he was impressed, for there he was, in the guise of an Old Testament king, enthroned above the lords spiritual and temporal, holding a sword and a Bible, which he was handing down to three kneeling bishops.

It was radical and provocative, for hitherto, bishops had conferred spiritual authority on kings, not the other way round. Once more, he found himself admiring Anne's audacity – and her vision. It had been one of the things that had brought them together, and it might yet save them now.

That evening, they watched a satirical play parodying the Apocalypse.

'It's by Master Moryson, Cromwell's man,' Harry murmured to Anne. 'Crum believes that plays are the perfect means of setting forth to the people the abomination and wickedness of the Bishop of Rome, and all the monks, friars, nuns and suchlike, and to declare to them the obedience my subjects owe me.'

Anne's eyes gleamed as she watched the Four Horsemen cavorting menacingly on the stage. Again, he felt warm towards her. Maybe they would make a son this year.

Harry was beginning to regret having made that alliance with Francis.

'He's done nothing for me!' he complained to his Council. 'I have not forgotten his refusal to consider the Princess Elizabeth as a bride for his son.'

'Most of Christendom does not regard her as legitimate,' pointed out Norfolk, blunt as ever.

'I don't need you to tell me that!' Harry barked. 'But I thought Francis would be a bulwark between me and my critics. Now he has joined them.'

'But without France, who in Europe will befriend your Grace?' Cranmer asked.

Harry hesitated. 'I am beginning to favour a new alliance with the Emperor.'

Several pairs of eyes were staring at him in astonishment.

'There are insurmountable obstacles to that,' Suffolk pointed out.

Cromwell smiled. 'Sometimes, my lord Duke, it is politic to take a pragmatic approach. Since the falling-out with the Emperor, England's trade has suffered.'

'Master Secretary's merchant friends have been at him,' Norfolk muttered.

'Indeed, they have,' Cromwell said smoothly, 'and we would do well to heed them because on their enterprise rests England's wealth. The Emperor can only be relieved that his Grace's friendship with King Francis has cooled. He too might be glad of a new alliance.'

'Not with his aunt banished to the country,' Norfolk tutted.

'She has only to say the word and her troubles will be over,' Harry said testily. 'Really, I would not have her be an obstacle to a new accord with Charles. You may have noticed that I have been making a great fuss of Chapuys to win his goodwill.' He frowned, remembering how wary the ambassador had been. Damn the man, he was still setting himself up as Kate and Mary's champion!

That week Henry had the oath put again to Fisher and More, and again they refused to take it.

'They are traitors and deserve death!' Anne reminded him, again and again, desperate for their voices to be silenced for ever.

'They will be tried,' he told her. 'The law will take its course.'

'No one must challenge the legitimacy of our son,' she said.

He looked at her, his eyes widening. 'Our son? You mean . . . ?'

'Yes, Sir, I am with child!' she told him triumphantly.

He took her hand and kissed it. 'I thank God!' he declared. 'You must look after yourself, Anne. We dare not risk losing this one.' He wished he could feel more optimism, but he had been here many times before.

His mind was torn; he could settle to nothing. In his heart, he knew that prosecuting More and Fisher, two of the best men in his kingdom when they weren't setting their faces against him, was a very serious step to take. If they were condemned, as the law required, would he be condemned too, by the rest of Christendom?

Yet they had refused to support him, refused the oath, and doubtless were inciting others against him. He had not forgotten that Fisher had been one of those who had supported the Nun of Kent. How could he let them get away with it, when others had died for their disobedience? The answer was that he couldn't. After all, it was not his fault that they were traitors.

Seized with sudden rage, he sent for Cromwell. 'I will not tolerate More and Fisher defying me. They must face the consequences. Have them put on trial!'

* * *

Cromwell had just brought Harry the news that Fisher had been condemned to death when an usher entered, bowing, and handed him a note.

Cromwell raised his eyebrows. 'Your Grace will be interested to hear that the Bishop of Rome has made Fisher a cardinal. His red hat is on its way.'

Harry snorted. 'He'll have to wear it on his shoulders then, for, by God, I'll have his head before it gets here!'

Later, when he was alone and his anger had cooled, he stood at his window watching Anne playing with her dogs in the garden. He hoped she was sensible of all he had done for her.

As Cromwell entered his study, Harry looked up from his desk and laid down his quill.

'It is done?'

'Aye, Sir. The Bishop looked the very image of death as they led him out to his execution. It's what months of rigorous confinement do to a man.'

Harry steeled himself. He would not show pity.

'He emerged wearing his finest clothes, declaring that it was his wedding day. On the scaffold, he insisted he was dying to preserve the honour of God.'

'What of the honour of his King?' Harry flared.

'The world knows whose cause is the more righteous,' Cromwell said smoothly.

It did not take long for Harry to discover that he was wrong. There was widespread outrage at the beheading of such a saintly man, and a bishop at that.

When Anne lost the child, in a welter of blood and tears, Harry's heart sank like a leaden weight. Was it a judgement on him? But he could not believe that. He had done God's work in his kingdom and he was reforming a corrupt church. He had freed himself from an incestuous wedlock. How could the Almighty frown on him?

He sounded out Cromwell, in the strictest secrecy, on the possibility of an annulment.

'Your Grace,' Cromwell said, seeming not at all perturbed, 'I am of the opinion that dissolving your marriage would be seen as an admission that you were wrong to divorce the Princess Dowager. Half of Christendom would expect you to return to her, on the grounds that she is your lawful wife.'

Harry stroked his beard and sighed. 'You are right, Crum. I don't want another scandal. And I have gone too far now to turn back.'

Sir Thomas More was tried at the beginning of July and also condemned to death.

'Fortunately,' Cromwell reported, not noticing how stricken Harry was feeling, 'our new Solicitor General, Master Rich, was able to give evidence against him, after your Grace sent him to take away Sir Thomas' books.'

It had been a cruel deprivation, Harry reflected, but necessary, for it had been a warning that worse would follow if More did not take the oath.

Cromwell was in full flight, in a triumphant mood. 'Rich pretended friendship to him, He put a case to him that, if it were enacted by Parliament that he, Rich, should be king and that it should be treason to deny it, would it be an offence to contravene that Act? Sir Thomas stated that it would be treason. Then Rich proposed another case, arguing that since your Grace is constituted Supreme Head of the Church upon earth, why should not Master More accept you as such? More said that the case was not the same, because Parliament can make a king, and depose him, but a subject cannot be bound in the case of supremacy, for the King cannot make himself head of the Church. Thus, he condemned himself out of his own mouth. He denied it, of course. He said that he had never said anything to incriminate himself in all his interrogations, so why would he have made such an observation in conversation with Rich?'

Harry's eyes narrowed. Had Rich lied? And if so, had it been at Cromwell's behest? 'What did Master Rich say to that?'

'He stood by his testimony. Then Sir Thomas said, "If this oath of yours be true, then pray I that I may never see God in the face." He said he was sorrier for Rich's perjury than for his own peril.'

'*Was* it perjury?' Harry demanded to know, toying with the idea of showing mercy to his old friend. Truth be told, he shrank from signing More's death warrant.

'Rich swears it was not.' Cromwell was not looking him in the eye.

'Then I pray he is not forsworn.'

He signed the warrant, resentful of Anne for her ability blithely to order new gowns for their imminent progress in the western shires while his heart was in a turmoil over More. He had been looking forward to their journeyings, anticipating the hunting and the hospitality. Yet there was to be another purpose to his travels, for he was resolved to win hearts for his religious reforms. Men of note who had been supporting his policies were to be favoured with visits; the goodwill of traditionalists was to be won over.

On 5 July, at the head of a vast train of courtiers, servants and baggage, Harry and Anne travelled west from Windsor to Reading. It was the day before More was due to be executed, and Harry could eat little at dinner in Reading Abbey that night. He felt sick to his stomach.

Needing to be distracted on the day the sentence was carried out, he went hunting. When he returned, Anne was waiting for him.

'More is dead,' she said, looking happier than she had done in days. 'He said he died your good servant, but God's first.'

Harry could not bear to see the triumph in her face. In that moment, he hated her.

He sat down, his heart racing. 'You are the cause of his death!' he snarled, jabbing a finger at her.

'He was a traitor and deserved it,' she flung back. 'It was not I who denied your supremacy!'

'Give me a son and justify what I have done for you!' he seethed, and was gratified to see Anne burst into tears and flee from his sight.

He sat there until darkness fell and the candles guttered. He could not be bothered with her now. All he could think of was how the world would judge him for More's death, for the man had had an international reputation. The love of his people meant everything to Harry, and he wanted the approbation of Christendom too. He saw now that, in the white heat of his rage, he had imperilled both. Worse still were his deep feelings of regret and remorse.

Yet he could never admit that to a living soul.

Anne was making strenuous efforts to please and divert him from darker thoughts. Relenting, he graciously permitted Lady Rochford to return to court, thinking it would please her. But she was soon complaining that her sister-in-law was no longer her friend. And soon there was proof of it, for that summer, to Harry's fury, there was a public demonstration at Greenwich in support of the Lady Mary – and Lady Rochford was one of several ladies involved.

'But why?' Anne cried. 'How could she play so false?'

Harry could guess. Lady Rochford's father, Lord Morley, had been close to Bishop Fisher. It was easy to see why she had become alienated from the Boleyns, like many others. But he said nothing, fearing to provoke another tirade, for Anne's tantrums were erupting more frequently these days. He clapped Jane and the other silly women in the Tower.

It was balm to Harry's troubled soul to ride through the glorious vistas of the West Country to Sudeley Castle, where he and Anne were to stay a week. In the summer sunshine, his state of mind gradually improved. He found pleasure in hosting feasts for the ladies, and secretly bedded a couple of them too. Noticing to his dismay that he was beginning to go bald, he had his hair cropped close to his head and commanded all the men at court to follow his example.

Cromwell joined him at Sudeley late in July, having come to arrange for royal commissioners to visit all the religious houses in the west. In a buoyant mood, Harry rode on to Tewkesbury, Gloucester, Berkeley Castle, and Thornbury Castle, which had once belonged to the treacherous Buckingham. Presently, the long cavalcade entered Wiltshire, where he and Anne spent three nights at the great house of Wulfhall as guests of Sir John Seymour.

Harry was much taken with the Seymours. Sir John's sons, Edward and Thomas, were rising stars of the court – and ambitious too. Well, there was nothing wrong with that. Their sister Jane was maid-of-honour to Anne, as she had been to Kate before her. She was a quiet, pale young woman, still unwed at twenty-seven, and there was a gentleness about her that Harry found attractive. Seeing her in the bosom of her family, and seeing how they all loved her, his interest was piqued.

One evening, after the feasting was over, he watched her slip away from the chamber where the company was gathered.

He would go after her, he decided, and get to know her better.

He looked sideways at Anne, who was laughing rather too loudly at one of Sir Francis Bryan's lewd jokes.

'If you will excuse me,' he said to Sir John Seymour, 'I will take the air in your glorious garden for a while. I can feel one of my headaches threatening.'

His host and the company made to rise, but he stopped them with a gesture. 'It is not often that kings can enjoy the luxury of solitude.'

He saw her before she saw him, a slender figure seated on a bench, her head in its bejewelled gable hood bent as if in prayer. He wondered why she had absented herself.

He stole forward, thinking how peaceful it was in this beautiful place, and how he envied Sir John his country life, his hearty wife and his large brood. In that moment, the burdens of state seemed too heavy to bear. He had chosen a hard course for himself, he thought bitterly. Yet he had had no choice.

Jane leapt to her feet, startled at his approach, and he pretended to be surprised to see her. She made to leave, to let him enjoy the peace alone, but he stayed her – and suddenly their eyes locked. She looked like a frightened faun, ready to leap away.

He smiled kindly at her. 'Sit with me a while. Don't look so afraid. I don't bite.'

She sat down again and shivered.

'What a beautiful garden,' Harry said. 'So peaceful. There's a sense of timelessness here. This is the true England; its essence does not lie in courts or cities. Do you understand what I mean, Jane?'

'I think I do, Sir,' she replied. 'I love it here.' He was impressed by her sincerity.

'You prefer it to the court.'

'It is my home, Sir.'

'It is rare to find someone who leans towards a quiet life,' he said, remembering More in the bosom of his family. 'Sir Thomas More was one such,' he found himself saying. 'I envied him his happy home and his leisure to study.'

Jane looked at him nervously, yet there was something challenging in her gaze, something that made him question the rightness of the punishment he had meted out to More.

He swallowed. 'I loved and respected him.'

Jane said nothing. He felt he had to justify himself.

'The world knows who was the cause of his death!' he barked, more harshly than he intended. Again, she remained silent, and he saw there were tears in her eyes.

'He defied me,' he said, still feeling the need to explain. 'He was my friend, but he defied me, and people think the worse of me for it.'

'I am very sorry for your Grace,' Jane murmured.

He drew in his breath, closing his eyes. 'So am I, Jane, so am I. All that I have done, all that blood spilt, has been for nothing, for still I have no son to carry on my great work of reformation.'

'Her Grace may yet bear you a son,' she said hopefully.

'I pray for it daily! The Emperor demands that I restore the Lady Mary to the succession, but he's a fool. Set a woman upon the throne and, if she marries a subject, there will be much jealousy, and factions warring at court. Let her marry a foreign prince, and what then of England? This great realm reduced to a dominion of France or Spain!

Loyal, true-born Englishmen must shrink from the prospect. I could weep when I think of it.' He felt on the brink of it now. 'Jane, I need a son!'

'I pray for it daily, Sir,' she declared. He was too choked to answer her, so they sat there for a while in silence.

'Your family has lived here a long time,' Harry said at length, when he could trust his voice to be steady.

'Yes, Sir. Seymours were living in Savernake Forest back in the fourteenth century.'

Henry nodded. 'I like your parents. They are genuine people. That is a rare thing.'

'I know, Sir,' Jane agreed, shivering again.

'I have kept you out too long,' he said, rising. 'Forgive me. There is a gentleness in you that induces confidences, Jane.'

Jane had risen too. 'We all need someone to talk to sometimes, Sir.'

'Would that I could talk to you more often,' he said, looking down at her and thinking how different to Anne this woman was. Calming, gentle – just what he needed when he was so beset with the cares of sovereignty. Their eyes met again, and something sparked.

'I . . . I am always ready to listen, Sir,' Jane stammered, and hastened towards the house, dropping a quick curtsey at the door.

'Good night, Jane,' he said.

'Good night, Sir,' she murmured, and fled.

As he sat up late, playing cards with his host, he brought the conversation around to her.

'You have a fine brood, Sir John. I envy you.'

'Aye, Sir, I have been blessed, and I pray that your Grace will be too.'

'I'm forty-four, man, and still I have no son. There's precious little time to get a large brood now.'

'Maybe God will surprise you,' Sir John said, throwing down his hand. 'Your Grace has won!'

Harry grinned and scooped up his winnings. 'Your daughter Jane is as yet unwed, I see.'

'She's a good girl, but no great beauty. Suitors haven't come flocking.'

'Yet she has charm, and she is kind. Many men would account those essential qualities in a wife.' Harry sighed, reflecting on Anne's lack of kindness; she had charmed him once, but these days he had to make himself respond to her. 'I like a woman with a gentle nature.'

'There was a suitor once, but his mother was against the match.' Sir John's ruddy cheeks flushed an even deeper hue. 'Your Grace knows why.'

Harry nodded. He was well aware that his host had caused scandal by bedding his own son's wife, but that had been years ago. 'We are both men of the world, John. These things happen. It seems that Edward has forgiven you.'

'I hope so, but can I forgive myself?'

'Best to let bygones be bygones.' Harry yawned. 'I must to my bed. Thank you for your splendid hospitality – and thank your good lady. Her pies were excellent!' He smiled; he could taste them now.

Soon after they returned to Windsor, Anne invited Harry to sup with her. The table was laid with the finest cloth and set with gold and silver plate; the wine sparkled in the candlelight, and the dishes laid out before him looked delicious. Anne wore a low-cut black gown he liked, the one with gold-embroidered biliments, and she had the pearls he had given her around her slender neck, framing the great B pendant she proudly favoured.

She should have looked enticing, but she was no longer the alluring young woman who had captured his heart. She was thin and she was ageing, and he was tired to satiety of her. She had never learned the decorum befitting a queen; she still upbraided him for his infidelities and dared to argue with him in public. Small wonder that she had never been popular. But for her, Harry might now be forging an alliance with the Emperor.

What needled him most was that she was still doing her best to influence public affairs. Her views were strident and her temper such that he dared not contradict her. Tonight, though, she was all smiles – and immediately he was suspicious. What did she want now?

She surprised him. 'Darling, I have wonderful news – I am with child again.'

Now he could forgive her everything. If she was carrying his son, he would never forsake her; even if he no longer loved her, he would honour her as the mother of his heir.

'Darling!' he exclaimed, embracing her, thankful that all those nights when he had pressed himself into service had not been in vain. He kissed her tenderly. 'This is the best news you could have given me!'

Suddenly, her mood changed.

'What is it?' he asked, alarmed that she should be disturbed at such a delicate time.

She raised sad eyes to him. 'I cannot tell you how afflicted I feel when I think that, if the Emperor ever invades in support of Katherine, our children might be excluded from the throne for the sake of the Lady Mary.'

'You must not worry, Anne,' he soothed. 'If he comes, we will be ready for him!'

'Sir!' Her voice was sharp. 'The Lady Mary will never cease to trouble us. Her defiance of your just laws has only given courage to our enemies. I pray you, let the law take its course with her! It's the only way to avert war. What profit can Charles gain when there is no one to fight for? He needs our trade and our friendship.'

Harry was appalled. 'You are asking me to send my own daughter to the scaffold.'

'She is a traitor, and a danger to you. While she lives, our son will never be safe!'

'I cannot go so far,' he said, feeling desperate. 'Maybe just a threat to have her executed will serve as an effective warning to the Emperor.'

Anne said nothing, but tears were streaming down her face and she was trembling.

He could not have her upset, not now.

'You're right,' he said heavily. 'It shall be done!'

The next day, he visited her before dinner. 'I have just come from the Privy Council. I declared to them that I would no longer remain in the trouble, fear and suspicion engendered by Katherine and Mary. I said the next Parliament must release me by passing Acts of Attainder against them, or, by God, I will not wait any longer to make an end of them myself!'

'What did they say?' Her eyes were aflame.

'They looked dismayed, but I told them it was nothing to cry or make wry faces about. I said, if I am to lose my crown for it, I would do what I have set out to do.'

'It was well done, Harry,' she said. 'It is the only way to secure the future of our children.'

'Yes, but, by God, at what a price!' he cried. Inwardly, he knew he could never bring himself to shed his daughter's blood, whatever the cost to Anne and himself. And, from her expression, he knew she could tell that he was already wavering.

Freed from his marital obligations, and secretly relieved about it, Harry began to pay more attention to Jane Seymour. She seemed nervous about receiving his addresses, and he wondered if they were welcome, but he reasoned that she was most likely fearful of Anne finding out, for Anne's moods were volatile these days.

He pressed Jane to become his mistress.

No, she said, and no again. She was saving herself for the man she would marry. He had heard that before, but in Jane's case, he believed it. There was no guile about her.

Very well, he would be patient. Few women ever refused the King. He could afford to wait a little.

If he had thought that Anne's pregnancy would restore the tenderness between them, he was grievously mistaken. Inflated with pride in her condition, she was insufferable, and he took to avoiding her.

The Boleyns and their faction were exultant and all-powerful. But they had made many enemies, Norfolk for one, despite the ties of kinship. He and Anne traded insults with a viciousness that shocked Harry. And Cromwell, once Anne's friend, had been alienated too. He remained outwardly friendly, but Harry knew they had quarrelled and that she had threatened to have him beheaded – Chapuys had told him, rather gleefully, as he recalled. But now no one could touch her – and there was news from Kimbolton Castle, where Kate was living out her miserable existence.

'She is dying, your Majesty,' Chapuys said urgently, following him down a gallery at Greenwich, looking desperate. 'Permit her to see the Princess, I beg of you.'

'No,' Harry replied, hardening his heart and angry at Chapuys' use of Mary's forbidden title. 'If I let the Lady Mary visit her mother, they will plot against me.'

'I think not, Sir,' Chapuys bridled. 'The Queen is too ill.'

'The Queen is in excellent health,' Harry corrected him, bristling. 'The Princess Dowager is ailing. May God grant her rest.'

'Allow me to go to her!' the ambassador begged.

'No!' Harry bit his tongue, remembering that he was supposed to be courting Chapuys. 'Understand my position, my friend.' He placed an arm around the other man's shoulders and steered him towards the privy chamber. 'Those two have defied me. They have broken my laws and resisted my commands.'

'But the poor lady is dying!'

'It is God's will, and we must not question His wisdom. While she lives, I fear there will always be an obstacle to my friendship with your master.'

'The Queen is not the obstacle!' Chapuys protested. 'Your Majesty knows very well who is!'

Always it came back to Anne. Pregnant or not, she was a liability.

Harry relented. There remained in him some small core of affection for Kate, for all that had once been between them. 'Go to her if you want. You are right, she is no threat to me, and she can't live long.'

Chapter 27

1536

The letter danced before his eyes, the words blurred by his tears.

Kate was dead. And among her pathetically few possessions, which had been forwarded to Harry, was her last letter to him.

Lastly, I make this vow, that mine eyes desire you above all things. It was that which had made him weep. Then he read on, and his sorrow turned to rage when he saw that she had signed the letter, defiant to the last, *Katherine the Queen.*

Pity died in him. He was glad that she was dead. Now the way was clear to an alliance with the Emperor. 'God be praised,' he muttered. 'We are free from the threat of war.'

Anne was exultant. She insisted that she and Harry hold court wearing yellow to demonstrate their joy at being rid of their great adversary. As the trumpets sounded a fanfare, Harry triumphantly carried the Princess Elizabeth into the chapel for a solemn Mass. Afterwards, he took great pleasure in showing her off to his courtiers. At two, she was an intelligent child with a sharp wit, and charmed them all. She sat on a cushion at the banquet, wearing one of the pretty satin gowns Anne had chosen for her, and clapped her little hands as the dancing began. It took a lot of persuading to get her to go to bed.

Harry was in a good mood. Kate was with God, Anne was with child, and the Emperor was free to offer his friendship. The world had not rocked on its axis because of the break with Rome, and England was poised once more to play a leading role in Europe.

There was just one thing troubling him. Mary was ill, having taken the news of her mother's death grievously. Harry's instincts told him he ought to go to her, but he was still angry with her – and he feared to arouse Anne's volatile temper, especially when her pregnancy was progressing so well. So he sent privily for reports and was relieved to hear that, although devastated by grief, Mary was out of danger.

It had been some time since Harry had jousted, but he had kept himself fit with other sports and was almost as trim-waisted and broad-shouldered as he had been twenty years ago. It was time to enter the lists again. The weather was fine for January, and he intended to take full advantage of it.

The stands at Greenwich were packed. As he cantered, fully armoured, down the tiltyard, lance couched, the spectators were on their feet, roaring their encouragement. The speed was exhilarating; there was nothing like it. His opponent was charging towards him at a similar rate. He braced himself for the impact. And then, all of a sudden, he was flying through the air, unable to save himself, and crashing to the ground. As his mighty steed fell on top of him, crushing the breath out of him, he heard cries from the onlookers and the thud of running feet. They got the horse up, then hands were lifting his visor, scrabbling at his armour.

'Your Grace? Are you hurt?'

'Your Grace, speak to us!'

'I am all right,' he muttered, somewhat dazed with shock.

'You fell so heavily that it is a miracle you were not killed.' That was Suffolk. 'In fact, Norfolk thought you were dead and hurried off to tell the Queen.'

'Send someone after him,' Harry croaked, as he was helped to his feet. It seemed that his whole body was a mass of aches and pains, but he was able to limp back to his tent and raise a hand to reassure the anxious, staring spectators that he was himself again – although he was feeling anything but.

His physicians were summoned and examined him thoroughly. 'Your Grace has taken no hurt,' they pronounced. 'We thank God that you did not sustain an injury to your head. Truly, He has you in His keeping.'

'You have to face it, Harry, your jousting days are over,' Suffolk said later. 'I've had to give it up. You should try riding or walking instead.'

Resting on his cushioned chair, nursing his pains, Harry glowered at him. 'I suppose I must admit it: I am growing older. We both are.' He bent and rubbed his calf. 'This damned leg is more painful than anything.'

'It will get better,' Charles soothed.

'Aye, I suppose so. And now Crum is plaguing me about Kate's funeral. She's to be buried at Peterborough with all the honours due to the Princess Dowager of Wales, but your pestilential mother-in-law, Lady Willoughby, is complaining about that. She wants to attend with your wife.'

'My wife will do as I command.'

'Then let her go, but I want no demonstrations on the day.'

He donned mourning, out of respect. After all, Kate had been his sister-in-law and they had lived as man and wife for many years. He ordered a requiem Mass to be said at Greenwich. Beforehand, he sat brooding restlessly in his closet, grief and guilt warring in him.

He needed a diversion.

He went to the window to see if there was anyone in the Queen's privy garden below – and there she was, Jane, the person he most wanted to see, the one good soul who could ease his tortuous thoughts. He hastened downstairs and, before Anne could spy them from her window, hastily bade Jane come up to his privy chamber.

At the sight of her, standing in the doorway, her sweet face and sympathetic expression, he knew she understood how he was feeling. He pulled her down on his lap and buried his face in her shoulder, just as, years ago, he had gone to his beloved mother seeking comfort.

The nearness of her was irresistible, and soon he found himself stirring. He sought her lips and she let him kiss her, but when his hand strayed to her breast, she caught her breath.

'Sir, you should not . . .' She giggled nervously.

The door opened, and there stood Anne, her face a mask of shock.

'How could you?' she wailed.

Harry set Jane aside and leapt up.

'Go!' he commanded, and she scuttled away. 'Darling, I am sorry.' He tried to look contrite.

Anne was weeping hysterically. 'You have no idea how you have hurt me!' she sobbed. 'The love I bear you is greater than Katherine's ever was, and my heart breaks when I see that you love another.'

'It meant nothing,' he said.

'Nothing? I saw you with my own eyes.' Suddenly, her hands flew to her belly. She looked panicked.

He was alarmed. 'What is it?'

'It is the distress you have caused me!' she cried.

'Just be at peace, sweetheart, and all will go well with you,' he soothed. 'Think of our son!'

'It's a pity *you* didn't!' she flung back, and left him standing there, open-mouthed.

Later that day, his son was born dead. A stillborn foetus of fifteen weeks' growth, they told him.

He was in too much agony of mind to spare Anne. 'A boy!' he wept. 'There could be no greater discomfort to me or my realm.'

'*I* was in peril of my life,' she protested. 'And you have no one to blame but yourself, for it was caused by my distress of mind over that wench Seymour.'

Fury gripped Harry. 'I will have no more boys by you,' he said icily.

'What do you mean?' she cried.

He glared at her. 'I see clearly that God does not wish to give me male children. I do not want to discuss it now. I will speak to you when you are up.' With that, he left her to her tears.

Back in his privy chamber, he received the condolences of his gentlemen, noticing that Rochford looked stricken. Harry was so distraught at his loss, and so angry with Anne, that he could barely respond. Now he could see what had been staring him in the face for a long time. God was again displeased with him.

'I was seduced by sorcery into this marriage,' he moaned, 'and for this reason I consider it null. I believe I might take another wife.'

They stared at him in amazement, for it was rare for him to declare his inmost thoughts to them, especially on such a subject. It was a measure of how distressed he was.

Will Somers was regarding him sadly. 'There's plenty more fish in the sea, Harry.'

'Go away, fool,' he growled.

Bryan rested his one eye on him. 'I've long feared, Sir, that the Queen has a defective constitution that prevents her from bearing healthy children.'

'Was she even pregnant at all?' Carew asked.

'How dare you say such things!' Rochford flared.

'Enough!' Harry snapped.

He sent for Jane late that night. She came to him in the dimness of the deserted Chapel Royal as he sat weeping in his pew, unable to control his distress. He felt her arms go around him.

'She lost my boy!' he sobbed against her shoulder. 'I know I will have no sons with her. I see clearly that God does not wish to give me male children. Jane, help me! I am in great fear that I have again incurred His wrath. Those miscarriages did not occur without good reason: they were manifestations of His displeasure. I fear my marriage with the Queen is as displeasing to him as my unlawful union with Katherine.'

'Alas, Sir, I wish that I could help you,' she murmured, resting her head on his, 'but I am not learned in these matters.' She hesitated. 'Would putting away the Queen restore your credit with God? It would leave you free to make another marriage, to a wife who could bear you sons.'

Harry nodded. She had gone straight to the heart of the matter. 'I am aware of that, darling.' He gripped her hand. 'I'm no longer young, Jane. I can't afford to wait much longer for God to send me a son. I must talk to Cranmer urgently.' He drew her tightly into his arms and kissed her. 'I do love you, Jane. You give me sound advice.

Look, I have a gift for you.' He reached into his pocket, drew out a roll of velvet and placed it in her hands. She unravelled it to find an emerald pendant and a matching ring with a great stone. She drew in her breath. 'Emeralds stand for purity and faith,' he said.

'I do not know how to thank your Grace. They are gorgeous. You are so good to me. I have not the words to show my appreciation.'

He bent forward and kissed her gently. 'I would give you the world. And when we are alone together like this, Jane, you should not be calling me "your Grace" or "Sir". I am Harry, your humble servant.'

She wound her arms around his neck. 'Yes, Sir . . . I mean, Harry.' They laughed, but he still felt sad.

'What can I do to make you feel better?' she asked.

He gazed at her with yearning. 'Comfort me,' he said. 'Help me to blot out the pain I feel.'

She tightened her arms around him. 'How can I do that?' For answer, his mouth closed on hers needily. 'Come to bed,' he murmured.

It happened just twice. Twice only, and it was not enough. But, early in February, he had to leave Greenwich and go to York Place for the Shrovetide celebrations and the new session of Parliament. He left Anne behind, which meant that he had to leave Jane too, but he frequently took his barge along the river of an evening to visit her. His love for her was flowering, a beautiful bud opening out towards the sunshine. It was a good thing, a fine thing, nothing like his dark, obsessive passion for Anne. Already, there was gossip about them.

In late February, when the daffodils bloomed, he sent Jane a letter with the gift of a purse of gold sovereigns.

'Your Grace, Mistress Seymour would not accept it,' the messenger told him. 'She knelt, she kissed the letter, then she returned both to me, declaring that she could accept a dowry from your Grace only when she found a husband.'

Harry was again impressed by Jane's virtue.

'Pray return to her,' he commanded. 'Tell her I will not visit or speak to her except in the presence of one of her relatives.'

To please Jane, he decided to appoint her brother Edward a Gentleman of the Privy Chamber. He had no doubt that Edward and Thomas Seymour, ambitious young men, striving for advancement, were urging their sister to please him. Their friends, Carew, Bryan, the Exeters and the Poles – conservatives all – were encouraging the affair and continually criticising Anne in Harry's hearing. The days were gone when he would angrily have reprimanded them. When they were reunited at York Place, even Jane spoke out against Anne, about her unkindness, her shrewishness, her scorn towards him. Anne had torn a locket bearing his picture from Jane's neck, with some violence. He recoiled when Jane showed him the weal on her throat. Clearly, Anne was realising that her day was done – and was fighting back.

Harry longed to have Jane in his bed again, her loving arms around him, but she had kept him at a distance since those two glorious nights, and now would not even let him kiss her. He liked that in her, even as he ached with desire and frustration.

He spoke to Cromwell, perplexed as to how he was going to conduct his courtship, and how it would progress if he could not even see Jane in private.

'I can help your Grace.' Cromwell smiled, ever resourceful. 'I can vacate my rooms at Greenwich, which afford that secret access to your privy lodgings, and Sir Edward and Lady Seymour can stay there and act as chaperones when you visit the lady. You will be able to enter through the gallery without being perceived.'

'Crum, you're a marvel!' Harry exclaimed.

The arrangement worked well. The Seymours kept to the inner chamber when Harry came to pay his chaste addresses to Jane. At first, it was enough just to see and talk with her, and he restrained himself from importuning her for more than she cared to give. What Anne made of her absence he did not know – and did not care. Yet even this degree of privacy did not prevent gossip.

'Messire Chapuys has heard rumours,' Cromwell reported, after a council meeting late in March. 'I told him that I believed your Grace has decided henceforth to live more chastely, and not change wives again.' He grinned.

Harry paused. Change wives again? The thought kept occurring to him, an insidious worm burrowing into his brain. But how? Cromwell had warned that divorcing Anne would be seen as an admission that he had been wrong to put away Kate – and it could compromise the legitimacy of Elizabeth, his sole heir.

'It is clear,' Cromwell was saying, 'that Chapuys has no great opinion of Mistress Seymour's virtue, just as he takes a dim view of the morals of most Englishwomen. But I set him right on that.' Harry was mightily relieved to hear it.

There seemed to be no way out of his marriage, and the rift with Anne could not be allowed to go on. True, she might be a barrier to an Imperial alliance, but he had no option but to fight for Charles' recognition of her as queen. It would be the ultimate vindication of all he had done.

He was gratified to see Anne confining her energies to the domestic sphere, spending lavishly on new attire for herself and Elizabeth. He entered her bedchamber one evening to find the bed heaped with bolts of purple cloth of gold, black and tawny velvet, carnation and white satin, pieces of lambskin and miniver, kirtles of white satin and black damask, nightgowns, cloaks and slippers.

'You'll have me bankrupt,' he observed, whereat she flashed a smile at him. It was the old Anne, the one who could tease and charm him, and suddenly he felt a surge of lust. Maybe they could make a son again! He ended up tumbling her amid the velvets and satins, caring not that he might spoil them. Afterwards, she lay looking up jubilantly at him, clearly believing he was hers again. Well, let her enjoy her fantasy, if it kept her sweet towards him.

'The Emperor,' Cromwell said, as Harry walked with him along the gravelled paths of the privy garden, out of earshot of the other courtiers, 'is now so eager to conclude an alliance with your Grace that he is prepared to be conciliatory. It is reported from Italy that he has prevented the Bishop of Rome from excommunicating you.'

Harry was relieved to hear that. The sentence of excommunication drawn up by Clement had never been promulgated, although the threat had remained, and his councillors had feared that Clement's successor, Pope Paul – who was showing evidence of being a far stouter opponent to Harry – would do just that. Harry was grateful, therefore, for Charles' intervention. It was an encouraging sign.

'The Emperor has indicated through Chapuys that he is willing to support the continuation of your Grace's marriage to Queen Anne, if you will have the Lady Mary declared legitimate.'

Harry bent, frowning, to pluck some heartsease for Jane. 'You favour this alliance, Crum?'

'I believe it is vital to England's security and prosperity. The London merchants have suffered through this rift with the Empire, for that is where they have their markets. They would welcome it. Even the Boleyns and their friends are resolved to abandon their hopes of a new *entente* with France and support an understanding with the Emperor.'

Harry had heard Anne say as much.

Cromwell lowered his voice. 'Your Grace should know that the Queen upbraided me for vacating my rooms for the Seymours. Sadly, she is hostile towards me these days. We fell out last year over the closure of the monasteries. She wants them reformed or turned over to charitable or educational purposes.'

'A noble aim,' Harry observed, 'but a vain one.'

'Especially in the face of all the lewdness and corruption we've uncovered. They will soon be swept away, the small houses first, and the larger ones to follow. Her Grace should think about how it will benefit the treasury.'

Harry's eyes gleamed at the thought of the untold cartloads of treasure that would soon be trundling his way – and of putting a stop to subversive monks and nuns secretly supporting Rome.

He knew that Anne now hated Cromwell. She had even urged him to have the secretary executed, and had her almoner preach a sermon on Passion Sunday, urging that wicked ministers be hanged.

But Harry had shrugged it all off as a woman's spite. He would never forsake Cromwell.

Determined to pave the way for an Imperial alliance by securing Charles' public recognition of Anne as queen, he invited Chapuys to attend him at Greenwich Palace on Easter Tuesday. Rochford was to afford him a warm welcome at the gatehouse and, well primed, Cromwell was then to appear, saying that the King had invited Chapuys to visit Anne and kiss her cheek – a great honour conferred only on those in high favour.

Harry was not bothered about the probability of Chapuys ignoring this summons. He had a better manoeuvre in store.

Rochford escorted the ambassador to Mass in the Chapel Royal. When Harry and Anne entered the royal pew in the gallery above the crowded nave, they could see the two men waiting below. Anne had her instructions too. When she and Harry descended the stairs to make their offerings at the altar, Chapuys was standing behind the lower door. Deftly, Harry moved so that the ambassador could not but come face to face with Anne, who swept him a deep curtsey, as if to the Emperor himself. He had no choice but to bow in response.

Anne was exultant. 'At last! At last!' she breathed, when they returned to the royal pew. 'I shall look to speak to him at dinner in my apartments.'

Chapuys, however, failed to turn up.

'Why does he not enter, like the other ambassadors?' she asked, dismayed.

'It is not without good reason,' Harry told her, inwardly seething, although not with her. He and his Council had been debating the advantages of an alliance with the Emperor against one with France, and Harry was now inclining more strongly towards the latter, because Anne might yet bear a son and he would not tolerate Charles dictating conditions in return for acknowledging her as queen. Yet he had just learned that Cromwell, eager to please his merchant friends, had progressed the negotiations with Charles and gone too far too soon without consulting him. He boiled with the impertinence of it.

When he met with Chapuys that afternoon, he drew him into a window embrasure so that they could talk privately, carefully excluding Cromwell. Drawing himself up to his full majestic height, he made a point of showing himself cool towards the mooted alliance, much to Chapuys' evident consternation.

'The Emperor must apologise for his past behaviour towards me and acknowledge the Lady Anne as my Queen – and in writing,' Harry insisted.

Cromwell had heard him – as he intended – and was shaking his head furiously. Both knew all too well that Charles would never agree to such humiliating terms.

Later, when Chapuys had withdrawn, looking thunderous, Cromwell tried to remonstrate with Harry.

'Be off with you, Crum!' Harry snarled. 'You've caused enough trouble. I don't know what you were thinking of. By St George, the Queen warned me you were working against me. It seems I should have listened to her.'

'But Sir, you wanted this alliance. I was only doing my best to implement your wishes.'

'Is that so?' Harry was working himself up into a rage. 'It seems, rather, that you chose to ignore them! And we know what happens to those who do that.'

Cromwell fled, sweat pouring down his brow.

That evening, Harry received word that the minister had been taken ill and gone home to Stepney. A likely story!

He had calmed down when Cromwell returned to court five days later, miraculously restored to health, and was ready to resume their old, easy relationship. What he was not prepared for was Cromwell and other councillors falling to their knees before him, looking grave and, yes, utterly terrified.

'Your Grace,' Cromwell intoned, still kneeling, 'it is our heavy duty to inform you that we have uncovered evidence of misconduct on the part of the Queen. The alleged offences are so abominable that we who have conducted the examination have been quaking at the thought of the danger in which your Grace has stood and realised that, on our duty to you, we could not conceal them from you. We can only praise God that He has preserved you.'

Harry was so stunned that he started to tremble uncontrollably. 'What misconduct?' he barked, his voice emerging as a croak.

Cromwell seemed to hesitate. 'Certain of the Queen's ladies have testified that she has betrayed your Grace, and with more than one man.'

Cuckolded! What? He was the King, and *no one* cuckolded the King. How dare she! He felt his face grow hot. 'Who?'

'We are still investigating, Sir,' said Sir Anthony Browne.

Harry tried to collect himself. His head was buzzing, and he could feel one of his headaches threatening. 'Show me the proofs,' he demanded.

Cromwell rose, drew from his bosom some papers and handed them to him. Harry scanned them quickly. They were depositions, all from women who served Anne, and seemed to consist chiefly of malicious gossip. His heartbeat resumed its normal pace.

'Gentlemen, I thought you were statesmen,' he said scornfully, masking his shock that things had gone this far. 'I marvel that you pay heed to such silliness. You know how catty women can be.'

'These are not the whole of it,' Cromwell said, his piggy face an alarming shade of white. 'There have been other allegations.'

'The state papers are full of them!' Harry snapped. 'The Queen is not liked. People have been making allegations about her for years, and all are false. You know that!'

'Indeed, Sir. But these ladies were sufficiently concerned to come to us.'

'That's as may be,' Harry said, 'but this drivel proves nothing!' He shook the papers in Cromwell's face. 'I thank you, gentlemen, for your concern.'

He was about to dismiss them when Cromwell spoke again. 'Will your Grace give us leave to investigate further?' he asked. 'This is not just about adultery; it touches on something far more serious.'

Harry hesitated. Inwardly, he was dismissing the matter as a cunning ploy of Cromwell's to unseat Anne. And yet it now occurred to him that, if grounds for divorce could be found, it might provide a way out of his marriage. The thought of Jane lying in his bed or smiling at him with their son in her arms hardened his resolve. 'Yes, Crum,' he said. 'I charge you all to make further inquiries, trusting that you will investigate the whole business.' He watched as they rose to their feet and filed out.

Could it be true, or was it really just malicious gossip? If true, then with whom had Anne betrayed him? Lying awake that night, he asked himself repeatedly who would have dared. She was the Queen, by God! But the depositions had seemed so petty and trivial that it was impossible to make a judgement. Clearly, his councillors had not got any other proper evidence

Even though it might play to his advantage, he shrank from the possibility that Anne had been unfaithful. If she had, he would have to act, and thereby publicly brand himself a cuckold. How could his pride stomach it?

Yet how would he live with not knowing while the Council's inquiries proceeded? How could he act normally with her when he was wondering if others had known her as intimately as he did himself? How could he look at the courtiers who flocked to her chamber for the pastime afforded them there without wondering if it was one of them?

He tried to be rational. The Queen of England was rarely alone. It would be difficult, all but impossible, to keep any illicit liaison a secret. She would have needed the co-operation of at least one of her women, maybe one who had testified against her, yet it was barely credible that Anne would have taken such risks. She knew that only Harry stood between her and her enemies, so why would she betray him, jeopardising everything for a few stolen hours of pleasure? He could not believe that she had committed adultery because she was desperate for a son. He had got her with child often enough.

By the time the clock over the gatehouse struck three, he had resolved not to allow himself to believe any of it – not yet. He would wait and see what further investigation could uncover.

After his night of torment, Harry forced himself to be calm and composed, and faced his councillors again. This time, Lord Chancellor Audley asked if he might have leave to appoint two special commissions to inquire into crimes committed in the counties of Middlesex and Kent, and to hear any cases according to law.

'Their purpose, Sir, is to determine if there is a case to answer and whether it should proceed.'

'I am aware of that,' Harry snapped. 'Very well, go ahead.'

'Our only wish is speedily to ascertain the facts for your Grace's peace of mind,' Cromwell soothed. 'All will be kept secret until sufficient evidence to justify a prosecution has been gathered.'

'*If* it is gathered,' Harry said sternly.

'I can authorise the Chancery to issue the necessary documents in your Grace's name,' Audley told him.

'Very well,' Harry repeated, rising. 'But be careful not to impugn the Queen's honour, and thereby mine, unless you have very good cause to do so.'

Chapter 28

1536

Harry tried to carry on as normal. He treated Anne with every courtesy and told her he was taking her with him to inspect the new fortifications at Dover and Calais at the end of April. Yet he sensed that she had noticed a distancing on his part, and he was watching her closely for any sign of unwonted favour towards other men. There was none, or no more than usual. He visited her bed and did his duty, for England still needed a future king.

At Cromwell's behest, he agreed to summon Parliament without delay.

'Everyone will think it is for the business of the dissolution,' the minister murmured in his ear. 'But it will be useful to have the lords in session in case anything comes of this matter of the Queen.'

Afterwards, as they were leaving the council chamber, Harry pulled him aside and waited until they were alone. 'Have you discovered anything further yet?'

Cromwell gave him a heavy look. 'We are still examining members of the Queen's household and have yet to substantiate certain allegations. If they prove true, your Grace might consider what course you wish to take. I have taken the liberty of discussing with the Dean of the Chapel Royal possible grounds for an annulment.'

Harry flinched, remembering how fraught it had been trying to disentangle himself from Kate. 'What grounds?'

'Means could be found to end the marriage, I am sure.'

'But if she has betrayed me, she has committed treason!'

'Then it would be up to your Grace to decide her fate,' Cromwell said smoothly. 'There are no precedents in England for a queen being convicted of criminal conversation.'

'The penalty for treason is death,' Harry reminded him, his voice like a stone.

'And for women,' Cromwell replied, 'that means burning.'

Harry's chest contracted. He could not do such a terrible thing to Anne, could not bear the thought of the body he had worshipped being consumed by the cruel flames, could not consign her to such hideous agony. Yet what if she had played him false with that same body? He must harden his heart. He was the King, and it was his duty to uphold the law, especially when the offence touched him so nearly. Inwardly, he was shaking.

It suddenly occurred to him that, if Cromwell was looking into an annulment, he could not have sufficient evidence to prosecute Anne.

'It seems you do not have proof of treason,' he challenged.

'Alas, Sir, I fear I will have it soon. And if the Queen is convicted as a traitor, then surely your Grace will be looking to have your marriage dissolved and her daughter disinherited.'

Harry was shocked. 'Bastardise Elizabeth, my only lawful heir?'

'Only until you remarry and beget a son.'

'By God, Crum, you get too far ahead of yourself!'

Cromwell looked pained. 'Does your Grace think I would go so far without good cause? I assure you, there will be evidence.'

There was.

At the end of April, their faces full of trepidation, Cromwell and other Privy Councillors attended Harry in his chamber and laid before him a list of charges against Anne, along with the depositions of witnesses, most of them Anne's ladies or Cromwell's spies. Steeling himself, he read them, first in disbelief, and then with mounting rage.

The Anne portrayed here was a monster. She had not only taken numerous lovers, but had conspired with them to murder him so that she could marry one of her paramours and rule England in

419

Elizabeth's name. Harry felt sick at the revelation that one of her lovers was her own brother, Rochford! Another was that puffed-up musician, Mark Smeaton, who was always hovering about her chamber. It was so incredible it was hard to believe that it was true – but here was the evidence to prove it.

'The proofs are damning, are they not?' Cromwell said at length, looking mournful.

Harry could not speak. Anne had plotted his death – Anne, whom he had loved with a passion, whom he had elevated far above her station and honoured with marriage, risking his kingdom in the process! Plotting the death of the King, the Lord's anointed, was high treason, the most heinous of all crimes, and it was invariably – and rightly – punished with the greatest severity. Even he, the King himself, would have no choice in the matter.

His head was spinning, his heart thudding dangerously. He feared he might die. He could not credit her wickedness. He had been duped, made a fool of. How could she have stooped so low?

He could have killed her with his bare hands, would have done so had she been in the room with him.

'Have any of them confessed?' His voice sounded strangled.

'Not yet, but Lady Rochford laid the evidence against her husband, and Smeaton is being questioned tomorrow,' Cromwell revealed.

'Rochford is a lecher, but that he should commit . . . such an abomination . . .' He could not utter the word.

'I think your Grace will find that he has committed every depravity known to man,' Sir William Fitzwilliam sneered.

'And Francis Weston. He's one of my gentlemen, and I thought him happily wed.' Harry had loved Weston, shared his passion for music and sport, and honoured him with the Order of the Bath.

'He is wanton, Sir, and had his filthy way without conscience.'

Harry shuddered. He could see why Anne would have fallen for Weston, who was young and handsome, but Sir William Brereton? Yet another of his gentlemen who had betrayed him! It was galling to think of the honours he had showered on Brereton. The man was a womaniser, but that Anne should have consorted with him . . . He was nearly fifty, hardly a court gallant!

As for Smeaton, how could she have so forgotten herself to take that varlet to her bed? What good were handsome looks without breeding? What had she been thinking?

They were waiting for Harry to let them know how he wished them to proceed.

Ill as he felt, with his heart jumping about alarmingly, he was determined to have the pot stirred to the bottom. 'Question Smeaton, then report back to me,' he commanded.

The knowledge of Anne's crimes hung like an invisible weight around his neck. There was to be a tournament to celebrate May Day, yet he could take no pleasure in the prospect. He tried to focus on affairs of state and decided that he would pursue the friendship of Charles after all. He wrote to his envoys at the Imperial court, ordering them to press the Emperor to agree to an alliance without conditions, and insisting that he acknowledge the validity of his marriage to Anne. Even now, that was important. He also wrote to Francis, demanding that he abandon his new alliance with the Bishop of Rome unless the latter agreed to revoke all actions against England. He was determined to force the European powers and the Church of Rome to recognise that he had been right to put away his first wife and take a second. It did not matter that Anne was now under a cloud of suspicion and might not be queen much longer. It was his own actions that must be adjudged right. Inside, though, he was sickened to his stomach.

He knew where to find the comfort he needed. Jane had opened her chaste arms to him after he had learned of the accusations against Anne, and he knew she would do so again. She was a haven of calm in a turbulent world. He did not feel for her the obsessive need he had had for Anne, but that seemed tainted now. Jane's gentle charms were exactly what he wanted in a woman.

He crept along the gallery to her lodging. 'Jane, I have to talk to you,' he said. The Seymours made obeisance and hastily withdrew into their bedchamber, leaving the door ajar. Harry shut it behind them.

Jane smiled a welcome, poured wine for them both, and drew up a stool facing his chair. 'You are troubled, Sir,' she said, resting her hand on his.

'Alas, I am weighed down with cares,' he sighed. 'I am dealing with a serious matter concerning the Queen. My Council has questioned her women and other witnesses, and the matter now appears so evident that there can be no room for doubt.'

'Oh, no,' Jane murmured. 'What has she done?'

'She has been conspiring my death!' he growled. 'She has taken lovers and conspired with them to murder me. That is high treason, Jane, the most heinous of all crimes. Today, in Council, we had no choice but to conclude that the Queen is an adulteress and a regicide, and deserves to be burned as a traitor.'

Jane shrieked in horror. 'Oh, but Harry, that is a terrible death!'

'It is a terrible crime!' he barked, and saw her recoil. 'Jane, you have a kind heart, but Anne does not deserve your sympathy or anyone else's. She has even betrayed me with her own brother.'

Jane gasped.

'And with a low-born musician.'

'Mark Smeaton?'

He was startled. 'How do you know that?'

'I assumed it, because he is always hanging around her chamber. I thought she had rebuffed him.'

'It was a pretence, I am certain of it. He is now being questioned at Master Cromwell's house, for it is believed he can tell more.'

Jane was gulping down her wine as if seeking oblivion. 'I am more sorry than I can say that the Queen has committed these wicked crimes,' she said, rising unsteadily and putting her arms around Harry, her soft bosom pressing against his cheek. 'It is hard to credit that anyone, let alone the person who is supposed to love you the most, could stoop low enough to do such dreadful things to him who is not only her lord, but her sovereign.'

Harry squeezed her hand and drained his goblet. 'Jane, I did not come here solely to rail against her. I came for another purpose entirely, but now is perhaps not the moment.' He looked at her intently, then drew her closer to him, kissing her temple. 'Or perhaps it is the right time,' he murmured, then drew back and looked her in the eye. 'When this is over, Jane, will you marry me?'

He had thought about it several times over the past days. Now, it seemed like the obvious, the perfect solution to his troubles. Jane would be his place of refuge. With her, he could enjoy the peace and harmony that had eluded him with Anne. With her, he could be healed, be the King he was meant to be.

Jane's lower lip trembled. 'Oh, my dear Harry!' she whispered.

'I love you, my darling,' he breathed, holding her gaze, 'and this time it is a true, pure and honourable love, not the obsessive love I had for Anne. I was mad then, but I am older and wiser now. I offer my hand to you, not as your King, but as your humble suitor. Say you will have me!'

He saw her hesitate and willed her to say yes.

'I love you,' she said, and he almost wept. 'I will marry you, but there is something I desire you to promise me first.'

'What must I do?' he asked, the knight errant in him rising to the occasion.

'Swear to me, I beg of you, that you will not send Anne to the fire. I should feel that it was on account of me and, whatever she has done, I could not live with myself knowing that her agony had made me queen.'

He frowned, but he could not be angry with her. 'Very well, Jane,' he said at length. 'Mercy is an admirable quality in a queen. I swear that she shall not be burned.'

Jane threw her arms around his neck and kissed him. 'Thank you, thank you, Harry! I will be honoured to be your wife; nothing could give me more joy!'

He crushed her to his chest as his lips closed on hers. In that kiss there was passion and longing, but also pain.

'There could never have been a proposal more timely,' she said.

Harry paused, uncomprehending.

'I believe I am with child,' she told him, and he was suddenly overwhelmed by the most blissful hope and joy.

'Are you indeed?' he asked in wonder.

'I am almost certain. Another week, and I will miss my third course.'

'Heaven be praised!' he cried. 'A son to crown our happiness. A blessing from God. An heir for England!' He kissed her with renewed fervour.

It would not be long now before matters came to a head. Anne, he thought, had guessed that something was amiss. He was avoiding her company as much as possible, fearing he would not be able to contain his rage. When they did meet, he made a supreme effort to rein it in, and he was aware that she seemed distracted. She had Elizabeth with her at Greenwich and was spending an unusual amount of time with her – she, who had never been overly maternal. Had she realised that these might be the last days she would spend with her daughter?

Hot fury seized him. She was not fit to be in the company of an innocent child!

He sent word that Elizabeth was to return to Hatfield immediately with her household. And there was Anne, with their daughter in her arms, accosting him as he stood at his window looking down at a dog fight in the courtyard.

'How could you send her away?' she shrilled. 'I see precious little of her as it is.'

'You never cared enough to complain before,' he retorted.

'Please, Harry, I beg you – let her stay with me.'

Elizabeth was beginning to look distressed. Her lower lip trembled.

'You are upsetting her,' he said coldly. 'Have her gear packed and stop making a fuss. She has been at court for long enough. The air is healthier in the country.'

Anne sniffed and bore Elizabeth away. Harry turned back to the window, but he was too agitated to register the fight in the court-yard below.

He cancelled the trip to Calais. He would have cancelled the tournament too, but for the fact that the court always celebrated the festival of May Day. He did not sleep well on the eve of it. He could not stop wondering what was happening at Cromwell's house, where Smeaton was being questioned. Would the musician's testimony clear Anne's name?

The tiltyard at Greenwich was packed with cheering spectators when he took his place next to Anne in the royal gallery. At his nod, the jousting commenced. Sir Henry Norris led the defenders while Rochford was the leading challenger. Harry could hardly bring himself to look at him, imagining him doing unspeakable things with Anne. Instead, he cheered on his beloved Norris, the trusty head of his Privy Chamber. When Norris' steed became uncontrollable, he lent him one of his own horses. Beside him, Anne was sparkling with jewels and apparently enjoying herself, but her laughter was brittle and there were dark shadows beneath her eyes. Did she suspect something?

A messenger in Cromwell's livery was bowing at his elbow, handing him a letter bearing the secretary's seal. He broke it and read that Smeaton had accused them all and confessed to his own guilt. Worse, he had incriminated Norris too. The words danced before Harry's eyes. Anne really had rutted with that low-born Smeaton! But with Norris? He could not believe it. How could Norris have betrayed him? There must be a mistake.

Blindly, he blundered to his feet and stalked out of the gallery, unheeding of Anne's astonished gasp and the stares of his courtiers. He had to know the truth.

He summoned six of his gentlemen and ordered that they ride with him to Whitehall, as his palace of York Place had just been renamed. He beckoned to the captain of his guard.

'Arrest Sir Henry Norris and bring him to me!' he commanded.

It was unheard of for the King to interrogate a suspected traitor; anointed sovereigns ought to distance themselves from anyone tainted by even the suspicion of treason, but he would not be satisfied until he had spoken to Norris himself. The very idea of his friend betraying him seemed preposterous, unbelievable. It occurred to him once again that Cromwell had concocted these accusations as a means of neutralising Anne, his enemy. But that too was preposterous. Crum would never do anything that so touched his master's honour; he was too faithful a servant.

By the time the horses were saddled, Norris, divested of his armour, was kneeling on the grass before Harry, a guard on either side. 'Your Grace, I beg of you to tell me why I have been apprehended?'

'Certain charges have been laid against you,' Harry said coldly. 'We ride to Whitehall. Mount your horse and accompany me.'

Norris obeyed, looking petrified.

As they spurred their steeds, Harry could not contain himself. 'Norris, have you not always enjoyed great favour at my hands?'

Norris stared at him, clearly alarmed. 'Of course, Sir. I am most grateful—'

'And have I not honoured you with my friendship?'

'More than I could ever have hoped for, Sir.'

'Then why have you betrayed me with the Queen?'

Norris looked dumbstruck. Harry could almost believe that his surprise was genuine.

'I swear to your Grace that such a thing never entered my mind. I have never betrayed you.'

'Evidence has been laid against you.'

'Sir, it is all lies!' He sounded panicked.

Harry wanted to believe him. 'If you are guilty, and confess it, I will spare your life and your property. Just tell me the truth!'

'Sir, I have nothing to confess!' Norris protested. 'I will submit myself to trial by combat to prove my innocence, if you will allow it.'

Harry was having none of that. 'No, you will stand trial like the rest.'

'The rest?' Norris looked aghast, but Harry had swivelled in the saddle and beckoned his guards. 'Take him ahead to Whitehall,' he commanded.

That evening, he ordered that the five men accused of treason be incarcerated in the Tower pending their trials. The arrests took place the following morning as rumours spread like flames through a frightened court.

'Everyone is asking who will be next,' Cromwell reported. 'Speculation is rife!'

'Have the Queen taken after dinner,' Harry ordered. 'She shall go to the Tower too and be tried. See that your case is watertight, Crum.'

He had hardened his heart against Anne and the men who had consorted with her. They had dealt him a mortal blow with their unspeakable crimes. He doubted his pride would ever recover, for the whole world would know that she had found him wanting as a man. What price then his magnificence?

Late that afternoon, Cromwell came to tell him that the Queen was in the Tower, installed in the apartments she had occupied before her coronation, thousands of years ago, it seemed.

'She was hysterical, Sir. She protested her innocence, of course, but it will avail her nothing against the depositions. We have set women to watch her and report anything compromising she says to the Constable.'

Harry waved him away, suddenly feeling choked. 'Enough, Crum. The matter grieves me too much.'

Left alone, he gave way to tears, thinking back over the years with Anne, the passion, the power games and the long holding-off. He remembered her ambition, her cool rejections in the early days, her cruelties to Kate and Mary. He should have known then that she was a she-devil. But he had been enchanted, bewitched! He could never have dreamed how far in wickedness she was steeped. These affairs of hers had been going on for years. Her French ways . . . He shuddered. He could believe anything of her now. God knew what other crimes she had committed or plotted.

He mastered himself and sent for his son Richmond, who had this day joined the court, unaware of the dramas unfolding there.

The boy knelt before him, a gangling youth of seventeen who had a passing look of Harry himself at that age. If Jane lost her child, or proved as barren as Kate and Anne, Richmond would be the sole hope of England. He had been raised like a prince and educated for greatness. Harry would have him legitimated and name him his heir. Henry IX. And, by St George, the people would accept him!

'Welcome, my son,' he said. 'I wished to see you and give you my blessing.' He rested his hand on Richmond's golden head, then clasped him to his breast and began weeping again. 'My boy, you and your sister Mary are greatly bound to God for having escaped the hands of that accursed whore, whom I fear would have poisoned you both had she had the chance.'

Richmond hugged him and stood up, coughing. Harry watched him, suddenly concerned. He had heard his own brother cough like that, one Christmas, many years ago. Surely God would not be so cruel as to take this boy too in the flower of his youth?

'Are you ill, my son?' he asked.

'A summer cold, Sir. It is nothing.'

'I will give you one of my remedies,' Harry said, rising and opening his cabinet. 'I made it myself and have found it most effective.'

'Thank you, Father,' the lad replied. 'God give you good night.'

Unable to face being alone, Harry sought out Jane. She seemed full of fear.

'Sir, what is happening? The court is in an uproar.'

'The Queen has been arrested. This is no business of yours, darling, and I want you distanced from any scandal. Carew has offered you his house at Beddington and I am sending you there until things have died down.'

'But—'

'No buts, Jane. You must go tonight, and not be embroiled in this. Do not fret. Think of our child.' He patted her belly.

'Will you visit me?' She looked frightened.

'If I can. Now go, and God be with you.' He watched her leave with a deep sense of loss. Now he would be truly alone to face the scandal and the humiliation.

Knowing the shameful truth of what was soon to be revealed about Anne's criminal activities, he could not bring himself to appear in public. He kept to his apartments or his privy garden, seeing only his closest ministers.

What could he do to restore his honour and his reputation as a virile, all-powerful king? The question tormented him. In the end, he decided it would look well if he were to be seen surrounded by admiring ladies. Anne's women were still twittering around, he had been told, terrified lest they be implicated in her crimes and not knowing whether to stay at court or go home. Ostensibly, there was the possibility that she might be adjudged not guilty and return in triumph, so he could not dismiss them yet. Therefore, during those harrowing days when she was in the Tower, he invited some of them to join him in his barge for lamplit evening banquets on the Thames, serenaded by his musician and singers. He chose those ladies who were the most beautiful and bade them wear their richest gowns. They clustered around him in the balmy dusk, all vying for his attention. Usually he would have enjoyed the flirtations, but inwardly he was in turmoil, veering between wanting Jane and trying to come to terms with Anne's betrayal.

He spent his nights lying awake, wondering what other crimes Anne had committed and how many men she had slept with in reality. He kept thinking back obsessively on how she had flirted with the courtiers who flocked to her chamber. She had never been so amorous with *him*!

One night, when sleep again eluded him, he rose from his bed and began writing a short play, *The Tragedy of Anne*, in which he portrayed her having illicit congress with all and sundry. Steeling himself to go out again, he took it with him to a dinner at the house of the Bishop of Carlisle, accompanied by many ladies and putting on a hearty front, as if his Queen's infidelity troubled him not at all.

'I am well rid of her,' he said sagely to the Bishop, as they dined on roast peacock and pigeon pie. 'Between ourselves, I believe now that more than a hundred men had to do with her. Indeed, I long expected something like this.' He showed his host the tragedy. 'You know that she and her brother laughed at my compositions, deeming them foolish things?'

The Bishop perused the manuscript. 'That was wickedly unjust, Sir. This is the best play I have seen.'

'Thank you.' His words were balm to Harry's bruised soul. 'Of course, it can never be performed, but it did help me to write it all down.'

Among the guests was Chapuys, who cornered Harry after supper.

'May I offer your Grace my commiserations on the Queen's treachery?' he asked, with what looked like genuine sympathy.

Harry was having none of it. 'Many great and good men, even emperors and kings, have suffered from the arts of wicked women,' he observed, determined to wear his horns lightly.

Chapuys looked sorrowful. 'Even so, I am sorry that your Majesty has been the victim of evil persons.'

Harry scowled at him. He did not intend to be seen as a victim.

Although he had been expecting the news, he nevertheless received a jolt when they told him that Norris, Weston, Brereton and Smeaton had all been condemned to death. It rendered the outcome of the coming trials of Anne and Rochford a foregone conclusion, for how could they now be found innocent? The executioner had already been sent for. Not for Anne the flames or the hewing of the axe, but the cleanness of a sword, wielded by the expert executioner of Calais. Harry had resolved to grant her this one kindness out of pity – not just to honour his promise to Jane, but also because Cromwell was worried about the English hangman bungling his task and inciting sympathy for Anne. The world, after all, would be riveted; it was not every day that a queen was sent to her death.

'But your Grace should not show mercy yet,' Cromwell urged, sitting with Harry in the privy garden in the fading dusk. 'We need the Queen's co-operation, to smooth the way for a new Act settling the succession on your heirs by a future wife. Her marriage must be annulled, and the Princess disinherited on account of her uncertain paternity.'

Harry bristled. He loved his daughter. 'Anyone can see she is mine!'

'Of course, Sir, but there will inevitably be those who cast doubt, and a disputed succession, another war of the roses, is the last thing England needs.'

Harry would never cease to be haunted by the spectre of dynastic conflict. Cromwell was right. Jane's son must succeed unchallenged.

'And you can find the means to end this marriage?'

'Yes, Sir. I have canon lawyers looking into it. But we will need the Queen's consent and I fear she might not willingly agree to the disinheriting of her daughter. We may need to bargain with her.'

'Bargain? How?' The very idea! Convicted traitors were dead persons, not fit even to plead.

'Norfolk is to preside over the trials. I will order him to have her sentenced to be burned or beheaded at your Grace's pleasure. I think you'll find she will agree to an annulment in return for the kinder death.'

Because of their high rank, Anne and Rochford were to have the privilege of being tried by their peers, in the King's Hall within the Tower. The public were to be admitted; justice must be seen to be done.

On that Monday, Harry could not concentrate on anything. He had no doubt what the verdict would be, yet he could not quite bring himself to accept that this was actually happening; that it was Anne who was at the bar.

'The sentence is death,' Cromwell informed him in the afternoon. 'As arranged, she is to be burned or beheaded at your Grace's pleasure. And Rochford will die too. Both protested their innocence.'

Harry was trembling, his heart pounding. The body he had longed to possess was to be brutally butchered. No matter what Anne had done, he could not efface the memories or the glory of the heady years of their courtship. They would always be with him, long after she was gone. How had it ended like this?

He mastered himself. Cromwell was waiting, frowning.

'Sir, there was a stirring at Rochford's trial. His wife had deposed that the Queen had made certain disparaging remarks about your Grace, and they were written on a paper, which was shown to him. He was ordered to say if she had uttered those words, but not to reveal what they were. But he read them out, denying she had said them.'

'What words?' Harry growled.

Cromwell cleared his throat, clearly embarrassed. 'That your Grace was without vigour and could not beget children.'

'What?' Harry leapt to his feet, seized with fury. 'How dare he? Now people will think it true! Am I not a man like other men? Am I not? Have I not sired four children on her?'

'But he denied that she had said it, Sir.'

'No matter. People will believe it. It'll be all around London and the court by now.' Humiliation upon humiliation! 'By God, he has deserved death for that alone!'

Wanting Jane to be nearer to him, for Beddington was inaccessible by barge, he had sent her to More's old house at Chelsea. Now he dispatched Sir Francis Bryan to her with the news of Anne's condemnation.

That evening, he arrived at Chelsea to dine with Jane, having had himself rowed along the Thames with an almost festive air of pageantry. He found her distracted and fretful, and had all to do to soothe her and reassure her that she was not the cause of Anne's death.

'Comfort yourself,' he urged her. 'As soon as she is dead, we will be married, and then our child will be born.'

'People will think it done in indecent haste,' she protested.

'It is a necessity. The succession must be assured. I am forty-five and getting no younger.'

Jane still looked doubtful, but, as usual, she deferred to his greater wisdom. He liked that. Anne would have kept on arguing. Anne! He was sick of the thought of her.

Two days later, Cromwell came to his closet to inform him that the men had all suffered execution. Five heads had rolled.

'Did they confess their guilt?' he barked.

'Only Smeaton.'

'Damn him! Damn them all!'

He dismissed Cromwell and sat down by the hearth, his mind in turmoil, his anger rising. He should not have been so merciful. They should have suffered the full penalty the law demanded for traitors – even Rochford!

All he wanted now was for this vile business to be over. Tomorrow, Anne would die too, then he would be free to marry Jane – and the world would be a better place.

Cranmer arrived late in the afternoon. Harry laid down the book he had been trying to read. 'Yes, my lord Archbishop?'

'It is done, your Grace. I have declared your marriage to the Queen null and void, which renders the Princess Elizabeth illegitimate. The Queen's proctors did not challenge my decision.'

'There were no grounds for doing so,' Harry observed, thinking of how cruelly this day's work would affect Elizabeth, an innocent child. Yet he had had no choice: the succession must be assured to Jane's son. After so many disappointments, he did not dare to consider that the child might not be a boy. The Seymours, he reminded himself, were an abundantly fruitful family.

'The terms were explained to them quite clearly,' Cranmer said, 'and they signified the Queen's consent.'

'She knew, as did I, that my relations with her sister created a barrier to our marriage, but we both chose to ignore that.' Harry sighed. 'Passion is blind, Thomas.'

'I think, your Grace, that the lady was not thinking so much on the barrier to the marriage as upon the manner of her death.' Cranmer's tone was stiff, his expression even more lugubrious than usual.

'It was once said that she was braver than a lion,' Harry recalled, ignoring the implied reproof, 'but her courage now seems to have deserted her.'

'On the contrary, Sir, she is facing death with great courage, I am told.'

'You were ever her champion, Thomas, but you know where your loyalties should lie.'

'It was a cruel choice,' Cranmer persisted.

'Blame Cromwell!' Harry snapped. To his horror, he saw that Cranmer's eyes had filled with tears. 'By St George, man, she is not worth your sympathy!'

'No, Sir. But I had a good opinion of her and find it hard to believe her guilty of all those dreadful crimes. And she has been a great champion of reform.'

Harry's eyes narrowed. 'You deny her guilt? Twenty-seven peers, her own father among them, condemned her!'

'I do not deny it. I am just shocked – and I am truly sorry for the misery and trouble into which she has cast your Grace.'

'Hmm,' Harry grunted, mollified. 'You can go to her if you like. Hear her last confession.'

'Thank you, Sir,' Cranmer murmured, and hurriedly withdrew.

Harry was plunged into turmoil when he learned that Anne's execution was to be postponed for another day because all was not yet ready at the Tower. He even found it in his heart to feel sorry for her. What if she had been ready for death, and now had to summon her courage all over again? What was it like, being granted more sweet hours on earth and counting them down as they sped inexorably towards their end?

The next day, the fatal day, he donned black mourning and spent the morning in prayer. The execution was to be at nine o'clock. When the hour struck, he heard the boom of a distant cannon. It was over.

Anne was no more.

Inexplicably, he found himself weeping.

Chapter 29

Soon afterwards, he heard footsteps approaching his closet. That would be Cromwell, back from the Tower.

'Your Grace, the Queen is dead,' he reported. 'She died bravely.' He sounded oddly impressed.

Harry rose from his knees, his legs feeling as if they had dissolved. Anne, dead at thirty-five. It was barely believable. For a moment, all he could think of was that enchanting girl with the jewel-threaded dark hair and the inviting eyes. Oh, she had bewitched him with her sorcery – and those others too, let him not forget!

'It was swift?' he asked.

'It was over before you could say a Paternoster. She asked the people to pray for you and said you had always been to her a good, gentle sovereign lord.'

'Did she admit her guilt?'

'She said she would not speak of that, but asked people to judge the best.'

Damn her! Infuriating, right to the end. And now everyone would wonder if she had died an innocent woman. Oh, she had been clever!

'Send to Lady Bryan at Hatfield,' he commanded. 'Order her to keep the news from the Lady Elizabeth and protect her from gossip. There is time enough for her to learn the truth about her mother when she is older. For now, she is of too tender an age.'

He spent the day in seclusion before visiting Jane in the evening. At the sight of her, so demure and comely, his heart leapt. The mother of his son! Soon, the world would know that his heir lay beneath her girdle. As yet, there was barely a hint of it.

Early the next morning, at Hampton Court, they were formally betrothed, and the world seemed to right itself. Their marriage was solemnised quietly ten days later in the Queen's closet at Whitehall, and afterwards, looking terrified, Jane, still wearing her white satin wedding gown, took her place on the consort's throne next to Harry's beneath the canopy of estate in the presence chamber.

He had dressed magnificently for the occasion. At forty-five, he prided himself that he still cut a fine figure of a king. His waist was narrow, his chest broad. Yet his mirror showed him that age was encroaching. He was losing his hair and his face had coarsened. The frustrations and stresses of the last years had left their mark, and not only on his appearance. Where he had once been open-handed, liberal and idealistic, he was now contrary, secretive, combative and changeable. He knew it, but could not help it, or the temper that erupted in him with increasing frequency. It was the price, he assured himself, of his greatness – and the frustrations and mishaps he had suffered.

He lay with Jane that night, glorying in their closeness, and feeling that he had come from Hell into Heaven. He longed to possess her again, but held off for fear of harming the child. But, oh, it felt good to have her caress him, and to run his fingers over her sweet body.

His abstinence made no difference. The babe came too soon, in a rush of blood. Harry could barely stem the tears. He felt desperate. Was he never to father a living son, even with Jane, whose right to be his wife God Himself could not dispute?

He sat by her side, holding her hand.

'I am more sorry than I can say,' she sobbed.

'It was God's will,' he sighed.

'Oh, my darling,' she said, 'I would not have had this happen for the world.'

They went to Greenwich for Whitsuntide. There Jane was proclaimed Queen and followed Harry in procession to Mass, with a great train of ladies following her and the whispering courtiers crowding around. Later that day, she dined in state, flanked by her brothers, Edward, newly created Viscount Beauchamp, and Thomas. Of the two of them, Harry preferred Thomas for good company, but there was no denying that Edward was the finer statesman, and he was now rising high and enjoying great influence at court. He was haughty, reserved, yet, for all his dignity, under the thumb of his strident wife, Anne, whom Jane disliked.

'She is too overbearing,' she complained. 'She makes me feel small.'

'By St George, I'll not let her,' Harry declared. 'I fear your brother is too much of an idealist to make a stern husband.'

'He is a moderate man.'

'Aye, and all for reform, but his real talent lies in his military capacity. He will make a great commander.'

'I am pleased that he can serve you well,' Jane smiled.

Both brothers were in attendance when Harry and Jane sailed by barge from Greenwich to Whitehall and Jane entered London in state. As Harry stood on deck to take the salute from the four hundred guns lined up along Tower Wharf, he saw her shudder and knew that she was thinking of Anne, now rotting in her grave in the chapel of St Peter ad Vincula, just yards from where their vessel rocked on the Thames. He steeled himself not to think of that. The Tower was looking festive today, its walls gaily hung with streamers and banners. None would have guessed at the tragedies that had been played out behind them only last month.

Jane had recovered herself when he led her in procession to Westminster Abbey to attend High Mass. The next morning, as she stood in the gallery above the gatehouse at Whitehall and waved him farewell as he rode off to open Parliament, he congratulated himself on having chosen so loving and dutiful a wife. She would never be drawn into discussions about religion or politics; she was compassionate and pious. If she seemed aloof, even haughty, he knew it was because she felt at a disadvantage beside the great lords and ladies of the realm; she was, after all, merely the daughter of a knight. Yet she bore her royal honours with dignity.

He was planning a splendid coronation for her, to take place in October. A great barge, built along the lines of the famous bucentaur of the doges of Venice, was to be constructed; it would bring her from Greenwich to London, where she would be received with magnificent pageantry and music.

Harry was pleased to see Jane determined to enforce high moral standards in her household, especially after the scandals that had brought Anne down.

'I insist on having my ladies modestly attired,' she told him one night after he had beaten her at cards, and they had fallen to discussing appointments to her new household. 'They must wear trains three yards long and girdles set with two hundred pearls. No one is to appear before me in a French hood.' There was no need to ask why.

Her modesty did not preclude her dressing magnificently and delighting in the jewels Harry gave her. She had gasped when, one night in bed, he placed around her neck an emerald and ruby pendant designed by Holbein, whom Harry now employed as King's Painter and who had also designed the exquisite gold drinking cup that had been his wedding gift to Jane. It was decorated with their initials entwined in true lovers' knots and her new motto, 'Bound to obey and serve'.

Watching Jane playing with her white poodle as they relaxed in the privy garden after Parliament had risen for the day, Harry felt pride in her enjoyment of simple pleasures as well as the luxuries he could give her. On the bench beside him lay an impressive piece of embroidery with her needle stuck in it. She was always stitching away when they were private together. Now she was bending down, inhaling the sweet scent of the flowers in the railed beds, gardens being her passion. She was an excellent hunter too. He admired that in a woman. Yes, he had chosen well. He felt blissfully contented.

It was a lovely summer, given over to celebrations and entertainments, with masques, hunting trips, river pageants and a firework display. It was almost like old times, and Harry even appeared in disguise as the Sultan of Turkey at a joust and banquet. He stopped short, however, of taking part in the tournament. Those days were over, he reflected sadly.

'Harry, forgive me, but I must ask again. Could you see your way to bringing the Lady Mary back to court?' Jane looked up from her stitching. 'I would have someone of high rank to make merry with.'

Harry suppressed his anger. He knew that Jane's sympathies had long lain with Mary; twice already, she had begged him to forgive his daughter.

'No,' he said, shifting in his chair, aware that his doublet was uncomfortably tight, for he had put on weight. 'I'm sorry, darling, but I will not receive her until she has acknowledged her mother's marriage to be incestuous and unlawful, which she is obstinately refusing to do. No, Jane, don't look at me like that. I intend to put an end to her disobedience.'

Jane regarded him unhappily, but she did not protest. It was not in her nature to gainsay him. Still, she did not give up. Over the next few days, she pleaded gently with him to forgive Mary.

'You have a kind heart, sweetheart, but Mary is my daughter and I will not have her defy me. I love her, but I love my honour more.'

Mary, however, continued to defy him. Just like Kate, stubborn and unreasonable! No, she would not do as he demanded. How could she betray her mother?

He would not allow a chit of twenty to flout him.

Cromwell offered to act as mediator and Harry soon became aware that a fair amount of cajoling and bullying was being used to browbeat Mary into submitting to his will. It worked. In the end, just as he was wondering how he would proceed against her if she continued to disobey him, she capitulated.

'She should have done so at the outset,' he grumbled.

'But now she has signed her submission,' Jane replied, 'so will you not be reconciled to her? She is your daughter, and I am sure she is longing to be restored to your favour.'

Harry looked down at her, so kind and innocent, and his heart melted. 'Oh, sweet Jane, I cannot refuse you.' Truth to tell, vexed with Mary though he was, he had missed her company during the long years of estrangement. And it had all been Kate's fault – Kate, who had poisoned their daughter's mind against him.

He took Jane to visit Mary at Hackney. He was forcibly struck by how small and nervous his daughter was, and shocked that she looked a shadow of her former self. She had been such a pretty girl, with beautiful red hair and the freshness of youth. Now, as he raised her from her deep obeisance, she looked ill and haunted, and she was much too thin.

'My most dear and well-beloved daughter!' he breathed, clasping her to him and fighting off tears. 'I have brought your good mother, Queen Jane, to meet you.'

Mary went to kneel, but Jane took her hands and embraced her.

'You cannot know how good a friend you have in the Queen,' Harry said.

Mary smiled at last. 'I know I am much beholden to your Grace,' she told Jane.

Harry led them into the great chamber and bade Mary be seated between him and Jane. He swallowed, feeling guilty despite himself, having belatedly realised how precious this dear child was to him. 'I deeply regret having kept you so long away from me,' he said, and at that Mary's composure broke and tears streamed down her face.

'Oh, my dearest father, how I have missed you,' she wept.

Harry was choked. 'I will not let it happen again,' he promised. 'We must forget the past and look to the future. There is nothing I would not do for you, my child, now that we are in perfect accord again.'

He gave orders that Mary's household be reassembled and recalled her old governess, Lady Salisbury, to court. He sent gifts of money and gowns. He even summoned Elizabeth for a visit. At nearly three, she was a forward child with a sharp wit and her mother's eyes, but very winning and all him in her colouring and her Roman nose. At the sight of her, he was filled with affection, and regret that she should be motherless at such a tender age, tainted with the stain of bastardy. He could have restored her in blood, yet he dared not, for

440

nothing must be allowed to prejudice the succession of his children by Jane. Instead, he made much of Elizabeth, vowing to do his best for her.

Also at court was Harry's niece Marget Douglas, his sister Margaret's daughter, whom he had brought south a decade back to serve Kate, and who had stayed on to wait on Anne and was now chief lady-of-honour to Jane. She was the same age as Mary, but in contrast to her wan cousin, Marget was beautiful, with a cloud of red hair and perfect features. That, and her royal blood, made her one of the greatest prizes in the marriage market. One day soon, Harry planned to make a splendid match for her, one that would bring some political advantage to himself.

When Cromwell informed him that Marget had been involved in a secret love affair with Norfolk's younger brother, Lord Thomas Howard, he was furious; and when it was discovered that they had precontracted to marry without seeking his permission, wrath seized him.

'Such presumption amounts to treason!' he roared, banging his fist on the table and making even Cromwell quake visibly. 'Send them to the Tower. I'll have their heads for this!'

Parliament was just then in the process of drafting a new Act of Succession, which disinherited Elizabeth and vested the succession in Harry's children with Jane. When Cromwell brought him the draft to approve, Harry was still seething over Marget's misconduct and still in two minds over whether to send the errant couple to the block. Thomas Howard had already been attainted by Parliament and sentenced to death. Could he consign his niece to the same fate?

Jane, of course, was begging him to spare them.

'She is your niece, Harry! They were young, foolish and in love. The Tower is lesson enough for her, surely, especially after what has just happened there.' Her voice faltered.

It pleased him to give way. After all, the naughty lovers had not, by their own independent declarations, bedded with each other. No real harm had been done. And he wanted to make Jane happy, for her to think him merciful. All the same, he ordered that it be deemed treason for anyone to deflower a lady of royal blood or wed her without his permission.

It was time, Harry decided, to reward Cromwell for the great services he had rendered to the Crown. That July, he conferred on him the accolade of knighthood, created him a baron – my Lord Cromwell of Wimbledon – and appointed him Lord Privy Seal in place of Anne's father, Wiltshire, who had gone home to lick his wounds. He also made him Vicar General and Vice Regent of the King in spiritual matters, and entrusted him with responsibility for the dissolution of the monasteries. There had rarely been a mightier subject, he reflected – or a more able one.

Cromwell now controlled all the major offices of government, which would enable him to put into effect the sweeping reforms that would free Harry from many of the chores of personal rule and lay the foundations for an efficient modern administration. The man was a wonder! His influence was everywhere, and nowhere more evident than in Council. Yet Harry had made it plain, subtly or otherwise, that Cromwell functioned only with his royal support and approval, and that it was he who held the upper hand in the relationship. He knew he was no easy master, especially when he was in one of his bad moods.

'You're not fit to meddle in the affairs of kings, you villain, you knave!' he shouted one morning, when Cromwell had come to his closet without his papers. He bawled out Master Secretary at least twice a week, and sometimes could not restrain himself from knocking and pummelling him about the head or shaking him like a dog. And every time, Cromwell slunk out of the chamber with a merry countenance, as though it did not matter, straightening his gown and cap, happy to pay the price for ruling the roost. He knew that, beneath his irascible, violent rages, Harry liked him.

Harry did not like Stephen Gardiner. The Bishop of Winchester was another at whom he lashed out on occasion. Despite his acceptance of the royal supremacy, Gardiner was a religious conservative. There was no love lost between him and Cromwell, and Gardiner strongly disapproved of his rival's reforms and his interference in church affairs. This was not just a professional feud, but an acrimonious personal conflict, and each was eagerly awaiting the chance to bring down the other.

It was Harry and Cromwell who laid down new doctrines for the reformed Church of England, treading a middle road between the teachings of the Catholic Church and the more radical beliefs of the reformers.

When Harry tried to explain them to Jane one hot afternoon, as they sat fishing in the ponds at Hampton Court, she looked doubtful.

'Harry, I do not understand these changes.' He knew she clung to the old religion in her heart.

'Sweetheart, this new Act states that the Scriptures are the basis of true faith, and that the body and blood of Christ are really present in the Mass. It says that Christians may be justified by faith and good works, and not by faith alone, as the heretics hold.'

Jane's pale features relaxed a little. 'But what of images? What of the saints?'

'Images may be used as remembrancers, but not as objects of worship in themselves, for that would be idolatry. And the saints are to be honoured as holy examples and as a means of furthering our prayers. You may invoke their intercessions and observe their holy days, as ever. You see, darling, nothing has really changed, except that pardons and indulgences from Rome are banned.'

With anyone else, he would have been far less patient or accused them of questioning his wisdom. But with Jane he was a better man, the king he ought to be. Under her gentle influence, he tried to be kinder, less irascible. He knew he could be an old bear at times, but he could not help himself. He was as he was.

Jane was smiling uncertainly. Harry left it and turned back to his fishing. Presently, they returned to the palace and he accompanied her to the Queen's chamber for some pastime. As the courtiers flocked around them, the musicians began playing and cards were laid out. Sitting opposite Jane, Harry began to deal. Then Cromwell walked in and bowed.

'Your Grace, you will be pleased to know that the order is given.'

Harry nodded, well satisfied. He saw Jane looking at him questioningly.

'Madam, my Lord Cromwell has arranged for the closure of the smaller monasteries,' he told her. There were murmurs of approval from the gentlemen standing around. Jane looked horrified, but said nothing.

Harry retired to his closet with Cromwell to discuss the scale of pensions that were to be awarded to the displaced monks and nuns, thinking of the vast estates and revenues of the abbeys that were soon to be diverted into the treasury, doubling his income and increasing his power. They could be used to finance his building projects and the purchase of new properties. Then there were the wagonloads of jewels that were coming his way, all removed from crucifixes, shrines and altar ornaments, along with a wealth of plate.

'Crum,' he said, 'I mean to distribute some monastic lands to win the support and loyalty of men with influence or those who are wavering. I am setting up a new Court of Augmentations under your control, to implement this. Give priority to important courtiers, then to the lords temporal and spiritual, then knights, gentlemen and household officers. The rest can go to those merchants, lawyers, doctors and yeomen who aspire to becoming landed gentry. Thus I will bind all ranks to me in gratitude and loyalty.'

'Are they all to pay for the privilege, Sir?'

'Mostly, Crum. It will depend on who should be well rewarded.'

Cromwell's eyes gleamed. 'We shall see how many men of affairs are prepared to compromise their principles for the sake of gain.'

'I do not envisage too many protests,' Harry replied. 'If I know my nobles, they will all be falling over themselves to buy monastic lands and use the building materials to raise grand houses for themselves. Wolsey would have been proud of me. He always said that the best way for a king to control a military aristocracy was to make them compete in emulating his magnificence.'

'And ruin themselves in the process!' Cromwell chuckled.

'Better that than plotting for the throne,' Harry grunted, his eyes narrowing as he realised that there might yet be opposition to his reforms. He was counting on the greed of his lords to counteract that.

Richmond was dead. It was Norfolk, the boy's father-in-law, who brought Harry the bitter news, coming upon him as he was sitting in his garden in his shirtsleeves on a warm July day, reading the latest reports on the closure of the monasteries.

'What is it, my lord?' he asked, noticing that Norfolk's face looked more lugubrious than usual.

The Duke knelt. 'Your Grace, your dear son has departed to God.' His voice was uncommonly gentle.

'No!' Harry cried out, unable to take it in. 'Not my boy, my beautiful boy!'

'I am so sorry. My poor daughter is distraught.'

'He was my hope, my heart.' Harry was rocking back and forth in his misery. 'What happened? He had just a slight cough when I last visited him.'

He had installed Richmond in apartments in the new palace of St James, and they had spent a happy afternoon hunting in the park, like any father and son. Harry had cherished those moments – and now they would never come again.

'My boy, my boy!' he moaned. 'He was just seventeen. He had all his life ahead of him. He was destined for greatness. And now . . .'

He felt a hand on his shoulder. Norfolk, that gruff martinet, was making a clumsy attempt to comfort him.

With a tremendous effort, Harry pulled himself together and gripped the Duke's arm. 'Speak of his passing to no one. I will not have men saying that I sire only weak sons. While I have no lawful heir, I wish to avoid speculation about the succession. Failing any issue by Queen Jane, I intended to make Richmond my successor and would have had him declared so by Parliament. But now . . .' Now the tears did fall.

Norfolk nodded.

'Have his body wrapped in lead and conveyed secretly to be buried with your ancestors at Thetford Priory,' Harry ordered, mastering himself and realising how difficult it was going to be to hide his terrible grief. His son, his brave, debonair son, gone for ever . . .

But there was Jane. To her, he could unburden his tormented heart; on her sweet bosom, he could weep until he was dry.

Of course, the news got out. Soon, the entire court was talking about Richmond's death and hasty burial, and looking askance at Harry, clearly wondering what grieving father would have had his child so meanly laid to rest.

Now that there was no longer any need for secrecy, Harry felt driven to exonerate himself. In Council, he turned on Norfolk. 'Why did you not have my son buried with the honours due to him?' he erupted, as the lords, to a man, glared at the Duke.

Norfolk got up and stamped towards the door, his face puce with rage.

'Methinks his Grace ought to be sent to the Tower for such a dereliction of duty,' Cromwell said loudly.

Norfolk turned. 'When I deserve to be in the Tower, Tottenham shall turn French!'

Harry would not meet his eye. He knew himself to be in the wrong. 'I spoke out of turn,' he said. 'Perchance the Duke mis-understood my orders. My lord, you will forgive the hastiness of a crazed father.' He paused, as Norfolk nodded and sat down again. 'When Thetford Priory is dissolved, as it will be, let my son's body be moved to Framlingham Church, where many of the Howards lie. And let his interment there be attended with all due honour.'

'I will see to it, Sir,' Norfolk said, mollified.

The next day, Harry departed with Jane for Dover to inspect the defences. The jaunt through Kent, with overnight stops at Rochester, Sittingbourne and Canterbury on the way, which he usually enjoyed, did nothing to lift his spirits.

They spent the rest of the summer hunting, enjoying good sport, in bed and out of it. Harry felt somewhat rejuvenated, and it was all down to Jane, yet it nagged at him that she had not conceived again. Surely God could not be frowning on this marriage too? Or was he himself, at forty-five, now past the age at which men were wont to be fertile? The thought horrified him.

'I feel myself growing old,' he confided to Chapuys as they strolled through the empty tiltyard at Whitehall. 'I doubt whether I will have any children by the Queen.'

Chapuys shook his head. 'It is early days yet, your Majesty, and you are a man in the prime of life. There is no reason why God should not grant you a son and heir.'

'Then I pray He does not delay too long!' Harry said fervently.

He continued to do his duty – and his pleasure – vigorously, and joyfully.

It was time to plan Jane's coronation.

'I intend to perform wonders!' he told her, looking up from a selection of pattern books from Italy and France. 'I've selected the most sumptuous furnishings for your sojourn in the Tower before your state entry into London, and I've got carpenters hard at work making Westminster Hall ready for the coronation banquet. I suggest, darling, that you set about ordering your coronation robes. I will have my tailor bring you some materials to look at.'

Jane gave him her sweet smile, but he could tell that something was wrong. She was like a nervous little bird, seeing dangers everywhere.

'What ails you, darling?' he asked, pulling her close to him.

'Nothing.' She returned his kiss. 'I just keep thinking that life is so perfect that something is bound to go wrong.'

'Nonsense!' he laughed. 'There is nothing to fear. You will have a wonderful day and the people will love you!'

There was even more reason to celebrate. Jane was with child again.

Harry was overjoyed. He could not do enough for her. Her every whim was to be gratified. She must not over-exert herself in any way. He fussed over her like a mother hen.

'Going to play midwife, Hal?' cackled Will Somers from his cushioned stool in the corner of Harry's chamber.

'Be off with you,' Harry grinned.

'It's good to see you so happy, old friend,' Somers replied. 'It'll be a prince this time, I'll wager. Chip off the old block!'

Harry cuffed him good-humouredly.

Bed sports, of course, were forbidden to him now. It was frustrating, especially at his age, when he felt he had no time to lose, and he held out for as long as he could bear it before doing what he had become accustomed to doing when his wives were pregnant.

He could not help himself. The urge was rampant in him, as it always had been. A pretty face, a smile, a swelling bosom – it took little to arouse his interest. Love didn't come into it. In that respect, he was Jane's alone. He took care to couple only with the few women he could trust not to talk; the wives of courtiers, or the Queen's maids who, desirous of making a good marriage, had reason to keep silent. Even so, he was aware that his reputation was well known, and that it had even been said that all it took to please him was an apple and a fair wench to dally with. His mouth pursed prudishly. He did not want Jane hearing things like that. And he would not hurt her for the world, especially at this time. He had seen what her father's incestuous infidelity had done to her family.

It was safer occasionally to take his pleasure with women of the lower classes. It was well known that they enjoyed it more than their well-bred counterparts – and they were almost always grateful for a few gold coins in reward. One day, Harry was on the road near Eltham Palace and met a pretty wench riding pillion behind a man who turned out to be her lover. He took an immediate fancy to her and bowed in the saddle.

'Good day, Mistress.'

The couple stared at him in awe. They knew who he was. But when his eyes fixed appreciatively on the girl's bosom, the man's gaze became hostile. Harry made a quick decision and pulled her onto his horse. Ignoring the fellow's shouts of protest, he rode off with her to the palace, where he found her a more than willing partner, so willing, in fact, that he decided to keep her in his lodging for several days before dismissing her. That, he thought, would be the end of it. But her paramour, a troublemaker called Webbe, had the audacity to make a formal complaint to the Council. It was quickly hushed up, of course. The woman was returned to him, and money changed hands, while Harry resolved to be more discreet in future. It would only be for a short time. In the late spring, Jane would be his again.

Chapter 30

1536

Harry's worst nightmare became reality that October when a great rebellion broke out in Lincolnshire and the north, where the old ideas remained entrenched among the gentry, who fiercely opposed the King's religious reforms. He knew, from the first alarming reports, that this was the most serious threat to his authority he had ever faced, and he immediately began preparing to lead an army against the rebels. At Greenwich, he had the tiltyard converted into a workshop and set his armourers to repairing his rusted old armour that had been taken out of storage. He would teach these traitors a lesson, by God!

His blood ran to ice when further reports made it clear that the rebellion was spreading through the north at an alarming rate – and that he did not have sufficient forces to deal with it.

'We must play for time,' he told his councillors.

Jane sat enthroned beside him as he gazed down on the sea of bared heads before him and announced how he would deal with the rising and suppress the rebels. The applause was deafening.

Suddenly, Jane rose, and the acclaim died away. As Harry stared at her, she fell to her knees before him, her face flushed. Not a whisper could be heard. He frowned. What mummery was this?

'Sir,' she said hoarsely, 'Sir, I beg you, for the sake of peace and of those of your loving subjects who regret the passing of the old ways, please think kindly upon the monasteries. I urge you to restore those you have closed. It is wrong for subjects to rebel against their Prince, but perhaps God has permitted this rebellion as a punishment for the ruin of so many churches.'

Harry glared at her, shaking with fury, embarrassed and mortified. That his meek wife, a mere woman, should challenge his policy, and in public, was deeply insulting. It was as if a lamb had roared. She should have realised that queenly intercessions were invariably agreed upon beforehand, to enable a king to rescind an order without losing face. But now here she was, kneeling before him, looking up to him with those scared pale eyes.

The old bear in him took over. How dare she side with the rebels? 'You forget yourself, Madam!' he snarled. 'This has nothing to do with you. I might remind you that the last Queen died in consequence of meddling too much in state affairs. Go and attend to other things!' He pointed to the great doors.

Cheeks aflame, Jane got unsteadily to her feet and curtseyed, then hastened through the throng, the ranks of courtiers parting for her, staring, smiling, murmuring behind their hands.

He soon regretted his outburst. The pain in Jane's eyes stayed with him. He would make things right between them later, yet he feared that something precious had been broken, something that might never mend. Damn the woman, why had she dared to speak out?

Making a false show of strength, he sent north an army under the command of Norfolk and Suffolk, with instructions to use conciliatory measures. And he postponed Jane's coronation.

It was as well. Early in November, she sent for him, which was unusual. She was in her bedchamber, her ladies informed him, seemingly unable to meet his eye. A sense of dread gripped him. He knew, before she broke the news to him, that she had lost their son.

'It is God's will,' she said gently, tears welling. 'I am so deeply sorry.'

'What do I have to do to placate God?' Harry cried, balling his fists. 'This marriage is pure, without any impediments! Why does He withhold sons from me?'

Jane looked so desperate that he felt as sorry for her as he did for himself – and for England. 'We must pray, and we must try again,' she said.

'How many times have I heard that?' he sighed.

'I am so sorry, Harry. I took the greatest care.'

'I know.' He sighed and patted her hand. 'It is not your fault.' But was it his?

He had no time to grieve. He had a rebellion to deal with. He was gratified to see most of the nobility rallying to the Crown, proof that the Reformation and the Dissolution were widely supported, at least in the south. It was the northern lords he feared and the vast numbers of followers they could command. If Norfolk's bluff were to be called, there was a very real danger of civil war breaking out. These rebels were on a mission to turn back the clock and spare the monasteries. They were calling their rising 'the Pilgrimage of Grace', and thousands were flocking to the banners of the hotheads who had started it all – banners that bore the Five Wounds of Christ.

Harry burned with indignation. They were attacking his authority as king, his supremacy over the Church and his wisdom in pushing through his reforms. Worse still, they threatened the peace of his realm, which he had striven to maintain ever since Flodden. He waited in a fury of impatience to hear what the dukes had achieved.

'The main objective is to make them disperse,' he had commanded. 'Agree to their demands and make them go home. Offer them all royal pardons.'

He had no intention, of course, of letting them get away with it. The promises and the pardons would be worth nothing. They would learn what it meant to defy their King.

In December, a truce was reached, with Norfolk, in the King's name, agreeing to all the rebels' demands, among them a request that the Queen be crowned at York, and dangling before them the royal pardons that Harry had no intention of putting into effect. But soon it was being reported that the pilgrims, as they called themselves, were still banding together.

It was Thomas Wriothesley who suggested inviting Robert Aske, one of the rebel leaders, to court for Christmas. Harry liked Wriothesley, for all the young man's insufferable pretensions to greatness; his father, Master Wrythe, had been a mere herald, but the son had changed his name with a view to bettering himself. He was Gardiner's man, for Gardiner was his patron and had furthered his career at court, where he had attracted the attention of Cromwell. It pleased Harry to call Wriothesley his 'Pig', just to bring him down a peg or two.

Where other councillors had urged him to deal gently with the rebels, Wriothesley had been the only one to criticise that policy.

'Bring Aske to court, your Grace, and lull him into a sense of false security,' he urged. 'That way, he will get his men to disperse. Then you can deal with them more efficiently.'

Harry liked that plan. He saw no reason why it should not come smoothly to fruition.

In October, he had invited Mary back to court, where he and Jane welcomed her warmly. He was dismayed to see how nervous she looked, and shocked when she fainted during the reception, with the whole court looking on, aghast. But he raised her, walked her up and down, and assured her of his fatherly love, and Jane was wonderful. She took Mary by the hand and treated her as an equal, refusing to go first through a doorway. She persuaded Harry to assign Mary fine lodgings in the royal palaces, even though he had not anticipated that his daughter would live permanently at court. Now, she could, if she pleased.

Harry was aware that too much lay between him and Mary for theirs ever to be an easy relationship. He had forced her to choose where her loyalty lay, and she had chosen her mother against him – and neither could forget that. And yet he loved her, and it grieved him to see her so forlorn, for all the kindness she had received. If only she had been more dutiful, more amenable, in the past.

'She is an anxious soul,' he observed to Jane across the supper table one evening. 'She is always suffering from one ailment or another. Women's problems, I suspect.'

'Her life has not been easy,' Jane observed, then stopped, reddening. 'I'm sorry, I meant no criticism.'

'If she and her mother had not been so stubborn, it would have been otherwise,' he replied.

'If she could make a good marriage . . .' Jane began. But they both knew that Mary's bastardy stood in the way of that, and Harry would never stoop to giving his daughter to a commoner.

'I am considering several options,' he lied. 'For now, let her rejoice in the reversal in her fortunes. She was thrilled with the gowns I gave her; she has always loved fine clothes. She has money for her charities and to reward those who do her kindnesses, and she can hunt, gamble, dance and make music to her heart's content. She should be content for now with all that.'

He would address the problem of finding her a husband, he resolved. At twenty, Mary should be married. Fortunately, she was still an innocent where men were concerned. She knew no foul or unclean speech. He had not believed it, and only last week had charged Sir Francis Bryan to test her virtue by using a lewd word while dancing with her during a masque. Mary had failed to react, to Harry's astonishment and Bryan's amusement.

He raised the matter of her marriage with Cromwell.

'I do not foresee a problem,' the minister said. 'Many princes would be glad to ally with your Grace, and the Lady Mary is comely.'

That was putting it diplomatically. She was small, spare and button-nosed with a prim mouth like Harry's. In looks, however, she resembled Kate, with that firm chin. But her Tudor lineage should compensate for her lack of beauty.

'Finding a husband for the Lady Mary would be to your Grace's advantage,' Cromwell said, after a thoughtful pause. 'If she bears sons, the succession would be assured.'

'But they would be of some other man's house,' Harry protested.

'They would be of your blood, Sir.'

'True. But the Queen may bear a prince soon. Let us trust in that.'

* * *

454

It was a bitter winter, so cold that the Thames froze. Wrapped in furs, Harry and Jane rode on horseback through the gaily decorated streets of London to a service in St Paul's Cathedral, then galloped across the ice-clad River Thames to Greenwich, to the delight of the crowds who came to see them. Christmas was kept with impressive solemnity and splendour, marred only by news of the death of the Queen's father, Sir John Seymour. But Jane put on a brave face. Mary and Elizabeth were at court, and she made every effort to ensure that both enjoyed themselves, hiding her private grief.

And there, looking somewhat bemused amid the magnificence and the revelry, was the Yorkshire lawyer, Master Aske, out of place in his good black worsted gown and his old-fashioned long hair. Harry took care to make much of him, walking with his arm around the man's shoulders and acting like a good friend rather than a king. Of course, he would pay heed to the rebels' concerns; of course, he understood why they had risen; of course, he forgave them. Aske went back north convinced that his sovereign was on his side.

1537

In January, another uprising broke out in Yorkshire and this time Harry was prepared – and hell-bent on vengeance. He sent orders that martial law be imposed in the north, and commanded Norfolk and Suffolk to suppress the rebellion, sparing no one.

He was feeling vicious. News had just come from Italy that his cousin Reginald Pole had not only accepted a cardinal's hat from the Bishop of Rome, but had also published a vile tract condemning Harry as a heretic and adulterer. Worse still, the Bishop of Rome had appointed Pole to organise a European offensive against Henry while he was occupied with the rebellion.

'This is treason of the worst kind!' Harry shouted across the council board. 'His family shall suffer the consequences.'

'But they have done nothing wrong,' Gardiner protested.

'Not that we know of,' growled Suffolk.

'Your Grace would be wise to keep them under surveillance,' Cromwell said. 'You will recall my warning you of the risk that my Lady Salisbury and her other sons might unite with the Exeters and the conservatives against you.'

'Lady Salisbury has condemned Reginald Pole's tract,' Norfolk pointed out.

'Words are cheap,' Harry spat. 'Have them all watched, Cromwell. Given the chance, to be revenged on Reginald, I would execute them all and be done with them.' He sat there, glowering.

God, it appeared, was still on Harry's side, for in March, Jane told him that she was with child again.

They were in bed together, and he had been intent on making love to her, but he drew back. 'You are sure?'

'I have missed two courses. There can be no doubt. I now know why I have been feeling tired, and why my breasts are tender, but I am very happy!'

He embraced her gently. 'Sweetheart, I have prayed for this! Maybe Heaven is smiling on me after all. A son to crown my victory – a blessing given by God.' His kiss was full of joy. 'We must take the greatest care of you this time.' He postponed her coronation, determined to spare her any undue strain that might threaten the child. He had had no intention, of course, of having her crowned in York, but he promised her that, after the child was born, she would go to Westminster and have the most splendid coronation ever seen.

'You are so good to me.' Jane kissed him. 'But I want only you – and our son. That is enough for me in this life.'

The Pilgrimage of Grace had been ruthlessly suppressed, a sure sign of divine approval. Two hundred rebels had been executed; Aske had been hanged in chains at York. Norfolk and Suffolk were in high favour, and other lords who had been active on the Crown's behalf were basking in their King's gratitude. Harry was exultant, knowing himself to be stronger, more powerful and more respected than ever before.

That spring brought warm weather. He had been determined to ride north to overawe the subjects who had dared rebel against him, but he was suffering from a great sore in his leg, which oozed pus. His physicians bandaged it up and advised him not to travel in the heat of the year. It was frustrating, but it could not be helped.

The doctors, it seemed, were perplexed as to what was causing him such pain. He had suffered a similar ailment some years before, yet had soon recovered. Maybe this flare-up had something to do with that fall from his horse last year. The worst of it was that both legs were affected, one more than the other. The pain was sharp, like hot knives, but he would not give in to it. He had ever been an active, sporting man, and had no intention of becoming an old greybeard, moaning by the hearth with his leg up on a stool.

He was aware that he had not been so active of late and that he was putting on weight. He must change his way of life now – yet how could he do so when it hurt to walk? Riding a horse was bearable, though, and he took care to go hunting regularly, driving himself on when his doctors were urging him to rest. He ignored them. As a monarch, he could not afford to be seen to be losing his grasp.

But the pain worsened, and soon he had no choice but to keep to his chambers. The physicians tried numerous remedies, and he devised some of his own, but to little effect. For a man who had always been fastidious and sensitive to smells, the condition was distasteful and humiliating. Only Will Somers could keep up Harry's spirits when his leg was paining him – Will, who was always there to cheer him in his darkest hours.

'They're all speculating about what's wrong with you, Hal,' he said. 'Can't count the number of times you've been dead and buried.'

'That's treason, fool,' Harry scowled.

''Twas not I! It was Exeter. He said you'd die one day, all of a sudden, for your leg will kill you, and then we shall have jolly stirrings!'

'Begone, varlet!' Harry roared, then, as Will slunk to the door, he called, 'Did Exeter really say that?'

'As sure as I stand here!'

'It is treason to predict the King's death. Do you think he means me ill?'

'Nah! He's more of a fool than I am. Hey, Hal, there's a French merchant here to see you, with the latest bonnets, trimmings and fripperies from Paris.'

Harry sighed. 'Send him away. I'm too old to wear such things.'

Will eyed him up and down cheekily. 'You could have fooled me, ha ha! Strikes me that's a fine bonnet you have on, and a lot of trimmings you must have chosen to wear?'

'Very well, send him in,' Harry groaned, 'if only to shut you up.'

The merchant spread his wares for Harry to see – and Harry liked what he saw. He ended up buying a rich collar, a hat, fur, linen and a mirror, and felt much better for it. A king ought to look like a king, he reminded himself. He was not dead yet.

Finally, his leg was better, and he celebrated by taking Jane on a short pilgrimage to Canterbury, where they made offerings at the magnificent shrine of St Thomas Becket.

As he knelt there, Harry's eyes narrowed. What was he doing here? This was no saint, but a rebel. Becket had been a traitor to his King. He had defied him and been justly punished when those four knights, loyal to their sovereign, had burst into his cathedral and slaughtered him. That, of course, had been a reprehensible and sacrilegious deed, but justice had been done. Aware of Jane on her knees beside him, eyes devoutly closed in prayer, Harry stared at the jewels adorning the shrine. There glinted a ruby once donated by a long-dead King of France, big as an egg. One day, he promised himself – and that not too far in the future – it would be his, along with all the other gems that had been donated to honour this treacherous renegade.

* * *

Back at Whitehall, in determined anticipation of the birth of an heir, Harry commissioned Holbein to paint a vast mural of the Tudor dynasty on the wall of the privy chamber, behind the throne. Every day, he went to see how the work was progressing. It was magnificent. The figures of himself and Jane, with his parents behind, were life-sized. It brought a lump to his throat to see his beloved mother; even now, he could still weep for her loss. He wished he had known her better, as an adult; with her to guide him, he was sure he would have been a finer human being. Instead, he was like his father, suspicious and crafty – and there was too much of his lusty grandfather in him.

Cromwell came up behind him as he admired the mural, with Holbein standing by impatiently, clearly wishing to get on with it.

'Don't mind me, Hans,' Harry said. 'It's exceptional, is it not, Crum?'

'It takes the breath away, Sir. And your Grace dominates the piece, as you should. Those approaching the painting will feel abashed and annihilated by its power.'

Harry scrutinised his portrait, in which he stood with feet firmly apart, hands on hips, gazing out with steely authority. This was the image of himself he wanted to project. 'Copies should be made of this likeness,' he said. 'Let every loyal subject have one on display in his house.'

'A state portrait,' Cromwell said. 'There will be popular demand for it, I promise you.'

Holbein waved his paintbrush impatiently. 'Your Grace, my workshop will be happy to help.'

'Good man,' Harry said, leading Cromwell away. 'Now, Crum, about the works at Hampton Court. The Queen is to be confined there. I want Queen Anne's old rooms ready by late summer.'

Cromwell looked dismayed. 'Even I cannot work such a miracle, Sir. There is too much work to be done if all trace of that lady is to be eliminated.'

'Have the men working around the clock,' Harry insisted.

'Even then, they will not be ready. Might I suggest that her Grace uses the Lady Katherine's old lodging overlooking Base Court?'

Harry scowled. 'I'd rather not have my heir born there, but it is an airy, spacious chamber. Have it prepared and made sumptuous.'

Jane's pregnancy was progressing well. She was now wearing open-laced gowns, and a joyful *Te Deum* had been sung in St Paul's and churches throughout the realm when the child inside her quickened.

But it was now June and the hot weather had brought a virulent outbreak of plague to London. Harry fled with the court to Windsor, where a terrified Jane began an over-rigorous observance of holy days and fast days, much to his concern. He could not believe how fearful she was of the sickness – she was worse than he was, if that was possible.

'Her Grace told my wife she fears she will lose this precious child,' Suffolk said. 'I would indulge a woman's fears in such circumstances. To be plain, she has cause to be scared. In London, I hear, the pestilence is killing off a hundred victims every week.'

'By God!' Harry exclaimed, alarmed. 'Summon the Council. Forbid anyone from the City to approach the court. I had best cancel my plans for a hunting progress. The Queen, being but a woman, will not want me to go so far from her. If she is frightened by rumours spread by fools in my absence, it might affect the child. I shall confine myself to short hunting trips and stay within sixty miles of her.'

He was content with that. He was in good spirits, happily anticipating the birth of his son. For it would be a son. All the doctors and astrologers had said so.

His good mood dissipated when he learned that the hot-headed young Earl of Surrey had punched the Queen's brother, Edward, now Lord Beauchamp, in the face within the verge of the court. There was bad blood between them, especially since Harry had had to warn Surrey to cease flirting with Beauchamp's wife, but any act of violence in or near his palaces was to be punished with the greatest severity; anyone who drew blood was liable to lose his right hand. He liked Surrey, who had been a great friend to his late beloved son Richmond, and no blood had been spilt, but he could not let such a misdemeanour pass, and ordered the twenty-year-old Earl to be brought before him.

'What possessed you to behave thus?' he barked. 'You should know better!'

Surrey flushed. 'My Lord Beauchamp suggested that I was sympathetic to Master Aske and his rebels. My Lord Cromwell here knows that is a lie.'

'My lord of Surrey speaks truth,' Cromwell said. 'He is utterly loyal to your Grace.'

Harry was inclined to be sympathetic. 'You shall be confined to your chamber at Windsor for two weeks. Use the time to reflect on curbing that temper of yours.'

As a glowering Surrey was led away, Cromwell bent to Harry's ear. 'He's been in a bad mood since Lady Elizabeth FitzGerald was sent to join the Lady Mary's household.'

Harry's eyebrows shot upwards. 'She is but ten years old!'

'It is not a romantic affection, I understand, but a platonic one. Your Grace should read the poem he has composed to "Fair Geraldine". It draws on Petrarch's love poems to his Laura.'

Harry obtained and read the fourteen-line sonnet. It spoke to his heart, calling to mind the love he had for Jane, a love that made him happy. He thanked God that, at forty-six, he had been granted such a gift.

Jane took to her chamber at Hampton Court as summer began to wane. There were no cases of plague nearby, but to minimise the risk of infection, Harry moved with just his riding household to Esher, where he took up residence in Wolsey's old house to await news of the birth. There was no point in his being at Hampton Court, for no man, even himself, was allowed to enter the Queen's lodgings during her confinement. It irked him because he knew that she would be fearful and pining for him. Dammit, he was the King and could do as he pleased. But one scathing look from that dragon of a midwife, and he had gone meekly off to Esher.

In a fever of impatience, he issued orders for a Garter stall to be prepared at Windsor for his son. He could not wait to hold his heir in his arms, to show the world that he was able to sire a lusty boy. George Boleyn's slur still rankled.

At last Jane's travail began. Harry sent frequently to Hampton Court to learn how it was progressing, becoming increasingly worried. Day followed night, and then it was night again, and still the child was not born. He felt like kicking the wall in frustration.

Will laid a hand on his arm. 'Peace be, Hal. All will be well. It's either a babe her Grace has in there, or a great pudding.'

But then, oh, praised be Heaven, came the summons, in the small hours of the morning. His son had been born. The Queen was well after her long ordeal and asking for him.

Desperate as he was to go to them both, he remembered his duty and knelt to thank God, who had sent him this great gift. Then he was leaping on his horse, feeling like a young man again, and galloping through the Surrey countryside to Hampton Court, mad with impatience.

'Make way for the King!' the guards cried as they led him through the crowds who had gathered in the galleries to congratulate him and express their joy. Then the door to the Queen's lodging was flung open. There Jane sat, propped up on pillows, her long fair hair spread about her shoulders, his son in her arms.

'Darling!' he cried, looking down in awe on the fair infant in his new swaddling bands and reaching out to take him. He was jubilant, weeping with joy as he held his heir for the first time. 'He is perfect,' he pronounced, gazing in wonder on the solemn little face, the pointed chin – just like Jane's – and the prim little mouth, his own to the life! 'I cannot ever thank you sufficiently, my darling.' He noticed that Jane's eyes were dark-ringed, proof that her labour had been hard. 'I trust you are all right.'

'I am tired,' she smiled, 'but the midwife assures me I will make a speedy recovery.' Harry looked up to see the dragon watching him, as if he might drop the child. He beamed at her.

Outside, they could hear cheering and see the glow from bonfires. The kingdom was erupting in celebration already.

And so it went on, all night and through the days that followed. The people had hungered for a prince so long that there was as much rejoicing as at the birth of John the Baptist. The *Te Deum* was again sung in St Paul's, and a two-thousand-gun salute resounded from the Tower; church bells pealed out triumphantly, more bonfires were lit, the Lord Mayor arranged for free wine to be distributed in London, and everywhere there were processions, street gatherings and civic feasts. Meanwhile, royal messengers were speeding to all parts of the realm with the joyful news that England had an heir. The spectre of civil war, which had haunted Harry's dreams for so long, had retreated.

The Prince was christened three days after his birth, on a mild October evening. The magnificent torchlit procession was led by knights, ushers, squires and household officers, followed by bishops, abbots and the clergy of the Chapel Royal, the entire Privy Council, the foreign ambassadors and many nobles. Then came the Lady Elizabeth, carried in the arms of Lord Beauchamp and clutching her brother's richly embroidered white baptismal robe and the chrysom oil. The Prince followed, lying on a cushion held by the Marchioness of Exeter, with Norfolk supporting his head and Suffolk his feet, all walking under a canopy of cloth of gold supported by four gentlemen of the Privy Chamber. The child's long velvet train was carried by the Earl of Arundel, who was followed by the nurse, Mistress Penn, and the midwife, looking even more dragon-like in her green finery. The Lady Mary, who was to be the Prince's godmother, walked behind, attended by many ladies. There were four hundred people present, despite Harry having restricted the numbers for fear of plague, although that was mercifully abating now.

He had transformed Wolsey's old chapel into a lavish architectural masterpiece with a beautiful fan-vaulted ceiling painted blue and gold, with drop pendants, piping cherubs and the royal motto, 'Dieu et mon Droit', on the arches. But he was not there tonight to see his son baptised amid such splendour. This was the godparents' day, by tradition, and he stayed behind with Jane, who was lying in her state bed, clad in an ermine-trimmed mantle of crimson velvet, waiting to receive her new-made little Christian and call him by his name for the first time.

Sometime after midnight, they heard Garter King of Arms crying out loudly: 'God, of His almighty and infinite grace, give and grant good life and long to the right high, right excellent and noble Prince Edward, Duke of Cornwall and Earl of Chester, most dear and entirely beloved son to our most dread and gracious lord, King Henry the Eighth!' This was followed by the sounds of the procession returning, and soon the chamber was crammed with people. Harry watched exultantly as Lady Exeter tenderly placed the babe in Jane's arms.

'My sweet son Edward! May God bless you all the days of your life.' Jane kissed him, then Harry took him, unable to stem the tears.

'Fair son, I bless you in the name of God, the Virgin Mary and St George.' He looked up with wet eyes and saw emotion in many faces.

When the young Duchess of Suffolk had borne Edward back to his nursery, refreshments were served – hippocras and wafers for the nobility, bread and wine for the rest – and Harry gave alms to be distributed among the poor who had gathered at the palace gates. It was nearly morning before the guests kissed the hands of the King and Queen and departed.

Three days later, Edward was proclaimed Prince of Wales.

The next day, when Harry visited Jane, he was dismayed to see her looking pale and drained.

'Her Grace has been very sick and suffered a looseness,' the midwife said, looking not so dragon-like now, but rather flustered.

'Is it something she has eaten?' Harry asked anxiously.

'She did ask for quails in a green sauce, and we served them to her.'

'By St George, you should not have suffered her to eat whatever she in her fancy called for,' he fumed.

'Sir, she is the Queen. She would not be gainsaid.'

'And you, woman, are in charge here!' He was gratified to see her blench.

He tried to cheer Jane with the news that he had created her brother Edward earl of Hertford and knighted Thomas Seymour, a lusty young fellow, in great favour with the ladies, but, Harry suspected, shallow and unscrupulous, and bitterly jealous of his older and more serious brother, in whose shadow he seemed doomed to live. He did not, of course, express this view to Jane as she lay there nauseous and drained.

After three days, however, her sickness eased and she was able to take pleasure once more in little Edward, with Harry looking down proudly on them both. He still could not quite believe that he had a son at last, and was full of happy plans for the boy's future.

Then, to his consternation, Jane suddenly became very ill. It wasn't the dreaded childbed fever, for there was no fever. She was struggling to breathe. He watched helplessly as the doctors leaned over her, perplexed. It seemed there was nothing they could do but wait for her to rally. But her breathing became ever more laborious, until they had to raise her to a sitting position to ease the pressure in her chest. All Harry could do was sit beside her, squeezing her hand, willing and willing her to get better. Surely God, having granted him such happiness, would not snatch away the beloved source of it?

But God was not listening. Jane's lips, then her fingertips, turned blue as she gasped her life away. And then she was gasping no more.

Numb with shock, Harry stumbled from the room and called for his barge to take him to Windsor, where he lurched into his bedchamber and slammed the door, shutting himself away to mourn in private, raging and weeping at cruel Fate that had taken the thing he most loved, yea, even more than the motherless child Jane had left behind.

Chapter 31

1537

He had never known what it was truly to mourn a wife. Full court mourning for a queen had not been decreed since the death of his mother thirty-four years ago, but Harry was too broken to deal with anything, so Norfolk, as the Earl Marshal, had taken charge of everything. Mourning was issued to everyone in the royal household, and clothes of blue, purple and white, the colours of royal grief, were made for their master, who was barely able to step out of his nightgown. For three weeks, the doleful obsequies and ceremonies continued.

Cromwell gently informed Harry that Jane's body had been dressed in gold tissue and laid out in her presence chamber, with a crown on her head and rings on her fingers. The Lady Mary, acting as chief mourner, and the ladies of her household were taking turns to keep vigil on their knees beside the bier, while dirges were sung and Masses offered for Jane's soul. Her body remained there for a week before it was coffined and moved to the Chapel Royal, which had been hung with black cloth and filled with the religious images she had loved.

In November, in the presence of many pensive hearts, Jane was carried in solemn procession to Windsor, with great pomp and majesty, to be buried in a new vault in the choir of St George's Chapel. Harry was not present. He stayed in his bedchamber, praying for Jane's soul or weeping on his bed, missing her desperately, longing for the sound of her gentle voice or a glimpse of her comely face, never to be heard or seen again. He had Holbein's portrait of her hung beside his desk, but it did not do her justice;

even a master could not capture the living essence of her. Yet it was all Harry had. And all he could do for Jane was order Masses for her soul.

He vowed to raise a splendid tomb for them both. It would bear an effigy of Jane sweetly sleeping, surrounded by marble figures of children with baskets of the flowers she had adored. His effigy would lie beside hers, their hands clasped – their dead, stone hands. The thought brought the tears to his eyes again.

But life had to go on. After the funeral, he emerged from seclusion. People remarked on how well he looked and how bravely he was bearing his sorrow. He knew they lied for his comfort. He was gaining an alarming amount of weight, for grief and his bad legs had prevented him from taking any exercise. His glass showed him looking old and pallid in his deep blue mourning. Yet he put on a brave countenance and was as merry as a widower might be, and as strong as a king should be. No one must know how deeply his loss had wounded him.

'Your Grace?' It was Cromwell, framed in the closet doorway, wrapped in furs against the November chill.

'What is it, Crum?' Harry asked testily, for he was finding it hard to concentrate on the state papers piled up before him.

Cromwell hesitated, never a good sign. Harry braced himself for what was coming next.

'Far be it from me to intrude on your Grace's grief, but you might consider that having just the one son does not necessarily secure the succession. We, your councillors, are all too aware that infants can easily be carried off by childhood ailments.'

'A fact of which I too am more than aware!' Harry barked. He too had been fretting about the Prince. Not that the boy was unhealthy – far from it – but he had wondered if losing his mother might somehow have had an injurious effect on him.

But he was far from ready to think about providing Edward with a brother.

'We urge your Grace to frame your mind to a fourth marriage, for the weal of your realm,' Cromwell carried on, relentlessly.

Harry glared at him. 'By God, man, are you all made of stone? The Queen has not been in her grave a week!'

'Sir, we all feel for you. But it would be prudent to safeguard the succession. I have already taken the liberty of drawing up a list of suitable foreign princesses.'

'Well, you can tear it up!' Harry snarled, dangerously near to tears. How could he bear another woman in the bed he had shared with Jane? How could he perform that act? He had nothing in him to give.

'Sir, the marriages of kings are matters of state, not of the heart. This is a political necessity!'

'By God, I swear I'll have your head!' Harry shouted, pulling off his bonnet and swiping Cromwell about the pate with it. 'Get ye gone, you base blacksmith's son! What do you know about the hearts of princes?'

His rage subsided as soon as Cromwell had scuttled out. He knew his ministers' concerns were real. He saw the wisdom in his taking another wife. But how could he frame himself to it?

Yet he must. He had a duty to his realm.

'I know I must marry again,' he sighed. 'I have one son, and I must ensure the succession by siring others.'

He was at supper in his chamber with Mary and Cromwell. He had sent for his daughter, saying he needed some female company to lighten his spirits.

Cromwell looked up eagerly. 'There are great advantages to be gained by a foreign alliance, Sir.'

'I'm not so old,' Harry said. 'I'm only forty-six, and I must be the most eligible catch in Christendom.'

'Indeed, Sir. Many ladies would be delighted to be honoured by your hand, but I have been looking into the matter, and the problem is that, just now, there are very few suitable brides available. Some are of the Protestant persuasion, and others are not politically desirable.'

Harry waved a dismissive hand. 'Well, look around, look around. I'll rely on your judgement, Crum.'

1538

It was a miserable winter. When Mary went back to Hunsdon, taking Elizabeth with her, Harry felt bereft. He was torn by grief for Jane, remorse for that time he had publicly reprimanded her, poor, gentle soul, dread at the prospect of taking another wife in her place, and fear that Edward might die. Not until the spring did he establish a household for his son at Hampton Court, under the governance of the redoubtable Lady Margaret Bryan, who had cared for Mary and Elizabeth.

He created a splendid suite of apartments for the Prince. In the presence chamber stood the magnificent cradle of estate in which the heir to England was shown off to privileged visitors, who approached via a processional stair and a heavily guarded watching chamber. Harry's terror at the thought of losing his precious son drove him to lay down stringent rules designed to eliminate all risks to the child's health and safety. It was not only illness he feared, but poison or the assassin's dagger. Even the greatest nobles had to obtain written permission from Harry himself before approaching the Prince's cradle.

He was beginning to wonder if it had been a good idea to have Edward living at court.

'No member of the Prince's household is to speak with any person suspected of having been in contact with the plague,' he instructed Cromwell, as they drew up yet more ordinances. 'Nor may they visit London without permission during the summer months, lest they carry plague. Any servant who falls ill must leave the household at once.'

Cromwell wrote it all down.

'The Prince's chamberlain is to supervise his robing, his daily bath, the preparation of his food and the washing of his clothes,'

Harry continued. 'All the Prince's food must be tasted for poison. The walls and floors of the rooms, galleries, passages and courtyards in and around his apartments are to be swept and scrubbed with soap thrice daily. Everyone is to observe the highest standards of personal hygiene.'

Cromwell raised his eyebrows. 'Good luck with that. Wolsey tried again and again to enforce such standards, but in vain. They even had to paint holy crosses on the walls to stop men pissing against them.'

Harry sniffed in distaste. 'Nevertheless, in this crucial matter, my will must prevail! See to it, Crum. And write down that everything that might be handled by the child is to be washed before he comes into contact with it. And I want no pages in his household because boys can be careless and clumsy. By St George, the court is an unsanitary place and I'm beginning to think that the pure country air is far healthier for the Prince.'

'I agree with your Grace,' Cromwell said gravely.

The sumptuous lodging was soon closed up and Edward's household was moved to the country and the various nursery palaces in the Thames Valley where his sisters had spent their growing years. Harry was sent frequent reports on his progress.

'There was never so goodly a child for his age,' he told Mary, as they competed at the archery butts during one of her visits to court. 'He's shooting out in length and is so strong that Lady Bryan thinks he will stand early.'

'I wish I could see him more often.' Mary's blunt features looked wistful, and it occurred to Harry that it was high time she had a child of her own. But no match he would have deemed suitable had presented itself.

That spring, when he was hunting at Royston, north of London, he had Edward brought to him. The child was seven months old now and so like his mother it was almost painful to look at him. He did not shy away from Harry's big, glittering figure, but held out his arms, crowing and chuckling. Harry played with him, shaking the gold rattle he had brought him and dandling him on his knee, then, cuddling him in his arms, he held him up at a window so that the crowds outside could see him. No wonder they cheered, for their Prince was one of the prettiest children to be found anywhere. He was strong, healthy, adventurous and full of promise. Harry was even impressed to see him throw a temper tantrum when Lady Bryan came to take him back to the nursery.

'He's certainly got spirit!' he observed.

'Indeed, he has, Sir!' With the struggling Edward in a vice-like grip, Lady Bryan bore him off.

Harry returned from the progress full of plans for his son's education and for the most adventurous building project he had ever undertaken.

'I want a palace to rival the French King's at Chambord,' he told Suffolk over supper one evening. 'Creating it will take my mind off my grief and enhance my reputation.'

Suffolk smiled. He was fifty-four now. Years of good living had aged him, and he too was getting fat. Long gone were the days when he and Harry had charged at each other in the lists. But he was Harry's oldest and greatest friend and, as such, enjoyed the freedom of being able to speak his mind.

'When will you ever stop building, Harry? Aren't sixty houses more than enough for you?'

'More like seventy!' Harry laughed.

He took Suffolk to Ewell in Surrey, deep in the heart of his vast honour of Hampton Court. Nearby, there had been a village called Cuddington, but Harry had had it razed to the ground. 'My palace will stand here,' he said, pointing to the wasteland and the piles of rubble. 'It will be the most amazing palace ever to be built. No one has yet seen anything like it, so I am calling it Nonsuch.'

He pulled the plans from the scrip hanging from his saddle and passed them to Suffolk. The Duke unrolled them.

'It's not very big. Just two courts.'

'It will be a hunting lodge and a private pleasure house. The outer court will look like my other palaces, but the inner will draw on the architecture of Italy. They are very advanced there and I hope to attract some of their finest masons and painters for the project.'

'Aye, I can begin to envisage it,' Suffolk said. 'And by the time it's finished, Harry, you might have a new queen to share it with.'

Harry gave a bitter laugh. 'There's only one woman I want to share it with, and she is gone from me.'

His plans for Nonsuch were thrust to the back of his mind that May when the hole in his leg closed up and the evil humours that usually leaked out of it were trapped. He had never known such agony. He was black in the face and speechless with pain, and his physicians clearly had no idea how to alleviate it, for all their soothing words. He read plainly in their faces that they feared he might die. He himself was past caring as the torture continued relentlessly for twelve dreadful days, during which he knew he was in great danger.

Then, suddenly, the wound broke open and a torrent of disgusting matter poured out of it. Within hours, Harry was sitting up in bed, eating a hearty meal.

'That was a close thing, Hal,' Will observed, strumming a lute discordantly. 'Your courtiers were expecting you to leave us, and were debating who should be your successor: a babe or a grown woman. Give me the babe any day!' he cackled.

Harry was not laughing. He was appalled to realise that his will and pleasure would have no force when he was dead. 'Their allegiance should be to the Prince and no one else. God, let me live until he is grown!'

He was up and about within days. The world must see that there was life in him yet!

His physicians urged him to take things easily. 'That wound could close again,' Dr Butts warned. 'We must keep a close eye on it.'

Cromwell had been busy searching out possible brides. 'King Francis seems amenable to a marriage alliance,' he murmured in Harry's ear as they watched a game of tennis. 'His ambassador is here to discuss the matter with your Grace, if you will grant him an audience.'

'I suppose I must,' Harry grumbled, but inwardly he was pleased at the prospect of a new friendship with France. It would act as a buffer against the machinations of the Bishop of Rome.

The Sieur de Castillon bowed low. He was well dressed, smooth and practised at diplomacy. He showed Harry some exquisitely painted miniatures of several French ladies.

'This is Madame de Longueville, a widow with two sons.'

Harry squinted at it. 'Hmm. Very comely. But she looks rather small. I am big in person and have need of a big wife.'

Castillon smiled. 'Ah! Then look at this one, your Majesty. She is Madame's sister Louise. Take her, she is still a maid, and you will be able to shape the passage to your measure.'

Harry laughed heartily, clapping Castillon on the shoulder, then turned his attention to the other likenesses.

'By God!' he exclaimed. 'I trust no one but myself. The thing touches me too near. I wish to see them and know them some time before deciding.'

Castillon raised his eyebrows. 'Your Majesty, I hardly think King Francis will permit his kinswomen to be paraded like hackneys at a market.'

Harry bridled. 'Surely it is not asking too much for these ladies to come to Calais to meet me?'

Castillon's voice was cold. 'Maybe your Grace would like to mount them one after the other, and keep the one you find to be the best broken in. Is that the way the Knights of the Round Table treated women in your country in times past?'

Harry gave a nervous laugh, feeling his cheeks flushing with shame. 'I meant no offence, on my knightly honour.'

He did not feel so warm towards France after that, and that summer, France and Spain signed a truce that left England dangerously isolated. Harry was hoping to shift the balance of power by pursuing a marriage with the Emperor's niece, the beautiful Christina of Denmark, Duchess of Milan, a widow of just sixteen. He dispatched Holbein to Brussels to paint her portrait and was entranced when he saw it. His grief for Jane would always be with him, but life had to go on – one look at the divine Christina's lovely, sweet face had convinced him of that. Once again, he was an ardent swain, ordering his musicians to play love songs deep into the night and having romantic masques staged at court.

'Go to Brussels, my Pig,' he commanded Wriothesley. 'Tell the Duchess that I am a most gentle gentleman with a nature so benign and pleasant that no man has heard many angry words pass my mouth. Wrap up the marriage contract.'

He waited in a fever of impatience. But when Wriothesley returned, he looked like a man on whom the severest blow had fallen.

'What did she say? Is the treaty drawn up?' Harry asked sharply.

'Your Grace, I fear it is not. Alas, the lady declared that if she had two heads, one of them would be at your Majesty's disposal.'

He was momentarily speechless. The saucy wench! The insult stung, though. He was not a monster. Anne had betrayed him in the most vile ways and he had dealt with her as she deserved. If this was a ploy to gain better terms, the Duchess had gravely miscalculated. He would not be honouring her with his hand.

In a bad mood, he departed on another hunting progress, making a detour to the south coast to visit his ports and havens, still smarting at Christina's impudence.

'I have found another possible bride for your Grace,' Cromwell announced one morning, as Harry emerged from the Chapel Royal after Mass.

Harry signed for him to walk with him along the gallery, out of earshot of his lords and gentlemen.

'Sir, I believe an alliance with one of the German states would be politic, to counterbalance the pact between the Emperor and the King of France.'

'But most of the German princes are Protestants,' Harry objected.

'Aye, but all would leap at the chance of an alliance with England. The Duke of Cleves has two unmarried sisters, Anna and Amelia. I have heard that Anna's beauty exceeds that of Christina of Denmark as the golden sun outshines the silvery moon. It might be worth pursuing the matter further. Like England, Cleves has broken with

Rome, and although the Duke is of the reformed faith, his sisters have been brought up as Catholics by their mother.'

'Hmm,' pondered Harry. 'Yes. I can see the wisdom in this. Dispatch envoys to discover more about them – and send Holbein to Cleves to take the likenesses of the princesses. By St George, Crum, I think you have the sow by the right ear.'

He remembered saying much the same thing to Cranmer all those years ago when he had been desperate to free himself from Kate so that he could marry Anne. And look where that had ended! But this Anna would be different. He felt it in his bones. God would smile on him this time.

When Harry returned to court in the autumn, Cromwell informed him that a man called John Lambert had been arrested for promoting the heresies of Luther.

'These Protestants must be stopped,' Harry said.

'Aye, and I hope your Grace will make an example of him and expose his beliefs as false and dangerous, and in so doing defend the true doctrines of your Church.'

'By all means,' Harry said. 'But how shall I do that?'

'He has appealed to you to judge his case in person, so I thought a public trial, with your Grace sitting in judgement, might be politic. You are skilled at theological debate and no one is better placed to defend the true faith.' Cromwell was clearly fired up at the prospect.

'It is unprecedented!' Harry replied. 'My judges act for me.'

'Your noble father once held a debate with a condemned heretic, to save his soul.'

Harry was warming to the idea. He did not doubt his ability to demolish this Lambert's arguments. People would see for themselves that their King was worthy to be the Supreme Head of the Church. And, more important than anything, he might be able to save the wretch from eternal damnation.

'Very well. Let it be proclaimed. I will deal with this dangerous fool as he deserves.'

As he had anticipated, crowds of spectators gathered on the tiers of scaffolding that had been specially erected along the walls of the great hall at Whitehall to see him seat himself beneath the canopy of estate on the dais. He had dressed all in white, for purity, and was flanked on one side by his purple-clad bishops and on the other by peers, judges and the gentlemen of the Privy Chamber.

Lambert was brought before him, under guard.

Harry spoke genially to him. 'Ho, good fellow, what is your name?'

'It is John Nicholson, your Grace, but I am known as Lambert.'

Harry frowned at him severely, leaning forward. 'I would not trust you, having two names, even if you were my brother. But you are my subject and I want you to have the opportunity of understanding the error of your ways and come back into the fold of the true faith.'

'I knew that your Grace would be a fair and just judge!' Lambert cried. 'I see it is true that no man can match you for wisdom and integrity.'

'I did not come hither to hear my own praises!' Harry barked. 'Do you believe in the doctrine of transubstantiation?'

Lambert hesitated. 'I deny it.'

'I warn you,' Harry frowned, 'that you will be condemned to the stake if you persist in this opinion.'

'But, Sir, I know it to be the right one!'

'You *know* that, in the face of all the doctrines of the true Church, which were drawn up by wiser men than you? Ha! Perhaps you would like to justify such an extravagant claim?'

And Lambert did. After five long and weary hours of arguing, Harry had to face the fact that his attempt to save the ingrate's life was doomed to failure.

'Would you live or die?' he exploded, his patience exhausted. 'You yet have free choice.'

Lambert, still standing, glared at him defiantly. 'I will not recant.'

Harry stood. 'That being the case, you must die, for I will not be a patron of heretics.' He watched as Lambert was led away to a fate that did not bear imagining.

'There is but one recourse left for a fool such as he,' he told Cromwell afterwards. 'Burning gives a heretic a taste of the fires of Hell to come, a last chance to recant before death. Let Lambert be burned over a slow fire, to give him more time to repent.'

When the dread punishment had been meted out, Cromwell reported that the man had faced death with courage. 'As the flames took him, he cried out, "None but Christ!"'

'Another soul lost to damnation,' Harry murmured. 'No one can say I did not try to save him.'

He felt beset. There was religious dissent on both sides, Popish Catholics and Protestant heretics. Lady Salisbury, her sons and their cousins, the Exeters, were still under surveillance. Harry had been close to his mother's kinsfolk since childhood, but these days he no longer trusted them, remembering that royal blood ran in their veins and fearing that they might yet try to seize his throne.

Cromwell was even more suspicious of them. He viewed them as reactionaries, an ever-present threat to the new order he had masterminded, and to his own position. So when he presented Harry with a formidable array of evidence that the Poles and the Exeters were plotting treason, Harry was aware that an ulterior motive might be at play.

But there were the proofs, in writing, before him, chilling him to the heart. Some of the most damaging information had come from Lord Montagu's younger brother, Geoffrey Pole, who had clearly been desperate to save his own skin. That there had been a conspiracy could not be doubted. However, it appeared to have been plotted ineptly and the traitors involved had been unbelievably indiscreet. Could they be as malicious and as organised as Cromwell asserted?

Then Lady Salisbury's castle was searched by royal officers, who found a silk tunic embroidered with the royal arms – undifferenced, as if they belonged to a reigning monarch. Harry was now sure that the Poles and the Exeters had been plotting to put Lady Salisbury on the throne, and that they had conspired to assassinate their King, the most heinous crime a subject could commit.

They must suffer for it; Harry was determined that his kinsfolk would never again have an opportunity to unseat him. He sent Exeter to the Tower on a charge of compassing his death and plotting to usurp the throne; and with him went Lady Exeter, Lord Montagu, his brothers and their mother, the aged Lady Salisbury, all accused of conspiring with Exeter. Harry even ordered that the young sons of Exeter and Montagu be confined with them. Privately, it grieved him to proceed with such severity, but anger and outrage outweighed any family loyalties. What of their loyalty to him, their King?

On a cold December morning, Exeter and Montagu faced the executioner's axe. Lady Exeter, her son Edward Courtenay and young Henry Pole remained in the Tower with Lady Salisbury, all attainted as traitors by Parliament.

It was a quiet Christmas. Harry was in no mood for celebrating, shaken by recent events and feeling very lonely. Jane had been gone for fourteen months now and he still missed her dreadfully. Grief would steal over him like a dark shadow waiting to engulf him. He longed for something good to happen, to lift his low spirits.

1539

Harry was dismayed to learn that the Emperor and King Francis, those two great enemies, had signed a new treaty, agreeing to make no further alliances with England. It left his kingdom vulnerable. He should take steps to find new allies, or lure either Francis or Charles away from the other.

'Your Grace must see this.' Cromwell came bustling into his closet, as he sat there, frowning, and handed him a document. His face was ashen.

Harry saw the heads of St Peter and St Paul on the seal that was attached to the scroll by a silken cord.

He had been excommunicated. The Bishop of Rome, apparently shocked at Harry's treatment of his relations, had published Pope Clement's sentence of anathema, isolating him from all faithful

Christians and calling upon the princes of Europe to dethrone him.

Harry shrugged and gave the document back to Cromwell. 'Nothing that man does has the power to scare me,' he declared.

He would not let it matter to him. He had been a good son of the Church – and been treated appallingly. He would not be intimidated into undoing all the good work he had done to re-establish true religion in England! He would not believe that other monarchs would take Rome's exhortation seriously.

But he knew this threat from his enemies was serious.

'We must take measures to resist an invasion,' he told his Council. 'We must strengthen our defences and order musters up and down the land.'

'We should also keep close watch on those of a conservative persuasion,' Cromwell urged. 'Get rid of Sir Francis Bryan.'

'What has Bryan done?' Harry looked up. He knew that Cromwell itched to remove free-thinkers like Bryan and replace them with his own men.

'He bends with the wind and cannot be trusted. Sir, replace him as Chief Gentleman of the Privy Chamber with Anthony Denny. He is highly educated and a humanist with a sincere affection for God's word.' Denny, of course, was one of Cromwell's protégés, and it was clear that Master Secretary was looking to secure yet another foot in the Privy Chamber. So be it. Denny was a sound man, while Bryan was unpredictable.

'I seem to recall that Denny began his career at court in Bryan's service,' Norfolk observed tartly. 'Yet I am sure he would not flinch at supplanting him.'

'I have no doubt he will make himself indispensable to your Grace,' Cromwell said hastily.

Harry harrumphed, weary of this constant wrangling among his councillors. He left them to their business and, taking advantage of the sunny January weather, summoned some of his gentlemen for a game of bowls. But he was in a testy mood and was not best pleased when Sir Nicholas Carew won.

'You were ever the cheat,' he ribbed him, only half in jest, whereupon Carew rounded on him in fury.

'I marvel that your Grace is such a bad loser! You always have to win!'

Harry stared at him, unable to credit his insolence. 'Get ye hence. I will not see your face in my court again.'

'With pleasure!' Carew shouted, and stalked off, watched by Harry and his astounded companions.

Harry shook with anger all the way back to his apartments. He could not let Carew get away with such *lèse-majesté*. What had possessed him to act thus? He had long been one of Harry's boon companions, but these days he was short-tempered and difficult. There had been an aggravating dispute over some lands in Surrey that Carew had refused to exchange for royal estates, in response to Harry's request. Once, he would not have hesitated.

When, later that week, Cromwell produced treasonable letters written by Carew at Beddington, Harry found it easy to believe he had been involved in the Exeter conspiracy. And so Carew, that false friend, followed Exeter and Montagu to the block. Traitors all!

That spring, Harry pressed on with his reforms. Knowing that his subjects were more inclined to the old religion than the new opinions, he had Parliament pass the Act of the Six Articles, enshrining the doctrines of the Church of England in law. It marked a return to more traditional religion, making him more popular than ever, although it found no favour with the radicals who wanted him to go ever further with his reforms.

'They'd make a Lutheran of me,' he grumbled to Norfolk and Gardiner, who led the conservatives at court. 'I hear they are calling the Act "the whip with six strings". Two of my bishops have even resigned.'

'Some might say your Grace has gone too far already,' Gardiner said reprovingly. 'I support the Act prescribing the death penalty for anyone denying the sacraments, but I cannot approve of English Bibles being available to all and sundry in every parish church and the laity reading and interpreting the Scriptures for themselves.'

'Calm down, my lord Bishop,' Harry retorted. 'It is my intention that men be allowed to read the Bible only for their own personal edification and so that they may instruct their children the better.' He rather liked the title page of the new 'Great Bible', which showed him enthroned, handing down the Word of God to his subjects, the fount of all spiritual virtue and authority.

'I can't see what all the fuss is about,' Norfolk said. 'I never felt any desire to read the Bible myself.' Gardiner gave him an exasperated look.

'Gentlemen,' Harry soothed, 'let us remember that we are discussing the Word of God. It should be available to all men to read. I will not be moved on this.'

Harry could not drag his eyes from the portrait of Anna of Cleves. The one of Amelia lay discarded on the table. In his hand, he held a miniature in an exquisite ivory frame in the form of a Tudor rose. The Lady Anna was indeed beautiful – if the limning was a true likeness. But Harry's envoy in Cleves had written that Holbein had captured the ladies' images to the life.

This might just be the woman Harry had been looking for, the one who would help him forget his grief for Jane and bear him sons. He looked on the demure, delicate, half-smiling face before him and was entranced.

'Proceed at once with the marriage negotiations!' he instructed Cromwell.

He was in jovial spirits that summer, busily extending the vast honour of Hampton Court, his private enclosed hunting domain that stretched across thirty-six square miles of the Surrey countryside. Containing several royal residences, it was intended to make hunting easier for him. His legs were no better; the problem was escalating, and his increasingly long periods of immobility had made him grow yet heavier. He did not like to look in his mirror these days, but closed his eyes when his barber, Master Penny, was shaving him or trimming his hair and beard. If he opened them, he would see an old man reflected before him.

He did not travel abroad so readily these days, but was constrained to seek his sport and pleasure nearby. All his mounting blocks were being raised so that he could get on and off his horses easily. In some of his hunting chases, he had ordered the erection of small timber-framed standings with outdoor galleries, where he and his companions could wait for the deer to be driven through two lines of nets below and then shoot them. He ensured that there were always ladies present, and was the perfect host, providing little banquets for them. He prided himself that, whatever age and infirmity had done to him, he could still charm the fair sex.

In June, he had a river pageant staged on the Thames at Whitehall. The riverbank was crowded with people and small craft filled with ladies and gentlemen, come to watch a mock battle between two barges, one manned by actors playing the Bishop of Rome and his cardinals, the other by the King's champions. Watching with Mary and his courtiers from the roof above the privy stairs, Harry roared with laughter as the Pope and his cronies were tipped into the Thames. They were all saved, for he had instructed his bargemen to pick them up.

It was a beautiful day, but there was something missing, and that something, Harry knew, was a beautiful woman at his side. Well, that would soon be remedied. He thought longingly of the Lady Anna.

The Duke of Cleves was eager to be friends with England and signed the marriage treaty in September. Later that month, his envoys arrived to conclude the alliance. During the eight days they spent at Windsor, an ebullient Harry laid on feasts and hunting expeditions in their honour, then took them to Hampton Court, where he ratified the treaty. When they had gone home, he began preparing for the arrival of his bride. His heart was hers already; he kept her portrait in his bosom or by his bed at night. He had a smile on his lips and a song in his head. He felt rejuvenated, exalted, ready to live again.

Full of gratitude to Cromwell for finding him such a bride, he allowed him his head in reforming the Privy Council, much to the chagrin of Norfolk and other conservatives, who bitterly resented his dominance.

'Pay them no heed, Crum,' Harry counselled, after one particularly acrimonious session. 'You are right. Promotion should depend on merit, not on birth. Those lords who hold office do so only on account of their abilities. I will not carry lightweights in my government.'

Harry was more powerful now than ever before. His proclamations had just been invested with the same force as an Act of Parliament, and he had granted himself the authority to pronounce on matters of religious doctrine.

'Oh, Hal,' Somers said mournfully, 'are we all going to have to genuflect to you now?'

Harry buffeted him affectionately. Will was the one friend he could depend on. He was that rare creature at court, a man of integrity and discretion who refused to become embroiled in faction fighting and never took advantage of his privileged position. Thanks to his barbed jests, Harry had been made aware of abuses within his household and been able to instruct Cromwell to eradicate them. And Somers was always on hand to offer comfort whenever Harry's legs gave him trouble and forced him into tedious inactivity, as they did that winter.

'It grieves me to see you limping so much, Hal,' he commiserated, as Harry gratefully sank down on a bench after presiding over what had seemed an endless audience.

Harry reached for his lute and began to strum a love song. 'I'll be a new man again when the Lady Anna comes.'

He frowned when he learned from his envoys that, some years ago, Anna had been absent from the ducal court for many months, and no one had been able – or willing – to tell the envoys why. His suspicions were immediately alerted. Had she been ill? And had her illness been of such an intimate nature that people had been ordered not to speak of it? If she had been suffering some women's malady, could it have affected her ability to bear children?

He was even more concerned when informed that his envoys had been thwarted in all their attempts to meet Anna and her sister. They had only seen them from afar, and swathed in such voluminous hoods and cloaks that they could not be seen at all. It was not the custom for well-born ladies to parade themselves in public, the envoys had been told. At length, however, the princesses had appeared at a court function and Harry's fears that something was amiss with them had been somewhat allayed. Yet still something was bothering him.

In his court there was a certain Mistress Gilman, a Fleming whom he employed as a painter. He dispatched her to teach Anna some English – of which Anne knew little, apparently – and entrusted her with a secret mission to befriend his bride and find out the truth about her illness. He was thankful to receive a letter from her, saying she believed there was no cause for concern. Much relieved, he resumed his joyous preparations for the wedding. Everything was ready for Anna's arrival. The Queen's apartments at Hampton Court and elsewhere had been refurbished. Her household was ready and waiting to serve her. Harry had sent two of his richest beds to Rochester and Dartford, where she would stay on her way to Greenwich. They would be married there at the start of the Christmas season, and then enjoy twelve days of lavish celebrations together. Anna would make her state entry into London on New Year's Day and be crowned at Westminster Abbey on Candlemas Day. The courtiers had already ordered a wealth of fine clothes and Harry was happily planning his wedding outfit.

He had long since forgiven his niece Marget for her clandestine betrothal. When Thomas Howard died of fever in the Tower, just after Jane's death, Harry had taken pity on Marget, who was also ill, and sent her to Syon Abbey to recuperate. Now he brought her back to court to serve as chief lady-of-honour to his new Queen. There was a new gravity about her, a wistful sadness in her beautiful face. Like him, she had been mourning a lost love for two long years; unlike him, she had no one in view to heal her. He resolved to find her a husband as soon as possible.

Norfolk had persuaded him to accept as maids-of-honour his pretty nieces, Katheryn Howard and Mary Norris, and his great-niece, Catherine Carey, Mary Boleyn's daughter. When Catherine curtseyed to him, Harry had to hide his shock, for it was like looking at his reflection. By St George, it must be clear to all whose daughter she was! But where, in the man, the same features had lent beauty, to the girl they did no favours.

He could not acknowledge her. Under the law, she was William Carey's daughter. Her mother had made that disastrous second marriage and moved to Calais with her soldier husband. Thank God Harry didn't have to see her at court, for she would be a walking reminder of her sister Anne. Oh, what a tangled web those Boleyns had woven, like predatory spiders – and he had been caught up in it. He shuddered.

No, it was best to leave well alone. He did not need any more complications in his life.

Chapter 32

1539

Harry sent the Lord High Admiral, the Earl of Southampton, with a great company to Calais to welcome the Princess Anna and escort her across the sea to England.

'You are to cheer my lady and her train, so they think the time short on the journey,' he'd instructed. 'Teach her to play the card games I like – that will help.'

He was looking forward to a Yuletide wedding, but the weather intervened. Storms and adverse winds kept Anna in Calais. Christmas came and went, and Harry could take little pleasure in the lavish festivities or even in the stunning portrait of the Prince presented to him by Holbein on New Year's Day. He was sick with impatience.

1540

When, at last, that morning, he was brought word that Anna had landed at Deal in Kent and was now on her way to Rochester, he could wait no longer. He would play the knight errant and hasten to his bride to nourish love. He would go incognito, for surely she would know him instinctively.

Summoning five of his gentlemen, he provided them all with marbled coats and hoods that had been used for a pageant, the same as he was wearing, and set off that day for Kent, braving the awful weather and taking with him a gift of furs for his lady and some royal robes.

At the Bishop's Palace at Rochester, his heart pounding in

anticipation, he ordered that he be announced to the Princess Anna as a messenger come from the King with gifts. In her chamber were a dozen German ladies dressed after a fashion so heavy and tasteless it would have made them appear frightful even if they had been beauties, which they most certainly were not. But it took only a cursory glance to notice that, before Harry's eyes fixed on Anna, who was standing by a window, looking down on a bull-baiting in the courtyard below. She turned towards him.

Dear God! She was not at all as she had been described. It was as if her portrait had been twisted and distorted. Painted full-faced, it had not shown the over-long nose and chin or the hooded eyes. Nor could any portrait have conveyed the distinct fishy smell of unwashed body linen – and worse – that emanated from the lady. He recoiled in disgust.

Holding his breath, he stepped forward and embraced her, assuming that she had guessed who he was – until he registered the outrage in her face and quickly muttered something about bringing her gifts from the King. Flushed with anger, she disengaged herself from his embrace and turned back to the window.

His fantasy had gone badly wrong. It was time to reveal himself. He withdrew to another chamber and ordered his gentlemen to bring his mantle of royal purple and his bejewelled bonnet. Then he made a grand entrance and was gratified to see the confusion and dismay in Anna's face as she and her women hurriedly sank to their knees. She tried, in broken English, to greet him properly, but failed, and he, racked with disappointment, lacked the will to help her.

They dined together that night. Harry had deputed the genial Sir Anthony Browne discreetly to instruct one of the German frights to have a quiet word with Anna about washing herself properly, and was relieved to find that she appeared to have taken the advice.

As they sat at table, making stilted conversation through Mistress Gilman, who was acting as interpreter, Harry began to see that Anna had a certain charm of manner, although it did not compensate for her want of beauty. She could not play, sing or dance, for such accomplishments were considered immodest in women in her country; nor was she learned. It had evidently not been thought necessary for her to master any language other than German. Instead, she had been taught to read, to write and to sew; she said she spent most of her time sewing. She had never been hunting, and her preferred exercise was a sedate walk in the gardens. How, Harry wondered, had anyone considered her fit to preside over his court, one of the most brilliant and cultivated in Europe?

Yet she did have some evident personal qualities. Her manner was regal. He soon gleaned that she was kind and good-humoured, amiable without being overfamiliar, and pathetically anxious to please him. She had been trained to do her humble duty as a wife, though he suspected she might be entirely innocent of carnal matters. It would be his unpleasant duty to enlighten her. He spent a sleepless night envisaging what that would entail.

The next day, Harry left Rochester as soon as courtesy permitted, having given the furs to Sir Anthony Browne to present to Anna. Later, as they sat in the boat on the way back to Whitehall, he could contain himself no longer and turned to Sir Anthony.

'I see nothing in this woman as was reported of her, and I marvel that wise men could make such reports as they have done.'

Browne looked nonplussed. 'I am very sorry that your Grace finds himself in this difficult position.'

'Others are going to be even more sorry!' Harry growled.

Cromwell was hovering in the gallery that led from the jetty to the royal apartments.

'How does your Grace like the Queen?' he asked, grinning.

'Nothing so well as I was led to expect!' Harry snapped. 'If I had known as much before as I know now, she would never have come into this realm.' He was remembering the gift of boar pâté that King Francis had unexpectedly sent him for Christmas – a sure indication that he wished to renew his friendship with England, rendering the alliance with Cleves completely unnecessary. If only he had taken heed then. But he had been blinded by infatuation – and with a portrait, by God! There was no fool like an old fool.

Cromwell seemed to have shrunk into his furs. He was visibly sweating, despite the January chill.

'I am grieved to hear that,' he croaked. 'Did she misbehave herself?'

'No, but I like her not!' Harry stumped off, leaving Cromwell to stew. This was all his fault and he would make sure he suffered for it.

That afternoon, the court moved to Greenwich, where the wedding was to take place. At noon the next day, to the sound of trumpets, and with Norfolk, Suffolk and Cranmer in attendance, Harry rode in procession through Greenwich Park towards the vast throng that had assembled on Blackheath for Anna's official reception. He was mounted on a horse trapped in rich cloth of gold and pearls, and clad in a cloak of purple velvet embroidered with gold and tied with great buttons of diamonds, rubies and Orient Pearls, while on his head was a jaunty bonnet rich with jewels. He could have choked to think he had ordered these clothes for what he believed would be the happiest of occasions. He had not thought he would be having to force a smile and a brave face to the world!

Presently, he saw Anna's procession approaching from Shooters Hill. As she came towards him on her magnificently caparisoned steed, he saw that she was wearing an outlandish gown of cloth of gold cut in the Dutch fashion, with no train. He doffed his bonnet and moved towards her, putting on – he hoped – his most loving countenance, and saluted and embraced her as the people cheered loudly.

'My Lady Anna, welcome to England!' he cried, so that all could hear, and he bowed in the saddle.

'Your Majesty, I am both honoured and joyful to be here,' she replied, bowing too.

Together, they rode back amid cheering crowds towards the pavilions that had been set up for them. Holding his hands to a brazier, Harry called for spiced wine to warm them both, picked at the banquet laid out for them, and presented his councillors to Anna. Then he and his bride mounted their horses and rode to Greenwich

Palace, followed by their retinues. Alighting in the outer court, he embraced and kissed her.

'Welcome to your own,' he said, then tucked her arm into his and led her through the great hall and upstairs to her lodgings, where he gratefully bade farewell to her. As he hastened along his privy gallery, his ears were blasted by guns being fired in celebration.

He had behaved impeccably, but the strain was getting to him.

'I cannot marry her!' he told his Council the next morning. 'There must be some way out of it.'

Cromwell was shaking his head. 'Sir, I fear the marriage contract is watertight.'

Norfolk and Gardiner were watching Cromwell with ill-concealed satisfaction, obviously revelling in his discomfiture.

'Am I served by fools?' Harry barked. 'Look again! Find a way! And put off the wedding until you do.' He watched mercilessly as Master Secretary gathered up his papers and scuttled from the council chamber.

'I have sat up all night and gone through the contract and legal precedents again and again,' Cromwell reported the following day, when the lords reconvened. His face was drawn, his clothes unchanged and his cap askew. 'I am sorry, Sir, but there are no grounds!'

'Then break the alliance,' Harry spat.

'Your Grace, it is too late to do that without giving great offence and provoking a hostile reaction. I fear the marriage must go ahead.'

Harry gave him a look that would have felled a lesser man. 'Very well.' His voice was icy. 'I will submit to the fate to which you have condemned me. Gentlemen, it is sometimes a sorry thing to be a king. Princes have to take what is brought them by others; only poor men can make their own choices. At this moment, I wish I was a poor man – and I have you to thank for it, my Lord Cromwell.'

Three days later, he dragged himself reluctantly from his bed to make ready for his wedding. He stood there seething, almost on the verge of weeping, as his gentlemen dressed him in a furred gown of cloth of gold with great raised flowers of silver. Around his shoulders, they draped a cloak of crimson satin embroidered with large diamonds, and placed a rich collar about his neck.

Before he emerged from his lodgings, he summoned Cromwell.

'My lord, if it were not to satisfy the world and my realm, I would not do what I must do this day for any earthly thing.'

It was a small comfort to see Cromwell turn white. 'Your Grace . . .'

'Unless you have thought of a remedy, Crum, you had best stay silent.'

Turning his back on the minister, Harry summoned his nobles and made his way to the gallery that led to the chapel closets. There he dispatched some of his lords to fetch the Lady Anna. She arrived wearing another Dutch gown of rich cloth of gold patterned with large flowers of great Orient pearl, with her long fair hair loose beneath a gem-studded gold coronet. She made three low curtseys to Harry, then he led her into the Queen's closet, where Archbishop Cranmer was waiting for them. It was like going to his doom.

Filled with distaste and dread, he slipped the ring on her finger. It bore her new motto, 'God send me well to keep'. She would have need of such prayers, he thought viciously.

And now they were man and wife. Feeling sick, Harry could not bring himself to partake of the spices and hippocras that were being served to the wedding party. He went off to his privy chamber to change while Anna was escorted by Norfolk and Suffolk to hers. She was still in her wedding gown when he rejoined her to walk in procession to his closet for Mass. Afterwards, they dined together, Anna having changed into a gown like a man's, furred with rich sables, and a German headdress encrusted with stones and pearls. She accompanied Harry to Vespers and supped with him. Afterwards there were banquets, masques and revels.

All too soon, it was time for the ceremonial putting to bed of the bride and groom. While Harry was still an ardent swain, he had ordered a new bed for the occasion. It had seemed a good idea at the time to have it adorned with the initials H and A and erotic carvings, but the sight of a priapic cherub and a pregnant one, intended to inspire lust and promote fertility, now made him shudder. Stoically, clad in his furred nightgown and bonnet, he suffered his gentlemen to escort him to Anna's chamber, as the ushers cried, 'Make way for the King's Grace!' Anna lay in the bed, looking like a frightened rabbit, as Harry climbed in beside her and the courtiers filled the room. They lay together, not touching, as Cranmer blessed the nuptial couch, sprinkled it with holy water, and prayed that they might be fruitful. Then Harry gave a curt nod and everyone departed.

He turned towards Anna.

'Would you like some wine, Sir?' she asked.

'I think I've had enough,' he said. 'Maybe we can have some later.'

Holding his breath, in case Anna had not remained mindful of the advice about cleanliness, he reluctantly drew her rigid body into his arms, steeling himself to assault the fortress, like a seasoned warrior. 'Do not fear me,' he murmured. 'I know how to please a lady as a gentleman should.'

He was surprised to feel himself stir against her. And then it came to him. He did not have to consummate this marriage. If he failed to do so, he would have grounds for an annulment. The realisation made him dizzy with relief.

He must go through the motions, nevertheless, make a show of willingness. He reached a hand under the covers, pulled up Anna's night-rail and laid his hand on one of her breasts.

He drew in his breath. It was not firm like a maiden's should be – and, by St George, he had felt many in his time – but slack and flabby like the breast of a woman who had suckled a child.

He felt the other breast. Just the same. Then his hand moved down to Anna's belly. It was soft and flaccid – as flaccid as he himself now was. And there were soft ridges – stretch marks, by God! – on either side. His suspicions deepened. They had sold him a harlot! This woman was no virgin. By God, he'd swear she had borne a child!

Anna was lying there silently, looking at him questioningly, playing the innocent! He was so angry that he did not trust himself to say anything.

'Alas, Madam,' he murmured at length, 'it seems I have indeed partaken of too much wine, and it has made me sleepy. I will come to you again another night.'

'Have I offended your Grace?' Anna whispered.

'How could you have offended me?' he muttered.

'All I want to do is please you,' she said.

He got stiffly out of bed and reached for his robe. 'I know that. If you would please me, Anna, then go to sleep and allow me to get some rest. Good night.'

He fastened the robe and crossed to the door, closing it silently behind him.

'How does your Grace like the Queen?' Cromwell ventured nervously, bustling into Harry's closet the next morning and placing a sheaf of documents before him for signature.

Harry rose, towering over him, glowering. 'I like her not!' he hissed. 'As God is my witness, I tried to move the consent of my heart and mind to love her, but I have not carnally known her – and I will tell you why!'

He began pacing up and down like a caged lion, ignoring the pain in his leg. 'She is no maid, which I discovered when I felt the looseness of her breasts and other tokens. It so struck me to the heart that I had neither will nor courage to prove the rest. I left her as good a maid as I found her. You have to get me out of this.'

Without giving Cromwell time to reply, he stamped out, retreated to his privy chamber and poured out his woes to Sir Anthony Denny, who listened with sympathetic horror. Harry then consulted Dr Chamber. If he was to plead non-consummation as a reason for dissolving the marriage, he was having no one saying that the fault lay with him.

'I cannot overcome the loathsomeness of the Queen's body,' he confided plaintively, 'nor can I be provoked or stirred to that act with her.'

Dr Chamber spoke soothingly. 'Your Grace, you must not force yourself, lest you suffer an inconvenient debility of the sexual organs. Give yourself a few days to acclimatise yourself to the Queen, and then I am sure things will be better.'

Harry thanked him. It was good advice.

He visited Anna's bed for three more nights, every time making a feigned attempt at the marriage act, then departing, not caring if she had realised that something was amiss.

He consulted Dr Butts. 'Alas, I have not been able to do what a man should do to his wife,' he confessed. 'I did not even take off my nightshirt. Even so, I had two wet dreams in my sleep on my wedding night, and I think myself well able to do the act with others rather than with her. What shall I do?'

Butts, his true friend for years, was a wise man. He looked at Harry searchingly.

'You want to be rid of the lady, I perceive. It is no secret. The whole court is talking about this marriage that is no marriage.'

Harry groaned. 'It was meant to be a secret. Now everyone will be laughing at me and pointing the finger, saying I lack vigour in bed.' That could not be borne!

'Methinks your Grace has complained of her to a lot of people, and gossip spreads fast.'

'It's no lie – I cannot bed her.' He told Butts what he had discovered on his wedding night.

The doctor frowned. 'I can see why your Grace was put off consummating the marriage.'

'I do not want people thinking I am impotent!'

'That's easily remedied.' Butts smiled. 'I and your other physicians will make it known, by subtle means, that the fault lies with the lady, not your Grace. In the meantime, my advice is to continue making a show of trying to make the marriage work – and get Lord Cromwell to find a way out of it!'

Harry took Butts' advice. He continued to visit Anna nightly and showed her every courtesy, even though he was still angry with her – or with her brother, rather, for lying about her being virtuous – and with Cromwell, for not having delved deeper. He himself had had his suspicions, had he not? He had sent Mrs Gilman to find out the truth, and she too had failed him.

Anna was making embarrassing attempts to please him and working hard at learning English. At his request she began wearing gowns in the English fashion, mostly of black satin or damask so that she could show off the jewels he had given her to greater effect. Some had been designed by Holbein in happier days and featured the entwined initials H and A. In the days after the wedding, courtiers had flocked to pay their respects to her. Now, Harry learned, her chambers were deserted.

He abandoned plans for her coronation, although he did arrange for her to make a state entry into Westminster early in February, sailing with her in the royal barge from Greenwich, attended by the nobility and guildsmen in a flotilla of smaller vessels. She received a thunderous salute from the Tower guns as she passed, and the banks of the Thames were crowded with cheering citizens. At Westminster Stairs, Harry helped her out of the barge, and they walked in procession to Whitehall Palace.

While there, he went to St James' Palace to inspect the newly completed state apartments. The chapel was almost finished. He gazed up at its magnificent ceiling, painted by Holbein to commemorate his marriage to Anna. There were their initials, badges and mottoes, with the date 1540. He gave a bitter laugh and turned away.

When April came, all breezes and sunshine, Harry forsook Anna's bed for good. There was no point in keeping up appearances. Their marriage was a travesty and everyone knew it. What Anna made of it, he neither knew nor cared.

Bishop Gardiner had invited him to a feast at Winchester House, just across the Thames in Southwark. Harry accepted, needing some merriment to raise his spirits. No doubt Gardiner would use the occasion to nag him about punishing heresy more harshly, but he could deal with that.

As he had expected, Norfolk was there and a whole army of Howards. It pleased Harry now to favour the conservative faction. He was still simmering against Cromwell, who had proved surprisingly useless in freeing him from Anna and had done nothing but bleat about the need not to offend the Duke of Cleves – as if Harry cared about that when both Francis and Charles were making friendly overtures.

He seated himself in the place of honour at the high table and gave himself up to the delights of eating. Yes, he knew he needed to lose weight. Chamber and Butts kept nagging him about it, and he had been shocked when his armourer told him that his new suit of armour would have to be fifty-four inches around the waist. But that could be deferred until another day. Tonight he intended to enjoy himself.

He was just tucking into some succulent roast swan when he saw her, a young brunette with a pretty face and the boldest eyes he had ever seen. By God, she was delectable! And she was smiling at him in an unmistakable way. He felt flattered to know that he could still attract a young maiden. The old Adam in him was not dead yet!

'Tell me, my lord of Norfolk, who is that young lady seated at the end of the table?' he asked. 'I've seen her at court. She serves the Queen.'

'That is my niece, Katheryn Howard, your Grace,' the Duke replied.

'Another of your nieces,' Harry said drily.

'This one, I assure your Grace, is nothing like the other.'

'Hmm. Her countenance is very delightful.' He beamed across at Katheryn. 'It is a pleasure to see you again, Mistress Katheryn.'

'Your Majesty does me great honour,' she said, with an enchanting smile. Norfolk and Gardiner were watching her approvingly.

'You are enjoying the feast?'

'How could I not, Sir, when your Grace is here?' She dimpled again, and he was lost.

'I see you are gracious of speech, as well as having excellent beauty,' he complimented her.

'She is virtuous too, Sire,' Norfolk added.

'It is a rare combination,' Harry observed. 'You are most fortunate, Mistress Katheryn, that Dame Nature has endowed you with such gifts. Tell me, how old are you?'

'I am nineteen, Sir,' she said.

'Oh, to be nineteen!' he sighed. 'Youth is so fleeting. Would that I were young enough to play the eager swain with such a beauty!'

'Oh, but your Majesty is not old! You are in the prime of life, Sir.'

He beamed at her, well pleased, certain that she was not just flattering him. 'I see that honesty too is among your virtues.'

He summoned a servitor and lifted his plate. 'Take these choice morsels to Mistress Katheryn. A token of our esteem, Mistress!'

'Oh, how kind of your Grace! Thank you!' Katheryn cried, as if he had given her the moon. He sat back in his chair, basking in her delight.

'And are you contracted to be married?' he asked.

'Oh, no, Sir.'

'She is pure and chaste and free from any matrimonial yoke, your Grace,' Norfolk said. Katheryn looked fleetingly sad. No doubt her lack of a dowry betokened a dismal future.

'You would be a prize for any man, Mistress Katheryn,' Harry told her.

He continued to exchange pleasantries with her and make jests for her amusement. She seemed to bask in his attention, and he saw that every eye in the room was fixed on her.

After dinner, he bade her sit by him.

'Are you happy in the Queen's chamber?' he asked.

'Yes, Sir,' she said. 'Her Grace is a good mistress.'

'Yes, she is an admirable lady.' His voice tailed away. Katheryn would have heard the rumours. Hopefully, she was too innocent to understand them.

When she told him she was proficient on the lute and virginals, he was greatly pleased, and delighted that she could sing and loved to dance. His heart went out to her as she confessed she could not go riding or hunting, as she had no horse. 'Alas, I am poor, your Grace. My lord father died in debt.'

'I know,' he said. 'I am sorry for you. Let's see what we can do about finding you a horse!'

He left soon after that, but not before lifting her hand to his lips and kissing it in the most courtly manner. 'I will see you again, Katheryn,' he promised.

'I should love that, Sir,' she told him and curtseyed low.

As his barge carried him back to Whitehall, Harry was in transports of delight. He felt young again, invigorated after being in such delightful company. Katheryn Howard greatly intrigued him. He had to see her again.

Gardiner proved most helpful. It was as if he had set himself to play Cupid. Harry had to laugh at the image that conjured up, of the fiery Bishop in the guise of a chubby cherub with wings fluttering, poised to shoot his arrow. Over the next two weeks, Gardiner hosted several suppers, feasts and entertainments for Harry, and Katheryn was always present.

Harry was no fool. He realised that Norfolk and Gardiner were doing their best to lure him over to the conservatives, taking advantage of his displeasure with Cromwell and the reformists who had urged the German alliance – and that they were dangling Katheryn as bait. Well, let them. His heart was his own. He would love where he wished. If they thought they could play him, they were mistaken: he would follow his head in matters of politics.

'I cast a fantasy on you the first time ever I saw you,' he told Katheryn, as they sat alone together late one evening after Gardiner had ushered the other guests from the supper table. 'What drew me was your extraordinary beauty and a notable appearance of honour and maidenly behaviour.' He placed his hand, laden with rings, on hers.

'Oh, Sir,' she said, 'I am not worthy of such praise!'

'But you are, Katheryn, you are! You have captivated me by your loveliness and sweetness, and your gentle face. You are so little and so precious to me! Your youth has rejuvenated me. I feel like a new man.'

He knew now that he was in love. Hopelessly, exultantly in love, when he had never thought to be so again. It was a heady experience for a man nearing forty-nine. And, to his great joy, his love was reciprocated; he was sure of it. Katheryn seemed bedazzled by him. She told him she longed to be with him, to serve him – while her eyes promised more. She revelled inordinately in the rich gifts he gave her, clearly never having owned such treasures. She welcomed his kisses, even as she gently moved his hands away from her body. She was no saucy wench to be tumbled lightly; she was a Howard, and royal blood ran in her veins. She was fit to be a queen.

All pretence of a happy marriage with Anna was abandoned as Harry revelled in his new love. He could not stop marvelling at her delightful countenance, her superlative grace, her diminutive stature that made him feel so protective of her, and her gentle manner. He leaned ever harder on Cromwell, determined to be rid of his unwanted Queen.

'I declare before God that she is not my lawful wife!' he stormed. He made his wishes known to Parliament, which dutifully petitioned him to look into the circumstances of his marriage, the Lords and Commons declaring that they had come to doubt its validity. Cromwell – Harry grudgingly gave him his due – was now at Westminster, working day and night with Parliament to find grounds for an annulment. To inspire him to greater efforts, Harry created him earl of Essex, with a hint of further rewards to come.

'Essex?' Norfolk exploded, when Harry gave him the news as they walked in the gardens at Greenwich. 'But that earldom was held by the Bourchiers, who were descended from King Edward the Third! Your Grace, I urge you, think again. This man is a blacksmith's son.' His lip curled in distaste.

Harry would not be lectured, and certainly not by Norfolk. 'You know my mind on this matter, my lord Duke. I reward on merit, not birth!'

But Norfolk and Gardiner, openly gleeful to have Harry to themselves, did not cease to disparage the absent Cromwell, asserting that it was not right for a subject to wield so much power, that he had gone too far in his religious reforms, and the people hated him.

Harry listened. Resentment against Cromwell was building in him too. He found himself inwardly agreeing with the conservatives. Had not his father often warned him about over-mighty subjects? He had banned his nobles from keeping private armies and had never allowed any one man undue influence. Harry remembered him saying that it was those factors that had helped to bring about the civil wars.

If Cromwell got him out of this mess, he would be grateful, although he might not forget who got him into it. If he did not . . .

Chapter 33

1540

On May Day, Harry and Anna watched the customary jousts from the new gatehouse at Whitehall. Among the challengers was Thomas Culpeper, a personable young man who was fast becoming one of Harry's favourite gentlemen. He was debonair, witty and always kind and solicitous when Harry's leg was plaguing him. Harry had come to look upon him with a fatherly affection. True, there had been that nasty business last year when Culpeper had been accused of rape and murder. Some common folk, simple villagers, had complained to the Council that he had defiled one of their women while his companions held her down, and that he had then killed one of them as they tried to apprehend him.

Culpeper had denied it, and Harry could not believe he had it in him to commit such appalling crimes. He had granted him a royal pardon. His accusers had persisted, but the Council, believing that the villagers were just trying to get money out of him in redress, had sent them away unsatisfied and muttering calumnies about the King's justice. Harry knew then that he had been right to protect Culpeper.

Now he watched as the young man charged down the lists, and rose to his feet with everyone else when he was unhorsed. He held his breath as he waited for Culpeper to get up, and exhaled with relief when he did, noticing that Katheryn, who was attending the Queen, had tears on her cheeks. What a tender, kind soul she had.

Norfolk and Gardiner and others of their party, notably Sir Richard Rich, who had brought down Thomas More, had not ceased to press

Harry to dismiss Cromwell. Early in June, they came to him, their faces grave, as he was discussing a new litany with Cranmer.

'Your Grace, you must see these,' Gardiner said, laying some papers before him. 'They are the depositions of those who love you and will not see you disparaged by a traitor and a heretic. My lord, Cromwell means to rule you!'

Harry immediately suspected that this was a trumped-up ploy to bring down the minister. 'How so?' he asked.

'While your Grace is working by all possible means to lead religion back to the way of truth, Cromwell has become attached to the German Lutherans. It is clear that he has always favoured the doctors who preach such erroneous opinions and hinder those who preach the contrary. He has denied the Real Presence in the Mass – and he has presumed too far above his base and low degree.'

Norfolk interrupted. 'His chief servants have testified that, recently, when they exhorted him to reflect that he was working against the intentions of your Grace and your Acts of Parliament, he betrayed himself and said he hoped to suppress the old preachers and have only the new. He declared that matters would soon be brought to such a pass that even your Grace, with all your power, could not prevent it, but that his own party would be so strong that he would make you embrace the new doctrines, even if he had to take up arms against you. Sir, these are the depositions of his servants, who heard him say those words.'

Harry read them, wondering if they had been fabricated. But what he saw before him left him chilled to his soul. He found himself trembling with anger and indignation. That Cromwell should presume to dictate to him, the Supreme Head of the Church of England, who had protected his people from the very heresy the minister was intending to force on them . . . It did not bear thinking about. He could see now why Cromwell had manoeuvred him into that alliance with the Protestant German princes. No doubt he thought he could count on their support! What rankled most of all was that Cromwell had had the impertinence – the gall – to think that Harry would be his puppet!

He felt ill as he read the depositions. He had liked Cromwell, confided in him, trusted him with the most important business of his kingdom. But he had nurtured a snake in his bosom, by God!

'Arrest him!' he roared.

'Your Grace, I beg of you.' It was Cranmer who spoke. 'Do not forget that this evidence has been laid against Cromwell by his enemies. No king ever had so loyal a minister as he. Whom shall your Grace trust hereafter if you cannot trust him?'

'You would say that,' Gardiner spat at him. 'You are his creature.'

'We are all God's creatures,' Cranmer retorted mildly, 'and I ask only for justice for a man who has done so much for this kingdom.'

'By God, he shall have it!' Harry growled.

'He was arrested as he entered the Council chamber,' Norfolk reported to Harry that afternoon. 'The captain of the guard apprehended him, and I and my lord of Southampton stripped him of his Garter insignia and his seal. He was shouting and swearing that he was no traitor as they took him off to the Tower.'

Harry sat silent, his heart heavy as a stone. He still found it hard to believe that Cromwell had turned heretic and plotted against him, but he had now questioned the witnesses himself and was satisfied that they spoke the truth. He had no compunction about letting the law take its course.

At the end of June, Parliament passed an Act of Attainder condemning Cromwell to death. Yet Harry stayed his hand, for Cromwell could yet prove useful by helping to secure an annulment of his marriage. He was eager to comply, of course, but if he thought it would win him a reprieve or a pardon, he was grievously mistaken.

The marriage was annulled by the bishops and by Parliament, on the grounds of Harry's lack of consent to it and a precontract made in childhood between Anna and the son of the Duke of Lorraine. Anna made no protest; in fact, she acquiesced with what, to Harry, seemed unflattering alacrity. In return, he rewarded her with a generous financial settlement, several fine residences, and the right to call herself his dearest sister, which gave her precedence over all the ladies in England after any future queen and Harry's daughters. She had handled herself so well, and been so amenable, that Harry suddenly discovered that he quite liked her, and invited her to come to court whenever she wished, since she had expressed the desire to stay in England.

That business disposed of, he directed that the sentence against Cromwell be carried out. He ignored Cromwell's last, frantic letter, and his final, desperate plea: *Most gracious Prince, I cry for mercy, mercy, mercy!* He had hardened his heart, and was looking to the future, not the past. Tomorrow, on the day of the execution, he was to be married to Katheryn Howard.

He had brought her to Oatlands Palace, a pleasant red-brick house in Surrey, and was brimming with heady anticipation. He was in no doubt that he would be able to give a good account of himself in the marriage bed; unlike last time, his body responded just at the sight of his lovely bride. But he could not forget that Cromwell was to die this day. Crum, who had been his right hand these past ten years. It wasn't easy to shake off the affection and true liking he had had for him, even though the wretch had betrayed him and gone over to the heretics. As he beheld Katheryn in her beautiful gown, said his vows before the Bishop of London and feasted afterwards, even as he claimed his bride in the ornate pearl bed he had specially commissioned from a French craftsman, his mind kept drifting to Tower Hill, where the public scaffold stood.

The next day, Surrey arrived to pay his respects to the new Queen, his cousin. 'The false churl is dead,' he reported. 'I witnessed the bloody deed. It is just that one who used attainders to spill the blood of others should be struck with his own staff.'

Harry felt anger rising. He was aware of Katheryn stiffening beside him. He did not want her upset on their honeymoon.

He took Surrey aside to a window embrasure. 'Have a care to the Queen's sensibilities!' he growled.

For once, Surrey had the grace to look chastened. 'Forgive me, your Grace.'

'Hmm. Now tell me, did he make a good death? Did he acknowledge his offences?'

Surrey hesitated. 'No, Sir. He prayed us all to bear witness that he died in the Catholic faith. He said that many had slandered him. He prayed that your Grace would long reign over us in prosperity. The executioner was not the usual one, but a ragged butcherly miser. It took three blows of the axe . . .'

Harry turned away, sickened.

'Sir,' Surrey said, 'the people were applauding you. You are more popular than ever, having got rid of this upstart tyrant.'

Harry waved him away, not wanting him to see the tears in his eyes. The conservatives must be rubbing their hands in glee and congratulating each other. He had already seen Norfolk, who was with the small household here at Oatlands, looking smugly triumphant. Had he been duped? Had they made an occasion to get rid of Cromwell?

The Catholic party was rejoicing, envisaging that Cromwell's fall was a victory for religious orthodoxy.

'It will drive the radical reformers underground,' Norfolk crowed one day at dinner.

Harry gave him a chilling look. He would not allow one faction to gain the upper hand. He meant to leave many of his old minister's men in post, and protect Cranmer from being unseated, for the Archbishop held similar religious views to the late minister, and was probably even more radical, if truth be told. Harry knew he had smuggled his wife into England from Germany. It was illegal, of course – the English clergy were sworn to celibacy, unlike their Protestant counterparts abroad – but Harry was not about to prosecute him for it; Cranmer was too valuable to him. But never again would he rely on any one minister, as he had on Wolsey and then Cromwell. From now on, he would rule alone, himself maintaining a balance of power between the rival factions of his court. And he would not trust a single man. Secrecy and surprise would be his watchwords; he would keep his own counsel, spin his own webs of intrigue, set traps, then pounce on the unsuspecting. He would rule on the precept that fear engenders obedience.

Katheryn's presence eased his inner turmoil. He was besotted with her, so amorous that he did not know how to make sufficient demonstrations of his affection. Unable to keep his hands off her, he caressed her openly, in public, far more than he had his other wives. He continued to shower her with gifts, including lands that had once belonged to Cromwell. He took delight in showing her off, and indulged her every whim. Never had he had a wife who made him spend so much money on dresses and jewels! Every day, she had some fresh caprice. Yet he did not begrudge her anything. Thanks to her, he was like a man reborn: his health had improved, and so had his temper.

He had not lost weight, but he disguised it well, he thought, with gorgeous clothes, and was gratified to see that it had become the fashion for gentlemen of the court, in emulation of their sovereign, to wear puffed and padded short gowns that were almost as wide as they were long – which looked very silly on some of them. He prided himself that he cut a magnificent figure in his finery, as a king should.

There were still in him vestiges of the golden youth he had once been. He could yet exert his famous charm, or show kindness and generosity when it pleased him. Only yesterday, feeling he had been over-harsh with two of his councillors, he had summoned them to his privy closet and reassured them that it was the matter under discussion, and not themselves, that had aroused his anger.

With Katheryn, he was a better king and a better person, he believed. She inspired him to live up to his ideals of kingship, which (he admitted to himself) he had sometimes failed to do. Reading his Bible in the garden one warm evening, as she frolicked with her lapdogs, he marked a passage on King Solomon's wisdom: *Let mercy and faithfulness never go from thee.* He was faithful, yes – no one could doubt his faith or his orthodoxy – but he had not always been merciful. Now, he would strive to be. He would not let anger rule him. Above all, he would never forget that, as Supreme Head of the Church, he had a special relationship with God. He was not only a king to be obeyed, but one to be worshipped. And he had been put on this earth to do God's work.

Katheryn was devout, but not as assiduous in her devotions as he would have liked. Still, she was perfect in every other way, and young enough to be moulded to his pleasure.

He had been touched when, seeing that his leg was paining him, she had taken his hand and suggested that he need not kneel to adore the body of his Saviour.

'You could receive the Sacrament sitting in a chair,' she said brightly.

'Darling,' he had countered gently, 'if I lay not only flat on the ground, but even put myself under the ground, I should not think that I am showing sufficient reverence to the blessed Sacrament.' At Easter, even though he was in agony, he had insisted on creeping painfully on his knees to the cross on Good Friday, and intended to keep on doing so while he lived. He would teach Katheryn by example.

He took pleasure in showing her his devotional books and the beautiful psalter he had recently commissioned from an illuminator who had done work for King Francis. As they sat poring over it in the garden at Oatlands, early in August, she exclaimed at the exquisite miniature scenes it contained.

'That's you, Harry, as King David slaying Goliath! And I like this one of you reading in your bedchamber, and the one of you with Will Somers.' Her small finger hovered over the page, pointing. 'But what is this you have written? What does it say?'

She was ill educated and could not read Latin.

'That is the thirty-seventh Psalm,' he told her, putting an arm around her shoulders. It says: "I have been young and now am old, yet have I not seen the righteous forsaken." And I have written "*Dolus dictum*", which means "A painful saying".'

'But you are not old, Harry!'

'I must seem ancient to you,' he smiled, willing her to deny it.

'Not at all! You are the handsomest of men to me.'

He rewarded her with ardent kisses for that, and watched her – so delectable in her low-cut French gown – as she skipped back to the palace to summon her maids for a game of hoodman blind. He did not begrudge her spending her days in one long round of pleasure, dancing and play, as she rejoiced and revelled in her new position. It pleased him that she had no interest in state affairs. It allowed him to forget them entirely in her presence, and that his treasury was all but empty. Things were so bad that he feared he might have to debase the coinage of the realm, so there was no money for a coronation for her.

Out of courtesy, Harry visited the Lady Anna at Richmond to inform her of his marriage, and was surprised to find her in a joyous mood and dressed in a new gown that actually became her. She served an excellent dinner and set herself to be a charming hostess, showing off the progress she had made in learning English. When it came to saying farewell, he realised he had really enjoyed himself, and promised to visit her again soon.

On his return to court, he reappointed to Katheryn's household many of those who had served Jane and Anna, including a horde of Howard relatives and dependents. Marget Douglas was again chief lady-of-honour. Jane's sister Elizabeth, who had married Cromwell's son Gregory, was among her ladies, as were Lady Rochford and Richmond's widow, Mary Howard. Seated in an arbour one fine day, Harry watched benevolently as Katheryn and her younger ladies ran about on the lawn tagging each other amid much laughter. He had chosen well for her.

The Howards now dominated the court. Katheryn's brother Charles had been appointed to the Privy Chamber, where her uncle, Lord William Howard, was already influential. Harry made Surrey a Knight of the Garter. He was aware that the ascendancy of the conservatives – among whom Norfolk, Gardiner and Pig Wriothesley were pre-eminent – was inflaming vicious resentment and jealousy among the reformers, whose party included Cranmer, Hertford and the latter's staunch friend and political ally, honest, able Sir William Paget. They were forever pressing Harry to make more radical changes in religion. Surrey, while he sided with his father against the Seymours, was an even more extreme reformist than Hertford, but, Harry sighed, he was a liability because of his wild, unpredictable streak. And Hertford was so high-handed that he was forever provoking squabbles within his own faction. Harry shook his head. Was ever king so beset? If Suffolk had managed to remain on good terms with both Norfolk and Hertford, why couldn't everyone else make the effort?

Take this morning, for instance. There had been faction fighting in Council, in his presence, if you please, with tempers running high as the lords vied for ascendancy, and no Cromwell to put a stop to it. Harry had bawled them out, but they would live to aggravate him another day. It now took all his will to play off the rival parties against each other, and beneath his outward mastery there was despondency. He knew not whom he could trust, and suspected that heretical ideas were infecting the minds of the more radical reformers. He was aware that many of his councillors were younger men, ambitious and aggressive, and although he liked to surround himself with youth and bask in its reflected glamour, the age gap was too wide to be easily breached in the council chamber.

It was vital to ensure that neither faction could ever be certain of him, and that all obeyed his dictates on religion, whatever their private persuasions, for the sake of unity.

'We shall proceed against those Catholics who support the Bishop of Rome, and against Protestants for heresy,' he had told his councillors. And when some young fool had dared to ask if his Grace was unsure of his religious position, Harry had left him in no doubt!

There were courtiers who tried to blind his eyes with obfuscation or manipulate him for their own profit. It had not escaped his notice that some councillors were in secret communication on matters of which they thought he had no knowledge. Well, they would learn that his eyes were everywhere, that he was still firmly in control of affairs, and that his authority was absolute and final.

Where once he had left administrative matters to Wolsey and later to Cromwell, he took care to keep a firm grip on them. Each day, he scrutinised state papers, read dispatches and letters, checked accounts – just like his father had once done – and made numerous amendments and marginal notes. He had commanded that, each Sunday evening, he be given a list of matters to be discussed by the Council in the coming week, and then drew up the agenda himself. Every Friday, Sir William Paget, his Principal Secretary, would write a summary of that week's meetings, which was presented on Saturday for his decision or approval. If a decision was needed more urgently, the Lord Chancellor would seek audience of him in the privy lodgings. Harry thanked God for the man's encyclopaedic memory, which retained details of every grant made to numerous petitioners and stored every snippet of information that might prove useful in the future.

The weather that summer was very hot. As Harry was out riding near Hampton Court, his gown and doublet discarded and slung across his saddle, he saw farmers bringing in the harvest and called a greeting to them.

''Tis a bad crop this year,' one informed him. 'There's been no rain these three months. And there be plague in London.'

'Plague? God forbid!' Harry doffed his bonnet and spurred his horse. Back at the palace, he ordered that everything be made ready at once for a progress, and took Katheryn away for an extended hunting trip through Surrey into Berkshire, skirting the capital at a safe distance until they reached Grafton in the county of Northampton, where they stayed for a week, doing what all lovers did on honeymoon.

At Ampthill, on the way homewards, Harry fell sick with a fever, plunging him into terror lest he had caught the plague, but Dr Butts told him that his legs had become infected. The doctors clustered around, looking worried, but he rallied. Then it was on to Dunstable, and when they returned to Windsor late in October, Katheryn had given Harry cause to hope that she might be with child. By then, thanks to her, he felt a new man. He rose before six o'clock, attended Mass, then rode out early to hunt, returning at ten to dine with her. In the afternoons, he attended to business. At night, he lay with his beloved, surprising himself at how lusty he felt. His leg was much better and he was hoping to lose weight with his new rule of living.

Two days later, they moved to Hampton Court. That night, Katheryn miscarried. Hearing her weeping piteously, Harry rose in the bed, his hand already reaching for his sword.

'What is it?' he asked. 'What is wrong?' Then he saw the blood. 'Oh, darling . . .'

She was sobbing uncontrollably. 'I am so sorry, Harry. So sorry! I wanted to gladden you with a prince. I'm so sorry . . .'

He folded her in his arms, swallowing his disappointment. 'There are many babes lost early on, as I well know. Do not distress yourself, Katheryn.'

His desire for privacy had become an obsession. Never certain of his health, he was determined that none should have cause to think he was losing his vigour and his grip on affairs, while greater privacy gave him the scope to manage any episodes of pain. He had shifted many of the functions of the presence chamber and council chamber to his privy chamber, leaving his presence chamber largely unused, apart from on state occasions. Consequently, the privy chamber was frequently overcrowded and no longer a place where he could resort for relaxation with his favoured gentlemen. Therefore, he had extended his private lodgings beyond it, and his life was now increasingly centred upon his bedchamber, to which only the most privileged had access. Already people were calling this suite of apartments his 'secret lodgings'.

He took to closeting himself there for days on end, rarely coming forth, even for Mass in the Chapel Royal, although his evenings were spent with Katheryn. He ceased to receive petitions in person, insisting they be submitted to the Privy Council, and ventured out only when it suited him, as when he took Katheryn to see the marvellous astronomical clock designed by Nicolaus Kratzer and installed in the inner courtyard at Hampton Court.

They gazed up at it in wonder.

'Look, sweetheart, it shows not only the hours, but the month, the date, the phases of the moon, the movement of the constellations in the Zodiac, and even the time of high water at London Bridge, which is most useful for travelling by river. And see there – it also shows the sun revolving around the earth.' Katheryn looked utterly bewildered, but she praised the clock enthusiastically.

They walked through the gardens to see the recently installed sundial designed by John Ponet, a fellow of Queens' College, Cambridge. It too showed the hours of the day, the date and the sign of the moon, as well as the ebbing and flowing of the sea, but again, Harry realised that Katheryn was only feigning interest to please him. Well, no matter! He tucked her arm in his and strolled back to the palace, summoning his dogs to heel. 'Here, Cut! Here, Ball! Come, sirs!'

Chapter 34

1541

Christmas had been celebrated with great magnificence, and on New Year's Day Harry had lavished jewels on Katheryn. Now the Lady Anna had arrived at court, bringing two superb horses caparisoned in purple velvet for the King and Queen. She showed no rancour towards Katheryn, who would not allow her to kneel, but embraced her warmly. If only Kate had behaved so amenably, Harry thought, beaming at them; how different things would have been.

That evening, after the three of them had supped merrily together, Harry retired to bed. The long days of revelry had proved unusually taxing for him, and he wished to preserve his strength. He left Katheryn and Anna to preside over the New Year festivities. The next morning, when he joined Katheryn in bed, she related how they had danced and drunk wine together.

'She is such a kind lady,' she enthused. 'I did not feel awkward with her at all.'

'I am glad of that, darling,' he replied, pulling her to him and nuzzling her throat.

At dinner that day, Anna again joined Harry and Katheryn, and there was more lively conversation and laughter. Harry presented Katheryn with a ring and two little lapdogs, then looked on with approval as she promptly gave them to Anna. When Anna departed later that day, both ladies looked quite wistful, and Harry embraced her warmly, telling her she was welcome at court at any time.

In February, to please Katheryn, he arranged for masques to be performed at Hampton Court, but when the day came, he was unable to attend. To his great alarm, the hole in his leg had suddenly become clogged, leaving him feverish and once more black in the face. He could see from their grave countenances that his doctors feared for his life. They quickly summoned surgeons to drain off fluid to relieve the swelling, but it was an agonising process, and he bore it with ill grace and clenched teeth.

Confined to his rooms because he was unable to walk, he snapped irritably at everyone and grew morose and depressed.

'I'll wager my councillors care not a toss what is happening to me,' he muttered to Will, who had remained faithfully at his side, trying to make him laugh when the pain became unbearable.

'Nay, Hal, they'll all be squabbling like schoolboys and getting nothing done. I'd have the lot of them whipped for their naughtiness.'

Harry grunted. 'I have an unhappy people to govern,' he complained. 'Time-servers and flatterers the lot of them! They look only to their own profit. But I know what they are plotting and, if God lends me health, I will take care that their projects do not succeed.'

'What projects?' Will asked, no longer jesting, but regarding his master curiously.

'They all want mastery over me, and over my kingdom! Well, they shall not have it. By God, I miss Cromwell. I know now that my councillors made false accusations and coerced me to put to death the most faithful servant I ever had.' A tear slid down his cheek. 'He was the best man in England. Cranmer was right. Who can I trust now? In whom can I confide? There is myself only.'

Will bent his head in sympathy. Then he began to strum his lute. 'Let me distract you, Hal,' he murmured.

'No! Begone!' Harry's misery was so great that he could not bear to listen to music, being consumed with grief, guilt and rage against those who had brought Cromwell down by their lies.

He remained shut away in his lodgings and ordered that many of his servants be sent home until he had recovered, as he didn't need them.

'People are complaining that the court resembles more a private family than a king's train,' Will reported.

'That's what I intended,' Harry snapped. 'I don't want people around me when I'm in this state.'

'Not even that pretty Queen of yours? Come, Hal, you'll be better soon.'

'Oh, cease your prattling!' Harry hissed.

Katheryn had asked repeatedly if she might visit him, but he had no intention of letting her see him brought so low and looking so old. For ten days, he kept saying no, until Will told him that there was gossip about a rift between them. At that, he relented. He was feeling better anyway. The wound had opened again and the pain had ebbed. With the leg bandaged, he could hobble around. He had himself dressed in a suit of crimson velvet and was sitting by the fire when Katheryn was ushered in. The sight of her, so fine and comely, raised his spirits instantly.

'Oh, Harry!' she cried, sinking to the floor by his chair, clutching his arm. 'I have been so worried about you, and when you would not see me, I feared that you did not love me any more!'

'Of course I love you, sweetheart,' he soothed, kissing her hand. 'I was very ill and did not want to worry you. But it seems you have been worrying anyway, and I never intended that. I trust you have been kept happily occupied.'

'Oh, yes. Master Culpeper said you asked him to keep me company from time to time, and he has been very kind. He has walked with me in the gardens and played his lute for me and my ladies.'

'He's a good fellow,' Harry smiled. 'I knew I could count on him to look after you. I am sorry I kept you from me. Just seeing your sweet face today has made me feel so much better. I think I will be able to go on progress to Kent after Easter, as we planned. Would you like to see how work is progressing on my palace at Rochester? And we could visit my houses at Otford, Knole and Penshurst.'

'I would love that!' Katheryn cried, clapping her hands, making him realise that life must have been very dull for her this past week or so.

He was inclined to indulge her when she begged to give some

succour to Lady Salisbury, who still languished in the Tower. 'I have heard that she lies in harsh conditions, with inadequate clothes and heat in this bitter weather,' she said, looking at him pleadingly.

'She is a traitor,' Harry reminded her. 'She is lucky that I let her live.'

'Forgive me,' Katheryn begged. 'I don't know what she has done wrong, although I do know you will have dealt her just punishment. But our Lord teaches us to be charitable to prisoners and I was but moved by her plight, as she is an old lady.'

Harry sighed. 'You have a kind heart, darling, but your sympathy is misplaced in this case. Lady Salisbury is my cousin and has a claim to the throne. Some years ago, her son, Cardinal Pole, wrote a treasonable treatise against me, for which reason he is now in exile in Italy. Not long afterwards, his brothers and their friends plotted to kill me. I had them executed and the rest of the family imprisoned in the Tower.'

'Was Lady Salisbury involved in the plot?'

'I am convinced of it. That is why she was condemned by Act of Attainder to lose her life and possessions. But, on account of her great age, I spared her the axe.'

'Your Grace is always most merciful,' Katheryn said, 'but, traitor though she is, it upsets me to think of her suffering such privations, for she is but human. Might I send her some warm clothing?'

Harry could not resist her. 'Very well,' he said at length. 'You may pay for it out of your privy purse.' It was the money he gave her for her pleasures.

'Oh, thank you, Henry! You are so kind!' she cried, rising and kissing him.

The court moved to Whitehall for Easter, and Harry was much his old self again, happily making plans for Katheryn's delayed state entry into London. She was to be presented to the citizens in a river pageant. Wearing white damask and cloth of gold, she carried herself as a queen should when she boarded Harry's barge at Whitehall Stairs and seated herself beside him in the cabin.

'You look beautiful!' he told her, taking her hand and holding it on his knee. The oarsmen pulled away and they were carried along the Thames towards Greenwich, past riverbanks crammed with cheering, waving crowds. He was in his element, smiling broadly from left to right, acknowledging the acclaim. At three o'clock, they passed under London Bridge and found waiting for them, in barges hung with tapestry and banners, the Lord Mayor and all the aldermen and crafts of the City. They escorted the royal barge past the Tower, where there were great salvoes of artillery, and when they arrived at Greenwich, all the ships docked there let off their guns in salute. The noise was deafening.

'A great triumph, darling,' Harry commented. 'My people love you.'

They enjoyed the progress that followed immensely, and Harry felt his old self again. And on their return, to crown his happiness, Katheryn told him she thought she was again with child. It was hard to express how overjoyed he was to be granted such a blessing so late in life. Bursting with gratitude, he resolved to have Katheryn crowned at Whitsuntide. The young lords and gentlemen of his court began practising daily for the celebratory jousts and tournaments.

His joy was dampened, however, when he received tidings of a new rebellion in Yorkshire, fomented by men who seemed bent on inciting another Pilgrimage of Grace. Harry feared that they were also plotting to restore the House of York to the throne. He acted speedily, and heads rolled.

With the crisis dealt with, he decided it was timely to plan a great progress to the north, to receive the submission of those who had rebelled against him in the Pilgrimage of Grace and the recent rising. Never having visited the northern parts of his realm, where he was just a name to the people, he wished to make a display of majesty and authority that would overawe and impress any disaffected subjects. To that end, he would take with him his richest clothing and the most sumptuous tapestries and plate from Whitehall. In case that were not enough to subdue his northern subjects, he was to be accompanied by a strong military presence.

Unnerved by the recent rising, and ever suspicious of any treason brewing, he remembered that the Countess of Salisbury still languished in the Tower under sentence of death. Despite her great age – she was sixty-eight – royal Plantagenet blood ran in her veins and she could still be a focus for malcontents who might try to overthrow Tudor rule while their sovereign was far away.

Hardening his heart, he ordered Lady Salisbury's immediate execution, ignoring Katheryn's desperate protests. After the sentence had been carried out, he learned that the headsman had been inept, and had hacked the Countess about the head and shoulders, butchering her in the most slovenly fashion. People were shocked, especially the Lady Mary, who had loved her former governess, although she did not complain to Harry. He was himself upset, for he would not have had the old lady suffer that way.

But he could now sleep more peacefully at night, for none of the old royal race remained, apart from the young sons of Montagu and Exeter, whom he was keeping in the Tower. Even so, he had been shaken by recent events, and was already in a foul mood when Katheryn confessed that she had suffered another miscarriage. He could not hide his displeasure, and avoided her company for a time lest he unleash his temper on her.

Not since the Field of Cloth of Gold, twenty-one years earlier, had Harry amassed such a retinue. When he departed for the north at the end of June, his train comprised five thousand horses, one thousand soldiers, the entire court, and two hundred tents and pavilions in which to accommodate those for whom there was no room in the houses where he was to stay. Katheryn – whom he had now forgiven – and Mary travelled with him, but Prince Edward was left behind, as was Elizabeth, and Cranmer, Hertford and Lord Chancellor Audley, staunch reformers all, remained in London to attend to matters of state.

Harry proceeded northwards via Hatfield, Dunstable, Ampthill and Grafton, hunting and hawking on the way. At every town and city he visited, the streets were gaily bedecked and people flocked to see him, and there were speeches, lavish receptions and banquets. He won hearts by exerting his charm and making himself accessible to all who sought justice. Progress was slow and hampered by storms. The roads became impassable, baggage carts got stuck in the mud and Katheryn became sick with the jolting of her litter. It took almost three weeks to reach Grafton, but then the weather cleared, and the vast train was able to press on to Northampton at a faster pace.

In August, Harry arrived at Lincoln wearing a suit of Lincoln green, preceded by his archers marching with drawn bows, the Yeomen of the Guard with their pikes and axes, his trumpeters and his drummers. After withdrawing into a pavilion to change into dazzling outfits of cloth of gold and silver, he and Katheryn rode in procession up the hill to the cathedral, where Harry formally pardoned the kneeling citizens for their disobedience during the Pilgrimage of Grace and the *Te Deum* was sung in celebration.

Then it was on to York. In the middle of September, they were welcomed there by the Archbishop and three hundred clergy. Two hundred rebels who had received pardons knelt in the street before Harry, offering him purses stuffed with gold.

He waited in York for the arrival of his nephew, James V of Scots, who had arranged to visit him there. And he went on waiting, growing increasingly angry and impatient. By the end of the month, James had still not appeared, much to Harry's chagrin. In the end, he gave up and moved east to Hull to plan fortifications, then returned south in slow stages to Hampton Court, arriving at the end of October. There he was informed that Prince Edward had been ill with a fever, but was now, to his immense relief, completely recovered. But the news had given him a bad turn and, to minimise the risk of further infection, he sent his son to Ashridge, one of the nursery palaces just outside London.

He was suffused with gratitude to God, who had spared his heir and given him such a beautiful, faithful wife, whose company, throughout the progress, had been a continual delight. He ordered that, on All Saints' Day, special services be held up and down the land to give thanks for the good life he led and trusted to lead with his jewel of womanhood, his rose without a thorn, as he called her.

On the day following, he arrived in the royal pew in the Chapel Royal for Mass to find a sealed letter awaiting him. The seal was Cranmer's.

He picked it up, puzzled as to why Cranmer had written to him and left the letter in such an odd place. As the Mass began at the altar below, he slipped it into his sleeve to read later when he was alone.

It shook him to his core. A courtier called John Lascelles had asked to see Cranmer in private, and informed him that his sister, who had served Katheryn before her marriage, had told him that, when they shared a dorter in the household of the Dowager Duchess of Norfolk, the Queen had been loose in her behaviour with one Francis Dereham, who was now her secretary. Harry remembered her appointing Dereham, a distant kinsman, to the post while the court was on progress in the north.

His frown deepened. He could not believe what he was reading. It sounded like malice on the part of a vindictive woman who had not been given a place in Katheryn's household. Moreover, he knew Lascelles for an ardent reformist; the man had served Cromwell and could have no love for an orthodox Catholic queen. And it was no secret that Cranmer wished to see the conservative faction toppled from power. No, Harry decided. He would not credit this, and he'd thank Cranmer not to bother him with spiteful gossip or hearsay.

He took his seat in Council the next morning, ready to castigate the Archbishop and make plain his displeasure. But when he saw Cranmer and all the other lords regarding him warily, almost pityingly, his heart lurched, remembering how he had initially dismissed the allegations that Anne Boleyn had been unfaithful.

'Your Grace should read these,' Cranmer said quietly, almost sorrowfully, and pushed across the table a pile of papers. Reluctantly, Harry picked them up and read, his throat tight. They were depositions from members of Katheryn's household.

It now seemed that she and Dereham had known each other well – too well. According to this testimony, which chimed with that of Lascelles' sister, they had once been lovers. And he had thought Katheryn an innocent!

Dereham, the arrogant bastard, had been heard to boast that, if the King died, he was certain that Katheryn would marry him. He had openly hinted at the favours she had granted him. He had floored a gentleman usher who objected to his remaining seated at table after the Queen's Council had risen.

How had none of this come to his attention before? Predicting the King's death was treason, and fighting within the verge of the court carried heavy penalties. Dereham had been lucky that no one had reported him.

But it was his casual boasts about having bedded Katheryn that pierced Harry to the heart.

'Is there any evidence that they have resumed their liaison?' he croaked, his head swimming.

'Not as such,' said Hertford, looking primmer than ever. 'But he has made clear his *intention* of doing so, and that is treason under the law. And there is some suggestion that the Queen was arranging secret trysts during the progress, with the help of Lady Rochford.'

'You need to find out more about that!' Harry barked, remembering how Jane Rochford had been well rewarded for laying evidence against her husband, George Boleyn, and his sister. Was this how she repaid him?

His eyes fixed on Norfolk, who looked as if he would rather be anywhere else. 'You told me she was virtuous!'

'That's what I believed, Sir, I swear it,' Norfolk protested.

'Then your stepmother could not have been very vigilant!' Harry snapped. 'And what's this about one Manox?'

'He was her music teacher.' Norfolk swallowed.

Harry barely heard him. He was reading the deposition that asserted that Manox had known of a mark in a secret place on the Queen's body. He himself knew that mark: it was in the crease between her thigh and her woman's parts, a place only a husband or midwife should see. He had kissed it, reverencing her as his wife, during one of their nights of joy. And she – he could not bear to think of it – had shown it to that scoundrel Manox, and to Dereham too, if other testimony was to be believed. She was not the pure young girl she had pretended to be. He had been grossly deceived!

Rage consumed him. 'By God, she shall suffer for this!' he roared. 'Bring me a sword and I will slay her myself!'

His councillors goggled at him, clearly unsure how to deal with this outburst, but he was too far gone in misery to care. Grief surged through him; he saw that he must lose the woman he had prized above all others, the darling of his old age. She had led him on, just like she had led the others, and she had duped him – and he, like an old fool, had been hooked like a fish. He could not believe it. Not Katheryn, sweet Katheryn, his darling . . . Hot tears coursed down his cheeks as rage gave way to devastation.

'By God, why should I have the misfortune to be cursed with such ill-conditioned wives?' he cried. 'And you're all complicit – you, Norfolk, and you, Gardiner, and you, Wriothesley. You all solicited me to marry her. You assured me she was pure! You should have known better! And now, what am I to do with her?' His voice shook.

'Sir,' Cranmer soothed, 'you should comfort yourself in the knowledge that the Queen's misdemeanours took place before you proposed marriage to her. She committed no crime. But we do have reason to believe that she once entered into a precontract with Dereham. If true, it would render your union with her invalid. You would be a free man.' His tone did not quite succeed in betraying his eagerness. Yes, Harry thought bitterly, free to marry another woman pushed into his path, this time by the reformers.

'Have the Queen confined to her rooms,' he ordered, mastering himself, 'and Lady Rochford with her. I want them both questioned closely, especially about Dereham and this question of a precontract. And arrest Dereham; find out what he can tell us. Then we will convene again.' He rose, noting the ill-concealed smugness of the reformers and the consternation of the conservatives, then he escaped to the privacy of his bedchamber and lay there weeping as he had not wept in years.

After suffering a dreadful, lonely night, tormented by thoughts of Katheryn in the arms of Dereham or being pawed by Manox, Harry felt the need for some spiritual comfort and went to Mass in the Chapel Royal. As he left afterwards, with his gentlemen in attendance, he heard Katheryn screaming.

'Your Grace! Sir! *Harry!*'

What was she doing in the gallery? She should be locked up!

Unable to stop himself, he twisted his head in her direction, then made to walk away, unable to bear the sight of her, whom he had loved so greatly.

'Harry! Listen to me! I *beg* of you!' she cried, and he hesitated. If he turned to her now, he could forgive her, take her back to his bosom and put a stop to this whole terrible business. But his anger, his grief and his sense of betrayal went too deep. Besides, she might not even be his wife. She might truly be Dereham's.

Sickened, he walked away, ignoring her cries for help. It sounded as if her guards had caught up with her and were manhandling her back to her apartments. She was wailing and howling, as if she knew that all was lost.

Cranmer had interrogated Katheryn.

'Sir, she was hysterical, in great fear for her life, and often incoherent. She denies everything, apart from bedding Dereham when she was in the Dowager's household. She insists she has never been unfaithful to you, and that there was never a precontract with him. She also avers that he never said he would wed her if your Grace died.'

Harry shook his head. She was doing herself no favours. Lying would not move him to mercy.

'If she would only admit to the precontract, there would be a way out for both of us,' he said dismally.

But Cranmer seemed reluctant to pursue that line of questioning.

Harry could no longer bear to be in the same house as Katheryn. The very air of Hampton Court seemed tainted by her promiscuity. He took himself off for a short hunting progress, seeking oblivion in the chase and the drama of the kill. When he returned, he put on a brave front, inviting those ladies who were not waiting on the Queen to a banquet and conversing gaily with them.

He was regaining his equilibrium. So far, he kept telling himself, the evidence pointed only to misconduct before marriage, which was not a felony and had definitely occurred before he began paying court to Katheryn. Aside from pretending to be what she was not, there was nothing to suggest that she had not loved him. All might not yet be lost.

But then Dereham, in the Tower, admitted that he and Katheryn had been precontracted. He swore he had not resumed relations with her after joining her household, nor had he looked for the death of his sovereign. It was what Harry had hoped to hear.

Precontracts could be annulled. He would ask Gardiner to do it, since he doubted Cranmer would be willing. He could imagine the arguments. But should he take Katheryn back, after she had lied to him and deceived him? Should a king marry a loose woman?

The answer was that he wanted her back, whatever she was. His loneliness and the emptiness of his bed were overwhelming. He could not face old age without her. She was his lifeblood.

Cranmer came to him one night after dinner during the second week of November, his face grave. 'Your Grace, we have questioned Dereham again and pressed him on whether he has had sexual relations with the Queen since her marriage. He denied it, as before, but he claimed that Master Culpeper had succeeded him in her affections.' He hesitated. 'And there is new evidence that Culpeper and the Queen were lovers.' His voice tailed off sorrowfully.

Harry felt himself falling to pieces. People spoke idly of their hearts breaking; he knew now what that really meant. Culpeper, whom he had loved like a son, had betrayed him. And Katheryn . . . It all became clear now. Her love for him had been a sham; she had given him fair words, flattered him, wheedled as much as she could from him, pretending to love him, when all the time she had been arranging secret trysts, cuckolding him, giving herself to a younger man. The memory of her laughter as she trailed her hair over him in bed came to him as if in mockery.

He stood up, his legs barely holding his weight. 'Find out if it be true,' he managed to say. 'I am for Whitehall. Have the court and some of my Council follow me there, while you and the rest conclude this business here.'

How he tottered to his barge he barely knew. He was veering between fury and desolation. He knew himself a broken man.

The councillors at Hampton Court sent regular reports, which he could hardly bring himself to read. Katheryn had admitted only that she had flirted with Culpeper, met him by the back stairs, given him gifts and called him her little, sweet fool – as Harry had often called *her*! His heart burned when he read that. They had shown her a letter she had written to Culpeper, signed *Yours as long as life endures*, but she had sworn she had not committed adultery with him, and accused Lady Rochford of having encouraged her to do so. When questioned, Lady Rochford had denied it and thrown Katheryn to the wolves, saying she believed that adultery had taken place. The lewd couple had met in her rooms with her standing guard, and also in the Queen's apartments. Once – Harry remembered the occasion – when he came to pay the marriage debt and found Katheryn's door locked, Lady Rochford had kept him waiting until Culpeper had escaped down the back stairs. He shook with outrage as he read that.

Cranmer reported that, under interrogation, the Queen's maids had given detailed depositions of what had been going on both before her marriage and during the progress, but none had actually witnessed any act of adultery. However, one had revealed that Katheryn had once met Culpeper in her stool chamber, and understandably the Council believed the worst, as did Harry. By God, they must have been desperate for each other to meet in such a rank place!

He sanctioned the arrest of Culpeper, commanding that the truth be got out of him by whatever means necessary.

This time, it was Hertford who brought the news.

'Your Grace, he confesses that he and the Queen met in secret on many occasions, but insists they never passed beyond words, although he meant to do so, as did she. Sir, this evil intent constitutes in itself high treason.'

'Do not presume to instruct me in the law,' Harry snapped, misery making him want to lash out.

'Forgive me, Sir. Culpeper insists too that the Queen was the prime mover in the affair, while Lady Rochford encouraged it and acted as a procuress. Sir, what would you have us do?'

His head in his hands, Harry knew he had to act the king, painful as it would be. 'Have the Queen's household broken up,' he instructed. 'Ask your brother to collect her jewels and return them to me.'

'What is to happen to the Queen?' Hertford ventured.

Harry rose and limped to the window, looking out on the slate-grey Thames. What was he to do with Katheryn? If she *had* intended to betray him, as Culpeper maintained, then she had committed treason and deserved death. But he could not contemplate executing her or putting her through a trial. He did not want to endure again what he had suffered only five years ago when Anne Boleyn had betrayed him.

'I may have the marriage annulled,' he said, turning. 'I will perhaps keep her in prison.'

He registered the dismay in Hertford's face. You jackal, Harry thought; you would have me behead her, for fear I might take her back.

'Sir, the penalty for treason is burning.'

'Again, you presume to instruct me!' Harry flared. 'I will send the Queen away to wait on my pleasure. Take her to Syon.' It had been one of the last abbeys to be closed down and was standing empty. 'And she is no longer to be called queen, being unworthy of the name. Lady Rochford shall go to the Tower.'

'I will arrange all,' Hertford said. 'Sir, there is another matter.

The Lady Margaret Douglas has been having secret meetings with the Lady Katheryn's brother, Mr Charles Howard.'

'Secret meetings?' Had his naughty niece not learned her lesson? 'Is that all?'

'Both say so.'

'By St George, am I always to be plagued by naughty, aggravating women? Have Cranmer reprimand her and remind her of her duty to me. And dismiss Mr Howard from the Privy Chamber; banish the pair of them from court. The Lady Margaret can go to Norfolk's house at Kenninghall. He owes me, by God!'

When Katheryn had been removed to Syon, Harry returned to Hampton Court. They told him that the Lady Anna was holding herself in readiness for him to recall her to his side. She would have a long wait, he thought, and sent one of his councillors to retrieve the ring Katheryn had given her.

Few members of the Howard family had escaped his wrath. There was now a whole cluster of them in the Tower, set to be convicted of misprision of treason for concealing the Queen's misbehaviour, and sentenced to imprisonment and the forfeiture of all their possessions. They were lucky to keep their heads!

The reformers were cock-a-hoop. The eclipse of the conservatives had left the Privy Chamber firmly under the control of the reformist party led by Hertford and Denny, who were no doubt congratulating each other and looking forward to remaining the dominant faction at court. But Harry was not letting them have things all their way. He meant to leave the Howards to fester in the Tower for a few months, perhaps a year, to teach them a lesson, then release them.

Norfolk and Gardiner were still at liberty, although he suspected that they had done more than anyone else to bring about his marriage to Katheryn, and that Norfolk at least had known of her past. The Duke had left court and gone to ground, doubtless aware that he would never again stand high in his master's good graces. Harry had received a grovelling letter from Kenninghall, in which Norfolk deplored the misconduct of his niece and other relatives and begged for some assurance of favour.

Sir William Paget knocked on the door of his study. 'Your Grace, I fear that Lady Rochford has found the strain of repeated interrogations so great that she has gone mad.'

Harry raised his eyebrows. 'Really?'

'Aye, and because of this fit of frenzy, she cannot legally stand trial.'

'But she must!' Harry insisted, aghast at being cheated of his revenge. 'She cannot be allowed to escape justice. Have my physicians treat her and report on her progress. Tell them to determine whether or not she is truly crazed.'

On 1 December, Dereham and Culpeper were arraigned at the Guildhall for high treason and sentenced to death. Harry could still not bring himself to contemplate condemning Katheryn to the same fate, and was even now fantasising about a reconciliation, so he commuted Culpeper's punishment of hanging, drawing and quartering to decapitation. The two wretches were executed nine days later and their heads set on spikes on London Bridge, as a warning to other would-be traitors.

During these terrible weeks, Harry could tolerate no company but that of Will and his musicians. He refused to see his councillors and insisted that they communicate by letter. He drowned his grief and shame in long, punishing days out hunting, and could not settle in one house for any length of time, but moved about restlessly. Christmas at Greenwich was a dismal affair, with only a small company in attendance. He forced himself to appear in public, but was pensive and melancholy during the feasting.

1542

On the first day of the New Year, Harry caught a glimpse of himself in the mirror as Penny was shaving him and was horrified to see how old and grey he looked. Katheryn had done this to him; Katheryn, who had so briefly given him back his youth. Once again, anger burned in him.

He sighed, dismissed Penny and picked up his Bible. It fell open at a passage he had marked in the Book of Proverbs: *My son, why wilt thou have pleasure in a harlot?* His tears blotted the page. This was how he was now, raging one moment, maudlin the next.

He had taken to solacing himself by indulging in food and wine. He knew he was growing heavier every day, but could not help himself. He had to have some pleasure in life.

'You're getting fat, Hal,' Will reproved, jangling his jester's bells in Harry's face. 'I do declare that three men could get inside your doublet.' Harry cuffed him and threw him out of the chamber. The jibe had touched him too nearly. But he must make an effort. He was the King; he could not hide for ever from his subjects.

He emerged from his apartments and once more took up the reins of government. It was hard, but it helped him to move forward. On the day Parliament brought in a Bill of Attainder against Katheryn, he distracted himself by entertaining sixty ladies to supper, making them great cheer and paying marked attention to Anne Bassett, a pretty young maid-of-honour on whom his eye had alighted before that first, ill-fated sight of Katheryn. He had allowed Anne to stay on at court, which had given rise to talk, of course, but he cared not – and Anne seemed not to care either, or her formidable mother, Lady Lisle. Their ambitions were transparent, yet only he knew they were futile. He liked flirting with Anne; he enjoyed her company – but he was in no mood to fall in love with any woman. His heart was still Katheryn's, more fool him. Still, it pleased his bruised vanity to have people see that he was attractive to a comely young lady.

In February, the Act of Attainder against Katheryn became law, condemning her to lose her life and all her possessions. The councillors had had a special stamp made of Harry's signature, and told him, in hushed tones, that they would use it to validate the Act, to spare him the pain of signing it.

He stayed them. Mindful that Katheryn had been given no chance to speak in her defence, he sent a deputation to Syon to offer her the opportunity of going to the Parliament house and clearing herself of the charges. He waited in fevered impatience, praying that she would do just that, enabling him to have the attainder repealed and take her back. Surely, she would seize this last chance to save herself?

The councillors stood before him, looking grave. 'Your Grace, the Lady Katheryn has declined to come to Parliament. She confessed to us that she has deserved death and asks for no favour except that the execution shall be secret and not under the eyes of the world.'

Harry buried his face in his hands. 'Why will she not accept this chance of rehabilitation?' he asked plaintively. 'How can I spare her if she professes herself guilty?'

'Sir,' Hertford said gently, 'in such a case, it would not be prudent to show mercy.'

'I am the King, the fount of justice and mercy,' Harry countered, glaring at him. 'I am inclined to have her imprisoned for life.'

The lords, reformists to a man, looked alarmed.

'It is not sufficient punishment for such heinous offences,' Denny ventured. There were urgent murmurs of agreement.

'Will your Grace be so lenient with her, when two men have died on her account?' Hertford asked.

Harry hesitated. If he spared Katheryn now, it would look like weakness. But how could he send a foolish girl of just twenty-one to a brutal death? How could he destroy the young body he had possessed and worshipped? Never, in all his years as king, had he faced such a hard, cruel decision.

He took a deep breath, reminding himself how she had played him false and cuckolded him, goading himself until rage seized him.

'Take her to the Tower,' he commanded. 'Go by closed barge, to avoid her being in view of the people. She shall die on Monday.'

He wept when they had gone, imagining how Katheryn would feel when she saw them arriving at Syon. Beyond that, he could not think.

The next day, Saturday, he authorised the signing of the death warrant. On Sunday, he ordered that Katheryn's confessor be sent to prepare her soul to meet its Maker.

He did not sleep that night, wondering how she was coping with the prospect of her imminent death. Early the next morning, he rose and knelt in his oratory, praying for her until he was sure that the time set for the execution was past. Then he waited for the lords who had witnessed it to report back to him, bracing himself for more pain.

'The Lady Katheryn panicked when we came for her and we had to force her to board the barge at Syon,' Suffolk related. 'Once we got to the Tower, however, she became calmer. Yesterday, she asked that the block be brought to her room so that she could practise making a good death. When she came forth this morning, she was so weak with fear that she could hardly stand, but she made a brave speech admitting that she had offended against God's laws most heinously. The end was swift; she did not suffer.'

But, by God, she must have suffered beforehand. Harry swallowed, making a mighty effort to master himself. 'And what of Lady Rochford?' Having seen no improvement in her hysterical state, he had demanded that Parliament pass an Act making it lawful for him to execute an insane person who had committed treason.

'She was calm and resigned when she mounted the scaffold. She confessed her faults like any sane person and did not seem at all crazed.'

He nodded. It was as he had suspected all along: she had been faking madness to save her neck.

'The Constable is having the bodies buried in the chapel of St Peter ad Vincula,' Hertford said. Katheryn would lie for all eternity next to Anne Boleyn, who had also betrayed her lord and King.

Harry crossed himself. 'May God have mercy on their souls.'

He rose, waved a hand in dismissal, and withdrew into his inner chamber, feeling like the loneliest, most wretched man on earth.

Part Four

Winter

Adieu, Madame et ma maistresse.
Adieu mon solas et mon joie.
Adieu, iusque vous revoie,
Adieu, vous diz per grand tristesse.

Adieu, Madame and my mistress,
Adieu, my solace and my joy!
Adieu until again I see you,
Adieu, I say, overcome by sadness.

(King Henry VIII)

Chapter 35

1542

By March, life at court was returning to normal. Harry hosted another banquet for the ladies. On the morning beforehand, he personally inspected the lodgings that had been prepared for them, going from chamber to chamber and checking the hangings and bedcoverings to ensure they were the best that could be provided. When his guests arrived, he received them with much gaiety and bade them heartily welcome, but took care not to favour any particular one, even though Anne Bassett was among them and making eyes at him.

Few others were, though. The Act of Attainder against Katheryn Howard had declared it treason for an unchaste woman to marry the King without first revealing her past. It was as if Katheryn's fate had put others off aspiring to the honour, Harry thought sadly, thinking that did not reflect well on the virtue of the ladies of the court.

As the months passed, his grief and anger abated, although he knew he would never be the same man again. In July, the court was diverted by news that the volatile Surrey had challenged one of the King's servants to a duel, provoking an enraged Harry to clap him into the Fleet prison. A fortnight later, after Surrey had written an abject letter to the Council admitting that the fury of restless youth had got the better of him and pointing out that he was not the first young man to have enterprised matters he afterwards regretted, Harry released him. The truth was, he liked Surrey. He admired his poetry, being a poet himself and having some understanding of the art – although the Muse seemed now to have left him, sadly.

Surrey had now eclipsed Sir Thomas Wyatt as the foremost court poet. Wyatt was rarely at court these days, having grown weary of being sent on diplomatic missions abroad. He made plain his desire to retire to the peace of his castle in Kent, but that autumn Harry insisted he travel to Falmouth in Cornwall, where an emissary from the Emperor would require a welcome and an escort to court.

He was grieved to hear that Wyatt never reached Falmouth, but had died on the way, at Sherborne in Dorset. How fleeting was life. Not twenty years ago, Wyatt had been lustily pursuing Anne Boleyn and provoking Harry's jealousy. It seemed so long ago now. They had all been young and ardent, not dreaming of the tragedies and dangers ahead.

Harry summoned Mary to preside for him over a feast in November, and was glad to see her looking so well and more confident. Yet he feared he was not good company, being preoccupied with deteriorating relations with Scotland. His nephew James was threatening an invasion, obliging Harry to send north a military force under Norfolk to prevent him and his army from crossing the border. Norfolk had seized his chance to regain his sovereign's confidence, and he and young Surrey, who was seeing military service for the first time, acquitted themselves well.

Early in December, news came blazing into court that the English had won a great victory over the Scots at Solway Moss. Norfolk boasted that it had been due to his expert leadership, although Harry suspected that Hertford, who had also been given a command, deserved some of the credit. He himself was jubilant, throwing off the last vestiges of his melancholy, and the court was gayer than at any time since before Katheryn's fall.

Then, to crown the English victory, came tidings of the death of King James. Harry could not mourn his nephew, who had been an aggressive neighbour for years. Instead, he rejoiced with his people, for Scotland was now in the hands of James' sole heir, the week-old Mary, Queen of Scots. The northern kingdom would be subject to yet another regency and should give England no further trouble.

Harry summoned his Council. 'My ancestor, King Edward I, tried in vain to conquer Scotland and bring it under English rule.

Yet I have conceived a plan to do just that through peaceful means. A marriage between Prince Edward and Queen Mary would unite the two kingdoms under my authority.'

There was a great thumping of the table in response. The lords could not contain their enthusiasm for the project. But the Scots, when approached, were violently opposed. Harry knew he faced a tough round of negotiations, yet the little Queen had to marry; she could not rule Scotland alone. Who better than young Edward, and a union that would put an end to centuries of strife and warfare?

1543

In February, Surrey returned south and disgraced himself again, celebrating the recent victory by rampaging through London with his wild cronies on a drunken spree. They outraged the citizens by smashing the windows of churches and aldermen's houses, and throwing stones at bystanders. The next night, they took a boat out on the Thames and shot pellets at the whores on Bankside.

Harry learned of this after the Lord Mayor complained to the Council, and Surrey was once more committed to the Fleet prison to learn to control his unruly will. Harry was exasperated with him.

'He is the most foolish proud boy in England,' he stormed at an embarrassed Norfolk, but affection for Surrey overcame his wrath, and soon the young Earl was a free man, and doing his utmost to regain his royal master's favour.

That winter, Harry's eye lighted on Lady Latimer. He had seen her at court, for she came to visit her brother, William Parr, one of his gentlemen, whenever she could safely leave her dying husband at their house in London. She was no giddy young girl, but a mature, well-educated woman of thirty. Harry was attracted by her intelligence as well as her comeliness. She was of diminutive stature, dignified and graceful, and always wore a cheerful countenance. Many courtiers praised her for her virtue.

Harry remembered her being born, for her father, Sir Thomas Parr, had served him, and her mother, a most erudite woman, had been one of Kate's ladies-in-waiting. Katharine Parr was Kate's god-daughter, named for her. Her brother William was one of Harry's favourite courtiers, and her sister Anne had waited on Katheryn Howard. The Parrs were a family with a long record of loyalty to the Crown.

But Harry had had good reason to distrust Lord Latimer, Katharine's second husband. He had joined the rebels during the Pilgrimage of Grace, and although he afterwards claimed he had been forced to it, Cromwell had had him watched. It was as well for Latimer that he had spent the years after the quelling of the rising working hard to regain royal favour. But he was very ill now, and Katharine would soon be a widow – a childless widow, and no wonder, having been wed first to a sickly boy and then an ailing man.

Harry watched and admired her from afar, weighing up whether he should approach her while her lord still lived. The matter was decided for him when, on a February day with a hint of spring in the air, she suddenly appeared in his privy garden.

She could not have chosen a worse moment.

He had been having a difficult day. It was the first anniversary of Katheryn's death and, unable to bear the jovial company in the privy chamber any longer, he had retreated to the solitude of his little banqueting house, where he had finally given way to the tears he'd been fighting back since dawn. He was weeping not only for silly Katheryn, whose life had been cut short through her own foolish wantonness, but also for himself and the miseries of unrelieved encroaching age. And then he heard a twig crack.

Ever suspicious, he heaved himself to his feet, his hand flying to his dagger, and stepped outside. And there, in his garden, stood a woman, looking as shocked as he felt.

'My Lady Latimer?' he stuttered.

'Your Majesty, forgive me! I got lost and there was this gap in the hedge . . .' She sank into a curtsey, visibly trembling. 'I beg your pardon for the intrusion.'

'No matter,' he said. 'I was praying for something to lighten my mood, and here you are. A serendipitous coincidence. Rise, please.'

She rose unsteadily. 'I am glad to have been inadvertently of service. I will leave your Majesty in peace now.'

'No, don't go,' he said. 'Stay a while and comfort a lonely old man.'

Her face registered astonishment. 'How can I be of service, Sir?'

'You can keep me company for a space,' he said, taking her hand and leading her into the banqueting house. 'Be seated, pray. I like to come here when I have leisure to enjoy some private time, because I am rarely alone. Would you like some wine?'

She accepted the glass warily.

'I trust you are well, my lady,' Harry said.

She smiled sadly. 'I am well, Sir, but my lord is not long for this world. That is why I have hardly been at court lately.'

'I am sorry,' he said. 'Death gathers all those we cherish. If you love, you invite pain.'

'I would rather know pain than never know love,' she said.

He drew a deep breath and wiped away a rogue tear. 'It is a year today,' he said, 'and I cannot forget her.'

'Time will heal you, Sir.'

'Forgive me,' he said, mopping his eyes. 'Sometimes, I think I will go mad. Half of me hates her for betraying me; the other half just wants her, desperately. I'm sorry, Madam, I should not be troubling you with my woes.' He tried to smile.

'You are not troubling me at all, Sir,' Katharine assured him. She reached across and pressed her hand on his. 'You *will* feel better. Just give yourself time.'

He did not withdraw his hand, but just sat there, thinking how kind and attractive she was. 'You're a good woman, Lady Latimer, and a comely one too. If I were ten years younger, I'd be pursuing you. Alas, what would you see in me now?' He found himself smiling.

'I see a very sad man who needs good cheer,' she replied, withdrawing her hand.

'And will you be the one to do it?' he asked, grasping it back.

'I think, Sir, that you have the strength of mind to do it yourself. It must be very lonely sometimes, having to make impossible decisions that you know will affect you adversely. Your Grace should find comfort in knowing that you did what you thought was right.'

He sighed. 'I would not have executed Katheryn, had it been left to me. I was persuaded that she should die, told I could not show leniency when others had suffered death for less, that I could not let my personal feelings sway me; that would have been to show weakness, and a king must always be strong. So, I was strong. But it does not stop me from having bitter regrets.'

Katharine's face was suffused with sympathy. 'I am so sorry that your Grace was plunged into that terrible dilemma, one not of your own making. I saw you with the Queen, saw how much you loved her. She did a terrible thing when she betrayed that love. It beggars belief.'

'My fool says she asked for what happened to her.'

'Your fool?'

He smiled. 'Yes, Will Somers. He knows all the secrets of my heart. He doesn't mince words with me. He keeps me rooted.' He paused. 'I do not like being a widower, Lady Latimer. Being married is a natural state for a man. God willed that I should suffer many mishaps in my marriages – but there were others to blame, of course. Yet I am still convinced that one day I will find true happiness in wedlock with a lady who will love me and never betray me. Someone like my dearest Queen Jane. And this time, I will choose her myself, and not take someone pushed into my path by the factions that blight my court.'

'Your Grace deserves such a rare person,' Katharine said. 'I pray you will find her.'

'It will not be easy.' He gave her a grim smile. 'I will take no stiff Catholics or anyone who has leant too far towards heresy. But I am not averse to a good theological debate, although few women are learned enough to take part, and some are too opinionated.' He paused. 'Do godly matters interest you, Lady Latimer?'

'I enjoy a friendly argument,' she said.

'And you like to discuss religious doctrine?'

'Yes, when I wish to have a point clarified to me. I am a great advocate of your Majesty's reforms. I admire you for breaking with the Pope. He is a greater persecutor of all true Christians than ever the Pharaoh of the Children of Israel was.'

Harry was impressed. 'By God, my lady, you have the sow by the right ear!'

He saw her shiver. Dusk had long since fallen and the evening was chilly.

'Your Grace, by your leave, I should return to my husband.'

'Of course, he said, clambering awkwardly to his feet, as she hurriedly rose too. 'Such wifely devotion is commendable.' He raised her hand to his lips and kissed it. 'It has been a physick to me, talking to you. I hope I may have the pleasure again soon.'

'It will be *my* pleasure, Sir. I'm glad that I was able to help.'

He had never thought he would take another wife after what had happened with Katheryn. Five wives were sufficient for any man, and there had been enough troubles in his marriages without inviting more. But here he was, contemplating matrimony again. In Lady Latimer, he knew he would find a safe haven. He wanted no more giddy girls or foreign princesses, just a quiet-spoken, good and virtuous woman who would be a companion and a comfort in his declining years. And she, he felt in his bones, was that woman.

He sent her a gift of gorgeous court gowns, fit for a queen and cut in the Italian, French and Dutch styles, with matching French hoods. When she read the accompanying note, it would leave her in no doubt of his honourable intentions. But more he could not do, not while her husband lived.

When she did not appear at court, he feared he had offended her, but then he learned that Lord Latimer had died.

He should have held back and waited until a suitable interval of mourning had passed, but he was nearly fifty-two, overweight and not in the best of health, and time was creeping up on him. He invited Katharine to court and began seeking out her company. She showed him all the proper deference and appeared to welcome his overtures, opening her warm heart to him. He became ever more impressed by her chastity, her wisdom, her learning and her devotion to the Gospel. Beneath the reserved exterior, he sensed there beat a passionate heart. Just the woman for him!

Mary joined him one March morning when he was playing bowls and waited until the game was finished. Then she strolled back to the palace with him, Cut and Ball trotting at their heels.

'Methinks, Sir, that you have taken a fancy to my friend, Lady Latimer,' she ventured – boldly, he thought, for Mary was prudishly reticent in such matters.

'Aye,' he grinned. 'But it is more than a fancy.'

'And that, my lord Father, is why I needed to speak to you. Did you know that Sir Thomas Seymour has been courting her since before her husband died and that he has been bragging to my ladies that they are to wed?'

Harry stopped dead on the path, feeling winded. Thomas Seymour! It could not be . . . Katharine would be wasted on that braggart. And yet, and yet – how could he possibly compete with such a dashing young man? What could he offer her?

The answer came readily. He could offer her a crown – but would she want it?

Of course she would! But he would have to move quickly. It would be easy to get Seymour out of the way; he could send him to sea on a naval exercise, or dispatch him on a diplomatic mission abroad. And then the field would be free for him to claim the victory!

Before he could take any action, Gardiner presented himself in Harry's closet. He and Wriothesley were ruthlessly seeking out heretics within the royal household, doing their best to bring down the reformists. Only this month, they had uncovered a nest of dissenters among the musicians of St George's Chapel at Windsor, which was too close to home for Harry's comfort. Even his favourite, John Marbeck, the gifted Master of the Choristers, had been incriminated, after heretical writings had been found in his house.

542

Gardiner and his cronies were now gathering evidence against other suspects.

Harry looked up to see Gardiner wearing a worried expression, not his customary combative one. What now? he wondered.

'Your Grace, it has come to my attention that you are paying your addresses to Lady Latimer, and I feel I must voice my concerns.'

Not another lecture! Harry groaned inwardly. First Mary, now Gardiner. By St George, the course of true love was never smooth!

'What is it?' he said testily. 'Speak, man!'

'I have reason to believe that she holds radical, if not heretical, religious views. I am told she entertains reformers at her house.'

'By God, so do I!' Harry exploded. 'And my daughter, who is as orthodox as they come, is a frequent visitor. Do you think *she* would have any truck with a heretic?'

Gardiner slunk away, murmuring an apology for having troubled his master unnecessarily. Harry tried to be fair. Gardiner might be overzealous in rooting out heresy, but he was loyal and he was a good son of the Church, invaluable in many ways.

But he just would not go away! In April, he was back, this time accusing Archbishop Cranmer of heresy. Harry listened wearily, knowing that Gardiner coveted Canterbury, and aware that there was probably a lot of truth in his allegations. He himself had long suspected that Cranmer had secretly embraced the Protestant religion. But he liked the man and would always be grateful to him for showing him the way out of his marriage to Kate. So long as Cranmer did not overstep the boundaries of Harry's Church – and he never had – he would protect him from his enemies.

'I myself will question him,' he said firmly. 'Ask for my barge to be made ready to take me to Lambeth Palace.'

Gardiner looked taken aback and seemed about to protest, but held his peace and scuttled off.

At Lambeth Palace, Harry did not disembark, but sent a message inviting Cranmer to accompany him on a trip along the Thames. When the Archbishop appeared, looking flustered, Harry beckoned him into the barge's statehouse and invited him to join him on the cushioned bench as the oarsmen pulled away towards Chelsea Reach.

Then he smiled at him. 'Ah, my chaplain, I have news for you. I now know who is the greatest heretic in Kent! Or should I say the greatest married heretic in Kent?'

Cranmer looked terrified. He was wringing his hands.

'There is no need to fear,' Harry assured him, placing an arm around his trembling shoulders. 'I have great love for your Grace, and what you believe in the privacy of your heart is of no interest to me, so long as you comply with my laws and the doctrines of the Church of England. But you should know that your enemies are trying to unseat you. Yet I will protect you, and to that end I authorise you yourself to preside over the inquiry into your alleged heresy. You may safely leave this with me.'

Cranmer still looked like a trapped rabbit, but he nodded, barely able to speak.

When Gardiner came again that afternoon and asked Harry for permission to arrest Cranmer, he granted it. As soon as he was alone, he summoned the Archbishop, determined to teach the conservatives a lesson.

'Take this ring,' he said, drawing it from his finger. It held Becket's ruby, which he had finally acquired when the saint's shrine had been dismantled. It seemed a fitting token to give to another beleaguered archbishop of Canterbury – although this one deserved it because he was loyal to his King. 'When they come to arrest you, give it to them. They will know, by that token, that you have my support.'

The next day, Gardiner was back, with Wriothesley, demanding to know why Cranmer had confounded them and evaded arrest.

Harry rose. 'Do you think I enjoy seeing my bishops at war with each other, my lord? I am sick to the stomach of the faction fighting in this court, and will not have an invaluable and devout servant like Archbishop Cranmer molested and hounded in this way! I command you to make your peace with him. Get out!'

No sooner had they fled his presence than Sir Thomas Seymour craved an audience.

'Your Grace.' He sketched a hasty bow, clearly a young man in a hurry. 'I have just come from Lambeth Palace and I really must protest against the lack of state the Archbishop maintains! His household is in no way adequate for his rank, and he knows not how to entertain in a style appropriate to his dignity. Might I urge, Sir, that his vast revenues be diverted to the Crown and replaced with a salary? That would be much to your Grace's benefit.'

Harry was astonished that one of Cranmer's own party was attacking him, but it was obvious that Seymour was out to curry his favour, hoping he would reward one who had suggested a new source of revenue. He studied the man, noting the swagger, the luxuriant red beard, the restless energy, and wondered what Katharine saw in this self-seeking rogue. Well, he had a score to settle with him!

'Thank you for drawing this to my attention, Sir Thomas,' he said smoothly. 'I will deal with it.'

Seymour looked crestfallen, as if he had expected more, but he took himself off. Harry then wrote a note to Cranmer and had it delivered at once. Later that morning, he summoned Seymour.

'His Grace of Canterbury asks you to present yourself at Lambeth Palace this afternoon,' he informed him, gleefully noting Seymour's astonishment. 'On your return, you will report to me.'

That evening, Seymour joined Harry in the privy chamber.

'Back so soon?' Harry asked. 'Had my lord Archbishop dined before you came? Did he make you good cheer?'

Seymour had the grace to look ashamed. 'I fear I have abused your Highness with an untruth,' he admitted. 'He feasted me most magnificently.'

'You see, the matter was easily rectified,' Harry said. 'You should have considered well before you made your complaint. I warn you, there shall be no alteration made to the Archbishop's establishment while I live!'

Seymour had the grace to look chastened.

'However,' Harry went on, 'as a reward for your diligence in coming to me with what you feared to be a matter of concern, I am sending you on an embassy to Brussels next month. Then you will report to Sir John Wallop at Guisnes and take up a new military command. We have need of men such as you to aid the Emperor against the King of France.'

If ever he saw a man's face fall, it was now. It was obvious, from the fleeting flash of enmity in Seymour's face, that the scoundrel knew he had been bested – and why!

When Seymour had departed, bowing low to hide his fury, Harry sat there humming, pleased with the success of his ruse. He felt sorry for Cranmer. Everyone seemed to have it in for him, one way or another. Well, Harry would do something to cheer him, for the man was sorely in need of it. He picked up his quill and wrote a private letter to the Archbishop, sanctioning the return of Mistress Cranmer, whom he believed had gone back to Germany.

Thwarted of bigger fish, the conservatives now struck at the Privy Chamber. Gardiner informed Harry that the Council had drawn up indictments against eleven of his servants, among them several trusted gentlemen, the Master of the Revels, Master Penny and even the royal cook. Harry was not impressed or pleased; he ordered the arrest of the man who had drafted the indictments and had him tried and convicted of perjury, then thrown into the Fleet prison.

Gardiner and his friends remained undaunted, determined to rid the court of radicals and heretics; their aim, Harry knew, was to eradicate all opposition to their party and suppress religious dissent. They would not find it easy, for the reformists were dominant and among them were several rising new men, including Sir William Paget who had one foot in every pageant. Harry had come to like him immensely and relied on him to screen most of his correspondence. What matter if the man enriched himself in the process and even (it was bruited) stooped to a little blackmail on occasion? He was honest at heart, and hard-working.

Harry had also come to rely on Sir Anthony Denny, another Humanist and lover of learning, and a man of great personal charm. His painstaking devotion to his duties endeared him to Harry, who used him as a buffer against a clamorous world and the petitioners who never ceased to make demands on him. Gardiner and his cronies loathed Denny, a radical who had the courage to speak out against this latest persecution of Protestants, but Harry would not have a word said to his detriment.

Harry himself, feeling his age and thinking increasingly on the prospect of divine judgement, was inclining more and more towards traditional religion; his heart was with the conservatives. He had ordered the publication of a book written under his direction, some of it in his own hand. Its true title was *The Necessary Doctrine and Erudition of Any Christian Man*, but people were soon calling it 'The King's Book'. It was the most orthodox and reactionary statement Harry had ever made on the creed of the English Church, and the radicals were vociferous in their protests.

'Some of the reformers say your book is not worth a fart,' Will remarked, lounging at Harry's feet before the hearth.

'I care not for their opinions!' Harry growled, prodding him with his slippered toe. 'They are but few men. Paget tells me that eleven twelfths of my subjects are faithful Christians.'

'That's not enough for our friend Gardiner!'

It was true. Gardiner was incessantly urging Harry to clamp down on wholesale reading of the Bible. But it was too late to turn back the clock. Being able to read the Scriptures in English had encouraged his subjects to think for themselves, and Gardiner feared that many had gone dangerously beyond the unquestioning obedience expected of devout Catholics.

Harry compromised, bidding Parliament condemn false and untrue translations and restrict the reading of the Scriptures to men of the upper and middle ranks of society, where at least one might hope to find a better-educated, more thoughtful level of understanding. Women, he decided, were best left to learn from their husbands at home, as St Paul had enjoined.

Katharine was now a frequent visitor at court and Harry was spending as much time with her as he could. He found their debates stimulating, especially those about religion, and was impressed anew by her erudition and sharp wits. Above all, he loved her company, and he had come to realise that she truly was the woman he had been waiting for.

He invited her to supper, just the two of them, alone. They talked of many things, but then he laid down his napkin.

'My Lady Latimer,' he said, 'you must be aware that I think very highly of you. You are a comely lady with many virtues and rare gifts of nature – all the things in which I most delight. You are a warm and stimulating companion. You exude goodwill.'

Katharine blushed. 'Your Grace, you flatter me.'

'I was never a flatterer,' he protested. 'I'm a plain man. I say what I think. And I think you are a woman I can respect, and that you would be a perfect queen of England.' He reached across and took her hand. 'Lady Latimer, I am asking you to marry me.'

She seemed momentarily tongue-tied.

'Oh, Sir, I am utterly amazed. I mean, I am not worthy,' she gushed at length. 'Your Grace does me too much honour.'

He squeezed her hand. 'You have every requisite quality, and we two get on well together, do we not? I have had many disappointments in my marriages, and some ill-conditioned wives, but I know we would accord well.'

'In truth, I do not know how to answer your Majesty. I am not long widowed. I was not looking to remarry so soon, if at all. And, given your Grace's health, I thought you just appreciated some feminine companionship.'

'By God, my lady, I'm not looking for a nurse, but a queen to grace my court and a wife to give me more sons! I want a mature and intelligent woman with whom I can enjoy good conversation, someone I can trust. And I know I can trust you. I'm lonely. I want a wife in my bed and at my board. And there is about you a certain glow. You have feelings for me, I think.'

He had poured his heart out, thinking it would melt hers. But she was looking doubtful. 'I do,' she said. 'I like your Grace very much, not just as my sovereign, whom I am bound to love, but as a friend. You have been so good to me and mine.'

'I hope you see me as more than just the fount of patronage?' he teased her.

'Of course! I would not have you think me mercenary, only grateful.'

'You have doubts? I am offering you the world.'

'Sir, I am indeed sensible of that,' she faltered. 'You have taken me by surprise . . .'

'I love you, my lady,' he said. He creaked to his feet, stooped down and kissed her gently on the lips. 'I would kneel to you if I could, my lady. It is my hope that you will make me a happy man.'

'Your Majesty's favour means everything to me,' she said. 'If you would grant me a little time to think and pray on the matter?'

He sat down, disappointed. 'Of course,' he said. 'But pray do not keep me waiting too long.'

He could barely contain himself. It was as if he was in the thick of the hunt and the prey was eluding him, and he was immersed in that moment when its capture became the most desirable thing in the world. Suddenly, his whole desire was to marry Katharine. He loved her; he prized her. She must be his!

She came to his lodging on an early-summer evening, wearing an elegant green velvet gown he had given her with a French hood of white satin. He rose as fast as his bandaged leg would allow him and held out his hands. 'No, Lady Latimer, there is no need to curtsey. Be seated.' He indicated the chair on the other side of the hearth, on which a great vase of roses had been placed.

'What beautiful flowers!' she said. 'I trust your Majesty is well?'

'Aye, and I hope to be even better soon. My lady, do you have something to tell me?' He held his breath.

She smiled at him. 'Yes, your Majesty. I am deeply honoured to accept your gracious proposal.'

He could have wept for joy. 'You have made me the happiest man in the world,' he said, his voice breaking.

Chapter 36

1543

They were married in July in the Queen's closet at Hampton Court, with Gardiner officiating and the whole world, it seemed, applauding. Among the twenty guests were Harry's daughters, Hertford and Marget Douglas, now restored to favour and bearing the bride's train. After the ceremony, the new Queen Katharine embraced Mary and hugged an excited Elizabeth, now nearly ten and already displaying the coquettish manners of her mother.

And so Harry settled contentedly into wedded bliss.

Katharine was quieter than any of the younger wives he had had, and they got on pleasantly. She had no caprices and made few demands on him. In bed and at board, she was loving and kind, and warmly sympathetic towards him when his bad leg incapacitated him. To his relief, he was able to play the husband creditably, and lead a fairly active life; and if he did not feel as rejuvenated as he had when he married Katheryn, he knew himself a lucky man, especially when Kate told him that their marriage was the greatest joy and comfort that could have come to her. Never, he thought, had he had a wife more agreeable to his heart.

He was proud to see her exerting her benevolent influence over the court and welcoming men of learning to her chamber. Her rare goodness made every day like a Sunday, which was virtually unheard of in a royal palace, and she was sound in her religious observances. She was forever scribbling down her thoughts, and when he read her private writings, he saw she was graced with a personal piety that had more in common with the teachings of Erasmus than those of Luther.

Kate soon gathered around her a circle of ladies who shared her love for learning and impassioned debate. One was Suffolk's young firebrand of a wife, Katherine Willoughby, an ardent reformist who kept a spaniel she had mischievously named Gardiner. Harry had to smile when he heard her calling him sharply to heel.

It did not worry him that Katharine's chamber might be a haven for radicals and reformist preachers, since she liked to encourage self-improvement and pious devotion. Whenever he joined her, he found everyone absorbed in virtuous study, reading, writing and applying themselves to extending their knowledge. It set a good example, even if it did arouse the undue resentment and suspicions of the conservatives.

But Katharine also enjoyed dancing and shared Harry's passion for music. One of his great pleasures was sitting in her chamber, listening to her Italian musicians and holding her hand. Simple pleasures. They were what a good woman brought to her lord.

There was plague in London that summer, and Harry issued proclamations forbidding the citizens to approach the court and courtiers to enter the City. Soon after his wedding, he took Katharine and Mary on a long hunting progress to the south and west of England. But the pestilence was still lively in the autumn when they returned. To Harry's great sorrow, Holbein was one of those who had succumbed. Visiting the master's workshop at Whitehall, he gazed on the last work he had commissioned – a vast painting of himself presenting a charter to the Barber Surgeons Company of London, which would now never be finished – and wept. How easily the tears came these days.

He began to seek out new artistic talent, though no one could replace the genius of Holbein. The best was a gifted native of Antwerp called Hans Eworth, whom he set to finishing off portraits Holbein had left incomplete. Kate liked Eworth and commissioned from him miniatures of herself and Harry. She also had a full-length picture of herself painted by another follower of Holbein, Master John.

Then Harry lured to England, with the inducement of a high

salary, a Dutchman, Guillim Scrots. Influenced by the art of France and Italy, Scrots was famed for painting costume in intricate detail. It was he who produced a most extraordinary portrait of the six-year-old Prince Edward.

Harry could not hide his dismay when he first saw it. It was uncommonly distorted.

'Your Grace does not like it?' Scots ventured, frowning.

'The Prince looks fat,' Harry complained. 'Elongated.' And then it came to him. 'It's an anamorphosis, of course!' He moved to the side and squinted at it, seeing the picture come into perspective. 'And a good one too! Holbein painted a skull in this fashion in his portrait of the French ambassadors. Well done, Scrots! I shall have it hung in Whitehall Palace. My courtiers will love it!'

Harry could not have wished for a better stepmother for his children. Kate was kind and supportive to them all, and they were quickly coming to love her. She had become close friends with Mary, who was only four years her junior.

'I mean to win the affection of your other children,' she had told Harry before they wed. Since then, she had invited all three to come to court whenever he permitted, and wrote regularly to them when they were absent, encouraging Edward to reply in Latin, at which he was making good progress.

'And Elizabeth has written to me in Italian!' she informed Harry, delighted. 'I must send her a gift. She ate something that disagreed with her and needs something to cheer her. And I will send Edward some money for his little pleasures. Oh, and Harry, you must see the suits of crimson velvet and white satin I've ordered for him!'

He beamed at her and kissed her hand.

He loved all his children, but Edward, the precious, long-awaited son, was naturally his favourite. The boy was growing up fast – he would soon be breeched – but Harry worried that he was small for his age. He had one shoulder higher than the other, and was short-sighted, but he was an attractive child with blond hair, grey eyes, an elfin face and a resolute, direct gaze, like his father's. On his recent

552

visits, Harry had been proud to see that, already, the boy was copying his mannerisms and stance, standing proudly with his feet firmly apart, hand on hip or dagger.

'Your Grace, we constantly urge the Prince to satisfy your Grace's good expectations,' Lady Bryan had assured Harry, more than once. Maybe that was why Edward was plainly in awe of him. On one occasion, when Harry and Kate had been visiting the boy at Hertford Castle, Harry had given him some jewels from the suppressed monasteries. Edward's face had lit up.

'Most noble Father, I thank you for these wondrous gifts, which betoken your great love for me. If you did not love me, you would not give them to me.'

'Of course I love you – you are my son as well as my heir,' Harry replied, embracing him. Yet he was aware that, to the child, he must seem a distant and awe-inspiring figure.

In October, when his birthday came, Edward was breeched and removed from the care of women. He did not seem moved at the departure of Lady Bryan and his nurses, and was sanguine about being given into the charge of the tutor Harry had chosen for him, who was supported by a staff of male officers.

'My son must have an education that befits him for kingship,' Harry had explained to each candidate he interviewed. 'It must be a classical education suitable for a modern ruler.'

The tutors he had summoned were all renowned Humanists, followers of Erasmus, Vives and More. The memory of More brought a pang to his heart; if More had not defied him, he would be here now, advising on Edward's curriculum.

The man he chose as the Prince's tutor was Dr Richard Cox, who had been Edward's almoner and had also worked with Henry on 'The King's Book'.

'Your Grace, I believe that learning should be enjoyable, and that a good teacher need resort only infrequently to the rod,' Cox said, placing a wad of paper on Harry's desk. They were in his closet, wrapped in furs against the cold winds rattling the casements.

'The carrot rather than the stick.' Harry nodded, remembering how old Skelinton had beaten him when he had erred. And yet he had reason to be grateful to the crusty old tutor, who had instilled in him a love of learning that had remained with him all his life. 'So, this is the curriculum you have drawn up?'

'Yes, Sir. As you instructed, there is a strong focus on languages, including Latin and Greek. His Highness will be taught Scripture, classics, philosophy, astronomy and all the liberal sciences.'

'He is highly intelligent and loves books,' Harry said proudly. 'I take it there will be time set aside for recreation and the manly sports.'

'Naturally,' Cox smiled. 'His studies will be supplemented by lessons in horsemanship, archery, fencing, tennis, music and dancing.'

'He will enjoy all of those,' Harry assured him. Inwardly, however, he was worried that, with his slight build, Edward would never be another sportsman like himself. But he was young; he would grow.

'I do not want him to learn in isolation,' he said. 'I intend to establish a small school for him, and I have chosen fourteen noble boys to share his education.'

He made sure he was present on the day the school opened. When he walked into the schoolroom at Ashridge, the boys all scrambled to their feet and Dr Cox rose behind his high desk on the dais. Edward, whose place was at the front, looked so much older now that he was out of his long skirts and had had his fair hair cropped close to his head – a real boy now! Next to him was Suffolk's son, Henry Brandon, and on the other side Surrey's heir, Lord Thomas Howard; behind stood Lord Lisle's son, Robert Dudley, and others, all sprigs of the nobility destined for a glorious future.

'Be good boys,' Harry bade them. 'Heed your tutor, for he is the best. Learn from him and be obedient, as I, your King, require you to do.' Fifteen little heads bowed as he limped to the door and left Dr Cox to it.

At Kate's request, Harry invited all three of his children to spend Christmas at court. The festivities began on 23 December, when her brother William was created earl of Essex in a glittering ceremony – rare these days – in the presence chamber at Hampton Court. The court then moved to Greenwich for Yuletide.

It did Harry's heart good to see Kate making much of his children, and to see them shake off their habitual dutiful reserve to romp with the revellers, as the Lord of Misrule presided over the merry disports. Harry himself joined in the games of hide-and-seek, shovelboard and prisoners' base, although he was grateful to sit down afterwards and enjoy a game of cards.

At New Year, Denny presented him with a clock salt he had commissioned from Holbein and Nicolaus Kratzer in the Italian style. Fascinated by anything mechanical, Harry soon found out that cunningly concealed inside it were an hourglass, two sundials and a compass. He was delighted and spent much of the day tinkering with it.

Kate was touched when Elizabeth presented her with her own very long translation of the Queen of Navarre's devotional poem, 'The Mirror, or Glass, of the Sinful Soul', for which she had embroidered a beautiful blue binding with a knotwork pattern in silver thread, encircling Kate's initials.

'Your Grace might have to rub out, polish and mend the words, which I know in many places to be crudely rendered,' Elizabeth warned, but Kate shook her head.

'Bess, I cannot tell you how much I appreciate the hours of work you have dedicated to the making of this wondrous gift. I shall treasure it always for that alone.'

Elizabeth's face flushed with pleasure.

1544

Harry's friendship with the Emperor had led inexorably to deteriorating relations with France. The threat of war had become a reality, and he had been building a string of defensive castles along the south coast in anticipation of a French invasion.

'But why wait for them to strike?' he asked his Council. 'Would it not be better by far if I invaded France myself?'

The lords were enthusiastic. Like their forefathers over many generations, they relished the chance of vanquishing England's traditional enemy – unlike their predecessors on the Council, who had once tried to curb Harry's ambitions. Brought up to lead men in battle, they were keen to prove themselves and win glory. Eagerly, they pressed Harry to declare war.

It was what he had wanted to hear. Even now, he cherished dreams of claiming his rightful inheritance, the fair kingdom of France, and being crowned at Rheims.

Before he could leave England, however, he must put his house in order and settle the succession. If he was killed in battle, his kingdom would be left in the hands of a child, and children's lives were precarious. Kate had been urging him to restore Mary and Elizabeth to the succession, arguing that it was only right that his own flesh and blood should inherit the throne if, God forbid, Edward did not survive. She did not, to his relief, press him to have his daughters declared legitimate, for that would have opened up a whole Pandora's box of controversies.

In February, at his behest, Parliament passed a new Act, settling the succession firstly on Prince Edward and his heirs, secondly on any children Harry might have with Kate, thirdly on the Lady Mary and her heirs, and lastly on the Lady Elizabeth and her heirs. Harry had insisted that the heirs of his elder sister, Margaret, who had died three years earlier, be passed over. He had no intention of uniting England and Scotland under Scottish rule, but was still aggressively pursuing his intention of marrying Edward to the little Queen of Scots. Not that the Scots were any happier at the prospect, but he was determined to overrule their objections, and by force, if need be.

But just as preparations for war were going ahead, his leg swelled up and laid him feverishly low once more. Kate, bless her, had her bed moved into a closet leading off his bedchamber, so that she could be near him and cheer him when he needed company. She ordered suppositories, liquorice pastilles, cinnamon comfits and plasters from his apothecaries for his ease and bade him rest his leg on her lap when he was able to sit in a chair.

'You're a good woman, Kate,' he told her. 'I thank God for you every day.'

'It is I who should be thankful,' she told him, squeezing his hand. 'He could not have sent me a more loving husband.'

When Harry eventually emerged from his privy lodgings in March, he was so weak on his legs that he could hardly stand.

'Your Grace,' Dr Chamber said severely, 'it is my belief that your great obesity is putting your life at risk. It should be urgently remedied!'

'And how shall I do that?' Harry snapped. 'I cannot exercise with this bad leg. I just sit down all day and drag myself around, so how can I get myself fit again?'

'Your Grace could try avoiding rich food and lavish dinners. And begin with just a little exercise each day. As you lose weight, you will be able to increase it.'

Harry glowered at him, even though he knew the doctor spoke truth. 'Go and leave me in peace. I will not brook being lectured!'

He tried to cut down the amount he was eating, but it was hard when the pleasures of the table beckoned. He tried to get up and walk about more, but he was still not fully recovered and his leg was agony. Yet he persevered. He must get fit in order to lead his army to France. The invasion was only weeks away. He had to be there in the saddle, in command, a warrior king like his martial ancestors, Edward III and Henry V.

His illness, and the pain, made him bad-tempered and prone to lashing out at anyone who irritated him. And no one was irritating him more at this moment than the Scots! Not even the thought of his enemy, King Francis, could rouse in him as much anger as he felt towards those northern savages who were simply refusing to see that the union of England and Scotland would benefit everyone.

He had had enough. It was time to make them see sense. He placed Hertford and John Dudley, Viscount Lisle, another radical, in command of his forces and sent them marching north to force the

Scots to agree to the proposed marriage alliance. On his orders, they sacked Edinburgh and ruthlessly laid waste the Scottish lowlands.

'Hah! The Scots do not like this rough wooing!' Harry chortled, reading the latest reports. 'I'll wager they'll come around soon enough.'

'Then the Prince can marry their little dumpling of a queen!' Will cackled.

'And Scotland will come under my rule!' Harry said, rubbing his hands.

When Audley died in early spring, Harry made Pig Wriothesley Lord Chancellor, and himself invested him with the Great Seal of England in the privy chamber. He had chosen Wriothesley because he was vigorously opposed to heresy, and as a counterbalance to the influence of the powerful reformist party. The conservatives needed such a champion.

After languishing in prison for a year, John Marbeck and the Windsor heretics were condemned to burn, but Harry valued Marbeck's playing so highly that he pardoned him, which did not go down well with Gardiner, and he had to consign the other wretches to the flames to placate the Bishop.

Then the Council discovered that Gardiner had shielded his Papist nephew Jermyn from prosecution. The nephew was sent to the block, and Gardiner's dominance was fatally undermined. Suffolk had almost persuaded Harry to proceed against him as a traitor, but the Bishop's friends in the Privy Chamber sent him a warning of what was about to happen.

Gardiner came running to Harry, putting him in mind of Lady Suffolk's dog coming to heel.

'Your Grace,' he cried, falling to his knees, 'I have come to confess my great fault in covering up the crimes of my wicked, unworthy nephew. I fear I was blinded and led astray by the ties of kinship. I acknowledge myself guilty of misprision of treason and beg for your mercy and forgiveness.'

Harry stroked his beard, his eyes on the man abasing himself before him, and considered what to do. It was fortunate for Gardiner that he had arrived just after a letter from Hertford, who was clearly not making as much progress in Scotland as Harry had expected. He was angry with Hertford and ready to have his revenge by favouring his enemy.

'Get up, my lord Bishop. You have behaved in a foolish, misguided way, but the real traitor has been punished and your family has suffered enough. Consider yourself pardoned.'

He felt deep satisfaction to see Gardiner babbling his thanks and kissing his hand fervently. It pleased him to play off one faction against the other and show them who really wielded power in England. But, of course, he had to balance his gesture by showing favour to the reformers. He summoned Cranmer.

'My lord of Canterbury, I have conceived the idea of an English Litany, a book of common prayer for use in our churches, and I want you to write it. I know of no man who has a better turn of phrase.'

Cranmer blushed at the compliment. 'This is an inspired idea, Sir. I will be honoured to write such a book.'

'You will be in good company.' Harry smiled, taking a small volume bound in gilded leather from his bosom. 'The Queen has published a book, *Psalm Prayers*, which she has selected and para-phrased herself.'

'The Queen has published a book?' Cranmer was surprised.

'I believe that no woman has ever done so before in England,' Harry told him. 'You should read it. The prayers are most erudite, and there is one for my success in France.'

'It was a happy day for England when your Grace married that blessed lady,' Cranmer smiled. 'She is a true friend of the Gospel.'

'I'm having her prayer read out in St Paul's at the service of intercession before we sail for Boulogne,' Harry informed him.

'I myself have your Grace's enterprise continually in my prayers,' Cranmer assured him. 'God will surely aid you.'

Harry was still determined to lead the invasion himself. As the time for his departure drew nearer, he was infused with a new zest for life.

There were a few details that needed to be attended to before he left, however. At the end of June, he and Kate were present at the wedding of Marget Douglas to Matthew Stewart, Earl of Lennox, in the Chapel Royal at St James' Palace. Lennox was one of the few Scots peers who supported Harry's plan to unite the two kingdoms under English rule, which was why Harry had bound him to himself in this alliance. After the wedding, he was to return to Scotland to plot on Harry's behalf. It would be a dangerous mission, because the government in Edinburgh might brand him a traitor, but he was confident he could raise support for the alliance among the nobility.

Marget made a lovely, radiant bride. It was an arranged marriage, but for the young couple it had been love at first sight. Harry was pleased for them and hugged his niece warmly after the ceremony.

'A safe harbour at last!' he murmured in her ear. 'I never thought to see this day, after all your naughty adventures.'

'Neither did I, Uncle!' she retorted with feeling, smiling impishly at him.

Early in July, Harry appointed Kate Regent of England during his absence in France. Hertford had been relieved of his command and summoned south. He was to remain in England and serve in a subordinate role as Lieutenant of the Realm.

Harry also made new arrangements for the education of his son, appointing a respected Cambridge scholar, Dr John Cheke, to assist Dr Cox.

'Denny recommended him to me,' he told Kate. 'He is perfect for the role. He was the first ever Regius Professor of Greek at Cambridge and Butts says he has one of the most outstanding minds of our time.'

He was gratified to learn that Edward had quickly taken to Dr Cheke, and soon he arranged for him to take over from Dr Cox as senior tutor.

Elizabeth was proving as bright and thirsty for learning as her brother; she was an honour to her sex. She was proficient on the lute and virginals and had proved so precociously able in languages and the classics that Harry, at Kate's behest, appointed a brilliant young man called William Grindal as her tutor, while Roger Ascham, another fine Cambridge scholar, took it upon himself to act as her academic mentor. Under their influence, she thrived. Privately, Harry wondered if she was the most intelligent of his children. No, she could not be; he was fooling himself. She was a girl, and girls could never be as clever as men. They had not the wits for it. Yet when he looked into those brilliant dark eyes, he wondered.

It pleased him to see Kate encouraging the children in their studies. It was she who had persuaded Mary to translate Erasmus' *Paraphrases of the Gospel of St John* into English. Mary had made a good start, but she was plagued by intermittent ill health – hysterical women's ailments, as far as Harry could make out – and so Kate had called in Nicholas Udall, the former headmaster of Eton College, to help her finish the project, and she had met the costs of publication. Harry had not been happy about Udall working with his daughter. Three years ago, the man had been forced to resign his post, having been convicted of buggery with some of his pupils. He had been condemned to death, but he had friends at court, among them Wriothesley, who had persuaded Harry to commute the sentence to imprisonment. Udall had spent a year in the Marshalsea before being released.

'He is now a reformed man,' Kate assured Harry, 'and he should be given a fresh chance in life, for there is no doubting the excellence of his scholarship.'

Mary, of course, had no idea why he had been imprisoned, and Harry was not about to embarrass or upset her by explaining.

In the middle of July, Harry kissed Kate farewell and sailed for Calais, having made detailed plans for his campaign and sent ahead maps and instructions for his captains; his broad knowledge of fortifications, warfare and military strategy had served him well.

With his armour burnished to perfection, he had ridden at the head of his forces towards Dover, loudly cheered by the crowds who had come running to see him, for the war was popular in England, with all ranks of society. While Harry was commander-in-chief, the redoubtable Norfolk, now seventy-one and pathetically grateful to be of use again, was to serve as lieutenant general of the army in France, and Suffolk, now sixty, was given command of the forces that were to lay siege to Boulogne, their first objective. Taking the town would give Harry a convenient bridgehead into France.

His councillors and his doctors were worried that his bad leg and unwieldy bulk would prove drawbacks, yet he felt merrier and in better health than he had been these seven years, reinvigorated at the prospect of taking the field again. Full of energy, he rode from Calais into French territory at the head of his army on a great courser, a heavy musket laid across his saddle; behind rode an officer carrying the royal helm and massive lance. Many marvelled that any man could lift a weapon of such huge dimensions.

At Boulogne, Harry had his army lay siege to the town, and throughout those long, tense and exhilarating days, he remained active from dawn until dusk. From England, Kate wrote to say how she rejoiced in the news of his good health. Nevertheless, as the siege dragged on, his leg became so painful that his armour had to be cut away to relieve the pressure.

He wrote to Kate as often as his limited leisure permitted, and she kept him regularly informed as to what was happening at home. She was staying at Hampton Court with his children, and assured him they were all, thanks be to God, in good health. Later, he was alarmed to read that there was plague in London, but Kate had taken the children away on progress, and had decreed that no one who had been in contact with the pest was to venture anywhere near anyone from the court, on pain of her indignation, unless they wished to be punished at her pleasure. But the sickness soon abated, and she was able to return to Greenwich in August. That was one less worry for Harry.

Boulogne fell on 14 September, and he entered the battered town in triumph, glorying in the moment. But the campaigning season was over, and there could be no more advances made this year. Reluctantly, he returned to England, to be greeted by joyful celebrations and the loving arms of his wife. Revelling in the adulation and the glory, he was confident that this was just the beginning and that he would go on to win France itself. It was happening at last!

1545

To mark the passing of the Act of Succession, Harry had commissioned a great painting of himself and his heirs. On a bright March day he stood admiring it as it hung in his magnificent presence chamber at Whitehall, where he had sat for it. It was truly masterful, and he himself was at its centre, enthroned. The artist had rendered skilfully the richly decorated ceiling, the wall panelling, the pillars embellished with antique grotesque work and the embroidered cloth of estate. But it was the figures that drew the eye. Prince Edward stood at Harry's knee, while to the right, on a lesser chair of estate, was Jane, who had given him his heir. It was fitting that it was she who appeared in the picture, rather than Kate, and Kate, sweet soul that she was, had made no objection. To either side, beyond the pillars representing legitimacy, stood Mary and Elizabeth.

Harry smiled to himself, well pleased, and stumped off to his bedchamber to read some dispatches. Sitting by the fireside, he found himself feeling feverish, and before long he was burning up so alarmingly that he had to summon his physicians. They urged him to go to bed and anxiously examined his leg, which was beginning to throb. Helplessly, he resigned himself to another bout of agony.

He could not be seen to be ill or losing his grasp, not with the vultures on the Council ready to tear each other apart, given the chance. He remained behind closed doors and commanded his councillors and servants not to make public the true state of his health.

'There's a lot of speculation,' Will reported, serious for once. 'Friend Gardiner fears you will not live until my lord Prince comes to man's estate.'

For once, Harry did not fly into a fury over his death being discussed, treason though it was even to imagine it. He shared

Gardiner's fears. He had inadvertently caught a reflection of himself in a window by candlelight and been horrified to see an old man with a bloated face in a skullcap and bonnet. Time had lain its hand on him. The grave beckoned.

But he must live until Edward was of age. He could not leave his son, in his tender years, to the mercy of the wolves who bayed for each other's blood.

He made an effort. He had them dress him and emerged, limping badly, into the court. Chapuys had been waiting for an audience, so Harry saw him that morning, and was disconcerted to see his old sparring partner carried in in a chair because of a gouty leg. Yet Chapuys was regarding *him* with concern.

'I am sad to see your Majesty so broken down,' he commiserated. 'I too have been slightly unwell. It is depressing at our age.'

Harry thought Chapuys looked as broken down as he was.

'I have had a fever,' he admitted. 'By St George, I felt ten times better in France than I have since my return.' Suddenly, his head was swimming. 'To be plain, I am not feeling well enough to continue with this audience, Eustache. I crave your indulgence – and your discretion.'

Chapuys bowed his head. 'You can rely on me, Sir.' Harry nodded as he summoned the ambassador's bearers back and watched him being carried out.

He was in no doubt that the truth about his health would be all over Christendom in half an hour.

He dragged himself back to his chamber, and there he stayed for days, locked in melancholy, unresponsive even to Will's witty jests. He dressed only to attend Mass, and occasionally roused himself to play cards with Hertford or Lisle. All the time, he was trying to come to terms with the dismal fact that he was doomed to be an invalid for the rest of his life – a bitter prospect for a king who had once been such an active and renowned sportsman.

'Of all losses,' he lamented to Will, 'time is the most irrecuperable, for it can never be redeemed by money or prayers.' He was feeling despondent and could not rise above it. Even reading was difficult, for his eyes kept blurring, and Kate urged that he order himself some new gazings from Germany. The frames were made of gold or silver and clipped onto the nose; the lenses, cut from rock crystal, came from specialists in Venice and were most effective. Yet being obliged to use them only darkened his mood. Maddened by inactivity and pain, he was more irascible than usual, aware that he was often of one mind in the morning and of quite another after dinner. Nothing pleased him, and his attendants approached him warily, obviously terrified of offending him or irritating him further.

In the end, of course, his iron will asserted itself. He could not sit idle for ever; it was not in his nature. He forced himself to carry on, heaving himself onto his horse and riding out to the hunt, or with his hawk on his wrist, trying to cover as many miles as he used to do before this damn leg laid him low. He played bowls as often as he was able and moved from house to house with restless frequency. The only people he felt he could confide in were Will, Dr Butts and Cranmer. Not Kate, for he wished to spare her worry. She was precious to him and must be protected.

Chapter 37

1545

One evening in spring, Kate joined Harry in his library. He left Gardiner and his clerks to their scribbling at the desks in the corner, and kissed her hand in welcome.

'I trust I find your Grace better today,' she enquired.

'Worse, if anything, Madam,' he said peevishly. 'I have received reports of new heresies and that doesn't help.' He saw Gardiner glance up briefly, then caught Kate looking coldly upon him. She did not like Gardiner.

'You should not be bothered with such things when you are unwell,' she said. 'And, if others took a more tolerant view of reform, there would be no need for them.' Her words were clearly meant for Gardiner's ears.

'And what do you mean by a more tolerant view, Madam?' Harry asked.

'Ease the restrictions on reading the Bible. Let each man – and woman – follow their conscience . . . Be more tolerant!'

'By God, Madam, we'd have religious anarchy – every man with his own opinion, and few qualified even to have one. No, it won't do. Now, Kate, forget about that. I wanted to show you this.' He opened a large book of architectural drawings. 'I fancy building a palace in the classical style.'

She took the book. 'These are from Italy?'

'That is Bramante's Tempietto in Rome. And that is the Palazzo Farnese. What a wonder it would be to have buildings like that in England.'

'We don't want new-fangled foreign buildings in England!' piped up Somers, who had been lurking behind Harry's chair. 'What's wrong with good, honest oak and brick?'

Harry cuffed him. 'Go away!' he ordered, and Somers slunk off into a corner, where he picked up a book and pretended to read it, upside down.

Smothering giggles, Kate turned to Harry. 'Will you build anew or alter an existing palace?' But he was testy with her, angry at her presuming to lecture him on his religious policies.

'I am tired,' he said. 'Farewell, sweetheart. I would rest now.' He closed his eyes, pointedly. When he opened them, she was gone.

But Gardiner was standing there, all bristling concern.

'Your Grace, I could not help overhearing what the Queen said.'

Harry scowled. 'A good hearing it is when women become such clerks, and much to my comfort in my old age to be taught by my wife!'

Gardiner was all sympathy. 'I marvel that the Queen should so far forget herself as to argue with your Majesty or dispute your learned judgement in matters of religion, which excels that not only of the princes of our age, but also of doctors of divinity. It is an unseemly thing for any of your Majesty's subjects to reason and argue with you so malapertly, and grievous to me to hear it.'

Harry nodded, feeling increasingly ill done by.

Gardiner was in full flight. 'It is dangerous and perilous for a prince to suffer such insolent words at a subject's hands. If they are bold to contradict their sovereign with words, they might well try to thwart him in deeds. And, regrettably, your Grace, I have reason to believe that the religion the Queen so stiffly maintains does not only wish to overthrow the government of princes, but also teaches that all things ought to be in common.'

'What religion?' Harry barked, astounded. 'The Queen is as devout as I am!'

'Alas, if I am not mistaken, she has embraced the Protestant heresy. I have long suspected it, and there are indications and ominous signs that I am right.'

'I do not believe it,' Harry declared, but already he was casting back in his mind for any hint or clue that would support Gardiner's allegation. And then he remembered something Kate had written in one of the letters she had sent when he was in Boulogne. It had struck him as odd at the time, but he had dismissed it as nothing, believing her sound in her beliefs. She had committed him to God, in the hope that he would long prosper on earth and enjoy the kingdom of the elect in Heaven.

The elect. That was the word that had troubled him. It called to mind the heresies of the Swiss reformer John Calvin, who believed in predestination, and that God had chosen His elect before He created the world, and that they were the only souls who would attain Heaven. It was an extreme Protestant view.

His heart contracted. Surely Kate, his beloved Kate, could not be a heretic? No, no, he could not deal with another disgraced wife – or bear the thought of her losing her hopes of Heaven. Nor could he contemplate her suffering the punishment for heresy. Having two wives beheaded had been bad enough, but burning . . .

He had to know the truth.

'Such pernicious beliefs,' Gardiner was saying, 'are so odious, and for princes so perilous, that I make bold to say that the greatest subject in this land, speaking those words that she did speak, and defending those arguments, would deserve death.'

'My lord Bishop, we must determine the truth of this matter,' Harry said, clutching Gardiner's sleeve. 'I command you to draw up a warrant to have the Queen arrested and questioned.'

Gardiner looked just like a cat that had a mouse cornered, and Harry was certain he was out to destroy Kate. It was time he and his fellow zealots were taught a lesson, as surely his accusations would be proved nonsense. And, in the process, his own mind would be put at rest. And Kate would be warned of the peril in which she stood.

A day or so later, with no word from Gardiner (whom he assumed was gathering his proofs, whatever they might be), Harry summoned Kate to his chamber, intending to test her himself.

'I was in no fit state to listen to you before, sweetheart, so now, I pray you, speak your mind on religion,' he invited. They were quite alone. Even Will was absent.

She launched straight in. 'You have worked marvels, Harry, but there are those who feel you would be a Papist without the Pope. It is as if you have put a stay on reform, and now there is this persecution. People should come to Christ through love, not fear.'

'But if they fall into heresy, they will not come to Him at all,' he said gently.

'Yet where is the line between reform and heresy?' she asked. 'How are we to know who is right?'

'Through reading the Scriptures, prayer and a good grounding in theology,' he said.

'But both Catholics and Protestants could say that.'

'Kate, we are talking about salvation. Tell me, do you believe that it is predestined?'

'No,' she said, emphatically enough. 'I believe we can achieve it through our faith in Christ.'

'Is that all?' He watched her closely. 'Do we not need to do good works in this world to attain salvation?'

'Of course we should.'

He nodded, not wholly satisfied, but fully resolved, this time, to spare the woman he loved, even if she was guilty.

That evening, having sat brooding for hours, he sent for Dr Wendy, who had been one of his physicians for the past five years, and had a bedside manner that invited confidences.

'I need to unburden myself to you,' he confided. 'I am worried that the Queen is lapsing into heresy. She has become a doctress, always dictating to me what I should do, and I can no longer put up with it, if only for her own good, for I know that her enemies are working against her. Wendy, I charge you, on peril of your life, not to utter this to any creature living, but I will not give way to their demands. Her Grace is to be arrested, but my intention is only to have her questioned, for I expect her to clear herself. If she does not, I will intervene and stop the examination, for I intend her no harm.

I wish only to bring home to her the danger she is risking.'

Wendy was thoughtful. 'Could your Grace not just have warned off her enemies?'

'I need to be sure of my Queen. And when I am, those who are trying to destroy her shall feel my displeasure.'

Harry was dozing in his chair when he was suddenly roused by a dreadful shrieking somewhere outside his open window. On and on the wailing went. Someone – a woman – was in terrible distress. Rubbing his eyes, he struggled to his feet, hobbled to the open casement and leaned out, then realised that it was coming from Kate's apartments. By God, it was Kate herself, he was sure of it.

Had Gardiner sent guards to arrest her? No, he would have warned Harry first. So what was wrong with her? Had she had some terrible accident?

He could barely stand, let alone walk, as his leg was bad today, so he sent Dr Chamber and Dr Butts to discover what was amiss.

Presently all went quiet, and Harry wondered what was happening. Was Kate all right now? Then the screaming began again. You would have thought she was being murdered.

He could bear it no longer. Summoning two of his Gentlemen Pensioners, he had them support him as he made his way to her chamber.

'Kate! Kate!' he gasped, out of breath. 'Help me to that chair.' The two men heaved his bulk into it.

Kneeling on the carpet, with Dr Wendy crouched beside her and the other doctors looking on helplessly, Kate stared at him through her tears, her face ravaged, her hood askew.

'Kate, what ails you?' he asked. 'I could hear you in my lodgings. I was worried for you.'

'Oh, Sir.' She drew herself up and clasped his hands as if they were a lifeline. 'I fear your Majesty is displeased with me and has utterly forsaken me.' Tears streamed down her cheeks.

'And why do you think that?' He kept his voice gentle.

Her hands trembling, she picked up a document from the floor and gave it to him. It was the warrant for her arrest. He stared at it.

'How did you get this?'

'I found it in the gallery, your Grace,' Dr Wendy said. 'I thought one of her Grace's people had dropped it.'

'The fools!' Harry barked, without thinking. 'I did not mean it to go this far. I just wanted to have my doubts resolved. Kate, tell me truly: are you a heretic?'

She looked at him, horrified. 'No, Sir,' she said firmly.

His eyes searched her face for any sign that she was lying, and found none. 'Darling, calm yourself. Nothing bad is going to happen to you. Be at ease now. Help me up, sirs!'

The two Gentlemen Pensioners sprang to attention.

'Good night, darling,' Harry said, as he limped to the door, leaning heavily on them. 'Be at peace. We will talk at length tomorrow.'

'Good night, Sir,' Kate sobbed, still on her knees.

The next morning, she arrived unannounced in Harry's bedchamber as he was chatting with his gentlemen.

'Madam!' he greeted her. 'This is a pleasant surprise. Do be seated.' Denny hastily vacated the other chair by the fire and Kate took it. She had dressed becomingly, and Harry's eyes fixed appreciatively on her low bodice and the cleft between her breasts. He was not so old and decrepit that he could not appreciate a woman's charms.

But that must wait until later. 'So, Madam, have you come to talk about religion again?' he challenged sternly. 'Are you going to resolve my doubts? For you have said things to me that are capable of more than one interpretation.'

'Sir, I did not intend for you to take my ignorant utterances that way!' she cried. 'Your Majesty knows as well as I do what great imperfection and weakness God allotted to us women, and that we are ordained to be inferior and subject to man as our head, from which head all our direction ought to proceed; and that, when God made man in His own likeness, with more special gifts of perfection, He made woman of man, by whom she is to be governed, commanded and directed. Her womanly weakness and natural imperfection ought to be tolerated and aided, so that, by man's wisdom, such things that are lacking in her may be supplied.'

Harry nodded, impressed by her very proper humility.

She smiled at him. 'Since God has appointed such a natural difference between men and women, and your Majesty is endowed with such excellent gifts and ornaments of wisdom, and I am a silly poor woman so much inferior in all respects of nature, surely your Majesty does not need my poor judgement in religious matters? I would always defer to your Majesty's wisdom, as my only anchor, supreme head and governor here on earth, next under God.'

Harry frowned. He would not be cozened by her flattery. 'By St Mary, you know very well that you have disputed with me. You have become a doctor, Kate, to instruct me, rather than being instructed or directed by me.'

She was quick to protest. 'You have very much mistaken me, Sir, for I have always been of the opinion that it is very unseemly and preposterous for a wife to take upon herself to instruct her lord; it is her part to learn from her husband and be taught by him. And, where I have been so bold as to dispute with your Majesty, I have not done it so much to offer my opinions as I did it to divert you with debate, so that you might be distracted from your pain and find some ease. And I hoped that, hearing your Majesty's learned discourse, I might receive some profit from it.'

Suddenly, the world had righted itself, as Harry realised that his fears had been groundless. Damn Gardiner! How dare he cast doubts on Kate's integrity!

'Is that so, sweetheart?' he replied. 'And tended your arguments to no worse an end? Then we are perfect friends again! Come here.'

She came to him and he embraced and kissed her, not caring that his gentlemen were looking on, grinning. 'It has done me more good to hear those words from your own mouth than if I had been given a hundred thousand pounds. I will never again think ill of you in any way.' He kissed her hand.

* * *

The following afternoon, it being a fine day, Harry invited Kate to join him in his privy garden. They sat in the little banqueting house, chatting over a flagon of wine, and she told him about the progress she was making with a second book of prayers and asked his opinion about her selections.

Both looked up as they heard the tramp of marching feet. Kate gasped in alarm as it came closer, and Harry rose, consumed with fury.

The iron gate opposite was suddenly flung open and, brandishing a document, Lord Chancellor Wriothesley marched into the garden at the head of a large detachment of the King's guard. Ignoring the pain in his leg, Harry stamped over to him, outraged.

'What do you think you are doing, my Lord Chancellor?'

Wriothesley fell to his knees, looking terrified. 'I came to arrest the Queen, Sir.' His voice came out as a squeak.

Harry snatched the document. It was a warrant for Kate's arrest, stamped with his sign manual. 'Knave! Arrant knave! Beast! Fool!' he thundered. 'Get out of my presence!'

Wriothesley fled, the guards running at his heels. Harry limped back to Kate, still seething with anger, although he attempted a smile.

'You seem somewhat offended with my Lord Chancellor,' she said shakily. 'I cannot think what just cause you have, yet maybe he was acting in ignorance. I pray you most humbly to be lenient with him.'

'Ah, poor soul,' Harry said, shaking his head, 'you little know how evilly he deserves this grace at your hands. On my word, sweetheart, he has been an absolute knave to you. Let him be.'

'As it pleases your Grace,' she said, pouring another goblet of wine. Harry would dearly have loved to see Gardiner's face when Wriothesley told him that their scheming had been trounced.

He was saddened when, in May, Chapuys informed him that his health would not permit him to continue in his post and that he would shortly be departing from England for good. They sat there in

Harry's privy garden, two incapacitated ageing men, waiting for the sunset.

'I shall miss you, old friend,' Harry told him. 'We have not always seen eye to eye, but I like to think we have been civilised about it – and that you have been fair in your reports of me.' He gave the ambassador a wry smile.

'I hope so too,' Chapuys said, with the hint of a grin that told Harry he had been bluntly honest.

'You have always performed your duties well, and I have come to trust you,' Harry said. 'I shall write and tell the Emperor as much, and that you are irreplaceable. But I doubt not that your health will be better on the other side of the sea.'

'I thank your Majesty.' Chapuys sounded choked. 'Might I have your permission to say goodbye to the Queen and the Princess Mary?'

Harry chose to ignore his unlawful use of Mary's former title. 'By all means. You were ever Mary's champion, even when she was being an infuriatingly froward daughter!'

'Some might say she had good cause,' Chapuys countered, and there they were, at it again, just like in former days. Harry's eyes misted with tears, for this would be the last time.

'Go in peace, old friend,' he said, extending his hand to be kissed.

'Farewell, your Majesty. I shall keep abreast of affairs in England during my retirement. It has become a second home to me.'

Kate was sad that summer, mourning the death of her young step-daughter, Latimer's girl. Harry wished he had more time for comforting her, but the war between England and France was still rumbling on. In July, when a French fleet began harrying the south coast, he rode down to Portsmouth to review his fleet and oversee operations.

Learning that two hundred French ships were lurking off the Isle of Wight, he gave the command for his flagship, the *Great Harry*, to lead his fleet out of the Solent to do battle. The night before she sailed, he dined on board with Lord Lisle, now Lord High Admiral, and Sir George Carew, the Vice Admiral. Some of those present were concerned because the English had only eighty ships.

'We were outnumbered at Agincourt and vastly so at Flodden,' Harry reminded them. 'Our English soldiers perform better under pressure.'

They still looked doubtful.

'We'll trounce the French and send them packing,' Lisle declared bullishly.

'Aye, we'll show them the might of English sea power.' Carew grinned.

'I see my fleet is in capable hands,' Harry smiled. 'A toast to you, gentlemen!'

The next morning, he stationed himself on the roof of Southsea Castle surrounded by many of his retinue, and with Lady Carew, wife of the Vice Admiral, standing beside him. There was a slight awkwardness between them because she was the daughter of Sir Henry Norris, the friend who had betrayed him with Anne Boleyn and gone to the block for his treason. Harry sensed a certain animosity, but the lady was respectful enough, and eager to see her husband acquit himself well.

They watched from the battlements as the English fleet glided past in stately formation. With a sudden crack, Harry's great ship, the *Mary Rose*, fired her starboard guns at the French galleys and then manoeuvred around to attack from the port side. As she turned, however, there was a violent gust of wind and she keeled right over and, before Harry's horrified eyes, began to sink. He watched transfixed as, with terrifying speed, she disappeared beneath the waves. He could see men floundering in the water, hear their shouts and yells, and witnessed some being dragged under by suction from the sinking ship. Near at hand, he heard Lady Carew screaming her husband's name, for he was aboard that vessel.

'Oh, my gentlemen! Oh, my gallant men!' he cried, trembling with shock, as he turned to comfort her, holding her close to his doublet as her shoulders heaved. Other ships were racing to the scene of the disaster, but there was nothing they could do. The *Mary Rose* had disappeared.

Later, they informed him that all but thirty-five of the five hundred men on board had perished, including Carew. He sat in his chamber at Southsea Castle, stricken, for the loss of his great ship with so many brave hands had been a terrible blow. Not even the news that his remaining fleet had sent the French packing could cheer him.

He spent the rest of the summer on a hunting progress with Kate. His councillors had ventured to suggest that he should not go away at such a time, but he was having none of it.

'I have such trust in the valour and affection of my subjects that I know I can safely leave the defence of my kingdom to them,' he declared. 'Have regular reports sent to me.'

At Guildford, late in August, he was watching an archery contest when Suffolk sat down beside him on the stone bench. He looked old and grizzled, another reminder that their glorious youth was long gone, but his eyes were alight at the prospect of leading another expedition to France.

'And will you go too, Harry?' he asked.

Before Harry could answer, the Duke suddenly clutched his chest and his ruddy complexion turned alarmingly pale.

'What is it, Charles?' Harry cried in alarm, as the gentlemen dropped their bows and came running. 'Fetch a physician!' he commanded, his heart pounding. But it was already too late. Suffolk had slumped forward, and when they raised him, they knew he had gone from them, just like that.

Harry drew back. He had loved Suffolk like no other, yet death held great terrors for him and he could not bear to be near a dead body. He rose, crossed himself, and limped back to the castle, tears streaming down his face.

That evening, he summoned the Council. 'For as long as my lord of Suffolk served me, he never betrayed a friend or knowingly took unfair advantage of an enemy,' he told them. 'None of you could say as much,' he added, his gaze bearing down on conservatives and reformists alike.

He sat down, sighing and near to tears. He felt old, defeated. 'We cannot do the late Duke too much honour. He shall be buried in St George's Chapel at Windsor, near the sepulchre I will share with Queen Jane, and it will be at my expense. See to it.'

'This will come hard on his widow and his sons,' Gardiner said. 'Young Henry Brandon is only eleven. It is a tender age to inherit a dukedom.'

'Lady Suffolk is more than capable,' Denny pointed out.

'Indeed, she is,' Harry added, thinking of that virago whom Kate loved as a sister, and her unruly dog Gardiner. 'She can continue to rule over Suffolk's estates until the boy is of age.'

'What of France, Sir?' Paget asked. 'Now that Suffolk has died, there is only my lord of Norfolk in command over there.'

'And he is incompetent!' Denny rapped. 'He takes too much upon himself, disobeying your Grace's orders.'

'Recall him,' Harry snarled. 'Send Surrey in his place. And trouble me no more today. I would be alone with my grief.'

Norfolk stood in front of him, looking mutinous.

'You have been called home because you abandoned Boulogne and withdrew to Calais, acting cleanly in contravention of my commands!' Harry raged.

'We had no arms and no provisions,' Norfolk bit back. 'It's madness to think that we can hold Boulogne.'

Harry was incandescent. 'I will be the judge of that! In future, my lord Duke, whatever you do, you must study to seek my honour, which has been somewhat touched by your conduct. Now get out of my sight!'

His wrath abated when Paget brought him glowing reports of Surrey's acts of valour in Boulogne. But not for long.

'He has repeatedly put himself at unnecessary risk, Sir,' Paget fretted, only days later.

'Write to him, Sir William. Tell him from me that he is not to court danger, but act with prudence. Add that I commend his courage and his loyalty. If only the rogue would calm down!'

'Your councillors are becoming concerned about his lavish overspending, and that he is inefficient in administering Boulogne.'

'Tell him he must put his house in order and account to me for his spending.'

When Paget had gone, Harry sighed and turned back to Kate's book of prayers and meditations, which had just been published. It was strongly evangelical in tone, but he was relieved to find that it did not overstep the bounds of orthodoxy. He smiled to himself, well satisfied.

In November – as if he had not suffered enough losses this year – Sir William Butts died. Harry grieved for his friend and physician, on whom he had come to rely, not just for cures, but also for intellectual stimulation. He appointed Dr Wendy in his place, but Wendy lacked the learned stature of Butts. Harry's loss was brought home to him that winter, when he suffered another bout of illness and none of his doctors seemed to have a clue as to what to do for him. By Christmas Eve, he felt so unwell that he began to fear he might be dying.

That same day, he had himself carried to Westminster and addressed Parliament, having had a presentiment that it might be for the last time. Kate had begged him not to go, but he had overridden her. There were many things he wanted to say to his subjects while he still had the chance.

The House of Lords was packed to the rafters, for word of his coming had gone ahead and the Members of the House of Commons had crowded in as well. Harry seated himself painfully on his throne.

The Speaker bowed to him. 'We welcome your Majesty most warmly to this House, and all of us gathered here wish to thank you for maintaining peace in this realm these thirty-six years and for being a careful and benevolent father to your people.

Feeling humbled, and quite emotional, Harry nodded graciously at him. 'I am grateful to you, Mr Speaker, for reminding me of my duty as sovereign, which is to ensure that I nurture in myself such excellent qualities and virtues as a prince ought to have, of which gifts I recognise myself both bare and barren.' He gave the lords a wry smile. 'But for such small qualities as God has endowed me with, I render to His goodness my most humble thanks, intending with all my wit and diligence to acquire for myself such notable virtues and princely qualities as you have alleged to be incorporated in my person.'

He paused, then fixed his gaze on them, taking in every man in the chamber. You could have heard a leaf fall.

'Now, since I find such kindness on your part towards me, I cannot choose but to love and favour you all, affirming that no prince in the world more favours his subjects than I do you, and no subjects or commons more love and obey their sovereign lord than I see you do me, for whose defence I will spend all my treasure and risk my person. But although we are in this perfect love and concord, this friendly amity cannot continue unless both you, my lords temporal, and you, my lords spiritual, and you, my loving subjects, take pains to amend one thing which is surely amiss and far out of order, which I most heartily require you to do.'

He leaned forward in his seat, ignoring the throbbing in his leg, and spoke sternly. 'Charity and concord are not amongst you, but discord and dissension bear rule. St Paul wrote to the Corinthians: "Charity is gentle, Charity is not envious, Charity is not proud." Behold then, what love and charity is amongst you when one calls another heretic, and he calls him back Papist and hypocrite? Are these tokens of charity amongst you? No, no, I assure you that this lack will be the hindrance of the fervent love between us, unless this is healed.

'Alas, how can poor souls live in concord when you preachers sow debate and discord in your sermons? People look to you for light and you bring them darkness. Amend these crimes, I exhort you, and set forth God's word truly, both by true preaching and giving a good example, or else, I, whom God has appointed His vicar and high minister here, will see these divisions extinct and these enormities corrected, according to my true duty.'

Another pause, to let that sink in, then he girded himself to speak from the heart.

'I am very sorry to hear how irreverently that most precious jewel, the word of God, is disputed, rhymed, sung and jangled in every alehouse and tavern, contrary to the true meaning and doctrine of the same; and I am even as sorry that the readers of the same follow it so faintly and coldly. For of this I am sure, that charity was never so faint amongst you, and virtuous and godly living was never less prevalent, nor was God Himself, amongst Christians, never less reverenced, honoured, or served. Therefore, as I said before, be in charity one with another, like brother and brother! Love, dread and serve God, the which I, as your Supreme Head and sovereign lord, exhort and require you; and then I doubt not but that love and league shall never be dissolved nor broken between us.'

His voice caught as he sank back in his chair, exhausted. An excited murmuring spread through the Parliament chamber and then erupted into spontaneous and prolonged applause. Harry rose and bowed; his eyes blinded by tears. He almost had to fight his way out.

'To us that have not heard your Majesty often,' one young Member of Parliament told him, 'it was such a joy and marvellous comfort as I reckon this day one of the happiest of my life!' Harry smiled at him and clapped him on the shoulder.

1546

He recovered, but in February, he was again laid low with a fever, which confined him to his apartments for three weeks. While convalescing, he drew up plans to aid the universities of his realm, which had lost revenues as a result of his reforms.

'At Oxford,' he told Kate, who was sitting at his bedside, embroidering, 'I shall re-found Wolsey's Cardinal College and rename it Christ Church. It will teach theology, Greek and Hebrew, and its chapel will serve as a cathedral for my new see of Oxford. The first Dean is to be Dr Cox, Edward's old tutor, and I myself will act as Visitor, if God gives me strength.'

Kate looked delighted. 'I have long hoped that you would establish your own university. It will be a fitting memorial to you and your great learning.'

'I'm not dead yet,' Harry jested, at which she looked horrified. He chuckled at her dismay. 'I know what you meant, Kate. I want to be remembered as a patron of learning. Which is why I am founding a new college, to be called Trinity College, at Cambridge. Did you know that, in 1540, I endowed five professorships at Cambridge, in Greek, Hebrew, civil law, divinity and medicine?'

'How could I not know? Your fame is bruited far and wide. I heard of it when I lived in Yorkshire!'

By the middle of March, Harry was out of bed and losing money at cards to his courtiers. Soon afterwards, he was well enough to attend a meeting of his Council, only to be met with protests over the great landed endowments he had given to his new colleges, especially on the part of those who had been covetous of university estates since the Dissolution.

'Sirs,' he rebuked them, 'I tell you that I judge no land in England better bestowed than that which is given to our universities, for by their maintenance our realm shall be well governed when we are all dead and rotten.' A shiver went through him as he said the words. Not yet, he prayed. Grant me life yet!

But, despite his leg paining him a little, he was better, even if his face bore the hallmarks of his suffering.

Kate was writing another book, to be called *The Lamentations of a Sinner*.

'Be careful not to make it too radical,' Harry warned her. 'Gardiner and his allies are rooting out heresy again. It is a dangerous time to preach the cause of reform.'

'I will be prudent,' Kate promised.

One spring afternoon, not long afterwards, Gardiner came bustling into Harry's closet. 'Your Grace should know that I have had Dr Edward Crome questioned about preaching heresy.'

'That preacher my courtiers are flocking to hear?'

'The very same, Sir. I have reason to believe that he is part of a secret Protestant circle based in London. If we press him, he may reveal their names.'

'Then have him questioned again,' Harry said. 'Root them all out!'

Two days later, Gardiner returned. 'Under interrogation, Dr Crome has named his associates. Some are your own courtiers, Sir, and there is a woman, a known troublemaker, called Anne Askew. She is a self-confessed Protestant and has connections at court. She is even acquainted with some of the Queen's ladies.'

Harry spied the zealous gleam in Gardiner's eye. He could see where this was going, that it was another attempt to unseat Kate. Well, he was having none of that!

'May I have her arrested and questioned?' Gardiner was waiting impatiently.

Harry exhaled. 'Very well.'

He spent the next two days fretting that the Askew woman would say something to incriminate Kate.

The next he knew, Sir Edmund Walsingham, the Lieutenant of the Tower, was standing before him, almost wringing his hands, complaining that the Lord Chancellor himself and Sir Richard Rich were torturing Anne Askew.

'The woman would not talk, your Grace, so they had me stretch her on the rack. When I saw she was at the end of her endurance, I went to untie her, but my Lord Chancellor was furious because she had given them nothing, and ordered me to strain her again. I refused because she was so weak that I thought she might die.' He swallowed. It was a serious thing to disobey the Lord Chancellor, but torture was illegal in England unless sanctioned by the King or his Council and certainly, no one had asked Harry to authorise this.

'My lord threatened to report my disobedience to your Grace.

Then he and Sir Richard Rich threw off their gowns and began to turn the rollers. Mistress Askew suffered their cruelty till her limbs were almost pulled asunder, but they did not take her down until she was nearly dead. Then they laid her on the bare floor and continued to interrogate her. When it was over, I hastened here.'

'Did they obtain the consent of the Privy Council to this torture?' Harry asked.

'No, Sir.'

He was enraged. Both Wriothesley and Rich were Privy Councillors and should have known better than to break the law. But, of course, they had known there would be opposition from the reformists.

'Undoubtedly the woman has been handled too severely. Sir Edmund, do not fear. I readily pardon you for disobeying orders. Go back and see to your prisoner.'

Harry knew he could not save Anne Askew. The woman was a relapsed heretic. But when he learned that Wriothesley and Gardiner had had one of his favoured gentlemen, Sir George Blagge, arrested and sentenced to burn for heresy, he was appalled, for he had a great affection for the young fool. Blagge was his Pig these days, as he had come heartily to dislike Wriothesley, for whom he no longer used that affectionate nickname.

'Oh, my Pig, my poor Pig! The bastards! I knew they would do for him,' he moaned to himself.

But others had heard the news too. Sir John Russell, the Lord Privy Seal, was announced not a half-hour later.

'Your Majesty,' he said, his tone urgent, 'on behalf of many of your Privy Council, I come to beg for mercy for Mr Blagge.'

'Am I to show mercy to a heretic?' Harry croaked.

'He's no more a heretic than I am, Sir, and many in your court,' Sir John replied. 'His words have deliberately been misinterpreted by those who think only of their own ambitions. Your Majesty can only gain in stature and reputation in exercising your prerogative of mercy.'

Harry nodded. He had been shown a way forward.

'You have done well to come to me,' he said. 'I will pardon him. And, Russell, thank you.'

Sir John rose, made his reverence and hurried away.

Harry summoned Wriothesley. 'How dare you arrest a Gentleman of my Privy Chamber?' he stormed. 'You will draw up a pardon here and now, in my presence. Then I will sign it and you will go and release Sir George and send him back to me. Do you heed me?'

Wriothesley nodded like a frightened rabbit.

Blagge returned to court that afternoon, looking like a man who had been granted Heaven.

'Ah, my Pig!' Harry cried. 'Are you safe again?'

'Yes, Sir,' answered Blagge, 'and if your Majesty had not been better than your bishops, your pig had been roasted by now!'

Anne Askew went to the stake in July, but that was the swansong of the conservatives. Hertford returned from the wars soon afterwards and formed a powerful alliance with Lord Lisle that eclipsed the influence of their enemies. Harry was no fool. He knew the reformists were out to secure control of the government after his death. Hertford, of course, was in a strong position as the uncle of the future King.

Seeing this formidable coalition, Norfolk, aware that his influence was dwindling, swallowed his pride and attempted to ally himself with the Seymour faction. Harry was happy to sanction the proposed marriage of the Duke's daughter Mary, Richmond's widow, to Sir Thomas Seymour. He had not forgotten that Seymour had once pursued Kate, and although she had never given him cause to suspect that she had had any feelings for the rogue, he still could not help regarding him as a rival. Marriage to Mary Howard would put an end to that.

But Surrey then professed himself violently opposed to the match, just as he refused to countenance one between his own daughter and Hertford's son. Nor was Mary Howard in favour of marrying Seymour. By St George, those Howards were a troublesome lot!

Chapter 38

1546

These days, because of his failing health, Harry spent most of his time in the privacy of his secret lodgings and rarely stirred out of his chamber, unless it was to walk in his privy garden. But even that pleasure was dwindling, for his legs gave him so much pain. He had lost his appetite for feasting and the flesh on him was falling away. There was no need to diet: the huge, gorgeous gowns and doublets hung on him.

He did not want the world, or the courtiers who waited outside in the presence chamber, to think him enfeebled or see what a shadow of his former self he had become. Apart from his gentlemen and servants, the only people he suffered to see him were Kate, a few trusted councillors, and the occasional ambassador, and all by his special commandment.

He knew from Will that speculation about his health was rife, and that his doctors were worried. He dared not look far into the future, for at times, especially in the long, wakeful reaches of the night, he could see none. Yet he would not give in. He refused to hear any mention of death and behaved as if he had many years ahead of him, ignoring the pain in his legs and driving himself to lead as normal a life as possible.

It would have been easier if he could walk, but that was becoming increasingly impossible. He had two chairs made with poles fitted on either side, so that he could be carried to and fro in his galleries and chambers. One was covered in quilted tawny velvet, the other in gold velvet and silk, and both had embroidered foot rests. They were kept with his maps and pictures in his study, which was now called the chair house. Because he could no longer negotiate stairs, he had a lifting device with a pulley installed.

He had no doubt that, behind closed doors, the power struggle for the regency was intensifying. Unlikely alliances were being formed, men coming together through self-interest or fear. The Seymours, allied with the Dudleys, were easily the dominant faction, and Harry was content that it should be so, for no one was better fitted to govern the Prince than his uncle of Hertford; but it was clear that the conservative opposition would not be giving in without a fight.

Surrey, however, seemed to have his own agenda, and in some ways to have lost touch with reality: he kept falling out with lords and courtiers on either side of the divide.

'He wants to gain control of the Prince himself,' Hertford warned Harry when he came to report on affairs that summer. 'Or rather, he thinks his father should.'

'I'd rather stab Surrey than see the government in the hands of the Howards,' commented Blagge, who was in attendance, and no wonder, for Surrey had insulted him more than once.

Harry was not unaware that Hertford was nervous about his enemies prevailing and had made sure that many of his clients and supporters were constantly in attendance on him. Hertford was on poor terms with everyone except Lisle and Paget, and at particular loggerheads with Wriothesley, who had switched factions as soon as he realised the conservatives were losing ground. Everyone was on a knife-edge. Lisle struck Gardiner during a fierce dispute in Council, obliging Harry to expel him from the court, but he was soon back, unrepentant; soon afterwards, so Will told Harry, Lisle and Hertford had used violent words against Gardiner and Wriothesley. From the privacy of his secret lodgings, Harry struggled to maintain control over the warring parties, but he was growing exhausted with the effort.

In August, after the Emperor had turned cold and peace with the French had finally been declared, Harry roused himself to receive the

Lord High Admiral of France, who had come to England to ratify the treaty. But Harry was too infirm to go to meet him. Instead, Prince Edward, with an escort of eighty gold-clad gentlemen and eighty Yeomen of the Guard, rode out to greet the Admiral at Hounslow. Harry watched from his window as they left, impressed by the boy's horsemanship. Approaching nine years old, he already had a kingly bearing.

After Edward had conducted the French Admiral to Hampton Court, he deputised for Harry on several occasions during the ten days of receptions, banquets, masques, dances and hunting trips that followed, and Harry was proud to hear that he had shown off his skills at Latin and on the lute. It was galling not to be present himself and take part in the pageantry he had once loved, but he was just not up to it. He did receive the Admiral in the presence chamber and had himself carried to Mass with him in the Chapel Royal. He was well enough to be present at an open-air reception, and even able to stand under a great silk pavilion, but after a while he had to lean on the shoulders of his guest and Cranmer.

When the celebrations ended and the French departed, Edward returned to Hunsdon. Harry embraced him tightly as they said farewell, fearing he might never look on his beloved boy again. Then he departed on his usual hunting progress with Kate, but did not stray beyond the Thames Valley, keeping to remote houses so as not to be seen by his people. Not so long ago he had revelled in their love and delighted in showing himself in public. He could have wept to think of what he had become.

At Oatlands, he shot from a standing as the deer were driven past him; then at Chertsey, he felt fit enough to ride with the hounds after a stag. For days on end, he enjoyed the chase, and began to believe he was not as decrepit as he had feared. But he was disabused of that hope in September, when he set out for Guildford and realised he had overdone things and could not go on. Having been helped into a closed chariot, he retired to Windsor and the progress was abandoned.

Confined to his bed again, fevered and in pain, he ordered that it be given out that he had a cold. In fact, as he could tell from the physicians' faces, he was in great danger and feared they had given up all hope of his recovery. Yet, miraculously, he rallied once more, and was soon out hunting and hawking, and as much in command of affairs as ever.

In October, he appointed Denny Groom of the Stool and Head of the Privy Chamber.

'The word is that his advancement betokens your support for his friend Hertford,' Will reported, as he perched on his stool, cracking nuts.

'Let them speculate,' Harry sniffed, easing his leg on the footstool, 'but I will not have it said that I favour one party above the rest. I shall have to do something for the conservatives now.'

He was tired to death of playing off one faction against the other. The matter was taken out of his hands, however, for in November, Gardiner refused point-blank to accede to Harry's very reasonable request to exchange some episcopal lands for royal estates. When the Bishop next came seeking entry to the privy chamber, Harry had him sent away. Clearly in a panic, Gardiner sent a message asking if Sir William Paget might speak for him, but Harry refused to grant Paget an audience. Gardiner would have to accept that he was in disgrace. It was his own damn fault.

In the middle of November, Harry moved to Whitehall to take the medicinal baths he usually had at this time of year, and which had always proved efficacious. As he lay soaking in the aromatic water in the huge sunken marble bath, one of his grooms informed him that Gardiner was without, craving an audience.

'No,' he said. 'Now, help me get up.'

Will told him that Gardiner was haunting the outer chambers of the palace, hoping to see Harry, but Harry remained adamant.

'I will not see him,' he declared.

'He's now endeavouring to be seen in the company of your favoured councillors, so that no one will believe he is disgraced,' Will reported a few days later.

At the beginning of December, Harry's secretary handed him a letter from Gardiner, who was again craving an audience and belatedly agreeing to the exchange of lands after all.

'Tell him,' Harry growled, 'that I see no cause why he should molest me further. Instruct him to arrange the transfer of the property through my officers in the usual manner.'

There was no way in which he was going to support the conservatives now.

It was a mild winter. Harry went to stay at Oatlands, where he felt well enough to go out riding once more. But just as he was feeling more optimistic and beginning to enjoy himself, he felt the shivers that normally warned of a bout of fever.

Not again, please God! But he soon knew he was not mistaken.

For thirty hours, he learned later, his doctors had battled to keep him alive – and he had been so far gone he had not known it. And yet, to everyone's amazement, including his own, here he was, well again, or so he assured himself. But although he was up and dressed, he still felt very weak.

'In case any light rumour may rise to the contrary,' he told his Council, 'my ambassadors abroad are to give out that my fever was merely the result of some grief in my leg. They must stress that I am now, thanks be to God, well rid of it, and will be better for a long while.'

He prayed it would be true.

Hertford and Lisle came to him, their faces grave.

'Your Grace, we bear evil tidings,' Hertford began. 'Sir Richard Southwell, who is close to my lord of Surrey, has felt it his duty to lay before the Council evidence about his lordship that touches his fidelity to your Grace.'

'What evidence?' Harry barked, ever alert for treason.

'It seems clear that Surrey has traitorously schemed to be king.'

'What? He has no claim to the throne!'

'No, he does not. But his sister, the Duchess of Richmond, when questioned, revealed that he had said that the Seymours and other new men had no love for the nobility, and if God called away your Grace, they should smart for it. Then she gave testimony that Surrey had replaced the coronet on his coat of arms with a crown, flanked by the initials H.R.'

Henricus Rex. Henry the King – a title that was Harry's alone.

'By God!' He was almost speechless. To think he had nurtured such a viper in his bosom, loved him and protected him from himself . . .

'We sent men to search Surrey's house,' Lisle continued, 'and they found armorial glass, paintings and plate bearing the arms of Edward the Confessor, which Surrey claimed he bore by right of descent, even though Garter King of Arms had ruled that King Edward was not in his pedigree. In the end, Sir, we were forced to conclude that Surrey had conspired to murder us all, depose your Grace and take possession of the kingdom.'

'That is not all,' Hertford put in – as if this were not enough to condemn Surrey to eternal damnation. 'When the Duchess's marriage to Sir Thomas Seymour was mooted recently, and Surrey feared your Grace would command it despite his objections, the Duchess deposed that he decided to use it to his family's advantage. He told her that, when your Grace sent for her to congratulate her on her betrothal, she should – forgive me – use her feminine wiles on you, become your mistress and wield as much influence as Madame d'Etampes does on the French King. She says she was outraged and protested that she would cut her own throat rather than consent to such a villainy. She and her brother fell out over this, and I believe it was her enmity towards him that has made her incriminate him.'

Harry was outraged. 'How dare that varlet look to manipulate me! Tell me, is Norfolk involved in this treason?'

'We believe so, Sir.' Hertford and Lisle contrived to look mournful. Had it not been for the proofs that had been found, Harry would have suspected that they had contrived to ruin the Howards to leave their own way clear to the regency. But those proofs were damning. It was hard to believe that Norfolk had betrayed him, but Surrey could hardly have attempted the throne without his father's collusion. Harry shuddered to think how narrowly he had escaped from their treacherous scheming, and sent up a fervent prayer of thanks to God for preserving him from the malice of traitors. Then, resolutely refusing to remember how loyally Norfolk had served him all his reign, he hardened his heart.

'Have them both arrested at once and taken to the Tower,' he commanded.

There was no protest from Surrey, but Hertford showed Harry a letter that Norfolk had sent to the Council from his prison.

I have always shown myself a true man to my sovereign, he had written, *and I think surely there is some false man that has laid some great cause to my charge, or else I would not have been sent hither. I have great enemies.*

Reading it, Harry almost wavered, knowing the last statement to be true. But he had been thoroughly shaken by the revelation of the Howards' treason and was in no mood to heed Norfolk's pleas.

With the collapse of the conservative faction, there was no doubt now that, when the time came, the regency would be entrusted to the reformists.

Harry moved by slow stages to Whitehall for Christmas. By the time he arrived, he was feeling very ill. The court was to be closed, he decreed, and he sent Kate and his daughters to spend Yuletide at Greenwich.

'I want you to make merry,' he bade them. 'Do not worry about me.'

When he kissed Kate a loving farewell, he wondered if he would ever look on her face again. He gave Mary and Elizabeth his blessing and saw tears in the eyes of all three as they left him.

He passed the festive season in seclusion, while his favoured councillors and attendants kept everyone else at bay, especially (he realised) those whom they feared might exert undesirable influence over him, and, at his own wish, ensured that little information about his condition reached the outside world.

He had drawn up his will before he left for Boulogne in 1544. It chimed with the provisions of the Act of Succession, except it expressed his desire that, in the event of Edward, Mary and Elizabeth all dying without issue, the crown descend to the granddaughters of his beloved sister Mary.

On the evening of St Stephen's Day, he summoned Hertford, Paget, Lisle and Denny to his chamber, and asked for the will to be read to him. He then had himself propped up on pillows and drew up a list of sixteen councillors – reformers all – to serve on a Council of Regency. That way, they would likely be united in a single purpose and would serve his son's interests rather than their own.

'Be aware that this is to be an equal coalition,' he said sternly, looking Hertford in the eye, knowing how ambitious he was. 'No one man is to wield power. And Gardiner is not included because he is wilful and not meet to be about my son.' Hertford bowed his head.

Harry lay back after the lords had gone, wondering if he had done the right thing. How many of the councillors he had chosen were not only eager for ever more radical reforms, but also secret Protestants? Had he prepared the way for a Protestant government?

He thought not. All had shown themselves loyal supporters of the Church of England and the reforms he had introduced. And they were loyal, which could not be said for some of the conservatives! Indeed, there was no real opposition and no other choice open to him.

He knew that his arrangements for the regency ran contrary to Hertford's expectations, and he had ordered Paget to stamp the will with his signature and keep it safe. Paget would surely see that his wishes were carried out.

Harry gritted his teeth to stop himself from crying out. It was New Year's Day and he was again stricken with fever. His leg was sheer agony, and the doctors were now cauterising it. He bore the agony with stoicism, but it was torture.

When it was over, he was told that the Queen and the Lady Mary had returned to Whitehall and were asking to see him; but he would not, *could* not, let them see him like this. And Hertford was against it. He knew that Harry had once considered naming Kate as regent, and he was clearly determined to prevent that. He need not have worried. It was better that men have the ruling of a young king and his realm. Kate had been handsomely provided for; it had been Harry's pleasure to reward her for the great love, obedience and chastity he had found in her.

Although he was confined to his sickroom, he followed reports of the proceedings against the Howards closely. He knew his instincts about Norfolk had been correct when, on the day before Surrey's trial, the old Duke admitted his guilt in concealing his son's treason. Even so, Surrey spoke up vigorously in his own defence at his trial, but his case had been prejudiced from the start because of his father's confession. He was found guilty as charged, and Harry sent to the peers who were sitting in judgement on him, authorising them to condemn him to death.

After the trial, his health improved a little. He ordered French saplings for his garden, hoping to see them grow into trees. He gave audiences to both the Spanish and French ambassadors and said he was sorry that his incapacity had prevented the speedy dispatch of their business. He made plans for Edward's investiture as Prince of Wales.

Norfolk and Surrey were attainted by Parliament and Surrey was beheaded on Tower Hill. But Harry was too weak to sign Norfolk's death warrant. He had suffered a relapse and could not even hold a pen.

He knew that he was dying. He saw his confessor and received holy communion. He was not wholly in command of himself when Sir Anthony Denny bravely defied the law and warned him that, in man's judgement, he was not like to live and should remember his sins, as every good Christian man should do.

'The mercy of Christ would pardon all my sins, though they were greater than they be,' Harry croaked.

'Would your Grace like to speak to any learned man?' He heard Denny through the mists of whatever lassitude had him in its grip.

'Dr Cranmer,' he said. 'But I will first take a little sleep, and then I will advise upon the matter.'

'Summon Cranmer from Croydon,' he heard Denny say. Then everything was a blur.

He heard someone murmur, 'He was undoubtedly the rarest man that lived in his time,' and wondered if he had died already.

Then another said, 'We speak of him as a god, but he was no saint. He did many evil things.'

'Aye, but in all the histories, you will not find one king equal to him.'

'Great Harry!' someone said. 'Look at him now.'

And then – or was he imagining it? – he heard a woman's voice he would have recognised anywhere, a voice stilled these ten years. 'Your wife I cannot be, both in respect of my unworthiness, and also because you have a queen already. Your mistress I will not be!'

Anne! And he remembered, most vividly, the enchantment she had cast, could feel, even now, the thrill of pursuing her. It was as if the years had rolled back, and he was again in the vigour of his manhood, racing in the saddle, his black-eyed beauty laughing at his side.

After that, there were more voices, all talking at once, it seemed, echoing down the years. He knew them all. Kate, declaring she had never been Arthur's wife; Wolsey, promising an annulment; Cromwell, crying for mercy; Katheryn, screaming in the gallery; and Jane, sweet Jane, fighting for breath. No, no, he moaned inwardly.

He was aware of someone – Cranmer, he thought – taking his hand and asking, from far away, if he died in the faith of Christ.

Somehow, he summoned the strength to wring that hand as hard as he could. It was finished. He could lay down his sceptre and give up the struggle. Knowing that Heaven lay ahead, he embraced the darkness.

THE ENGLISH ROYAL HOUSE 1547

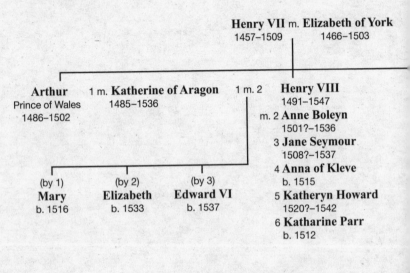

Henry VII m. Elizabeth of York
1457–1509   1466–1503

Arthur
Prince of Wales
1486–1502

1 m. **Katherine of Aragon**
1485–1536

1 m. 2

Henry VIII
1491–1547

m. 2 **Anne Boleyn**
1501?–1536

3 **Jane Seymour**
1508?–1537

4 **Anna of Kleve**
b. 1515

5 **Katheryn Howard**
1520?–1542

6 **Katharine Parr**
b. 1512

(by 1)
Mary
b. 1516

(by 2)
Elizabeth
b. 1533

(by 3)
Edward VI
b. 1537

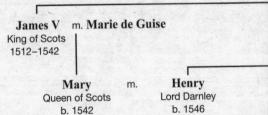

James V   m. **Marie de Guise**
King of Scots
1512–1542

Mary   m.   **Henry**
Queen of Scots   Lord Darnley
b. 1542   b. 1546

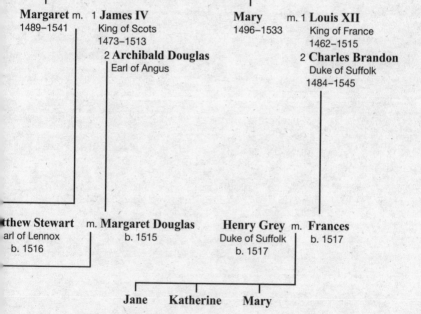

Margaret m. 1 James IV
1489–1541   King of Scots
          1473–1513
         2 **Archibald Douglas**
           Earl of Angus

Mary   m. 1 **Louis XII**
1496–1533   King of France
          1462–1515
         2 **Charles Brandon**
           Duke of Suffolk
           1484–1545

tthew Stewart m. **Margaret Douglas**
arl of Lennox   b. 1515
b. 1516

Henry Grey m. **Frances**
Duke of Suffolk   b. 1517
b. 1517

Jane   **Katherine**   **Mary**

597

Author's Note

Having written six novels on Henry VIII's wives, each from their point of view, I have long been saying that it was about time Henry VIII had his say in a novel all to himself. I'm delighted that my publishers agreed, and here it is, written entirely from his viewpoint.

I must confess to feeling a certain trepidation in writing a novel about Henry VIII. He is such a famous, larger-than-life subject that I was wondering if I could ever do him justice. There are so many aspects to his story that it was hard to choose which ones to develop for the book, and there was a cast of hundreds, many of them historical titans, to bring to life. No pressure there!

Fortunately, I have spent many decades researching Henry VIII and the extraordinary dynasty his reign cements, and I was able to draw extensively on that research for this novel. Given constraints on length, and in the interests of keeping narrative pace, I have sometimes telescoped events or simplified the politics and the religious controversies of the day. Nevertheless, the issues that gripped and exercised the early sixteenth century, and Henry in particular, are presented authentically. All views expressed in the book reflect the opinions of the period.

Many fascinating figures passed through Henry's court and shaped his life, both personal and political. In this novel, I have prioritised those who were important to his story or help us to understand different aspects of his character. I have used contemporary sources extensively to underpin and embellish the story, although some have been used out of context, and archaic language has been modernised in places.

Some of my tale is, of course, speculative. I have based Henry's feelings for his wives and others on contemporary evidence, although that does not always record people's emotions or motives. We don't, for example, know when Anne Boleyn agreed to become his wife. In this, and in many other places, I have made informed guesses. My own theory is that Henry's matrimonial career was shaped in part by the loss of his mother, Elizabeth of York, who personified the late-medieval ideal of queenship, and that she was the benchmark against which he judged his wives.

Readers may wonder why I have credited Katherine of Aragon with eight pregnancies, when usually six are listed. But in one of his letters, Henry refers to her fifth month as 'her dangerous times', and we know of no documented pregnancy that ended at that stage. The word 'times' being plural, I have speculated that there were at least two late miscarriages.

My novel *Anna of Kleve* was written from Anna's point of view, so I used the German form in the title. Henry called her Anna, but the English called Kleve 'Cleves' or 'Cleveland', hence my use of 'Anna of Cleves' here.

Why 'Harry'? It was an affectionate name sometimes used by, and for, Henry VIII, and I felt that the use of it made him more accessible and human. The book's UK title, *The Heart and the Crown*, reflects the extent to which his passions and emotions drove him and were at times in conflict with the political man. The US title, *The King's Pleasure*, reflects how the will and pleasure of the King held sway over all his subjects, for it was seen as the will of God working through the monarch.

I very much hope that this novel gives some insights into the mind of a brilliant, autocratic, vain, intellectual, ruthless and romantic king who changed the face and institutions of England for ever and whose memory is still vividly alive five centuries after he lived.

Writing this book posed a tremendous challenge, and I owe a huge debt of gratitude to everyone who has supported me throughout the project. Huge thanks go to my amazing commissioning editors, Mari Evans and Frances Edwards at Headline, and Susanna Porter at Ballantine, and especially to my fantastic editor, Flora Rees, who heroically compared the text to more than three thousand pages in the Six Tudor Queens series to ensure that there were no anomalies. I wish also to express my warm appreciation to the publishing teams on both sides of the Atlantic, especially Caitlin Raynor, Jessie Goetzinger-Hall, Lucy Upton, Kathleen Quinlan, Melissa Sandford Folds and Megan Whalen. It's my pleasure also to thank all the other incredibly talented people who work in production, design, marketing and sales, not to mention all the booksellers, bloggers, events managers, printers and distributors who get my books out to the wonderful readers who buy them and post such lovely comments online. Heartfelt thanks to you all – and, of course, to Rankin, my beloved husband, without whom there would be no books!

Alison Weir, Carshalton, November 2022

Dramatis Personae

(In order of appearance or first mention.)

Henry VIII ('Harry'), King of England
Will Somers, Harry's fool
Katharine Parr, Queen of England, Harry's sixth wife
Elizabeth of York, Queen of England, Harry's mother
Mrs Anne Luke, Harry's nurse
Henry VII, King of England, Harry's father
The Lady Margaret Beaufort, Countess of Richmond and Derby, Harry's paternal grandmother
Mary Tudor, Harry's younger sister, later Queen of France ('the French Queen') and Duchess of Suffolk
Margaret Tudor, Harry's elder sister, later Queen of Scots
Arthur Tudor, Prince of Wales, Harry's deceased elder brother
Katherine of Aragon, Dowager Princess of Wales, Arthur's widow, later Queen of England and Harry's first wife
Catherine Tudor, Harry's youngest sister
John Skelton, poet, Harry's tutor
William Blount, Lord Mountjoy, courtier, humanist scholar, later chamberlain to Katherine of Aragon
(Sir) Thomas More, lawyer, humanist scholar, later Lord Chancellor
Desiderius Erasmus, humanist scholar
Edward IV, King of England, Harry's maternal grandfather (reigned 1461–83)
Charles Brandon, later Duke of Suffolk, courtier
Arthur, legendary King of Britain
Sir William Brandon, Charles' father, late standard-bearer to Henry VII

Richard III, King of England (reigned 1483–5), brother of Edward IV and Harry's great-uncle

Giles Dewes, Harry's languages tutor

(Sir) William Compton, courtier, later Chief Gentleman of the Privy Chamber and Groom of the Stool

(Sir) Edward Neville, courtier

Edmund Audley, Bishop of Salisbury

William Warham, Archbishop of Canterbury

Pope Julius II

Doña Elvira, duenna to Katherine of Aragon

Isabella I, Queen of Castile, mother of Katherine of Aragon

Ferdinand V, King of Aragon, father of Katherine of Aragon

Juana, Queen of Castile, older sister of Katherine of Aragon

Richard Foxe, Bishop of Winchester, Lord Privy Seal

Philip I (of Burgundy/Habsburg), King of Castile, husband of Queen Juana and son of the Holy Roman Emperor Maximilian I

Eleanor of Austria, daughter of Philip and Juana, later Queen of France

Maximilian I, Holy Roman Emperor

Edward III, King of England (reigned 1327–77)

Henry V, King of England (reigned 1413–22)

Catherine of York, Countess of Devon, Harry's maternal aunt

William Courtenay, Earl of Devon, her husband, Harry's uncle

Perkin Warbeck, late pretender to the throne

Cecily of York, Harry's maternal aunt

Anne of York, Lady Thomas Howard, Harry's maternal aunt

Thomas Howard, Earl of Surrey, later 2nd Duke of Norfolk

Lord Thomas Howard, his son, Harry's uncle, later Earl of Surrey and 3rd Duke of Norfolk and Earl Marshal, husband of Anne of York

Bridget of York, nun at Dartford, Harry's maternal aunt

James IV, King of Scots, husband of Margaret Tudor, Harry's sister

Henry Courtenay, son of William Courtenay, Earl of Devon, and Catherine of York, and Harry's cousin, later Earl of Devon and Marquess of Exeter

The Pole family, descendants of Harry's late maternal great-uncle George, Duke of Clarence, Harry's kinsmen

Edward, Earl of Warwick, late son of George, Duke of Clarence

George, Duke of Clarence, brother of Edward IV and Richard III, Harry's uncle

Richard Empson, adviser to Henry VII

Edmund Dudley, adviser to Henry VII

Lady Catherine Gordon, widow of Perkin Warbeck

Gutier Gómez Fuensalida, Spanish ambassador

St Thomas Aquinas, theologian and philosopher

William the Conqueror, King of England (reigned 1066–87)

Luis Caroz, Spanish ambassador

Thomas Wolsey, chaplain, later Lord High Almoner, Archbishop of York, Cardinal and Lord Chancellor

John Fisher, Bishop of Rochester

Edward Stafford, 3rd Duke of Buckingham, Harry's distant cousin

John Howard, late 1st Duke of Norfolk, father of Thomas Howard, 2nd Duke

The Princes in the Tower, Harry's maternal uncles: Edward V, King of England (reigned briefly in 1483), and his brother Richard, Duke of York

St Edward the Confessor, King of England (reigned 1042–66)

The Black Prince, Edward of Woodstock, Prince of Wales, son of Edward III

George Talbot, 4th Earl of Shrewsbury

Sir Robert Dymmock, King's Champion

John Islip, Abbot of Westminster

Louis XII, King of France

William Cornish, Gentleman-of the Chapel Royal, Master of the Revels

Anne Browne, first wife of Charles Brandon

Margaret Mortimer, her aunt, second wife of Charles Brandon

Sir Thomas Boleyn, later Viscount Rochford, then Earl of Wiltshire and Ormond, Lord Privy Seal, father of Anne, Mary and George Boleyn

Elizabeth Howard, his wife, daughter of Thomas Howard, 2nd Duke of Norfolk

(Sir) Henry Guildford, courtier

(Sir) William Fitzwilliam, later Earl of Southampton

Henry Stafford, late 2nd Duke of Buckingham

Margaret Plantagenet, daughter of George, Duke of Clarence, sister of Edward, late Earl of Warwick; later Countess of Salisbury

Sir Richard Pole, her husband

Edmund de la Pole, Earl ('Duke') of Suffolk, Harry's maternal cousin

Richard de la Pole, Harry's maternal cousin, nicknamed 'the White Rose'; Yorkist pretender

Fray Diego Fernandez, confessor to Katherine of Aragon

Will Wynesbury, Lord of Misrule

Stillborn daughter of Henry VIII and Katherine of Aragon

Henry Bourchier, Earl of Essex

Elizabeth Stafford, Lady FitzWalter, sister of the Duke of Buckingham

Anne Stafford, Lady Hastings, sister of the Duke of Buckingham and Harry's mistress; later mistress of William Compton

George, Lord Hastings, husband of Anne Stafford

Robert Ratcliffe, Lord FitzWalter, later Earl of Sussex, husband of Elizabeth Stafford

Elizabeth Poyntz, Lady Mistress to Henry, Prince of Wales

Henry, Prince of Wales, first son of Henry VIII and Katherine of Aragon

Margaret of Austria, Regent of the Netherlands, daughter of the Emperor Maximilian I

Sir Thomas Knyvet, Chancellor of the Exchequer

Thomas Butler, 7th Earl of Ormond, chamberlain to Katherine of Aragon

Jane Colt, first wife of Sir Thomas More, mother of his children

Alice Middleton, second wife of Sir Thomas More

Pico della Mirandola, Renaissance philosopher

Pietro Torrigiano, sculptor

Raphael Sanzio, painter

Guido Mazzone, sculptor

Michelangelo, painter and sculptor

Benvenuto Cellini, sculptor

Thomas Grey, 2nd Marquess of Dorset

John Colet, Dean of St Paul's, humanist scholar

Pierre Terrail, the Chevalier Bayard, French knight

Louis I d'Orléans, Duke of Longueville, French general, Grand Chamberlain of France

Pope Leo X

Charles, Infante of Castile, later Charles I of Spain and Charles V, Holy Roman Emperor; son of Philip I of Castile and Queen Juana

Guillaume de Ghislain, Maximilian's champion

Juan, late Infante of Spain, brother of Katherine of Aragon

Elizabeth Grey, Charles Brandon's betrothed

James V, King of Scots, Harry's nephew

Philibert II, Duke of Savoy

Anne Boleyn, Queen of England, Harry's second wife

Etiennette de la Baume, Harry's mistress

Stillborn second son of Henry VIII and Katherine of Aragon

The Borgias: the family of Pope Alexander VI

Jane Popincourt, maid-of-honour to Katherine of Aragon

(Sir) Nicholas Carew, courtier

Elizabeth Bryan, his wife, sister of Sir Francis Bryan; Harry's mistress

Dr John Chamber, Harry's chief physician

Elizabeth Stafford, wife of Thomas Howard, 3rd Duke of Norfolk, daughter of Edward Stafford, 3rd Duke of Buckingham

Mary Boleyn, daughter of Sir Thomas Boleyn and later Harry's mistress

Bessie Blount, Harry's mistress

Sir Thomas Bryan, vice chamberlain to Katherine of Aragon

Thomasine Haverford and Cecily Swan, laundresses to Katherine of Aragon

Stillborn third son of Henry VIII and Katherine of Aragon

George Boleyn, later Viscount Rochford, son of Sir Thomas Boleyn

Francis I, King of France

Claude de France, Queen of France, his wife, daughter of Louis XII, King of France

Charles III, Duke of Savoy

Sebastian Giustinian, Venetian ambassador

Governatore, Harry's favourite horse

(Sir) Francis Bryan, courtier

Giles, late Lord Daubeney, owner of Hampton Court

Mary, second daughter of Henry VIII and Katherine of Aragon

Agnes Tilney, Duchess of Norfolk, wife of Thomas Howard, 2nd Duke of Norfolk

Lady Margaret Bryan, Lady Mistress to the Princess Mary and later to Harry's other children; wife of Sir Thomas Bryan and mother of Francis and Elizabeth Bryan

Henry, Earl of Lincoln, eldest son of Charles Brandon, Duke of Suffolk, and Mary Tudor

Archibald Douglas, Earl of Angus, second husband of Margaret Tudor

John Stewart, Duke of Albany, Regent of Scotland

Lady Margaret ('Marget') Douglas, daughter of Archibald Douglas, Earl of Angus, and Margaret Tudor; later Countess of Lennox

Sir William Kingston, Constable of the Tower

St Thomas Becket, saint and martyr (murdered 1170)

Sir William Sandys, courtier

Friar Dionysio Memmo, musician

Martin Luther, German theologian, founder of the Protestant religion

Francis, Dauphin of France, eldest son of King Francis I

Guillaume Gouffier, Seigneur de Bonnivet, Admiral of France

Richard Pace, Harry's secretary

(Sir) Henry Norris, courtier, later Chief Gentleman of the Privy Chamber and Groom of the Stool

Cardinal Campeggio, Papal Legate, Papal Protector of England

Third daughter of Henry VIII and Katherine of Aragon

Nicolaus Kratzer, astronomer and mathematician

Charlemagne, Holy Roman Emperor (d. 814)

Louise of Savoy, mother of Francis I, King of France

Henry Fitzroy, bastard son of Henry VIII and Bessie Blount; later Duke of Richmond and Somerset

Gilbert, Lord Tailboys, husband of Elizabeth Blount

William Carey, courtier, husband of Mary Boleyn

Germaine de Foix, Dowager Queen of Aragon, widow of King Ferdinand V

Diego Fernández de Córdoba y Mendoza, Count of Cabra, Spanish nobleman

Fadrique Álvarez de Toledo y Enríquez, Duke of Alva, Spanish nobleman

Henry, Lord Stafford, eldest son of Edward Stafford, Duke of Buckingham

Ursula Pole, his wife, daughter of Margaret Plantagenet, Countess of Salisbury

Henry Pole, Lord Montagu, eldest son of Margaret Plantagenet, Countess of Salisbury

Geoffrey Pole, son of Margaret Plantagenet, Countess of Salisbury

Reginald Pole, later Cardinal, son of Margaret Plantagenet, Countess of Salisbury

John Longland, Bishop of Lincoln, Harry's confessor

Elizabeth Tailboys, daughter of Henry VIII and Bessie Blount

Marguerite of Valois, later Queen of Navarre, sister of King Francis I

Antonio Toto, architect

Dr Thomas Linacre, physician, tutor to the Princess Mary

Juan Luis Vives, Spanish educationist

Father Richard Fetherston, chaplain to Katherine of Aragon

James Butler, heir of the Earl of Ormond

Lord Henry Percy, heir to Henry Percy, 5th Earl of Northumberland, later 6th Earl of Northumberland

Mary Talbot, daughter of George Talbot, 4th Earl of Shrewsbury, and later wife of Henry Percy, 6th Earl of Northumberland

Pope Adrian VI

Pope Clement VII (Giulio de' Medici)

Henry Parker, Lord Morley, scholar and translator

Jane Parker, his daughter, and wife of George Boleyn, Viscount Rochford

George Cavendish, Cardinal Wolsey's Gentleman Usher

Master Fermour, merchant of Calais

Edmund Mody, Harry's footman

The Lytton family of Knebworth

Edmund, Duke of Somerset, Harry's deceased younger brother

The Beaufort family, Harry's paternal ancestors

William Fitzalan, 11th Earl of Arundel

John de Vere, 14th Earl of Oxford

Thomas Manners, Earl of Rutland, Harry's cousin

Isabella of Portugal, Empress, wife of the Emperor Charles V

Giovanni di Maiano, sculptor

(Sir) Thomas Wyatt, poet and diplomat

Elizabeth Brooke, his wife

Sir John Russell, courtier, soldier and diplomat

Bess Holland, mistress of Thomas Howard, 3rd Duke of Norfolk

Don Diego Hurtado de Mendoza, Spanish ambassador

Henry, Duke of Orléans, second son of King Francis I

Hans Holbein, painter

Gabriel de Grammont, Bishop of Tarbes, French envoy

Elizabeth Wydeville, Queen of England, wife of Edward IV and Harry's maternal grandmother

Joan Lark, Cardinal Wolsey's mistress

Infanta Maria of Portugal, daughter of Manuel I, King of Portugal, by Maria of Aragon, sister of Katherine of Aragon

Trastamara dynasty, ruling family of Castile

William Tyndale, religious reformer, translator of the Bible

Dr (Sir) William Butts, Harry's physician, humanist scholar

Sir Edward Seymour, courtier, brother of Jane Seymour; later Viscount Beauchamp, then Earl of Hertford

Henry Carey, son of William Carey by Mary Boleyn

Francis Weston, courtier

Eustache Chapuys, Imperial ambassador

Thomas Abell, chaplain to Katherine of Aragon

Stephen Gardiner, Harry's secretary, later Bishop of Winchester

Edward Foxe, Harry's almoner

Thomas Cranmer, reformist cleric, later Archbishop of Canterbury

Simon Fish, heretic

Black Joan, first wife of Thomas Cranmer

(Sir) Thomas Cromwell, Harry's Principal Secretary, later Lord Privy Seal, Lord Cromwell and Earl of Essex

Niccolò Machiavelli, Italian author of The Prince

Elizabeth Wyckes, late wife of Thomas Cromwell

Anne and Grace, daughters of Thomas Cromwell

Gregory Cromwell, son of Thomas Cromwell

A physician to Cardinal Wolsey

Gertrude Blount, Marchioness of Exeter, wife of Henry Courtenay, Marquess of Exeter

William Brereton, courtier

(Sir) Thomas Wriothesley, Harry's secretary, later Earl of Southampton and Lord Chancellor

William Peto, provincial minister of the Observant Friars

Father Elston, Observant friar

Sir Thomas Audley, Lord Chancellor

Mark Smeaton, musician and courtier

Monsieur de la Pommeraye, French ambassador

Eleanor Paston, wife of Thomas Manners, Earl of Rutland

Mary Howard, daughter of Thomas Howard, 3rd Duke of Norfolk, later wife of Henry Fitzroy, Duke of Richmond and Somerset; Harry's daughter-in-law

Françoise d'Alençon, Duchess of Vendôme, mistress of King Francis I

John Bourchier, Lord Berners, the King's deputy in Calais

Charles, Duke of Orléans, third son of King Francis I

Henry Howard, Earl of Surrey, son of Thomas Howard, 3rd Duke of Norfolk

Dr Rowland Lee, later Bishop of Coventry and Lichfield

Thomas Heneage, courtier, later Groom of the Stool

Friar John Forest, confessor to Katherine of Aragon

Sir John Gage, Harry's vice chamberlain

Frances Brandon, daughter of Charles Brandon, Duke of Suffolk, and Mary Tudor

Henry Grey, Marquess of Dorset, husband of Frances Brandon

Katherine Willoughby, second wife of Charles Brandon, Duke of Suffolk

Maria de Salinas, Lady Willoughby, mother of Katherine Willoughby, Duchess of Suffolk

Thomas, Lord Burgh, chamberlain to Anne Boleyn

Elizabeth, daughter of Henry VIII and Anne Boleyn

Anne Boleyn, Lady Shelton, aunt of Anne Boleyn

Elizabeth Barton, 'the Nun of Kent', prophetess

Stillborn son of Henry VIII and Anne Boleyn

Joan Ashley, Harry's mistress

Pope Paul III

Philippe de Chabot, Seigneur de Brion, Admiral of France, French envoy

William Stafford, second husband of Mary Boleyn

Madge Shelton, Harry's mistress, cousin to Anne Boleyn

John Houghton, Prior of the London Charterhouse

Richard Reynolds, monk of Syon Abbey

Miles Coverdale, reformer, translator of the Bible

Richard Moryson, Thomas Cromwell's propagandist

Sir Richard Rich, courtier and politician, later Solicitor General

Henry Parker, Lord Morley, scholar and translator

Sir John Seymour, father of Edward, Thomas and Jane Seymour

(Sir) Thomas Seymour, diplomat and soldier, brother of Jane Seymour

Jane Seymour, Queen of England, Harry's third wife

Sir Anthony Browne, courtier

John Kite, Bishop of Carlisle

The executioner of Calais

Anne Stanhope, wife of Sir Edward Seymour

Lord Thomas Howard, younger son of Thomas Howard, 2nd Duke of Norfolk

William Webbe and his paramour, who became Harry's mistress

Robert Aske, one of the leaders of the Pilgrimage of Grace

William Wrythe, herald, father of Thomas Wriothesley

Lady Elizabeth FitzGerald ('Fair Geraldine'), muse of Henry Howard, Earl of Surrey, and later the wife of Sir Anthony Browne

Francesco Petrarch, Italian scholar and poet

Laura, his lover

Edward, Prince of Wales, Duke of Cornwall and Earl of Chester, son of Henry VIII and Jane Seymour

Mistress Sybil Penn, his nurse

Louis de Perreau, Sieur de Castillon, French ambassador

Marie de Guise, Madame de Longueville, later Queen of Scots and wife of James V

Louise de Guise, her sister

Christina of Denmark, Duchess of Milan

William, Duke of Cleves, brother of Anna and Amalia of Cleves

Anna of Cleves, Queen of England, Harry's fourth wife

Amelia of Cleves, her sister

Maria of Jülich-Berg, Duchess of Cleves, their mother

John Lambert, heretic

Edward Courtenay, son of Henry Courtenay, Marquess of Exeter

Henry Pole, son of Henry Pole, Lord Montagu

Sir Anthony Denny, courtier, later Chief Gentleman of the Privy Chamber and Groom of the Stool

Master Penny, Harry's barber

Susanna Gilman, painter

Katheryn Howard, Queen of England, Harry's fifth wife

Mary Norris, niece of Thomas Howard, 3rd Duke of Norfolk, and later the wife of Sir George Carew

Catherine Carey, daughter of Henry VIII and Mary Boleyn

Lord Edmund Howard, younger brother of Thomas Howard, 3rd Duke of Norfolk, and father of Katheryn Howard

Bourchier family, earls of Essex

Thomas Culpeper, courtier

Francis, son of the Duke of Lorraine and later Francis I, Duke of Lorraine

Margarete Preu, second wife of Thomas Cranmer, Archbishop of Canterbury

Elizabeth Seymour, sister of Jane Seymour and wife of Gregory Cromwell, son of Thomas Cromwell

Charles Howard, courtier, brother of Katheryn Howard

Lord William Howard, younger brother of Thomas Howard, 3rd Duke of Norfolk

Sir William Paget, later Privy Councillor and Harry's Principal Secretary

John Ponet, fellow of Queens' College, Cambridge

John Lascelles, courtier

Mary Lascelles, his sister

Francis Dereham, Katheryn Howard's kinsman and secretary

Henry Manox, Katheryn Howard's former music master

Anne Bassett, maid-of-honour

Honor Grenville, Lady Lisle, her mother

Mary, Queen of Scots, daughter and successor of James V

Katharine Parr, Lady Latimer, Queen of England, Harry's sixth wife

William Parr, her brother, later Earl of Essex

John Neville, Lord Latimer, Katharine Parr's second husband

Sir Thomas Parr, courtier, father of Katharine Parr

Maud Green, his wife, lady-in-waiting to Katharine of Aragon

Anne Parr, his sister, maid-of-honour

Edward Borough, Katharine Parr's first husband

John Marbeck, Master of the Choristers

Sir John Wallop, soldier and diplomat

Hans Eworth, painter

Master John, painter

Guillim Scrots, painter

Dr Richard Cox, tutor to Prince Edward, later Dean of Christ Church, Oxford

Henry Brandon, son of Charles Brandon, Duke of Suffolk, and Katherine Willoughby, later 2nd Duke of Suffolk

Lord Thomas Howard, son of Henry Howard, Earl of Surrey

John Dudley, Viscount Lisle, Privy Councillor, Lord High Admiral

Robert Dudley, his son

Jermyn Gardiner, nephew of Stephen Gardiner, Bishop of Winchester

Matthew Stewart, Earl of Lennox, husband of Lady Margaret Douglas

Dr John Cheke, tutor to Prince Edward

William Grindal, tutor to the Lady Elizabeth

Roger Ascham, Cambridge scholar

Nicholas Udall, former headmaster of Eton College

Donato Bramante, Italian architect

John Calvin, Swiss religious reformer

Dr Thomas Wendy, Harry's physician

Sir George Carew, Vice Admiral

Dr Edward Crome, preacher

Anne Askew, heretic

Sir Edmund Walsingham, Lieutenant of the Tower

Sir George Blagge, courtier

Claude d'Annebault, Lord High Admiral of France

Sir Richard Southwell, courtier

Anne de Pisseleu d'Heilly, Madame d'Etampes, mistress of King Francis I

Various nobles, Privy Councillors, gentlemen of the Privy Chamber, Esquires of the Body, courtiers, knights, Members of Parliament, judges, chamberlains, household officers, heralds, royal servants, clergymen, clerks, Yeomen of the Guard, Gentlemen Pensioners, Barons of the Cinque Ports, constables of the Tower, ambassadors, envoys, lawyers, physicians, Masters of the Revels, musicians, children and choristers of the Chapel Royal, Lords of Misrule, painters, grooms, ushers, messengers, ladies-in-waiting, maids-of-honour, midwives, admirals, soldiers, sailors, mayors, civic officers, citizens, merchants, common people, apprentices, boatmen, rebels and whores.

Timeline

1485

– Battle of Bosworth; Henry Tudor defeats Richard III, the last Plantagenet King, and becomes Henry VII, first sovereign of the royal House of Tudor

1491

– Birth of Henry VIII

1494

– Prince Henry created Duke of York

1501

– Marriage of Arthur Tudor, Prince of Wales, and Katherine of Aragon

1502

– Death of Prince Arthur

1503

– Prince Henry created Prince of Wales and betrothed to Katherine of Aragon

1509

– Accession of Henry VIII
– Marriage and coronation of Henry VIII and Katherine of Aragon

1510

– Birth of a stillborn daughter to Henry VIII and Katherine of Aragon

1511

– Birth of Henry, Prince of Wales, to Henry VIII and Katherine of Aragon
– Death of Henry, Prince of Wales

1513

– Henry VIII invades France
– Battle of the Spurs; Thérouanne falls to Henry VIII
– James IV of Scots killed at the Battle of Flodden, a decisive victory for the English

- Tournai falls to Henry VIII
- Birth of a short-lived son to Henry VIII and Katherine of Aragon

1514

- Henry VIII breaks the alliance with Spain, makes peace with France and marries his sister Mary to Louis XII of France
- Birth of a short-lived son to Henry VIII and Katherine of Aragon

1515

- Death of Louis XII of France; accession of Francis I
- Thomas Wolsey, Henry VIII's chief minister, made a cardinal

1516

- Death of Ferdinand of Aragon
- Birth of the Princess Mary, daughter of Henry VIII and Katherine of Aragon

1517

- Martin Luther publishes his ninety-five theses in Germany and inspires the Protestant Reformation

1518

- Birth of a short-lived daughter to Katherine of Aragon and Henry VIII

1519

- Death of Maximilian I, Holy Roman Emperor
- Election of the Holy Roman Emperor Charles V
- Birth of Henry Fitzroy, bastard son of Henry VIII by Elizabeth Blount

1520

- Henry VIII meets Francis I of France at the Field of Cloth of Gold

1521

- The Pope bestows on Henry VIII the title Defender of the Faith

1525

- Henry Fitzroy created Duke of Richmond and Somerset
- The Princess Mary sent to Ludlow for two years

1526

- Henry VIII in pursuit of Anne Boleyn

1527

- Henry VIII questions the validity of his marriage to Katherine of Aragon and asks the Pope for an annulment

1528

- Cardinal Campeggio, Papal legate, comes to England to try the King's case

1529

- The legatine court sits at the monastery of the Black Friars in London; Katherine of Aragon appeals to Henry VIII for justice; the case is referred back to Rome
- Cardinal Wolsey falls from favour
- Sir Thomas More appointed Lord Chancellor
- Eustache Chapuys appointed Charles V's ambassador to England
- Reformation Parliament sits (1529–36)

1530

- Henry VIII canvasses the universities for their views on his case
- Death of Cardinal Wolsey

1531

- Katherine of Aragon banished from court
- Thomas Cromwell emerges as Henry VIII's chief minister
- Submission of the clergy to Henry VIII

1532

- Sir Thomas More resigns the office of Lord Chancellor
- Death of William Warham, Archbishop of Canterbury; paves the way for the appointment of the radical Thomas Cranmer
- Anne Boleyn becomes Henry VIII's mistress
- Anne Boleyn created Lady Marquess of Pembroke
- Henry VIII and Francis I meet at Boulogne

1533

- Henry VIII secretly marries Anne Boleyn
- Parliament passes the Act in Restraint of Appeals (to the Pope), the legal cornerstone of the English Reformation, making the King the highest authority on all legal matters
- Anne Boleyn appears at court as Queen of England
- Cranmer pronounces the marriage of Henry VIII and Katherine of Aragon incestuous and unlawful, and confirms the validity of Henry's marriage to Anne Boleyn
- Coronation of Anne Boleyn

- Birth of the Princess Elizabeth, daughter of Henry VIII and Anne Boleyn

1534

- The Pope pronounces the marriage of Henry VIII and Katherine of Aragon valid
- Oath of Supremacy administered to leading subjects
- Imprisonment of Sir Thomas More and John Fisher, Bishop of Rochester, for refusing to swear the Oath of Supremacy
- Anne Boleyn bears a stillborn child
- Parliament passes the Act of Supremacy, making Henry VIII Supreme Head of the Church of England, and the Act of Succession, making the children of Queen Anne the King's lawful heirs

1535

- Executions of John Fisher, Bishop of Rochester, Sir Thomas More and several Carthusian monks
- Henry VIII and Anne Boleyn undertake a major progress to the west of England
- Henry VIII visits Wulfhall, the Seymour family home
- Henry VIII begins courting Jane Seymour
- Thomas Cromwell and his commissioners compile the *Valor Ecclesiasticus*, a record of the wealth and income of the monasteries

1536

- Death of Katherine of Aragon
- Anne Boleyn miscarries a son
- Anne Boleyn arrested and imprisoned in the Tower
- Anne Boleyn tried and condemned to death for treason
- Anne Boleyn's marriage to Henry VIII dissolved
- Anne Boleyn beheaded in the Tower of London
- Betrothal of Henry VIII and Jane Seymour
- Marriage of Henry VIII and Jane Seymour
- Jane Seymour proclaimed queen of England
- A new Act of Succession settles the succession on Jane's children by the King
- The Lady Mary signs her submission, acknowledging her mother's marriage incestuous and unlawful
- Henry VIII reconciled to his daughter

- Thomas Cromwell appointed Vicar General
- The Pilgrimage of Grace (1536–7)
- The Dissolution of the Monasteries begins (1536–40)
- Act of the Ten Articles of Doctrine passed

1537
- Birth of Prince Edward, son of Henry VIII and Jane Seymour
- Death of Jane Seymour
- Henry VIII begins searching for a fourth wife

1538
- Treaty of Nice between the Emperor and the King of France leaves Henry VIII in political isolation
- Henry VIII excommunicated by the Pope

1539
- Treaty of Toledo between the Emperor and the King of France further isolates Henry VIII
- Act of the Six Articles of Doctrine passed
- Henry VIII sanctions the translation of the Bible into English
- Henry VIII opens negotiations for a marriage with Anna of Cleves
- Henry VIII signs the marriage treaty (4 October)
- Anna sails to England

1540
- Meeting of Henry VIII and Anna of Cleves at Rochester
- Official reception of Anna of Cleves at Blackheath
- Marriage of Henry VIII and Anna of Cleves
- Henry VIII begins courting Katheryn Howard
- Thomas Cromwell attainted in Parliament
- The marriage of Henry VIII and Anna of Cleves formally annulled by Act of Parliament
- Execution of Thomas Cromwell
- Marriage of Henry VIII and Katheryn Howard

1541
- Henry VIII undertakes a great progress to the north
- Fall of Katheryn Howard

1542
- Execution of Katheryn Howard
- Death of James V of Scots; accession of Mary, Queen of Scots

1543

- Marriage of Henry VIII and Katharine Parr

1544

- Henry VIII's forces invade Scotland; the 'Rough Wooing'
- Henry VIII invades France and successfully besieges Boulogne

1545

- The *Mary Rose* sinks

1547

- Death of Henry VIII; accession of Edward VI

Reading Group Questions

- *She had been everything a queen should be: beautiful, kind, fruitful, charitable, open-handed and devout.* The novel opens on a desperately sad little boy mourning the loss of his mother. What shadow does the death of Elizabeth of York cast over Harry's life? To what extent do you feel that his search for a perfect queen was an attempt to resurrect her presence, and with this paragon of virtue held in his mind, could he ever have been satisfied?

- Harry and his father, Henry VII, have a tense and volatile relationship. What do you think Henry VII's true reasons were for keeping Harry so close to him throughout his teenage years? Was it worry for the safety of his only heir, or did he see something concerning in Harry's capricious nature? What about Harry's relationships with his own children, after the tragic loss of so many infants, and of his illegitimate son?

- *Arthur, in Heaven, had stolen one final march on him and was enjoying the greatest thing of all: their mother's presence.* Harry's jealousy and resentment of Arthur continues beyond his brother's death. As Prince of Wales and then King, Harry ultimately takes everything that was to have been Arthur's, and laps up his noblemen's compliments, but do you feel he is still constantly trying to prove himself? Where else do you see this intense competitiveness in Harry's character and personal and political relationships?

- Harry is undoubtedly the centre around which the court rotates, but various other characters hold their own – for a while – within his orbit. From Will Somers to Thomas Cromwell, Cardinal Wolsey to Eustache Chapuys, who really stood out for you and why, and whose stories most intrigued you?

- Harry's obsessions with architecture, art and science allow Alison Weir to weave evocative descriptions of the culture of the Tudor court into the novel. Through these descriptions, Harry's conversations with characters such as Thomas More, and the ground-breaking curriculum created for his young children, what are we able to learn about the rich intellectual background to Harry's life, and his thirst for knowledge?

- Very few people could speak with true honesty to Harry, but those who did had a particularly fascinating relationship with him. What are your impressions of his sister Mary, the French Queen, and his childhood friend – and ultimately her husband – Charles Brandon? As recurring characters from the Six Tudor Queens series, how does seeing them through Harry's eyes change or develop our view of them? Who else was able to command Harry's attention and why did these relationships, particularly with his closest advisers, turn so sour?

- If you've read Alison's Six Tudor Queen novels, what new understandings have you found from hearing Harry's side of their stories? What do we as readers learn about the behind-the-scenes machinations to which the queens themselves were never privy to? Does it increase your sympathy for women such as Anne Boleyn and Katheryn Howard, and the pressure both were under, in different ways, from Harry's obsession? Who do you think he found the most contentment with in the end, and why?

- *He had never known what it was truly to mourn a wife.* The loss of Jane Seymour in 1537 is a turning point in Harry's life, when, for all his power, he could not command her to live. And it comes at a moment when his main ambition – the birth of a healthy son – has finally been achieved. How do you think her death changes Harry, and what impact does it have on the court and society around him?